THREE COMPLETE NOVELS

Piers Anthony
and
Robert E. Margroff

Dragon's Gold

Serpent's Silver

Chimaera's Copper

WINGS BOOKS
New York • Avenel, New Jersey

This 1994 edition is published by Wings Books,
distributed by Random House Value Publishing, Inc.,
40 Engelhard Avenue, Avenel, New Jersey 07001,
by arrangement with Tor Books.

Random House
New York · Toronto · London · Sydney · Auckland

Printed and bound in the United States of America

Library of Congress Cataloging-in-Publication Data

Anthony, Piers.
[Selections]
Three complete novels / Piers Anthony & Robert E. Margroff.
p.   cm.
Contents: Dragon's gold—Serpent's silver—Chimaera's copper.
ISBN 0-517-10012-6
1. Fantastic fiction, American.   I. Margroff, Robert E., 1930–
II. Title.
PS3551.N73A6   1993
813'.54—dc20   93-25128
                                                          CIP

10 9 8 7 6 5 4 3

CONTENTS

CONTENTS

Dragon's Gold

Contents

Prologue

T HE FUGITIVE DID NOT know that his arrival at the small Rud
farm was preordained. He would have scoffed at the notion,
had he been told. All he knew was that his injured leg hurt abominably, that
he was so filthy he was disgusted, and that he was too tired to fight or flee if
discovered.

It was night again. He had hardly been aware of the passage of time since
his escape, except for the awful sun by day and the cruel chill by night.
Dehydration and shivering, with little between except fear and fatigue.

Yet this was a decent region, he knew, if viewed objectively. He heard
froogs croaking loudly in the nearby froogpond, and corbean stalks rustling
in the breeze. Appleberries and razzelfruits perfumed the air and set his
stomach growling. The natives claimed that these bitter fruits could be
charmed to become sweet, but he refused to credit such impossible claims.
He was not yet so far gone as to believe in magic! But they certainly looked
good! Hunger—there was another curse of the moment!

But thought of food had to be pushed aside, as did dreams of a hot bath
and a change of clothing. He had come here, he reminded himself sternly, to
steal a horse. He hated the necessity, for he regarded himself as an honorable man, but he seemed to have no choice.

He crept nearer to the cottage, orienting on its single faint light. How he
hoped that there would be no one awake to challenge him! He did not know
how close the Queen's guardsmen were, or how quickly they would appear
the moment there was any commotion. How ironic it would be to die igno-
bly as an unsuccessful horse thief!

He paused, studying the light. Far off there sounded the trebling screech
of a houcat. His pursuers had lost the trail last night, and he doubted that
they would swim the river to pick it up again. There were hazards in that
water as bad for guardsmen as for thieves, and only a truly desperate man

would have been fool enough to risk it. Perhaps the guardsmen thought him dead already. This fool, for the time being, was almost safe.

He came close and peered cautiously in the window. A slender girl sat reading by the flickering light of a lamp. He gazed at the coppery sheen of her hair, and the planes of her somewhat pointed face, and the gentle swell and ebb of her bosom as she breathed. How lovely she seemed! It was not that she was beautiful, for by his standards she was not, but that she was comfortable and quiet and clean. A girl who read alone at night: what a contrast to the type of woman he had known! There was an aura of decency about her that excited his longing. He could love such a girl and such a life-style, if ever given a chance.

For a moment he was crazily tempted to knock on the window, to announce himself, to say, "Haloo there, young woman, are you in need of a man? Give me a bath and some food, and I shall be yours forever!" But he was not yet so tired that no reason remained. If he did that, she would start up and scream, and the guardsmen would come, and it would be over.

He ducked past the window and tiptoed to the barn. He held his breath as he tried the latch on the stable door. It opened easily, without even a squeak. This was a well-maintained farm. He felt a certain regret that this should facilitate the theft of an animal. It might have been more fitting to steal from a sloppy farm, but a squeaky door would have been an excellent guardian.

From inside came the scent of horse and hay. He felt around in the dark just past the door and found the halter exactly where it should be. The arrangements in good Rud barns were standard.

There was the snap of a broken twig. He turned.

She stood there in the wan light from the window, garbed in a filmy nightdress and a shawl. The first thing he noticed was the way her firm slim legs showed in gauzy silhouette.

The second thing he noticed was the pitchfork she held at waist height, aimed at his chest.

He swallowed, trying to judge whether he could dodge aside quickly enough to avoid the thrust of those sharp tines, and whether he retained the strength to wrestle the implement away from her. And if he did, what, then? How could he hurt a girl he would rather embrace? Perhaps it was a trick of the inadequate light, but her eyes seemed to be the exact color of violets back on his native Earth.

"Speak!" she said. "What is your business here?" Her voice sent a thrill through him; it was dulcet despite its tone of challenge.

What use to lie? He hated this whole business! "I came to steal your horse. I would rather have stolen your heart." And what had possessed him to say that?

"You are a thief? A highwayman?"

She hadn't thrust her fork at him. That was a good sign. He decided to tell her the rest of it. "I'm not an ordinary thief, not even a good one, as you can see," he said with difficulty. "I just had to have a horse. I know you won't believe that I'm not a criminal."

"Why didn't you come openly to my door, then?"

"I—I looked in your window, and saw you reading. You were so—so *nice*! I thought you would scream if you saw me. I—I'm a fugitive from the Queen's dungeon. I know that doesn't make me a hero, but maybe it carries a bit of weight."

"You have round ears," she said, her voice assuming a soft, strange quality. "You cannot be of this planet. Certainly you are no ordinary thief. Introduce yourself, Roundear."

She seemed to have no fear of him, only a certain caution. It was almost as if she had been expecting him! "John Knight, of Earth," he said.

"A name may be an omen, Knight," she said. She smiled a mysterious witching smile and lowered the fork. "You may call me Charlain. We shall be married on the morrow."

He stared at her. Then, tentatively, he smiled. She returned the smile. Then, unaccountably, he laughed, and she laughed with him.

She took him inside the house and gave him a bath and some food, and when he was clean and fed she kissed him and took him to her bed. He was so tired that he fell almost instantly to sleep despite the presence of her warm body beside him. He didn't even care that this might be a ruse to lull him, so that she could safely turn him in to the Queen's guardsmen. He had to believe in her.

Thus did John Knight first encounter the woman he was to marry. She practiced fortune-telling, so had known he was coming: a round-eared man who was a fugitive from the Queen. She had told no one of this vision, so knew that his arrival was no trap by the Queen. She had known that the man would be completely unprepossessing, but would be the one she could truly love, and that though he had known a woman before her, he would never know one after her.

They married on the morrow, in a secret ceremony, and that evening he was enough recovered to remain awake in her bed for some time. Their life together had begun abruptly, but had an unspoken understanding that was at times mysterious and at other times thoroughly natural to him.

The following year their round-eared baby was born, and two years after that their point-eared baby.

The prophecy that John Knight had not known about was on its way to fulfillment. His life was relatively placid after he settled; not so, that of his children.

I /

DRAGON SCALE

THE ROAD WOUND LIKE a twisting dragon's tail. Through rank underbrush and skeletal trees. Past boulders the size of cottages. Along a sparkling mountain stream bordered with high piles of debris left by the late spring floods. It did not look like the setting for the beginning of the fulfillment of a long-term prophecy.

Two slim figures walked the road, carrying travel-sacks and leading a donkey. One was sixteen, tall enough to be handsome were it not for his round ears. The other was fourteen but looked twelve, with pointed ears. Both wore the garb of Rud rustics: heavy leather walking boots, brownberry shirts, greenbriar pantaloons, and lightweight summer stockelcaps whose long tips ended in tassels of blue and green yarn. They could hardly have looked less like folk destined to commence the fulfillment of a significant prophecy.

Kelvin, the elder one, played on his mandajo as he walked, picking out the accompaniment to "Fortune Come a-Callin'," a Rud tune of great antiquity. The three-stringed lute of Rud could be beautiful when properly evoked, but Kelvin was not playing it well. Some had magic that related to music, and some did not; some thought they had magic when they did not. Kelvin was of the latter persuasion, but he wouldn't have cared if he had realized. His thoughts were far away.

Jon, the younger one, brushed back long yellow hair. A stranger, looking at Jon's alert greenish eyes and large ears and face that showed no hint of a beard, would have dismissed this as a lively boy. The stranger would have been mistaken, for Jon was Kelvin's sister. Because it could be dangerous for a girl to go alone into the countryside of Rud, the parents had tried to restrict her to the farm and village. But Jon was an adventurous sort, always eager to go out exploring. Realizing that she could not be restrained, they had finally yielded with two stern strictures: always go in company with Kelvin, and go as a boy. That suited Jon just fine, for though she would die rather than say it, she looked up to her brother, and wanted to share his activities. She also rather liked masquerading as a boy, for though her parents had been happy to have a girl, Jon herself envied the freedoms and prospects of the other sex. She had become almost letter-perfect at the masquerade, but now nature was playing on her a disgusting trick. Her hips were broadening and her breasts were swelling. It was getting harder to look the part, and it would be impossible without her solid shirt. What would she do when her rebellious front became too pronounced to conceal? She was disgusted, and the very thought put her in a bad mood.

Now Jon peered into the underbrush and up into the branches of the trees, looking for trouble. She carried a sturdy leather sling whose pocket held a carefully positioned rock of the required squirbet-braining size. Just let one of those creatures show its snoot now . . . !

"Fortune come a-callin', but I did hide, ah-oo-ay," Kelvin sang with imperfect pitch. "Fortune come a-callin', but I did hide, bloody saber at my side, ah-oo-ay, ah-oo-ay, ay."

"You call that old pig-gutter you're packing a saber?" Jon demanded. She spoke with deceptive good humor, her eyes wandering over to her brother. To the dark handle of the war souvenir protruding from its worn and cracked scabbard.

Kelvin lowered his instrument. His thoughts leaped ahead to the deepening gloom and the forbidding mountain pass. "We're not riding either," he said, referring to another verse.

"No, but we would be if you hadn't let that horse dealer swindle us," Jon said. She lifted the halter and made a grimace of distaste at their pack animal. "A horse to ride would be great, but you, you jackass, had to buy a jackass!"

"I thought," Kelvin said lightly, his attention focusing a bit, "that I could put two of them to work. You and Mockery."

"Mockery's the name for it!" Jon snapped. "Anyone but you would have been put off by the name, but you had to go and hand over our last two rudnas for it!"

"Jon, Jon, show faith in thy elder," Kelvin teased. "We hadn't the money for a horse, and Mockery was cheap. We'll need his strong back, and yours, to pack out all the gold we'll find."

Jon made an uncouth noise. "If he ever lets us load! It took us half the morning to get our pitifully few supplies strapped to his ornery back. He's got a kick like a mule! I suppose when we want our tent, he'll start all over."

"Not so, little brother Worrisome Wart!" Kelvin always referred to her in the masculine, maintaining the masquerade; what started as a game had soon enough become second nature. "It's only that he's jealous. *We* have the lighter loads. Smart animal, Mockery. Smart enough to know when we're in dragon country. Anything that smart, including me and possibly ye, knows the danger."

"Do we, Kel?" Her voice was almost pleading.

Kelvin narrowed the bluish eyes that seemed almost as strange as his rounded ears, in Rud. This was not like Jon. Usually she tried with pretty good success to appear more recklessly masculine than any ordinary boy could be. Until today she had seemed if anything too confident. What was bothering her?

"Jon, if you're afraid—"

"Ain't that!" Jon snapped. "Not any more than you are, anyway. But curse it, Kel, if I'm going to get et up by a dragon, I at least want a chance."

"Few people have a chance," Kelvin retorted. "Dragons are big and strong and mean. If you run into one, it will devour you fast. Once it bites off your head, which I'm sure it will do early on, I can promise you that you will hardly feel a thing."

"Great!" Jon said, not appreciating the humor. "So we just stay away from it?"

"That's all anyone with any sense does. Or," he added, giving a slight nod at Mockery, "any*thing* with sense."

"But dragons have been killed, haven't they?"

"A few times by heroes with armor and war-horses and lances. You know that, Jon. A few have fallen, but not to the likes of us."

"But if we had a good sword, and a war-horse, and a lance—"

"We'd get et, just the same," Kelvin said confidently. "You ever see me ride a war-horse? Or use a sword except for hacking brush? It takes training, Jon; it doesn't just happen."

Jon subsided into silence as they plodded on. The road was becoming narrower with every mile. The debris piles were getting higher and higher. Now the mountain walls seemed to lean inward. The sun hid its face behind the peak of the mountain to the west. The air became noticeably cooler as the bird and animal sounds became more hushed and were heard less often.

"I don't like this place," Jon said, looking about at the tangled masses of trees the flood had left. "It's ugly."

"Nobody comes here for a picnic, Jon. Riches aren't found in the nicest places. If we're to get gold, we have to put up with ugliness."

Jon flushed a little and looked away. Now and then something Kelvin said did have a noticeable effect. But he wondered whether he should caution her about showing any color; that was a trait associated more with girls, and could give her away. He decided to keep quiet; Jon didn't like to have her female mannerisms pointed out. There was a certain irony in this, because in truth she was becoming a rather pretty figure of a girl when she let herself be.

Kelvin estimated the time. It was getting to be late in the afternoon. Soon they would stop to build camp, and then early tomorrow they'd find gold. Or at least they'd search for it. If the spring floods had washed it down from the high mountains, they might find nuggets of it along the stream. That was their hope; that was what made this an adventure instead of just a chance to explore. A chance for Jon to be a boy—perhaps one of the last chances, for soon there would be no easy way to conceal her nature.

He wondered how he would feel if he knew that he was really a girl, and would have to resign himself to becoming a homemaker and never going out exploring again. He shuddered; he knew he would hate it. He wished he could at least express some sympathy for Jon, but he couldn't; it would come out all wrong, and she would be furious.

"Gods, Kel, look what I found!"

He blinked as he strained his sight to see what shone so brightly in Jon's hands. His eyes were not the best; if Jon's curse was being a girl, his own was being inadequate in various ways like this. Jon had reached down into a clump of ugly brown weeds, and now held something that filled her cupped palms.

Carefully, Kelvin took it from her, bringing it close enough for a decent focus. It was a scale that could have come from a dragon's neck. It had the heft of gold, and some luster through the grime. It could be very valuable.

"It's a dragon scale, isn't it? Isn't it?" she demanded, hopping about in her excitement.

"Easy, Jon, easy," he cautioned her. "Don't shout or do anything to attract a dragon's attention. This could be fresh, and—"

"Think I'm crazy?" Jon asked. Then, "It is, isn't it? Gold that migrated to the scale from the nuggets swallowed by the dragon? It's just as the books said! Just like the shellfish that get metal in their shells from ingesting bits of metal and then become unfit to eat! We're lucky, oh so lucky!" She was dancing again.

Kelvin stopped her with an upraised hand. "Quiet, fool! The dragon could be in hearing distance!" For the scale of a dragon meant danger as well as wealth, and suddenly he was quite nervous about this aspect.

"Around here?" Jon whirled happily. "If that's so, why isn't smart-ass Mockery a-rearin' and a-rarin' and kicking up his heels? You know dragons shed scales! It probably happened weeks ago."

"Yes," Kelvin agreed. "But we can't be sure. We can't be sure it's not lurking and waiting for us."

Jon gave him a look of contempt. She had always been bolder than he. "Hah. Do you think that was just dropped?" She pointed to a pile of dried dragon dung.

Kelvin looked at the bits of white bone sticking out of the dung, and shivered. That, he thought, could be the remnant of a human being.

"We have to be careful, Jon," he said. "We have to check around here to make sure there's no fresh sign. If a dragon's been around in the last day or so, we want to move out. If we don't find fresh sign, we'll set up the tent, cook the squirbet you bagged, eat, and get a good night's sleep. Then, first thing tomorrow, we'll search." His hands felt clammy as he put the scale into a pocket of his pantaloons. The very notion of a nearby dragon gave him the cold sweats.

But Jon was already climbing a high mound of rocks and weeds and piled-up tree trunks. As usual she did not appear to have heard a word Kelvin said.

2 /

DRAGON IRE

CONTROLLING HIS FEELINGS AS much as he could, Kelvin petted Mockery and made plans for putting up the tent and cooking the squirbet Jon had knocked over earlier during the day. He took off Mockery's pack, put hobbles on the beast, went to the nearest sapling, and cut a sturdy tent pole with his incredibly dull sword.

"I found another! Two more!" Jon cried from halfway up the pile.

Kelvin's heart leaped. He controlled it. Careful, careful, he thought. Move too fast, make too much noise, and the two of them could become bones in dragon dung. Were those other bones human? Had the dragon eaten the last intrepid gold-hunters to brave this place?

"Kel, there's six of them! All in a bunch, and stained! The dragon must have been in a fight with another dragon."

So that was why so many downed trees, Kelvin thought. The flooding river hadn't done it all; dragons had added to the carnage of this region. He shivered in spite of himself as he imagined the size of the beasts. Two of them? That would account for the ground being grassless over there and for the dirt showing. Where would the loser go afterward, he wondered, and thought again that he really should be curbing Jon's noisy explorations.

"Let's make our camp now, Jon. Please." He hated sounding like a coward, but the possible presence of a dragon made him feel very much like one.

Jon ignored him, clambering nimbly on up the rockpile. *She* had no foolish concern about monsters!

He picked at a blister on his hand as he waited for her to finish with the pile and come down. Just how was their tent to be constructed? And what would they eat? The appleberry bushes had been savaged, too; even his most ardent charm was unlikely to make their fruit edible here.

"Kel, I've found . . . ." Jon's voice trailed off, forcing Kelvin to look around for her. He spotted her atop a jumble of boulders piled amidst tree trunks, the rock coated with decomposed vegetation and sandy soil from the river bottom.

"Kel, I see . . . I think I see the dragon!"

"What!"

"The dragon. I think it's dead. It's dead, Kel! It got licked in the fight. All those scales! We're rich, Kel! Come on up, and . . . oh-oh."

"What is it, Jon?" His heart thumped. His throat dried instantly.

"Oh, Kel, it's alive, but I think it's almost dead. I think we can kill it and—"

"Jon, come away from there!" If the dragon was alive, but badly injured, they might be able to escape.

"A fortune, Kel! A fortune! Kel, I'm going to sling a rock at it."

Total folly! "No, Jon, no!" Kelvin croaked, his throat so tight with fear he could hardly speak.

But the intrepid little sister was already twirling her sling. With the skill of long practice and a natural knack she let fly and followed through with her usual "Got him!"

Kelvin couldn't speak; his horror had closed off his throat entirely. He held his breath as Jon stared down the opposite side of the pile. What was she seeing there, anyway?

"It sees me, Kel," her voice came back, rising with sudden alarm. "It's awake. It—Kel, it's coming for me!"

Kelvin's voice tore loose from his constricted throat. "Run, Jon, run! Back here!"

He heard the scramble as Jon moved. Her head appeared at the crest. She seemed to be moving slowly, but Kelvin realized that this was really the effect of his terror: the world seemed to have slowed almost to a standstill. Now it came to him: this huge pile of debris had been kicked up by the fighting dragons!

Fighting? Then why wasn't the loser dead? A dragon never left prey or an enemy alive; he would chew it to bits just out of spite, even if he wasn't hungry. Dragons *liked* to kill, to make blood splatter! Everyone knew that! When they fought each other, the loser always died, because no dragon ever fled from anything. It couldn't have been a fight!

Then what had happened? Obviously this dragon had been only sleeping. But why had it scratched up such a mountain of refuse? For he was sure now: the natural hill here had been enhanced by more than flood refuse. Dragons were known to be as lazy as any other creature; they saved their energy for important things like pursuing prey and fighting and—

And mating. He remembered the stories now. The mating of dragons was almost indistinguishable from a fight to the death. It seemed that the females never did mate voluntarily, so the males had to run them down and subdue them and rape them. It was said that the effort of doing this tired out a male dragon more than any other activity, and that some dropped into deep sleep on the spot. That must have been the case with this one. Probably it would have slept for several more hours if Jon hadn't jolted him with a rock on the snoot.

But even a tired dragon was a worse threat than any other living creature. There was no telling how long this one had had to recover; it might have slept for several days, and now be largely restored, and plenty hungry. And they, like the fools they were, had blundered in, thinking the scales that had been torn off in the ecstasy of rut meant that the dragon was gone.

Jon was coming down the ragged slope, slip-sliding across slime-slick stones. The dragons probably hadn't even noticed the havoc they wrought on the landscape! The male had finally tamed the female, probably holding her down with his huge teeth and claws while it rammed into her torso. There would be blood galore, his as well as hers. Once the male's urge was spent, his grip would have relaxed, and the female would have torn free and departed. This was the one encounter in which dragon did not kill dragon; she had to go gestate, and he had to let her go. So, worn but satiated, he slept where he lay . . . until this moment.

With a cry of despair and fright elevated to unadulterated terror, Jon turned and dropped, screaming as she slid through loosely piled debris and river-borne brush. She had fallen into a hole in the pile!

But her cries were drowned out in a moment by the loudest and most drawn-out hiss Kelvin had ever heard or imagined. It was the sound of the biggest, most dreaded reptile ever to slither through a nightmare. Then a scrabbling noise, as huge claws dug at smooth rock to find a foothold. No worn-out dragon, that!

Kelvin looked wildly around for safety, spotted none, and turned to his faithful steed. The donkey, amazingly enough, was chomping grass. Obviously the animal was stone-deaf; this was the first time Kelvin had realized it.

"Kel, Kel! He's going to get me, Kel! He's going to get me! He's climbing up, Kel! He's climbing!" Jon's former boldness had been completely dissipated; now at last she understood what he had feared when he saw the first golden scale.

What does one do when one's sister is in dire danger from a menace that cannot be opposed? One does what little one can.

Raising the old sword in his already sore hand, Kelvin rushed madly for the pile. A tree trunk lay next to some smaller rocks and made a regular staircase that Jon had followed. Kelvin's running feet found it of their own accord. Panting, he reached the spot where Jon had fallen, looked down between stacked rocks and tree trunks, and saw her frightened face.

"I can't get out in time, Kel!" she screamed tearfully. "I'm trapped! Save yourself, Kel! Save yourself!"

Kelvin, in a rear portion of his mind, recognized this as one of his sister's better ideas, but somehow he wasn't satisfied with it. Whether he would have taken her up on it he could never afterward be certain, for at that moment the golden-scaled, elongated snout of the dragon appeared over the pile's top boulder. The thing was simultaneously awful and beautiful: deadly living gold. He had known that dragons were monstrous, but from this range that was an appalling understatement. He judged that this one could swallow both of them in a single gulp. He could not see the main torso, but guessed that its size must be equivalent to that of six or seven large warhorses. No wonder so few men had ever dared face such a creature! The wonder was that any who had done so had survived.

The monster levered itself up on gigantic scaled claws. Its entire head was now visible, and the front of its body. Kelvin could see the crest on the head and the short, leathery wings. He knew he should be afraid, but his emotion seemed to have shorted out that stage, leaving him strangely clearheaded.

Kelvin raised his sword. His arm shook so that he seemed to be fencing. He wished he had scoured off the rust and put a razor edge on the blade. He couldn't imagine what he could do with a sharp clean sword, let alone this dull dirty one, but now was not a good time for imagination anyway.

Ping!

His arm went numb. Something serpentine and leathery and wet curled three times around his sword blade and twice around his wrist. He lurched backward in horror—and was promptly pulled forward by the long, forked tongue.

Some sword! he thought, insanely hacking with the edge of his free hand at the tongue's forked tip. The edge of his hand came down precisely right, and he yelped with pain and disgust as he numbed his own wrist. The dragon seemed unaffected by the hand chop that had all but fractured Kelvin's good right arm. He got his feet wedged in a crack of a boulder and pushed back.

The tongue uncurled from his arm, and the sword went with it, up and into the cavernous mouth. Those teeth—they were the size of short swords! The breath—a poisonous hot wind from a fetid swamp.

Kelvin was falling backward. Then he saw the sword spinning in midair, and he heard a splatting sound. The dragon had simply spit out Kelvin's best and only weapon. And now . . .

The ground closed in about him. He was falling through the same hole that had swallowed Jon! His arms spread out reflexively to catch hold of the edges, but his fingers only tore out hunks of brush and sand. His descent slowed, but did not stop.

There was an "Ooof!" of protest. He had landed on something soft. His sister's body had filled out more than he realized.

They scrambled to separate. It was dark in this hole and smelly.

"You hurt?" he whispered.

"Just bruised," she gasped. "You?"

He didn't answer, for he heard a scrabbling sound on the rock overhead.

Could the beast move the boulders? Could it dig them out? How tired was it?

"Kel—"

"Quiet!" he hissed. Surely the dragon *could* dig them out, since it had formed this miniature mountain. But *would* it? In its fatigued state it might decide it wasn't worth the energy it would take to roust out these two little morsels.

"There's a hole here," Jon whispered. Already she was reverting to normal, ignoring his strictures.

Kelvin felt Jon's hand in the dark, and she moved it to the place. There was indeed a hole—an aperture formed by two large tree limbs near ground level. A way out, possibly, but not necessarily to safety. If the dragon discovered it, he could reach in with that long tongue and lick them out as if they were only ants!

This hole was more danger than help! Kelvin tried to think of a way to seal off the opening and keep the dragon's sinuous tongue outside. His hands went out in quick desperation and snagged on a broken branch. He felt along the branch and encountered a smooth, rounded surface. Further investigation informed his senses that here was a boulder that wasn't supporting anything. If he and Jon could somehow move it and use it as a plug for the hole . . .

"Look!" Jon whispered, nudging him urgently.

In the dim light he saw the dragon's clawed foot, just as it lit on something with a sound like a bursting bladder. A moment later there was a loud hiss; then the frantic snort and squeal of a suddenly alert donkey.

"There goes Mockery," Kelvin said. He had an ugly picture of the donkey in the jaws of the dragon, and he hoped the monster would hurt his teeth on the hobbles. Mockery was unable to run; if only he hadn't put those restraints on!

But he realized that this just might have saved his life and Jon's. The dragon had found easier prey.

Jon whimpered. Kelvin hardly noticed, but suddenly he realized that his sister was worming on past him, blocking his light.

"What—Jon . . . ?"

"I won't let it! I won't let it!" Jon screamed. "It can't have Mockery. Mockery's ours!" Evidently she had had a change of heart about the worth of the animal.

Kelvin grabbed hold of a slim leg above and below a boot top and pulled her back. "You want the dragon to discover this hole?"

Jon subsided. Kelvin breathed a silent sigh. Now, if the incipient scream of the donkey didn't set her off—

He felt a foot on his back. "There's a root here," Jon said. "Or something. I think it can get back up."

A loud hiss that sounded like escaping steam drew his attention back to the hole at ground level. The dragon had moved. Now he could see the little donkey hobbled near the riverbank. It no longer mattered whether Mockery could hear; certainly he could see and smell! The donkey's eyes were rolled back, the nostrils flared.

Then suddenly there was a loud hiss as the dragon's awful, golden-scaled head moved directly over the animal. Slowly the long, serpentine neck lowered, hunching, and the mouth gaped to display the deadly teeth. The forked tongue shot from the mouth and just touched the donkey's flank.

Throp!

It was a magnificent donkey kick that landed with stunning accuracy on the huge snout. A man would have been killed by that strike, or a war-horse disabled. The dragon didn't even seem to notice. Seemingly bent on tasting before devouring, it closed its front teeth in a dreadful snap on Mockery's tail. The tail came off in a little shower of blood.

Kelvin closed his eyes, dreading what the dragon would do next. There was nothing he could do except let it happen.

"Bite my ass, will you! Take that!"

Kelvin's eyes popped open as the childish scream of defiance ended and a walnut-sized projectile struck the dragon's bloodred eye. The rock seemed to go into the eye like a froog into mud, then eject and lodge just under the eye's huge lower lid.

The dragon let out a hiss that hurt Kelvin's ears. The neck twisted the head around to stare at the pile of debris and at the small human figure. A great claw lifted to the lizard face and delicately flicked out the rock from beneath the eye's lid. The slow thought processes were almost evident. This tiny creature was trying to attack!

The dragon hissed again as the neck went back in striking position. *This is the end of Jon,* Kelvin thought, for the moment too stunned to act.

Then Jon jumped down into the hole, landing on him. Kelvin felt the wind go out of his chest, and a heel bruised his left ear, and a foot hit his hand. He was glad his sister didn't weigh more than she did!

"I got him, Kel! Got him in the eye! Right in the big, bloody eyeball!"

"You've gotten us killed," Kelvin gasped as soon as he could talk. "That thing might have been content with the donkey, but now—"

Nearby snorting interrupted him. A huge, open nostril was sucking up dust at the ground-level hole. Certainly the dragon smelled them now! In another instant the tongue would intrude, would search them out, and then . . . dragon fare!

"Jon, help me roll this boulder!" Kelvin strained at the rock, trying to get it between them and the flaring nostril. He strained, and then he remembered a broken branch he had felt before that might serve as a pry and a smaller rock that might serve as a fulcrum. Quickly he got the smaller rock and the branch positioned, and got Jon's small hands on the branch next to his.

"Heave, Jon, heave!"

He strained until he saw stars. Beside him, Jon groaned. The rock quivered ever so slightly. It was free—broken free of the dirt. Now if it would just *move.*

"Kel, it's got me!" Jon said. At that moment Kelvin realized that a rough and living rope had shot to the side of the boulder and fastened on Jon.

"Where does he have you?" he asked quickly.

"M-my leg."

"Hang on to me. I think—" He threw his back into the effort and then all his weight, buttressed by hers. The dragon was pulling her, and that was actually helping them to put pressure on the lever. It had to be now, he thought, or else there would never be another chance.

The boulder moved. Kelvin scraped up a bit more strength from somewhere and put all he had into it.

The boulder rolled grudgingly over the soggy ground. Now if only—

It had! The boulder had partially blocked the hole, and—

"I'm free, Kel! It let go! But—"

A terrible hissing outside—and something moved next to Kelvin's shoulder. He jerked away with revulsion, even though he knew what it was and what they had done.

The dragon's long tongue was *under* the heavy boulder—a rock the weight of perhaps two very large men, or one very small donkey. The tongue was pinned!

The tongue vibrated at its unpinned tip. Saliva rained into their enclosure, and a breath that was dizzying in its putridity came with a most stomach-turning gagging sound.

"We got him, Jon! For now! Let's get out of here before he forgets how he's hurting and starts using his legs to roll that rock off his tongue!" For though the dragon could readily have moved the rock with its legs or even its head, it was too stupid to make that connection. It was trying to free its tongue by reflex, snatching it back into its mouth. That way would never work!

Jon led the way. They helped each other out of the trap and to the top of the pile where Jon had first sighted the dragon. The beast lay almost level with their faces, its eyes glaring hatred. Kelvin stared back, almost hypnotized by its stare.

Jon picked up the fallen sword and handed it to him. "You've got to, Kel. If you don't, it may get loose. Or it could just die here."

Kelvin's urge was to flee immediately, but he realized she was right. If the dragon was truly pinned, and never figured out how to escape, it would die a lingering death that shouldn't be wished even on a monster. If it did escape, the two of them and the donkey would be in immediate danger, for the dragon would sniff them out and pounce on them long before they got home.

He took the old sword, held it tight, and considered the best place to attack. An eye, probably, but would the sword penetrate all the way to the beast's brain?

Gnash!

A large clawed foot came up as he hesitated, striking within an arm's length of Jon. Jon leaped back and almost slid down the hole again.

The sword was inadequate, Kelvin concluded. He needed a lance.

"Jon, that long tent pole I cut—can you bring it to me?" Kelvin didn't dare move, in case the dragon decided to ignore the pain of its tongue and rip free; then he would have to try with the sword, however hopeless it seemed.

"What do you want it for?"

Damn her impertinence! "Just get it! Hurry!"

From the corner of his eye he watched her scamper. He stood just outside the range of the monster's leg. It was unnerving to be this close, but if he retreated farther he would not be in position to strike at the eye if that became necessary.

Jon paused to examine Mockery's tail stump. "Jon, Jon, Jon!" Kelvin said to himself in frustration. But finally she brought the pole.

He used the sword to sharpen the end of the pole to a near needle point. The dragon's eye watched him with unnerving intensity. Did the monster know what was coming? If so, why didn't it simply wrench out its tongue and free itself? That would be less painful than a stake through its eyeball! But of course it was an animal, unable to plan ahead. No creature as powerful as a dragon needed much in the way of intellect, ordinarily.

It would be better if he could fasten the sword to the pole. But then there was a haft on the sword that would surely stop it from penetrating. The pole, if he put his weight behind it, would stab through the jelly of the eyeball and on through, into the pulsing, seething brain.

Suddenly Kelvin felt faint. The vision of that brain—could he do it, even to save his own life? Could he kill so messily in such cold blood?

Jon watched as he put down the sword. Her face bore a peculiar and undefinable expression. "Kel, let me do it."

"No. It's dangerous, and I doubt you're strong enough. I'm not even sure that I'm strong enough."

"That's what I'm afraid of. You look as if you're about to conk out."

"No!" Stupid sister! Kelvin took the pole firmly in his hands, balanced it until it felt right, took a deep breath, and ran the few steps to the dragon. Staring into the bloodred eye and trying to visualize the location of the brain in that reptilian head, he drove the pointed stake with all his strength.

The point hit true. The eye was so large that it would have been difficult to miss.

It went through the pupil, sending blood and gray stuff squirting back at him.

There was a frightful scream. The dragon's head jerked violently. The pole snapped up into the air, hauling Kelvin with it, for he was so frozen with fear that he could not let go. Then his hands lost their grip and he flew. He had a glimpse of Mockery and the river and trees.

There was the sensation of air moving across his face. He knew he had done all he could. Had it been enough?

He felt only a timeless waiting, as for unknown hands . . .

3 /

MEMORIES

"MAMA, WHY ARE MY ears so small and so round? Why aren't they like yours? Why are they like Daddy's?"

He sat in the bath and put questions to his beautiful mother. Even as a small child, he knew what a lovely creature she was. Her hair was the hue of copper, and her eyes of violets. Her skin was translucently white, and her ears were large and pointed. What more could a child ask for?

"Because, my dear, you are very special," she said.

"Special, Mama?" He knew she didn't mean it to hurt, but it always did. He didn't want to be special, he wanted to be normal.

"Your father is special. That is why you are, too."

"But . . . why?"

"He's from another world, dear. A world just a little bit different from ours. There are many such worlds, many such existences, universes. They lie side by side, touching as the skins touch on an onlic. Each skin subtly different, yet subtly same. We can't see the worlds that interpenetrate ours, but they are there, and they are real to the people or beings living there."

"There?" He didn't understand her explanation at all. He only knew that he hated the pungent taste of onlics.

"Here. All about us. Your father talks of atoms and the great spaces between the stars, but the wise ones in our world have different explanations."

He looked around their cottage, at the furniture and at the water he had splashed from the tub onto the polished yellow wood floor. "Here? Another boy? Another boy in another world in another tub?"

"Perhaps many boys in many vessels on many worlds touching and almost a part of ours. It has to be. That may be how myths start, and superstitions, and stories and tales from the imagination. It's the closeness, the nearness, the very near identity." Her fingers, so strong and shapely, soaped

22

his chest. "You'll understand when you're older, dear. When you are old enough to begin to fulfill the prophecy."

"Prophecy? What's that, Mama?"

She dried her hands on a towel, crossed the room to his father's desk, opened it, and took out the vellum-covered book with the bloodstain on its cover. She brought it to him, opened it, and turned the pages so he could see the strange, straggly letters.

"This," she said, "is the Book of Prophecy. It was written long, long ago by Mouvar the Magnificent, who saw ahead, and who wrote ahead, and who became godlike in the process. Mouvar, who fought the great battle with the dark sorcerer, Zatanas, and who will live, some say, forever, if Zatanas does not finally kill him and eject his essence from our continuum. I'm going to read to you some of Mouvar's words written long, long before your father and I were born."

"Is it about me, Mama?" Excitement tingled his hands and feet as though he had grasped an electric bug and been shocked.

"Yes, darling. It's about you. It's in rhyme, like all the prophecies. It doesn't give your name, but it's about you." Squeezing one of his small hands in her larger, stronger hand, she read:

> *A Roundear there Shall Surely be*
> *Born to be Strong, Raised to be Free*
> *Fighting Dragons in his Youth*
> *Leading Armies, Nothing Loth*
> *Ridding his Country of a Sore*
> *Joining Two, then uniting Four*
> *Until from Seven there be One*
> *Only then will his Task be Done*
> *Honored by Many, cursed by Few*
> *All will know what Roundear can Do.*

"That's pretty, Mama. What does it mean?"

"That you will fight dragons. That you will rid Rud of its tyrant Queen, Zoanna, daughter of Zatanas. That you will first join two of the Seven Kingdoms, then unite with four. That you will finally join and unite into one land *all* the Seven Kingdoms."

"How will I do that, Mama?"

"When the time comes, you'll find a way. It's prophecy. Prophecy may be misunderstood, but always comes true. Always. If not in our world, in another almost like it."

"True about dragons, too?"

"Yes, darling. About dragons, too."

"Dragons . . . with claws and teeth and a long tongue and scales?"

"Yes, darling. And the scales will be gold, just as in the story I read to you."

"And will I marry the princess and will we live happily together ever after in a great big palace? Will we have servants and courtiers and jesters and acrobats and ponies?"

"You may," she said with an affectionate smile. "But the prophecy leaves us to guess about such details. I don't have the complete prophecy; no one does. Bits of it are scattered around the globe. Some talk of gloves, and some of round-eared girls, but those may not be valid aspects of it. But I know enough to know that you are the one."

He pondered that. "Did you know all the details when you married Daddy?"

She laughed. "I hardly knew any, dear. I simply knew that I had to marry a roundear if I was to have a roundear child, and even then the chances were only even. I hoped he would be a good man."

"You *wanted* a roundear son?" he asked incredulously.

She drew him into her and kissed the top of his left ear. "I did indeed, Kelvin! But had I known he would be you, I would have wanted him even without the prophecy."

He found himself crying, and she held him close, comforting him. But these were not tears of grief, but of relief. Now, finally, he could accept being special. He had secretly feared that his point-eared little sister had arrived because his mother was unsatisfied with him.

His father finished twirling the rope and tossed it over the peg. A jerk of the line and the peg shot from the ground and followed the rope to his hands.

"All right, Kelvin. Now you try."

But Kelvin had his hands over his eyes. "It's magic, Daddy! It's magic!"

"It's *not* magic!" Stern blond eyebrows, stern face. "Magic is simply natural law that hasn't been explained. There's no such thing as magic in this world or any other. Do you understand?"

"Y-yes, Father." He watched the adult roundear, frightened, as the lasso was placed in his hands.

"Now you practice, and you practice, and you practice. This is the only skill I had before I went into the army, and it's the one skill I can leave you with."

"What good is it, F-father?"

"You saw me lasso the cow the other day."

"Yes, but she would have come anyway."

"Someday there may be something that won't. Now you hold the loop in this hand, and—"

They worked at it for a very long time, but finally he could rope the peg nearly as well as could his father.

* * *

The door flew open with a bang, scaring Kelvin as he played with fortune cards on the cottage floor. His father rushed in, trailing a cold wind and a swirl of snow. He limped across the room, favoring the leg the wild bull had kicked long ago while he was trying to separate it from their cow.

Mama looked up from the coat she was mending, her expression the one she wore when she was expecting something to happen that happened.

"Charlain, I saw them again," his father said, taking his mother's hand. "They've tracked the rumors to the village. Now I *have* to go. I won't endanger you and the boy any longer!"

His mother lodged the needle in the coat sleeve, stood up, and put her arms around his father. They held each other for a while. By and by she said, "Your travelsack is ready. Will you take the horse?"

"I can't take your horse," his father said. "I couldn't take it the first time I came here, and I can't do it now. You'll need it for plowing. Those cursed tax collectors . . ."

"I'll fix you a lunch."

Kelvin looked at his father and together they watched his mother go into the kitchen. Suddenly his father was kneeling by him, holding him up against his chest. A noise came from that chest, or perhaps his father's throat, and it was not a sound a big, strong man was supposed to make.

"Don't cry, Father."

But his father merely said, "Son, I want you to listen. Listen to me now, even if you never have before. Your mother's head is filled with nonsense. Don't believe her, son. In my world they understand—about atoms and the spaces between atoms. That prophecy is nonsense. Foolish! You're just a boy, son. You won't have to fight a dragon and fight with a sword and lead armies the way she says. If I can, I'll come for you someday. All three of you. If we can, we'll go home to my world. It's not as nice as this world in some ways, but then in other ways . . ."

"Father—" He felt confused, lonely, and scared. What was happening? Why did his father have to leave?

"It will be, son. It must be. Promise me you won't try to live out her prophecies. She's a fine woman, but—"

"Here's your lunch," Mommy said. She held out a small packet that gave forth the smell of freshly baked bread, and a jar of the bright red razzlefruit wine that Kelvin was not yet allowed to try.

"Charlain, oh, Charlain!" his father said, and then the two were hugging as though there was never to be any more of it.

"I don't want to go. I really don't. But—" There was such anguish in his father's voice.

"It might as well have been written," she said. She seemed so calm, so certain of her facts. "It's as true that you have to as . . . as the prophecy itself."

"Yes." He smiled, wiping at his eyes. His tone seemed to add, "But we both know I don't believe in that nonsense."

"Kelvin," Mommy said, placing her hand on his head, "you stay inside and keep an eye on your sister. Play with your cards. Read your fortune, and your father's, and mine. I'll come back to you before it is suppertime."

Kelvin watched them out of the house and into the barn where the horse was kept. When they did not immediately emerge, he did what his mother had told him and sat down with the cards. His sister, only two years old, was sleeping, so she was no trouble.

He looked at the painted pictures and swirling symbols on the cards. Could these tell anything about what the future would bring?

"Sometimes," Mommy had said, "if you look at them and think about them."

"Nonsense," Daddy had said gruffly. "Nonsense. All of it nonsense. Don't you believe her."

But Mommy had countered Daddy with a conspiratorial wink. She knew what she knew, however tolerant she was of the ignorance of others.

The woodsman's face was grim when he brought the news. Watching him and his mother, Kelvin felt that she really didn't look surprised. She looked, in fact, much as she had the day his father left.

"Nothing much to bury, ma'am. They cut the big bits into little bits, the filthy highwayman or whoever did it. The wild things had been feasting, but it was no wild thing that was to blame."

She nodded, understanding perhaps more than her son did or could imagine. After a painful pause, she said, "I dreamed it would be you, Hal Hackleberry. You to bring me the dread news, and more."

"Ma'am?"

"Charlain. I want it to be Charlain again." She picked up a stockelcap that his father had sometimes worn under protest, patting it as though it were alive. She looked at what she was doing, then back at the woodsman.

"He didn't believe," she said. "Never. Never once, even after Kelvin happened. He just wouldn't believe."

The woodsman shifted his feet. "I understand, ma'am. Some men are like that. It's nothing against them, you understand."

"I know. Not against them. Some things just have to be. Would you care for some wine?"

"Why . . . yes, ma'am, I would. But—"

"But I have already grieved," she said. "I knew when he left that I would never see him again in this life. I grieved, and now . . . now I am ready."

"Ma'am?"

"For a new life. A life that maybe was only interrupted for a time."

Kelvin was surprised to find tears dripping from his face. The woodsman might be a good man, he thought, but Daddy—Daddy was special.

"Roundear, Roundear, Roundear," taunted the circle of reddish faces. They moved closer, reaching out to poke Kelvin in the stomach and ribs with stiffened fingers.

"You stop that!" cried eight-year-old Jon. Her fists were clenched, and she was all fury as she turned round and round to face the tormentors. But the harder she shouted, and the more angry she got, the bolder the teasing became. "You stop that or my brother will fight!" Jon told the biggest and roughest boy of the bunch. "You're just jealous 'cause he can charm the berries better'n any of you!"

"Jon!" Kelvin said with alarm. But he knew there was no stopping her youthful indignation. It was true that he had developed a way with plants, being able to encourage them to flower and to sweeten their fruit, but that wasn't anything he cared to advertise. His natural father would have called it magic, therefore invalid.

"He's a hero! A big hero! Mama said!"

"Fight? Fight? You want to fight, Roundear?" the thirteen-year-old with the tooth out in front demanded.

Kelvin shook his head, remembering what father John Knight had said about the stupidity of human beings fighting. *Only if there's no other way, son. Only if there's no other way.*

"You're afraid," said the bully. "Aren't you?"

"Yes." Kelvin said it before he thought. He always spoke the truth except to his mother when they were pretending.

"Ha! Some hero! Come on, boys, let's go to the pond and skip rocks."

Kelvin breathed a shuddering sigh of relief.

"He'll fight *you,*" Jon said. "And he'll lick you, too."

"Jon, shut up," Kelvin muttered. But he knew that the unsayable had been said. Now, as his father had said, there was really no other way.

"Your mother's a witch, Roundear!" the big boy said, pushing his face close to Kelvin's. "Your sister's a nasty little froog, and you're a scared and stupid squirbet."

"Sticks and stones," Kelvin said, reciting the charm his real father had taught him. "Sticks and stones may break my bones, but words will never—"

The fist landed on his cheek, hurting terribly. The boy was all strength and no bluff, and happy to demonstrate it.

Kelvin hit back, almost by reflex. By good luck he hit the bigger boy on the mouth. The boy stood back, putting a hand to his bruised lips where a trickle of blood showed.

"Now you'll get it!" the boy exclaimed. He leaped at Kelvin, swinging with one hand while he grabbed with the other. Kelvin tried to twist aside, and that was partially effective as the fist grazed his ear, but the boy's other hand caught him and hauled him roughly in. Kelvin tried to jerk away, and only succeeded in winding himself into a tighter hold. He pushed forward, the only way he was free to go, and this overbalanced the bigger boy. Their feet got tangled together, and they fell on the ground.

They rolled over and over, while the other boys cheered their hero and Jon shouted advice, mostly inappropriate. Perhaps it looked like a good fight from outside, because of all the motion, but it was really just Kelvin trying desperately to get away while the big boy sought to pin him in a position for some more effective punishment.

Kelvin was getting the worst of it. Now the bigger boy was on top of him, hitting him more often and with greater force. Kelvin was losing his ability to avoid or fend off the blows, and each one hurt awfully.

The bigger boy paused. "You eat horse dung, don't you, Roundear!"

This was Kelvin's chance to capitulate, cutting down on his punishment. But he couldn't lie, even now. "No."

Fists rained down on his face, bruising, hurting, scaring him silly with the thought that he might lose teeth or even an eye.

"I'll help you, Kelvin!" Jon cried. She piled onto the bully's back, fists raining as hard as an eight-year-old girl could manage.

The bully was distracted. It gave Kelvin a chance. He struck upward, his fist catching the bully's turned head.

He had scored directly on the nose. Blood exploded from a rupture. *"Aahhhh!"* the big boy screamed.

Now his face, so close and ugly, was turning as red as the blood from his nose. Kelvin had won the fight, amazingly, for the bully was unable to do anything except react to the pain and horror of it. It seemed that it had never occurred to the bully that *he* might get hurt. The other boys would not interfere, for there was a code: it had to be one on one. Jon had violated it, but she didn't count, being a girl.

But in that moment before it broke up, a bright shaft of sunlight lit the bully's features, turning them to gold, and that was the image that was to remain most firmly in Kelvin's memory. Because that color was—

Dragon's gold.

Jon and Kelvin had been working beside Hal, their replacement father, grubbing out some tree stumps so that they could plant more grain. The sound of horses' hooves on the hard road and a plume of summer's dust warned of the approach of guardsmen.

Hal nodded toward the woods. "Better you get out of sight, Kel, just in case." He was not their natural father, but he was a good man, and had always treated them well and looked out for their welfare. Charlain had chosen well, both times she married.

"I'll go with him," Jon said.

Hal glanced at her. "Maybe that's best. You're growing up, girl, and there's no telling what guardsmen might do."

Jon flushed, hating to be reminded of her nature. But it was true: the Queen's guardsmen had been known to do things to young girls that couldn't be done to boys. That might be part of what she hated about being a girl.

They went behind some duckberry bushes and crouched, waiting. Kelvin breathed on the leaves and stems, and the bushes moved to provide better concealment. Shortly the guardsmen were there on their war-horses, talking down to Hal.

"You're behind on your taxes, farmer!"

"It's been a bad year."

"You'll pay a fine. A big fine."

"I'll get the money. But if I sell our horse, there'll be no money to buy more seed grain." He patted the large gray animal hitched to the stump. Hal was kind to animals, too, and worked well with them.

"That's your worry, farmer." The guardsman's voice rang with contempt. "Scum like you have to pay. If you don't pay, we set fire to your house and seize your boy to sell in the boy market."

"I'll pay." It was evident that though Hal was technically subservient, he had no real respect for the agents of the Queen. "I just have to chop some wood, and—"

But the big guardsman's face was turning redder and then golden in the rays of the sun. Squinting through the bushes, Kelvin began to see him with a snout like that of a dragon. What was the big difference between a guardsman and a dragon? Both brought destruction on common folk!

The matter of dragons was looming larger in Kelvin's mind. He feared them terribly, but their scales were gold, and represented wealth that could free the farm of debt. He would really have to do what he had talked about to Jon. They would have to leave here and go after gold.

Dragon's gold.

4 /

HIGHWAYMAN

"Jon! Jon!"

The girl looked up at him with eyes that shone from her face nearly as brightly as what she held in her bloody hands. What she held was palm-size yellow gold, and had belonged to the late dragon.

"Gee, Kel, I thought you were dead!"

"So you were getting the gold anyway." What kind of creature was this sister of his? Sometimes it seemed to him that if anyone was a changeling, it was Jon.

"Well, I couldn't reach you very well, and I thought I might as well start getting the scales. They come off hard, Kel. It's going to be a lot of work."

Kelvin wormed his way off the tree branch, held himself poised, then swung clear and dropped. He lit with a shock to his feet and legs that surprised him. Dragon scales, he remembered, were far from soft, even if gold was supposed to be a soft metal.

"I looked about some," she continued. "There's a funny little patch of berries—"

"You didn't eat strange berries!" Kelvin exclaimed, alarmed. "You know that many of the wild plants out here are poisonous!"

"Of course I know," she said in an aggrieved tone. "I can't charm them into edibility the way you can, with your round ears. I didn't eat any. But for all I know, they might be good, so I saved a few to show Mommy."

Kelvin relaxed. At least she had had some sense! "But what's strange," she continued, "is that they look, well, tended. Almost as if the dragon was taking care of them. His prints are all around the patch, and there's a path leading to it, which is how I found it. A dragon path. I was going off to—you know." She never liked to refer directly to natural functions, partly because she couldn't perform them in quite the manner she deemed proper for a boy. "So I followed this path, because it was easy, and there was this patch, almost like a garden, and the dragon could've tromped all over it, but didn't. Isn't that funny?"

It was indeed! Why would a dragon protect a simple patch of berries? "You did right to save some," Kelvin said. "Dragons know about some things we don't."

Feeling trembly and far from good, he let his legs collapse beneath him. He sat down on the flat area between two short wings. The dragon's tongue was still protruding from its mouth and entering the debris hole, but now a long pole was embedded in its left eye socket. Evidently he had scored on the brain, but he shivered to think how close a call it had been. If he had not thrusted hard enough, or if the dragon's death throes had hurled him into the trunk of a tree instead of onto a branch . . .

Could he really have a charmed life, the way his mother insisted? She had been right about his magic with plants, after all, and if he really *was* destined to be the hero of the prophecy, then this was not the coincidence it seemed. Yet his father had been such a practical man, making so much sense, that it was hard to believe he could have been wrong about magic.

Jon came close, bringing Kelvin's sword. "You get them off, Kel. It's far too much work."

"For you, you mean," he said, disgusted.

"Uh-huh. You're the biggest, so—" Then her composure disintegrated. She flung herself into his arms, almost stabbing him with the sword. "Oh, Kel, I thought you were *dead,* maybe, and I couldn't even reach you!"

He felt her tears soaking into his shoulder. So it had all been an act, her nonchalance. Unable to help him, she had gotten to work, hoping he would recover, and when he had, she tried to remain tough, but wasn't able to carry it quite all the way through. How glad he was of that; she had almost fooled him!

In a moment she recovered her composure. "Oh, I'm getting all icky," she said. "I'm sorry."

"I'm not," he said. "Do you think I like the notion that you don't care at all what happens to me?"

"But it's not manly to cry."

"Jon, someday you're going to have to accept the fact that you're not—" She cut him off with a bad word.

He dropped that aspect. "Anyway, I'd sure cry if *you* got killed. But you're right; we've got to get to work here. There's a skinning knife in the pack. I'll use that and you use the sword and with luck we'll get the job done."

"When?" Jon asked somewhat sourly.

"Before nightfall if you work hard. You're not going to be girlishly squeamish about dirty work, are you?"

"No!" She hefted the sword, suddenly ready to use it.

"I thought not. Here, let me see how it works." He took the sword from her, stuck it under the nearest scale, and pried. Grudgingly, it came up. Then he cut at the leathery flesh holding it.

This would take longer than nightfall, he realized. Even a dead dragon was tough!

He hacked the scale free and held it up. "There we are—easy as pie." He returned the sword to her and went to fetch the knife.

He was correct. Three grueling days later they had finished as much of the unpleasant task as was possible without turning over the dragon, and were on their way out of the pass. It was just as well, for the huge carcass was decomposing, and the vultures were circling ever lower; soon the attention of other predators or even men would be attracted, and that would be no good for the two treasure-hunters. They had to get away with their prize, and back to the farm unobserved.

Bobtailed Mockery was in tow with two very heavy travelsacks. They had scraped the scales as clean of attached flesh as possible and washed them in the river, but still some odor accompanied them. Jon had to walk behind Mockery and swat the biting flies that landed on the beast, because the donkey threatened to dislodge the load when tormented by flies he could no longer flick off with his tail.

"Do you think we should have dumped all our stuff?" Jon asked. "Those pans and those blankets were still good, even if Mockery did roll on them in the river."

"We can buy more. One scale should buy all the pans and blankets we'll need in our entire lives."

"If we don't live too long," Jon said, liking the notion.

"Of course, Brother Wart."

They plodded on. They were out of the pass now and the sun was shining and it looked to be a glorious day for two rich youngsters. Kelvin was thinking that they hadn't much of a worry in the world. A few scales would pay off the errant taxes on the farm, and a few more would cover all the luxuries Charlain might want, and Hal, too, though Hal was a man of simple tastes. They would turn the scales over to him for safekeeping; he was honest, and would not cheat anyone.

Suddenly a huge black war-horse appeared as if by magic in the road ahead. It bore a man clad all in black. Some bushes swayed at the side; the man must have been lurking there. He leveled a sword that flashed golden in the sun and looked extremely sharp.

"Your property or your lives!" the man said in the time-honored manner of the highwayman.

Disaster! Kelvin swallowed. "We're without coin," he pleaded in the traditional way of the waylaid traveler. He knew that the brigand would check the travelsacks in a moment.

"No coin, just scale," the man said with the certainty with which Charlain announced anything after a look at the fortune cards. "What'd you two do, find a dead dragon?"

"No—" Kelvin started.

With a sudden swish the man's sword tip slashed through the lashings on Mockery's pack and sent the sacks falling. Golden platelets came loose from their stacks and rained down. Mockery went into a bucking protest.

Kelvin choked. He grabbed his sword, yanked it from its scabbard, and—

Watched as it spun through the air in response to the highwayman's quick and expert backhand motion. "Don't try that again, sonny, or it's your life! You!" he snapped at Jon. "Drop that sling, or you'll eat your ears!"

Mention of ears reminded Kelvin to check his own. Fortunately he had remembered to pull down the stockelcap, covering them. Years of getting beaten up had made this an automatic reflex, just as was Jon's concealment of her female attributes.

"Gods curse you, highway horse excrement!" Jon exclaimed.

The bandit swung round to her. "You do what I say, cubwhelp, or—"

Jon's sling started its defiant circle, but before she could let fly, the horseman had leaped his horse to within arm's reach and was leaning down, grabbing the girl by her shoulders. Once, twice, the bandit shook her, and Jon's head tossed helplessly and her long yellow hair flopped out of the cap. Then the highwayman thrust her aside.

Jon lit in the road and immediately scrambled back to her feet. She had dropped the sling as the bandit reached her, and now her face was very pale.

"You look like a damn girl!" the highwayman muttered. "Maybe I'll just lop off some of that hair."

Jon said a word that would have gotten her a hiding even at their liberal home. The bandit laughed. "But appearances can be deceiving, eh? Spoken like the man you'll someday be!"

He had not caught on! Kelvin gave a heave of relief. Bad as their situation was, it could have gotten worse.

"Both of you, load that scale back on that beast! Tie that strap together again so it holds," the highwayman snapped. "And hand your own packs up here!"

They worked, Kelvin knowing that his own face must resemble Jon's. If only the outlaw would make some mistake!

Finished, scales all in place on Mockery's and the war-horse's broad backs, the bandit rode over to Jon. Leaning down, he grabbed the girl and swung her up in front of him on the saddle.

"I'm taking this one to market," he said to Kelvin. "An overseer's whip will teach him manners. Snarly whelp!" He cuffed Jon, who had managed by a clever twist to bite his hand.

Jon said something that Kelvin did not hear but brought another cuff. Reacting at last to this new threat, Kelvin leaped for the war-horse's bridle.

He grabbed the rein and raised an arm to try to deflect a blow from the highwayman's sword. He saw a twisted dark face, lips pulled back from yellowed teeth, an old red scar that reached from the right corner of the villain's mouth to the edge of his gaunt cheek below his right squinty eye.

A moment later he found himself lying in the partly filled ditch as a bird sang somewhere and the drumming of the war-horse's hooves pounded off in the distance. Once again, Kelvin had been absolutely ineffective.

5 /

CAPTIVE

JON HAD CEASED STRUGGLING hours ago. She had realized very early that the more she resisted, the tighter the highwayman gripped her, and it would not be long before his hand or arm encountered aspects of her that were not normal for a boy. She now rode docilely ahead of the bandit on the huge black war-horse. Waiting, she told herself repeatedly, her chance to escape cleanly.

"Not so chipper now, little foulmouth?" the highwayman asked. It was a taunt, she knew, not a question. "You know where I'm taking you? You know what's going to happen to you?"

"You said the Boy Mart," Jon said. She knew of it. Runaway boys, delinquent boys, boys seized for their fathers' nonpayment of taxes, possibly even kidnapped boys were sold like livestock to be slaves. To work someone's plantation, or mine, or to row a galley. It was all legal in Rud, and boys remained slaves until they reached the legal age of manhood: twenty-five. Quite a number, it was said, failed to live to that age.

There was, however, one thing worse than the Boy Mart. That was the Girl Mart. The girls, it was said, generally lived out their terms, but hardly wanted to. The lucky ones became housemaids or servant girls, but many were sold to brothels or to sadistic old men. Suicide was the leading cause of death among them. Already Jon knew that if she didn't manage to escape, she had better protect her secret, because the Boy Mart was the better bet.

"Yes, the Boy Mart," the bandit repeated, taking her silence for natural dread. "Best thing in the world for you. The *only* thing in the world for you." He laughed. Jon looked around at the towering cliffs and the stunted trees and the new twisting path that led through brambles and brush and on into more bleak land. It was semidesert ahead. That was what was called the Sadlands—a region fit only for scorpio-crabs, giant spiders, and snakes. Outlaws such as this one reportedly lived there, though why they should choose to do so was a mystery.

Well, perhaps not so big a mystery. Since honest folk stayed well clear of the Sadlands, that made it relatively safe for outlaws. If they had good horses, as this one did, they could range pretty far out, raiding better regions and returning. There was a story that an outlaw had aggravated the Queen once, and she had sent a party of guardsmen into the Sadlands after him, and they had never returned. Maybe it wasn't a true story, but it had an authentic ring. Actually, the Queen's guardsmen were little different from criminals at times, so maybe they had simply gone into business for themselves. Maybe this one was one of them.

"Whoa," the highwayman called, pulling on his reins.

Jon made her decision to fight, to the extent she was able without risking betraying her nature. Whatever the outlaw wanted, he was not going to get much cooperation.

The bandit slipped a dark bandanna over her face. "Can't have you seeing where we're going for the night, whelp."

So that was it! The outlaw was not very smart for telling her, Jon thought. One way or the other she was going to see through the bandanna, or over it or around it. Since she was destined for the Boy Mart, she probably would not be hurt if she behaved; then when she escaped, she could tell Kelvin where the highwayman's hideout was, so they could steal back their gold.

But the bandanna was tight. Twice folded over her eyes, it let in not a bit of light. The outlaw, unfortunately, knew his business.

The horse resumed its steady walk. Jon thought they were going uphill, not down, then down, not up. But she wasn't sure; it could be the other way around. She tried to edge a hand up to the bandanna, but got it slapped down promptly.

"None of that, I tell you," the bandit said. He didn't even sound annoyed. Maybe he took such efforts as a matter of course.

But she had to see, Jon thought. She *had* to.

An insect buzzed loudly near her left ear. She shook her head, and as she did, an idea struck.

Her ears. She could wiggle her ears. Girls weren't supposed to do that; therefore it was one of her proudest accomplishments.

If she could wriggle her ears just enough, the bandanna just might be coaxed down a bit. The right side of the blindfold wasn't folded evenly at the top. If she could work the single thickness down, she could see through it. If the bandit didn't stop her.

Slowly, Jon turned her head until her right ear was directed frontward. The outlaw might not see it now. With luck.

"Flies bothering you? Here!" The highwayman's slap almost took her head off. Her breath hissed in with pain—but while she shook her head in reaction, she made her right ear twitch.

"Huh, missed the fly, hit your face. Hah."

Had he seen, Jon wondered? Could *she* see, now that the bandanna had slipped a little?

Through her right eye she picked up a little light. She could make out the bright sunlight and its sheen on two towering rocks—one on either side of the horse. They were going a different way than into the Sadlands. This was back the way they had come! So the bandit *was* trying to deceive her!

Now she detected the scent of the bilrose tree, and remembered the grove they had passed through earlier. Then she heard water, and knew they were back at the river.

The horse was taking another road, into the mountains. It was the only turnoff place near the river; Jon was certain because she had walked every step into dragon country. It went up above the village of Franklin and then into the mountains and then somewhere she had not been.

The horse plodded now. The outlaw was taking his time. That meant he felt secure from discovery.

They were up in the mountains, and Jon knew the road they had taken. The highwayman had said he didn't want her to see where they would spend the night, and now he seemed satisfied that she didn't know where they had gone. So the camp or cave or whatever must be close. How criminally clever, to have a hideout close to a traveled road, while pretending to stay far away!

Now she heard the *clip-clip-clip* of the war-horse's hooves on rock. Then they were definitely going down a steep path. The outlaw's hand clamped on her shoulder just as she seemed about to pitch off headfirst.

"Well, we're here," the highwayman said. With that, he pulled the blindfold off.

Jon blinked. A rude log cabin was there, set in a box canyon. Cactus trees were nearby. It could indeed be the edge of the mountains in the Sadlands. The outlaw expected her to think they had ridden on and that this place was far away from where they had left Kelvin.

Kelvin? What had happened to him? Was he struggling out into the Sadlands trying to track the highwayman down? He would get himself lost and die of exposure! Kel was a decent brother, but sometimes he was short on common sense.

But now was not the time to worry about Kelvin, whom she could not help. Now was the time to think about herself. Once she got free, she could see what she could do for Kelvin.

"Marta! Marta!" the highwayman called, startling Jon. "Come look at what I brought."

A big, slovenly woman with a wart to the side of her large nose appeared in the doorway. She could almost be this outlaw's sister, judging by her looks. But the way the two embraced indicated otherwise. It seemed odd that a violent criminal should have affection for a stupid fat wife, but it was evidently so.

"Another boy?" the woman said, her voice as abrasive as her appearance. "Can't you do better than that? There's a glut of them on the market; they don't fetch the prices they used to."

Jon knew what *did* fetch good prices: girls. She had to protect her secret!

"I did do better, woman!" the outlaw said cheerfully. "Take a look at these." He held out scales that still had some messy flesh attached, despite Kelvin's and her own best efforts.

"Uck! What?"

"Scale, love, scale! This one and his brother found a dead dragon and pulled its scales off. They've loaded them for me. In those bags on the donkey and in here." He tapped his saddlebags.

"A *dead* dragon?"

"Must have been. The pup and his weakling brother were still alive."

"Some people have all the luck!"

"Yah. *Us!*" Laughing at his own supposed wit, the highwayman shoved Jon stumbling to the back of the cabin. A rough cage stood there with open door.

Jon knew better than to argue. She climbed inside the cage and watched him lock the door.

"She'll bring you a few corbeans and a jug of water," the highwayman said. "You sleep on that old blanket in the corner. And don't try to escape!"

"Suppose I do?" Jon asked, morbidly curious.

"Then I'll slice off your legs and leave you for the wild houcats and the bearvers. That's if I'm in a good mood. If I'm in a bad mood, I'll do something mean. Har, har, har!" He really thought he was being funny.

Jon sat in the cage and stared at the back of the cabin, knowing that it wouldn't be smart to try anything now. She might be able to pry out part of the cage and squeeze through, but that would surely make noise, and they would be alert. The highwayman might indeed be expecting some such attempt, and have a punishment in mind. He wouldn't cut off her legs, for that would ruin her value on the Boy Mart, but he might rip off her clothes and beat her. Except that once he ripped off her clothes, he wouldn't beat her, he'd think of something worse.

The light faded. The woman brought her a plate of stew that smelled somewhat like urine, and a jug that smelled of the liquor it usually held, but now it had only water. The woman did not bother to speak, only motioning her to stay in back of the cage while she set the food inside.

After the long and rough day Jon had had, the stew did not taste nearly as bad as it might have. She ate and drank.

Then she became aware of the need to relieve herself. Would they let her out at least to urinate? But if they did, they would surely watch her, and that would be extremely awkward. If she tried to stand and do it like a man, she'd only get her pantaloons soaked, and they'd know. But if she didn't get out pretty soon, she would have to soil herself right here in the cage.

She pondered, and decided on a course that had a better than even chance of success. "Hey, I gotta go poop!" she called out in the crude masculine manner.

"Just stand up and do it through the slats," the highwayman said, laughing.

"Not in my house!" the woman exclaimed angrily. "It stinks bad enough already!"

"Then *you* take him out," the man said.

"I don't want no woman watching me!" Jon protested loudly. "What do you think I am?"

"Aw, she's seen it before," he retorted. "We sure aren't going to let you loose outside!"

The woman got up. She fetched a length of rope from a peg on the wall. "He won't be loose." She came and opened the cage door. "Put your head in this," she said, showing a noose at the end of the rope.

Jon obediently put her head forward, and the noose slipped over. The woman tightened it just enough to be snug on the neck. "You try to run, you know how fast this'll tighten," she said.

"I know," Jon agreed. She would be choked in an instant. She climbed carefully out of the cage and walked across the room to the door. The woman had the other end of the rope coiled twice about her hand; she would not let it slip accidentally, and could twitch the noose tight at any moment.

It was getting dark outside. The woman showed the way to a rotten log some distance from the house. There was a trench beyond it, and the smell made clear its purpose.

Without a word Jon pulled down her pantaloons just enough and stuck her bottom out over the trench. She put one hand down in front as if to direct the aim of a member there. The dusk and the hand effectively concealed that region of her body. Fortunately she did have solid as well as liquid wastes to deposit, so the woman had no reason to be suspicious. Men did squat when they had to do both.

The woman proffered something white. It was paper—a fragment of some old wrapper. Jon took it and used it, then quickly pulled up her pantaloons, as if embarrassed that any male anatomy might show before a woman. It would have been far more awkward if the highwayman had come with her, for then she could not have justified her concealment.

They returned to the house. She had made it! They had thought she might try to escape, but she had just wanted to get her business done without destroying her masquerade. Escape had to wait on a better opportunity. Meanwhile, she would have to go easy on what she drank, so that she wouldn't need to urinate again until she could do both together. Until darkness, again, if she didn't manage to escape first.

Back in the cage, she lay down on the smelly blanket and peered out through the cracks in back at the canyon wall outside. By twisting her head to the side she could just manage to see some stars.

When the highwayman and his wife slept, she could get up and pry her way out and escape. If she could do it silently.

But when she slept, she was so tired that she never woke till morning. Her chance to escape had passed. She would be stuck with her luck in the Boy Mart.

6 /

HERO

K ELVIN RECOVERED HIS SWORD from the ditch, sheathed it, and began what he knew was going to be a long walk. The war-horse's hooves had made plenty of tracks, but the road got harder ahead and the tracks vanished. It was hot and it was uncomfortable and his head hurt.

He would have to have help. There was no way he could rescue Jon by himself. No way that he could even hope to find the highwayman. He had to get to Franklin. That was where the Boy Mart was. The highwayman had said he would sell her, and he wouldn't ride to some more distant market when Franklin was convenient. Kelvin hoped. But when he did get there, what could he do but get himself arrested and sold along with his brother?

There had to be help somewhere. Guardsmen were not to be trusted since the start of the reign of Queen Zoanna, but once they had been good and dependable defenders of the land. Things had been different back before his father's time. His father—his natural father, John Knight—had run afoul of the Queen in some way, and that had led perhaps to his death. Kelvin had a morbid curiosity about that, but it wasn't something his mother liked to talk about.

He would have to go to the guardsmen's barracks outside Franklin and tell about the highwayman and ask and hope. He would have to be very polite and servile, because otherwise he would be seen as a runaway and a vagrant and taken to the Boy Mart as merchandise.

The bandit probably had a shack out in the Sadlands, Kelvin thought, sniffing the spicy scent of bilrose blossoms from the grove ahead. He would take Jon there, and then tomorrow take her to the boy market. There Jon would be sold, to work at something hard and degrading and unworthy of her sharp brain. If she managed to conceal her sex. That was a special problem, and Kelvin didn't know what complications it would lead to, but it made it all the more urgent that she be rescued promptly.

He thought of Jon, hiding her nature, and being forced to work at hard labor until she was twenty-five years old. Not all boys survived that long, and Jon would have twice as much trouble. The rich merchants and plantation owners and shipping company masters supported the Queen in order to keep the custom alive, so they could have cheap labor. Other lands had long since rid themselves of every type of slavery, except (some wits claimed) that of matrimony. Rud was a fit land for a hero of prophecy to start!

He didn't feel like a hero. Not now that he was out of dragon country, and not even before. It was all nonsense, this prophecy. His father had said as much, and he had believed. Many, many times, he had believed in the invalidity of the prophecy, despite his mother's certainty.

But he had slain the dragon, a perverse thought came.

Luck! Just dumb luck. If there hadn't been that haven in the debris pile, that rock and that stout branch, a deaf donkey . . .

But how, then, do you think prophecy works? It's the stacking of fortune cards, the loading of prediction dice. One has a little extra bonus in the game folks call life.

He shook his head. He didn't like the way his thoughts were going. It must have been that blow the bandit had given him. That and the heat. It was pointless to argue with himself!

Ahead were the two sentinel rocks flanking the road, like waiting highwaymen. Such imagery came readily now! Straight ahead were the Sadlands, while dragon country was back the way he had come, and the road to Franklin was to the right and across the bridge.

He had no choice but to go right. It was almost as if it had been prophesied. But that laugh was ringing somewhat hollowly in his mind now.

The appleberry bushes by the bridge parted just as he got there and a large, woolly, red-coated bearver waddled out. The animal looked at him, sniffed, caught the scent of dragon's blood, and turned and ran.

Kelvin heaved a sigh. If he had been forced to face the bearver in a bad mood with only this old sword, he knew he would have ended up as the bearver's meat.

That's no way for a hero to think!

Who's a hero?

I'm a hero.

Shut up!

He had to keep walking even though he was tired and depressed and everything seemed crazy and hopeless. His tongue felt swollen and his head whirled so that everything shimmered in the heat haze. He had to go under the bridge and wash his face and get a drink.

His legs felt like cooked lengths of pasta stalk, wobbly and weak. Slowly he made his way down to the water. A mooear raised its handsome big-horned head, sniffed, caught the scent of dragon on him, and abruptly turned tail and went.

Dragon is good for one thing, anyway.
That's more than I am right now.

He knelt on the muddy bank and looked at his reflection. He had dirt all over his clothes and all over his face. He should wash both body and clothes before going into Franklin, he realized. Otherwise he would be arrested as a vagrant for certain. Then he would go to the Boy Mart, but not as a rescuer. Jon would cuss him out roundly, before they were separated forever by the auction.

He scooped up some of the water and drank. It was muddy-tasting, but very cold, like snow from the high mountaintops. His hands tingled and hurt from their contact with the cold.

If only he had some money, he thought. If only . . .

He stripped off his clothes, sloshed them in the river, tossed them aside, and then went to work on himself. Without soap, it was difficult, but he scrubbed himself with his wadded-up clothing and managed to get some of the dirt off each. The dragon's blood had accumulated on his boots and was caked and noisome; that was his hardest struggle. When he was done he was shivering blue, with welts and bruises showing up much better now that their covering of grime was gone, but at least he didn't look as if he had just wallowed in a mud hole and rolled around in dragon filth.

As he was redonning his garments, something scratched his right hand. He looked in the hip pocket of his pantaloons and found a single golden scale. It was the first dragon scale Jon had found. He had slipped it into the pocket and forgotten it.

So at least I can't be arrested for vagrancy. Not as long as I hold that.
Luck!
Stacked cards. Weighted dice.

He had to get on to Franklin.

As he started back up the bank he spied a battered plant. The mooear had trampled it when fleeing. But this was no ordinary growth; it was a shade-blooming spicerose! Those were extremely rare and valuable, because the scent of their blooms was supposed to send the one who sniffed one into a few minutes of utter ecstasy.

There was a rose, on a broken stem. Kelvin lifted the flower and sniffed. It had a very pleasant aroma, but it didn't transport him. Either the story of the power of a spicerose was exaggerated, or he was immune to it. As a roundear he had a number of attributes that differed from those of pointears, including his facility with plants; this could be another example.

Too bad he couldn't heal the trampled plant! But his magic, if such it was, was limited to facilitating health in a living plant; he could not restore a dead one. He felt guilty, because if he hadn't come down under the bridge, into the shade that the spicerose required for its blooming, the mooear would not have spooked and the fine plant would not have been damaged.

Well, he might help the rose a little; he could save the flower, and breathe a second blooming into it for some other person, later.

He tucked the rose into a pocket, where the direct sunlight would not touch it and destroy it, and resumed his climb.

As he reached the road again, he felt better than at any time since the highwayman rode off and left him in the ditch. Maybe the spicerose *had* buoyed him!

As he started walking he wished that he had his mandajo. He didn't feel like playing or singing, and yet it would be company. Alas, the highwayman had it, along with the donkey and the gold and his sister.

A squirbet chattered at him from an oaple tree.

He looked up at the fuzzy, short-tailed rodent and thought how good the last one had tasted. Jon had been responsible for that: Jon and her sling.

Well, at least he could eat one of the fruits of the tree. Oaples weren't the most luscious fruits, but he could make do. He reached up and put his hand on a low-hanging one. "You are the oaple of my eye," he said to it. "I long to eat your delicious substance. May I pluck you?" He tugged, and in a moment the tough stem let go. Like most fruiting trees, this one was subject to flattery. Kelvin knew his father would have said it was superstition, that he just knew how to pick the ripe ones, but the fact was that any fruit Kelvin touched tended to ripen and sweeten when he praised it, and to turn sour when he condemned it. His mother had the same ability, and she had no hesitation about calling it magic. "Of course it is, dear! My family has always been good with plants." Which meant, he reflected, that his round ears were not after all responsible. Did it matter?

He plodded on, step by step, eating the oaple, trying harder and harder to think that the prophecy his mother so firmly believed in would enable him to win out. To believe that his mother was correct. After all, if she was right about one thing, why not another?

His lovely mother, Charlain. His homely, sturdy, decent stepfather, Hal. What were they doing now? Kelvin and Jon had planned for an exploration of a week's duration; it had taken them two days to reach the dragon, three more to get the scales off, and this was the sixth day. They would not even be missed until tomorrow or the day after. Unless Charlain read the cards, and realized. But what could she do, assuming that the cards worked? No, this was Kelvin's own mess to muddle through, somehow.

After an eternity on the road, he brushed sweat from his eyes and saw the grimy barracks building ahead. He dreaded what was likely to happen there, but he knew he had to do it. He was, after all, supposed to be some kind of hero.

* * *

"Ho, ho, ho! Took your little brother, did he? Said he'd take him to market, did he? Heh, heh, ho!" The burly guardsman clasped his sides and wiped at the tears running down his florid cheeks.

Kelvin swallowed as he looked at this blue-and-gold-uniformed representative of law and order. He was at the guardhouse outside the village of Franklin. Beyond the guardsman were others, similarly uniformed, similarly slovenly. Open collars and dirty undershirts seemed to be the order of the day. Even if the guardsmen were competent, they were an unlikely lot to ask for help. But he had to do it. Hanging on to his slipping courage, he persisted: "You do arrest highwaymen?"

"Certainly, my boy, certainly. Every now and then when one of them doesn't divide the loot."

"Shut your fat mouth, Carpenter!" a guardsman wearing sergeant's stripes ordered. He glared at the man until he sobered, then swung round to Kelvin.

"Tell me, boy, was there anything of value taken?" His tone was freighted with contempt. "Besides that valuable brother of yours?"

Kelvin thought quickly how not to lie. He hadn't actually said Jon was a boy, just that the outlaw was taking Jon to the Boy Mart, and the guardsmen had jumped to the obvious conclusion. He knew that if he told them about the gold, they would lose what little interest they had in justice and go for the wealth. "Our donkey, sir. We paid out two rudnas in good coin for him. He's bobtailed, and he's deaf. Stone-deaf, sir, though we didn't know that when we bought him."

"Deaf? A deaf donkey," said the first man Kelvin had spoken to. "A skinny boy to act as a scullery hand or stable boy! A skinny boy and a deaf-as-stone donkey. Ho, ho, ho!"

"Carpenter!" roared the sergeant. "The next time you bray like that you'll do a donkey's work! You hear?"

"I hear ye, Sarge."

"Sergeant! Sergeant, you impudent jackass!"

"Sergeant," the man agreed after a pause.

Kelvin looked from private to sergeant and then about the small guardhouse. Only one face, that of a young guardsman only a couple of years older than Kelvin, showed any sign of sympathy. He thought he would prefer to talk to this man, but the sergeant was staring straight into his face.

"You know the consequences of lying to a queen's guardsman, don't you, boy?"

"I, ah, yes, sir."

"I can hang you or cut off your ears or cut off anything else I fancy. A guardsman must not be lied to—especially by scum. You understand?"

"Y-yes, sir."

The sergeant paused, glaring at him, and Kelvin thought to himself that he recognized him as one of the tax collectors who had come to his farm.

"What did this highwayman look like, boy?"

Kelvin thought fast. "He wore black, and he had a black horse."

"That describes half the highwaymen in Rud. What else?"

"A—a scar. From here"—his finger traced a line on his face—"to here."

"This scar—was it deep red?"

"Yes, sir."

"Cheeky Jack!" Carpenter said suddenly. "That rascal owes me a drink or six! I thought he moved out to the plains, and here he is, plying his trade just like he's been since the day he left the barracks!"

"Carpenter," the sergeant said evenly, drawing his sword, "stick out your tongue."

"What?" Carpenter's face paled. He had evidently pushed the sergeant too far this time.

"Stick out your fool tongue. It's flapping too much. I believe I should shorten it."

"No, Sergeant. Please!" The man was really frightened.

"Are you refusing a direct order?"

"N-no."

"Stick out your tongue!"

Carpenter's tongue protruded from his bulbous lips. He looked sick. He wasn't laughing now. Sweat stood out in globules on his greasy forehead. Kelvin was suddenly conscious of the odor the man exuded of cheese and beer and a long-unchanged undershirt. Here he had been concerned about his own appearance, and the guardsmen were just as bad!

The sergeant's sword rose and flicked, its point just lightly pricking the man's tongue. A single drop of blood fell to the unswept floor of the barracks. Carpenter's eyes rolled, their whites showing in terror. It was obvious that the sergeant could have done much worse damage if he had chosen to.

"Let that be a reminder," the sergeant said, sheathing his blade. "Now you," he said, turning quickly to Kelvin. "Get out."

"Sir?"

"Out!"

"But this Cheeky Jack—will you catch him?"

"Out! I don't want to see your baby face again. Ever. And, boy, if I find you've lied to me, whatever happens to your brother will be nothing compared to what I'll see happens to you. You understand me, boy?"

"Y-yes." There went hope, he thought.

"Then get!"

Kelvin ran outside, looking wildly around at the dusty road and the collection of houses and shops on the adjoining street. There was no help anywhere. For him or for Jon.

A burst of laughter from the guardhouse set him walking. At the end of the street was a shade tree and a bench, empty for the moment. He made for it, reached it, and sank down on it with a sigh that made him feel much older. Sixty, perhaps. He sat and gazed at the grass, wishing the sergeant were under it. If only he had such magic, to rid Rud of such monsters! If only there *were* such magic! He'd give anything to have such power instead of this worthless prophecy that was only getting him in trouble.

"Ah, there you are! I was hoping I'd catch you."

Kelvin rose, ready to run, but it was the young guardsman he had seen watching him. The man was empty-handed and looked human. Of course after Carpenter and that sergeant, *anyone* would look human.

"Stay there. I'll pretend I'm chewing you out for sitting where only guardsmen are allowed to sit. It's not a law, but the officers have made it one. Some such as Carpenter would beat you for sitting here."

Kelvin stared at the fellow, but there was no mockery in the man's manner. The guardsman was leaning over, staring him directly in the face.

"We're not all like that. The trouble is, with such as Sergeant Kluff, we have to pretend to be. If I didn't, well, then I'd be beaten, or worse. I'd like to help you, but I'm not sure I can. You go into Windmill Square and find my father. He's got the biggest, widest shoulders of any man you ever saw. He looks like me, but heavier and older, with graying hair. You talk to him. His name's Morvin Crumb. I'm Lester Crumb. Friends call us Mor and Les Crumb. Crumbs, it's said, from the same loaf."

"I'm Kelvin Knight Hackleberry. Friends call me Kel."

"Knight? What an interesting name! I wonder if it means anything, prophecy-wise. Well, go to Windmill Square. Just follow that side street." He nodded with his chin. "Wait by the speaker's platform and eventually my father will show. He's a rough man, and stern, but you'll like him. Most people like Mor Crumb."

"I—I thank you," Kelvin said. He felt overwhelmed by this unexpected kindness.

"You just do it, Kelvin Knight Hackleberry." Les Crumb gave him the friendliest smile yet, a smile made brighter by a ray of sunshine that momentarily turned his face to the color of a dragon's sheen.

"Maybe, just maybe," Les added as Kelvin started to get up, "Father can help you to recover your brother."

7 /

GAUNTLET

KELVIN SAT ON A bench in the park called Windmill Square and listened to his growling stomach. It was getting louder than the sounds of the gathering across the square! It was difficult to decide whether his worst complaint of the moment was hunger or fatigue, but the longer he rested, the more the balance shifted toward hunger. He had eaten only the single oaple this afternoon, and there were no fruit-bearing plants in sight. What was there to eat? He had to wait here until Mor Crumb showed up; if he left even for a few minutes, he might miss the man. And if he cared to risk it, where would he go for food? To some shop where they would charge him so much that he would have to use the dragon scale for money, and then they would cheat him of most of its value? No, he really needed some honest help, and the young guardsman's father seemed like his best bet. But when would the man ever show?

He gazed up into the beenut tree nearby. Maybe there would be some beenuts. They were not his first choice of food, because of the extreme difficulty in cracking them open, but they would certainly do for now, and the tree was close enough to the bench so that he could watch it from there. This was the remnant of a once-magnificent tree, with thickly spreading foliage to the sides, but a sadly marred trunk. Lightning had wounded it, leaving an oozing cleft. As a gust of wind moved the leaves about, he saw into that cleft. There was something wedged in it that reflected a glint as the sunlight briefly penetrated to it.

Curious, as well as hungry, Kelvin got up and walked to the tree. None of the people in the vicinity paid him any attention. The ground beneath it was a tangle of weeds and briers; no one had come here recently. But there, at about twice the height of a man, was the wedged object. It seemed to be some kind of heavy glove, with metallic reinforcements.

Well, where there was one glove there might be a pair, and gloves could always be useful. Kelvin suppressed his fatigue and set about climbing the tree to reach it.

The bark was rough, so that he found fingerholds and toeholds. He hauled himself up, and in due course reached the glove. He took hold of it and hauled it out of its cleft. It was more than a glove; it was a massive gauntlet, fashioned of good quality dragon leather, with reinforced studs of silver metal across the knuckles. That was what had reflected the gleam. This must have been one expensive piece of equipment when new!

He felt around for the companion glove, but couldn't find it. He climbed higher and inspected this entire part of the tree, but there was nothing. Just this single gauntlet for the left hand. How strange that it should have been left here alone!

Still, half a pair was better than none. Might as well use it. He shook it out to free it of whatever bugs might have taken up residence inside, and slipped it on his hand. The thing fit marvelously well; it was as though it had been made to his measure. It seemed about time that something went his way!

He climbed down. His right hand felt the abrading roughness of the bark, but his left hand was quite comfortable. The gloved fingers gripped with surprising accuracy and force, greatly facilitating his descent. His hand felt as if it had infinite power.

He reached the base. Now he observed the beenuts scattered on the ground, dropped by the tree. Those should be edible; maybe he could after all crack some open and get a meal of sorts.

He picked one up and brought it to his mouth. His teeth clamped on the hard shell and bore down, but it would not give. This nut was too tough for him; he would have to bash it open with a rock.

Naturally there were no rocks around. No big sticks, either. Well, he could bash it with the haft of his sword. Of course that would probably either make it explode into far-flung fragments that would be lost in the briers, or crush shell and nutmeat into one inedible mass. What he really needed was a nutcracker.

He held the nut between the thumb and forefinger of the gauntlet and squeezed, wishing it could be that easy.

The nut cracked.

Kelvin did a double take. Oh—he had probably happened on a flaw, catching it just right. He picked out the meat and put it in his mouth. It was slightly bitter, but tasty enough. Had he picked it fresh from the tree, he could have charmed it into a better taste, but the fallen nuts were beyond his power to improve. However, he was not about to climb way up to the tips of the bearing branches to reach growing nuts; he would probably fall and break his neck if he tried.

He picked up another and tried it similarly, between the gauntlet's thumb and forefinger. This one cracked open as readily as the first. Good enough!

He tried the third with his right hand. He got nowhere. He tried it between his teeth, but it was impervious. He tried it with the gauntlet, and it opened as if its shell were made of paper.

Now, this was interesting! He experimented, and verified that the glove had power that the rest of him lacked. When he linked his right hand to the gauntleted left and squeezed, carefully, his right soon was hurting, while his left never felt the pressure. Apparently the glove amplified the power of any motion his fingers made—enormously.

He reached out to grip the tough bark of the tree. He squeezed—and the bark crumbled. He put several nuts in the glove and squeezed hard—and they compressed so quickly and thoroughly that juice spurted. What remained when he opened his hand was just dry mash.

Kelvin gathered as many beenuts as he could hold and returned to the bench. There he methodically cracked them open and ate them, feeling steadily better as his stomach got back into business. What a discovery this gauntlet was! How strange that it had remained lodged in that cleft, and nobody else had noticed it or, if they had, bothered to fetch it down. All the people here, constantly passing through, yet none of them really looking at the tree! Who would have thought that the accidental acquisition of a single glove could have brought him a decent meal!

"Young man—"

Kelvin jumped, turning. The man facing him had the reddest countenance he had ever seen. His shoulders were as wide as the rest of him, and the rest of him was as broad as the back of a war-horse. His ears shone pinkly at the lobes and had little tufts of dark hair at their tips.

"Morvin Crumb?" Kelvin asked after a moment, recovering from his surprise. He had gotten so involved in cracking nuts that he had tuned out the world!

"That's right, youngster. And you're—"

"Kelvin Knight Hackleberry. Your son said—"

"Yes, I know." Morvin brushed a pile of beenut shells from the bench and sat down beside him. Then, speaking in a conspiratorially low tone, he said, "We've had a small group of vigilantes here in Franklin. Crumb's Raiders, we call ourselves. Now and then we can help someone, but it all depends on who they are and how bad they deserve help. What's your loss?"

"My sister," Kelvin said, thinking of nothing else. "A highwayman named Cheeky Jack has her, and—"

"A girl? How old is she?"

"Fourteen. But she—"

The man shook his head sadly. "Then it is already too late to help her. Don't you know what outlaws—and guardsmen, too, for that matter—do to girls that age?"

"Yes, but she's masquerading as a boy. So with luck Cheeky Jack doesn't know."

Mor considered. "So you two aren't entirely naive about traveling, then?"

"Not entirely," Kelvin agreed. "But we still got ourselves into real trouble. If that outlaw finds out—"

"Better hope he doesn't. Then at least she has a chance."

"He said he was taking her to—"

"Yes, yes." The man rubbed his bristly chin. "The highwaymen stock the Boy Mart all the time. We've had little luck in preventing it."

"Then—"

"Maybe. If Les can help. He's a good lad. Too good for the likes of the Queen's guards."

"Then why—"

"Listen, Hackleberry, we may not have much time. The speaker up there on the platform has been trying to stir up trouble." He jerked a thumb, indicating the region. "He's a windbag, and none of us noticed what he was saying until we started noticing the crowd. He's got about twelve listeners besides several Raiders, and that's too many if—"

"I don't see any guardsmen." Kelvin looked about. All he saw were farmers.

"They come disguised. And there are informers."

"Do you really think—"

"Any moment. That's why we have to leave. Now."

A clatter at the end of the park caused them to turn. Three guardsmen, one of them Private Carpenter, another Sergeant Kluff, were bearing down on the platform and the speaker.

"You, Speaker, you're under arrest!" the sergeant shouted. "And you, Crumb and the boy, you're under arrest, too."

Crumb's eyes stood out in his red face as he bellowed back: "Good people, none heard me speak today! I was but listening to the talk and enjoying the shade! There's no cause for my arrest!"

"None for mine, either," Kelvin squeaked. He hardly sounded like any hero now!

"Boy," Crumb said, "they mean to slay us. I'll fight them, but they're mean. That sergeant's fast! I want you to hold back and watch your chance. Maybe I can get one or two of them, and if I do, you get away. Hear!"

"I need your help!" Kelvin gasped.

"*I* need someone's help," Crumb said, disgusted. "They must have followed you."

"If I had a good sword—"

"Lad, this is nothing for a boy, this is something for a man. Get away if you can. Save yourself, and then maybe some other time you can save your sister. Or somebody's sister."

Kelvin picked up his old sword. He raised it in his right hand and the gauntlet on his left and tried to look as defiant and fierce as Crumb. "Now I'm armed," he said, but his attempt at a bold statement came out as another squeak.

"Look at the fool!" cried Private Carpenter of the pricked tongue. "Thinks because his name is Knight he's a warrior. You protected by magic, boy?"

"Gods," Crumb exclaimed, staring at Kelvin. "Hackleberry, that gauntlet —where did you get it?"

"Found it in the beenut tree," Kelvin replied, wondering at the man's intensity. "It was in the wood where the lightning struck."

"Lightning? Lightning! Gods! Hackleberry, off with your cap!"

"What?"

"Your stockelcap, man! Off with it!"

Hesitantly, then defiantly, Kelvin reached for his cap. He pulled it off, feeling it yank at his ears.

Crumb gave a great sigh. "A roundear! Could it be the Roundear of Prophecy, come at last?"

"That's just a wild story!" Kelvin protested. "I'm no hero!"

"We'd better assume it's valid, because otherwise we're finished," Crumb muttered. Then his voice rose, booming across the square. "The Roundear of Prophecy came to lead our fight!"

"But—" Kelvin protested weakly.

"Treason!" shouted Sergeant Kluff, taking a step forward.

Now Crumb's stance and voice took on the appearance and sound of the seasoned orator. "Good people," he cried in a voice that really carried, "are you willing to live and let your children and grandchildren live under the rule of a tyrant? We've got a champion here—or the start of one. Think! Act! Now!"

Suddenly hands were raised and the three guardsmen were surrounded.

"Back! Back!" the sergeant ordered. "Back, or I'll split the lot of you!"

But the man was given a hearty shove in the back and he stumbled forward. Crumb backed away, calling over his shoulder. "Hackleberry, lad, I want you to take my sword."

"But—"

"Just take it, son. Don't think about it. Just think about your left arm and using it to protect yourself."

Kelvin feared his legs would go out from under him, they felt so rubbery, but he took Crumb's sword and let Crumb take his. Crumb looked at him and made a motion. Carpenter and the other guardsman were suddenly grasped by willing hands. Only the sergeant remained free.

Then, to Kelvin's astonishment and alarm, Crumb did an amazing thing. Sheathing the old sword, he said, "You take him, Hackleberry."

"W-what?"

"The sergeant here. Or would you prefer to battle all three?"

"At once?" Kelvin squeaked, terror constricting his throat again.

"Look how scared he is," said the sergeant. "He can't take me, gauntlet or no gauntlet."

"Think left hand, Hackleberry," Crumb whispered.

Kelvin hardly had time to think. As the sergeant's blade swished out, he raised the gauntlet in what he knew was a futile effort to stop him.

With blinding speed the gauntlet got between the sergeant's blade and Kelvin's otherwise unprotected face. He felt nothing but a slight tap on his wrist. Then the sergeant's blade rebounded.

Kelvin looked at his intact left hand. That hand should have been lying on the ground! He took a deep, shuddering breath, raising that hand again as the sergeant drew back his blade for another strike. The man's teeth were gritted; he intended to make sure that he lopped off Kelvin's entire upper section this time!

The blade struck forward. The gauntlet moved like a snake striking a bird. It caught the blade, then wrenched the sword expertly from the sergeant's hand.

Kelvin, numbed by this occurrence, still managed to raise Crumb's sword, posing its blade in front of the man's throat.

"Still don't believe it's his gauntlet, Sergeant?" Crumb asked the disarmed man.

The sergeant looked at the sword point, at Kelvin's trembling arm, then turned pale as the belly of a froog. He dropped to his knees. "Don't slay me. Don't!" he pleaded.

"Slay him, Hackleberry!" Crumb ordered.

Kelvin's hand shook. "I c-can't!"

"He needs slaying. He would have slain you, and me. And any other who got in his way. He enjoys slaying. He has no mercy, and deserves none. You know that!"

Kelvin did know that. Still he couldn't do it. "I—"

"Hackleberry, is it possible that you don't know the meaning of that gauntlet?"

Kelvin shook his head. He had never felt more certain that he was unsure of anything.

"Gods!" complained Crumb. "What do they teach younguns these days? It's a gauntlet once owned by Mouvar the Magnificent, he who wrote the Book of Prophecy. You *have* heard of the book?"

"Of course." Some of Kelvin's uncertainty was replaced by ineffective indignation.

"And you do remember the story of his battle with Zatanas, Prince of Evil, sorcerer and father of our unwanted Queen?"

"They flew," Kelvin said. "According to legend."

"And Mouvar dropped his gauntlets. When they are found, Zatanas will be properly vanquished."

Now Kelvin remembered. There had been such a story in another section of the fable Charlain had read to him. He had not made the connection before. Could this really be one of those fabled gauntlets? "According to legend," he said weakly.

"Right. What else?"

" 'And the gauntlet great shall the tyrant take,' " he quoted. It seemed impossible that this could be one of those! His father, John Knight, had always pooh-poohed such legend, despite his mother's belief, even though the legend was the reason his Charlain had married him. Could she be right, after all?

"That's the scripture, lad!"

"The gauntlets are supposed to contain the souls of brave and powerful knights."

"Right! With them, you cannot be defeated."

"But—" Belief was starting to seep in. "But I have only one."

"A detail," Crumb said. "Maybe both gauntlets were seeking you, and this is the one that found you. Now is the time for you to take command. To lead your people. To excise the sore on this our gentle land."

"I, uh—"

"To start with, what are you going to do about this?" Crumb lightly touched the sergeant with his foot.

Kelvin looked at the man groveling before him. So this was what it was like to be a hero and a puppet of prophecy!

"I—I give him his life." It was what any hero would have done in any old storybook.

"You *what?*"

"I g-give him his life, if he—"

"Hackleberry, hero or no hero, you've got rocks in your fool head!" Crumb took back his sword with a sudden grab. Then, as the sergeant made a triumphant half-leap with an extended knife, Crumb swiftly and expertly deprived him of his head. He gave a quick signal and the men holding the other two guardsmen used daggers on their charges in silent unison.

"You," Crumb said to Kelvin, "have an awful lot to learn about being a hero."

Looking at the two dead men oozing blood, and at the headless, spurting body of Sergeant Kluff, Kelvin felt a sudden great illness.

The beenuts he had so avidly consumed chose this moment to erupt from his mouth.

A moment later, Kelvin stood clutching his aching stomach. The park and the men and the body were whirling round and round and round.

Learn to be a hero. Learn to be a hero.

If he could. If only he could!

8 /

BOY MART

JON LOOKED AROUND AT the circle of boys. Some were older than she was, and some were her own age. But she looked younger, because she was not a boy. How long could she maintain her masquerade? Here there seemed to be no private place for natural functions, and if they required the boys to strip . . .

The boys clustered around her the moment the guards closed the door and departed. She had only a moment to look around, noting the small barred windows. There were three pails in the corners; one seemed to contain water for drinking, and the other two—

Oh, no! They were what served for elimination! Right out in public. That was certain disaster for her.

So this was the Franklin Boy Mart, she thought as she wondered what she was going to say to the crowding boys. At least, this was one of the holding pens. The odor was bad; the boys were all dressed in rags, and seemed not to have bathed for weeks. Still, she hadn't had a bath either, since Mockery rolled in the river. Her dirt was now excellent protective costuming; she did look like one of these boys.

"You," the biggest, meanest-looking boy said, poking her in the stomach with a thumb. "You know who's boss?"

"Not me," Jon said. It would do her no good to fight here. If she fought anyone, it would be whoever purchased her. If she couldn't manage to escape first.

Her answer seemed to puzzle the boy. "You new? This your first time?"

"Yeah," Jon said, trying to get some masculine husk into her voice. "I've never been here before."

"Newly pressed?" another boy asked. This one was a bit shorter than the first, but looked just about as mean.

"Newly brought by a highwayman," Jon said. "I've always been free. Never bound."

"Lucky!" the big boy said.

Jon examined the faces. Most, underneath their dirt, seemed unnaturally hard. Village boys didn't usually look as though they never laughed.

"I'm Bustskin," the big boy said. "I'm boss until somebody knocks me down."

"Boss of what?" Jon asked.

"Here."

"Here? This room?"

"Yeah."

"That's not much."

"You want to challenge it?"

"No. You're the boss."

"You sure, Newskin?"

"Newskin? What's that?"

"You. When you're new, just ready to be bound. Newskin."

"Oh. Yeah, I don't want to fight anyone. I had enough fights before I got here."

"Yeah? Who with?"

"The highwayman. And a dragon."

"Dragon?" Bustskin was incredulous. "You?"

"And my brother. We both fought it."

"Liar."

Jon considered. She didn't like being called a liar. She might have to fight this fellow, lest the boys take her retreat as a sign of unboyishness, but she didn't want to. She was older than he took her for, and she did know a trick or two that she had taken pains to learn after being so ineffective when trying to help her brother in the past; she just might be able to surprise him and knock him down. But her risk was much greater than just victory or defeat. If she won the fight, but her clothing got torn and revealed her nature, she would be a worse loser than he. What was the course of least danger?

"You going to let me call you a liar, Newskin?"

Jon shrugged. "You could lick anyone here," she said, hoping he wouldn't notice the change of subject.

"Yeah. And don't you forget it, Newskin." The big boy half turned, as though to leave, then suddenly slammed a rock-hard fist into her stomach.

Jon doubled over, gasping.

"That's just for being a liar. For being a Newskin."

"Fight! Fight! Fight!" several of the boys chanted.

Jon found tears in her eyes. That fellow could really hit! At the same time, she was thankful he hadn't struck her in the chest. How awful it would be to be bound with him on the same plantation! Judging by Bustskin's darkened skin and ruddy complexion, he had never been in a mine, and he didn't look as if he had ever rowed a galley. Chances were he would get a foreman's job bossing field workers, and just possibly he would survive to reach twenty-five. If someone didn't slay him first.

"You going to fight, Newskin?" the bully asked.

"Don't do it, Jon! Don't!"

Jon blinked. It was a red-haired lad she remembered from the village. He was a decent sort, but had been given up for a tax penalty a year before. His parents and brother and sisters had all cried.

But he represented perhaps a worse threat to her than the bully did. Because he had called her by name. He knew her—and therefore knew she was a girl. If he gave her away—

"Tom? Tom Yokes?" She had hardly recognized the boy, so changed was his appearance. He had scars on his arms and legs; both his eyes were blacked. "He did this to me," Tom said, indicating the scars and his eyes. "If I couldn't lick him, then you sure can't. I'm bigger than you, and stronger."

Because he was a boy. He had avoided reference to age, knowing they were the same age, so as not to betray her. He was keeping her secret.

Jon wished fleetingly that her brother were here. Kelvin didn't like to fight, but he could when he had to, and he was almost as big as Bustskin. Bustskin deserved a lesson.

But she was not the one to give him that lesson. Not now, not this way. Slowly Jon straightened, letting go of herself. Her stomach still hurt. She hadn't balled her fists, and she knew that with Bustskin standing there so eagerly that it wouldn't be wise.

"Tom . . . can I talk to you?" she asked. "Over there in the corner?"

Tom nodded.

"You win, Bustskin," Jon said. "I ran away from home. I was caught by someone on a black horse. I never saw a dragon and I never learned to fight."

Several of the boys broke into a halfhearted cheer. It irked her to lie. Kelvin, she knew, would have stuck to the truth or kept his mouth shut. She really respected Kelvin for that, but she just couldn't do it herself.

Bustskin drew back his fist and waved it in front of Jon's mouth. "I should hit you once or twice for lying to me."

"You did," Jon said.

"No, Bustskin, don't!" Tom cried.

Bustskin whirled on him. "You want some more, Redhead?"

"N-no. We're going to be sold soon, Bustskin. Now's not the time to fight. Besides, you've licked everyone here."

"Yeah, I have, haven't I?" Bustskin turned and clapped another boy on the back. "Let me tell you about the girl I had on the Finch plantation. She was the overseer's daughter and she brought us slops. One day when she came too near and the overseer was away, I reached out and—"

As he spoke, he turned again and reached out by way of illustration, grabbing the closest material available: Jon's dirty brownberry shirt. This could not have been accidental; probably he intended it as one final humiliation. He hauled in and up, pulling it out of the waistband. The material was too tough to tear, but the jerk did cause her to stumble forward, and as her head came low, he pulled the shirt up over her head, blinding her.

There was an abrupt silence. Quickly Jon brought down her shirt, but she knew it was too late. They had seen.

"I'll be damned!" Bustskin exclaimed. "It's a girl!"

Jon tried to bluff it out. "So I didn't want them to know," she snapped. "It's not so bad, being sold as a boy. You don't have to tell."

"Tell? Hell!" Bustskin's eyes were round. "I've got better things to do with a girl than tell!" He stepped toward her. "Give me some of that skin, honey. I don't have to talk about what I did to that plantation girl; I'll *show* 'em!"

"Not with me, you don't!" Jon retorted.

"Oh, yeah?" He grabbed for her again.

Now Jon really had to fight. She kicked him in the shin, knowing the pain would be enough to double him over. But he was tough; he only winced, and hung on, hauling her into him again. "Let's just get those pants down," he said, pawing at her pantaloons.

Jon brought up a knee, aiming for the groin. But the bully was streetwise, and twisted his torso to the side, so that the blow missed. He caught her raised leg and held it, drawing on the pantaloons, pulling them down around her bottom.

"Yeah, that's nice, very nice!" he grunted, his hands squeezing at her buttocks as he continued to work on the pantaloons. The other boys watched, fascinated by the proceedings. Most of them were young enough so that this would be their first such experience.

"You can't do that!" Tom Yokes protested, trying to interfere.

Bustskin paused just long enough to slam Tom in the gut with a backhand fist. "You knew her—and didn't tell!" he said savagely. "I'll pulverize you— after I finish with her!"

Tom clutched his front, his breath knocked out. It was clear that he was unable to fight the bully, no matter how proper his instincts were. But this distraction gave Jon time to regroup.

When Bustskin turned his attention back to her, she let him have a prime smash in the nose, just the way Kelvin had done it to another bully years before.

But again the bully's experience saved him. Even as her arm moved, he jerked back his head, and the blow only caught him on the mouth. It smashed his lip against his teeth, and the lip started to bleed, but the injury wasn't serious enough to make him pause. Meanwhile, Jon's knuckles stung; teeth were hard!

Now the line of battle was at her thighs, as Bustskin struggled to get her pantaloons the rest of the way down and she clung to them to keep them up.

Her head thrashed back and forth, her hair flying out, and she kicked her feet, but could not break free of the bully's grasp. She saw Tom retreating to the door, and with a fraction of her mind wished he had been just a little bit bigger, stronger, and bolder. He was a decent kid; that was his problem. He couldn't have helped her much anyway; if he had hauled Bustskin off, another boy would have hauled Tom off, and held him until Bustskin was through with her.

Slowly and erratically, the pantaloons came down, until finally they were all the way off, and she was bare-legged. Another snatch, and her ragged underpants were torn off. The watching boys could have been zombies for all the expression on their faces; it seemed that most of them had never before seen the thighs of a fourteen-year-old girl.

She kicked at the bully, then hunched over and butted him with her head, but he simply shifted his grip, threw her down, and pinned her to the floor with his body. Now he started working on his own clothing, to get the essential section open for business. It was evident that he had not been making up the story of the overseer's daughter; he knew how to get a girl down.

She snapped at him with her teeth, but this, too, was ineffective. Now he was ready below; he used a knee to wedge her legs apart. She was worn out from fighting; she could no longer resist him. But she refused to give up; she continued to squirm as much as she was able, hoping for a chance to hit him where it would do the most good.

Then the hulking shape of a guard loomed over them. A ham-hand caught Bustskin by the collar and hauled him literally up in the air. "A girl!" the guard exclaimed. "You idiot! Don't you realize that a virgin girl is worth ten times as much as you on the open market? You know what the penalty is for ruining value like that?"

Bustskin swallowed. His hands went to his front. He was getting a glimmer of the penalty.

The guard dropped him, staring at Jon appraisingly as she scrambled for her pantaloons. Obviously he had seen everything he needed to. "Definitely prime," he said. "We'll get a bonus for this discovery! Come with me, girl."

Jon really had no choice at this stage. She drew up her pantaloons and followed the guard to the door.

There Tom Yokes stood, cringing. "Sir, remember—"

The guard paused. "Yeah, you did call us," he said.

"They'll kill me now, if—"

"Okay, you get a separate cell," the guard decided. "Come on out."

"It was the only way—" Tom said to Jon as they left the cell.

She touched his hand briefly. "I know."

Then she was hustled off to the section that was the holding pen for the Girl Mart, while Tom was taken to his solitary cell. She didn't know whether she would ever see him again.

9 /

GIRL MART

THE BOY MART had smelled of unwashed bodies and manure-coated boots. The Girl Mart was cleaner, but Jon feared it more. Boys were sold for work, but girls could be bought for play, and that could be much worse.

The boys had been rowdy and rough. The girls were quiet—too quiet, for it was the silence of despair.

Jon found herself in a dusky chamber where eight or ten girls sat, each isolated by her own thoughts. She had endured the impersonal preparations: the stripping by a matron, inspection of her private parts to verify that she was healthy and was indeed a virgin, a stiff shower and scrubbing, and garbing in a rough smock and slippers. Now she stood before the desolate girls of all ages, feeling naked under the smock, for she had no under-clothing anymore. Obviously girls were supposed to be rendered naked at short notice so that buyers could appreciate their assets.

She had salvaged one small vestige of her pride, however. She had saved the handful of dragonberries in her pocket by putting them in her mouth. She hadn't needed or wanted those berries; she had done it simply as a matter of principle, to prove that they could not fathom *all* her secrets or deprive her of all her possessions. Actually, the berries tasted awful, though she neither chewed nor sucked on them; her cheek had become numbed by their presence. But she had carried them past the gauntlet of inspection and changes, and so they represented her small victory. After all, they could have been gold coins if she had had any to save.

She took a step forward—and reeled, abruptly dizzy. She almost fell, then caught herself, then reconsidered and collapsed to the floor.

An older girl got up and came to her. "I know it's rough, honey, the first time. Did they beat you?"

Jon opened her mouth, but couldn't speak. Instead the sodden berries dribbled out.

"God! Don't tell me—!" the girl exclaimed. "Are those what they look like?" She squatted to pick one up. Her smock hiked up over her knees, and Jon saw that she, too, was naked under it. "They *are!*"

"I just didn't want—" Jon said, but then her voice failed her again, and more berries slid out.

"Did you swallow any of those?"

"No, I just—"

"Grackle! Tanager!" the girl cried to the other girls. "Come here, haul her up, take her to the bucket and wash her mouth out good! Quickly! Maybe it's not too late!"

Two husky girls came and hauled Jon up by the arms. "But I didn't even swear," Jon protested weakly.

The leader girl laughed. "Swear! Who cares about that! Don't you know what those berries are?"

"No, I just found them near a dragon lair."

Grackle and Tanager got her head down by the bucket. "Take a mouthful, spit it out," one said.

Jon obeyed, and did it again, and again, until all trace of the berries was gone, though her mouth remained sore.

"I guess you'll live," the girl said. "What's your name? Mine's Thornflower."

"Jon, just Jon," Jon said, feeling somehow inadequate. Their names were so fancy!

"We make up our own," Thornflower explained, catching on to Jon's confusion. "To conceal our shame. So news doesn't get around about what happened to us, you know."

"Oh. But about those dragonberries—"

"They're poison! One of them makes a person sick, two puts her in a coma, three will kill her. You had a dozen in your mouth! Whatever possessed you to do that?"

"I'm just ornery. I wanted to hide something from them, just to prove I could do it, and the berries were all I had."

Thornflower shook her head. "I understand, I suppose. But dragonberries! Of all the things to put in your mouth! Why, just the juice from their hulls will make you sick."

"I know," Jon said wanly. "Now."

"You better pick a room and lie down. You need to recover your strength for the auction tomorrow, because if you're sick they'll think you're faking, and they'll beat you. No malingerers here! Which do you want?"

"I get a choice?" Jon asked, amazed.

"Any room that has a free bunk, if the other girl doesn't object. We're not boys, you know; we're halfway civilized."

Jon stood unsteadily and looked at the rooms. They opened off the main chamber, and each had two beds. Girls were lying on some, or sitting on them with their heads in their hands. The accommodations were much better than those of the Boy Mart, probably because the proprietors didn't want bruises or dirt to interfere with the marketability of the girls.

In one chamber a girl sat hunched in a corner, her hands over her ears. "What's the matter with her?" Jon asked.

"That's Flambeau. She's really bad off. She's a roundear. That's why she covers—"

"A roundear?" Jon asked, coming abruptly alert.

"You know, one of the offspring of some intruder from that other planet. They're pretty much like us, except for those horrible ears."

"I'll room with her," Jon said.

"She won't talk to you," Thornflower warned. "She just wants to die."

Jon stooped to pick up the berries that had washed out of her mouth. "Well, if these really do—"

"Say, that's one tough notion!" Thornflower said admiringly. "But don't let the guards know you gave them to her, because—"

"They'll beat me," Jon finished. "No one will tell?"

"No one will tell," Thornflower promised.

"Thanks. I like it better here than at the Boy Mart."

"You were *there?*"

"I was pretending to be a boy. Bustskin found out, and tried to—"

Thornflower sighed. "The first time's the worst. I remember mine, when I was ten."

"You were raped when you were ten?" Jon asked, appalled.

"The first time, yes. By a middle-aged man. He wasn't too rough, actually, but he was so dirty and clumsy, I felt like dying."

Jon glanced again at the huddled girl. "Is that why—?"

"Sure, I thought you realized. She's a roundear, so isn't worth much on the market, so the guards knew there wasn't anything to lose."

"The guards?"

"Didn't you know? No, I guess you didn't, because they don't do it to virgins, of course. Just to us who can't lose that kind of value."

"You mean—you, too?"

"All of us. Or at least any they want. If we cooperate, they give us little things, like extra rations or clean water. If we don't—well, then it gets ugly."

"And Flambeau—"

"Didn't cooperate," Thornflower finished. "She's new here, like you. She didn't understand."

"I guess I'm pretty well off, after all," Jon said, shuddering.

"Depends how you see it," Thornflower said, shrugging.

Jon thanked her, and went to the room. She sat down near the huddled girl. "Flambeau," she said.

There was no response.

"Flambeau, listen to me," Jon said. "My brother is a roundear."

Slowly the girl lifted her head. She had black hair and brown eyes, and would have been quite pretty if the hair weren't matted and the eyes swollen from crying.

Then she dropped her face again. "Don't tease me!" she said, and her body was racked with renewed sobs.

"No, he really is. I'm half roundear, too, only my ears came out like my mother's. When they said you were one—"

Jon stopped, because the girl's hands were clamped tightly over her ears, effectively blocking the sound.

Well, if she really thought she wanted to die, Jon would just call that bluff! She opened her hand and put it down under the girl's nose, showing half a dozen dragonberries.

Flambeau saw them. She snatched at them, surprising Jon. In a moment, she had swept up three and popped them into her mouth.

"Wait!" Jon cried. "Those are—"

The girl lifted her head again. She swallowed. "I know. Thanks."

Jon had not meant to have the girl really commit suicide! Now what was she to do?

Well, she could alert the other girls and have them haul Flambeau to the bucket and poke a finger down her throat to make her vomit up the berries. That would save her life. But to what purpose? If she really did want to die, maybe it was better to let her do it in peace. Jon knew how rough it could be on a roundear, because of Kelvin, and how it could be for a girl. So maybe Flambeau had reason.

Her alternative was to let nature take its course. She was in doubt, so she did nothing—which meant the second choice. She did not feel at all easy about it, but that was it. If she was cooperating in a death, maybe that was just the way it had to be, here in this awful place.

Lunch came. Thornflower supervised the doling out of portions of the rough bread and thin soup. It wasn't much, but no one complained; they were all aware of how readily and capriciously it could be cut off.

Flambeau remained on her bunk, where Jon had laboriously hauled her. The girl had a well-fleshed body, and would have been a real prize on the market if it hadn't been for her round ears. At least what little she would have brought would now be denied to the owners of the Marts. That was a very small consolation; Jon now wished she hadn't ever shown her the deadly berries. But what was done was done; she reacted as she had when she wasn't sure whether Kelvin had survived the dragon's toss: she went on with her business. What else was she to do?

But after about three hours, Flambeau stirred. She was alive! Jon went to her. "I'm sorry I gave you those dragonberries!" she cried. "I didn't think you'd really—"

The girl opened her eyes. "I found him," she said.

"What?"

"I found your brother. With the round ears. He's a hero."

Jon laughed. "You were dreaming! My brother's a great guy, but he's not really a hero. Just the notion of fighting puts him in a cold sweat, though he does it when he has to."

"Kelvin," she said. "He has a gauntlet."

"Kelvin doesn't have any such thing!" Then Jon did a double take. "How did you know his name? I never told you!"

"I was there. I ranged out from my body and found him. He was easy to find, because he's the only other roundear in the vicinity. All I could think of was what you said, so I just concentrated on those round ears, and suddenly I was there. He's handsome!"

"You what?" Jon understood the words, but they weren't making much sense.

"I went out and found him. I could see him and hear him, but I couldn't talk to him, because I was only a ghost." Then Flambeau did a double take. "What am I saying?"

That was better! The girl was as confused as Jon was. "You swallowed three dragonberries and almost died. I guess you could have been a ghost! But you weren't, because you recovered, and here you are. How do you feel?"

"Very weak," the girl said. Then: "My name is Heln."

"They told me—"

"My given name. After my roundear mother, Helen. Heln Flambeau."

"Oh." Jon was disconcerted. "I'm Jon. Jon Hackleberry."

"I know. Kelvin spoke of you. He means to rescue you.

"You dreamed all that?"

"I don't think it was a dream," Heln said.

"You mean to say that the dragonberries didn't poison you, they just sort of sent your soul out wandering for a while?"

"I suppose so. I didn't exactly wander, I could go anywhere I wanted. I just sort of flew, only I could get somewhere without even flying, just by *being* there. So I decided to be where there was that roundear you spoke of, just because—" She shrugged. "Now I don't think I want to die anymore. I —I got—something terrible happened, and I really wanted to die, but now I have something back that sort of makes up for it. It's as if I've entered a whole new realm, and what happened in the old one doesn't matter so much anymore. I've left that old, spoiled life behind. Now I want to live, and travel astrally again."

"Better not," Jon said. "Those berries kill most folk, and if you took too many, too fast—"

"Yes. I'll wait. But now I have something to live for. I want to meet your brother, in the flesh. Kelvin's nice. He's my age."

"He's nice," Jon agreed. Could she really believe this? She decided to be forthright. "Look, Heln, this is hard to believe all at once. I really don't know if you were dreaming or if you really did it. Could you tell me more about my brother?"

Heln smiled. "His eyes are sort of blue, and his hair brown. He's thin. He wants to rescue you, and get back some dragon scales, but he got all caught up in being a hero, because of the gauntlet."

"What gauntlet? He doesn't have any gloves!"

"He found it somewhere. I came along after that, so I don't know where, but everyone says it means he's the hero of the prophecy. I don't know what the prophecy is, though."

Jon realized that there was no way Heln could have known all that unless she had been there. Obviously she hadn't been there physically. So she must have been spiritually. "But the berries are poison! Why didn't they kill you?"

"I don't know. Unless—did your brother eat any?"

"No. Why?"

"Maybe they don't work the same on roundears. Maybe they kill the folk of Rud, but just separate the souls of roundears, because our metabolism is different. Where did you get them?"

Jon explained about the garden near the dragon.

"Why would a dragon tend a garden? Do they like to eat berries?"

"Those few little berries wouldn't feed a dragon more than a second!" Jon exclaimed. "They eat hot flesh."

"But they must have some reason to tend those gardens, if other dragons have gardens. At least that one did. Suppose it had the same effect on a dragon? Made it able to explore without going anywhere? Wouldn't that help it forage for prey?"

"It sure would!" Jon agreed. "I always wondered why it's supposed to be so hard to catch a dragon! When hunters get together in big parties and try to run a dragon down, the dragon's never there. We thought it was because the dragons heard them coming, but maybe—"

"I think we've just discovered the dragon's secret," Heln said. "No one knew about it, because the dragons are able to guard their gardens pretty well, and anyone who ate the berries died. Just as I meant to die, be-cause—" Here she faltered. It seemed that despite her words, she had not yet let go of the bad experience.

"Thornflower told me what happened to you," Jon said. "I'm sorry. I almost got, well, the same thing. So I guess I understand. But you know, the other girls seem to have survived it all right."

Heln considered. "Kelvin—would he—?"

"He wouldn't rape anyone!" Jon exclaimed, horrified.

"I mean, would he—would he be able to like a girl who—"

Oh. "I'm sure he doesn't judge by that sort of thing. I mean, he knows how bullies are. It wasn't your fault. And I came to you because you have round ears, like him. I think he'd really like you, if he met you."

"I'm glad. Because I think I really like him. He was so confused, but trying to do the right thing, instead of being so brutal the way the others are. Unsure of himself."

"That's my brother!"

"Yes. While the others—they don't seem to care anything about—they just use—"

"Yeah," Jon said, understanding. "He's not like them."

"But of course we're both going to be sold in the auction tomorrow. If only I could have told him! But I couldn't say anything to him; I was completely invisible and silent. He knows you're here, because someone told him, but—"

"Kelvin will rescue me somehow, I know it!" Jon said stoutly. "And then he'll get back our gold. And when he rescues me, I'll tell him to rescue you, too. I know he'll want to meet you, and you can help him so much if you can do that thing with the berries again." She paused. "But suppose they only work once? And the second time they really do poison you?"

"Next time I'll only take one berry. That's not supposed to kill a person anyway. I'll see if it works. But I think not today; they did leave me rather washed out."

"Well, you could be hungry, you know. You missed the noon meal."

Heln laughed weakly. "I suppose I could be. I'll make sure to eat all I can tonight."

IO /

AUCTION

MOST OF THE POTENTIAL bidders were buyers for the larger plantations. Here and there on the tiers of seats forming a half circle around the ring was to be seen a seaman in search of new galley hands. The seamen's blue shirts and trim sea trousers contrasted with all the brownberry shirts and greenbriar pantaloons. The seamen's flat, tight-fitting caps shone like white rocks in the tossing sea of bobbing green and yellow stockelcaps.

Back where Queeto sat, the noise was the steady murmur of men talking crops and the buying and selling of crophands. Feeling a sliver from the plank seat digging into his squat behind, tasting the bitter bile that always rose in his throat amid such surroundings, Queeto retreated into his favorite fantasy. In his mind the clouds of hatred roiled thick and black as he imagined himself with the money to buy boys for his own purpose. In this favored daydream he did not have an enlarged and humped back, but instead was straight and tall, with a high, black-crowned forehead. In fact, in this vision he resembled the one he was proud to acknowledge Master: Zatanas, Confounder of Righteousness, Defender of the Ugly and Misshaped.

At last the auctioneer made his appearance. Standing tall, dressed in black, he was almost the picture of an ancient prophet with his gray, flowing beard. He cleared his throat at the lectern, banged his gavel twice with reports like exploding skulls, and waited for silence. Then, having achieved it, he began.

"Some of you have come from distant kingdoms and may not know all of our Rud customs governing the Boy and Girl Marts. Some of our stock have been seized for nonpayment of taxes; others are convicted felons. Most were young vagrants who have been properly and legally impressed."

Queeto squirmed, reminded that he, too, had been a vagrant, though not one a bounty hunter would have taken for sale at a Boy Mart. As a lad, his had been a hard lot: tormented constantly by smooth-cheeked boys and ugly soldiers; in constant flight from those who knew he had stolen something; eating whatever and wherever he could. In those days he had to eat, unlike the days following Master.

"And now," the auctioneer was saying, "our first lot of six boys from MacGregor Plantation. Used for one season and now to be replaced with fresh hands. These still have a lot of work left in them, gentlemen, and seasoned as only MacGregor seasons them—"

In the center ring, prodded by the overseer's whip, six lanky boys with whip marks and protruding ribs walked the circle. Obviously they had been recalcitrant and repeatedly disciplined. Useless, because of one year of hardness, for Master's (and Queeto's own) exacting purposes.

The boys were sold to one of the smaller plantations. The purchaser was a man of such evil countenance as to be identified as such even by the approving dwarf.

Small lot followed small lot, and soon it was down to single, broad-shouldered farm boys seized for their father's nonpayment of taxes. Watching their misery, remembering the torments of his long-ago youth, Queeto felt a little, though only a little, avenged.

But none of these were quite suitable for Master. Queeto knew better than to buy any boys that weren't precisely right. He sighed; he would just have to report no purchases, this time.

"And now," the auctioneer announced, "the Girl Mart."

Immediately the lagging attention of the buyers revived. Even those who had no intention of bidding liked to look at the girls!

The girls were herded out, in their slippers and smocks. Most were motley, not attractive despite their youth and the management's evident effort to get them prettied up. It took more than the combing of the hair and washing of the face to make a hardened young slut into an attractive package! But a few were interesting. One had an excellent chassis and good face, marred only by a stockelcap someone had inexplicably pulled down around her ears. Another looked to be thirteen or fourteen, with good lines, long fair tresses, and a bearing that indicated her spirit had not yet been broken. She was exactly the kind Master wanted!

The auctioneer hauled a girl out of the bunch. "And what am I bid for this fine specimen of womanhood?" he asked rhetorically. "Let's start it at ten rudnas."

"Five," a seaman said.

The girl made a gesture at him with a finger. She was no innocent youngster! That of course lowered her value; the average buyer preferred to degrade a girl in his own fashion, rather than wrestle with one who had already been broken in. Queeto watched in silence.

Finally the auctioneer brought out the lively young one. Her yellow hair glistened in the sun, and her smooth skin was marked only with a purpling bruise across her face. Her cheeks were healthy and ruddy. She was full of the good red juice of life. Yes. Exactly what his appetite craved and the Master specified. Either sex would do, as long as it had the right attributes.

"And here's a fresh virgin, age fourteen, just turned in by a public-spirited citizen. She was caught trying to steal a donkey."

"I was not!" the girl retorted. Oh, she was a prize!

"Fourteen rudnas," the auctioneer said, acknowledging a bid from a wide-shouldered, red-faced man accompanied by two younger men on Queeto's right. "Who will make it twenty?"

There was a pause. This one was obviously worth more, but the buyers were still appraising her, deciding how high they should go. Meanwhile the girl, looking at the first bidder, did a double take. Did she know him? That could be good for her, or bad, depending on the nature of the prior contact.

"Twenty," a plantation buyer said. She would get plenty of use in a hurry if he took her home to the farmhands!

"Gentlemen, let's get serious," the auctioneer said. He whipped off the girl's smock, rendering her abruptly naked.

The body thus revealed was full-hipped but still light in the breasts. She was just coming into her prime, with some growing yet to do. Her half-defiant, half-chagrined attitude spoke more clearly than any words the auctioneer could say of her naivete. Oh, she was certainly a prize, probably abducted directly from some farmer's house!

There was bound to be heavy bidding here. Queeto decided to preempt it. "One hundred rudnas," he called. This was a princely sum, but money was of no consequence to him or to the Master. This borderline child would never again be at this stage of innocence!

"One hundred and two rudnas," said the big man.

Queeto was shocked. He hadn't expected to be bid against at this level. He had made a preemptive bid! But he hesitated only a heartbeat, then called, "One hundred and twenty-five."

There were gasps from all around, and murmurs, and even a few snickers. They knew he had gone over the limit for even the most delectable of young flesh. It wasn't a matter of money now, but of propriety. Why fatten the Mart's percentage beyond what was reasonable? Queeto clenched his teeth, and hoped the other man wouldn't force him into further embarrassment by bidding again.

The girl, still naked, was signaling frantically to the big man. She pointed to the girl with the cap. What was she trying to do, get him to bid on someone else? Well, the other man could have the capped girl, who was obviously concealing some serious flaw under that cap. Otherwise the auctioneer would never have put it on her.

"One hundred twenty-five going once," the auctioneer said happily. "One hundred and twenty-five going twice, one hundred and twenty-five going thrice. *Sold,* to the gentleman with the sack of gold between his shoulders!"

That was a punnish reference to Queeto's obvious hump. The auctioneer would not be so frivolous, Queeto thought, if he had known him to be an immortal.

The next girl up was that capped one. Suddenly, defiantly, she reached up and tore off the cap. The audience gasped. Her ears were round! That destroyed her value. No wonder it had been concealed. The auctioneer was furious; any play he might have made had just been destroyed.

There was only one bid for that one, of two rudnas, and the big man took her. Well, at least she was cheap! Queeto wondered what use the man would find for a nonvirginal roundear girl; no matter how sweet her shape, she simply wasn't worthwhile.

After the silently glaring young purchase had been placed, securely shackled at ankles and chained at wrists, into his specially appointed carriage, Queeto found the bile subsiding in his stomach. After all, he had prevailed, and the chattel was his. Perhaps it was just as well that the stupid man had bid against him, because it had given him a chance to prove that such opposition was hopeless. Such reminders were in order, periodically.

The wind out here on the open road blew fresh, carrying tree smells and grass odors. The stars shone down, twinkling. Owlarks hooted and whistled. Froogs chirped. Queeto smiled as best he could, thinking of Master, of good red juice, and of what lay in store for his purchase. A healthy, spirited virgin —that was the very best kind to degrade, because there was much more reaction for the effort. Master would be very pleased.

"Hold there!"

What was this? Three men. Highwaymen? Yes, all had bandannas round their faces. How did they dare? He thought all highwaymen knew that the Master's tribute could become the Master's vengeance if they molested one of his own. A stern warning should suffice.

Then, by the light of the stars, he recognized the big, broad-shouldered bidder at the Mart, and the two who had been with him. Obviously some amateur going into business for himself. The fool!

"I represent someone of great importance," Queeto said loudly. "If it's gold you want, I have little left after the Mart." Thanks, he thought, to the man's idiot bidding.

"It's not gold we're after," said the big man. "It's the girl."

"My master—"

"Damn your master!"

Queeto's shock was renewed. Such disrespect for persons of power was almost unheard-of! Had the man no concern for his health or his sanity, let alone his life? But he was in no position to fight; he would simply have to tolerate this affront, and make a full report to Master.

Queeto watched as the two stockelcapped young men sheathed swords, dismounted, and threw open the door to the carriage compartment.

"*Kel!*" cried the girl who had cost a fortune.

"Brother Wart," said the young man. That was odd indeed; why call a girl "brother"? Then, to the other, "She's shackled."

"Key, dwarf!" the big man ordered.

Queeto knew better than to argue. These were rough men showing little caution; anyone who would waylay a carriage of the Master would hardly hesitate to slay the Master's underling. He tossed the big man the key ring, who caught it and quickly transferred it to the slighter built of the thieves.

With a jingle, they released the girl. Then the big man cut the harness on the carriage's horse.

A moment later they were gone, one horse carrying double. Queeto was alone on a lonely road with an empty carriage. They hadn't even had the decency to steal his animal, he thought bitterly, but instead had left it for him to catch—or to try to catch.

"Damn!" Queeto said, wishing himself adept in magic. "Master isn't going to like this. Master isn't going to like this at all!" That was of course an understatement so gross as to be humorous, but he wasn't laughing. There was no telling against whom Master's rage would first strike.

II /

LEADER

Well away from the carriage, they slowed to a walk, so that the double-loaded horse would not be unduly fatigued. Kelvin, riding with Jon behind him, introduced her to his new friends: the father-and-son team of Morvin and Les Crumb. "They are members of the Raiders," he explained. "They oppose the Queen and her evil policies. But they have to operate in secret, or the Queen's guards will wipe them all out."

"What about Heln?" Jon demanded. "You bought her, didn't you?"

Morvin Crumb laughed. "How could we fail, after you signaled so strongly! Then when she took off her cap, and we saw she was a roundear, we understood. That had the incidental effect of ruining her value; the auctioneer was furious!"

"We had to hurry down with the money," Les agreed. "Otherwise we knew she'd be severely beaten."

"Then where is she now?" Jon asked.

"She was very tired," Kelvin said. "I think she'd been sick. She said something about eating dragonberries, and how glad she was to see me, and then she just, well, slept. So Mor carried her to his horse, and took her out to a hideout cabin he has in the wilderness, and got a girl to tend her, and that's where we're going now. How did you find her? Where did she come from? Why did she seem to know me?"

Jon explained about her discovery and removal to the Girl Mart, and how she had picked Heln Flambeau for company because of her round ears. "I knew right then she was the perfect match for you, Kel!" she said, and Kelvin felt himself blushing. Then she told of what she had learned about the dragonberries she had saved, and how Heln had tried to commit suicide with them.

"Suicide!" Kelvin exclaimed. "Why?"

"She had been raped, Kel. She's a delicate girl, always treated well before; when that happened, she just wanted to die. I told her it wouldn't make any difference to you."

"Of course it makes a difference!" Kelvin said. "Who did it? We'll have to kill—"

"I mean in the way you feel about her."

"But I don't even know her!" Kelvin protested, blushing again.

"You must have seen her ears—and her body," his sister said. "What more do you need to know?"

Kelvin shut up, knowing that she was baiting him. Indeed, he had seen her ears and her body, and been somewhat smitten on the spot, but hadn't wanted to admit it. "I—of course it wouldn't make any—if I—" He faltered to a stop.

"Just make sure you tell her that," Jon said firmly. "She likes you, Kel."

"But she never saw me before!"

"She saw you. The berries didn't kill her; they only sent her into a trance, and her spirit left her body and traveled around, and she saw you. She liked your ears, of course; there couldn't have been any other reason, could there?"

She was still teasing him. She was certainly back to normal! Kel did not protest any further.

But Mor Crumb was interested. "She traveled astrally? I thought that ability was lost centuries ago!"

"We think maybe it was her ears," Jon said. "That maybe the berries kill the folk of Rud, but only stun those with Earthblood, so their spirits can travel for a while. Maybe if Kel ate some berries—"

"No!" Mor cried with surprising vehemence. "He's the hero of the prophecy. We can't risk him on poison berries!"

"I told Heln she could be very useful, because she can travel anywhere, see and hear anything. That's why I signaled you to buy her."

"You did well, girl," Mor Crumb said. "The Raiders can really use a talent like that! We can spy on the guardsmen, on the Queen herself!"

"But if the berries are poison—" Kelvin said weakly.

"We'll have to find out what the minimum number is she can take that will let her spirit travel, without harming her," Mor said. "Obviously the effort takes a lot out of her, so we won't overdo it. But what a tool!"

Kelvin could see the point, but remained troubled. He didn't like thinking of a beautiful girl like Heln Flambeau as a tool.

They reached the cabin in due course. Mor knocked in a code pattern on the door, and the girl opened it, then slipped out and disappeared into the darkness. They went in.

Heln Flambeau was up, having recovered from her fatigue. By the wan, flickering light of a lone candle Kelvin saw her face, round ears and all. She had brushed out her black hair, and now it shone beside the candle, and her half-shadowed face was lovely. She had been bedraggled and then unconscious before, not presenting her best aspect; now, animate, she was beautiful.

Jon nudged him. Kelvin opened his mouth. "I'm, uh, beautiful," he said.

"You jackass!" Jon hissed.

Morvin Crumb burst out laughing. In a moment everyone was laughing.

Heln approached gracefully. "I'd like to be your friend, Kelvin," she said. "Did your sister tell you—"

"No difference!" he exclaimed.

". . . about the experience I had with the dragonberries?" she finished. Kelvin choked. "I did," Jon said.

"I saw you with the gauntlet. I realize you are a hero, but if there's any way I can help—"

"I'm no—" Kelvin began.

"You sure can!" Morvin said. "We need information on the whereabouts and activities of the Queen's guardsmen. If you can spy on them without their knowing—"

"I think I could," Heln said. "But I would need more berries, and I don't think I could do it too often, because it really took the strength from me, that one time."

Kelvin tried to get a grip on himself. "You actually saw me and heard me?"

"Oh, yes," she agreed. "Of course it was all rather confused, because you weren't explaining anything, you were just going somewhere, but everyone was saying you were a hero, and something about a prophecy, and I couldn't stay long. I never did this before, I mean going about in astral form, and I suppose I'm not very good at it."

"I'm not very good at being a hero!" Kelvin blurted.

She smiled. "I think we have a lot in common."

"Round ears," Kelvin said.

"That, too."

For some unaccountable reason he felt himself blushing again. He hoped the dim light masked it.

"We'd better bunk down here," Morvin said. "We're going to be busy, the next few days. You two girls better take the bed, and the rest of us'll lie on the floor."

They settled. Kelvin was tired, but also buoyed by the rescue of his sister, and by the discovery of Heln Flambeau. He had never dreamed of meeting a roundear girl, let alone a beautiful one his own age! And she liked him! It was almost too good to be true. He hated to think it, but it seemed that the highwayman's abduction of Jon had been a net blessing.

* * *

Morvin Crumb's face got very dark, his heavy eyebrows knitting together like dark caterpillars. He stared at the bedraggled farmer and the pinch-faced woman Kelvin guessed to be the man's wife.

"Say that again, Jeffreys," Crumb said, making no move as yet to dismount from his horse.

"They burned my barn. Ransacked my house. Carried away everything they wanted and smashed and destroyed the rest. We watched them from the woods."

"Damn, and I suppose that's just the start!"

"Must be," Jeffreys said. "I heard one of 'em say they would hit Al Reston next. You know what it's about, Morvin?"

"Revenge," the big man said.

"I—I smell smoke!" Jon said from the front part of Kelvin's mount. The big bay shifted on his feet and whinnied, as though he had caught the scent.

"That would be Gaston Hays," Morvin said. "Looks as if they're trying to get us all. All of us with the Raiders."

"Sir," Kelvin said, speaking determinedly. "If it's all because of me—because of what happened in the park—if it is, sir, perhaps I should, uh . . ." He swallowed. What had he been about to say?

Morvin glared at him, seemingly seeing into his very soul. "It had to come, youngster. Prophecy or none, slain bullies or no. We planted right, and now we reap the expected crop."

"They won't have killed many," the younger Crumb said, kneeing his dappled gray to within touching distance. "The Raiders were expecting it. Most have been setting watches every night for weeks, and every time there's trouble in the park everyone sets a watch."

"It's an excuse to play cards and read books late a'night," said Jeffreys. "Few will have been taken by surprise."

"Fewer yet, if I have my way," Crumb muttered, and Kelvin knew he was thinking of Heln, who remained back at the cabin. Obviously astral spying could do a lot to help them oppose raids like this. If they could learn exactly where and when each raid was planned . . .

"We will round up those who have suffered," Morvin said. "Then we disband Crumb's Raiders. What we have now we'll call Knights. That's appropriate, isn't it? Kelvin Knight Hackleberry Knights. Knights of the Roundear."

Kelvin felt himself blushing again. So absurd of Crumb—and yet there *was* the gauntlet.

"What does he mean, Kel?" Jon whispered. She was back in boy guise, feeling most comfortable that way, especially after what had almost happened in the Boy Mart.

Kelvin poked his sister lightly and explained all with a brotherly word: "Quiet!"

"We'll have to hide out for now," Morvin said. Kelvin realized irrelevantly that the man's chronically red face probably spared him the embarrassment of blushing; who would know the difference? "But when we can, we'll gather men and arms, and then, come good or come evil, we'll fight. This time to win!"

"What will you use for money?" spoke up Jeffreys' wife.

"What we have. What we can scrape up. If only we had some gold. Say half a dragon's worth!"

"I know where we can get gold!" Jon said, and immediately Kelvin wished his sister's captor had left her with a gag.

"That so?" Morvin asked. He sounded interested rather than disbelieving.

"My sister's just a child," Kelvin started, and promptly got Jon's elbow poked into his stomach.

"Let 'er speak, Hackleberry," Crumb said.

Jon sneezed, lightly, brushing some hair back under her stockelcap, and said, "Our dragon—the one Kelvin slew—"

"He slew a dragon?"

"Yeah. With a tent pole, right through the eye socket and into the old brain pan. That's where I found the dragonberries."

"Gods!" Morvin exclaimed. "And here he pretended to be afeard of a couple of mere guardsmen!"

That was exactly the reaction Kelvin had feared. He knew he was no hero, and that the dragon business had been mostly luck and desperation, as had the gauntlet business. What would he be in for now?

"Well," Jon continued blithely, "we packed out the gold, but Cheeky Jack's got it. He's the bandit who kidnaped me for the auction. I heard his name when—"

"Impressed you for the auction," Crumb said. "They don't call it kidnaping, because there's supposed to be a law against that. You wouldn't, eh, know where old Cheeky is hiding, would you, youngster?"

"You bet I would!" Jon said enthusiastically, while Kelvin cringed. He knew that more heroic business was coming up.

They saw Mockery grazing behind the lean-to shack, from the rim of the canyon nearly a quarter of a mile away. Morvin suggested an arrow to stop the equine's mouth, but Jon quickly protested, and Kelvin hastily explained that the donkey was deaf as a stone and unlikely to sound an alarm.

"In that case we'll slip down that steep bank behind those trees and come in from the southeast," Morvin said, pointing with his sword tip.

"Jack will be home. That's his horse," Jon said, indicating the black stallion hobbled near the door.

"Um, now, that one could make a bit of noise if we don't come in just right," Morvin said. "Any ideas?"

"My idea is that he won't," said his son. "Donkeys are the ones who make the commotions. Horses can be passed."

"Then let's pass," Morvin said. He turned to Kelvin. "Son, you got that gauntlet on right?"

"I think so, sir." Why was Crumb calling *him* son, he wondered? What must the man's actual son think?

"Good. Because I'll let you do the killing. You need the experience."

Kelvin swallowed in private agony. He had known that this was part of what leadership entailed. If there was one thing he did not want to experience, it was killing. Not even villains who would steal gold and sell his sister for a plantation hand.

"All right. Go," Crumb said, dispensing orders as naturally as everyone around seemed to take them.

After a downhill run, a careful descent, and a cautious walk, there was a silent crawl. They were almost to the black horse when Jack emerged from the shack and saw them.

"Well!" he said, his hand going for his sword.

"Take him, Hackleberry," Morvin said.

Kelvin found himself on his feet, good sword in right hand, gauntlet on left.

"Baby boy's brother," said Jack, "come to get his head split." He never had learned of Jon's deception.

"Get him, Kel!" Jon cried, sounding bloodthirsty.

Kelvin trembled, though he knew (he kept telling himself) how this should end. Magic was after all magic, and the fight in the park had convinced him that the gauntlet was that. If only it was for the proper hand!

"You fight with bare sword hand, sonny?" Jack seemed amused. "What's the mitten for? You going to use it to wipe something? Your nose, maybe? Perhaps your blood?"

"I'm ready, mister," Kelvin said. It was as brave a statement as he could muster. Yet the highwayman's taunts were making it easier.

"Are, huh? Well, in that case—" The sword swished and darted like a striking serpent.

To be caught and flung away with one lightning move on the part of the gauntlet.

Jack blinked and opened and closed his mouth like a fish drowning in air. "What—what—?"

Kelvin raised the tip of his sword to the highwayman's throat. "If you have anything to say, say it fast." *Because if this takes any time, I'll lose my nerve!* he thought.

"I didn't mean—I only wanted—" The eyes of the bandit were wild as they darted from sword tip to the face of the elder Crumb, to Jon's face, to his own sword still quivering in the trunk of a tree.

"Don't kill him! Don't!" It was a large slovenly woman standing in the doorway of the cabin.

"Watch her, men," Mor Crumb snapped.

Kelvin realized that this was the man's wife. Could he kill a man with a wife and maybe a child? Even such a man as this? After all, Cheeky Jack hadn't really hurt Kelvin or Jon, he had just taken their gold and sold Jon to the Boy Mart. All that evil was now being undone.

"You're sorry, aren't you? And you won't do it again?" Kelvin hardly realized what he was saying. He only knew that the Crumbs were watching him and that Morvin was trying to get him blooded: to shed his first human lifeblood.

Jack shook. "I never saw anything like that move! You just grabbed my blade right out of my hand! You must be—"

"You better believe it," the elder Crumb said.

The highwayman raised his hands, eyes now on the gauntlet. "It hardly seems fair. Magic—"

"You prate of 'fair'?" Crumb demanded. "You who attack nearly unarmed and unskilled boys? You who prey on them with no other object than enriching yourself? You who prey on the weak without a sign of conscience?"

"Kill me, then," Jack said, regaining a bit of defiance. "Kill me and get it over with!"

"Kill him, youngster!" Morvin said.

"Kill him, Kel!" Jon's shrill voice echoed the elder man's.

"Yes," the younger Crumb said. "Strike!"

Kelvin closed his eyes, bunched his muscles, and tried to will the deed. But Jack, trembling there with his bare arms raised, was now just as helpless as anyone he had ever slain. Villain he might be, but now he was helpless before a sword, and to strike now would make Kelvin feel like a murderer.

"Murderer!" the woman screamed, echoing his thought.

"Shuddup!" Mor said to her. "Another word, woman, and—"

She was silent. Kelvin could imagine the gesture Mor must have made.

"Go on!" Crumb said. "I swear I won't do't this time! Ye's got to do for ye'self!"

Do for myself and kill, Kelvin thought. Kill an unarmed man before a woman who loves him. This is how a leader acts?

Abruptly he lowered the sword point. "I give him his life," Kelvin said.

"What!" Crumb shouted, outraged. "Hackleberry, may I ask why?"

Because this hero wasn't cut out for murder, he thought. But he knew Morvin would snort at that.

"Because," he said, and fought to find some acceptable reason. "Because he's only a—a man. Only a highwayman. Only one bandit."

"What? Are ye daft?"

"Only one highwayman," Kelvin said, his mind racing with all the velocity of a slug. What was he trying to think of? "But there are others," he continued with sudden inspiration. "Many others—as your son has told me."

"What are you blathering about?"

"He can spread the word. He and his wife. About us. What we did today. We won't allow boys to be pressed any longer. Or girls. We won't allow anyone to rob and to steal and to kill as he has done."

"We'll do it! We'll do it!" the woman said.

Morvin silenced her with a wave. He raised a hand and rubbed his chin. "Hackleberry, I do believe you make a little sense. Let him spread the word to his friends, and if he's up to his villainy again, we disarm him and we gut him!"

"Right, sir!" Kelvin cried, weak-kneed with relief.

"Gods, but I believe you'll make a leader yet! Me, I'd never have thought of that."

Not that it mattered, Kelvin thought, but he wasn't sure that even he himself had thought of it. He had wanted to avoid killing, and somehow an excuse had come. An acceptable excuse, he had realized, even while making it, but nothing *but* an excuse.

Maybe, just maybe, there was something to the prophecies.

But somehow he still wanted terribly to doubt.

12 /

DRAGONBERRIES

"BUT I CAN'T EVEN try it without more dragonberries," Heln Flambeau protested. "We lost the rest of them at the Girl Mart. I'm willing to try, if we can get the berries."

Kelvin had hoped she wouldn't be willing, but he couldn't say that. What would he do if she ate the berries again, and this time they poisoned her? Maybe it had been a fluke before.

"Then we'll just have to fetch more berries," Morvin Crumb said. "Actually, we'll need the rest of the scales from that dead dragon, just to be sure we have enough gold. Jon tells me you only got them from the topside of the beast, the easiest place to reach."

Damn his big-mouthed little sister! Now they would have to go back to the dragon, and Kelvin didn't like the notion of bracing even a dead dragon.

"We'll take a full crew, so we have the manpower to turn the critter over," Mor continued. "We'll get them all this time, to be sure! And Jon will get a whole basketful of the berries at the same time."

"Yeah!" Jon said enthusiastically.

"I should come along," Heln said.

"No!" Kelvin cried.

"But why not, Kelvin? The berries are for me."

"I don't want you in dragon country! There could be another dragon!"

"Well, yes, but—"

"Gods, Heln, the thought of anything happening to you—"

"Then you do care for me," she said as if it were a discovery.

"Of course I—" But then he got all tongue-tied.

"He's right, Flambeau," Mor said. "Dragon country is no place for women."

"Now, just a minute!" Jon protested. *"I'm—"*

"Or children," Mor added.

That didn't sit any better with her. "Now, I won't let you exclude me! I found those berries, I know where they are!"

"Right. I said you're coming. Let's get on with it." He turned away.

Jon jumped for joy. Then she paused. "But what does that make me? If not a woman or a child—"

"A Knight," the man said as he moved out toward the horses.

"Oh. Yes." Abruptly pleased again, she hurried after him.

Heln turned to Kelvin. "Please, be careful, hero," she said. "I don't know what I'd do without you."

Kelvin felt himself blushing yet again. Why was he so helpless in her presence? She gave him chances without end to say something meaningful, but he always muffed it. "Uh, yeah," he mumbled, true to form, and stumbled off to join the party.

There were thirty of them now: all the farmers and townsmen who had called themselves Crumb's Raiders and now called themselves Knights of the Roundear. Dressed in their brownberry shirts, greenbriar pantaloons, and lightweight summer stockelcaps, they looked like anything but an army. Smelling of natural fertilizing agents, they didn't even have the aroma of an army, Kelvin thought as he rode along with the Crumbs, Mor and Les, and with Jon sharing his big bay mare. What an outfit, and what a mission! They were going back to dragon country to find the rotting carcass and get *all* the scales and all the berries.

"You play this?" Les asked, his horse sidling nearer.

"Huh? Oh." Lester held out the mandajo they had found in Jack's shack.

"A little. It's mine."

"Play it. Now."

Kelvin hesitated but a second to test the tension on the strings. He knew he was not the best minstrel, indeed, not better than mediocre, but he enjoyed playing and singing and felt comfortable doing it, and there was much to be said for pleasure and comfort after the disruption and tension of recent events. He strummed a little, then burst into his favorite theme:

"Fortune come a-callin', but I did hide, ah-oo-ay. Fortune come a-callin', but I did hide, bloody saber at my side, ah-oo-ay, ah-oo-ay, ay."

Jon got out her new sling and a rock. As on their first trip into dragon country—such a short time ago, and yet seemingly so long ago—she seemed alert for squirbets. Or, Kelvin thought uncomfortably, something larger.

"You say it's along this bank?" Mor asked, leaning down from the extra-big plow horse he rode.

Kelvin nodded. They should be seeing buzvuls soon, he thought, looking at the overcast sky for the dark scavenger birds. Normally buzvuls were said to be an ill omen.

"There!" Les exclaimed, pointing. At the same time, the stench of the rotting carcass reached them on the breeze. Kelvin felt his nose wrinkle and his stomach lurch. Somehow the odor made him feel even less like a hero or leader; he had no nose and no stomach for it.

"Yup, that's dragon stink," Mor said with a smile as broad as his back. He might have been talking about a gentle perfume, or—Kelvin's gut tried to lurch again—a toothsome delicacy.

"I wonder—the buzvuls aren't landing. They're just hovering in the sky," Les Crumb remarked, glancing up.

"Who cares?" Mor replied. "The body's there, there's still scale to gather. That's what counts."

"There was another dragon," Jon said. "We saw its tracks. It looked as though they fought."

"Or mated?" Les asked.

"Much the same thing, with dragons," Mor said.

Kelvin put away the mandajo in his horse's saddlesack. It was, after all, his. As usual no one had seemed to pay much attention to his playing. Mor and Les had come to the same conclusion he had: that the two dragons had probably been mating. Did that mean that the other would return to this vicinity? Farm animals, he knew, could require several matings before it took, and it could be the same with dragons. What would happen if the female came back and found men crawling over the corpse of her mate? The thought made him shudder, but no one else seemed concerned. Were they fools, or was he a coward? Somehow he didn't really like either alternative.

As they rounded the river bend, the word went back and forth from man to man, and soon all were craning their necks, reddened or dark-tanned as the case might be, as they strained to see the sight. Soon everyone who had been behind moved up front, leaving the Hackleberries and the Crumbs and Keith Sanders, the rabble-rouser from the park, and burly, graying Gaston Hayes.

Kelvin felt himself frowning. Something wasn't exactly right, but he couldn't quite pin it down.

"What is it, bold brother mine?" Jon asked brightly. As often was the case, Jon seemed to sense her brother's sensing.

Then he realized what it was. "The scales—they were scattered about like petals from flowers. I just had a glimpse, but—we didn't leave them like that. We loaded all we could onto Mockery, and stacked the rest neatly near the body. Wasn't that so, Jon?"

Her mouth grew tight. "Yeah."

"The other dragon!" Kelvin cried, his forebodings now assuming full force. "It's been here—feeding."

"You sure?" Morvin barked.

"The scales have been moved!"

"Maybe Jack?"

"He didn't know where the dragon was," Jon said.

"He could've smelled it," Mor pointed out.

"Then why would he scatter the scales instead of taking them?" Les asked. "Dad, I think—"

Abruptly he broke off, for a very live dragon's snout had appeared over the side of the dead one. Blood-stained jaws gaped, gobbets of spoiling flesh hung on the terrible teeth. The thing rose up on its front legs and issued a long and penetrating hiss. Its bloodred eyes seemed to fasten on them instantly.

"Gods!" Crumb muttered. If he hadn't taken the notion of a companion-dragon seriously before, he certainly did now.

"Run for your lives!" someone cried. It was, Kelvin realized a moment later, Keith Sanders. It seemed that the man was just as proficient at urging rabble to flee as urging it to fight.

"No! Stand and fight!" Lester called. His sword came out of its scabbard with the whisper of polished steel being bared for action. No coward, he!

The dragon gave a frightful snort that raised dust from the road's surface. It came charging, hard.

Men and horses scattered. Men shouted. Horses squealed. Men and horses screamed together as the huge jaws snapped, again and again. If there was one thing a dragon preferred to a rotting carcass, it was live meat. It also liked fighting better than sleeping. This dragon was having a ball.

The tail lashed, like a big, thick rawhide whip, knocking down horses and flinging off riders. The jaws crunched indiscriminately on men and animals. Blood and other bodily substances stained nearby rocks and trees and roadway. The dragon wasn't trying to feed, just to disable, so that the maximum amount of prey could be rendered helpless before fleeing. Then the feeding would be done at leisure.

"No! No! No! We've got to stand!" Lester called. "United, organized, disciplined—"

He was of course correct, and his military training helped him. But his words had all the effect of the proverbial cry down a dry well. Men, so eager to do battle earlier in the day, now fell over themselves and collided with one another following Keith Sanders' pusillanimous advice.

In that moment Kelvin realized that most men were just as cowardly as he knew himself to be. The difference between them was that he anticipated the things he feared, while others ignored them until it was too late. That didn't make him feel much better, but he did think his way was less foolish.

Meanwhile, the dragon was having a field day with cowards and bold men alike; it didn't care one way or the other about the social qualities of its prey.

Gaston Hayes brushed back gray hair from his face and raised his ancient crossbow. He aimed into the dust of the dragon's activity; his rheumy eyes squinted, and he squeezed the trigger.

The bolt went *thunk*. It had not even struck a dragon scale, but had lodged in a tree instead.

"Damn ye for cowards!" Morvin Crumb exclaimed angrily, addressing the running Knights. He moved out of the way of a horseman who seemed blind to his presence and all else but the way of escape. He adjusted the lance he carried. He had a polished, never-used lance that he had brought just for this unlikely situation.

Mor kneed his big plow horse out to meet the dragon. The lance lowered, aimed roughly at the creature's head. The whites of the horse's eyes showed, but he leaped a plow horse's ungainly leap at his master's urging. The dragon, who had been coming fast, wriggling almost comically from side to side, now put on its brakes. Its front feet locked and skidded. Its broad tail swished as it swung around and down, hard.

The tail caught Morvin Crumb across his chest. It struck the mailed vest he wore with a loud metallic clank. Crumb, big man that he was, went spinning like a child's tantrum-tossed toy. He lit in some nettlebushes, wind gone and senses fled, on his broad back.

So much, Kelvin thought fleetingly, for courage.

"Help him," Les urged Kelvin. "If we go in fast, maybe we can save him!"

"Yeah!" said Jon.

Looking at his sister's eager young face, Kelvin did what he felt he had to, and pushed Jon off their horse.

"What are you doing!" Jon protested. But she knew. What he was doing was putting little sister out of the way of danger—or as nearly out of danger as was possible at the moment. This act infuriated her, but it was necessary.

He and Lester charged at the side of the dragon. Just as they reached it, its enormous head snapped around.

Les delivered a quick, slapping sword low to the snout, the monster's eyes being far out of reach. The creature's great clawed forefoot rose and swept him almost casually from his mount. Les flew, and lit down in the bushes not far from his father.

Kelvin felt his gauntlet pull the horse's reins. The animal responded by halting abruptly. Kelvin saved himself from going over the horse's head by a sudden grab at the bay's tossing mane. His sword slipped from his fingers, slid by the horse's neck without cutting, and clanked harmlessly on the roadway. Desperately he tried shifting his weight to keep his seat. Hero, indeed! He could hardly even keep his seat!

Morvin was up now. Shaking his big head, he looked for the lance.

Kelvin found it, or rather his left hand did. The gauntlet wrenched his shoulder, reaching he knew not for what. He saw the ground come up at him and he had to fling out both hands to avoid striking his head. He lit with a thump that at another time might have brought forth a cry of agony. Clouds of choking, gray road dust rose around him. His left hand fought him, finally closing on a smooth shaft.

Kelvin forced himself to his feet, the shaft of the lance smooth in his right hand and gripped clumsily and higher up by his left. He felt dizzy. Because of the dust he could see neither horse nor dragon.

A great chilling hiss froze him. Terrible, swordlike teeth flashed directly overhead. Hot and carrion-scented air blew sickeningly into his face.

Glunk!

He felt the shaft driven into the ground. His left arm remained steady as he tried but failed to retain his balance.

Dust swirled. Stench overpowered. Saliva and blood dripped down on his face. The ground shook, heaved, and rocked. A great hiss was followed by a bubbling noise, which in turn was followed by a loud, gusty, fading sigh.

Barely conscious, Kelvin saw figures emerge from the settling dust. Mor and Les Crumb came to stand over him. Jon, coming up behind, looked as if she were crying.

"Ye did it again, son," Morvin said.

"Huh?" What a brilliant retort, the cynical back of his mind remarked.

"Look, lad!"

Kelvin struggled to his elbow.

He was lying, he discovered, in a messy bubble of thick, sticky, steaming dragon blood.

While above him, staring with a single fading eye, held upright by the lance that impaled its mate and entered the hidden recesses behind the socket, swayed the dead, nightmarish head of the once unconquerable dragon.

13 /

THE FLAW

"So this is the Kingdom of Throod," said Kelvin, sniffing the spicy smell of orlemon cakes that reached them from the bee-hive-shaped ovens. It was as hilly as Rud, but the trees and the crops were different, the trees running much to citrus.

"Good enough for me," Jon said from Mockery's back. She wiped some limfruit juice from her mouth, licked the rind, and then tossed the rind at a barking wolfox's pointed face. The wolfox promptly disappeared into the thicket of hazbert brush.

"You've got some treats in store," Lester Crumb said, riding up to their left. "I was here for nearly a month, once. Prettiest girls in the Seven Kingdoms."

"Girls, phooey!" Jon said.

Little sister, Kelvin thought, would soon enough be changing her attitude, once she got into a situation where boys behaved decently toward girls. Of course they always had behaved well toward certain girls. He wondered what Maybell Winterjohn, the prettiest and freckledest girl in school, had done since he left. If things had been different . . . but there had been no choice. But of course she would never have been interested in a roundear.

"A rudna for your thoughts," Heln murmured.

Kelvin jumped. He hadn't seen her ride up beside Jon. "I, uh, um, that is—"

"Why do you feel you have to blush every time the subject of women comes up?" she asked.

Heln, of course, was not turned off by round ears. That made her so obviously the girl for him that he wondered why he was unable to believe it. He blushed harder.

"I was only teasing you, Kel," she said. "I know it's hard for you to adjust to being a hero, just the way it's hard for me to live with the fact that I got—" But now she choked off.

"N-no difference!" he exclaimed.

"I think that's what I like about you—besides your burning red round ears—that you represent no threat to me," she continued after a pause. "You aren't like those beasts. You wouldn't ever—"

"Never!" he agreed fervently.

"Because I guess you know that it's likely to be a long time before I can —that is—you know."

And probably just as long a time for him. She had drawn a nice analogy, between his supposed heroism and her degradation. Both of them had had to do things for which they had been totally unprepared, and it remained difficult to adjust to the new realities. They were indeed well matched, in devious as well as the obvious ways.

He looked at her, and she smiled at him, and suddenly he wished he could just take her in his arms and do all the things with her that made him blush to think about but that he never had the nerve to take seriously. He felt his blush intensifying yet more. But then he saw that she was blushing, too, and that helped a great deal.

"Say—" Jon started.

"Quiet!" Kelvin and Heln said together.

"I hope I never get like that," Jon said, and rode on ahead, affronted.

"I hope she *does*!" Kelvin said.

"She's ready now—when she meets the right boy."

"Never!" Jon called back.

A blue and white bird different from any in Rud flew over, calling from its long beak: "Cau-sal-i-ty! Cau-sal-i-ty!" At least that was what it sounded like to Kelvin. That could only be the creature known as the primary bird. Rud's bluebins and robjays were so much more sensible; at home birds sounded like birds, not aged philosophers.

The road ran downhill, past a stone cairn dedicated to the memory of Throod's soldiery who had perished in the two-hundred-year-old war with Rud. It was discomfiting to imagine the shades of those soldiers out there on the grass in front of the cairn. What would they think, Kelvin mused, of the two Crumbs and two Hackleberries and one Flambeau come to their home-land for mercenaries to fight in a war that hadn't happened yet? Probably they would approve; after all, soldiers were soldiers. How many had ever fought in the name of a cause so noble or for pay so magnificent? Yes, they would have to approve.

Mockery made his mockery sound, and Lester looked over at him, and then at his father. Kelvin knew what the latter was thinking. They should have taken more men. With Mockery and the one pack horse loaded with scale, they could be in danger from highwaymen. But Throod for some strange reason was far more law-abiding than its neighboring kingdoms, especially Rud.

"Whoa," called Morvin suddenly.

They drew their mounts to a stop as the big man dismounted and crossed the road to a rough, wooden fence. He crossed the fence into a field filled with trellises supporting large yellow clusters of curapes. He spoke briefly to the farmer dressed in creaseless brownskins, paid him a full scale, and came back with his arms loaded. Kelvin took the fruit handed to him and popped and squirted the sweet tart ovoids into his mouth. Paradise, he thought, paradise. The most luscious fruit growing anywhere in the Seven Kingdoms, and yet the boys of Throod took up soldiering for the highest bidders in other lands. Strange, but then maybe Rud would look like paradise to someone who didn't know. Possibly the government here was not much different from Rud's, though all he knew was that they voted for officials and changed officials frequently. In civics class he had heard Throod's government described as "one weak step above anarchy." He hadn't understood that exactly, but then it had seemed probable that he would never need to.

"Recruitment House ahead," said Mor, wiping yellow juice from his mouth and pointing. "We'll order our men and supplies, show that we've got gold to pay for them, and then head back."

"By way of The Flaw," Lester said, verbally capitalizing. "Visitors have to see The Flaw while they're in Throod. Wouldn't be right if they didn't."

Mor made no reply other than a grunt as they rode on to the large, unadorned structure that was not unlike a barracks.

"I do hope Captain Mackay will be here as agreed," Mor said, worried. "He's supposed to have the men—experienced warriors *and* experienced officers—ready for us. But there's a saying that Throod mercenaries, though reliable, do get into scrapes. I remember last time I was here, back in the big conflict, when a third of the men were unavailable. Seems some of them had started a mercenaries' union to fix rates, and some liked the idea and some didn't. So add to the other reasons we lost and the Queen won the fact that we didn't get the right men."

Kelvin thought that if he had been a mercenary he would have wanted a union to fix rates. But then he hadn't been a paid soldier, wasn't now, and never would be. The mercenary's life of endless marches and battles until wounded too badly to function or continuing until either slain or too old to fight had no appeal. Better a farmer's life, or even the life of a tradesman.

They entered the door of Recruitment House and stood looking around at the scant furnishings and the dozen or so men. No one moved or spoke for a moment, and then the big, gray-haired man with one arm stood up from his table in the corner. He held out his hand, gray eyes meeting Morvin's blue.

"Morvin Crumb. I'm Captain Mackay. Welcome to Recruitment House and the Kingdom of Throod."

Morvin merely glanced at the empty sleeve. Good officers, after all, were traditionally warriors who had lost something in a fight. There were officers with patches over eyes, or with wooden stumps for legs, or misshapen shoulders, or deformed backs. Experience was what counted, and that with the training and leading of more able men to fight.

"You know why we've come," Morvin said. "This here"—he indicated Kelvin with a thumb—"is the Roundear. Kelvin, take off your cap."

Hesitantly, Kelvin reached up and pulled the head-covering off his straw-colored hair. He didn't like being placed on display like this, but he knew it was necessary. Jon and Heln were both now wearing stockelcaps, for different reasons, and he was glad of that.

"Glad to meet you, Roundear," Captain Mackay said, gripping his hand. It was a rough hand callused by years of sword wielding and horse handling. It was a large hand, which all but engulfed his.

"I'm not certain I'm the right roundear," Kelvin confessed. "But I do have this gauntlet I found, and it's evidently the one of prophecy. With it on, I just can't lose in a sword fight."

"And the gauntlet great shall the tyrant take. The magician bad, by the gauntlet had," quoted the Throodian. "Yes, one of the interesting prophecies, clumsy as their wording tends to be. Don't worry about whether you're the one or not, son. As long as you've got the gauntlet and people *think* you're the one, it helps. What really counts of course is something else— military tactics and men trained to carry them out. How are you on tactics?"

"I, uh—"

"Don't worry. You'll learn. And you'll have good officers, I'll see to that. Well, sit down and we'll make our plans."

Kelvin took the proffered chair, as did the rest of the party. It seemed to him that though he was supposed to be the hero of the prophecy, he did little but let others move him around. Still, it was sensible to sit here in this quiet place and make plans. That was true even if he had little to do with making them.

"We brought scale to get things started," Morvin said, waving away the amber bottle the captain silently indicated. "We'll need everything—swords, lances, shields, body armor, war-horses, the works."

"I understand," the captain said, pouring himself a glass and not offering the refreshment to Kelvin or Lester or Jon or Heln. "You've come to the right place. But the terms—"

"When we win, each man gets a choice of citizenship and land, or a mercenary's top wages plus bonus."

"And if the fighting lasts and the men need gold to send to their families?"

"More scale. There are more dragons where the last two came from."

"Last two? You went on a hunting expedition into dragon country?"

Morvin nodded. "We did that. But I've got to tell you, this roundear here slew both of them."

The gray eyebrows raised. Kelvin felt the steely eyes going over him. "You don't look like a warrior," he said.

"I'm not," Kelvin said. "But the prophecy and the gauntlet—they made the difference."

"Tell me how."

Kelvin took a deep breath. He had told the tale so many times in recent days that it was almost like reciting a piece. "When Jon, my younger sibling here, and I arrived in dragon country the first time, we were all on our own. Just Jon and me and the deaf donkey outside. I had a sword, but it was an old sword. Jon's the best with a sling, of anyone I've seen. When Jon saw the dragon, Jon thought it dead, and—" On and on with the familiar tale.

Captain Mackay listened intently. His eyes turned to fix on Jon, and it was evident that he understood her nature quickly enough, but he gave no overt indication. He was the kind of soldier who could keep a secret. Silently he motioned to the grizzled officers drinking at the other tables. They rose and came across the room. All stood listening raptly, now and then one or another breaking his silence with a brief and appropriate curse.

"And I never even knew until I regained consciousness," Kelvin concluded. "There he was, skewered right through the eye, just as the first had been skewered by the tent pole."

"Wizard's Teeth!" cried a bearded man with one ear missing and an ugly scar across his cheek. "That was some adventure! You're either the Roundear of Prophecy or the luckiest roundear in any of the Seven Kingdoms!"

"Yes, I guess that's so," Kelvin said. "But I don't *feel* special, and without the gauntlet—"

"You'll do just fine until another contender comes along," the captain said. "Personally I don't think anyone could be that lucky. It has to be the prophecy."

"I agree with you," Morvin said. "He just don't realize what he is yet."

"He's learning, though!" Jon piped up.

Kelvin gave his sister his customary light kick. His sister, experienced in his ways, drew her foot back under the table, and the captain gave a slight jerk as the kick connected.

But the grim oldster was smiling. "I, too, had a sibling once, Roundear. And whether this one be your blood sibling or your friend sibling, I know what prompted that kick."

"Blood sibling," Kelvin said. "Our father was a roundear, our mother a pointear, so the chances were even, and that's the way it happened: one of each. Then our father was killed, and our mother remarried."

"Who was your father?"

"He called himself John Knight. He was from Earth."

"I know of him."

"You do?" Jon exclaimed eagerly.

"That is to say, I heard of him. That was all." But by the way his jaw tightened, Kelvin realized that the man knew more than he was telling. Was it something bad? It couldn't be! Yet—

"About our business," Morvin suggested.

"Eh," the captain agreed, switching his attention. "The business will be concluded satisfactorily. I know my trade, Crumb."

"Mor. Mor Crumb."

"Mor."

"Yes, I'm sure you do." Morvin stood up. "If it's agreed, then, two thousand men and at least thirty good officers. With your men and our men when our men get trained—"

"It will be a battle," the captain said. "That Queen of yours—I'm not sure we have any edge. We could take 'em in regular combat, but they've got a magician that's as slippery as a greased eelshark, and twice as mean. So don't be thinking this is any pushover."

"We have a secret weapon," Mor said.

"Eh? Where?"

"I can't tell you that in front of your men."

The captain nodded. "You aren't bluffing?"

"No."

"Then tell me when you're ready. If it's enough to make up for the edge their magic gives them—"

"It may be."

"Then I trust we'll have a satisfactory outcome. I'll have the men and supplies ready in half a day. Come back here and we'll all ride together for Rud."

"Agreed," Morvin said.

"Then why don't you take these young folk sightseeing? Take them to see The Flaw."

"I had it in mind," Morvin agreed. "Come, Knights."

They trooped out. Kelvin, however, felt less than satisfactory. "You know we haven't tried using Heln for spying yet," he said. "It may not work."

"And then again, it may," the ruddy man responded. "If we can spy out their plans ahead of time, we can lick them every time. I'd call that a good edge."

"Still—" Kelvin said.

Heln put a fine fair hand on his arm. "It will be all right, Kel," she said. "Those berries didn't hurt me before, and now we have plenty of them. I'm sure I can do what needs to be done."

Kelvin was silent, still not liking the risk either to her or to their effort if this ploy failed. But again, what choice was there? He seemed to be fated to participate in things he didn't like or trust, again and again. Was this a hero's lot?

"The Flaw," Jon asked brightly. "It's near here?"

"Very near," Mor said.

"It's just a big old crack without a bottom," Jon said, giving Mockery's neck a pat as they walked past. "Who wants to see that?"

"You do," Lester said. "And so does your brother. Believe me, it's something you're never going to forget."

Jon snapped a rock from her sling into a tall oaple tree, disturbing a squirbet who was packing off a sugary nut high amid the branches. It was a for-fun shot, Kelvin knew, and not one that Jon intended to score.

"Schoolmaster used to tell us that when he brought out the strap," Jon said. "And you know, he was right: I never forgot. But maybe you're right. Maybe a dumb old hole in the ground is worth seeing."

"It's behind that high board fence over there," Mor said. "It's got slits you can see through. You can poke an arm and your head through if you've a mind to, but there's no sense in that. I've heard of women who've been jilted by soldiers dropping their engagement rings down there. Waste of good metal and precious stones."

In a moment they were at the barrier, some distance from others who had come to see The Flaw. Like the others, they approached the nearest openings in the fence. The sawn-out viewing place was chest-high on Morvin and Les, head-high on Kelvin, and chin-high on Jon. Heln was just the right height for it. Hesitantly and just a bit fearfully, on Kelvin's part, they looked.

Down, down at twinkling stars set amid velvety blackness. Now and then a bright object such as was seen in the night streaked through the black, trailing a long tail: a luminous tadpole in a froogpond of space.

Kelvin shifted his feet, half fearful that the solid ground would disappear beneath them. Then he looked over at open-mouthed Jon and Heln, and the big eyes of Mor and Les.

"The metaphysicians say it's a tear or a rip in the physical universe," Les said. "It's said that two universes, two realities, are here joined; that one bleeds or oozes into the other."

"And sometimes something or some*one* manages to cross," Heln murmured. "Like my mother—"

"Or my father," Kelvin finished, awed.

If the mood touched Jon, she flung it off. "I'm going to get a star," she said briskly. She hurled. The rock flew over the barrier and plummeted. A quick flash and it was gone.

"Didn't lead it enough," Jon said, and tried again. Again the flash in the adjoining starfield.

"You really think you'll hit a star?" Les asked, sounding amused.

"I will if I keep trying," Jon said.

"Not a star, Jon. They're too big and too distant. You haven't a chance."

"You sound like a schoolmaster," Jon said.

"I might have been," Les said. Then, giving Kelvin a nudge he felt in his back, he pointed to two dark-haired tourist girls a short distance away. "I bet those two are from the Kingdom of Aratex," he said. "Let's go talk to them."

Heln's hand clamped firmly on Kelvin's hand. She didn't say a word, but he received the message. "Some other time, maybe," he said.

Morvin laughed. "Maybe never, eh, son?"

But Kelvin didn't reply. He was too conscious of Heln's hand on his. He would be satisfied, he realized, if she never released it. But he couldn't say so. Maybe this was another flaw in his character—one that faintly echoed the amazing Flaw they had just experienced.

14 /

MESSAGES

"Now, I want," Morvin Crumb said, leaning over Kelvin at the writing table, "for this to be just right. Read what you've written."

Kelvin looked at Jon and Lester and the odd dozen or so Knights crowded around their outdoor table. He cleared his throat and read.

"To Her Imperial Majesty, Queen Zoanna of Rud. Your Majesty: Whereas you have seized power without popular mandate, and whereas your rule has become oppressive in the extreme, I, Kelvin Knight Hackleberry of Rud, the Roundear of Prophecy, call upon you to abdicate the throne and restore to it your rightful consort, King Rufurt, should he live, or someone of the people's choice, should Rufurt be presently slain or incapacitated beyond the ability to rule. You have seven days from the receipt of this message to announce your abdication. Should you not abdicate within that time, the Knights of the Roundear shall attack with all their magic-supported strength and fury, seize the imperial palace, and force your abdication, if need be, by sword point."

Morvin frowned. "It seems right, but—"

"It should be more insulting," Jon said. "Say, perhaps, 'Your Imperial Majesty, Usurper, Hag, and Meanie.' "

Les laughed, but his father seemed to consider it. "Perhaps," the elder said, "usurper might fit . . ."

"But we want her to agree!" Kelvin protested.

"Hmm, quite right. She won't, of course, but—oh, hang it, Hackleberry, just write 'In the Name of Freedom, I am.' "

"In the Name of Freedom, I am," Kelvin said, writing.

"There. Hold it. You got the wax ready, Les?"

"I have, Father."

"Then affix his signature."

Lester leaned over and deposited a drop of wax on the paper.

"No, no, not *there,* you idiot! Quick, scrape that off."

Lester scraped, using a knife blade. The wax came off cleanly.

"There, above where the wax was, write 'Kelvin Hackleberry, Roundear of Prophecy.' "

Kelvin did so, feeling uncomfortable about the prophecy part.

"Now date it. Anybody got the date?"

"It's June twenty-first of twenty twenty-four," Lester said.

Kelvin marked the date.

"Now fold in past the middle and overlap the edge."

Kelvin followed instructions.

"Now, Lester. Your wax."

Lester dripped wax, in a round, big circle. The wax made a small puddle across the overlapping edges.

Lester blew on it.

"Now, Hackleberry, your ear," Morvin ordered.

"You want me to—"

"Just *do* it, Hackleberry!"

With a sigh, Kelvin turned his head sideways and pressed his right ear in the wax.

"My, that looks like fun," Jon remarked.

"Hold it, hold it, hold it," Morvin snapped as Kelvin showed signs of bolting upright. "It has to set. All right, now up, carefully."

Kelvin raised his head. He looked at the paper. The impression was that of a round ear, more or less. That had been Morvin's idea, as had almost everything. He touched his ear. How smooth it now felt!

He glanced across the landscape, to the cabin where Heln was fixing food. He wished he could go feel *her* round and smooth ears, not to mention her round and smooth—

"Messenger!" Morvin shouted.

One of the Knights was almost instantly at his shoulder. Kelvin recognized him as one whose farm had been burned.

Morvin put the document in a message tube and capped it. "Deliver this to the imperial palace. Just call out, 'A message for the Queen,' and toss it to the gateman. Then ride out—fast."

"Aye, sir," said the Knight, giving them a faintly impudent smile. "I'm on my way."

As he left, Morvin remarked, "We have to get more discipline. Now, about these posters and handbills . . ."

All afternoon they were putting them up. They would ride to the edge of a village, find a likely tree, and while one of them kept a lookout for the

Queen's minions, the other nailed poster to tree. All the posters read the same, and by now Kelvin, if not Jon, was thoroughly sick of them.

Each poster said:

ATTENTION: A new day is coming and those who would help bring it about are invited to join with us in our demand that Queen Zoanna abdicate. Sign the petition and deposit it with your local representative Knight; he will tell you how you can help further by resisting oppression locally or by joining our ranks. We are all free people and will not long continue to suffer tyranny. Right and Prophecy is on our side!

(*signed*) Knights of the Roundear

Kelvin sighed as he nailed up another one. He was growing so tired! No one had told him that revolution would have so much tedious labor.

The distribution of handbills was hard work that soon became a bore. After the posters came the handbills, freely thrown from horses and placed also in many reaching hands:

PEOPLE OF RUD: Should the Queen not abdicate her position by the end of this week, we are at war. To join the right side, the winning side, see your local recruiter. Give any snooping soldiery short shrift or the long shaft, as appropriate. Join now, today, while you still can.

Knights of the Roundear

Some job for a hero, Kelvin thought, tossing the last of the flyers to a boy he almost recognized. And now, back home to the tent, and then another day of doing Crumb's bidding.

Snap! Snap! Snap! Plunk! Plunk! Plunk!

They were getting a little better, Kelvin thought, as he watched the arrows hit the scarecrow targets the mercenaries had set up. Most farmers, and some townsmen, did after all hunt for game. But in a battle, with other men for targets? He shivered, just at the thought of it.

"You're sure it's safe?" Morvin Crumb demanded. "We've tested those berries on animals, and you know every one of them died. I can't see that the shape of the ear should make that much of a difference."

"It's not just the shape of the ear," Heln said. "It's the Earthly ancestry. Those of us with round ears must be breeding true to our heritage, so are not affected the same way as the natives are. Anyway, I survived it before."

"Could be a fluke," Mor said.

"I'll just take one berry this time," she promised. "If I make it to astral separation, I'll do something simple, like—"

"I don't trust this either," Kelvin said. "To gamble on poison—"

"Like visiting my folks—and yours," she continued brightly. "To be sure they're all right."

Kelvin's protests dried up. Of course he wanted to know that his folks were all right! So, reluctantly, he acceded to the experiment. After all, they did need to know whether it worked reliably.

Heln solemnly consumed a single berry, from the horde they had harvested from the dragon's garden. Again Kelvin wondered why a dragon should have tended it so carefully. Of course the ability to separate astrally could be an immense advantage—but were dragons smart enough to realize that? Or did they simply like the feeling of astral travel? Maybe that was it; they did for recreation what they could have done for phenomenal power over their environment—because they were stupid creatures. A man would never be that foolish!

Or would he? Kelvin thought about some of the people he knew, and remained disquieted.

Heln sank into sleep. Then she stopped breathing. "She's dying!" Kelvin cried, horrified. He leaped toward her, though there really wasn't anything he could do.

"No, don't touch her!" Jon said. "She was like that before. It's the astral separation!"

"But she's not even—"

"That's the way it is. She looks dead, but she's not, quite. When her spirit returns, she'll recover. I'm sure. I think."

With that note of confidence, Kelvin had to be satisfied.

After an hour there was a tremor at Heln's breast. She was recovering!

Soon she was able to talk. "I did it!" she said. "I traveled to my folks, and they're all right. Then to yours, and they're all right. Only—"

"Only they need gold to cover the taxes," Kelvin said, with a dark glance at Morvin Crumb.

"No, they aren't being bothered about that. But I saw guardsmen camped around their farm. Not doing anything, just watching. What does that mean?"

Morvin slapped his thigh. "It means confirmation!" he exclaimed. "Just as I suspected! Your folks and their farm are a trap for you, Kelvin! They're waiting for you to visit home; then they'll nab you. That's why I didn't want you to go, not even to take them money they might need. The Queen's guards won't bother your folks as long as they remain bait—but you can't go back there."

Kelvin felt weak in the knees. The big man had been right all along, saving him from a horrendous mistake!

"I didn't know how much time I had," Heln continued. "So I looked around, and I found I could orient on people who were thinking of you, Kelvin. There were a lot of them, all friendly, but one was very unfriendly. So I went to that one, and it was Zatanas."

"Zatanas!" Morvin exclaimed. "The Queen's evil sorcerer!"

"Yes. He was talking with the dwarf, the one who bought Jon—"

"What did he say?" Morvin asked, almost drooling in his excitement.

"Something about how he had brought the roundears here—"

"*He* did it?" Kelvin asked, amazed.

"And something about lizards. Then my time ended, and my spirit was hauled back to my body. I'm sorry I couldn't have stayed a little longer. Maybe I should have eaten two berries . . ."

Then, exhausted, she slept again, but this time her breathing did not stop. It seemed to Kelvin that one berry had been quite risky enough; probably the new ones were more potent than the ones Jon had carried around squashed in her pocket, and then soaked in her mouth. Three full-strength dragonberries might very well have killed Heln!

Morvin looked at Kelvin. "That was a message we didn't expect!" the big man said. "Why should Zatanas make a claim like that? About bringing the roundears here?"

"And what does he want with lizards?" Kelvin added.

"It's beyond me! I only hope we don't find out the hard way!"

Heln slept the rest of that day, and on into the night. Obviously astral separation took a lot from her! Kelvin sat beside her for hours, finally working up the courage to take her hand. What a lot of information she had gathered, in that one brief hour of astral travel! But he remained worried about its effect on her health.

Mainly, though, he just liked holding her hand.

15 /

ZATANAS

THE LABORATORY WHERE ZATANAS performed his miracles was a veritable rat's nest of stacked caldrons, rolled-up pentagrams and other magical charts, old books of spells and sciences, and other traditional tools of the trade. The place smelled of a thousand herbs, intermixed with the scent of burned incense and charred bones. In the center of the room an owlhawk perched on a human skull held upright by a dagger stuck in the remaining neck vertebra. Another skull had been sawn lengthwise, one-half serving as an incense burner, the other as a receptable for some vile-smelling unguent. Light streamed in from the high windows, and yet the place was dark, as though the interior drank the light, or forbade its passage.

Zatanas, dark of visage, long of face and nose and claw, hummed contentedly to himself as he sat at a table and munched the simple repast that Queeto, his dwarf, had set out for him. Unlike Queeto, he still sometimes ate when the physical act of eating pleased him, as it did now. The meat tasted like dragon, he thought, though actually it was axoglatter, a particularly ugly lizard with a green skin that in the right light shone like the scales of a dragon.

"A little less strong and a little more rancid," Zatanas said, musing as much to himself as to the hovering dwarf.

"What, Master?"

Zatanas belched loudly and reached for the flagon of good orange wine on his table. The wine was specially spiced, as was most of the magician's fare. A little dried blood from the right sources added greatly to taste.

"I said," Zatanas said, "that the meat is aged to perfection. A little less aging and it would be tough. A little more and it would be leather."

"Thank you, Master," the dwarf said, widening his already wide mouth. He frequently responded like that, no matter what Zatanas said. That was one of his more endearing traits, and made it slightly harder to punish him properly when he erred. Zatanas had been furious at Queeto's recent loss of his purchase at the Girl Mart, but had elected for the time being to withhold action. When Queeto began to think of becoming impudent, then Zatanas would punish him for that error, restoring appropriate equilibrium to their relationship. The dwarf, knowing this, was meanwhile being extremely well behaved, as servile as he had ever been. That was good.

However, this matter of the abduction of the girl could not remain unattended. He would have to locate the culprits and deal with them in a manner that would discourage any repetitions. That meant that simple extinction was not enough; their deaths had to be public and horrible beyond any reasonable expectation. He knew their identities, of course; that wasn't the problem. The problem was bringing them down in precisely the right manner, an object lesson for all time in all the land.

First, however, he had to get hold of them. As long as they remained hidden in the wilderness, moving constantly about, he was unable to pin them down.

So Zatanas watched, and waited, unwilling to act until he could accomplish his full purpose in his own exacting way. He had patience; his ire, once incited, never cooled. Sooner or later the stupid round-eared boy would seek to visit his home farm, and walk into the trap, and the idiotic would-be revolutionist Crumb would try to rescue him, and then—ah, then it might begin.

Meanwhile, he had a rebellion to quell. He trusted that Crumb would not risk either himself or the roundear boy in a direct conflict. That was important, because he didn't want anything to happen to either, prematurely. It wouldn't make much of an impression if they both died coincidentally in battle.

Zatanas picked daintily at a foreleg with its three toes still attached and crunchy. "I have decided to hold a conference with my daughter the Queen."

"Will I attend, Master?"

"No. She doesn't wish for you to be in her sight."

Queeto frowned, his toad mouth and swine eyes making a face. "Why, Master?"

"Because you frighten her. She still thinks you're a demon from another world. I don't see any reason to enlighten her, do you?"

Queeto grinned more broadly than ever. He, as Zatanas well knew, liked being feared by royalty. In fact, he liked being feared by anyone.

"You tell her about the lizards, Master?"

Zatanas tossed the leg bone to the owlhawk. The owlhawk caught it in its strong beak with a snap and immediately set to pulverizing it. Zatanas swallowed more wine.

"Just what do you think you know about the lizards?"

The dwarf answered promptly, almost as though rehearsed: "That they are little brothers to the dragons, Master."

"Right. Most fortunately."

Zatanas rose and crossed the dimly lit room to the worktable. On it he had set up and molded hills and valleys of clay and dirt and sand. It was a perfect miniature landscape of the terrain for leagues about the castle. A carved palace occupied the same position in the miniature landscape as the castle they were in did the real landscape. There were miniature houses and even a miniature river that had to be continuously fed from a small spigot and a bucket behind the scene of distant hills and houses. All in order, a work of incredible delicacy that had taken many pains and much time.

"You see, Queeto, bringing roundears to this world was a mistake on my part."

"*You*, Master?" Queeto was properly incredulous that Zatanas could make any mistake, let alone admit to it, even in complete privacy.

"Yes, a possibly serious mistake," Zatanas continued, enjoying the effect on his minion. "You might call it a grotesque flaw." He smiled, appreciating a private joke. "I reckoned not with Mouvar and the force of his prophecies. But no matter," he said, waving the dwarf's concern away. "It's a mistake that my daughter and I will soon rectify."

"With lizards, Master?"

"With dragons, small friend. In this very place."

Queeto looked at him, baffled. "You and the Queen, your daughter— here?"

Zatanas rubbed at a speck of lizard dung on the tabletop. "She out there. You and I in here."

"Ah."

Just as if he understood. Remarkable animal, this. Almost as remarkable as dragons. Not quite as large, not quite as stupid.

"Queeto, little brother, remember what I told you about the magic that can be performed with miniatures?"

"Yes, Master. The doll that looks like an enemy and that you break so that the enemy breaks."

"Exactly. Well, here we have a small copy of the land and the palace and the houses and the river. Over there"—he pointed at the lush growth of transplanted shrubs forming a forest—"is where in our actuality is dragon country. If little brothers emerge from here, they will appear to us to be the size of real dragons in relation to the palace and the farms."

"I—understand, Master."

"Do you? Well, watch."

Taking a lizard from a cage, Zatanas set it among the plants. He then took a clay figure molded to look like a mounted knight with tiny sword and placed it in an open field. From a jar he took a bit of honey on a knife blade and applied it to the figure. He stood back, and soon a large fly was buzzing at the honey.

"Now!" he said, and dropped a pinch of herbal powder on the lizard.

The lizard raised its dragon head, sniffing. Its green scales seemed to flash gold; it raised its small hood. Suddenly it was running full tilt, wriggling from side to side.

The lizard reached the knight, pulled it down, and licked it with its long tongue. The fly, buzzing loudly, disappeared down the creature's throat.

"Now, what," the magician asked rhetorically, "do you suppose the real knight will look like when a real dragon steps on him?"

Queeto looked at the squashed clay. "Gooey," he said happily. "Blood making a crimson puddle, bones all white and broken, brains a pulpy pink mess."

"Exactly. And that's why I am going to hold a conference with the Queen. Her spies will locate the enemy, and there's where I'll have a dragon —or several dragons." He made an expansive gesture. "And that," he finished dramatically, "is how dragons doing my magical bidding will win the war."

Queeto's exclamation of servile appreciation of genius seemed almost genuine.

The Knights and the Queen's guardsmen were met in battle. Horses neighed or screamed, men cried challenges or curses or groans, swords clanged, crossbows twanged, blades and missiles made meaty clunking sounds. Dust rose in clouds beneath the horse's hooves and obscured everything that wasn't happening over a horse's length away.

War, Kelvin realized, was no more glamorous in practice than was dragon-fighting. It seemed to consist of flowing blood, billowing dust, and endless confusion. Where was the glory and the honor men spoke of? All he saw was phenomenal wasted effort.

He had trained for days to try to use his gauntleted left hand with his sword, but it was all but hopeless. In order to stay mounted he needed at least his right hand on the reins, and the left, even with practice, could hardly counter a sword swung with a good right arm.

Except, he discovered, under actual battle conditions. Then as in previous encounters, the gauntlet knew the threat, and countered sword blows, darting in to stab or disarm attackers. There was blood on the sword and the gauntlet, and Kelvin didn't want to look at either. Fortunately it made little difference. When a guardsman was close, the gauntlet knew before Kelvin did.

"Gods, but you're a fighter, Hackleberry!" Morvin Crumb said at his right. "Reminds me of me when I was your age."

Kelvin wondered what it would do to his image if he vomited—again.

Taking lives, even the lives of evil men who wanted to kill him, just wasn't the way it was presented in storybooks. At least, not for him. He was appalled by this whole business.

"Just got me another, Dad!" Lester said to the far side of his father. "Makes three."

"Four for me," Morvin said. "The lad here polished off half a dozen. Without, I think, a sweat."

Kelvin wondered whether Mor was being kind. Kelvin was sure he was bathed in cold sweat. If he had to think about more than guiding the horse and ducking an occasional blow, he would soon be exhausted. His left arm was beginning to ache. Without the gauntlet, he would have been finished long before.

"Bet this whole pass looks like one big rolling cloud," Morvin said with gusto.

Reminded of the dust, Kelvin tasted it. He spat, and the spittle didn't quite clear his chin. His left hand tingled and he knew another enemy approached.

"Gods!" Morvin exclaimed. "There's something—Gods!"

Kelvin's blade met an enemy's, deflected it, and lunged, nearly unseating Kelvin. He saw the guardsman, no older than himself, give him a stricken look, then drop his sword, slump forward, and slide from the saddle under their horses' feet.

"Seven," Lester said. He had moved past his father to Kelvin's back.

"Gods! Oh, Gods!" repeated the elder Crumb, delighted.

But Kelvin knew that it was little of his own doing. He had tried to intercept the enemy's blade, true, but his aim had been bad. He would have been skewered had not his gauntleted left hand shoved him over so that, losing balance, he had whipped his other arm about—so that the sword had made a completely unplanned and unexpected trick motion, deflecting the other blade and continuing with horrible force into the other man's body. Certainly it had looked clever, but the cleverness had all been in the self-willed gauntlet, which seemed determined to make a deadly fighter of him despite his ineptitude. This had been happening all along.

What would the gauntlet do if he threatened to vomit on it? Cut off his head?

"Kel! Kel! Wait!"

Kelvin's head snapped around. It couldn't be! But it was. Coming full tilt down the hill, Mockery, and on his back—

"Jon! Jon! Over here!"

Guardsmen started for the girl. Three of them.

Kelvin needed no gauntlet to put his steed into motion. He kneed the horse, turned its head, was yanked down by the gauntlet and thereby ducked a blow from his right. His horse made a leap over a crawling guardsman and a wounded Knight, and detoured around others not identified.

Kelvin yanked the reins, bringing it back on course. Then he was there on the hillside, and his sword was flashing and his reins lifted with his buckler as a blow almost took him across the face. It was amazing, the precision with which that gauntlet yanked him about, just so, so that every move was right.

A Knight on a black stallion flashed to his right, and then that Knight was confronting his attacker on his right hand as Kelvin lurched, pulled about yet again by the gauntlet, and his wildly flailing sword dealt with the man to his left.

Two bodies fell.

Kelvin sighed. Lester sighed, for what he was sure was a different reason. The bodies of their late foes lay unmoving in the dirt.

"Watch out, Kel!"

Jon's warning saved him just in time. He ducked, even as his left arm unsheathed the sword from its gory grip in the throat of a third foe and swung around to counter and disarm this fourth.

But the fourth attacker was no fool. He whirled his horse and fled.

"Jon, you idiot!" Kelvin exclaimed. "Why did you come here?"

"Heln remembered!" the girl cried.

"What's this?" Mor Crumb asked gruffly.

"She remembered about the lizards!" Jon said. "From when she saw Zatanas! So I had to come warn you!"

"What *about* the lizards?" Mor demanded.

"They're dragons!"

"What?" Kelvin was having trouble following this.

"And I saw them! 'Cause I knew to look! The dragons!"

"You saw dragons?" Mor cried.

"Three of them! Big brutes! Coming here!"

"I don't understand," Kelvin said, understating the case.

But suddenly Morvin Crumb did. "Sympathetic magic! Lizards are like miniature dragons! That evil sorcerer must've enchanted dragons by working through lizards!"

"I could see them from above," Jon continued. "Coming up the pass."

"You sure?" Kelvin asked, somewhat dully.

"I saw them!" Jon repeated. "Just as Heln said. Three lizards. 'Cause Zatanas didn't think you'd be fool enough to go into battle yourself!"

Kelvin turned to Morvin, baffled. "Does that make any sense?"

"It must, in some twisted way," the ruddy man said. "Gods! Nothing can face three dragons!"

"That's why Heln was so worried!" Jon said. "She'd been trying to remember all these days, and just couldn't, and then she saw a lizard and it clicked. So she told me, and I—"

"You did right," Kelvin said. "If those monsters catch us—"

"We'd better retreat, fast!" Lester said.

"Son, I think you're right. Kelvin, you get that horn to your lips and you blow the way I told you you never would!" Shaking in spite of himself, Kelvin lifted the polished ox horn Morvin Crumb had hung about his neck. Three long notes meant retreat, and would give the other Knights their location.

He blew. The sound came out and carried. *Whoomp! Whoomp! Whhhoooommmmp!*

Blowing it made his head swim. So did the heat. So did the action he had just seen.

"Come on, now," Morvin cried. "Uphill and fast! Dragons don't like heights, everyone knows that!"

Kelvin hadn't known that, however. Still, it probably made sense. Flying creatures liked heights, and the local dragons were landbound.

They turned their mounts uphill, donkey and Jon just ahead of them. Looking back, Kelvin saw other Knights, some of them barely holding on to their horses, coming at a gallop. Behind them a cheer sounded as guardsmen thought they had won.

"We were beating them!" a Knight exclaimed. "Why did you sound retreat? Now we're in disarray, and soon's they regroup they'll come after us and destroy us on the run!"

"Maybe, maybe not," Morvin said. "We got word there's—"

"Ahhhh!" someone screamed behind.

And there it was: a dragon riding out of the dust, with a man in its mouth. Then another dragon and another, shimmering gold and deadly.

"Run for your lives!" Lester cried.

They ran, all of them, including the donkey. Now no one questioned the wisdom of their sudden disengagement from the fray.

Panting, standing at the top of the steep hill and looking down into the pass where the dust roiled and men and horses were being slain and rapidly devoured, the Knights knew they had made their escape just in time. The pursuing guardsmen hadn't been that fortunate, for the dragons had come up behind them.

"The girl saved us!" Morvin exclaimed. "That division of the Queen's guardsmen—they'll never be the same!"

"But if Zatanas sent the dragons," Kelvin asked, musing it out, "wouldn't he have known that his own side would be in the way? Why would he do that?"

Morvin nodded. "Something doesn't add up. We'd better get right back, and your girl will have to eat another berry. We'd better spy on the evil magician, and find out what's he really up to."

Kelvin hated having Heln risk her life again, but realized that it was necessary. The dragon attack had been too near a thing.

16 /

DOUBTS

"I DON'T UNDERSTAND IT," Heln agreed. "Maybe that's why I couldn't remember about the dragons—I mean, how they related to the lizards Zatanas had. It seemed impossible that they could be the same, or that he would send dragons to ravage his own side as well as the enemy. So I suppose I just didn't believe it, until almost too late."

"Better take another berry and find out," Morvin said gruffly. "We can't afford many more surprises like dragons coming into the fray! I never guessed the evil sorcerer could control dragons!"

"But it's been only a few days since she had a berry," Kelvin protested. "We don't know whether it's safe for her to—"

"It isn't safe to go into battle against dragons!" Mor exclaimed vehemently. "Those could have been our boys as well as theirs getting chomped!"

Heln put her hand on Kelvin's. "I'm sure it's all right," she said. "I do feel woozy after a berry, but a good night's sleep helps, and I recover strength next day."

"I don't know," Jon put in. "You're losing weight."

Morvin's great fists clenched, but his voice was controlled. "Why don't you go outside and play, child?" he said to Jon.

"I'll try to eat better," Heln said, smiling tolerantly.

"You look just fine to me!" Kelvin said without thinking, distracted as he always was when she took his hand. Then, of course, he started blushing.

Heln smiled at him. "You're getting better at expressing yourself, I think," she remarked.

"Here's the situation," Mor said. "Our camp is closer to the site of the battle than Zatanas' den is, and we hurried, so I'm sure we got home first. But the evil sorcerer will be getting the news about the battle within the hour. If we can spy on his reaction when he learns, we may find out what we need to know. It's the best possible time; we know that it's no use wearing you out spying when Zatanas is asleep or eating or not doing anything special. We have to catch him when he's plotting against us; then we can counter his plots."

It did make sense, Kelvin had to agree. He hated to see Heln seem to die, but she did recover, and they did need the information. That business with the dragons had been entirely too close!

Heln settled on her bed and swallowed a dragonberry. Soon she sank into her coma. The others left, but Kelvin remained beside her, ill at ease. If only she didn't have to risk her life this way, to help their cause!

And if only he *could* express himself adequately to her! Instead of always being so confounded tonguetied. She had made it plain that she would be receptive to his advances, within reasonable limits. He felt so silly, bumbling about; but every time he tried to do something about it, he wound up blushing again.

"Gods, Heln, I wish I weren't such an ass with you!" he exclaimed aloud. She, of course, could not hear him; she had just stopped breathing. Her hand in his was growing cool; that had alarmed him before, and it troubled him now. It was so like death, this astral separation!

"I wish I could just take you in my arms," he said, venting his frustration aloud, because that made him feel marginally better. "I wish I could kiss you, and say, 'Heln, I think I love you, and I want to be always with you!' But I just can't! I know I'm a jackass, and I hate it, but my stupid tongue just tangles in my mouth and I blush—Gods, I wish I didn't blush!"

He looked at her, so deathly still. "How I would curse myself if you didn't wake!" he continued. "If somehow the berries—if the worst happened, and you—if I'd never even said to you—" Then everything clouded up, and he found himself bent over her cold hand, his tears flowing as he kissed it. "Damn, damn, damn!" he muttered brokenly. "If I'm a hero, they just don't make them the way they used to!"

Then, embarrassed anew, he pulled out his shirt tail and used it to dry off her hand. If she should ever suspect he had made a scene like this—!

Heln recovered consciousness as her spirit separated from her body. This was the third time she had traveled astrally, and she was learning its pattern. The first time she had been trying to die, and had thought her spirit was going to the afterlife. She had been amazed when she discovered otherwise, and then intrigued. Separation was actually an exhilarating experience; she was so free, with no body to drag after her or worry about! Of course she paid for it when she became physical again; Jon was right about her losing weight. She just couldn't seem to force herself to eat enough to make up for the energy she lost. Perhaps astral separation was part of the process of dying, and it was easier to die than to live. She had wanted to die, that first time; maybe that had made the whole experience easier. But the experience itself had gone far to restore her will to live, and, indeed, to participate in life as the woman she was, rather than as the object of degradation the guards of the Girl Mart had made of her. How glad she was that Kelvin was not at all like that! Every time he stammered and blushed, she liked him better.

She hovered above her body, gathering her presence, getting ready to make the jump to the evil magician's lair. Her vision cleared, and then her hearing. Kelvin was with her body, as he had been the last time; she really appreciated his loyalty. He was holding her hand.

"Gods, Heln, I wish I weren't such an ass with you!" he exclaimed abruptly.

What was this? He hadn't spoken before, as far as she knew. She decided to wait a moment more, and see what this led to.

"I wish I could just take you in my arms," he said.

Well! Apparently Kelvin could be much more expressive when he thought he was alone!

"I wish I could kiss you," he exclaimed. "And say, 'Heln, I think I love you, and I want to be always with you!'" he continued.

"Well, why don't you?" she asked, but of course he couldn't hear, because she had no voice in this state.

"But I just can't!" he added, sounding tortured.

Heln continued to listen and watch, until he completed his statement. When it was evident that he would say no more, she gathered herself for the jump to the other place. But she was thoughtful. She understood Kelvin better now; how could she make the best use of this explanation of his puzzling behavior!

Because of her delay, she arrived at Zatanas' residence just after the messenger left. She hoped she hadn't missed anything critical. She phased into the dusky chamber where the evil sorcerer and his dwarf henchman were.

"I don't like it! I don't like it at all!" Zatanas stormed, startling the owlhawk into flopping its great wings as it perched atop its human-skull pedestal. Queeto, too, looked scared.

"That messenger just now said we lost nearly two hundred guardsmen! To dragons. Dragons! What incredible, astounding luck! Black Star curses on the witless beasts!"

"But Master, didn't they attack the Knights? Didn't they get some of them, at least?"

"No!" The sorcerer looked as if he felt like taking out his anger on the dwarf, but managed to refrain.

"But why, Master?" the dwarf asked plaintively.

Zatanas chewed his lower lip, perhaps deliberately making himself hurt.

"Because, stupid dwarf, dragons destroy all men without natural discrimination. They have very small brains. Even smaller than yours."

"But you directed them with lizards. The images were dressed as Knights."

So that was it, Heln realized. The dragons had been guided to attack the Knights first—and of course the guardsmen would have quickly gotten out of the way. Heln knew that Morvin and Kelvin would be glad to know that explanation. Costumes were the key!

"Quite right," the sorcerer was saying. "But the infernal Knights were not present. Somehow they got out of the pass before the dragons came. And the guardsmen were still there, luxuriating in the Knights' rout."

"Then they *were* defeated, Master! The guardsmen had the ruffians beat!"

"That's what the guardsmen want to think. But not I. I think that somehow one of the Knights must have been above the pass and seen the dragons and called retreat."

Heln held her breath, before remembering that she wasn't breathing in this state. If the evil magician ever realized exactly how the Knights had known the dragons were coming—

"But—" the dwarf protested.

"Exactly. It shouldn't have happened. Next time it will *not* happen. Next time the dragons will see Knights and not be tempted by guardsmen."

"How, Master?"

Yes, how? Heln echoed. Morvin had been right: this was exactly the time to spy on the sorcerer!

"Through sensible intelligence. I intend to make good use of my daughter's spies. Her *official* spies."

"But your magic, Master. Can't you see ahead without—"

"No. The ingredients are missing for the spells. Anyway, you are confusing precognition with clairvoyance."

"What?"

"Seeing ahead is precognition. That magic I can do, when I have the right ingredients for the magic, which ingredients are so devious and perishable that I am chronically short of them. Seeing *around* is clairvoyance—knowing what is happening elsewhere without going there. That magic I lack. How I wish I had an astral propensity!"

"Master?"

"Oh, never mind! Mouvar, cursed be his memory, was precognitive, and he believed that there would be clairvoyance among men someday. But he was mistaken; only the dragons have it, and they're too stupid to take advantage of it, fortunately. What a waste it was, for Mouvar to have precognition, when *I* could have used it to conquer the planet! And the dragons—"

"Master, will the dragons do your bidding?"

"They will," Zatanas said grimly. "Everything will. In time."

"And the Queen's guardsmen will defeat the Knights?"

"They will be defeated," Zatanas said, "as surely as I am the supreme sorcerer."

Then Heln's time was running out, and she had to return to her body. She hoped she had learned enough; certainly she now had explanations for some mysteries. So the dragons *did* use the berries for astral separation, and Zatanas knew it—but didn't know about Heln's own ability to do it, too. And Mouvar had had precognition! That suggested that the prophecy Mouvar had made was valid. Still, why, then, did Zatanas have such confidence of his own victory?

Kelvin paced the outside length of the tent, the side farthest from the campfire. His mind was not on the scent of woodsmoke or the calling hoots and wails of wild things in the forest. Rather his concern was the sour bile taste in his mouth left by continual efforts to vomit.

It wasn't fear that caused his stomach to revolt. Not exactly. It was doubts. They formed and re-formed like the long, grotesque shadows of the Crumbs and two of the Knights on the other side of the tent wall.

What he was doing was right and just. He had to believe that. But the killing was as unheroic as slaughtering a farm animal. His gauntlet did it, and each time he felt sick. He wanted to escape the destiny the prophecy claimed for him, but that was according to all accounts impossible.

He sat down under a tree and looked at the moon peering like a yellow goblin face through the twisty dark branches. By and by he raised his hands to his eyes, and quietly, so as not to be heard and discovered, he wept.

It's hell being the victim of prophecy, he thought.

"Kelvin." He jumped; it was Heln's voice.

He tried to clean up his face, but it was way too late for that; she had seen. "You should be resting," he muttered.

"There is something more important," she said.

"The revolution," he agreed, and his stomach gave another twinge.

"That, too." She came close. "You don't look well, Kelvin; I'm concerned about you."

He shrugged. "I'm just not much of a hero, for sure!"

"I suppose the only thing harder than being brutalized is having to be brutal yourself."

He stared at her. Could she understand?

"I was raped," she reminded him. "I wanted to die. I tried to die. I think I felt as bad as you do now."

Surely so! "I guess I really don't have much to complain about," he said. "I guess I wasn't thinking."

She reached out and took his limp hand. "No, Kel, no! That's not what I mean at all! I mean I do understand! You're in a horribly difficult situation, having to do things you don't like at all, like going out into battle and killing people. You're a gentle person, you don't like to fight, and I see it tearing you up, just the way it would tear me up if I had to do it. And I wish I could make it easier for you."

"I—" But as usual he froze up, and couldn't have said what he wanted to say even if he had known what it was.

"Kel, I like you the way you are," she continued earnestly. "It's not just your round ears, and it's certainly not the prophecy. I liked you when I first saw you, in my first astral separation, when everyone else was hustling you along and you didn't know what to do, you just wanted to save your sister from the Mart. You gave me reason to want to live, because you were like me in the ears, and that helped a lot, but I think I would have liked you anyway. And I liked you even more when I just saw you, in my last astral journey."

"What?"

"Kel, I didn't go right away. I heard you talking to me—"

Oh, no! Kelvin felt the blush rising so hot and fierce that it threatened to make his face blister. He tried to retreat, but she hung on to his hand.

"Do you know what I have to say to that?" she asked softly. Her eyes in the shadow seemed huge, their brown turning black.

"If I'd known—I'm so sorry—" he stumbled.

She reached around him, embracing him, drawing him in close. "Kel, I think I love you," she said. Then she drew him in closer yet, and lifted her face, and kissed him.

It seemed almost as though he had separated astrally himself. Part of him looked down at the embracing figures from above, while another part of him simply floated in a tide of sheer bliss. What he had always wanted—and *she* had brought it to *him*!

At last she broke the kiss and gazed at him. "Now you may slap my face, if you wish," she said.

Caught off guard, he started to laugh. Then they were both laughing helplessly, clinging to each other for support. She felt phenomenally good that way, too.

"But there is a condition," she said as it ebbed.

"No difference!" he exclaimed.

"And that is that if I'm going to be close to you, I want you more like the hero you are supposed to be."

Now he felt dread. "I just *can't* enjoy killing!"

"Nor should you. I want you to assert yourself. *You,* not Morvin Crumb, are the Roundear of Prophecy! *You* should make the key decisions."

"But—he's the only one who knows—"

"Listen to him, certainly, but don't be governed by him."

"Uh, I suppose—"

"Make up your mind, hero, or I'll kiss you again."

"I, I just doubt that I can—"

She kissed him again.

When it was over, he felt pleasantly giddy. "I'll try," he said.

"See that you do," she said, smiling.

"Now we'll attack this guardsmen's barracks," said Morvin Crumb, pointing at the map. The heads of all those who had been designated officers nodded agreeably.

Kelvin swallowed. He thought of Heln's kisses. "Yes!" he exclaimed. "I mean no!" Even so, he surprised himself. *It's now or never,* he thought, knowing that Heln was right. *Now is the time for me to make my stand.*

The eyes of all the six strong men in the tent were turned to him. Morvin seemed amused; the others were either surprised or openly incredulous. They all knew that Kelvin was a mere figurehead.

"I don't understand, youngster," Pete Palmweaver said. He was the youngest and in many ways the most likable of the graybeards who had fought guardsmen before Kelvin's birth.

Now he had committed himself to an opinion; he had to follow through. "I may be a youngster to you," he said, "but I'm also the Roundear of Prophecy. I feel that I should decide what is done in my name."

They watched him, not indicating whether they were taking him seriously. He found that unnerving, but again he thought of Heln's kisses, and knew that they were rewards, not punishments, and he wanted to be worthy of such rewards. "I feel strongly that we should *not* attack there."

"Where, then?" asked Morvin, setting down his pointer, now looking less amused and sounding it.

Where? He had thought this out before, and decided, but now his mind threatened to go blank. He wrestled it back into focus. "We must move as close to the palace as possible. Bypass the barracks and attack here," he said, pointing with his finger to the area in front of the palace.

"That will be hard to do," Morvin said. "It will mean going over Craggy Mountain."

"We will do it," Kelvin said. "Instead of attacking Heenning, we bypass Heenning, and Dawlding, and Kencis. We move directly to Gorshen."

"I don't know, youngster. That's a pretty illogical move, seems to me."

"Maybe," Kelvin said, feeling inspired in this moment, "that's exactly what the Queen's strategists will think. They could have ambushes at any of those places. We can't afford to take the chance."

Morvin considered. "Just could be. Too bad we don't have any way to know for sure."

"Yes, too bad," Kelvin agreed, feeling on firmer ground. They had not spread the news of Heln's ability, because that would make her a high-priority target, and she was completely helpless while in astral separation. They had made it a policy not to send her on such missions unless they had reason to believe there was something significant to be learned, so she was not spying out the locations of the guardsmen this time. Morvin had declared that they could not afford to become too dependent on her information, and with that Kelvin heartily agreed.

"Hmm, you think they will expect us to attack the barracks at Heenning."

"I do." *And I, after all, am the Roundear,* he reminded himself.

"Well, I suppose we could give out the story that we planned an attack on Heenning, with subsequent ones in mind for the others," Morvin said. "Then we could do as you suggest. Just in case there are any spies."

"There aren't any spies," Palmweaver said.

But Kelvin wondered. He did not always trust the faces he saw turned to follow his every move when he strolled around camp. It occurred to him that Morvin didn't either. Maybe it was Morvin's notion to test for spies in this manner, to rout them out before they found out about Heln. Certainly he had the impression that Morvin didn't really mind Kelvin's assumption of power. Still, his doubts, about both their situation and his ability to lead, were not fading out.

17 /

QUEEN'S IRE

KELVIN LOOKED BACK AT the column of Knights following him and Jon and the Crumbs and Palmweaver. They had gone about two leagues and already the horses were noticing the steep ascent. No road here, only the paths made by deoose, meer, and other large game. The footing was rough; broken shale and fallen boulders made it hard on men and horses. The sky was overcast, threatening rain. Ozone made the air sharp, as did the needletrees' scent of aromatic green spice. Owlhawks hooted in the woods. A bearver lumbered across their path, its dark red coat blending subtly with the reddish moss that grew on the tree trunks and boulders.

"It's a long, long way to Gorshen, as I told you," Morvin said. "By now we could be at Heenning."

Yes, Kelvin thought, and an hour from now we could all be dead. But he did not say such to Morvin, mainly because he knew it wouldn't be expected of a tool of prophecy.

"What say, Kel?" Lester asked jovially.

"I say that we will take them by surprise at Gorshen."

"I sure hope you're right, brother mine," Jon gasped. She had insisted on coming along, but her enthusiasm was waning as she got tired.

At Heenning, a huge dragon reared its golden head, smacked its enormous mouth, and looked about the deserted barracks. Where were the brownberry shirts and greenbriar pantaloons of the morsels it had been driven here to find? It stepped on a fence, squashed a roof, and bit in two a large timber that had formed part of a now ruined catapult. The dragon always knew hunger and rage, but now it knew more. It also knew the growing frustration of having come so far and finding not the tasty bits that had somehow beckoned. How much better it would have been to dream

114

with some dragonberries, and range across the world and down into The Flaw with complete abandon!

Behind the big dragon were four lesser dragons that came barely above the rooftops of the barracks. They reacted as strongly. Dragons liked feasting and dreaming and mating, in that order, and combinations of the three when they could work it. They did not like hunger or boredom.

Tails lashed. Walls smashed. Timbers splintered. The strong smell of dragon urine and excrement mingled with the lesser odor of human beings. The smell of food. But where was it? The buildings were being demolished, but they were empty.

Then the breeze changed. The big dragon raised his snout, sniffing.

There, hiding on the hillside: *food*

As appetites sharpened, the dragons rushed for the blue-and-gold-clad men hiding behind bushes and trees and rocks. They brushed aside the little sticks that rained off their scales, and the larger sticks leveled at them by men astride horses. The dragons slapped their tails, gnashed their teeth, chomped, squashed, and ate.

There was food here after all.

The Queen's guardsman arrived on a lathered horse at the gate of the palace. He called to the gateman and was admitted, then was taken by a guard directly to the audience chamber.

Watching from the window of his quarters, Zatanas half guessed the meaning of the man's appearance. He took time only to clap on his pointed wizard's cap—an affectation that had once impressed his daughter—and then ran. He hurried down the three winding staircases to the little antechamber beside the room where the Queen held a hurried audience.

The Queen, of course, would know he was there, though he was hidden behind a curtain. He listened as the messenger told his disturbing story.

"O Queen, we deserted the barracks and waited, as commanded, but the enemy did not appear. The dragons *did* appear. They destroyed Heenning, as we expected they would, and then—then they found us."

"Do you mean to say," exclaimed the Queen, "that the dragons attacked guardsmen *again*?"

"Yes, Your Majesty. The enemy was not about. The dragons attacked. They destroyed us! There's not a guardsman alive who can stand up to a dragon!"

"Father!" the Queen called abruptly. "Father, come in here now and explain why you have done this to me!"

Zatanas took a deep breath, cursed himself for the foolishness of ever having a child, and went through the velvet curtain.

The Queen was a sight he would rather have missed. She sat on her golden throne, her skin red as dragon-sheen hair, and her eyes the color of dark green feline magic alight with the cometing yellow lights of intense anger. Her fingers gripped the carved arms of her throne like talons, and she looked more like a witch than a monarch. A witch from some land deep down through The Flaw, more inhuman than human. In short, his daughter in her natural state.

"My dear daughter and proudest materialization," he said in a suitably placating fashion, though he knew that little but dripping flesh would placate a dragoness, "the enemy is using magic. Mouvar's magic, cursed be his name. How else than by magic could they have known—"

"The question is, Father, why didn't *you* know? Are you a sorcerer or are you not?"

That again. Well, he wasn't about to plead lack of expertise! If she ever guessed that he wasn't all-powerful, she might decide to destroy him. She was his flesh, after all.

"I was depending on your spies," he said. "Why haven't they—"

"Foolish old fraud! My spies gathered their intelligence. The Roundear's Knights were supposed to have attacked Heenning. You stood here when they reported. You knew—"

"I knew what they said. But the Knights were not there, Your Majesty, as this man has just testified."

"Don't belabor the obvious! Then I suppose they are somewhere else?"

"Undoubtedly," he agreed with a certain irony. "The question is where."

"The question is why there should be a question at all!" she flared. "If you can't—"

They were interrupted by a second guardsman who burst into the audience chamber in the company of a guard. "Your Majesty!" the man cried, falling to his knees. "I beg to report that the Roundear Knights have attacked Gorshen! Caught unprepared, we were outnumbered, and—"

"Beaten?" the Queen supplied with deceptive calm.

The man hung his head.

After brief questioning that established the extent of the disaster, the Queen dismissed the others, remaining alone with her father. She inhaled.

Zatanas felt the Queen's eyes. "You—you unmitigated wretch!" she exclaimed. "I should have you castrated in the public square! *Why didn't you know of this?*"

"Think carefully before you threaten me, daughter," Zatanas said grimly, knowing that she was not given to bluffing. There was a time for placation, and a time for self-defense, and this was the latter. "It was my magic that made you Queen."

"Yes, magic made me Queen. *Roundear* magic! I used it then and I'll use it again."

"No, no, you mustn't." Now he felt desperate. "You must never use roundear magic again."

"Mustn't I?" The threat sounded in her tone.

"No, it's . . . risky. Better to destroy all roundears and all tools brought by roundears. Better my magic than—"

"Father," she said severely, "would you have me destroy my own magic?"

"No. No, of course not." What *had* he been thinking of? There would be no talking her out of this now. They faced horrible danger—all because he had slipped.

Looking very much his daughter, which was to say much like a dragon, she said, "I intend to use all tools and all persons to secure my throne."

"Of course, daughter. But with care, due care! Otherwise—"

"It's this roundear stripling who claims to represent the prophecy!" she exclaimed. "I'm going to use my spy in their camp to eradicate him once and for all. Then this nuisance will fade out."

"But you shouldn't waste an emplaced spy!" Zatanas protested.

"What good has he been to me so far? If he can't get word about the enemy's movements to me in time, I might as well use him in a manner that counts."

She was making a certain amount of sense, but Zatanas didn't trust this. It would be almost impossible to get another spy placed, once this one was exposed, and if he failed in his mission, as was quite possible considering the way the breaks had been going—

Still, this was better than risking the wrong kind of magic. It was true that the elimination of the enemy figurehead could have considerable impact, and perhaps so demoralize the upstarts that their effort would fall apart. "What do you have in mind, daughter?"

"I was always apt at poisons," she said briskly. "It will be nice to get my hand in again."

"Very good, daughter," Zatanas agreed.

Jon skipped a rock on the smooth stretch of creek. It hopped three times, as a well-skipped rock was supposed to. The circles formed and raced outward.

"I'll bet there's fish in here," Jon said aloud.

A Knight heard her and smiled. "You're probably right."

"If I had some equipment," Jon told him, "I could catch us some!"

"Not enough for the whole camp, you couldn't," the man said, coming over. His hair color was brick, and his name, appropriately, was Appleton. She had seen him around often enough. He was, she guessed, about three years older than Kelvin, and halfway handsome.

"But I'd enjoy trying," Jon said. "I get tired of just running errands for you fellows. I'd like to be doing something besides polishing boots and fetching firewood and spring water."

"I don't blame you," Appleton said, his hands still occupied with the rope he was braiding. He stood close to her, gazing out over the stream. "It does get dull here."

"I wish *I* had some magic!" she exclaimed. "I wish I was a Knight!"

"You're useful enough," Appleton said, abandoning his rope braiding. "But you know, you should try dressing your own way."

"How's that?" Jon asked, not understanding.

"Like a woman. You'd be a really pretty girl if you ever let yourself."

"I don't want to be a girl!" she said vehemently.

"Well, I could see your point if you were an ordinary girl. But even though you try to cover them up, I can see the lines of you. You would be no ordinary girl."

Something strange overtook her certainty. "I wouldn't?"

"Not at all! I tell you, you could start smiting hearts right here in this camp if you tried."

"Me!" she exclaimed derisively.

"You," he agreed, with no derision. "You've got the face, you've got the lines. Look at the way that roundear girl took over your brother. You're as pretty as she is."

"Never!" But she felt herself flushing.

"I'll make you a bet that if you borrowed one of her dresses, and walked out in the camp, you could beckon to any man here, and he would come to you."

This was beyond belief. "You're teasing me!"

"Am I? Then laugh this off."

And he took her by the shoulders, brought her into him, and kissed her on the mouth.

She was too amazed to react. She felt the pressure of his hands on her, so strong and firm, and his lips on hers, and she felt as if she were floating.

Then he drew his head back, and released her. "There," he said. "I'd be lying if I said that wasn't fun. But I suppose you'd better slap me."

"Wh-what?" Her knees felt like sodden reeds.

"I just made a pass at you," he said. "Because you're an attractive young woman. Now you slap me, because I shouldn't have done it. That's the way it is."

"I couldn't do that," she said, feeling faint. She had to sit down on the bank, before she fell down.

He sat beside her. "Well, maybe next time," he said. "A girl can't be too free, is all. Bad for her reputation."

"When I was at the Boy Mart, they found out and tried to, to—" she said, starting to babble and quickly stalling. She didn't know how she felt.

"Like Miz Flambeau," he said. "That's different. They do it to anything they can get their hands on. But among civilized folk, it's different. You're in no danger here."

"I don't know," Jon said. "It's a whole different realm. It's like magic."

Indeed, the notion of being an attractive young woman was like being a changeling, becoming something she had never thought to be.

"Magic is what you make it. I know the feeling. My granny was a witchwoman and spell-maker."

"Really?" Jon asked, impressed, and glad enough to change the subject. "She turned people into froogs and batbirds?"

"Hardly!" he said, laughing. He found a dry bed of red moss and sprawled on it. "She could mend a broken arm, ease the pangs of childbirth, cure barrenness, that sort of thing."

"Oh. No real magic."

"I wouldn't say that. She knew a thing or two, Gran did."

"About what?" Her attention was drifting back to the kiss, and her feelings associated with it, that still hovered about her like little vague clouds. Could she really be a girl—and like it?

"Oh, about our name fruits, for instance—oaples and appleberries."

"What did she do with them?" Really borrow a dress from Heln? How well would it fit her?

"Put magic into them. She could make a weak man strong or a strong man weak, and I learned from her."

"You did, huh? Magic?" Magic: beckoning any man, and making him respond.

"That's what I said, Hackleberry."

That brought her attention back to reality. She *wasn't* a girl, not any way it counted. Just as her brother wasn't a hero. "Could you help Kelvin?"

"Help him? In what way?"

Jon thought about the night she had seen Kelvin crying. "I don't think he's as brave as he could be. Or as strong."

"Hmmm. I could probably help him there, if that's true."

"You could?" And if it was possible to help her brother become brave, then it might be possible to help her become a proper girl.

"I think so. I know the spells. Let me fix him a stockelcap full of appleberries, and you take them to him. Only don't tell him they're magicked. If you do, they won't work."

"I won't tell," she agreed. "And he'll eat them. Kelvin never could resist a stockelcap full of fresh wild appleberries."

Kelvin was sitting on a log, staring glumly at a map and picking at a scab on his hand where a knife had slipped. Jon rode up on Mockery. Wordlessly Jon held out a stockelcap filled with ripe red and white appleberries.

"For me, Jon?" he asked, sounding surprised.

"Got lucky," she said. "Found a whole patch of them. Maybe not as sweet as you can make them when you do the picking, but pretty good anyway."

Kelvin eyed the berries. "It's awfully soon after lunch and my stomach's been bothering me."

"Appleberries should fix that right up," she said eagerly.

"You never brought me appleberries before. Usually I had trouble keeping you out of those I picked."

"I'm reformed," Jon said, "and you're important. Gol' dang it, Kel, can't I do something nice for my own brother?"

"Of course you can, Jon! Of course. But climb on down and we'll eat them together."

"They're all for you," Jon said. "I ate my fill where I found them."

"I should have known." But he hesitated.

"What's the matter, Kel?" she asked, concerned.

"This fool gauntlet. All of a sudden it feels warm. Matter of fact, it tingles. There aren't any of the Queen's own around, are there?"

"I d-don't think so, Kel." What was bothering him?

"Well—" Kelvin took the stockelcap with his right hand and placed it at the end of his log. But as he set it down, his left hand shot out and sent the stockelcap flying. The berries rolled into the dust under Mockery's snorting nose.

"Now, why did it do that?" Kelvin asked, annoyed. "That gauntlet ruined the treat you brought me!"

Jon wondered, too. Could the gauntlet object to Kelvin becoming brave? So that maybe he wouldn't need it so much?

Mockery didn't wonder. His nostrils flared. He lowered his head and began to eat appleberries.

Kelvin watched, frowning more deeply. "Jon, is there something different about these berries?"

"Different?" Jon felt apprehensive. If Kelvin knew, the magic wouldn't work, Appleton had said. But of course it made no difference now, because the berries had been spilled.

Mockery gave a jerk. His eyes rolled until the whites showed. He trembled from nose to tail and then, to Jon's complete horror, he slowly sank downward.

"Jon, what's going on?" Kelvin demanded. "What's the matter with Mockery? What—where did you get those berries? What's wrong with them, anyway?"

Jon was scrambling to get off the donkey's back. Then, sitting in the dust and looking at Mockery's closed eyes and protruding tongue, a horrible suspicion came over her. Mockery, she felt certain, was either dying or dead. She let that sink in until she not only believed it, she understood the cause. Then, painfully, she answered Kelvin:

"He said the berries were magicked—that they would help make you brave."

"Jon, your donkey's been poisoned," Kelvin said, looking into the animal's mouth. Then he looked from Jon to the donkey and back, a new expression sweeping his face.

"I didn't know!" Jon protested, starting to cry. "I didn't, Kel. Honest! I thought—oh, I was a fool!" Poor Mockery, she thought. Poor dear, deaf, faithful, brave, true Mockery. What had she done to him? What might she have done to her brother? The tears flowed faster.

"I believe you, Brother Wart," Kelvin said. "No need to cry."

"Yes, there is!" she cried. "He—he sweet-talked me, told me I'd make a pretty girl, and I believed everything!"

"Well, he was right about that much," Kelvin said. "You'd be as pretty as Heln is, if you tried."

"But it was only to fool me, so I'd bring you p-poison!" she said. "Oh, Kel, I'm so ashamed!"

"No need, no need, Jon! Anyone would have been fooled. We'll find him and—" His face turned grim. "Question him. Who was it?"

"Appleton. Oh, I hate him! I hate him!"

Kelvin blew on his horn, and every Knight within hearing dropped what he was doing and came.

But Appleton, of course, was not among them.

18 /

ROUNDEAR

"I'VE GOT TO DO it, Kel," Heln said. "You know that! After what happened—"

Kelvin nodded. "After they tried to poison me. That means that Appleton was a spy for the Queen, and we'd better find out if there are any others."

"Yes. I can scout around, astrally, and see if I can locate Appleton. But mainly, I'd better spy on Zatanas, and try to learn what mischief he's cooking up next."

"Better wait a bit," Morvin said. "They have scouts out, and we can spot those, but let them go. When the first one reports to the Queen, that's when we'll likely learn something from her or Zatanas. Timing is everything, in spying as in battle."

Kelvin had to agree with the logic of that. He certainly didn't want Heln taking such a risk for nothing. Also, it meant she could wait another day or two before eating a berry. He still hated to have her go into that temporary death.

Zatanas scowled his blackest and tried his best to look the part of the menacing warlock. His daughter, unfortunately, did not seem impressed.

"I want you to drain his blood," she said.

"But why? His blood is worthless to me. Only the blood of some truly innocent person, or a virgin of either sex, has the potency required for my magic."

"Never mind that. I want revenge. He was supposed to have destroyed the upstart, claimed he did, and what had he done but send a girl on a man's mission? No wonder it failed! Let him now take the place of the girl."

"Better I work on my invincibility spell. Your agent failed, and that is unfortunate, but then the Roundear was protected by magic."

"You think so?"

"I know it," he said. "Just as I know that no part of your agent—Applebee, was that his name?—is of any worth. Perhaps my lizards can feed on him. That should cause him some reasonable agony."

"You won't take his blood?"

"No. If you want him bled, use your royal torturer. That pig likes to waste flesh."

"But it's you he fears. He knows the royal torturer will harm only his body, whereas you—"

"I gave you my final word, daughter. I won't waste my time on worthless flesh."

"Stubborn old man!" she snapped, but she did not seem displeased.

"Bothersome witch!"

Perhaps they would not have talked that way if they had thought anyone could be overhearing.

The messenger arrived covered with dust and sweat, smelling of blood and horse. He was quickly ushered by the palace guards directly into the Queen's audience chamber.

"O Queen," the messenger cried, falling to his knees before her throne. "I beg to inform you that the Roundear's Knights are nearing Skagmore, but one day's ride from this palace!"

The Queen scowled at the messenger and then at Peter Flick, her latest, and weakest-chinned, consort. She liked her men servile.

"What do you think of that, Peter? The old man's magic isn't helping us."

"I say," Peter said with the high squeak that designated his excitement, "that now is the time! Use *roundear* magic against your roundear enemy. Do it now, Your Majesty, while there is yet time!"

He was saying exactly what she already wanted to do. She liked that in a man. If only her father weren't such a curmudgeon!

Nevertheless, she argued the other side of the case, hoping this would provoke a truly convincing refutation. "Prophecy," she said. "How can mortals, or even immortals, fight against it? Prophecy always works out."

"Not always as expected," Peter piped. "There's a roundear who is your enemy, but is he the only roundear? No, certainly not! You have one. One of your own, my Queen."

"Yes, so you've reminded me." Casually she tweaked one of Peter's very pointed ears. "So why do I hesitate?"

Peter looked at her with that abject lustful longing that was his prime attraction; he existed to treasure her mind and body as fully as was possible. So intense was his stare that she found her own passion responding; perhaps she would take him to her private chambers soon, and have her way with him. "Dare I remind you, O Queen? Dare I say that you have a, shall we say, an intimate relationship?" He licked his lips, being eager for intimacy himself.

"There is that," she agreed in an offhand manner. "But if the prophecy doesn't apply, then we lose."

"Well, maybe," he said, reluctant to concede such a possibility.

"If my best guardsmen and my father's magic don't stop the enemy, I will use roundear magic. But—"

"Queen, you *must* have a roundear fighting on your side. Only in that way can the prophecy be fulfilled to our—to your—satisfaction."

"Yes," she said. "There will indeed be a roundear fighting on our side. In the next battle. And he, dear Peter, will go equipped with the strongest possible kind of ages-old magic."

He licked his lips again, his desire for her causing him to flush and fidget. "Which is?"

"A mother's love."

"Uh, yes," he agreed, disgruntled.

She decided it was time. She reached out to stroke him in a sensitive region. "Come to my chambers now," she murmured, turning away.

"Yes, Your Majesty!" He was practically slavering with anticipation.

"They know we're near Skagmore," Heln reported as she recovered. She was still woozy, as she tended to be after astral separation, but knew she had to report quickly.

"Of course they do," Morvin agreed. "We let their spy go through. But what are they going to do about it?"

"They're going to use roundear magic," she said.

"But I'm the Roundear of Prophecy!" Kelvin objected.

"The Queen said she would have a roundear fighting on her side, at Skagmore, and that he would have the strongest possible magic—a mother's love."

"What does that mean?" Kelvin asked querulously.

"I don't know. She didn't say any more about it. She had this—this courtier, who, well, dotes on her, and they—well, it's not relevant. But it certainly seems as though they have another roundear."

"I don't know anything about any other roundear," Morvin growled. "But I do know of that palace flunky. The Queen's latest in a long line of panderers. She beds them until she tires of them, and then gets rid of them. There's a name for men like that."

"And for women like that," Les put in.

"I'm sure I wouldn't know it," Heln said delicately. "But that's all I got. They're worried about the prophecy, but think they can nullify it with this roundear. The Queen certainly didn't seem to be joking or bluffing."

"What of Zatanas?" Morvin asked. "He's the dangerous one."

"He's against it. He doesn't like the use of roundear magic, and tried to talk the Queen out of it. But if his magic doesn't stop us, then she'll use what she's got. Whatever that is. I wish I could have learned more, but I have no way to question them."

"You learned enough, girl," Morvin said gruffly. "We're well warned to be alert for the unexpected. Better rest now."

Heln made a tired smile and sank back on the bed, sinking immediately into a normal slumber.

Kelvin felt his stomach burn as they left the tent. Tomorrow—Skagmore, and the battle that would decide if they were about to push on for Sceptor and the palace. Heln had required him to assert himself, and he had done so, and saved the Knights much misery as a result, but still he hated this warfare. He just wasn't cut out to be a soldier!

"Fortune come a-callin'; and I did hide. Little devils at my side."

Kelvin jumped. Morvin was singing! This was uncharacteristic and unmusical, but the big man was definitely doing it.

Then the man laughed, seeing Kelvin's wonder. "Just making a point, maybe," he said. "I can see you don't much like this business, Hackleberry."

Kelvin could only nod agreement.

"Come to my tent. We've got some talking to do."

Kelvin followed him into his tent, feeling uneasy. When they passed the tent flap, he half expected to see Crumb's son or some of the designated officers, set up for a briefing. Instead there was only a large amber bottle.

Morvin picked it up and waved it at him. "Drink, youngster?"

"No," Kelvin said uneasily. He had tasted liquor and hated it. Whether this was a conditioned response because of what he had seen it do to others, or whether it simply tasted awful, he wasn't sure. It probably didn't matter exactly why the stuff was vile. He had learned that Heln felt the same way about it, so perhaps the stuff affected roundears differently than it did natives.

"You ever hear me tell about the old days?" Morvin inquired. "About fighting with the loyalists and the upstarts? We were winning, youngster, and make no mistake. Got about as far as Skagmore, and then—"

Kelvin felt a chill. Skagmore was to be the site of tomorrow's battle. Obviously Morvin was not just rambling. "Magic?" he asked, dreading the answer he knew was coming.

"*Roundear* magic, son. Took us by surprise. The roundears—not as the Gods intended, Hackleberry. Not as the Gods intended."

"Tell me about it," Kelvin said, abruptly twice as interested. If the big man knows about the roundears of the past . . .

"It was 'fore your time, but I remember it as though it were this afternoon. I killed roundears with my sword—did you know that?"

"I—I think I guessed it," Kelvin said. He sat down on the stool Morvin kept for visitors, and his hand reached out almost of its own volition to touch the battered map case. He knew that Morvin Crumb had been a good soldier, like his father before him and his son after him.

"Hard to kill, they were. Great fighters. But the worst of it was, they had magic. Weapons such as no sane mind ever imagined. Not swords and crossbows, no. Magical."

"Tell me," Kelvin repeated, eager to hear everything.

Morvin took a drink. He wiped his mouth on the hairy back of his hand and said: "Explosive thunders that blew apart men and horses. Lightning that struck with a red bolt and went right through men and war-horses and good solid armor. Oh, I tell you, Hackleberry, it was awful! And some of them flew—flew overhead, but not as birds fly. I saw two of them high in the sky pierced by crossbow bolts. I saw them fall to their deaths, Hackleberry. But then I saw another, equally high. This one controlled the lightnings. I saw men, horses, trees—just smoking red holes where the lightning struck. We ran and we ran. We had to. There was no fighting that."

"I understand," Kelvin said, and thought that perhaps he did.

"Do you? Do you really?" Morvin took hold of his arms and looked drunkenly into his face. "It was as if we were weeds and grass before a fiery scythe. Do you understand what it is to face such beings?"

"You say I'm one of them," Kelvin reminded him. It was the sharpest retort he had ever given Crumb.

Morvin looked at him hard and shook his head. "You may be one of 'em, son, but you haven't their magic. Not that I've seen, anyway."

"No," Kelvin admitted. Why did he feel that Morvin saw to his depths? Saw the fear he knew was there, however hard he tried to bury it? He swallowed a lump. "Not now, I haven't. Just a little plant-charming, and I guess that isn't the same. But—"

"But you will have, won't you?"

"I—I don't know." Tearing himself away, Kelvin pushed through the tent flap to the outside and the good, clean night air. It occurred to him in a rare flash of fancy that all he faced now were the uncaring and unknowing eyes of distant, unreachable stars.

19 /

SKAGMORE

"How bad do you think it'll be?" Jon asked.

"It gives me a deep chill," Heln answered. "They know we're coming, and when and where, so they'll be ready. They aren't bringing in the dragons this time, because we've been able to turn the dragons against the Queen's guardsmen too often, but they've got a lot of troops. I wish—"

"Me, too," Jon said. "But Morvin's determined to fight and win, and he's convinced Kelvin, so I guess it just has to happen. Men are such fools!"

"You're finally seeing the light!"

"I'm finally seeing the light," Jon agreed morosely. "What good can it be, to be a man, if you just go out and get yourself killed?"

"Not much. That's why there are women. To catch the men and make them settle down on farms and live decent lives."

"You like farm life? It bores me!"

"I like it a lot better than warfare or the Girl Mart!"

Jon nodded, seeing the point. "Still—"

"But it has to be with the right man."

"I don't have a man, right or wrong."

"But you're young yet, Jon! *I'm* young! We have time."

"Not if all the men get killed fighting!" Jon retorted.

"We just have to hope that the Knights win this battle, and don't get killed, and that then the Queen will abdicate and there won't be war anymore. Then I'll capture your brother, and you—you can find someone."

"Do you really think I—?"

"Of course! You're a pretty girl, if you'd just let yourself be!"

"When I tried to—to let myself be, I almost got my brother poisoned!" Jon said bitterly.

"He was a bad man. He was using you. But if you really went looking, you could find a good one."

"If any good ones survive the fighting."

Heln smiled. "I'll make you a deal, Jon. If we win this battle, then good men will survive. If we win, I'll help you all I can to be a completely female girl, and you'll give it a really honest try."

"I don't know—"

"You'd rather have the Queen win?"

That brought home the horror of the alternative. "If my being a girl-type girl can encourage our side to win, then it's a deal!"

"Every little bit of magic helps," Heln said. They shook hands.

Skagmore was particularly ugly. Faded army barracks, stripped paint, unrepaired fences, scattered refuse piles. Appalling. The place smelled, as only an army town could, of horse dung and latrines and unhauled garbage. Altogether unbeautiful.

The place was so still that one could hear the rustle of a bird's wing. Kelvin looked from Morvin to Lester Crumb and then at the rest of the accompanying Knights, their main force, and wondered. It was remarkable that this place, so near to their ultimate goal, was deserted. The enemy *knew* that the Knights were coming; Heln had spied on the messenger's delivery of word to the evil Queen. But the enemy didn't know that the Knights knew they knew. So this apparent vacancy could only be a trap.

And were they to walk right into it? Yes, they were, for that was the only way to spring their countertrap. They had drilled for this. To lure the enemy into open battle in a seemingly advantageous position, so that they would attack with confidence, and carelessly. Then—

Kelvin felt his stomach twist. They had planned so carefully, but it was risky. Suppose their surprise didn't work? Suppose something went wrong? Then what?

There was only one answer: they had to make sure that nothing did go wrong.

So they moved down into the town, seemingly innocently, commenting loudly about the marvel of its emptiness. "We scared them off!" "They knew they couldn't win!" "See if there's any food left in the storehouse!" That sort of thing, also rehearsed.

They rode all the way into the town square. Then the trap sprang. Horsemen were suddenly racing down each alley, pikes ready, swords drawn. The enemy plainly outnumbered the Knights, and were now closing in for the quick kill.

Kelvin raised the signaling horn and blew the blast that signaled the formation of the phalanx. Now his fear was dissipating into excitement. *This had to work!*

The Knights formed a close living fence with shields joined at the edges and spears raised and ready to stab. They had never separated far; a formation had been maintained, of its special loose kind, so that each man had only a few feet to step to reach his key position. In the center the horses waited, secure until the line should burst. Archers and crossbowmen formed a line between the horses and the spearmen. In practice it had seemed impenetrable; now it seemed less so, but it was ready.

They had picked up many recruits in the past few weeks. Many of them were without horses, and a few without even swords. But their mercenaries had taught the recruits well, and the knowledge that it was their land they fought for gave even the least experienced men courage. The Queen, obviously, had no respect for farm boys turned fighters, and the guardsmen evidently proposed to cut them down without mercy.

Arrows rained from the advancing foe, as the Queen's archers stepped from their concealment behind the horsemen and aimed their shafts over their vanguard. Almost casually, because of the practice they had had, the Knights raised shields and stopped the missiles that sought their blood. The rattle sounded like hail. The barrage that should have cut down as much as a third of the force at one stroke, and demoralized the rest, brought no casualties and no demoralization. The phalanx remained tight and strong.

With a great cry that rose like a wave at sea, the men in blue and gold uniforms threw themselves hard against the waiting phalanx. They met much fiercer resistance than they had anticipated. Men cried out as waiting spears stabbed through their bodies. More came, for they could not stop their impetus. These were met by the strokes of swords. The enemy formation was crashing against the wall of shields and breaking like a wave across a rocky shore. Still they came, seemingly maddened beyond reason, still not believing that the Knights were fighting back so effectively.

Bows twanged. Missiles flew. Blue and gold uniforms sprouted feathered barbs. But the sheer mass of the charge had its effect, and the phalanx lost cohesion. Brown-and-green-clad Knights cried out here and there, dropping their arms, dying as bravely as any soldier.

The phalanx had done its work. The thrust of the charge had been broken, and three or four guardsmen were down for every Knight lost. Still they came, and came. The guardsmen outnumbered the Knights by as much as ten to one. This was worse than Morvin's worst projections! The Queen had thrown all her reserves into this effort, holding nothing back, and that threatened to make the trap effective after all.

Now Kelvin and the Crumbs were fighting from their steeds. Kelvin was glad that Jon had been banned from this engagement; it would have been terrible to have his little sister see their end! Immediately he condemned himself for thinking so quickly of defeat. They were supposed to win!

Kelvin's left hand, with the gauntlet, knew what to do. He had learned how to make it hold a sword, and it was now fighting with that sword so expertly that any surviving observer would have thought him left-handed. But gradually his left arm grew tired. The hand was powered by the gauntlet, but the arm was not; it obeyed the imperatives of the hand, but at the cost of increasing fatigue.

In a brief lull, realizing that even the gauntlet could not save him if his left arm became too tired to follow its dictates, Kelvin changed sword for shield in his left hand, and took the sword in his right. He had no magic there, but did have some training, and at least that arm was relatively fresh.

Now, you devils, come on, he thought, maneuvering his horse away from corpses. His stomach had no qualms now, despite the bleakness of the likely outcome of this encounter; he was ready for the next stage of the fray.

Suddenly there were three guardsmen before him, each mounted. They were charging him as if he were a magnet.

Mor Crumb saw the situation and angled across to engage one of the attackers. Les Crumb moved too slowly, and was knocked off his mount by a lucky blow from the second. The third reached Kelvin, striking at him.

Kelvin's sword blade missed as his gauntlet raised the shield and deflected the enemy's sword. Now they fought, and steel clanged against steel. Each blow and counter shook Kelvin's whole arm and shoulder and the shock seemed to reach right through to his mind, dulling it.

Kelvin was tiring. Now it was not merely his left arm; it was his whole body. Battle was hard work! He wished he could get out of this, just quit fighting and go home to the farm, but of course he could not.

There was something else bothering him. His opponent's face—young, determined, and somehow enormously familiar. He racked his brain in the midst of the fight, but all he could think of was that the stranger bore a slight resemblance to Jon. That was impossible, of course; Jon was a girl, and this one was a man, several years older than Kelvin himself.

Then the other made a deft move, and Kelvin was unhorsed. He landed hard, twisting about, and saw the enemy sword swishing down at his unprotected face. His shield was pinned partly under him, no help now.

His incredible gauntlet let loose of the shield and snapped across to grab the naked blade.

The stranger did not release his weapon. Kelvin's left hand jerked.

Crash! The stranger hit the dust beside him, his sword flung wide. Now neither combatant was armed with a blade.

The stranger raised his head, as jarred by his fall as Kelvin was. For a moment they sat face-to-face, staring at each other. There *was* a resemblance to Jon, or somebody like her, a resemblance that bothered Kelvin as much as the notion of imminent defeat and death.

Now, in his fatigue, he saw something else. It had failed to register before, but on the right hand of the stranger was a gauntlet identical to his own.

The other man moved—and Kelvin's left arm jerked up. His gauntlet met the opposite gauntlet and grasped it. He felt the effort down the length of his worn-out arm. The two gauntlets were struggling against each other—the two that should be a pair!

Back and forth, up and down and around, the gauntlets and the trapped hands struggled, stirring up sweat and dirt. Kelvin saw exhaustion on the other man's face, and fear. The stranger felt the same exhaustion and fear Kelvin did, but was a similar captive to his gauntlet!

The other gauntlet pulled his down, as if seeking to pin it to the ground. Kelvin reached with his right hand to help, and met the left hand of the stranger.

Their two bare hands grasped and squeezed and struggled and fought, exactly like the two gauntlets, but more weakly.

Suddenly there was a noise close at hand. Horsemen—but of which side? Kelvin was too weary to raise his head. Too weary to really think. So, it seemed, was the stranger. The battle had devolved to their four struggling hands; little elsewhere seemed important.

Their bare hands weakened, and fell apart. Human flesh had met its limit; they could fight no more.

But the gauntlets still fought like scorpiocrabs in a bottle.

Other figures came to stand by the combatants. One person or the other was about to be struck down. Which one would that be? It hardly seemed to matter.

It seemed to Kelvin that there would never be, could never be, an end.

Mor Crumb maneuvered his war-horse as close to his son as he could. Les, on the ground, guarded somewhat by his well-trained horse, was either dead or unconscious.

"Oh, please, Gods, if Gods there be, let him be only unconscious," Mor mumbled as he simultaneously fought off two attackers.

Neither Les nor the gods made a sound.

Mor finished the attacker on his left with a well-aimed thrust. The guardsman on his right got through his guard, to the side of his shield, and sliced his left forearm.

Mor felt the sharp sting and the wetness and knew he was wounded. But the mailed vest he wore was still doing its duty and the shield remained strapped securely to his now bleeding arm. "Oh, ye would, would ye? Well—"

He barely got his sword around, saving his face and possibly his head by the slimmest margin. He felt the swish of the enemy's sword and felt his left ear sting. He had lost part of the ear from that blow. How much, he couldn't now be concerned about.

Somehow his sword deflected the guardsman's, and then, with less science than he felt he usually commanded, he got his blade under the other's helmet and drove upward.

"Ahhhh!" The man fell, pierced to the brain. Part of his nose had been lobbed off by the blade's keen edge.

Now to see to his son.

Lester was still lying there, his face turned upward.

"Damn ye, you've got to be all right!" Mor shouted. It was a foolish thing to say, and he realized it. Where was help? There had to be help for them. For *him,* Morvin mentally amended. For Lester. For his precious son. If Les didn't live, then all of this was for nought. It was for Lester and Lester's future children, if any, that this war was being fought.

A horse wheeled to his left. Mor jerked on the reins.

A brownberry shirt and greenbriar pantaloons, much dusted and a little smeared with blood. A freckle-faced boy who should be out working his father's fields and whom Mor remembered they had left with the main force at the edge of town.

"We have to retreat," the boy said. "There's too many for us!"

"Greenleaf, is that you?"

"Yes, sir."

"Yes, *Mor.* Show a little respect!"

The boy managed a faint smile. A good lad, this. Mor recognized him from their training sessions. Greenleaf had been as clumsy as Kelvin Hackleberry without his gauntlet, but then had learned. As they all had to learn.

"Les," Mor said, indicating his fallen son. "I'd like to get him out of here. He got clubbed by the flat of a blade. He will live, I think. If we can take him to safety."

"I—I'll see what I can do, s—Mor." Then, turning his head slightly, Greenleaf called, "Broughtner! Over here!"

A dapple gray war-horse joined them. This one was ridden by a craggy-faced, ruddy-complexioned fellow who had some months ago been working hard to be a Franklin's ne'er-do-well.

"You called, Greenleaf?"

"Les, he's down."

Broughtner arrived. "Um, I see."

"Can we take him back?"

"Can try."

"You'll do more than try!" Mor told them. Then, simply because it seemed the appropriate thing to do, he began to swear.

"Look out!" Broughtner cried. In the same instant, Mor's horse gave a terrible scream and started to collapse under him.

Mor got his head twisted around as he fell. He saw the big guardsman who had ridden in at them and the pike that had been deflected downward by Broughtner's blade. The pike had gotten his mount right behind the rib cage.

He had allowed himself to forget that they were still amidst the battle!

Mor hit the ground and rolled over as a war-horse's big hooves tried hard to trample him. Then the big guardsman was coming down to join him and Les. As he fell with flailing arms, Mor saw that his intestines had been split.

"Good work, Greenleaf!" Broughtner called.

"Uh, uh, uh," Greenleaf said, shuddering at his own act.

Saved by a boy and a man whose previous destiny had been to drink himself to death. The ignominy of it! But better alive, better alive than dead.

"You look a bit battered, Mor," Broughtner said.

Mor stood up, shaking his head. It did have a buzz in it, he discovered.

"You'll need Les's horse," Broughtner said. "Better cut the throat of this one."

Mor reluctantly had to recognize the man's good sense. Better do it now, he thought, before the animal suffered more.

He placed his sword tip against the horse's neck, drew back, and mentally called upon whatever gods there were for strength. "Sorry, old friend," he said, and swung hard at the vein he knew was pulsing just beneath the slick hide.

The horse gave a very loud sigh. Blood spurted, catching Mor's face and sword arm. He moved back, wiping at it, refraining from cursing because it wouldn't do to curse his dying equine friend.

"You certain he's alive?" Broughtner asked.

Mor gave him a hard look. "Can't you see that I just killed him?"

"Your son. Not your horse."

Gods! For a moment he had actually forgotten.

Moving as swiftly as his wounds and weariness permitted, he knelt by Lester as Broughtner caught and held the horse. The mount neighed, but steadied under Broughtner's hand.

"Lester, Les, speak to me, speak to me!" But there was no response.

He raised the head a little, and there was blood. Not a lot, not as much as soaked his own clothing, but some. Internal bleeding—how bad was it?

He drew off a gauntlet, wishing again that he might wear the gauntlet the Roundear had. *That* glove was—

The Roundear! Where was he? Mor lurched up, gazing across the battle. There was no sign of Kelvin Hackleberry!

"Find the Roundear!" he panted. "We can't lose *him*!"

"Yes, Mor." Greenleaf cast about, searching.

Mor returned his attention to his son. He felt under the brownberry shirt, trying to find a heartbeat.

"If he's dead, we'll have to leave him," Broughtner said.

Damn the man! "He's alive!" he snapped.

"Then get him on the horse. This horse. You take his."

It took almost all Mor's strength, but he placed his hands underneath Les's arms and hoisted his body up to Broughtner. He had never before felt so incredibly weak! It must be the bleeding, and the drinking last night and the fact that he hadn't really slept. *I've gotten old,* he thought sadly. *But I recognize it.*

Broughtner took Les and positioned him in front of him on the horse. Meanwhile, Greenleaf returned, spreading his hands: he had been unable to locate the Roundear.

"I can't fight this way," Mor complained. "You two will have to watch out for me."

"We will," Greenleaf said.

Mor wished that he could feel as confident.

"The Roundear!" Broughtner cried. "There he is!" He wheeled his horse, almost knocking Mor down.

Mor strained his eyes. He counted six guardsmen riding hard. Slung over the neck of the leading horseman's mount was a slight figure wearing the green and brown. No wonder Greenleaf hadn't spotted Kelvin; he had been draped across an enemy horse!

"After them!" Greenleaf cried, his own dismay sounding.

"No! No, they've got him," Broughtner said. "We can't even catch them, let alone overcome them. Best we get back to the others with the word. Best we get back alive."

Mor grabbed hold of the man on his son's warhorse and levered himself up to a mounted position. His head whirled. He all but slid off. Any notion he had of pursuing was obviously futile.

"Yes," he said reluctantly. "Too many guardsmen. Too many for us to fight anymore."

"We've got to retreat, regroup," Broughtner said.

"Yes. Regroup," Mor gasped. But he was thinking, even as he spoke, mostly of Les.

20 /

NURSE

I T WAS A SAD party that straggled back to the camp. Morvin Crumb was wounded, his son was unconscious, and more than half the Knights were missing.

Jon and Heln ran out together. "Where's Kelvin?" Jon cried, horrified as she failed to spot her brother in the group.

"Captured," Mor said wearily. Then he fell over in his saddle, and others had to catch him before he dropped from his horse.

Jon turned to look at Heln, and found the other's face a reflection of her own horror. Kelvin—captured! What would become of him?

Quickly they learned the details of Kelvin's loss. He had been carried off by several guardsmen, after apparently fighting against one with another gauntlet like his own. "That other—he had round ears!" a Knight said. "I caught one glimpse of him, before I had to defend myself from another charge."

"Roundear magic!" Heln said. "A roundear with a magic gauntlet! That's what the Queen meant!"

"If only we had understood better!" Jon said, her heart gripped by the horror and grief of her brother's fate.

"I must find him!" Heln cried.

Mor, now standing on the ground, propped by two other Knights, responded. "Girl, get that notion from your head! You can't go after him!"

"I meant—my way," she said.

"It's too soon, girl! You haven't recovered from the last time!"

"I love him!" she exclaimed. "I must find him!"

Mor glanced across at the stretcher on which his son lay. "I know how that is. Then do what ye must, girl—but only this once. It won't do him any good if you die from overdosing."

"I'll watch over her," Jon said quickly.

Morvin turned away. "Les—got to get a nurse for him—"

But there was nobody to tend the unconscious man. All the survivors were tired, many of them wounded; it was all they could do to take care of their own.

"Put him in our tent," Jon said. "I can watch two as well as one."

No one argued; they were glad to have her assume this burden, so that the others could collapse. They hauled the stretcher in and got the unconscious young man on Jon's bunk.

Then Heln ate a berry and lay down, and Jon watched both: the unconscious woman and the unconscious man. Both were so still it was as if they were dead. One should recover; the other—

Jon went to Lester Crumb and checked him more closely. There was a trace of blood on his lips, and more in his mouth; something had ruptured inside him and this was the only evidence. How bad was it? She had no way to know, but the fact that he remained unconscious did not bode well.

She decided to do the job right. There was no one else to do it, after all. She got a basin of water and a cloth and washed off his face. Then she stripped his clothing, discovering numerous cuts and bruises, and cleaned these off. She tied bandages around the bad ones, so that no further blood leaked, and formed a more comprehensive bandage for his head, because the whole side of it was one massive purple bruise. It looked as though the blow to his head had caused him to bite his cheek and tongue, and that was the source of the blood in his mouth; that suggested that he had no bad bleeding deeper in his body. That same blow had put him in a coma, and she could do nothing for that except make him comfortable. She covered him over with all the blankets she had, trying to keep his cold body warm, and hoped. Lester Crumb was a decent man, who had helped Kelvin and had always been courteous to Jon herself. It would be awful to have him die.

Heln was normal for this stage, lying as still as a statue, her breathing stopped or was so slight it wasn't evident. There was nothing more for Jon to do except wait.

After half an hour, Les groaned. Jon hurried across and took his hand. Was he pulling out of it?

He turned his head, choked, and spluttered out some saliva and blood. Jon grabbed his shoulders and helped him sit up so that he could cough and get his throat clear. He retched, and spat, and then sank back. She washed off his face again, and found that now it was hot: he was running a fever. But he sank back into a more natural sleep, and that meant that he was recovering. His color was better now, despite (or maybe because of) the fever; he was a handsome man.

Not long later he stirred again, and again she helped him sit up and retch. This time his eyes opened. "Thanks," he said, and slept again.

Then Heln began to recover, and Jon went to attend to her. By this time she was feeling very much the nurse; both her patients were improving!

For the next hour she shuttled between the two, doing her best to keep each comfortable. Heln woke and reported:

"I found him!" she said weakly. "They took him to the dungeon under the Queen's palace and dumped him there with two older men. I think they drugged him, because he never woke up, and somebody said something about how he would sleep for at least another day. He didn't look injured. So I think he'll be all right, and maybe the long sleep will even do him good. But we've got to get him out of that dungeon!"

"That's for sure," Les said, startling them.

Jon turned to him. "I thought you were sleeping."

He smiled. "I was, until I heard you two talking. I seem to be in the wrong tent."

"No, they brought you here so I could watch you," Jon said. "You were unconscious, and your father was wounded, and over half the Knights are gone and the rest in bad state, so—"

"I thank you. But now I had better get out. What happened to my clothes?"

"But you're feverish!"

"Not anymore, I'm sure. We Crumbs heal quickly."

Jon went and put her hand on his forehead. Sure enough, the fever was down. Maybe that was his little bit of magic. She explained about the clothes, and brought them back to him, then turned her back while he dressed.

He stood, and wavered, and she had to run to provide support before he fell. "I think you'd better lie down again," she said.

"No, I've got to consult with my father, plan strategy," he said. "With Kelvin captive—"

Jon could hardly argue with that. "Then I'd better help you walk."

"Ooo, my head!" he said. "I'm dizzy! I think you'd better."

"I'll be all right," Heln said. "Get him to Morvin. If there's any way to rescue Kel—"

Jon supported Les as he staggered out, and got him to Morvin's tent. There a strategy meeting was already in progress. The generals had the war map unrolled and were fretting over it.

"Son!" Mor exclaimed, lurching up to embrace Les. "How are you?"

"Some fool is still slashing about with a sword inside my head," Les said with a pained smile. "But Jon here got me patched up, and Heln has found out that Kelvin's in the Queen's dungeon, so I had to come here."

"The Queen's dungeon!" Mor said. "They haven't killed him?"

"Drugged him. They say he'll sleep for another day. So they can't be planning anything sooner than that."

"They've got their own wounds to lick," Mor said grimly. He looked terrible; the top part of his left ear had been sliced away so that he looked like half a roundear. His left arm was in a sling.

"There's not much we can do but surrender," General Jeffreys said. "The Queen's terms, total and unconditional surrender, aren't to my liking, but—"

"Ye talk like a fool!" Mor snapped. "Surrender unconditionally and she'll hang or imprison the lot of us!"

"She might not," Jeffreys said, looking sheepish and as though he wished he could be back on his farm.

"And I say she will! The officers, at least!"

"I—I agree with my father," Les said. His eyes did not quite focus, but his mind seemed sound. "I gather a messenger arrived while I was sleeping. That means the Queen knows our location, and this may just be stalling for time while she gets together another army to destroy the last of us. If we surrender now, we have to be prepared to flee Rud. Maybe some of us can survive in the Sadlands, a few can venture into dragon country, but most of us will have to get all the way out. I'm hoping that most of us can find our way to Throod. But—"

"You can be sure you'll be taken in," said Captain MacKay. "We Throodians don't abandon our friends."

"I appreciate that, Captain," Les said with dignity. "But my point is, that we could be better off *not* surrendering and being dispersed, with many of us executed out of hand. We might best stick together and fight on. The worst that could happen is that we'd get killed."

"When most of us could live, if we surrender," General Jeffreys said. "Understand, the word is gall in my mouth, but I'm trying to be practical. We have scant resources remaining to fight, and—"

"Har-rumph," said Mor, drawing attention back to himself. "I'm not prepared to say we surrender unconditionally."

"Why not?" General Saunders demanded.

"Because of the Roundear."

"He's captured. Imprisoned in her dungeon. He'll be killed, probably publicly. Even if we had the manpower to raid the dungeon, they'd just kill him before we could fight our way in. They'd like nothing better than to have us present our remaining troops for slaughter like that."

Mor nodded. "Hmm, I hate to agree with you, but I fear you're right. There's little we can do to save him."

"Yes, there is!" Jon exclaimed before she thought. Abruptly all eyes turned to her.

"Jon!" Mor snapped. "Why are you still here? This is a strategy conference! Go outside and—"

"Play?" Jon suggested, knowing that that was not what he had been about to say. "The Roundear you talk about is my brother! He didn't want to be a hero and fight this war. You, Mor, and you, Les, you forced it on him! He'd be back on the farm now, if you hadn't interfered!"

"She's got a point, Father," Les said. "She has a right to be here, and—"

"She doesn't know what she's saying!" Mor said. "She's only a girl!"

"Yes, a girl!" Jon agreed hotly. "And Kel's only a boy. But then, who else are you fighting the war for?"

There was a stunned silence. Jon leaped into it, determined to express her thought. "You told us over and over, Mr. Crumb. 'It's for the young, it's not for the old, that we're fighting this.' Everyone here heard you say it. Everyone in the camp!"

"She's right," Les said.

"Youngster," Mor said, looking sad, "if I could help your brother through direct action—"

"But you can! You can! He fought for you, and now you talk of abandoning him. What kind of people are you? What kind—"

"The realistic kind," Mor said. "We know the difference between fact and fancy. We can't—"

Without giving herself a chance to think, Jon ran at Mor, fists raised. She wanted to punch him into some kind of agreement, crazy as that was.

But Saunders caught her and held her. "What kind of respect is this, you gamin?" His face, normally so calm and solemn, was now fierce.

Jon felt all her madness go. Here she was trying to act like a man again, and succeeding only in childishness. She would be lucky if the general didn't shake her in humiliating fashion.

"Let her go, Saunders," Les said. "She has reason to react. It's her *brother* we're writing off. My father would react much the same if I were the one being deserted."

Mor started to speak, then paused thoughtfully. "Gods," he muttered. "It's true. When I saw you down, son, I couldn't think of anything but—"

Saunders' grip tightened briefly. Then he let go.

"You got anything to say, Jon?" Mor asked. "Anything we need to know?"

"I think we should fight," Jon said. "That's all I have to say."

"We?"

"We patriots. We who care about Rud."

"You're only fourteen, Jon, and female, but you may be right," Les said. "Maybe we should make an all-out effort. Tell the Knights we're making one last effort to take the capital, defeat the Queen, and rescue the Roundear."

"Are you daft?" Mor demanded of his son. "After all you've been through, you still want to fight? I wasn't going to suggest attack, merely that we not surrender."

"I don't want to fight at all," Les said. "But you've convinced me time after time, Father. We have to defeat this tyrant. We have to rid this land of its ugly sore so that it will heal and become fair and free once more. How many times have you said it, Father? How many?"

Mor looked away. "I don't want you to be killed, son. You came too close today! I don't want any more deaths. I don't want to surrender, but if we surrender now and get us to—"

"She'll never let us out. She'll want a formal surrender, with you and me and the main officers. Then you know what will happen? Then she will send us to the dungeons. If we ever get out from there, it won't be in any condition to fight anybody, and more likely just for execution. There's no reprieve in surrender!"

"I—"

"You know it's so!" his son said challengingly.

Jon kept her mouth shut. What a beautiful job Les Crumb was doing, arguing her case! She was glad she had helped him recover.

Mor swallowed, his big throat producing a gurgling sound. "You may be right, son. You may—"

"I say he *is* right!" Saunders said suddenly. "I say we'd *better* fight another battle and make it an all-out one. Even if we don't win, maybe we can force surrender terms."

"How can we win?" Mor asked, his face rigid. "They've got magic."

"No more than we had! Father, we've got *arms*."

"Um, maybe so. One all-out attack on the capital."

"She won't be expecting it now. Not after that last defeat. And she doesn't have that many guardsmen in good shape right now."

Mor turned to the map. As the big man traced a possible route of march and attack, Jon noticed that the river ran all the way into the capital. Why not go by the river, she wondered? But Mor was talking.

"We've lost a lot of ground, and a lot of lives. But if we start our march tomorrow and we're not stopped before we get there, four days will see us there."

"Four days?" Jon asked. "I thought it was only one day's ride from Skagmore to the capital."

"One day's ride for a messenger on a fast horse," Les explained. "Four days for a tired army, hauling supplies, foraging for food. The Queen's guardsmen will take longer than that, because they're licking their wounds and don't believe there is any need to return rapidly to the capital. That's our advantage: striking by surprise, at their weak spot: the capital whose reserves have been expended for the battle just past."

"I'll come along!" Jon said.

"No, you won't, girl," Mor said, turning on her. "Your mother needs to be sure of at least one child. If we fail, that's you. Before we leave, you are starting your march home. The same goes for the roundear girl."

Jon started to protest, but Les made a warning signal. She understood: Les knew that his father had gone as far as he would go, and that it was best to settle for that. And, she realized, Mor was probably right; this tough march and battle, using the remnants of their army, would be no place for two young women. She had to quit while she was ahead.

21 /

TRAVEL

JON WAVED AT THE Knights who had brought them to the road and were now riding back to the camp. *They didn't even give us horses!* she thought angrily. *They could at least have spared us two of the lame ones.* But then, of course, they would have had to lead the animals, and move slow, and find grain and water for them. Besides which, all the animals were needed by the army for this final effort. So they could travel faster than the guardsmen would, and fall upon the capital when its defenses were minimal. She didn't question that; it was her brother who stood to benefit.

Except that the Queen would surely have him killed the moment the attack materialized. What would they gain then, even if they won?

She brushed at some perspiration on her forehead, squinting into the morning mists, wondering why it had to be so hot, hoping the mists would soon rise. They had a long walk ahead.

Maybe, just maybe, they should go back, she thought. But she knew that no girls would be allowed along. Mor had made that absolutely plain.

"Are you thinking what I'm thinking?" Heln inquired.

"Yes, but they'd never let us do it."

"How could they stop us, if we went by a separate route?"

"Separate route?"

"Maybe you didn't know that my folks' farm is between here and the capital."

The capital! If they could get there ahead of the army and rescue Kelvin, so that the Queen *couldn't* kill him—!

Then Jon sobered. "I might sneak in, in the guise of a boy; I've had a lot of practice. But you could never pass for anything but a beautiful girl, and besides that, your ears—"

"But I want to save Kelvin as much as you do!"

"And how do you think you'll help him, if they catch you and rape you again?"

Heln was silent, and Jon was immediately sorry. She was sounding just like Morvin Crumb!

"I mean—" she started awkwardly.

"No, no, you're right," Heln said. "I really can't help him directly. But maybe I can help you to help him. If I eat a dragonberry, and spy out the terrain for you, so that you'll know exactly where to look and what to avoid—"

"Yes!" Jon exclaimed. "Then I could sneak in and free him, before the attack, and then when the attack started it would be easier to get out in the confusion!"

"But first you have to get there," Heln pointed out. "I know my folks would help, if we asked them—"

"Let's go!" Jon exclaimed.

But they were afoot, and that made the distance to Heln's folks' farm stretch out. They plodded step by step, resting when they had to, and gradually the mists lifted.

Ahead was the bridge. She remembered crossing it on the way to dragon country and adventure. How long ago that seemed! Why then, just weeks ago, she had been a child!

She touched the top of her pantaloons and her sling. At least Mor had left her that, she thought. It was a wonder it hadn't been confiscated for the war effort!

They walked on, this time not toward the Hackleberry farm, but toward the Flambeau farm. And by dusk, weary, dirty, and hungry, they reached it.

There was a flurry of amazed greetings as Heln made herself known. She explained how Morvin Crumb had purchased her, and freed her, but that she hadn't been able to communicate with them because that could have alerted the Queen's guardsmen to the whereabouts of the Knights.

"We wondered why they had guardsmen camped nearby, watching us," her father said. "They never did anything, just watched. Until they were called away a few days ago—"

"To fight at Skagmore," Heln finished. "And that's why we're here. This is Jon Hackleberry—"

"Hackleberry! You mean—?"

"His sibling. Jon needs to get quickly to the capital, to help rescue Kelvin, who is the Roundear of Prophecy. I said you'd help—"

"Certainly we'll help. The river flows right down there. We have a raft—"

"A raft!" Jon exclaimed. "Of course!"

So it was arranged. They had a great supper, and then Jon slept while Heln ate another berry. This was risky, because it was the third in as many days, but the need was great.

In the morning, Heln told Jon what she had spied. Kelvin was still asleep, but was supposed to wake soon. The two other prisoners were friendly, and would take care of him. She had studied the layout of the dungeons as well as she could, with all their approaches, and the city around, so was able to make a fair map. Jon now knew where the guards marched, and where the river bypassed their observation.

Heln's point-eared father took her down to the raft tied at the river's edge. "It isn't the fanciest craft," he said apologetically. "We made it to carry firewood down from the forest, and we just lashed the larger logs together with what vines we could find. I think it will hold, but—"

"It's great, sir!" Jon exclaimed. "Much better than I could make!"

"Then the Gods be with ye, lad, and may you rescue your brother just as he rescued our daughter." He set a bag of supplies on the raft.

"Thank you, sir." She didn't like deceiving these good folk about her nature, but feared they would not have let her go if they knew. She scrambled on and took up the heavy pole.

Flambeau untied the raft and shoved it out into the channel. The current caught it and bore it on, slowly rotating, until Jon managed to steady it by poling. She was on her way!

The novelty of it palled soon enough. All she had to do was keep the raft in the channel where the current was strongest, using the pole to push it away from the banks and shallows. Every so often it snagged, but all it took was work to free it. At this rate, she would arrive well before the Knights! She hoped.

A wave rippled up beside the raft. It didn't look natural. She hefted the pole, watching.

There was a great splash, and a sheet of water drenched her. Something the size of a small colt dived underneath the raft. The craft rocked, dipped, and swirled.

A bearver, Jon realized. Probably just playing, but maybe—

A shaggy red head broke the surface. The bearver looked at her, large ears laid back, seemingly considering.

This game was not nearly as much fun for Jon as for the animal. "Go 'way!" Jon called, splashing with the pole.

The bearver seemed not to notice. It dived.

Jon grabbed hold of the edge of her raft just as a loud thump sounded on the bottom, and the whole craft lifted. The thing bowed, the logs sinking down at the edges. "Hold, vines, hold!" Jon prayed. This was a sturdy raft, but it wasn't constructed for this kind of stress!

The support dropped out. The raft smacked the water. The vines parted. Jon found herself in the water with floating logs. She struggled, kicking out.

Then something grabbed her leg.

Now I'm finished, she thought as her head dipped under. All her grand notions of rescuing her brother, and she couldn't even get there without drowning! She inhaled water, and then her head was above water again, and she was choking and spitting it out.

The bearver's head broke water right beside her. It was a cub. An infernal brat!

"Shoo! Scram!" Jon said. She didn't think it intended to eat her. At least, she hoped it didn't.

The bearver blinked muddy-orange eyes. "Ooompth?" it inquired.

"I don't talk bearver," Jon said. "Beat it!"

The animal paddled along beside, far more comfortable in the water than she was.

Jon grabbed a floating log. She was a good swimmer, but the water was swift. She could tire quickly enough even if the bearver let her alone.

She had her sling tucked into the top of her pantaloons. She slid a hand down and got it. But she didn't have any ammunition.

"Shoo, bearver!" she cried, and smacked the creature right across the face.

The bearver looked surprised. Then it opened a large mouth, displaying sharp yellow teeth.

What have I done? What have I done? She wished she could undo what she had done, but of course it was too late.

The bearver shook its head, splashed water on her with a paw, and swam away.

Jon sighed, amazed at her luck. Apparently she had hurt its feelings more than its body, and it had retreated in a pique instead of advancing in a rage. A mature one might have reacted otherwise. She grabbed at a new log, and determined that she would rebuild the raft if she possibly could, adding new and stronger vines.

She was in luck. The main part of the raft remained tangled together; not all the vines had broken. Her bag of supplies was bobbing nearby. She clambered aboard the remnant, got the pole, used it to snag the bag, and then pushed for shore.

Landing the craft proved to be no problem. Repairing it was more difficult. Here there were no decent vines; she had to use the ones she had come with, and she didn't trust them.

She sat on the shore and opened the bag, pondering what to do. Inside she discovered really nice food: nuts, fruits, and bread, now sodden but still good. Heln's folks had been kinder to her than she had known!

She finally gave up on the notion of rebuilding the raft; she just didn't have the time to go in search of the necessary vines. At last, regretfully, she tied the bag of supplies to her waist, and launched out from the shore with a floating log with a vine looped around it.

The log promptly dunked her. When she climbed back on, it dunked her again. It wasn't nearly as easy to stay on a single log as she had supposed!

It's a long, long way, she thought. Could she make it? Could she make it there ever, let alone on time? She began, not for the first time this day, to feel really sorry for herself.

A stinging fly flew down and lit on her nose. Jon struck at it. She missed the fly but scored on her face. Her hand came loose from the vine she was holding, and then she was at pains to get hold of it again.

Was it going to be this way all the way, she wondered? She was very much afraid that it was. Still, she intended to get there, no matter what. She clung to the log and let the central current carry her. This wasn't much fun, but it was getting her in the right direction.

As it grew dark she found a sandbar, landed, ate some more from the bag —bless the Flambeaus!—stretched herself out, and lapsed into a fully exhausted sleep.

22 /

TOMMY

JON WOKE FOR THE second morning in a row feeling stiffer and sorer than she had ever felt before. How she wished that the bearver hadn't broken up her raft! She had managed to lash two logs together so that she could lie on them and float with some efficiency, but then the sun beat down on her back, and she had to spend much of the time in the water anyway. She had made, by her best estimate, adequate time, staying constantly in the swiftest current, but it was one wearing effort!

She crawled out from behind the log where she had slept, stretched, yawned, and rubbed her eyes. Blearily she walked to the nearest appleberry bush and proceeded methodically to eat her breakfast. She lacked her brother's finesse with ripening the fruits being plucked, but these were pretty good anyway. She was fortunate that these bushes grew all along the river, and even more fortunate that the bag of supplies the Flambeaus had provided had enabled her to remain all day in the river, not having to break to forage for food while traveling. That was perhaps the major reason for her moderate progress.

She discovered a few rounded stones near the bushes. She picked them up; they were just right for her sling. She didn't want to encounter a bearver again without ammunition.

As she made ready for yet another siege of log-clinging, her spirits dampened. *This is turning out to be one miserable adventure,* she thought. She chewed the last of the appleberries, relishing the taste less than she had on the first morning. *I'll never get to the capital, and if I do, what can I do? I haven't an army. All I've got is my sling.*

She felt sorrier for herself and more discouraged than ever before in her life. Why was she even bothering to try to be a stupid male-type hero? She wasn't even a male! The very notion of getting there in time, and then being able to sneak past the guards into the dungeon, and then get her brother out —what had ever made her think she could manage all that? The guardsmen

146

would surely catch her, and discover what she was, and she knew what they would do then. Maybe she should admit that her mission was impossible, and quit right now.

She wiped appleberry juice from her mouth and looked across the river. And her heart made a leap like that of a fly-snaring fish.

There was a boat. A small boat, containing one man. The man was hunched over, rowing, and two fishing poles stuck out of the back of the craft. As it drew near, Jon could see the man's gray hair and seasoned face. Soon he had pulled almost abreast of her.

Could she somehow wangle a ride? That would be an enormous help! Maybe she could, after all, make it in time. Then—well, she would worry about the rest when the time came. After all, she did know the layout, thanks to Heln's astral visit. What had seemed doubtful now seemed promising.

"Catching any?" she called.

The boatman paused in his rowing, tugging a large ear with freckled spots on it. "Eh?"

He couldn't hear well, Jon realized. She should have kept still and let him row right past. But curse it, she hadn't seen other than bearvers and mooear for the past two days, and she didn't know how far she had still to go. She was anxious for information and any help she could beg.

The boat's oarlocks squeaked as the old man resumed rowing, drawing closer. He was coming in to meet her. Jon waited, working out what she would say. She stepped a little nearer to the bank.

The boat bumped shore and the old boatman raised rheumy eyes to look at her. "Eh?" he repeated.

"I said, sir, I was wondering how far to the capital?"

"The capital's right over there, lad," he said, pointing a trembly hand at the opposite shore.

Jon blinked. The morning fog still hid the other bank. It might have been possible for her to float right by the capital and not know it!

"Uh, thanks," she said. Now she was uncertain again, because she had decided to worry about getting past the guards when she arrived, and here she was already! Did she really want to risk this? Did she have any chance, realistically?

The old man was looking at her speculatively, his forehead furrowed and his hand on his chin. "You wouldn't be one of the bound boys, would you?"

"Bound boy!" Jon kicked herself mentally. She had all but forgotten both her situation and her masquerade. She had indeed been sold in the Mart, and remained technically the property of the dwarf who had bought her, and of course the old boatman had taken her for the boy she pretended to be. "I'm not bound to anyone," she said, deciding it was true. Her delivery to the Boy Mart had been illegal, so nothing that had followed was legal, and anyway, she had been rescued. Certainly she had never been a bound *boy*!

"Not with the maintenance crew, then?"

"What maintenance crew?"

"What maintenance crew? My, you are a stranger, aren't you! The maintenance crew at the palace. The grounds maintenance crew. Never less than a dozen boys, cutting grass, trimming trees, repairing walks. You say you're not one?"

"I'm not," Jon said, wondering if he was an agent for the Queen. No, that was unlikely; the old man could hardly row his boat, let alone recapture a bound boy.

"Well, if ye are, I'm not blaming you. Dirty business, this bound boy business. Dirty business!"

"Yes, it is," Jon said. *Glad you think so, oldster! You could be my big break!*

"I've got a grandson got bound. Little skinny fellow. You know him? His name's Tommy. Tommy Yokes."

Jon felt her mouth open. Tommy? Here? The boy who had kept her secret at the Boy Mart, then summoned the guards so as to stop her from getting raped? She could hardly think of a person she would rather encounter, if she needed help getting into the dungeon undiscovered.

"I—I know him," she said.

"You do? Really?"

Jon nodded. "We went to school together after he moved to our village. I'm—" No, better not give her name, she realized; the old man just might recognize it, and know her for a girl. "A friend of his."

"Ye are! Why, that's something, that is!"

"Yes, it is. It really is. Is Tommy working with the maintenance crew?"

"He is. Has to. You see, he has no choice."

"I know. Once a boy's been sold into slavery—I mean, legally bound—"

"Ye had it right the first time, lad! The way the Queen squeezes the common workingman—"

"Could you row me across the river, Mr. Yokes? I haven't anything to pay you with, but—"

"I can row you. But ye'd best not go. Many a greedy hand in the capital would have you impressed, bound, and sold. You'd be working with Tommy, then, but you wouldn't like it much."

"I'm sure I wouldn't like it!" Jon agreed. "But I—I've business."

"But no money?"

Jon shook her head. "I'm sorry, Mr. Yokes. I'd pay you if I could."

Yokes scratched an ear again. "Maybe I can lend you a wee coin until you've seen Tommy from a distance. That what you want to do?"

"That's part of it."

"Yes, I can lend you a rudna. And if one of the guardsmen grabs you, tell him I'm your employer. Tell him you're checking on my grandson for me."

"I'll do that!" Jon agreed.

"Well, get in the boat."

Jon got in and pushed them free of the bank. The old man rowed. Straining her eyes, Jon could make out the piled-box affair that was the royal palace. She wondered if she would actually get there, and if she did, would she see Tommy and maybe find out a little more about Kelvin? It had now been three days since Heln had checked, and anything could have happened. Her brother might even have been moved to some other prison. At the moment she just couldn't be sure of anything. That was part of what made it such nervous business.

"Well, here we are," the old man called as their boat bumped the opposite shore.

Jon scrambled to get out. "Thanks, Mr. Yokes, and—"

"Here. Here's the rudna. Now, you be sure and look me up and tell me you've seen Tommy."

"I will, Mr. Yokes." The grandfather was as decent a man as the grandson!

"I'll be fishing all day. I fish all day every day. But I've a house over there. Just a shack, with a couple goeep staked out front. If you need a place to stay, you can stay with me and fish."

"Thank you. Thank you, Mr. Yokes. I've a brother—"

"Oh, then you're not alone in the world."

"No. Not quite."

"You're lucky, then. But if you need help keeping out of the Boy Mart, come to me. I'll help any young fellow I can."

"Thank you. Thank you," Jon repeated. She had never felt more grateful to anyone, or more guilty. This old man was giving her trust and help, and she was deceiving him about her nature and her mission. Yet, if he knew either, would he let her go into that danger? She couldn't risk it. She took the rudna, pocketed it, and prepared to climb out of the boat.

"One thing more," the old man said. "This being so early, the grounds maintenance crew will be at their camp back of the orchard. That's along the palace wall and then right. Just follow that big wall, but keep away from guardsmen and anyone else you see. Some of those fellows are real eager to 'press; they get a bonus for anything they bring in, you know."

"I'll remember," Jon said. She hardly needed that particular warning! She wondered whether her greenbriar pantaloons and brownberry shirt would identify her as from the country. Well, it was way too late to change.

She climbed out, bending over to hold on to the rim of the boat while she stepped to shore.

"Hold on, that won't do at all," the man said. "Not at all."

"What?" she asked, pausing with one foot out and one in.

"Got to patch up that tear in your shirt, or the whole world'll know."

Jon looked down. Indeed, her shirt was torn, and at the moment, the tear was gaping open, showing her bosom quite clearly. She had never worn an undergarment in that region, considering it unmasculine. "Oops." The material must have snagged on a sharp branch when she got dunked, because no normal stress would damage the tough fabric.

"I have needle and thread," he said. "I patch my own, you know, these days." He fumbled in a small chest, and brought them out.

Jon climbed back into the boat. It occurred to her that the man didn't seem surprised. "You knew?"

"I'm halfway deaf, but I'm not blind, child. I raised a son and a daughter, and I still know the difference atween them. You were doing such a good job of being a boy, I figured you might pass if you wanted to, so I let it be. I know a girl wouldn't dare go where you're going. But that tear's worse'n I thought. Here, I'll get it."

Jon sat still in the boat while he worked on her front, carefully sewing the tear closed. It wasn't the neatest job, but it was adequate, and it made it impossible to see through to her body. Though his hands had to brush her front frequently to complete the job, he took no liberties; he was just making sure the job was done right. He was like his grandson in this respect too: he could keep a secret, and offered help only when it was warranted.

"I—I don't know how to thank you, Mr. Yokes," she said as he finished and knotted and broke off the thread.

"Just make sure nobody else catches on," he said. "You're playing a dangerous game, girl."

She stood, leaned forward, and kissed him on his weathered cheek. Then, quickly, she stepped out.

"And she said she didn't know how to thank me," the old man muttered as she shoved his boat out into deeper water. He touched his cheek, then grabbed the oars. Jon had to smile.

Following the wall as the old man had instructed, she soon came to a squalid series of tents. Heln had not described these, which meant that they must have been set up in the last two or three days. Probably the boys pitched their tents in whatever section of the palace grounds they had to work on that day. As she looked out from behind a tree, she saw a large boy belaboring another with a stick.

"You going to work today, Tommy Yokes? Or are you going to hang back again and pretend you're sick?"

"I'll work," Tommy said, cringing back from the stick. "I know you're the foreman, Bustskin, but I can't work when I'm sick."

"You can try," Bustskin said, and poked his stick in the thinner boy's stomach.

Then the big boy turned—and saw Jon.

Suddenly Jon felt enraged. After all she had been through, after facing a bearver at very close range, Bustskin held little terror for her. She knew he would recognize her in a moment, and she knew what he would do then. She had a vision of Heln, huddled in her cell, the victim of rape. That enraged her further. What right did any male have to—

Bustskin's mouth opened. Tommy, spying her himself, reached for him, as if to stop him from going after her. Bustskin swung his fist backhanded, not even looking, and smacked him hard on the chest.

Then Jon's sling was in her hand, and she was putting a stone in it, and her arm was swinging forward, seemingly all in the same motion. Bustskin was wide open, because of his strike at Tommy.

The rock flung true. It struck Bustskin in the stomach, hurled with all the force Jon could muster. He doubled over, dropping the stick and clutching himself in surprise and pain.

"Get him!" Jon said, starting forward herself. She knew that if Bustskin got away, or even got a chance to yell, her effort would be all over.

The younger boy leaped on Bustskin's back and bore him to the ground. Tommy began pummeling him, as Bustskin tried futilely to defend himself. Jon picked up the stick, ready to knock the big boy on the head. But now Tommy seemed to require little help. He was raining blows on Bustskin, smashing into his chest, neck and face.

"Stop! Stop!" Jon cried. "He's unconscious!"

"I want him that way!" Tommy gasped. "I want him never to wake up!"

Such fury! Now that Tommy had a chance to get even, he was almost uncontrollable. But she had a more important task than beating up the bully.

"We have to tie him up and get him out of sight."

"Why? A lot of kids'll be glad he got what's been coming to him!"

"And a lot of guardsmen won't! I want to take his place."

"What?" He was dumbfounded.

"So that I can go with you through the palace gate, onto the palace grounds, and get inside the building. So that I can rescue my brother from whatever dungeon he's in."

Tommy looked at her, freshly amazed. "You're crazy! The guardsmen will kill you!"

"Not," Jon said evenly, "if I have your help. *Do* I have your help?"

Tommy grinned sickly. He looked at his enemy on the ground. "You've got more than that," he said. "You have my friendship—right up until a guardsman takes your life, and mine. Because once they find out what we've done here—"

That, Jon thought, feeling the chill of what she had gotten into, could be all too soon. But she shrugged it off. "Your grandfather sends his greeting," she said, as they got to work tying and hauling Bustskin. "I promised to tell him how you're doing, but now I think I'd better deliver you personally to him. There'll be no life for you here, after this."

"That's for sure!" he agreed.

23 /

KIAN

THE FIRST THING KELVIN was aware of was the smell: stale and musty. Then he heard the drip, drip, drip of moisture. His mouth tasted bad and his head ached. He placed a hand on the back of his skull and felt a lump, but he did not remember being hit. Slowly, hating the necessity, he opened his eyes.

Rock walls. Chains. Two faces, bearded and dirty, looking down at him. He felt around and discovered he was lying on straw. High overhead a barred window let in a little light that illuminated only this end of the cell.

"Welcome to the Queen's dungeon, lad," the man with the grayer beard said.

His gauntlet was gone, Kelvin discovered. That other fellow probably had the pair, assuming the two gloves hadn't destroyed each other.

"I'm the former King of this land," said the graybeard. "Not that it makes any difference now. Who, lad, might you be?"

Kelvin took a deep breath. So this was the rightful King of this land—King Rufurt! Somehow he had the impression that the King already knew Kelvin's identity.

And the other man—Kelvin's head whirled when he looked at him. The man's eyes were as blue as his own. That was what had caught his attention about his enemy, the one wearing the right-hand magic gauntlet. The enemy's eyes had been dark and blue, too.

And—this man had round ears!

"Recognize me, Kelvin?" the man asked in a husky voice. His voice seemed to choke as he said it.

"F-father?" Kelvin gasped.

Then, suddenly, he and his father were hugging each other. "I thought you were dead!" Kelvin said.

"It's a long story," John Knight said. "A long, long story. But we have plenty of time. Tell me how you come to be here. All we know is that you've been unconscious from the drug for two days; we were concerned that you would suffer amnesia or something."

Kelvin did not have amnesia. He told them everything. It took some time.

His father listened to all his adventures without comment. He did flinch when told of his wife's remarriage, but relaxed when reassured that Hal Hackleberry was a good man who had taken excellent care of all members of the family. He swore briefly and colorfully when told of Cheeky Jack's stealing the gold and kidnapping Jon. He was skeptical about the magic gauntlet at first, but then seemed to accept it. He was interested to learn of Heln, the female roundear. The forming of the Knights of the Roundear, and the subsequent battles, fascinated him.

John Knight asked many questions when Kelvin was done. Kelvin answered patiently. Finally his father began to talk himself, and then it was Kelvin's turn to be fascinated.

"Son, I've long hoped to talk to you this way, but I thought it unlikely that the chance would ever come. It's high time! You see, I was born in another—I suppose you could call it another existence. Things are different there. Not better, necessarily, just different. Many of the things that are here regarded as make-believe are normal there. Flying machines, horseless carriages, talking boxes, moving pictures, thinking machines, nuclear bombs. Fantasy here, but reality there. And in my world much of what is taken for granted here is regarded as fantasy. Magicians, prophecies, magic gauntlets, astral separation—I never believed in these things until too late. I suppose there's a leakage between the universes, somehow, so that the visions, if not the reality, cross over. People in this world imagine horseless carriages, while people in my original world imagine magic gauntlets."

The man paused, rubbing his eyes. "It is better in my world in some ways; many of us have conveniences that you can only dream about, literally. But it is also worse in some ways. We have pollution, crime, inflation—these become complex to explain, but they are nevertheless pervasive evils. So when I came here, I thought this world a paradise. It seemed so peaceful, so safe from such things as bombs—"

Kelvin could keep silent no longer. "How did you get here?" he asked. "To this world. Zatanas claims he brought the roundears here—"

"Zatanas! That old fraud? He had nothing to do with it! He just pretends he did, so that others will think him more powerful than he is. He's strictly a magic man, not an alternate-worlds man."

"I thought as much," Kelvin said. "But if it wasn't him, then—"

"How?" His father seemed to look backward into time, sorting it all out behind his suddenly closed eyelids. "They called it a 'clean atomic artillery shell,'" he said. "They said we were in no danger. Just testing, as they'd tested other weapons on other human sacrifices. We were soldiers, but not one of us wanted to be there, any more than the boys and girls sold at the

Marts want to be there. I was a platoon leader. There were twelve men in my squad, counting Mary Limbeck and Jeanne Donovan. The girls were the only ones who tried to pretend it was a lark. The shells were supposed to whiz overhead, but one of them didn't. I saw it coming in, yelled 'Hit the dirt!' and then . . . I suppose the other squad escaped, but us, we were right under. Somehow, someway, we ended up—"

"In Rud?" Kelvin asked excitedly. Now at last he was getting answers to questions he had had all his life, and he could hardly contain himself. The miseries of his bruised head and body, and his confinement in this dungeon, were for the moment forgotten.

"In Throod. At the lip of what you call The Flaw—that big, incredible tear right through the center of . . . existence. Anyway, we were there, wearing combat equipment. All twelve of us. We had on our uniforms. We each had a laser pistol and hand grenades. Four of us had jet-propulsion backpacks. None of us had radiation sickness, though at first we feared—"

"Radiation sickness?"

"Forget it. Or think of it as a hostile type of magic that causes people to bleed from unbroken skin and waste away and die, with no cure. Just let me tell you that we were all right. *All right!* That was our miracle, perhaps our first taste of magic. We set about living, and we found that we were in the one land where mercenaries were commonly recruited. We heard of some fighting in Rud. The two women, wouldn't you know, married locals and settled in Throod—"

"Heln's mother!" Kelvin exclaimed.

"I don't think so," John Knight said. "Every one of their children I know of had pointed ears. Round ears seems to be a patrilineal trait, here."

"But—"

"What was her mother's name?"

"Helen."

He nodded. "I may have an alternative explanation for you, in a moment. To continue: we brave ten men were out to get our fortunes."

"Fortune came a-callin'," Kelvin said.

"Right! Fortune came a-calling, and only the women hid—we thought. We ten went to Rud and to Rud's contemptible would-be Queen. Queen Zoanna, she calls herself, and I can well believe her father is the legendary sorcerer. She bewitched us, I tell you. Every one of us, but especially me."

"What did you do, Father?" Kelvin was breathless.

"What did I do? What weak men have ever done when confronted with the likes of her. She convinced me that the King here"—he jerked a finger at Rufurt—"was dead. I didn't know different. I fought for her, with my nine men. She got her kingdom and four of the men got their deaths, pierced by arrows or spears or lances. The six of us roundears who survived the campaign thought we'd lead rich and idle lives."

He shook his head. "Ha! We were fools. She distrusted us too much. She was devilishly clever in the manner she first divided us, then eliminated us. Me, she married; the others she imprisoned one by one. I, befuddled by her wiles, didn't catch on until it was too late, and I realized that I alone remained free—and I was in fact captive in the palace. I tried to leave, and could not. Then I knew what I should have known at the outset. I stormed at her, threatened to kill her. But I was a fool even then, for she had deprived me of my weapons. Before I knew it, guards had hold of me and were dragging me to the dungeon on her orders."

"But the Queen—" Kelvin started.

"The Queen. Yes, the Queen. She took a new consort, the first of a long line of them. She never made the mistake of choosing a strong-willed one again; each was a marvel of spinelessness. The latest is a jellyfish by the name of Peter Flick, a coward and a sniveler of the worst sort. Perhaps that's why she fell under the spell of her father, who claims responsibility for our being here. He was the only strong man remaining in her life. He gave her advice, and she killed—I call it murder, but she called it execution—my remaining men, one by one. You see, she still wanted something from me, and each time she asked for my cooperation and I told her to go to hell, she killed one of my men, and made sure I knew it. Finally, to save the last of the five, I agreed to do part of what she asked. It wasn't totally against my will, I confess. In that manner I bought his freedom; she swore to me that she would let him go, let him out of Rud unharmed, and I think she honored that. I never knew what happened to him after that, though I think I can guess now."

"I don't understand! What did you agree to do, and why do you think the Queen honored the agreement?"

"The two are linked, Kelvin. The Queen keeps me alive because she—we—have a son. It's not that she has any particular affection or loyalty to either of us, but her magician father advises her to maintain us both in health. Again, I never knew why—until I heard your story. The favor she wanted was for me to train our son in the way of roundear magic, as she puts it, and I think she honored her agreement to free my last man because she was afraid that if she didn't, and I found out, I would take it out on the boy. So she offered a life for a life—my man's life against our son's life. I did train our boy, and I did not try to turn him against his mother. I kept my part of the bargain, and now I am glad I did, because I see that she kept hers."

"But how can you know that?"

"Your roundear girlfriend—who do you think was her natural father?"

"Heln!" Kelvin exclaimed. "She—had a roundear mother, who had to give her up, and—"

But John Knight was shaking his head. "My surviving man was nicknamed St. Helens, after a volcano, because his temper—well, that's irrelevant."

"Helens?" There was the name, all right! "But—"

"Think it through, son. If you married a pointear and wanted to protect her from possible malice by the Queen, what would you do?"

Then it came to him. "They put out the story that it was the *woman* who was the roundear! So that the Queen's guards would not realize that the man had a child, or where he was—"

"And when things got too hot anyway, then he just disappeared, drawing away the pursuit—"

"And Heln's *pointear* mother remarried—just as my mother did! And Heln herself never knew—"

"That's the way it goes," John Knight agreed. "Surely St. Helens knew that his daughter would be safer in a point-eared family, and that her mother would take care of her, just as I knew that your mother would do the right thing. Surely it was painful for him, as it was for me, but necessary."

"Yes, Mr. Flambeau is a fine man," Kelvin agreed. "He protected her, but when the taxes got too bad, she volunteered to go to the Mart—and I guess I'm glad she did, even though she got—"

"There are aspects of the life of the good folk of Rud that none of us like," John Knight said gravely. "That's why the prophecy is so important, about the overthrow of the tyranny. I never believed that prophecy, but now I think I do. If you really are the one—"

"But you—how did you get free to—?"

"To sire you and Jon? Kelvin, I escaped once. My other son helped me, though I didn't ask him to. Apparently even the Queen could not eradicate all decency from him. He was only three at the time, but he managed to distract a guard so that my cell gate didn't get properly locked, and 'accidentally' let me get out. I'm proud to say that I destroyed every weapon that remained from my own world, with the exception of one flying unit, which I couldn't find but know the Queen has hidden away somewhere. And a few grenades and laser pistols. Your mother was—now, there is a *real* queen! She knew where I had come from, what I had been doing, and accepted me anyway. She was—*is*—the most beautiful woman I know, outside and inside. There, on that land with her, and with you and Jon, that was *really* paradise. But it couldn't last. I knew it couldn't. I heard of the spies coming, and I left you and my only true wife, and I took with me the grenades and the pistols. I used those weapons to defend myself. I left fragments of guardsmen, and suspect that those were found and identified as me. That's why the word went out that I was dead. Well, long life to Charlain! She deserves better than an otherworld roundear!" He paused, wiping his eyes.

Kelvin considered what he had learned. Now at last he knew the full story of his father's origin, and his own! But there was one other matter. He took a deep breath. "About your son—yours and the Queen's."

"Kian. Yes, fine boy, Kian. Or he could be. You met him under unfortunate circumstances. Perhaps when he visits you—"

"Visits me?" Kelvin could not conceal his surprise. "Here, in this dungeon?"

"Turn around and look," his father advised.

Kelvin turned, startled. There stood his opponent of the battlefield, the one he had fought gauntlet-to-gauntlet. Kian, blue eyes, blond hair, a light blond mustache, and round ears. Four years older than Kelvin himself. How had he failed to recognize him immediately as his half brother? Because he hadn't known he *had* a half brother!

Kian was now wearing the gauntlets as a pair. Did they work as well for him? If they did, he must be truly invincible, immune to anything short of a projectile. No swordsman alive could fight as well as those gauntlets could!

"Kelvin, brother," Kian said. His voice, too, was a little high-pitched, much like Kelvin's own.

Kelvin stood up from the bed of straw that served as furniture. He felt woozy, and his head hurt, but in a moment he steadied. "We are brothers," he agreed. No use denying it, and he really couldn't bear Kian a grudge.

"I'm glad you were not killed," Kian said. "You could never be my brother, dead, or my friend."

"Yes," Kelvin said. Was Kian as lonely as he, deep inside?

"You know about the prophecy," Kian said. "It refers to me. I'm to rid the land of Rud of a sore: your band of Knights, Kelvin. Now that the confusion engendered by the separation of the gauntlets has been abated."

Kelvin choked back an exclamation of astonishment. That was one enormously interesting interpretation! What would his mother Charlain have made of it? What had John Knight and King Rufurt made of it?

"We both have round ears, Kelvin," Kian continued. "My mother, the Queen, explained it to me."

Kelvin looked at his father, and his father shrugged. Then, seemingly taking pity on him, John Knight spoke.

"If prophecy isn't all nonsense, he could be right, Kelvin. But of course it could refer to you, too, or to Heln Flambeau. Who knows, where prophecy is concerned?"

"I did defeat you in battle," Kian said.

"No, you didn't!" Kelvin said hotly. "I fought you to a standstill!"

"He's got you there, Kian," their father said. "I think it has to be called a draw."

"Without the gauntlet you were wearing—" Kian started.

"And without the one *you* were wearing—"

Both broke off, and Kelvin had half an impulse to laugh. If the situation had not been so serious—

"You see, Kelvin," their father said, "Peter Flick has been after Zoanna to get Kian trained to the jet-propulsion backpack unit and the laser pistols —all the otherworld weapons left. I trained him in the background of our world, its philosophies and politics and technology, so he understands the principles, but not the specifics. He knows enough to know that if he tries to use that jet unit he's likely to break it or get himself killed in an accident, and of course he doesn't know how to charge the pistols. So my input remains necessary; that was one safeguard I kept. Kian's loyalty is to his mother, and he thinks he can't have it for an alien creature such as me. Right, Kian?"

Kian shook his head. "No. I would be loyal to you, Father, were you not the sworn enemy of my mother."

John Knight turned away, and Kelvin realized that he had hoped for a more positive answer. He had challenged Kian to agree that his own father was an alien creature unworthy of loyalty, or to disagree and to change sides; instead Kian had steered a careful course between the extremes. Kelvin had to respect that.

But Kian's face was stricken for a moment. Kelvin realized that Kian wished he did not have to choose between his father and his mother, and felt bad about doing it. Kian was free, and in the Queen's favor, but his course was not easy.

"We may be on different sides," Kelvin said, "but we're still brothers."

Kian flashed him a look of gratitude, then covered that, too. Obviously he could not afford much emotional attachment to the enemies of his mother, whatever his private inclinations might be.

"Well, isn't this cozy?" a new voice came. A man virtually pranced in, like a high-spirited pony. He came to stand beside Kian, his right hand on his sword. "The roundears united. Unnatural father and two unnatural sons."

"You scum!" John Knight exclaimed. He was suddenly at the bars, reaching through them like an enraged animal.

"What are you doing here, Peter Flick?" Kian inquired coldly. "Did my mother get tired of spanking your fanny and dump you in the dungeon with your betters?"

Kelvin saw the expression of wild fury pass from the face of his father to the face of the Queen's consort without losing anything in transition. A backhand across the face could not have been more effective. Flick's right hand went for his sword—but Kian's left hand shot out to intercept it halfway there. The gauntlet must have squeezed cruelly, for Flick clenched his teeth.

"One day you will go too far, alien spawn!" Flick gritted.

"I doubt you'll ever see it, rear-kisser," Kian retorted. "Now state your foolish business and get out; you're making the cell stink." He released the man's wrist and turned his back.

Kelvin couldn't help himself; he was getting to like his half brother. Naturally Kian didn't like the man who was taking his father's place in the Queen's bedroom, and because Kian was of the Queen's own flesh, he had immunity to the threats of the other. So he really wasn't being brave. But he had a very pretty turn of the phrase.

"I'm here to lay out the facts," Flick said. "Either you, John, cooperate in teaching Kian to use the magic flying harness and the magic lightning-makers, or your Rud brat here will pay. Neither Zoanna nor I have love for that one—Zoanna least of all. I remind you that the torturer's coals are hot. The chains are oiled. The spikes are very sharp. Finally, should all that fail, there is her dear old father and the use he has for youthful blood. For the boy's sake, you had really better cooperate."

Kelvin looked at his father and felt great fear. Would this man whom he hardly knew help his enemy in order to save him? Would John Knight let him be tortured? And what was that about the magician and his need for blood?

"You disgust me, you dragon dropping," Kian said, flashing a look of pure ire at Flick. "That is my brother you're threatening with torture!"

"Then you'd better help convince your father to cooperate," Flick said with satisfied malice. "You are the one who will benefit, you know."

"How can you trust me?" John asked. He seemed genuinely curious.

"Why, the usual way, of course. There will be expert crossbowmen watching. And of course you won't be allowed to touch the otherworld artifacts. You will stand back and direct Kian with your voice. And you will direct correctly, or—" He looked at Kelvin significantly.

Kelvin wondered if he could stand torture. He doubted it. The very thought made him ill. Looking at his father's clenched fist, seeing how much it was costing him, he still wished him to agree.

"All right!" John said. "All right! Tell her I'll do what she wants, but to keep her father out of it."

"Agreed," Peter Flick said, smirking. He danced on out.

"I want you to know I had no part of this ugly ploy," Kian said, his gauntleted fists clenching.

"I know it, son," John Knight said.

Kian turned abruptly and strode from the dungeon. Kelvin knew this was not anger but his effort to conceal his flush of pleasure at the term their father had used. Kian might hate Flick and the Queen's methods, but he was on the Queen's side, and had to maintain his composure.

24 /

IRONY

Heln couldn't stand the suspense any longer. It was now the fourth day since Jon's departure; had she made it in time? Were the Knights attacking as they had planned? And, most important, what about Kelvin? Was he still in the dungeon with the two older men, or had something worse happened to him? She had to know, even if she couldn't do anything about any of it!

She had explained to her folks about the dragonberries, and how they had helped the Knights fight. Her mother was concerned, but agreed that if the berries had worked several times before, they should be safe enough to try again. She promised not to panic when Heln seemed to go into a coma or even to die. She understood about youth and love. "After all, I loved your roundear father," she said gently. "I was grief-stricken when he had to go."

"What?" Heln asked, thinking she had misheard.

"It is time for you to know, dear. You were not completely adopted. Your father, not your mother, was the roundear. I always was your mother. I did not want to burden you with this knowledge before, but now that you have found a roundear of your own—"

"But *why*?" Heln asked. She had no memory of the one she had been told was her original mother. Now, abruptly, she had learned that the parent she thought adoptive was genuine, while the one she thought genuine was adoptive. Her mother, not her father, was natural. She had never suspected!

"The Queen's guardsmen were searching for a grown roundear man," she said. "I believe now, from what you have told me, that it was your friend Kelvin's father. But they would have killed any roundear man they found. It was just too risky for my husband to stay; too many people knew him, knew he was of foreign origin. So I moved with you to Rud, where they would never expect the family of a roundear to go, and he went the opposite way. I never heard from him again, and fear he is dead. But if they had caught him with us, they would have killed us too, just to be sure. Your father saved us by deserting us, just as Kelvin's father did. I remarried for the same reason Kelvin's mother did: to complete the concealment. We hid your ears, and I married Frond Flambeau, and that is the way it has been ever since. I'm afraid I rather threw myself at him; he was a good man, but plain, a widower, and it seemed to me he would be a decent provider. So I promised him everything he might wish in a woman, if he would keep the secret and treat you as his own. He agreed, and he did that, and I don't regret my decision, though I never really loved him. He even protected me by claiming that he was your natural father, from an affair with a roundear woman, so that no one would suspect you were the child of a hunted man."

"You—you made yourself a plaything of a man you didn't love—just to protect me?" Heln asked, horrified.

"For myself, too, dear," her mother said. "I needed the security. This land is not necessarily kind to a woman without protection. I never deceived Frond about my motives, and as it turned out, he needed a woman to manage the farm, and I think perhaps I was a more attractive woman than he might otherwise have had. Not all marriages are made in paradise, but they can work well enough when their basic aspects are understood. If you marry another roundear, you may face similar realities."

Heln thought about her ravishment at the Girl Mart. She had not told her mother of that aspect of her experience, but perhaps she suspected. Sometimes desperate measures were required to keep body and sanity together. Heln had pretty much thrown herself at Kelvin similarly, wanting a man who would understand about her ears and who would not try to do to her what the guards had. How could she blame her mother for choosing rationally and doing what was necessary to secure her situation? Frond Flambeau *was* a good man, just as Hal Hackleberry was, and it seemed that in each case attractive women had used them for their own purposes but rewarded them too. Heln knew that Frond Flambeau had loved her mother deeply from the outset, and had taken excellent care of Heln herself in order to be sure that her mother would never wish to leave him. It had been no choice of his to send her to the Mart! But Heln, feeling guilty for the extra burden her existence placed on him and the family, had insisted, and had paid a worse price than she ever expected, and received a better reward than she had dreamed of, in encountering Jon and Kelvin.

"I think I am ready for those realities," Heln said. "I always believed Frond was my father, and I see no reason to change my opinion now."

"I am pleased to hear you say that," her mother said. Her words were mild, but there were tears streaming down her face.

Then Heln took a dragonberry, and sank into her sleep of astral separation.

Soon she drew free of her body, and saw her mother sitting nervously beside that body, trusting that what Heln had told her was true, but nevertheless afraid of her seeming death. She was sorry her mother had to suffer this concern, but there was no other way.

She willed herself to the capital, and to the dungeon where she had found Kelvin before. She was horrified when she found the cell empty; where had they taken him? But a quick search located Kelvin and an older man: they were going up a dark, hidden flight of stairs. They were escaping!

But would they succeed in getting out of the palace and off the grounds? Heln moved about some more, scouting the vicinity. She found few guards; they seemed to have been sent elsewhere.

She lifted up above the palace—and froze in horror. She saw dragons— many, many dragons, huge and ugly, converging on the grounds. And beyond them she spied the Knights of Morvin Crumb's force; the Queen was evidently sending the dragons against them! That would be disaster!

Yet she could do nothing except hope that the Knights would realize their danger in time, and flee.

Where was Jon? Heln zeroed in on her essence, and found her in a field near the palace. She was with a boy Heln recognized: one who had been sold that day at the Mart. And with several others, marching in together. They were heading in toward the palace—and toward the dragons.

Finally Heln saw the strangest sight of all: a man flying through the air! She knew that was impossible, but there he was doing it! He was flying toward Jon. What would happen when they met?

Then Heln's time was up, and she was drawn rapidly back into her body. She had seen much, but she understood little of it, and she still didn't know what would happen. But with all those dragons rampaging, she very much feared the worst. She hoped that Jon would succeed in helping Kelvin, and not in getting herself chewed up by a dragon. What an irony, to have Jon getting so close, only to be walking into so many unexpected dangers!

Tommy fitted her out in a pair of bound-boy coveralls and a large floppy straw hat. On the back of the coveralls were the letters BB. The clothing smelled of sweat from the boy who had worn it previously, but fit as well as any was likely to. She was getting entirely too broad across the hips! She pretended that Tommy wasn't trying not to stare, feeling perversely flattered. If she managed to get through this mission alive, she might have more to say to him. Tommy was a nice boy, and he had helped her a lot.

Jon stretched her legs and arms. Snug only around the rear, and fortunately loose around the chest. Reasonably comfortable.

"I'll want to get in with my sling and some rocks," she said.

Tommy shook his head. "You think you can defeat guardsmen?"

"I can avoid them," Jon said, wishing she were more confident. "The sling and the rocks are for getting my brother out."

"You think you'll just knock a few guards out and then unlock a door? Assuming you can find a door?"

"I can find a door." She remembered the layout Heln had described well enough; that was not her problem.

Jon checked over the river rocks in the bucket Tommy had brought her. A couple she discarded, but most were of the right weight and size.

"I think," Jon said, "that if I carry the rocks and sling in the bucket and you push the wheelbarrow ahead of me and everyone else just goes in as usual—"

"The guards will notice you."

"You said that new bound boys come and go all the time."

"Yes, but the gate guards probably know when new boys are with us."

"Just let Jerry," she said, referring to the boy whose clothes she wore, "stay here and—"

"We'd be one short. They count, I'm sure."

Jon pondered. To be so close, and yet to be kept from entering! "Bustskin has to lead us," she said.

"He does if we're to get through the gate. The guards know him already. He struts."

"Hmmm. Leave Jerry here, and have Bustskin lead as usual."

"Can't be done."

"Why not?"

"He won't cooperate."

"We'll make him," Jon said.

"How?"

Jon looked at Bustskin's hard, somewhat battered face. Even if the boy would lead, the bruises and black eye might make the guards suspicious. If the guards questioned them, that meant she would be caught, and she didn't care to be caught. Not at all!

"The guards," she said seriously, "will have to be distracted."

"Take off your clothes," he suggested with a fleeting smile.

"Not distracted that much," she said, with as brief a return smile. She liked Tommy.

"I know. But how?"

Yes, how? How would a great hero handle this? "Um, maybe we could start a fire."

"They'd look, but they'd look back again."

Yes, he was probably right. The shift was abount to change, and they would soon have to move. She looked over at sullen Bustskin, and an inspiration struck. "Bustskin will have to escape, and Jerry with him!"

"What!" Tommy and bound Bustskin exclaimed in unison.

"We get all lined up to go through the gate. Then Bustskin starts running and Jerry right after him."

"I won't!" Bustskin said.

"Yes, you will," Jon said, "because there's going to be a slip noose around your neck, and Jerry running right behind you with the end of the rope."

"I'm not afraid of him," Bustskin said.

"And your hands will be tied."

"I'll yell," Bustskin said.

"And choke?"

"If I have to."

He probably would, she realized. The problem with Bustskin was that he was a terrible person but no coward.

She looked at the noose she had been making in the leather thong that had been part of the tent lashings. There had to be a way! But if they couldn't make Bustskin cooperate . . .

Then Jon, desperate for an answer, thought she saw one. "Jerry will have to run and get the guards to chase him. Bustskin will stay with us, with a knife at his back."

"It will never work," Tommy said realistically. "He'll yell the moment the guards are close enough to hear."

Jon faced Bustskin. "Listen, jerk. Remember what you tried to do to me, at the Boy Mart?"

"Yeah, and I'll do it again," he said. "The moment I—"

"So can you guess where my knife is going to strike first, the moment you make a peep? So that even if you get me caught, *you* won't be the one to do that thing, to me or anyone, ever again?"

Bustskin gulped.

"You doubt me?" she asked, fingering the blade of the knife and eyeing his crotch. "You think I'll have anything more to lose, the moment you squeal?"

"Uh—"

"Do you think it will be worth it?" she persisted.

He was silent. He knew she had a score to settle with him, and that the main thing holding her back was the fact that she needed his cooperation.

"I think Bustskin will cooperate," she said. "Maybe I hope he won't. Meanwhile, I'll carry this knife low, like this." She held the blade down flat against her thigh. "And move it like this." She brought it up suddenly to crotch level, the point spearing forward. "If I don't score the first time, I'll just try again. Even from behind, I should manage to skewer something." She lowered the knife, then repeated her motion, this time stabbing upward with full strength. The odd thing was, she was absolutely serious; her memory of what Bustskin had tried to do to her was very clear, and it was mixed up with the memory of Heln huddled on the floor. There was a vengeance owing!

"I'll do it," Bustskin said, sweating.

"You bet you will," she agreed. She turned to Jerry. "You can do your part?"

"I—I think so," said the pale boy with smaller than average ears. "They won't kill me. They'll just beat me and bring me back."

"Good," Jon said. Then, looking at the sun, "We'd better go."

Jerry walked with them as far as the gate. Bustskin led the troupe, Jon close behind, actually touching his rear every so often, which made him jump. Indeed, her knife was ready!

But when they got there, the gate was wide open and there were no guards. The sound of fighting rose from some distance away, and with it clouds of dust Jon now associated with a proper fight.

The battle, she thought, *has begun!*

With no other thought than rescuing her brother before the dungeon guards realized what was happening and killed him, she ran through the gate, across the lawn, and into the flower garden. She knew her way from here; Heln had described it.

Glancing back, she saw bound boys scattering in every direction. One, who just had to be Tommy, hesitated for a moment and then ran with the others.

Jon heaved a sigh. Of course Tommy had to try to save himself. But it would have been nice if he had decided to help her first, just to get her on down into the dungeons.

She paused. What was that? That roaring sound? That wasn't regular battle!

A figure hung in the air, then began moving slowly as she watched. It moved at treetop height—an otherworld sky demon such as the Knights had talked about.

No, no, no, she thought. They couldn't have discovered her presence. They couldn't have!

The figure kept coming, heading right for her.

There was only one thing to do. She would have to bring down the sky demon.

Jon hefted her sling, fitting a rock. She waited, teeth clenched, determined not to let the sky person close.

The figure came nearer, and with it a whooshing noise like a great wind from the nostrils of a gigantic flying dragon. Jon was terrified, but she knew that if this demon got her, her brother could be doomed.

25 /

INTERPRETATION

A	s soon as the guards had left, taking John Knight with them, Kelvin had set about trying to think of a way that he and King Rufurt might escape. It was obvious to him that his father was really powerless to resist Queen Zoanna. Certainly that was the case while he, Kelvin, remained hostage for his father's cooperation.

"I think," he said to the King when they were alone, "that we'd better act fast. Is there any decent soil here?"

"There's manure from rats, and slops," the King said. "But—"

"That will do. Gather a pile of it and wet it down."

"Look, young man, I may be a prisoner, but I'm still a king! I don't do that sort of work!"

Kelvin had forgotten the man's rank for the moment. "Okay, I'll do it myself. But time is of the essence."

"You have something in mind?"

"I have a few seeds I saved," Kelvin said, fishing them out of his pocket. "Some of them seem to respond better to roundears than to natives. If I can grow something special, it might help us escape."

"Impossible," the King said. "It would take weeks to grow anything, and there's no decent daylight here."

"Um, yes." Then Kelvin's questing fingers found the shriveled husk of the flower he had plucked. It had lain for weeks in his pocket, forgotten. He drew it carefully out. It was battered but intact: a desiccated spicerose. "But maybe I can revive this."

"You can speak to flowers?" the King asked, amazed.

"Oh, sure. Flowers and fruits like me, I don't know why."

"I recognize that species," the King said, excited. "That's the shade-blooming spicerose—one of the most prized flowers! I used to grow them in my chambers, but they would respond to only one gardener."

"Yes, that's why I saved it," Kelvin agreed. "A mooear trampled the plant and broke the stem, so I thought I might restore it when there was someone who could appreciate it. But then things got complicated, and I forgot."

"You can restore that rose?"

"Yes, I think so. They prefer shade, and we have that here, so—"

"I'll get the damp manure!" the King exclaimed. He busied himself, scraping the stuff up from the edges of the cell, while Kelvin cradled the dry rose in his hands, breathing on it. Already it was beginning to revive.

The King brought a double handful of fairly foul stuff. "Hold it there," Kelvin said. "I'll just put the stem in, and then talk to it . . ."

This time the King did as he was bid without protest. He held the manure, while Kelvin planted the rose in it, then cupped the faded blossom with his hands and whispered to it. "Oh, lovely spicerose, bloom again for me, if you please," he said to it. "I long for your rare fragrance."

"It's working!" the King exclaimed. "The petals are filling out!"

"Yes. But it won't last; it's been dry too long."

"Careful! When the fragrance comes, a single sniff can put you out."

"No, it doesn't affect me that way," Kelvin said. "I like the smell, but it doesn't put me into a dream."

"The glory and penalty of being a roundear," the King remarked sagely. "To have the power to restore a rare flower, but to be unable to reap its proffered reward."

"That seems to be the nature of heroism," Kelvin agreed with a shrug. "If I had my choice—"

They heard the steps of the guard returning. "But a native—" the King said.

"Yes. Pretend you want it, so he notices."

"I understand. Tell me when the rose is ready. I don't dare smell it myself."

The guard returned to his station outside the cell. He was bored, of course, just waiting until his shift changed.

Kelvin nursed the rose along. The petals filled out and pale red color came. The smell manifested. "Ready," Kelvin murmured.

"Hey, boy," the King said abruptly. "Save some of that for me!"

"No, it's mine!" Kelvin replied, playing the game.

"But I'm the King! I am entitled to the first sniff!"

The guard came alert. "What's that?"

"He's got a spicerose, and he won't share," the King said indignantly.

"A spicerose!" the guard exclaimed. "I don't believe it!"

"You fool," Kelvin said. "Don't tell *him*! He'll just take it for himself!"

"You bet I will!" the guard said, spying the rose. "Give it here!"

"But it's mine!" Kelvin protested.

"Give it here, or I'll club you on the head!" the guard said.

With obvious regret, the King brought the handful of manure and the rose to the bars. The guard leaned forward and took a deep sniff of the rose. His eyes glazed, his mouth curved into an idiotic smile, and he fell against the bars.

"Get his keys!" the King said urgently, holding the rose to the man's descending nose.

Kelvin reached through and grabbed the keys. Then he unlocked the gate, stepped out, and unlooped the rope he kept coiled beneath the waistband of his pantaloons. Made of lightweight thistlehemp fiber, it had gone unnoticed by his captors. He passed it around the body of the slumped guard and tied him securely.

"But we may need that rope," the King said, setting manure and flower down.

Kelvin agreed. So they tied the guard again, this time using strips torn from his own uniform. They hurried, because the blissful sleep produced by a spicerose lasted only a minute or two. This rose had been good for about two sniffs; now its petals were shriveling again. Its moment of glory was over, and there would be no reviving it again.

"You did well, rose," Kelvin said, and it almost seemed that the petals gave a final quiver before they curled up in death.

"Too bad it did not have a worthier subject for its joy," the King remarked.

"Now," Kelvin said, "maybe we can get out of here."

"Follow me," the King said, and started running full tilt up the stairs. The guard was stirring, but would be unable to free himself in time to do them any harm.

Kelvin followed, surprised at how fast the old King could run after months, no, *years,* of confinement. Perhaps all those exercises the King and his father did each day had kept them in better condition than even they could have hoped.

"This way," said the King, taking a branching flight of stairs. "This leads to the secret passage I had constructed. Even the Queen doesn't know."

The stairs took them to an apparent dead end. The King threw his weight against what appeared to be solid rock. At first nothing happened, but then as the King continued to push, his groans were answered by a louder groan. Slowly, protestingly, a heavy stone door swung in. It opened, at long last, on an empty room with dust and cobwebs and only a little light.

"But this isn't out!" Kelvin said, looking at the dirt-encrusted windows with dismay.

The King touched his elbow. "Follow me."

This time he led the way through a door he uncovered behind a worn tapestry hanging on the wall. This passage led outside, emerging at a solid clump of shrubbery. They had to force their way through it, and when Kelvin looked back, there was no sign of the exit they had used. This was a concealed escape the King had thoughtfully provided for himself back before Kelvin was born. Just in case events should make it necessary.

After a determined struggle, they stood outside in the strong sunlight. Kelvin took a breath of fresh air, untainted with dungeon odors, and smelled the spicy sweet scent of appleberries and other fruit. Then, as the song of a bird broke off in the nearby orchard, a strange roaring noise took its place.

Kelvin's first thought was a dragon. But then he realized what it was, even as he heard the King say, "He's teaching him!"

So they would see Kian fly, Kelvin thought. But should they risk it? Maybe they should just get away. By the time the practice session was over, they could be all the way off the palace grounds. But what would happen to John Knight, then? They couldn't desert him!

The roar became a whooshing sound as they suddenly saw Kian moving slowly across the grounds at treetop height. He looked thrilled but scared, his gauntleted hands clutching tightly to the harness.

Kelvin stared, hardly believing his eyes. The King, beside him, seemed as enraptured. This was true roundear magic!

As they watched, a small missile looped from the garden to their left. It was headed right for Kian's face. The gauntlets ripped the harness in their effort to intercept the missile, and caught it, but now the apparatus was out of control. The noise coming from Kian's back increased to a tortured whine. He shot up toward the palace's roof.

There was a sickening meaty smack when he struck.

Kian fell, his backpack unit smashed and smoking, twisting and turning in the air, until he landed on the hard cobblestones below.

Then there was silence, and a streamer of oily smoke.

Kelvin and the King reached Kian a few steps ahead of John Knight and his pursuing guards.

Kian looked up at Kelvin. Blood ran from the corners of his mouth. He made a wheezing sound. He tried to move, to sit up, but could not. His gauntleted right hand reached Kelvin's bare hand and held it, not squeezing.

"You're the one, Kelvin," Kian gasped. "The prophecy refers to you, not to me. I know that now."

"Don't try to talk, Kian," Kelvin said. He knew this was foolish; he should have run in the other direction. He could have escaped, and now he would be recaptured. Yet he could not desert his half brother in this time of tragedy.

The gauntlet seemed to grow warm in his hand. "I'm glad it's you, Kelvin," Kian gasped. "Take the gauntlets. Take them and . . ."

The eyes, so much like Kelvin's own, took on a glassy look. The hurt face relaxed. A sigh, ever so gentle, escaped the thin lips.

"Kian, Kian," Kelvin said, finding his eyes wet.

"Kian, son," said John Knight. He was there on the ground beside them, his fingers stripping off a gauntlet and feeling the wrist.

"Is he—?"

"There's a pulse," John Knight said. "He's not gone yet. If we can get help for him—"

From outside the palace grounds there was the clang of swords, the neighing of horses, and the shouts of men: the sounds of a wild battle just beyond the garden walls.

"I should never have let you use that harness, Kian," John Knight said brokenly. "They made me show you before you were ready. *She* made me. Your reactions were wrong! Those gauntlets tried to save you, but they aren't attuned to roundear science. They did exactly the wrong thing!" He seemed not to hear the battle sounds.

"Now I'll have to use these myself," John Knight said. With scarcely any comprehension, Kelvin saw his father remove the two otherworld weapons from short scabbards belted around Kian's waist.

What did any of this matter? The roundear magic had come close to killing Kian, and it was uncertain whether he would live or die. The prophecy had turned out to be purely a matter of interpretation, not anything to be counted on. Here they were, stuck in the middle of the palace grounds, surrounded by the Queen's guardsmen. What hope remained?

26 /

DRAGON SLAYER

KELVIN RAISED HIS HEAD and saw a guardsman aiming a crossbow at him. He had allowed himself to be distracted far too long with Kian; now he was helpless before the enemy. He didn't even have the gauntlet to defend him.

He reached for the left gauntlet, the one John Knight had removed from Kian's hand, the one Kelvin had used before. But he knew it was too late; already the guardsman's finger was squeezing the trigger. He couldn't possibly don the gauntlet before that arrow pierced him.

Perhaps, then, Kian had been right in his interpretation: he, not Kelvin, was the Roundear of Prophecy. Because Kelvin was about to be dead, while Kian still lived. If that was the way it was, then so be it; Kelvin had no time for fright or anger, just for regret. Heln would be sad . . .

A ruby beam hit the crossbowman in the chest and went right on through him, stabbing on out the other side. The man dropped, a smoking hole in his chest. His shaft fired into the ground.

Dazed, Kelvin watched, his hand still reaching for the gauntlet. What was happening?

A second guardsman started to raise his crossbow. Another red ray appeared, transfixing him. The man never uttered a sound as he dropped backward onto the grass.

Kelvin saw his father lower one of the weapons he had taken from Kian. His face was grim. Astonished, Kelvin realized that the magic lightning weapons—or laser pistols, as his father called them—were really as deadly as the legends portrayed them.

"Come," said his father, and raced for a flight of stairs that led to a balcony at the front of the palace.

Kelvin lurched to his feet. He looked at Kian, and realized that his half brother's fate was out of his hands; Kian would live or die as the prophecy decreed, and all Kelvin could do was leave him alone. He would only get himself killed if he lingered here, and the guardsmen would drag Kian to safety and medical care soon enough.

He snatched up the left gauntlet, then tore the right one off Kian's unresisting hand. Then he whirled and followed John Knight, his heart beating hard, the memory of Kian's glassy eyes and last words all too sharp. Kian might be his enemy, technically, but he hoped Kian lived. But Kian didn't need the gauntlets at the moment; Kelvin did.

King Rufurt was running too, panting as he struggled to keep up. Now the steps were slapping beneath Kelvin's feet, and then there were no more steps and the three of them were on the balcony.

Below the balcony were walks and a garden and a beautifully cared-for lawn. Beyond the garden fence, quite visible from here, a battle was going on. Men in blue and gold uniforms were battling hard against men in green pantaloons and brownberry shirts. Men were hurting and men were dying, as were war-horses and plow horses. The din of the battle carried clearly, especially the cries of the wounded and dying.

His side was winning, Kelvin thought, straining his eyes to see through the dust. He had never thought the Knights would come here to fight, after losing the battle at Skagmore! But maybe they hadn't lost; maybe the tide of that battle had turned after he, Kelvin, lost consciousness. Was that big man Mor Crumb? It seemed to be. And with him, Les! Victory was, after all, within their grasp!

A frightful roar shook the very walls of the palace. Below, bright gold monsters smashed walls, trampled men, and lifted huge snouts holding men in brownberry shirts impaled on swordlike teeth. Horses neighed and screamed as tremendous clawed feet came down.

Dragons! At least twelve! Several times as many as any living man had ever seen! How could this be?

Kelvin heard a gasp of astonishment and horror, and realized that it was his own. The beasts were at the back and flank of the Knights. The Knights of the Roundear—*his* men! They weren't touching the Queen's army, just his.

That explained how the dragons had come. Zatanas, the Queen's evil magician father, had summoned them, just as he had for the first battle.

He looked at the gauntlets he had taken from Kian. Were they really invincible? How could they defeat that many dragons? Yet the monsters had to be stopped. They had to be, or all was lost! He drew them both on, and they made his hands tingle with their special animation.

Kelvin looked at his father. John Knight was adjusting knobs on the otherworld weapons. He lifted one of them, aimed it like a crossbow, and pressed a trigger.

The red beam speared out. It jumped instantly to a dragon, whose head was lifted high, golden scales reflecting bright in the sun. The dragon was munching a mangled red thing that had surely been someone Kelvin had known and joked with. Blood was oozing down from the morsel between the sword teeth, dripping down from the dragon's golden chin, splattering across its golden breast. Dragon's gold—drenched in blood. There was a symbol of the Queen's rule!

But as the beam struck, the dragon's head disappeared in a puff of smoke and steam and dissipating vapor, leaving only a neck attached to a body. The body and neck settled downward as the tail lashed; the tail had not yet realized that the monster was dead.

"One," John Knight said.

Both Kelvin and the King simply stared. No wonder roundear magic was legendary!

The man aimed his weapon again. The beam lanced through another dragon, burning into the great body, the scales reflecting a coruscating splay of light before the heat penetrated to the vital heart and the creature collapsed.

"Two." Then, in rapid succession, "Three. Four. Five. Six."

Kelvin wanted to scream. Those beautiful, terrible dragons! They would never have come here on their own; they normally left men alone unless men braved their wilderness fastness. The evil magician had used the lizard magic Heln had described to compel them to come, and now they were dying. One after the other, the red beam caught their raised heads or exposed breasts. One, larger than the others, retained part of a ruined head with a wide hole through it where the nostrils and eyes had been. One, caught lower down, simply collapsed with a great smoking, bubbling hole in its throat. They all were going down!

"Seven," John counted. "Eight. Nine. That will even the odds. Now if number ten will get into position so I don't have to risk hitting a horse. . . ."

"I wouldn't have believed it possible," King Rufurt said. He was gasping for air, his chest still heaving from the run up the balcony steps.

Kelvin saw the magician before the rest of them. He appeared on the balcony with them, and his face was a study in fury and disbelief.

"My dragons! My lovely dragons! You're frustrating my dragons!"

John turned from the balcony edge, the offworld weapon still in his hand. He looked surprised to see the magician. Then, his face singularly grim, he raised the weapon.

At the same time, Zatanas raised his arms. He made a gesture and spoke a spell.

The red beam came from the weapon, stopped just before reaching its target, and made a bend. The beam went up into the sky and vanished. The magician stood there, unharmed. From a doorway behind him the hunchbacked dwarf emerged.

"What?" John said, amazed. He looked down at his weapon.

Zatanas pointed a finger. John Knight froze in the act of checking his laser pistol. He stood as still as a statue, seemingly locked in place.

King Rufurt moved. "Your evil sorcery—" he began.

The magician's finger moved again. King Rufurt froze in place, his mouth still open in speech.

This was potent magic! Kelvin knew that it was up to him to deal with the sorcerer. He raised his arms.

Once more Zatanas' finger moved. Kelvin felt a new tingle in all his body except his two hands, enclosed by the gauntlets. He could not move even an eyelid. He was off-balance, but his body did not fall. Only the gauntlets retained the power of action. But they held no weapon, and the magician and the dwarf were several horse lengths away, their backs to the balcony stairs. Despite the magic of the prophecy, Kelvin was helpless.

Suddenly a small white object struck the magician's pointed hat and head. Zatanas stumbled over to the railing, eyes unfocused, reaching a hand to the back of his skull. The pointed cap fell from his head, flipped over the railing, and dropped.

The dwarf ran to the magician and stopped him from falling too, bolstering him with outstretched arms. "Master! Master! What is it, Master?"

Behind the two, Kelvin saw a small figure drop out of sight on the stairs. Could it be? Had she come too? Suddenly Kelvin understood why Kian had gone out of control!

A great hissing sound came from below. A gigantic dragon reared its golden-scaled head up over the railing. Red eyes focused on the nearest human beings. Its mouth opened, gaping awesomely, and its long, forked tongue flicked out.

The dwarf screamed shrilly as the dragon's tongue yanked servant and master over the edge.

Kelvin found that he could move now, and he saw at a glance that his father and the King were similarly free. The sorcerer's spell had been broken by Jon's rock.

Without a thought for the danger of his action, Kelvin rushed to the railing, which was still dripping with dragon saliva, and looked down over the edge. The dwarf's shrill scream seemed to hang in the air long after it was uttered. Below were the mashed hedges and fences and men, and only the tail of the dragon as it ran around to the palace's east side.

It was John Knight who brought Kelvin's attention back to the balcony. The man's hand was on his shoulder, and the other hand pointed the offworld weapon at the golden tail. But no destructive beam emerged; it was pointless to make a strike that would merely wound, not kill.

"Father, I—" But Kelvin faltered. Could he tell John Knight about Jon? If the man learned about her sling, he would know what had happened to Kian. How would he react to that? What would he, Kelvin, do if that dread alien weapon were to point at his little sister?

"Damn," said his father. "A second earlier and I could have had him! But he did us a favor, that dragon did. Somehow he broke through the force field that held us. I don't understand magic, but I do recognize a force. A force field by any other name—"

"Kel! Kel! Kel!" Jon was running across the balcony. The sling was in her hands. Would John Knight see it and raise that terrible weapon now? If he did, could Kelvin or his gauntlets stop him?

The weapon did not come up. Jon ran right past John Knight and flung herself into Kelvin's arms. "Kel, Kel, I knew you'd come through alive! I knew it!"

"We haven't won yet," Kelvin reminded her. "There's still the battle. And the dragons."

"Speaking of dragons," John Knight said, still searching for one.

"How did you get here, Jon?" Kelvin asked, hoping to divert attention from the sling.

"The river," she said. "And a little help from some friends afterward. Brother mine, did you see that old magician reel when I conked him? I saved your lives, that's what I did!"

That did it! But John Knight merely turned to her and said, "I don't think you recognize me, just as I didn't recognize you at first. You have grown, and I think undergone a metamorphosis."

"A what?" Jon asked blankly.

"You were a girl when I last knew you."

She turned to Kelvin. "Who—?"

"I am John Knight," their father said. "You were named after me."

Her mouth dropped open. "But—"

"He didn't die," Kelvin said. "He was captured by the Queen. I found him in the dungeon."

"You were only two years old when I left," John Knight said.

"You have round ears!" she exclaimed abruptly.

He laughed. "Yours are like your mother's."

"So you must really be my—"

A hiss like that of escaping steam put all of their attention on the dragon peering over the balcony. The beast was looking at them, seemingly trying to decide which one to consume first.

"You use the laser like this, Kelvin," John Knight said. "Sight here, the same as a crossbow, squeeze this trigger, and—"

The bright red beam caught the dragon in its mouth and bore on through. As the beam vanished, so did most of the dragon's head. The rest of the beast collapsed into a golden pile on the palace's lawn.

"You really must learn to use this," John Knight said. "Ordinarily I'd say no, but now's the time, and if you don't finish off dragons before they finish your Knights, what's left for this land?"

Kelvin didn't know. He was astonished that his father was carefully placing the weapon in his hands.

"There's one! Watch until its head isn't in line with a Knight, then aim and press the trigger."

Kelvin shook, but his gauntleted hands were steady. He raised the weapon and squinted through the aperture, which, indeed, was not unlike a sight on a crossbow. The gauntlets animated his hands, making his aim confident.

He followed the dragon's head. He focused the cross so that it was between the creature's eyes. Then, firmly, of its own volition, his gauntlet pressed the trigger.

The dragon's head disappeared, exactly as the others had done.

"Good shot, Kel!" his sister exclaimed.

"You've got the warrior's eye and nerves," said his father. "Now I want you to get any others that are destroying your men. It's your responsibility, from now on."

"But—"

"You three go stop the dragons. I think we've gotten most of them, but we want to be sure. Tell the men the fighting's over. And, son, give me your word that when all of this is over, you'll destroy the laser. Get rid of it, as you get rid of dragons that destroy the people and the land."

"But the dragons don't really do that!" Kelvin protested. "They stay in dragon country, mostly. It's only when the evil sorcerer makes them come that they—"

John Knight smiled. "A conservationist! You, the dragon slayer!"

"But the dragons themselves aren't evil! They cultivate magic berries that—"

"I'll watch out with this other laser while you go out front. Your men will rally round you when they see it's you and the King. Kill any guardsmen who refuse to surrender. Only remember, it isn't good to kill helpless men."

"I'll remember," Kelvin said. It was evident that his natural father still didn't really believe in magic.

27 /

BLOOD SORCERY

HELN REVIVED, AND FOUND her mother waiting anxiously. "I saw them!" she exclaimed. "All getting ready for battle, and Kelvin escaping, and Jon, and dragons—"

"I'm so glad you're safe!" her mother exclaimed. "I was so concerned—"

"But they don't know about the dragons!" Heln cried. "Those dragons will destroy them! I must warn them!"

Her mother shook her head. "There is no way, my child. We are too far from the palace."

"I know, I know!" Heln said impatiently. "But if I don't warn them, they'll die! Kelvin, and Jon, and all the brave Knights! And if they die, I will too!"

Her mother only shook her head sympathetically.

"The astral separation!" Heln exclaimed. "That's the only way I can reach them instantly! I've got to go back, find some way to warn them!"

"But you said you can't speak to anyone in your astral state!"

"I can't, but I've *got* to, this time! I've just got to! Otherwise everything is over, for all of us!"

"But isn't it dangerous? You said you had to rest between—"

"I ate three berries the first time!" Heln said, suddenly impatient with caution. "They separated me for longer, and it took me longer to recover, but I *did* recover."

"Still—"

"Mother, *I've got to help!*"

Her mother spread her hands, knowing better than to argue further. Heln took another berry, and soon sank back into her deathlike state.

It was different, this time, because she had not yet properly recovered from the prior berry. It was as if her body was eager to give up the spirit, and the spirit eager to be free. She seemed to leap out of herself, finding herself spinning in the air above the house. Then she willed herself to the capital, and she was there, looking down on the palace grounds.

The battle was in full swing. Men in brownberry shirts were fighting the blue and gold guardsmen, and the Knights seemed to be having the best of it, perhaps because of the element of surprise.

Then the dragons came, and tore into the Knights of the Roundear. Heln screamed inaudibly as she saw people she knew getting crunched in those terrible golden jaws. She had to stop it—but she was helpless. She was only tormenting herself by watching this!

She sought Kelvin. Somehow she had to find a way to communicate with him, to tell him—what? That there were dragons attacking? He surely knew it already! What could she do, even if she could talk to him? She had been foolish to think she could make any difference, regardless!

But she was here now, and she had about an hour to use up. She could look around, and maybe she would learn something useful. At least she would have a better notion how the battle was going.

She found Kelvin on a balcony. He was talking with one of the older men who had been in the dungeon with him. As she came close, one of the men pointed an object at a dragon. Red light appeared, and the dragon's head puffed into smoke.

That was a weapon! A powerful roundear magic weapon, for the man had round ears! Kelvin had found a marvelous ally! But—round ears? Who could that man be?

The man aimed at another dragon, and killed it. Then, in rapid succession, several more. Heln almost felt sorry for the monsters!

Then the Queen's sorcerer, Zatanas, appeared on the balcony, with his dwarf henchman. He pointed at Kelvin and the men, and they froze where they were. The evil magician was overcoming them with his magic!

Heln went into a frenzy. *Stop Zatanas!* she screamed with all her being. *Go there, stop him, now!*

Huh? something responded.

Heln paused in mid-frenzy. Someone had heard her! Someone had answered! She oriented on that response, her spirit jumping instantly to that spot.

She paused, amazed. It was a dragon!

You heard me? she called to it, hardly believing.

The dragon's head whipped about, and its ears perked forward, as if it were trying to locate the speaker. It *did* hear her!

Actually, it made sense. She was using dragonberries for astral separation, and this was a dragon. If these monsters ate the berries, and used them for astral separation, they must have some sensitivity to the astral state. Maybe they could communicate with each other's spirits. So this one heard her, but because she wasn't another dragon, it was confused.

Well, she could certainly use this discovery. "Trouble by the balcony!"

she cried, knowing that it was her thought, not her voice, it heard. "Go stop Zatanas!" She wasn't sure how much of this the dragon could understand, but the urgency of direction and action should be clear enough.

The dragon turned and lumbered for the balcony.

Heln jumped there ahead of it. This time she spied Jon Hackleberry approaching the balcony. Jon saw Zatanas, and brought out her sling, and heaved a stone. Her aim was true, and the evil sorcerer reeled from a strike on the head. So Jon was succeeding in helping her brother! Maybe Heln's effort had been unnecessary.

The dragon reared below the balcony, lifting its golden head. Its tongue whipped out and wrapped about the magician and the dwarf, pulling both over the edge. It ran off with its prey as the frozen men recovered. Maybe she had helped after all!

Now Jon ran up. There was a flurry of introductions—and, listening, Heln suddenly realized what should have been obvious before. The grown roundear was Kel and Jon's father! The roundear from the other planet! No wonder he knew the roundear magic!

The man was showing Kelvin how to use the terrible dragon-slaying weapon. Then another dragon appeared at the balcony; perhaps it, too, had responded to her directive to the first one. She didn't know how broadly her thoughts were broadcast, or how sensitive the monsters were to them.

John Knight killed the dragon with the roundear weapon. Then he put the weapon in Kelvin's shaking hands and told him to use it on the next dragon. It was obvious that Kelvin was in no state to accomplish this; he seemed to be as much afraid of the weapon as of the dragons. Poor, dear, uncertain Kel! How she loved him!

"Hold it steady, Kel!" she cried, knowing he could not hear.

But *something* heard! She felt a quiver of response. Then Kelvin's hands became rock-steady. When he sighted another dragon, his aim was perfect, and he killed it.

What had responded to her this time? It hadn't been a dragon! Heln spread her awareness out, searching. She had to know exactly what her astral self could communicate with; it might make a big difference!

She didn't find what she wanted, but she did find a surprise. She was at the dragon she had first brought to the balcony—and it hadn't eaten the magician and the dwarf! It had brought the two to a hidden spot. Was it going to eat her now? She paused and listened, absorbing the scene.

Queeto dropped down from the slippery tongue and lit feet-first in a cluster of thornbushes. He seemed hardly aware of the smart of the scratches or of his torn tunic as he watched the sorcerer.

Casually, Zatanas was uncoiling the dragon's dark purple tongue from around his own waist. He seemed quite oblivious to the golden-scaled face overhanging him, puffing forth moist, rancid dragon breath.

"It w-won't harm us, will it, Master?" Queeto asked. He looked as though he had never been more frightened.

"It won't hurt *me,*" the sorcerer said, his voice carrying the strong conviction of the magic-protected. "Not my little brother."

"A spell protects us both, Master?"

"The dragon does my bidding." The sorcerer rubbed the back of his head where a red lump was showing. "Good thing it happened to be in the vicinity when I got struck; I hadn't summoned it."

Heln was mortified. Her effort had *helped* the evil magician? By bringing a dragon who carried him away to safety, when he would otherwise have been killed by the roundears? She should have left well enough alone!

The magician glanced about. "Let's go around to the courtyard and the three flights of stairs to our quarters," he said. "We've plans to make."

Plans? Heln knew she had to keep listening!

"But, Master, the dragon—"

"Ah, yes, the dragon," Zatanas agreed. He faced the monster. "You may go to eat more Knights. But not back to the balcony. Stay away from there."

As though it understood, the great beast drew in its tongue. Without a backward glance it strolled off across the grounds, knocking over statuary, crushing ornamental plants, hedges, and whatever it chanced to tread upon. Its great tail swished twice, and then it was doing the wriggle-run that in its small brother the lizard was so comical. It raced through the orchard, knocking aside bushes and splintering trees. Then, having reached the high wall, it stretched up, hooked its talons at the top, and pulled itself over. It perched there like a great, ungainly bird, then dropped out of sight.

Queeto sighed, evidently now feeling his scratches. A dragon was a sight to behold, and few men ever beheld them so close and lived to speak of it. Heln was impressed, too; Zatanas really did have power! He was now doubly dangerous, because Kelvin and his father thought the evil sorcerer was dead, and were no longer on guard against him.

"Come!" the magician said.

Meekly, Queeto followed him. The dwarf licked his lips, as though the sour taste of fear had been replaced by the eager, peppery feel of anticipation. Nothing seemed to be able to destroy Zatanas, or even hurt him, not even the most powerful beast alive. Whatever evil he planned was surely a horror Heln had to spy out!

"Hurry!" Zatanas snapped. "You waddle so slow!"

They had come now into the courtyard at the back of the palace where all the trade goods were normally brought: the special foods and furnishings and supplies.

Queeto was muttering, talking to himself as he scurried to catch up. "From here that roundear boy tried to fly. Dangerous, having the roundear man teach the roundear son to do that. I knew that, I could have told them, but the Queen wanted it for some fool reason. I wanted to watch, but the

Master had business, bringing dragons here to once and for all devour the Roundear and the Roundear's Knights. I could have told them that was even more dangerous, but did anybody want my opinion? No, nobody listens to Queeto!"

"Get moving!" Zatanas called back irritably.

"Only something happened that Master hadn't anticipated," the dwarf continued to himself, evidently getting some satisfaction from the narration. "The flying roundear boy fell, and the roundear man got the roundear weapons. I could have told them that something like that would happen! That lightning-hurler stick—look what it did to the dragons! Master had to stop that! But then he got conked on the head by a stone from nowhere—"

"Stop that muttering!" Zatanas exclaimed. "You drive me crazy with your nothing-comments!"

Queeto shut up, and followed the sorcerer up the three flights of stairs. By this time he was puffing too hard to mutter anyway. But Heln had learned some interesting things. She had seen the flying man, going right toward Jon, but had had to return to her body too soon. Now she knew that the man had fallen. Knowing how apt Jon was with her sling, Heln could piece together what had happened. Jon was making her presence count!

The stairs at the back of the palace led up to the sorcerer's quarters. Heln saw that three other flights ran down from those quarters to a secret anteroom adjoining the Queen's throne room. The sorcerer was really set up for spying!

"Hate these stairs!" Queeto wheezed briefly as his short legs carried him to the top. He sounded almost like the choking breath of the dragon that had carried them. He surely would have preferred to have the dragon carry them all the way here, if he hadn't been so afraid it was about to eat them!

An owlhawk greeted them with a squawk. Its huge yellow eyes looked for food, its talons pulling at first one and then the other leather thong that bound it to its perch.

Zatanas went straight to a dusty old book. He opened it, scanned its yellowed pages, then set it aside. He took a pinch of powder, tossed it in the air, and said, "Abidda bebop teevee a zee hop." At least, that was what it sounded like to Heln.

Smoke puffed as yellow grains of powder settled. A picture formed as the sorcerer held his arm out toward it and furrowed his uncapped forehead.

In the picture were Queeto and Zatanas, as well as the three others. It was the way things had been on the balcony, but now the view was from a spot that took in the balcony and part of the stairs.

On the top stair a small figure twirled a sling and sent a stone flying at the imaged magician's head.

The stone struck. The sorcerer staggered. Queeto helped him. The dragon came. The long tongue snaked out. It wrapped itself around the magician's waist, then Queeto's. They went over the side of the balcony.

Heln was amazed at the accuracy of this vision; it showed exactly what had happened! Jon was quite recognizable as she ran up to join the others.

"Master! Master!" Queeto cried. "It's her! It's the girl I bid upon! The virgin girl the brigands took from me! The Roundear's sister, Master!"

"Yes," Zatanas said calmly. "I thought it might be. The fool came to help her brother."

"Will you bleed her, Master? Will you bleed all her blood out and skin her alive while she screams with horror and shrieks with agony?"

The magician's hand reached down to pat the bald spot on Queeto's head. *"We* will bleed them, little brother. I will put the silver needle into the virgin's arm, and you will catch the blood as it drips, drop by tasty drop, into the golden urn."

"Oh, Master!" Queeto said, licking his lips. "That makes me so happy!"

It hardly made Heln happy! This was worse than she had feared. They planned to capture Jon and take her blood!

"And at the same time we will bleed the other," Zatanas continued. "Not of his blood, but of his strength. As the sister weakens, so will the brother. So, too, may the roundear father."

"Like the lizards and the dragons, Master?"

The clawlike hand patted his head again. "Exactly like the lizards and the dragons, Queeto. This is the nature of sympathetic magic, of blood sorcery. It is the way I brought the roundears from Throod to Rud to help my daughter secure her throne, a generation ago. Stick-figure men, but the real ones had to follow, because the stick figures had round ears. Only it will not be dragon appetite the Roundear feels, but weakness, and then much, much pain, until finally, at long last, we allow him death. He cannot escape it, for it will stem from his blood sibling, whom we shall control absolutely. His gauntlets will not avail him then, and neither will the roundear weapons."

"Oh, Master! I wish we could make it last forever!"

"We will try, little friend. We certainly will try."

Abruptly, Zatanas returned to his book and began turning pages.

Heln, appalled, drifted from the chamber. She had to warn Kelvin of the threat to his sister, and to himself! But how could she? Not through the dragons, certainly!

She returned to Kelvin. He was now on the field, holding the roundear weapon, looking for dragons to slay. Jon was with him, but Heln was sure that the evil sorcerer was devising some way to abduct her. Kelvin's gauntlets would protect him, but Jon had no such security. They had to be warned!

But how? Heln's time was ending; soon she would be drawn back to her body, and she knew that it would not be safe to take a third berry. The second one had worked too well, sending her out too strongly; a third might vault her out so far she would never return. She had to do what she had to do now.

What about that response she had felt before, the one she had been trying to identify, when she found the dragon and Zatanas instead? It had been near Kelvin, but it hadn't been Kelvin himself.

"Where are you?" she cried desperately. "Answer me!"

She felt the response! It was near Kelvin again. She jumped over to it, and found herself hovering right in front of him, as if he were holding her with his gauntlets.

The gauntlets . . .

"Is that you, gauntlets?" she asked. "Do you hear me?"

She received the feeling of agreement. Was she imagining it? It was so hard to tell! At least the dragons could move in the direction she sent them, so she could tell by their actions. But these gloves—

"Left gauntlet, *lift!*" she exclaimed.

Kelvin's left arm came up, as though he were waving. He looked startled.

She could do it! She could command the gauntlets! It must be because she was another roundear, and they were attuned to roundears. That was why only roundears could use them; back at the camp, Kelvin had tried lending his left gauntlet to other men, but their hands had been rent by pain when they tried to don it. The gloves accepted *only* roundears.

But now she felt the first slow tug of her faraway body. She was about to leave; she had only a few seconds left. There was no time to try to make the gauntlets signal in air or write a note; what could she do?

The second tug came, drawing her away. "Zatanas' lair!" she screamed. "Gauntlets, Jon will be in Zatanas' lair! Take Kelvin there, when—"

But now the third pull was drawing her back, and she could say no more. How she hoped the gloves understood! If they could somehow guide Kelvin, so that he could save his sister before her demise brought them both low. . . .

28 /

SYMPATHETIC MAGIC

JON TIGHTENED HER GRIP on her sling as the horseman approached, but it was one of the Knights. The swirling dust had made it uncertain until the beast and its rider had drawn quite close.

"Gods!" Les Crumb exclaimed, recognizing them at the last second. "It's the Roundear! And Jon! And—"

"And your rightful King!" exclaimed Greenleaf as he strode on foot with bared and bloody sword. His dead horse lay next to the wall surrounding the palace grounds, as did half a dozen dead guardsmen.

"Then—" Lester began.

Kelvin raised the laser. "We've won!" he shouted. "With this weapon I can slay any dragon, any guardsman!"

"Hold up," Mor protested. "I haven't figured out what Jon is doing here, let alone all the rest. I sent the girls home—"

Through the dust rode a guardsman with raised sword, ready to chop. He was almost upon a startled Greenleaf before Kelvin acted. The red beam reached out, took away part of the Queen's wall and the man's sword and sword arm. The guardsman screamed as his horse barely missed running down Greenleaf.

They waited until the horse and one-armed rider had vanished in the swirling dust. Then Lester reached down and grabbed Kelvin's arm. "Come, Kelvin! There's dragons and foe to be slain!"

"But—" said Jon.

"You, girl, and you, Your Majesty," Mor said, "you should be safe here. See to it, Greenleaf, and—" He paused as another figure loomed from the dust, but this one wore their colors. "We'll be back. See that these two are kept safe until we end the fighting."

Then he and Kelvin were away in the dust, leaving Jon and King Rufurt and the few Knights who had appeared.

Jon wanted to swear. Here she was, the hero who had helped destroy the magician and his apprentice, and helped save Kelvin and John Knight *and* the King. Here she was, being treated like a child or, worse, a girl who had to be protected.

"It shouldn't take long," King Rufurt said. "The guardsmen won't want to fight magic, and the dragons will either have to retreat back to dragon country or be slain. We've all but won!"

Jon knew the King was right. That was, after all, what Kelvin's father had said, and who, after all, would know better? Still, there was an awful lot of noise, and a lot of fighting remaining. She wished she could be at Kelvin's side, or at least somewhere where she could watch Kelvin. If only Kelvin had given *her* a fancy weapon! But such a thought, she knew, had never occurred to him.

Dust was so thick that it was hard to see even the nearer Knights, though so far she had recognized every one who came up. She wiped at her tearing eyes and drippy nose, hating the dust. Battle dust took the glory right out of it! That, and all the gore. Maybe it would be better just to be a girl, and leave the mess to the men. She had never actually fought in battle with a sword.

Jon felt a man's hand on her shoulder. Looking up, she saw a Knight on a horse. How had he come so close without her being aware of him? It was not one she recognized.

"Want up on the horse?" the man asked.

Why not? Maybe she would get to fight after all. Just so she could say she had done it, when this was over.

She threw her leg up as the man hauled on her. In half a breath she was astride the big war-horse. This reminded her of the time she had been on a black stallion with another man's big arm around her.

Another man?

She twisted to look in shock into the dark face, seeing the scar under grime, the gleam in the man's eyes. That could mean only one thing. The man was an enemy, and one she recognized!

"Che—" she started to say.

Cold steel touched her throat. "Shut up, or I'll decapitate you right here and throw your head to your friends. Keep your mouth shut, don't struggle, and you'll live to be of some use. *My* use."

It was humiliating and scary, but what could she do but keep silent? One little squeak on her part, and she felt certain the highwayman would do what he threatened. How had the bandit gotten here, and dressed like a Knight? Had he learned that she was not the boy he had sold to the Boy Mart? Of course she couldn't ask! All she could do was keep her mouth shut and try to stay alive.

Jon felt the horse leap forward, and then King Rufurt and the Knight guarding him were behind and there was dust swirling all around. An open section of wall loomed ahead. With a single tremendous leap the war-horse cleared the rubble. Behind them were shouts and the sounds of another horse.

The man holding her swung around. He slashed quickly at their pursuer, and then as the man drew close, he stabbed.

Greenleaf fell soundlessly from his horse, pierced through the heart. Jon stifled a cry; if only she had thought to jog the bandit's arm or something, she might have saved the Knight! She was a helpless female after all.

The palace's walls loomed. Then they were behind the palace, in the courtyard, the horse halting in response to the quick pull on its reins.

"Down!" Cheeky Jack ordered. "Slowly."

Jon moved slowly, the sword at her throat.

Her captor swung down, dropped the reins, and slapped the war-horse's flank. Jon saw with astonishment that the beast raced into the orchard where broken branches and downed trees suggested a dragon had been. As it neared the first trees, the horse started to change. It seemed to grow in size. It developed a lizard's tail and a snout. It was turning into a dragon!

Jon shook her head, hardly believing what she had seen. Had she really just ridden a dragon? She couldn't have! Yet now a dragon was scrambling over the orchard wall.

The highwayman laughed, and it was a cackle. As she looked, startled, at Cheeky Jack's face, it seemed to melt and flow. The scar vanished. The hair changed from black to dark gray. The nose elongated. The chin became sharp and protruding.

In a moment it was the evil sorcerer who stood there.

Had she realized his true identity, she would have screamed warning at the outset, no matter what! But she had been sure he was dead! How could he have survived the attack by the dragon?

The dragon. But the magician could tame dragons! *That* was how he had survived!

"Wh—what are you going to do with me?" Jon asked. Then she remembered to add "Zatanas," so as not to aggravate him further. If he merely kept her prisoner for a time, hoping to use her to bargain for his life when the Knights won—

Again the cackly laugh. "I shall use you, of course, in my magic. I shall use your blood and your skin and your bones and your eyeballs and your stupid little soul. I shall use you to gain, once and for all, full control over this, my rightful land."

Jon shuddered. She felt certain that whatever else the black magician might be, he was as powerful as he was insane.

Regretfully, Kelvin sighted the laser at the charging dragon. His gauntlet steadied his aim, and squeezed the trigger. The red beam went out like the finger of a deadly lightning god.

The dragon collapsed in a golden pile, its head mostly disintegrated.

Kelvin felt real regret, and he hoped this was the last such killing he would have to perform. They had now ridden down three dragons. The real hero was the pair of gauntlets, which made his aim perfect. But he wished the dragons had fled back to dragon country, so that no more had had to be destroyed. There was a lot of dragon's gold on the battlefield, and some Knights were already hacking away at the precious scales, taking their spoils, but how much better it would have been to leave the dragons alone in their own haunts!

Kelvin squirmed in the saddle. It was a nice warhorse, and nice accouterments. The Crumbs had captured it for him. But all he really wanted was for the fighting and killing to stop. The guardsmen hadn't a chance against him, and once the word got out, they would realize it. How many guardsmen had charged him and been slain? How many had seen him destroy dragons, and had ridden to spread the news? Roundear magic was indeed the key to victory!

"I think," Kelvin said, "that I weary of the fight." That was a dragon-sized understatement!

Lester frowned. His father, some distance away, had not heard, and therefore did not bellow his customary protest. "You want to go back to Jon and the King? Until this is over with?"

Kelvin nodded.

"All right. I'll cover for you. I'll get Father away from here, and when we're out of sight, you go back."

Kelvin appreciated Les's help. The elder Crumb had become so obsessed with the fighting that he seemed not to want to stop. Not that Mor killed guardsmen who weren't trying to kill him, but he didn't avoid meeting them either. For Kelvin to drop out of the fighting before the guardsmen had accepted defeat must be barely understandable to Les, and not at all comprehensible to Mor.

Already, Kelvin felt guilty. "But maybe I should—"

"No, I understand," Les said. "I get pretty sick of it myself. I almost got taken out at Skagmore, you know. Father dragged me back unconscious, and your sister nursed me back to consciousness. She's some little woman, when she wants to be."

Kelvin laughed shortly. "But she doesn't want to be! That's the problem."

Les shrugged. He shaded his eyes with a hand. "Over there!" he called suddenly. "Behind those trees! Someone in a guardsman's uniform!"

"Let's get him!" Morvin cried, wheeling his horse around. The Crumbs raced for the trees at full gallop. There was a cry of dismay from the trees; evidently the guardsman had hoped to remain undiscovered. Kelvin could understand that.

As he watched them, he felt a tingle in his gauntlets—both hands. Usually this meant danger, but now there was no danger. Once, his left gauntlet had lifted of its own accord when there was no enemy to fend off. Now the tingle was back, with no visible threat.

Kelvin locked the safety mechanism on his laser the way his father had done, and holstered it. It still didn't feel comfortable hanging from his waist.

The Crumbs disappeared among the trees. Was the tingle for them—a danger they faced?

As though in answer, the gauntlets grew warm. He felt them tug at the horse's reins. They were up to something, and he could not afford to assume they were mistaken. They often seemed to know best.

As the horse turned, the right gauntlet slapped its flank. The steed leaped forward, and proceeded to a full gallop away from the trees and the Crumbs.

He was going back to join Jon and King Rufurt—but the gauntlets were doing it, not himself. Were they tired of battle, too?

Then the gauntlets turned the horse again. An opening appeared in the wall, and they were racing for it.

Kelvin barely remembered to flatten himself and nudge the horse with his knees before the leap. Then they were over, on the palace grounds. Broken hedges and flowers and a tipped-over statue showed where another beast had run. A war-horse, or a dragon? Where were the gauntlets taking him, and why?

A man lay dead on the ripped-up lawn. As they raced by, Kelvin recognized the dead one as Greenleaf. How had he come to be here? Whom had he been chasing, and who had slain him? But the gauntlets did not slow the horse.

They were at the side of the palace now, approaching the rear and the courtyard. He recognized the side of the balcony and its stairs. The balcony was now empty, and there seemed to be no living thing near the stairs.

The horse's hooves clattered on cobblestones. The gauntlets pulled the reins. Now they walked, to another flight of stairs. The gauntlets, almost uncomfortably hot now, urged him to dismount. They had never before shown so much will of their own!

Kelvin swung out of the saddle, left his steed to wander or wait as it wished, and raced up the stairs. He slowed his steps as he neared the top. He felt uncomfortably weak and light-headed—weaker than he had felt at any time except when he was sick. He must have gotten more tired than he thought! Maybe that drug they had given him to make him sleep so long had weakened him. He had been quite active recently, and maybe shouldn't have pushed his limits.

An owlhawk tethered on a skull flopped its wings and snapped its beak as he entered a darkened room thick with unusual and unidentifiable smells. What *was* this place?

For a moment he stood weakly swaying in the doorway as his eyes adjusted and his gauntlets all but burned his hands. Then he saw the magician and the dwarf. The two he had thought devoured by a dragon! And—

Shock struck him, even as the sorcerer made a puff of pink-colored smoke appear. "Jon!" Kelvin whispered. "Jon!"

For there was his sister, strapped to a table. She was very pale. A needle was in her arm, and her blood was dripping into a golden vessel held by the hunchbacked dwarf.

Kelvin had sworn to protect her—and look what had happened! They were bleeding her to death!

Zatanas was mumbling something, gesturing as he had on the balcony. Instantly Kelvin felt frozen, paralyzed by the power of magic. His natural father had tried to convince him that such magic did not exist, but on this matter John Knight had been horribly mistaken.

Kelvin remembered the laser weapon in its holster. If he could reach it— if the gauntlets . . .

The sorcerer made a gesture. Instantly the mystery weapon slid from its holster and floated in midair. The laser turned, steadied before Kelvin's nose, poised there briefly like a hummerfly, then retreated as suddenly to the magician's waiting hand.

"An interesting toy," Zatanas said, moving the laser to a vacant shelf and dropping it. "But against me, worthless. It's not true magic, you see. Not like mine."

Kelvin tried to speak. There was no sound from his lips. In his ears, steadily, was the drip, drip, drip of his sister's lifeblood.

"I really hadn't expected you to be fool enough to come here," the sorcerer continued. "That is why I devised a demise for you that would strike wherever you were, inescapably. But this is even better."

Kelvin still stood, feeling weaker and more hopeless every moment. Why couldn't he even try to fight this man?

"Let me explain for you one of the basic principles of sympathetic magic," said Zatanas. "Like affects like. As your sister and you share a parentage, so you share a bond greater than that of strangers. As her blood leaves her and she weakens, you weaken, too. Slowly, slowly, over a good long time. It would be inartistic to rush it! Every stage must be properly savored. When we skin her, you will feel some of the agony. When we pluck out her eyes, your vision will weaken until you are blind. When we—"

But Kelvin had ceased to listen. He was thinking only of Jon and the gauntlets, and of the necessity, somehow, someway, to overcome this horror. Yet he remained powerless.

Drip, drip, drip, drip . . .

29 /

QUEEN

JOHN KNIGHT ROAMED THE palace rooms, searching. He had not told the Knights (he found the name entertaining) what he intended to do, knowing that would only have diverted them from the necessary business of winning the battle. This was an aspect of it he just had to do himself.

He was looking for the Queen. His son and hers lay outside, perhaps receiving the medical attention he desperately needed, perhaps already beyond the power of any such help. The Queen was not directly responsible for Kian's situation, but she was certainly indirectly responsible, for she had set him up to fight the Knights, and that had brought him crashing down. It was ironic that it was Jon's daughter's slung stone that had done it, but it had had to be done, because once Kian mastered the flying harness and the laser pistols, he would have destroyed the Knights and ended the threat to the Queen's evil dominance. John had had deep reservations about showing Kian the proper use of these items, but with Kelvin in the Queen's power, he had had no choice. Now the weapons had changed sides, and he had his daughter to thank for that, and only hoped that this had not cost him Kian's life. His hatred for the Queen was built upon such matters as this: that she had set John Knight's children to fighting each other.

He wondered whether he was quite sane, to hate her so. Yet he knew that the Queen and her consort had to be destroyed. They had brought this fair and wondrous land almost to total ruin, and if allowed to live would wreak further evil. It was Zoanna's nature to bring destruction on others; that was why she herself had to be destroyed.

Yet he had thought he loved her, once. Certainly he had fallen under her spell for a time. Her body—

John Knight shook himself. He could not afford to be distracted by that! The woman he had more truly loved was Charlain, even though he had had to leave her. So now he would eliminate the Queen, and if he lost his own life in the process, well, that would leave Charlain's life less complicated. She had remarried, thinking him dead, and he could not fault her for that. She and her second husband had done a fine job with the children, both of them.

He entered another room, a ballroom where once he had danced with the Queen. Crystal chandeliers hung above, and along the walls were heroic life-size statuary of royal family members from ancient days, and the floors were polished inlaid rare woods. What happiness he had had here for a time, when he had supposed himself a kind of king! He had thought he had the love of a beautiful Queen!

He paused, searching with narrowed gaze, holding the laser ready, willing himself to hate her as he had hated her every day of his imprisonment. As he had hated her when she acceded to Flick's demand that Kian try to be the Roundear of prophecy. As he had hated her when she forced him to train Kian. As he had hated her when Kian fell.

His eyes rested momentarily on a doorway he didn't remember, and a shimmer there made him think "ghost." Then she was there in all her beauty, undimmed by twenty years, hair undone, dressed in the filmiest of nightgowns. She beckoned him, and his hate evaporated; it was impossible to oppose such a creature! He knew that magic, another aspect of that sorcery he had tried not to believe in, kept her eternally youthful in body, if not in mind. Suddenly it didn't seem to matter. Despite himself, he took a step forward.

The floor vanished beneath his feet.

He landed in a painful heap, the laser still in his hand. Something struck his wrist, and his fingers opened involuntarily. The laser clattered to the floor. Something struck him on the head, dizzying him.

"Go ahead, Peter, finish him!"

It was her voice. Hers! He blinked, seeing her now, trying to see the reality he knew was there.

She stood before a reflecting mirror that sent her image up to the mirror placed in the ballroom, and to this cellar, too. She was no ghost! She remained hidden, physically, while her image supervised the action here. The floor had not simply dematerialized; above him, in the ceiling, was the opened trapdoor.

It had been a simple trap. Mirror and trapdoor. Planned for him since he agreed to teach Kian? Or just here, waiting for its time of need? Waiting for John Knight to come seeking her? Waiting for the laser in his hand and his heart full of hate? The Queen was evil, but no fool. She had known he would one day attempt to take her life.

As his sight cleared, he saw Peter Flick standing over him. The Queen's cruel consort had the sword turned flat side toward him, ready for another swing.

"Finish him, Peter! Use the edge!"

Was that the woman he had loved? No, it was just the illusion, the reality of her as deceptive as the mirror image. Magic enhanced her, and always had. He had fought so hard against a belief in magic because he had wanted the illusion to be real. He had tried, even after his first imprisonment, to believe that it was real. That refusal to accept magic had even misled Kelvin, and now—

"I want him to suffer," Peter said.

"Fool!" she retorted. "That man is dangerous! Finish him!"

John Knight tried putting his hands out, to brace himself against the floor. The floor seemed to spin. Then there was agony, as Peter Flick trod heavily on his right hand. He felt Flick's full weight. He heard a snapping sound, and knew that his trigger finger had broken.

"He can live a long time yet," Flick said. "Just as long as I'm willing to let him. Let's keep him alive a while and enjoy him, love."

"Peter," Zoanna said icily, "remember who you are! *I* am the one to say, and I say kill him."

John Knight realized that because the Queen wasn't here physically, being present merely in mirror image, she had to act through her consort, and Flick was taking advantage of the situation. Evidently the man was too stupid to realize what that would cost him, the moment the Queen didn't need him anymore. He saw Flick's evil grin, and then he saw him pick up the laser.

"No! No!" John said. He was trying to play for time; he wasn't really that weak.

"Yes, yes," Flick taunted. "Yes, I will fix you with this. That's more appropriate, don't you think? To be slain by your own offworld weapon. Offworld magic, offworld science, as you call it—it's all the same to me."

"Peter, that's dangerous!" the Queen said.

Peter Flick examined the weapon, turning it over and over in his delicate fingers. His hands were more accustomed to the touch of fine linen and fragile art objects.

"You don't know how to use it!" the Queen said. "Remember what it did!"

"I'm remembering. I think I'll start with his legs."

John watched his enemy turn the laser until it pointed at his feet. He saw the grin he had come to know so well, and knew that Flick would take his time squeezing the trigger. More time than he needed.

He watched the finger start to tighten. He took a deep breath and kicked out. His heavily booted foot struck Peter's left kneecap.

Peter gasped and lost his balance. His arm came up. His finger tightened involuntarily.

The ruby beam cut halfway through the supporting column at John's back. A chunk the diameter of a dragon's neck vanished. It left a hole between the column's base and the rest of it.

The column dropped, its end smoking. It twisted sideways and fell, breaking apart in segments.

But Flick was not paying attention. His finger still pressed the trigger, and the beam still shone. It raced on, cutting a trench through the overhead floor. Flick's right arm went all the way back as he fell.

The ceiling gave way with a crack louder than a pistol shot. Bits of statuary rained down. The floor sagged where a jagged, zigzag cut had been made. It shook, starting to collapse from the center.

It was coming down, John realized. The ballroom floor was crashing down on Peter Flick's head!

"The Queen was right," John said as he scrambled for the relative safety of an arch. "That thing is dangerous."

Then, with a crunch like that of a gigantic dragon's jaws, the ballroom floor gave way completely and crashed into the basement.

John Knight saw Peter Flick caught under the descending roof. The man had not had the wit to seek immediate shelter. Dust rose in choking clouds so thick that John could not see, and his ears felt as muffled as his eyes, and it was hard to breathe. He curled up, covering his ears as well as he could, closing his eyes, and putting his mouth against his shirt to inhale.

Finally, as the noise ceased to reverberate and only a great ache remained, he crawled through the settling dust to the region where Flick had disappeared. There was a large timber there now, with something sticky beneath it. The laser had stopped showing; evidently the weapon had been crushed, too. Well, he had planned to dispose of it anyway, in due course.

That left—

"Zoanna!" he called gently.

There was no answer. He strained his eyes to see in the dim light coming through a break from above. The entire palace must have collapsed, or at least the main section. The wings, including the one where Zatanas had his quarters, might still be standing. The evil sorcerer had to be eliminated, too, for he was the power behind the Queen.

"Peter. Pe-ter." Her voice, very faint.

Damn her! So he would have to kill her after all! Why couldn't she have been crushed with Flick? John didn't have his laser now, or even a sword. He would have to kill her with his bare hands, and he wouldn't have liked that even if his right hand hadn't been crushed.

He felt his way over broken picture frames, torn canvases, chunks of statuary, and wads of drapes. He located her by the sound; she thought it was her consort coming.

He saw her left arm, pinned by part of a fallen column. Her mouth was wide now, as were her eyes, but there was no blood that he could see. She appeared to be hurt mainly by shock. This was the real Queen, the physical one; the mirrors had been broken.

"Peter," she said. "Peter, help me." It was her old voice, almost. The voice that had weakened him and hypnotized him. It was a voice as could work enchantment even without the help of magic.

He knew he should throttle her. But he couldn't do it one-handed.

"There's a passage," she said. "Trapdoor. River. Escape."

Did she know to whom she spoke? Did she even know where she was? Her eyes seemed to suggest no, but her words could be taken either way.

He hardly knew where he found the strength, but he worked until he pulled her arm free. She had been lucky; the full mass of the column had not come down on her. It had fallen across statuary that supported most of its weight. He only needed to excavate around her arm, making more room, to work it free.

The arm hung loosely from her shoulder. Certainly it was damaged, but at least it was there. He got one of his own arms around her and helped her to stand, bending slightly because of the sagging ceiling here. Her body was light, and its contours sweet against him; how he wished that—

"Trapdoor. There. There," she said. Her good arm pointed to the far right corner of the room, and at a statue of a dead hero whose head was now detached and whose sword arm was broken. That seemed appropriate!

He half dragged, half carried her as he made his way step by step to the spot she indicated. When he got there he had to put her down and drag aside the statue. Then he had to pull back the rug with its fighting-dragons motif, to strain to lift the trapdoor by its iron ring.

When the trapdoor opened all the way, he gave out an involuntary groan and almost plummeted head foremost down the crumbling wooden and moss-grown stairs. The cool, moist air of an underground river came up to meet him. Of course—the capital was beside a river, and this would be a tributary.

He shook his head, fighting off the dizziness that assailed him. Somehow he got her to her feet again. Somehow he got started down the stairs. It seemed a long, long way down. Longer than he had ever climbed down before. He felt weaker and weaker by the second, as though his blood were leaving him. But his body was intact except for his broken hand; he wasn't bleeding.

"Raft. Raft," she said. "Hurry. Hurry."

He hardly knew what to answer, and didn't try; he needed all his remaining strength to do the job.

Step by step, downward, they went. Her thigh against his, her body close against him. She was a middle-aged woman now, and surely she had no magic enhancing her anymore, yet she was alluring in every aspect. He couldn't hurt her!

His feet slipped, and he stopped, steadying himself with grim determination. Then he went on, step by slow step down, and she went with him.

At the bottom of the first flight there was a landing, then a second flight of stairs. John dragged them down. At the bottom of the second there was another landing and a third set of stairs. How deep *was* the stream? But finally they were there at a crumbling and moss-covered dock. There was an old raft tied here that appeared to have remained for an eternity.

He stopped, tottering, half collapsing on the dock. He felt the water lapping, lifting and lowering about him, and he knew he hadn't finished, but he was too exhausted to do any more.

Now she seemed to be supporting him, bearing him up, helping him onto the raft. His feet obeyed her, as once his whole body and mind had done. Now this foot, now that foot, and now he seemed to be on the raft with her and she seemed to be lifting a pole attached there by a rope, and she seemed to be poling them out into the current.

He struggled to sit up, to make sense of what was happening. He thought he heard a splash.

Pulling himself up to sitting position, he saw a string of silvery bubbles in the dark water behind the raft. Nothing else. He was alone.

He was too weary and disoriented to think or ponder anything. He couldn't even feel the pain in his hand.

The raft drifted. It passed between rock walls covered with eerily glowing moss that gave a strange green color to everything. The stream didn't seem to be flowing into the river that served the capital.

John Knight moved on to an unknown and perhaps unknowable destination.

30 /

RECOVERY

K ELVIN WATCHED THE BLOOD dripping into the golden urn, feeling, thanks to Zatanas' magic, that it was his own blood as well as his sister's. Jon, wide awake, unable to move because of the straps, whispered softly, "Kel, Kel, save me."

"Yes, why don't you save her, Kelvin Roundears?" Zatanas inquired. It was almost as though he expected an answer.

"He can't, Master," Queeto said, and swished the blood in its vessel, shaking all over as he croaked his laughter. "Not ever. Not him. He can't move, Master. And he's getting weaker. Weaker and weaker and weaker!"

Kelvin knew that the vicious dwarf was right. Queeto was having his revenge for the way they had taken Jon from him, after the sale at the Mart. There would be no mercy there. But if he willed the gauntlets to move, and if they did so, and brought along the rest of his body . . .

But there was little use. Zatanas had his laser on a shelf and he hadn't acquired a sword or even a dagger since leaving the palace balcony. There was little even the gauntlets could do as long as Queeto and Zatanas stayed out of reach. Only if he could reach them, he thought. Only if—

A great crashing, splintering noise came from below the floor. Clouds of dust rose in the room, books fell, glassware rattled. Something crashed over and made a foul stink.

The room shook violently. Almost as if a quake had come.

Queeto stumbled back, still on his feet but losing his balance. He pulled the golden vessel away from the tube in Jon's arm, splashing Jon's blood on himself. His hump seemed to pull him over, on his back, against Kelvin.

Instantly the gauntlets acted. Pulling Kelvin's unfeeling arms along, the gauntlets fastened on the dwarf's thick throat.

"Master! Master!" Queeto cried. His short, powerful arms reached back but couldn't stretch to the gauntlets and Kelvin's arms.

Kelvin willed strength to the gauntlets. Never before had he wanted to destroy any living thing as badly as he wanted to destroy this dwarf!

Queeto made a choking sound. His eyes bulged. It was magic strength squeezing the life out of him. But the gauntlets did not wait for him to suffocate; they crushed so hard that his neck collapsed, and he was dying.

Zatanas struggled up from the corner where he had been flung. His breath came in shallow, whispering drafts. His eyes bulged in sympathy with the dwarf's.

"Lit-tle bro-ther," he whispered. "Like links like. The spell I cast—it's affecting us!"

He choked, wheezed, and gasped horribly. On his feet, he rose unsteadily to his height. He began to raise a hand to gesture.

"Kel," Jon whispered. It wasn't much, but it distracted him for a moment. He had to save her!

Kelvin felt a bit of strength. He could move now! He concentrated, trying to aid the gauntlets in their grisly task. He put all his remaining strength into it—and the terrible fingers crushed in so hard that they pulped the tissues of the dwarf's neck, and Queeto was abruptly dead.

Zatanas tottered. Then, with no sound, no real warning, dwarf and master crumbled into unequal piles of dust. Only their clothing remained with the dust rising up from it and then settling down again.

Kelvin stepped on the dwarf's clothing and the dust as he fought to get to Jon. It was only his own weakness that slowed him now, instead of the sorcerer's magic, but that was enough. He struggled to her, almost falling, and clawed at the needle in her arm. He hauled on it, trying to pull it out; the gauntlets were clumsy for this.

He wrenched it out, and blood flowed across her arm. He reached down for the dwarf's sash and brought it up to make a tourniquet for her arm, but couldn't get it right, and still the blood flowed.

"Just untie me," she said. "I'll take care of my arm."

He put the gauntlets on the straps, and the gloves ripped the straps apart. Jon sat up unsteadily, and put her free hand on the wound, stanching the flow at last. Then she glanced at the floor, where the dust was. "Kel, what—?"

"Dust," he said. "Magic kept them alive, and now magic has destroyed them. The prophecy was right: 'And the gauntlet great, shall the tyrant take.' You remember those words, Jon?"

She raised her gaze. "Well, you saved me, Kel. But the Queen may still be lurking."

Kelvin picked up his father's weapon from the shelf. He made certain the safety was on, then placed it in the holster.

The room shook. More books hit the floor. More glassware trembled and fell. The odor got worse. The floor seemed to give a little. Below, something creaked and grumbled.

"The palace!" Kelvin said. "I think it's collapsing!"

The owlhawk fluttered. The poor creature was a victim, he thought, just as Jon had been.

He untied the leather thongs holding the bird to its grisly perch on a human skull. He watched it fly to the window overhead, then go through to its freedom.

He put his arm under Jon's shoulders and helped her sit up. His strength was returning, but hers was not. "I'm so tired, Kel," she said. "So very tired."

"Yes, I know." He had felt the power of the linkage, and knew exactly how tired she felt. He understood how the evil magician had died when the dwarf did; the magic transference was potent.

Jon pushed her legs over the side of the table. "We have to get out of here, Kel," she said faintly. "Before they—" She nodded at the dust. "Before they return to life."

"They won't return to life," Kelvin said. But he had seen and felt the power of Zatanas' magic; now he was no longer sure of its limit.

Jon rubbed at a cheek. "They won't, will they? Never again. You—you've killed them." Yet she, too, sounded uncertain.

"Say rather that the gauntlets killed them. Lean on my shoulder and I'll walk you out."

"I'm very weak, Kel."

"I know." *How well he knew!* "But you'll make it. We both will." He hoped. His confidence in things was only a shadow of what it had been, back before they went hunting for dragon's gold.

It seemed to take forever to cross the room and descend the stairs. In the courtyard, his superb warhorse waited for them, the only living creature remaining there.

Jon, recovering slightly, pulled herself up to the front of the saddle, while Kelvin sat behind her with the reins. It was good to be mounted again; this entire region made him nervous. Of course the evil sorcerer was permanently dead! Yet, somehow . . .

"Master! Master!"

"Courage, little brother apprentice. We will regain our bodies. Do as I do."

Dust motes drifted in the silent room. Slowly they settled downward. Heaps of dust began drifting together, eddying into larger and larger clumps.

More dust swirled, coming together. Slowly the particles attached to others of their kind. Bit by bit, a skeleton formed. A shape that was as yet nothing *but* form.

A lizard, escaped from its cage, raised its head, flared its hood, and scuttled for the corner.

With agonizing slowness, the skeleton assumed greater solidity. Other dust particles attached to it. A figure began to shape. It was a faceless mannequin, and then a faceless corpse. Tiny whirlwinds moved about the floor, sucking up dust that had once formed the sorcerer Zatanas.

"Master! Master!"

"Try, Queeto. It is your only chance."

Now other dust particles at the other side of the room began to move. Slowly, slowly they lifted, then swirled, then formed. "Master! Master! I'm doing it!"

"I knew you would. Apprentice like Master, always." The dust whirlpool swirled, moving hither and yon, questing for dust in obscure corners.

Slowly, ever so slowly, the two bodies formed.

"Will there be enough, Master? Will there be enough?"

"There will be. If not enough from us, then enough from other sources. Dust is dust."

"How much time, Master? How much time?"

"Enough. Work, Queeto, work!"

Now the body of Zatanas lay stark on the floor by a broken gold vessel and a slash of crimson. An opened book lay almost beneath the magician's form. Hair grew, fingernails, eyelashes. But the body did not breathe.

Queeto's hump was finished. His short legs and powerful forearms appeared as they had in life. The whirlwinds fed the form at an increasing pace.

"When can we enter, Master? When?"

"When the bodies are set. For now they are only forms. Mine is almost ready; yours is not."

The body of Queeto emerged from the dust. Organs, blood and bone, ugly, misshapen, monstrous, all dust. But the dust was being set by the solidifying action of agglutination. Magic was converting it to form. Soon it would be living flesh.

"I'm done, Master! I'm done! I'm whole!"

"Almost. There must be time for setting."

The owlhawk's shadow touched the window. Then it was inside the room, diving for a lizard on the floor.

The lizard ran into a pile of clothing. The owlhawk swooped, caught the lizard up in its talons, and carried it to its perch. It lit on the skull, opened its beak, and with one swift motion bit the lizard's head off.

"Master! Master!"

"It will go away. It must!"

The owlhawk devoured its repast. Another lizard crawled along the wall. The big bird flopped its wings, scattering dust, dislodging particles, making of two apparent corpses two apparently faceless mannequins. But it caught its prey.

"*Master!*"

"It will go away, Queeto. We can live again as long as there is our dust."

Again the owlhawk returned to its perch. Again it devoured its dripping repast, this time more slowly. Bits of lizard blood and lizard juices dripped from its opened beak.

"Master! Master!"

"When it has fed, it will sleep. Owlhawks sleep in the day."

The bird finished its second lizard, rotated its head, and stretched its wings.

"Master, it—"

A third lizard ran along a shelf of glass bottles and retorts. This was too much temptation. The owlhawk flew, talons extended. The wings stirred up dust in a swirling cloud. The talons touched the lizard, and needle claws sank into its greenish sides.

The blood dripped as the bird dropped, lizard clutched in its claws. As it dropped, its wingtips fanned and brushed bottles and glassware.

A beaker fell. A bottle tipped, rolled off the shelf, and burst explosively on the floor. Another bottle followed.

Fanned by the commotion, the dust figures collapsed inward on themselves.

Unperturbed, the owlhawk carried its prey to its longtime perch. Green flames shot from the broken bottle. They rose high, crackling, giving off smoke.

"Master! Master!"

"Fear not. If I live, I will bring you back. If not as Queeto, then as an object. A magical staff, or—"

"But, Master, I don't want to be a staff!"

"You will take what you will get! Cursed bird, I will enter you and—"

The bird lifted from its perch, dropping the mangled lizard in its wake. It rose to the highest shelf, its wings dislodging boxes and containers and bottles that fell and burst with hideous noise.

Now it was flying for the window, and outside.

"Master! Master!"

"Cursed bird, why didn't it wait?"

Now the room was filling with dancing green flame. The flame grew, devouring what it reached. Clothing charred and blackened. The owlhawk's perch burned, and so did the dust.

"Master, Master, I fade."

"Oh, the ignominy of it! Destroyed by a bird!"

"*Mas-ter. Mas-t-er . . .*"

The green flames licked up the walls, shot out of the windows, and then onto the roof.

Soon the crackling flames were being witnessed by nothing living, semi-living, or with any hope of living.

Epilogue

THEY GATHERED IN THE great tent that had been pitched on the Hackleberry farm, the temporary headquarters of the new government while the palace was being rebuilt. The Hackleberries and the Flambeaus had met, and liked each other, and were cooperating in the plans for Kelvin's marriage to Heln. King Rufurt had decreed that all back taxes on both farms were excused, in return for the services that members of these families had rendered in restoring the rightful government. The scales from the slain dragons had become part of the royal treasury, and were backing the new currency and paying for the rebuilding and all other obligations. A program of tax reform was being instituted, so that no longer would farmers be impoverished by taxes, and of course the Boy and Girl Marts were abolished.

Yet certain mysteries remained, and it was to investigate these that they were here. They had discovered, because of certain remarks made by Heln's mother, that a person who touched Heln while she was astrally separated could pick up some of what her spirit was doing. Indeed, it was possible to communicate with her when she knew that the person was there to hear; she could not see or hear the person when her spirit was elsewhere, but she could send her thoughts to that person through her unconscious body. They had tried it experimentally, Kelvin lying beside her and holding her hand while she separated, and he had received an ongoing narration of her experiences.

After the palace had burned down, workers going through the wreckage, preparing the site for the new palace, had discovered flights of stairs descending to a nether dock, where a subterranean river passed. There were signs that suggested that John Knight and Queen Zoanna had fled the collapsing palace by that route, and taken a boat down the river. But the stream did not flow into the surface river that flowed by the capital; it wended its way elsewhere. Men had searched as far as they could along it, but it wound so deviously through its channels that they had been unable to trace it far, and their labors were needed for the work on the new palace. There had been no sign of either John Knight or the Queen; possibly they had drowned, or floated far away. But it was necessary to know their fate, for if John Knight lived, Charlain's marriage to Hal Hackleberry was in question, and if the Queen lived, the kingdom itself was in danger. So now, a week after the victory of the Knights, Heln was going to explore the river labyrinth astrally, and Kelvin was going to report her findings as they occurred. Everyone who counted was here for this quest.

Heln swallowed a dragonberry. "Stay with me, dear," she said to Kelvin as she sank back on the bed.

"Always, dear," he agreed. He held her hand firmly and sat on a chair beside her. Much had changed, but this had not: the use of the endearment still caused him to blush. The others pretended not to notice.

"I wish I had someone to call me 'dear,' " Jon murmured. She was seated on Kelvin's other side. She remained pale from her loss of blood, and was weak, but was otherwise in good condition.

"What about that boy who helped you get into the palace grounds?" Les Crumb asked, standing on her other side.

"Tommy Yokes?" She smiled briefly. "I liked him, but he went back to his girlfriend the moment the King freed the bound boys." She shrugged. "I guess I wasn't cut out to be anyone's girlfriend."

Kelvin's eyes were closed, as Heln's breathing slowed and her hand grew cold. But though he felt the impact of the transference, he remained conscious in the tent. Jon was speaking quietly, so that only those closest to her could hear, but he was one of them.

"When I was knocked out in battle," Les said, "I felt myself sinking down and down, and I did not know whether I would ever rise up again. When I woke I couldn't move at all, and I felt terrible. But then I felt a hand cooling my brow, and I knew someone was taking care of me, and I knew that if I recovered I would owe that person my life."

"That's silly," Jon said. "Your father brought you in. I only helped clean you up."

"Yes. I was delirious. My thoughts made no sense. When I opened my eyes and saw you, it was as though I had never seen you before. You were absolutely beautiful."

"Oh, shut up," she said, embarrassed.

"That vision remained with me after I recovered," he continued. "You are as lovely this moment."

"What are you saying?" she asked, disturbed.

"I thought your interest was elsewhere. After all, you are young. But you showed great courage when you went to rescue your brother. When it seemed you were dying, I—"

"Please, I don't like to think about that blood."

"When you recover, if—what I'm trying to say is—you don't seem that young anymore, to me—"

Jon finally got his drift. "You mean—you see me as—as—".

"As a woman," Les finished. "And if you were to find it in you to consider me as a man—"

Then Kelvin received the first signal from Heln. "I'm at the underground river now," he said, verbalizing her thought as he received it. There had been stray murmurings in the tent, from several conversations; now it was abruptly quiet. "I jumped to this site as soon as I got fully separated, but now I shall have to move more slowly, or I might miss something important. I hope you are receiving this, Kel."

There was a brief wave of mirth in the tent; obviously he was receiving it. He kept his eyes closed, to concentrate entirely on her thought.

"The water winds about," he continued, speaking for her. He began to glimpse it himself: the dark water, the cold cave walls. "It splits into several channels, but I see they merge again farther down, and there's only one big enough for a boat. I'm following that one. I'm sort of flying just above the water, moving faster now; I'll spot any boat if it's here."

She was silent for a time, evidently having nothing to report as she followed the buried river.

"You mean it?" Jon whispered, and Kelvin knew she was not talking to him.

"With all my heart," Les whispered back.

There was a disturbance at the tent entrance. "Am I permitted?" Kian asked. "I know I was on the wrong side, but those are my parents you seek."

"Permitted," King Rufurt said gruffly. "You behaved as you had to, and you are Kelvin's kin. We are glad you survived."

It grew quiet again. Kelvin could tell by the sound of his sister's breathing that she was deep in thought. Les Crumb had certainly caught her by surprise! But Kelvin remembered how the man had remarked favorably on her; it seemed he had been serious.

"I just don't see any boat," Kelvin said for Heln. "The current seems stronger now; I suppose it could have carried the boat quite far. I've traced the river a long way—oh!" She was uncommunicating for a moment; then: "It drains into The Flaw! The Flaw! The water just, just—falls in. Into the starry dark! I don't know how far I can follow it, there; I think it's not safe for me."

"Get away from there!" Kian cried. "Zatanas said something about The Flaw once—it's an astral bridge as well as a physical one!"

Get away! Kelvin thought as hard as he could, hoping he could reach her. So far the communication had all been one way, but if it was humanly possible to reverse it—

"Suddenly I'm very nervous," Kelvin said for Heln. "I don't trust this place at all. I'm going back up the river; maybe I missed something."

Kelvin heard a general sigh of relief. They had thought that only Heln's body was vulnerable when she separated, because she had no control of it then, but now it seemed that there were places her spirit could not safely go.

"I am feeling weak," Jon said. "Would you help me walk back home, Les?"

"Certainly." There was a smaller disturbance as they walked from the tent, Les supporting Jon with his arm about her waist.

That was interesting, Kelvin thought. Ordinarily his sister would have fainted rather than admit any feminine weakness. But of course she had lost a lot of blood, and a week wasn't nearly time enough to replace it.

"I *did* miss something," he said for Heln abruptly. "Not the boat; I'm afraid that's gone, and if they were in it, they're gone, too. But there's another channel of the river, or maybe it's a tributary. I must have overlooked it because I was going the other way, and it comes in at an angle. It's actually larger than the other; the caves are rounder here, almost polished, as if this is an artificial channel. And it leads—oh!"

Every breath in the tent seemed to be held. Kelvin strained to see what Heln was seeing, and made out a round door of some sort.

"There's a door here, perfectly round, like round ears," she said, chuckling. "I'm going through; it can't stop me, though it seems to be locked tight. Inside—it's a chamber, in the shape of a sphere, and there's—why, there's a parchment sitting on a table. Let me look—yes, I can read it! It says: *To whom it may concern*—I suppose that's me!—*if you have found this cell, you are a roundear, because only a roundear could penetrate to it without setting off the self-destruct mechanism.*" She paused. "I *am* a roundear; this message is meant for me! But this chamber must be hundreds of years old! How could it—oh, I'd better keep reading it! *I am Mouvar*—"

"Mouvar!" King Rufurt exclaimed.

"And I am a roundear."

"A roundear!" everyone exclaimed.

"But because the natives look with disfavor on aliens, I masked my ears so that I could work among them without hindrance. I used the technology of my home frame to set things straight, then retired, for it was lonely. I set up the prophecy of my return, or the appearance of any roundear, to facilitate better acceptance in future centuries. The tools of my frame are here, and you may use them as you find necessary. If you wish to contact me directly, seek me in my home frame, where I will be in suspended animation. Directions for using The Flaw to travel to the frame of your choice are in the book of instructions beside this letter. Please return any artifacts you borrow. Justice be with you."

"Mouvar—a roundear!" Mor Crumb exclaimed. "Suddenly some funny things make sense!"

"There's another pair of gauntlets," Kelvin said for Heln. "And something that looks like a roundear weapon. And a jar of seeds—they are labeled 'Astral Berries'—and something labeled a levitation belt, and—oops, my time is running out; I must return."

Then, after a moment, "That's funny! They're kissing! I didn't know they felt that way about each other!"

And, finally, Heln's hand warmed, and Kelvin knew she was waking.

"Kissing?" King Rufurt asked. "No one's kissing here! What does she mean?"

Then Heln's eyelids flickered. "Did—did you hear?" she asked Kelvin.

"Everything!" Kelvin agreed excitedly. "You found Mouvar's retreat! He was a roundear!"

"Yes—but I think not from our fathers' world. He spoke of frames, and that big book of instructions—I think The Flaw leads to many worlds, and on some the people have pointed ears, and on some round ears—"

"We'll learn it all, now we know the chamber exists!" King Rufurt said.

"Not necessarily, Your Majesty," Mor Crumb rumbled. "I don't know much about alien magic, but I know what 'self-destruct' means! Only a roundear can get in there!"

"But we have roundears!" the King said.

Kelvin exchanged a glance with Heln. "We shall do as we feel best," Kelvin said. "Those tools are too powerful to let loose on this world. We've already gotten rid of the bad government; we don't need even the gauntlets Mouvar lost anymore. In fact, I'll be happy if I never kill another dragon."

"The dragons guarded the astral berries," Heln said. She was weak from her experience, but animated. "They should continue to guard them, so that if things get bad again, centuries hence, the berries will be there for the next Roundear of Prophecy."

"Then I'll appoint you Guardian of the Dragons!" the King said. "You can use the berries to check the whole of dragon country, and warn me of any poachers; we shall take the gold only of dragons who die of natural causes. We won't use Mouvar's magic at all."

"If I may—" Kian said. He was bandaged and weak, but intense.

The King looked at him. "I don't think we could afford to trust you with—"

"My father—and my mother," Kian said. "They were in that boat on that river. They must have floated into The Flaw. They must be in some other world—some other frame, as Mouvar calls it. If I could go there to search for them—"

"That seems fair," Kelvin said. "You know the danger, Kian. You may never return, if you lose yourself in The Flaw."

"I realize the danger," Kian said. "But there really is no place for me here, and if I have a chance to find them—"

"Granted," King Rufurt said quickly. "Heln will read the instructions for you, so you can travel through The Flaw."

"Thank you, Your Majesty," Kian said.

"Now I am very tired," Heln said.

"Everybody out of the tent!" the King said, and immediately there was motion as the people moved out. "We have much to think about, and much yet to learn." And the King, too, departed, leaving Kelvin alone with Heln.

"But one thing more, before I sleep," she said.

"Anything!" Kelvin agreed.

"Just give me what Les is giving Jon."

"What?" But then he caught on, and bent down to embrace her and kiss her.

Serpent's Silver

Contents

Prologue

HELN KNIGHT HACKLEBERRY LAY back against the pillows. Her brown eyes were closed, and her bosom heaved shallowly. Her shiny black hair framed her lovely oval face. She was as beautiful as she had been on their wedding day, seven months ago, Kelvin thought.

He lay beside her, squeezing her calloused yet very feminine hand. They were on their new bed in their new home, but they were not alone, and this was no pleasant interlude.

He glanced up at his sister, Jon, who was unusually silent. Then his gaze passed Jon's normally smiling husband, Lester, who was quite serious now. He wished again that he hadn't let them talk him into this.

She has to! It's your father and your brother! Jon had insisted. *They've been missing four months!* When had Kelvin Knight Hackleberry ever been able to argue his manly little sister out of anything? She was correct, of course, but that did not make him feel any more comfortable at the moment.

Heln's hand was growing cold now, as if she were dying. Oh, it was so like death, this astral traveling—death from poisoning. Indeed, dragonberries did kill pointears; only roundears like Heln could survive them, suffering just the partial death of soul-separation. They were never sure of the safe limit, and he hated the risk. If she died, he would go with her into death, he thought, if that was the only way to be with her always.

His hand tightened on hers, but she did not stir. It was fortunate that he could experience some of her thoughts and share her experiences, he thought, while she was in this state. He could even communicate with her while her spirit traveled, freed by the magic that had once been the secret of the golden dragons. So he knew she wasn't really dead—not as long as her mind touched his.

Now he started receiving her thoughts. "I'm back at the underground river now," Kelvin said for her. He had become like a thing his father had

213

once told him about: a radio receiver. He tuned in on the words and repeated them without conscious volition. In this manner she shared her experience with those standing by her body.

Kelvin became aware of her sensations: the cold cave walls drifting by, the passages twisting, splitting, merging. The dim glow of lichen on the walls, somehow distinguishable from the lamplight in the room the four of them occupied. Images in her mind and his, overlapping yet distinct. He remembered another device his father had talked about: the receiver of words and pictures known as television. Perhaps he was becoming like that, too. But he could not show the pictures to the others.

"The Flaw! The Flaw! I see it now!" He was speaking for her, but he saw it, too: the water falling, falling into a darkness filled with stars.

He willed her away from that dread void, thrilling to its menace. "The other room! The other room!" he cried.

Then she was taking him, through her awareness and his, through the round, solid door. Perfectly round: rounder than round ears! They floated into the metallic chamber that only roundears such as the two of them could enter without causing its destruction. That was what the parchment there claimed; they had read it only partially during her prior visit here, but he believed it.

They hovered together above an open book on a table, and a box the size of a closet. The walls of the box were lined with dials and what appeared to be clocks. Kelvin recognized the sort of instruments his father had talked about: they were gauges and controls that somehow ordered things to be done.

"He left here," Kelvin/Heln said. "Into the other frame. He stepped in here to follow the path of your father. It will still work for us. We can cross the astral bridge through Mouvar's magic. To where Kian and your father are."

For Kian was Kelvin's half brother. They had been on opposite sides, and had fought. Though they were friends now, Kian's guilt had led him to go on the risky tour through the dread Flaw, searching for his lost parents. He had not returned.

Heln and Kelvin entered the box. The vision became a blackness so deep it shimmered. There was something like a crash of soundless thunder; then a streak of fire that split their existence. Stars appeared, shining all around and through and into them. Existence whirled, collapsed, and expanded. Time and place ceased to have meaning. Then they were . . .

Moved. Into a hazy chamber closet like the one they had entered. The closet wall with its clocks reappeared, forming out of the confusion. The image needed tuning; it seemed to be far away. But even as Kelvin thought of that, the sights and sounds and smells of the new location came into clear focus. They had arrived—where?

Two sets of footprints crossed from the closet to a rock wall, where a large round metal door stood ajar. It might have been the same door they had just entered—but that one was closed. The footprints might have been their own—but they were going in the opposite direction, and in any event, Kelvin and Heln were not here physically. So these could be John Knight's and Kian's prints.

They began moving, bodiless but with direction. Kelvin smelled grass, and heard the songs for birds and the tinkling of what might be metallic chimes. This was an intelligible world, then.

They paused, Heln sensing the way. There was a metal rope ladder anchored to a solid ring in the cliffside. The ladder descended into a large tree that seemed similar to the beenut tree where Kelvin had found his magic gauntlet. That was a good sign! They swooped down to the roots of the tree and along the ground.

Heln in her astral state seemed to be drawn to a location or person of her choice. In this she was like the magnetic compass his father had described— or the magic needle that pointed always to The Flaw.

As Heln followed the pull of the brother Kelvin had first met on a battlefield and tried to kill nine months before, he looked around to the extent this form allowed. He saw or sensed displayed in a tall oaple tree the source of the chiming. Three silver spirals hung from a branch and produced the sound when the breeze twirled them. They looked like snakeskins, he thought uneasily: silver serpent hides that were stiff and dry yet also shiny and bright.

Now they were traveling across a wide valley, mountains, and rolling farmland similar to that of Rud. On and on interminably—but then swooping abruptly, hawk-fashion, to a palace on a river bluff. They entered the palace and drifted through spectacular halls filled with art objects, some of which seemed familiar. On down carpeted hallways, polished corridors, and banistered stairs. To—

A dank, dark, foul-smelling place that seemed made for fear. Kelvin jerked with shock.

"What is it, Kel?" his sister asked, hovering over his body. He had stopped talking, alarming her.

"Dungeon," he said. Indeed it was, exactly such a dungeon as Kian's mother, the evil Queen Zoanna, had used to confine Kelvin and his father and Rufurt, the good king of Rud.

Now he could see in the dim light that came through the high barred windows. There was his father, John Knight, haggard and dirty. There was his brother, Kian, in no better shape. And a third man, battered, blood-spattered, lying on the floor, propping his head with his arm, evidently too weak from loss of blood to do more.

Standing between them and a barred door was a wide man wearing a silver crown. Kelvin focused on the man's face.

"Rufurt!" Kelvin whispered.

But no, this Rufurt had round ears, as did the prisoners, while their Rud counterparts had ears as pointed as Jon's and Lester's. The Rud king's face, even after years of imprisonment, had a jovial appearance around the jowls that nothing could quite erase. This nearly identical face was taut and grim by comparison.

Yet a part of his mind shrieked: *It's Rufurt!*

At the king's gesture a man in uniform unlocked the cell, entered, and bent over the wounded man. John Knight grabbed the bars, seeming about to speak. Undeterred, the torturer pushed the unfortunate man's head down on the floor and twisted it sideways. Then he brought out a silver tube, held it above the prisoner's ear, unstoppered it, and tilted it carefully. Something silvery oozed out and flowed, undulating, into the man's ear.

The guard paused only long enough to make sure the vial was empty. Then he let go of the prisoner and stepped quickly away. He got out of the cell as if afraid of something.

The prisoner pulled his face from the grime of the floor. His hand came up to touch his ear, as if it itched. It seemed that he was not sure why the guard had departed without beating him again. Or that he was afraid to think about it.

Then his look of perplexity darkened into something else. He clawed at his ear as if trying to wrench it out of his head. His eyeballs rolled back until only the whites showed. He screamed. It was a horrible sound, signifying something infinitely worse than pain.

The king made a ghastly smile that was all the more horrible for being on King Rufurt's face. "Silver's not so nice, now, is it, Smith? Now that the little beastie's chewing in you?"

Little beastie? Kelvin hoped he misunderstood.

The man shook all over, from head to foot. His eyes stared wildly, seeming ready to pop out of his face. His arms and legs spasmed. He screamed again, as if trying to vomit out his tongue, while the other prisoners looked on with drawn faces. The screaming continued, diminished, because the man could not take enough of a breath to make it loud.

"We must go back. We are going back," Heln said with Kelvin's mouth. With that the dungeon faded and slipped sideways. They were pulled, as though by elastic, back to the chamber, into the closet, through darkness and stars. It happened so swiftly as to be instant; their minds seemed to shatter.

Then they were home. They were on their bed in their room, with their closest friends looking down at them. Where their bodies had been all along.

Kelvin sat up, turning to his wife. That horror—

Heln's eyelids flickered. Her big, soft brown eyes opened to stare into his blue ones.

"Oh, Kelvin, we must help them! We must!"

"But—"He thought desperately, an enormous fear threatening to swallow what passed for his courage. "I have things to do here. There's the prophecy."

"And you will fulfill it, dear, you will. But you are a hero and a roundear. Only a roundear can journey to the chamber as Kian did. Only a roundear can make the trip we just did."

"You can't go," he said, being firm. Immediately he knew in his most cowardly secret self that he had misspoken. He should have said "we," including himself as well as her.

"Oh, Kelvin, you're so brave! I knew you'd want to go to that other world and rescue your father and your brother! I knew you just couldn't do anything else!"

Yes, he thought glumly. Yes—but what had he done to deserve this hero mantle? He had never wanted to be a hero. Jon had wanted to and he had not. Now, because he had lucked out on one step of a prophecy, they thought he couldn't fail at anything.

"Don't worry, we'll take good care of her," Lester said, his boyish smile broadening.

Kelvin knew that Lester and his sister would do that. He had no decent excuse to get out of another mission of foolish attempted heroism. He wished that he had never agreed to let Heln take that astral trip.

Yet that prisoner, with the appalling silver beastie in his ear—was that the fate awaiting John Knight and Kian, if someone didn't get them out of the dungeon? Kelvin was sickly certain that it was, and that he was the only one who could do anything about it. He was a coward, but he had to act.

I /

SACRIFICE

K IAN REACHED THE BOTTOM rung of the metallic rope ladder and looked down. From the chamber entrance the ladder had appeared to disappear into the top of a very large beenut tree. It still did. The rope was of a material different from any he had seen before, and it seemed to grow out of the trunk where the spreading branches formed the crown.

Well, he had been a tree climber as a boy. He was twenty-one now, and it had been some time since he had practiced, but he remembered. What fun it had been, peering in the windows of the palace from his secret perch and watching the comings and goings of the sycophants and courtiers!

This was a different world—but perhaps not too different, he thought as he clambered easily down the close-set branches of the beenut tree. The vegetation of this frame seemed exactly like that of his own. His half brother had climbed a similar tree in the park in Franklin and discovered a gauntlet with remarkable properties. Kian now wore an identical pair.

The armored gloves made climbing easier, but he could hardly say how. Well, yes, he could: he found that he could easily hang on to a branch by just a couple of fingertips, feeling no strain. It was as though there were muscles in the gauntlets aiding every move his hands made. Because he was a roundear, he knew, they worked just as well for him as for Kelvin.

He let go of a branch and dropped the remaining distance to the base of the tree. Catching his breath, he looked up but could not see the ladder or the cliff face with its open metal door. The secret was well hidden; he realized that he should mark the spot well in his mind, in case he ever wished to return to his own world.

The birds sang just as they did at home. There was no difference, so far, in anything. He found himself surprised, even though he knew this was the nature of the frame worlds. His grandfather Zatanas had tried instructing him on the nature of reality and what he called the magic art: worlds might differ, but not the fundamentals of nature and magic.

More recently Kian had read the parchment book he had found in the chamber before taking the gauntlets and the alien weapon, and launching his own adventure. Each overlapping world, he had learned, was almost like the ones touching it, but with small, subtle differences. "You may even meet yourself, or someone like yourself," Lester Crumb had said.

Kian shook his head. That didn't seem unreasonable for others, but he knew that his father would not be duplicated here. John Knight, after all, had come from a distant frame where they called the world "Earth." He had never figured out quite how his father had crossed over; it seemed to have involved war magic of a sort not understood in Rud. But John Knight was unique—and therefore so were his sons.

Kian had gone only a short distance along the stream, admiring its blue water and leaping fish, when another sound reached him: a tinkling, musical note.

He paused, trying to locate the source. It seemed to come from a large oaple. He walked that way, staring hard into the branches where three long silver belts or spirals hung and twisted in the river breeze. Twirling, they touched each other to produce the sounds.

When he reached the tree he discovered that the belts were indeed spirals. Each had the apparent fragility of snakeskin, but was metallic except for an underlay of leather. They were silver, too: real silver, in a pattern like that of overlapping scales. He removed a gauntlet, fitted a thumbnail under a scale, and tried to pull the scale loose. It remained fast: the organic and inorganic were seemingly one.

Kian considered. Could he still find the large beenut tree and the ladder? Yes, he had marked the fact of the river making a sharp bend, and certainly such a large tree—one big enough to laugh at floods, if trees could laugh— was readily found. The chimes, whatever they were, might be to mark the upcoming bend.

He tested the scale of one of the skins with the point of his knife. It came away silver. Silver like that had to be very pure!

Could snakes here have scales of silver, in the same way that dragons back home had scales of gold? No, that hardly made sense. Dragons were virtually immortal beasts with powerful gizzards. The gizzards ground up weighty stones that the dragons swallowed in the course of centuries to pulverize their food internally. The food was rough, because dragons hardly chewed anything that no longer struggled, and even those big stones got worn away. They contained gold, and that gold migrated in due course to the brightly shining scales. Thus the gizzard was the key to the dragon's gold. But snakes—who could imagine them with gizzards? They swallowed their prey whole and let their digestive juices handle it. No stones in them!

He went on. When he judged it was noonday, he stopped to rest and eat the lunch Jon had packed for him. "Don't tell Les," she had whispered. "He complains that I'm not feeding him well. I don't want him to grow a paunch like his father's! He just might be jealous." Kian had smiled and teased her in the manner Kelvin was always doing. She was easy to tease and to be with —this boyish, pretty girl whose ears were pointed, though she was Kelvin's sister.

Thought of his ears caused him to pull down the lightweight stockelcap. He wore it for concealment. Only a fool would choose to wear such a thing on such a warm day! Yet he might meet someone, and if this frame was not totally unlike home, his round ears would set him apart. Pointed ears had always been considered natural, and round ears unnatural. Best that he wear the cap despite the discomfort.

He checked himself with the little mirror Heln had slipped into his travel-sack, first adjusting the stockelcap, then smoothing his light blond mustache. It was essential to pay attention to appearances regardless of what frame he was in! He knew, and had known since near infancy, that he had a striking figure and a reasonably handsome face. There had been a time when that was important to him, and perhaps someday such a time would come again.

He resumed his journey along the road. At home this path would have taken him through the mountainous region near Franklin. Not far from dragon country. He smiled. Well, he wasn't about to venture into dragon country, if that existed here! Unless, of course, his father and mother existed in this world, in such a region.

Soon he would have to swallow one of the dragonberries in his pack and see if they worked. Not even Heln knew about these. If the berry made him sick, as it did most people, he would take no more. But roundears could eat them and not be poisoned, not fatally, anyway. The berries enabled Heln to take flight astrally, her spirit homing in on some distant person or place while her body slept. Because she was a roundear—and Kian was a roundear, too. He, his half brother, Kelvin, their father, and Heln were the only folk he had ever encountered with ears of this unnatural shape. What an advantage, if the berries worked for him!

The road forked. Impulsively he followed the side branch into the mountains. He felt more comfortable this way, though he could not have said why; after all, at home it would have taken him into the domain of the dangerous wild things. Maybe he was just trying to be an adventurer, as his father was: someone who would choose the wild way.

A deoose crossed his path soon after lunch, and a bit later a fleet-footed meer bounced out of the bushes and then across the path in sprightly leaps. Red moss was on every tree; it was really still much like home. Possibly there were dangers similar to those in his own frame. At this stage he preferred familiar dangers!

As if in response to his thought, a bearver reared up from some appleberry bushes and greeted him with a loud woof. Then, perceiving that he stood his ground, it came out on the road and began a stalking advance.

Kian started to draw his sword, which was a properly polished blade his mother had chosen. But bearvers were large and unreasoning beasts, dangerous at all times. He knew he might be able to kill it, but he also knew that the chance of that was slight. One swipe from that huge paw could disarm him, gauntlets or no, and then—why hadn't he fled the moment he saw the predator?

Even as he foolishly drew the blade, another thought occurred. What about the alien weapon he carried? That might scare the beast so that it would think better of charging him. No known opposition could cow a bearver, but the unknown might.

Kian drew the weapon from its soft, curved alien scabbard. He pointed it, letting the gauntlet on his hand control his action. Then he tried to tell the glove to aim ahead of the beast, rather than trying to destroy it. This was partly because if the weapon were only partially effective, the effort would enrage the beast, making things worse, and partly because he preferred merely to scare it away if he could, and partly to see whether he had this kind of control over the gauntlets. He was in trouble, granted, but if he got out of this he might learn something that would help him the next time.

He—or the gauntlet—aimed the weapon. His—or its—finger squeezed. From the bell-shaped muzzle there came a series of sparks and a low hissing. The bearver gave a bark and charged.

Kian didn't have time to consider. The gauntlet straightened the weapon, this time taking dead aim, and pressed the trigger. And again the result was a few sparks and hissing. There was no evident damage to the bearver.

What was this, a toy?

Disgusted and now thoroughly scared, Kian dropped the weapon and leveled the sword. But the bearver, unpredictable as always, now swerved in its charge. Kicking its big heels back in a frolicsome manner, it made an ungainly leap over to the side of the road and plowed into the fringing bushes. It paused to look back, seeming almost to grin; then it woofed comically and disappeared.

"Bearvers will be bearvers," Kian remarked, weak with relief. It was a common saying at home. A bearver might decide to eat a person, or it might simply amuse itself by scaring a victim into loosening his bowels. He was thankful that his bowels had only twitched as the monster charged, and that his pantaloons were not in need of washing. He had escaped both death and shame, this time.

Now the road was descending into a valley, a lush region that should have held farms. There was nothing of the sort. In another oaple tree hung another of the spiral chimes. Parchment-thin yet curled into stiffness.

He stared at the silver and listened to its tinkle while he ate a few appleberries. A chill ran up and down his back; he had a feeling that something was wrong. Through the mists far below in the valley, among rocks that had rolled down over the centuries, he could see a movement. People—maybe a crowd. From this distance they seemed short and broad, reminding him of Queeto, his grandfather's dwarf apprentice. In the midst of the crowd, a little to the front and grasped by either hand, was a taller, slimmer person. It was hard for Kian to see, but this could be a woman or a girl of normal stature.

He strained his eyes, wishing that he could make things out better. The dwarfs gathered with the prisoner—for so she seemed—at a spot between two upright rocks the size of horses. Two of the dwarfs did something that produced a flash of silver. Then all the small people withdrew, leaving the woman or girl apparently shackled between the two stones. The small ones disappeared the way they had come.

What was this—a human sacrifice? It had that aspect! Was the woman a criminal? The dwarfs magical creatures? Just what had he come upon? It was probably a bad idea to interfere—but for all he knew, the woman could be his mother. Surely not—yet how could he be certain?

Half running, wishing he had a horse, he descended the slope in as fast a fashion as he could manage. He did not know how long the woman would be there, or what sort of danger he might face. He just had to *know,* lest he forever regret it.

When he broke through the bushes and faced her at close range, he was startled by her beauty. Her slim arms were stretched on either side, tethered by chains of silver. She had long blond hair, and deep blue eyes, and a figure that—

"Leave! Oh, leave!" she begged. He had no difficulty understanding her, because she used the language of home. Her head bobbed in the direction of a perfectly round hole in the side of the cliff. "Before it comes! Before it slithers out and devours us! Please!"

"You need help," he said, drawing his sword. Her lips were lying to him, he thought, while her eyes were speaking truth. She did not want him leaving her to some terrible fate.

"No! No! It will come soon! The appointed one! The one that always comes!"

"You're intended as a sacrifice?" He went closer, sword in hand.

She tossed her head, her hair flipping from her left ear and exposing it for the first time. Now he understood: *she was round-eared!* Round, not pointed! As it was back home, so it must be here! Roundears either hated for being different or at best barely tolerated.

"It's coming!" she cried. "I hear it!"

Indeed, there was a strange slithery sound coming from that hole. The whisper of it sent the hairs on the back of his neck tingling.

"I'm not afraid of it, whatever it is," he lied. This was surely worse than what he had faced before! And what was it, anyway? A burrower the size of a bearver? A tunneler through solid rock? Whatever it was, the size of that hole made him shudder. He fixed his eyes on the dread aperture and waited, knowing that whatever appeared was not going to run or tease.

So suddenly as to be startling, a large silvery snout thrust from the hole, just in time to catch a ray of sunshine that lighted the cliff's face. Then a flat silvery head emerged, followed by a long, long, undulating silver body. It was a serpent as large around as a war-horse!

A serpent covered all over with silver scales—surely real silver! Just as at home a dragon's scales were real gold. This serpent must be the overgrown version of the snakes from which the silver skins had come. It was as large as the legendary anaconda John Knight had told about. Kian had thought that to be a mere story. Some story! This thing could swallow a man and his war-horse together!

Kian doubted it could help, but he reached for the alien weapon he carried. His hand slapped only the holster; the weapon itself was gone! He had neglected to pick it up after his encounter with the bearver. The weapon, worthless though it might be, was back there on the road.

"Run! Run!" The girl was shaking with terror, and whimpering, but still she tried to warn him away.

Not a chance! His legs wouldn't work for him now. His gauntlets and his sword had to work together to save them. With the gauntlets, he had to believe, there was at least a chance of accomplishing something.

The serpent emerged sinuously all the way from the hole, lifted its head, and reared back. The eyes swayed above his own. A long, drawn-out hiss like that of a salivating dragon came from the mouth. Then that dread mouth opened, revealing dagger-length crystalline fangs. Drops of clear liquid fell to the ground, spattering and hissing and emitting little puffs of steam. Where the drops struck grass, the grass writhed, turned black, and crumbled into ash.

What a beast! What a monster! At least as formidable as the dragons! Wait till Kelvin heard about this—if Kelvin ever did hear about it. If Kian survived to tell him! If!

The beady black eyes looked into his. They held him as the body writhed behind the head, getting into better position for attack. The head and fangs moved closer. The body coiled around under that elevated head as if independent of it, the tail section undulating in unnerving fashion.

Kian found himself staring into bottomless pits. Beady eyes? Now they were windows into some kind of hell! He saw, peripherally, the open nostrils and the bright spots reflecting from the flashing scales. He felt overwhelmed!

He shook his head, trying to clear it. This was magic! The magic a snake used to immobilize its prey. All the prey had to do was break that gaze and flee, and the snake would not be able to catch it, but somehow that seldom happened. Now Kian understood why. He *couldn't* break the gaze!

The snout darted suddenly, along with the long, flat, enormous head. The mouth opened wide, the fangs dripping their corrosive poison. The girl screamed.

He tried to snap out of it. He tried to raise the sword. The gauntlets, unaffected by the serpent's spell, raised his unresisting arms and his sword-hand for him.

The left gauntlet grasped the lower jaw of the serpent. The right gauntlet swung the sword hard at the serpent's eye. The blade rebounded from silver scales, leaving a barely detectable groove. His arm felt the jolt, and pain lanced through his shoulder.

The serpent's head went back again. It was not hurt, but now it seemed more cautious. Perhaps it distrusted anything that resisted the power of its mesmeric gaze.

His brother, Kelvin, had slain dragons by driving a sharpened pole and a heavy lance through their eyes and into their tiny brains. This serpent's eyes were smaller than a dragon's and no easy target, despite their hypnotic power. He had no lance, no pole. His sword was worthless against any part of the serpent except the eyes, and he couldn't get a clear shot at them!

Now something else happened. His left hand, within the gauntlet, began suddenly and severely to hurt. It was as if he had thrust his armored hand into a fire! His hand—and the gauntlet—were being injured by the serpent's venom!

The left gauntlet dropped from his hand and landed on the grass. His hand continued to hurt, still burning. His right hand still held the sword— but what could he do with it? The angle was wrong; he could not get at that eye with a side slash, and he could not orient properly for a stab with the point.

Hissing the hiss of a thousand lesser serpents, the monster bared his fangs again and prepared for the final strike.

As if in a dream, Kian heard the drumming of a war-horse's hooves. He heard a voice, a man's, screaming something that sounded like: "Back! Back! Into your hole, you worm!"

He would gladly retreat, if he only could!

A whistling sound filled his ears, and that, too, was coming from outside the range of his trapped vision. His eyes remained locked by the serpent's; only his ears were free.

Belatedly he realized that it was to the serpent the man was yelling, not to Kian.

Help of some sort had arrived. But was it soon enough, or strong enough? Could it break the spell that held him, and give him even a slight chance to survive?

2 /

IN-LAW

THERE WAS AN ABRUPT knock on the cottage door. Heln gave Kelvin a startled look, then put down the dough for the exotic dish she was making: an appleberry pie whose recipe had been in both their families. "Who?"

Kelvin shrugged. He was putting things together in a travelsack for the journey he didn't want to make. Yet it was expected of him, and he did feel obliged to rescue his father and half brother. It wasn't as though he wouldn't have the laser and the gauntlets that had saved his life numerous times. Kian should have taken the laser, the only operating laser in the Seven Kingdoms. Instead Kian had chosen the unfamiliar and alien weapon found in the hidden chamber. Possibly he had also taken along the levitation belt the chamber still held. But Kian had almost been killed while using a flying device from his father's world. Of course, that was partly because Jon had felled him with a stone from her sling. Still, it showed the hazards of flight! So if the term "levitation" meant what they thought it meant, neither he nor Kian wanted any part of it.

"I expect Jon to come over," Kelvin said as Heln wiped off her hands and started for the door. "She and Lester won't let me start out alone, or with just you and my horse." He added to himself: *But I wish all of you could come along. All of you all the way to wherever Kian and our father and our terrible former queen have gone.* Because all of them had more actual courage than he did, though no one ever spoke that truth openly. Especially Jon, whose nature at times seemed more like that of a big brother than a little sister. That had changed substantially when she got together with Lester. Still—

Heln made a face at him for joining wife and horse in the same breath, though in truth the two were of similar value in many Rud families. She often made faces like that, and despite her worst effort she remained as pretty as ever. Tongue out in a mock spell of insult, she went to the door and heaved at the heavy latch. It released with unaccustomed ease and the door jerked open—leaving her making a face at the visitor.

"Heln Hackleberry?"

She jammed her tongue back in her mouth and put her face straight, too late. She would have blushed, but instead she paled. The stranger at the door was a formidable sight.

He was a big, rawboned man with a stockelcap pulled down around his ears despite the heat of the summer day. He was approximately Hal Hackleberry's age, with a big ugly nose and black beard, dirty clothing, and a travelsack on his back. He wore a formidable sword.

"Yes, I'm Heln Hackleberry," she said, stepping back. Kelvin, fearful of robbery or worse, positioned himself for a quick rising and charge. "Mrs. Hackleberry."

"You won't recognize me," the stranger said with considerable understatement. "You never laid eyes on me before. Adult eyes, that is."

Heln frowned. Kelvin held his position. This didn't sound like robbery, but . . .

Abruptly the man reached up and pulled off his stockelcap. His ears popped into view. They were large and red—and round. As unpointed as her own and Kelvin's.

"I'm Sean Reilly, nicknamed St. Helens," he said.

"St. Helens!" she gasped. "You—"

"Right, girl. I'm your father." His dark eyes swept past her to Kelvin. "And you be the Roundear of Prophecy, son?"

Kelvin and Heln looked at each other. Kelvin felt as though the floor had vanished.

"A Roundear there Shall Surely be," the man said. "Born to be Strong, Raised to be Free."

"Fighting Dragons in his Youth," Heln continued faintly. "Leading Armies, Nothing Loth."

"Ridding his Country of a Sore," the man said, reciting the prophecy of Mouvar. "Joining Two, then uniting Four." He looked directly at Kelvin.

"Until from Seven there be One," Kelvin said reluctantly. He had been thrilled by the prophecy as a child when his mother had told him about it, but as an adult, he had been wary of it. "Only then will his Task be Done."

"Honored by Many, cursed by Few," the man concluded. "All will know what Roundear can Do."

Kelvin experienced the old embarrassment. "I've heard it all my life, but I'm not sure that it applies."

"Hmpth. I'm not sure either, son. But you did slay dragons in your recent youth, and you did, to your great credit, rid Rud of the sore that was her queen."

He had indeed—but the accomplishment had been far less heroic than the prophecy made it seem. Kelvin was afraid that any further testing of the prophecy would get him killed. So he changed the subject. "You're really Heln's father?"

"You doubt my word?" the man demanded gruffly.

"I don't know you," Kelvin said with some asperity. Ordinarily he would not speak this way to such a formidable stranger, but the man's attitude and round ears had shaken him. "How can I know whether your word is good?"

"Maybe I should go elsewhere!"

"No, no, come inside," Heln said quickly.

Kelvin could hardly protest. If Heln believed in this man, there must be something to it. Certainly there were few roundears in Rud!

St. Helens entered, and Heln closed the door. He looked around the cottage, as if evaluating it.

Now Kelvin began to see certain trace similarities between St. Helens and Heln. Nothing tangible, just hints in the lines of the face and the manner of gesture. This, he fought to realize, really was Heln's father: the last male survivor of John Knight's twelve-man squad from unlikely round-eared Earth.

"I've come from the kingdom of Aratex," the man said. "I've come to visit my daughter and my famous son-in-law. But I've come for a purpose."

"You have?" Certainly it was easier to accept this formidable man than to doubt him. St. Helens and Mor Crumb were about the same size, Kelvin decided, though Mor's girth was greater and St. Helens seemed all chest and muscular arms. There was a wildness about this giant's appearance and manner that reminded Kelvin too much of men he had only pretended to command in the war.

"I'm here to lend you my age and experience. 'Joining Two' might as well mean Aratex and Rud. You agree?"

"It might," Kelvin agreed. But it might also mean any one of the other kingdoms. Or, as was the way with prophecy, the words might mean something else entirely. He had speculated once that they might refer to his marriage with Heln, or the marriage of his sister to his friend Lester.

"Things are right in Aratex. The dissatisfaction is great. Together we can do it, son."

"You mean annex Aratex?" Kelvin asked numbly.

"Annex is a good word. So is invade."

Kelvin shivered. The thought of going to war again, of risking everything he had so narrowly gained, and in an unnecessary war at that, was just more than he cared to contemplate. He feared that his face gave him away.

"You know about Blastmore, of course?" St. Helens inquired. "Rotten excuse for a king. Good chess player, but otherwise rotten. In his way he's as bad or worse than your former queen."

"I, uh, heard reports," Kelvin agreed. "He has a witch to keep people in line."

"Old Melbah. Ghastly hag! She goes up to Conjurer's Rock, waves her fingers and shouts gibberish, and everybody faints. People there are real cowed—afraid to do anything on their own. With help, well, that's a different matter."

"I've heard she controls the elements through magic. Wind, water, fire, and earth. That she can make the wind blow, the water rise, the fire burn, and the earth tremble."

"Superstitious nonsense!" St. Helens flared. "Are you really my commander's boy? John was a skeptic."

Kelvin found it difficult not to flinch. Indeed, his father had been a skeptic! John Knight had maintained that all magic was superstition. But that had changed after Zatanas the sorcerer had demonstrated his power. No one would have disbelieved, after seeing what Zatanas could do! But this attitude of St. Helens was exactly what was to be expected in a member of John Knight's crew, and went far to confirm the man's authenticity.

"I, uh, haven't made any plans to invade Aratex," Kelvin said after a moment. "I have something else to do that may take time. My father and half brother are in another frame, and in trouble. I have to try to help them before—"

"Yes, yes, I reckon they'll come in handy. Is it true that the queen escaped?"

"I'm not sure. Kian thinks she's alive—or he did before he left. Heln couldn't find her astrally, so maybe she's dead."

"Or at least out of action. As far as this frame's concerned."

"I—suppose." Kelvin still wasn't comfortable with the concept of multiple frames, though he certainly couldn't doubt them. The implications—

"Well, we'll just have to go together. You'll need my help, and later we'll make plans together for Aratex."

"Go? You mean with me?" Kelvin felt new alarm. "Into that other frame? That other existence? Only roundears can enter the chamber and make the trip."

"I know." St. Helens smiled and tweaked one of his own very prominent ears. "I've got the tickets on either side of my thick Irish head. Don't worry, you and I will do just fine."

3 /

OUTLAW

A S THE SERPENT TWISTED around in the direction of the disturbance, a rope with a large loop at its end sailed neatly over the wide, flat head. A gigantic black war-horse with a large dark-featured man in the saddle made an abrupt turn in front of Kian. The noose tightened, yanking the head to the side.

The serpent swayed but did not fall. It darted at the horse just as the rope reached its limit. Obviously the serpent found the noose no more than a nuisance—an irritation that would quickly be dealt with.

The man in black brought down a sword on the serpent's snout. The horse leaped with instinctive dread, barely escaping the dripping fangs. The two actions were beautifully coordinated, so that instead of sinking its fangs in flesh, the monster received a smart rap on the nose.

Kian felt the spell relax as the serpent's eyes pulled away from him. He was standing there, wearing one of the magic gauntlets, holding his sword. Meanwhile, a total stranger was doing the fighting. This wouldn't do. Kian had to act while he had the chance.

The girl screamed again, apparently in fear for the horse and the heroic rider. But both were safe. The flank of the horse swept on by, and the great head struck the grass just in front of Kian.

Now the rider was circling a tree, the rope still attached to the serpent. The slack went out of the rope and the horse backed as the rider jumped down and ran on foot, charging the serpent with a long spear. It was no dragon lance, but it was a far more effective weapon than a sword in this instance.

Kian's right gauntlet dropped the sword, pulled his arm to the left gauntlet on the ground, and replaced it on his hand. The poison was still in it, and the pain resumed in his left fingers. Yet he knew he had to endure it. *Good gauntlet! Good gauntlet! Make me brave as Kelvin! Make me brave!*

Kian did not know what he could do, if anything. But he had to try. He ran to the side of the serpent, waving his sword and shouting something unintelligible even to himself. The notion of frightening the monster this way seemed ludicrous, but it was all he could think of. If he could distract it so that the other man could attack it more effectively—

Now the spear was flying through the air, right toward one of the serpent's eyes. It struck near the lid of the eye and bounced off. With a clatter it alighted almost at Kian's running feet.

The gauntlets acted. They had the spear by its shaft and his sword stuck in the ground before Kian had quite stopped.

A forked tongue darted from the great serpent's mouth. Then the head snapped upright. The rope that held it snapped like a thread. The head swiveled to orient on the dark stranger, who was retreating after casting his spear.

Galvanized by the gloves, Kian's arm moved. The spear flew upward. This time it struck true, right in the center of the serpent's dark eye. The razor-sharp point and balanced heft of the weapon had effect; the specially forged spearhead plunged deeply in. The serpent jerked all along the length of its body, and gyrated, moving its head violently, but the spear remained in place.

The gauntlets hauled Kian forward. With no wasted motion they reached for the moving silver wall. Then, to his complete surprise, they propelled him into a handspring that landed him on the monster itself! They prevented him from pitching off the rounded hill that was the serpent's back and tugged with astonishing insistence at his arms.

Kian found himself running along a slowly moving and abruptly sharply jerking surface. *He was riding the serpent!* The scales were slippery, and threatened to cause him to slide off at any moment, but he never slackened his pace. The gauntlets wouldn't let him! On and on, ascending the slope of the thrashing monster.

Now he was on the huge, tossing head! How had he gotten here? He was at a dizzying height, and slippery blood was spattered across the silver, making his footing even more treacherous. Indeed, he skidded, unable to handle the violence of the head's motions.

His feet went out from under him. But the gauntlets were straining to reach the spear's haft. The left glove, overriding the pain of his hand, grabbed the edge of the eye. The right glove captured the shaft of the spear.

The serpent vented a deafening hiss of anguish and threw back its head. The left gauntlet shifted its grip as Kian's body slid entirely off the snake's head. He found himself pulling on the spear with both hands, hanging in midair. But the spearhead was barbed; it would not come out without inflicting far worse damage than it had on entry. The serpent's head twisted, rotating sidewise—and the spear angled straight up. Still the gauntlets clung, and now the weight of Kian's body bore down on the spear and rocked it back and forth, so that it dug yet deeper into the socket.

Scarlet blood spurted, some of it onto him. But he could not let go. Acid drops flew from the bared fangs, hissing where they struck. One drop of it struck Kian's face on the left cheekbone. It burned like fire. Still he clung, unable to do anything else. Relentlessly the gauntlets forced the spear inward, rocking it, questing for the serpent's brain.

The head snapped about with such violence that even the blood-soaked gauntlets could no longer hold. Kian screamed as he was hurled through the air. The ground came up to smash him. He grabbed at it, and the gauntlets helped him. Pain seared him as he somersaulted and lit somehow on his feet.

A weaving silver hill nudged against him. Another shoved him out. He was still among the coils of the serpent! He scrambled awkwardly to his feet and ran away, heedless of direction, trying to get clear of the body of the serpent before he was crushed by it.

A loop of rope landed on him and tightened. Kian was hauled in a new direction, helplessly. In a moment he found himself up against the horse. The stranger was there, slapping something cold against his face.

The pain abated. Kian raised his left arm with its gauntlet, and the stranger put the medicine on its burn; instantly the brown spot disappeared, and so did the burning in Kian's hand.

Now at last he could orient on his surroundings. He saw by the scuff marks that the stranger had used the rope to haul him away from the thrashing serpent; he might otherwise have been crushed, as he had had no idea where he was going. He owed the stranger his health or his life!

"You are one brave warrior!" the man exclaimed. "First you scored on the eye after I missed; then you ran right up the thing's neck and drove it in for the finale! I never saw nerve like that!"

"I—"Kian said, trying to protest. It had hardly been bravery!

"But you got disoriented by the venom, so I lassoed you out. I knew you couldn't see well anymore. The stuff gets in your eyes and your brain, so that even when you win, you lose. That's a bad burn! But we got the salve on in time; you should be fine now."

"The gauntlets did it," Kian said. "I—I only followed where they led."

"Gauntlets! They're magic, aren't they? No wonder! Must have come from Mouvar."

"Mouvar? You've heard of him?"

"Hasn't everybody? Where've you been?" The stranger took his hand. "Not that it matters. The name's Jac. Smoothy Jac, they call me. Best skin thief in the Seven Kingdoms. And you?"

"Kian. I'm—a stranger." He was looking at the admitted outlaw's round ears. Round ears—could they be common here?

"Native to Hud? Or from one of the other six?"

"N-no." Rud at home; Hud here. Still seven kingdoms.

"You know the girl?"

He started to shake his head; the pain was not nearly as bad now, and the burning had become more of a freezing sensation. Then he realized that he did know her. Or almost did. Back home that face, that beautiful face, and the curvaceous form with the definitely jutting breasts had belonged to a girl his mother had wanted him to marry: Lenore Barley.

"You look as though you do."

"Eh, someone. Almost the same." But Lenore had pointed ears, he remembered, and this one's ears were as round as his or Kelvin's or John Knight's, if he still lived in this land, or the outlaw's. Truly, it seemed that round ears belonged here.

Then Jac surprised him. "Damned flopears," he said. "Sacrificing a slave girl any rich man would pay a fortune for!"

Oops! "You deal in slaves?"

"No! I *was* one! I deal only in releasing them. King Rowforth, cursed be his imperial name, is the reason there's still slavery. His wife, good woman that she be, would like to end it. But I suspect you know that as well as I."

"No, I didn't. I'm really a complete stranger." He managed to sit upright on the grass, turning to watch the weaving coils of the dying serpent. He was still recovering from the horror just past, and adjusting to the newness of this situation.

"We wouldn't dare try to take the skin before sundown, and by that time the flopears will be here," Jac said. "Besides, no war-horse foaled could ever carry a skin weighing as much as that one. It's a shame; there'd be a fortune. Release a lot of slaves with what that'd bring."

"The girl," Kian said. "We'd better release her." That should have been the first thing he did, but he had needed time just to get himself together.

"If we do, the flopears will try to follow us."

"After facing that," Kian said, nodding at the huge serpent, "I'm not much scared." Who were the flopears? Was there really a third kind of ear?

Jac went to fetch his horse, which had wandered during their dialogue, and Kian retrieved his sword and ran back to the girl. Up close she looked even more like Lenore Barley. She always had been a pretty girl, but he hadn't wanted to marry her. It had been his mother's idea. At home he had always thought Lenore aristocratic and vain, not at all like the friendly kitchen women and serving maids. But now, as he looked into this sweet face, he wondered if he should not have married Lenore despite her upbringing.

With one easy swing of the sword the gauntlets cleaved through the chain, first on the left, then on the right. The chain came away clean and bright: genuine silver. "Oh, thank you! Thank you," the round-eared girl exclaimed, her bosom heaving in maidenly excitement.

"I'm, eh, a stranger," Kian said, trying not to be too obvious about what he was noticing. "From out of this world, you might say. You?"

"Lonny Burk, originally from Fairview. I'm afraid the tax collector took me directly to the flopears. They want a sacrifice each year and they want her to be a stranger, comely, blond, and"—she hesitated momentarily, blushing—"virginal."

"Then you've never actually"—he hesitated, then went bravely on—"been a slave?" Slave boys were routinely beaten, to break their spirits; slave girls were routinely raped until they stopped resisting. He tried to tell himself that this was irrelevant to his assessment of her, but his inner self didn't see it that way.

"I told you. I was never taken to the Mart. To please the flopears and collect the most silver, the agent kept me safe. Even so, he made me an offer —to take me out of the line if I agreed to—you know—and not let on. But I knew he was married, and he was so ugly and smelled so bad I knew I'd prefer the serpent."

"Perhaps you made a fortunate choice." Because, he thought, if she had chosen otherwise, they would never have met, and then he would never have realized that Lenore Barley was the girl he should marry. Lenore—Lonny's near counterpart. "You mentioned flopears. Were those the short people I saw here before—"

"You don't know about the flopears?" she asked, amazed.

"As I said, I—"

"They can freeze a mortal person in his tracks just by looking at him! That's why we can't resist them."

"A mortal person?" he asked, surprised at this term. "But all of us are mortal!"

"Yes," she agreed unhelpfully.

He was rubbing her wrists where the circulation had been restricted by the shackles when Jac appeared, leading his horse. "I'm heading back to the Barrens before the flopears come back. You two want to come?"

"If—we can ride," Kian said.

"Oh, don't worry about Betts," Jac said, patting the war-horse. "She can carry all of us. Only no skin, blast it, and I'm afraid not even that chain. Enough weight is enough for her."

"These Barrens—"

"Blank, worthless land inhabited solely by outlaws and other dangerous creatures. Surely you've heard of it?"

"Yes." Back home it was the Sadlands; here it would, of course, be almost the same.

"Well, climb on. You, missy, ride in front of me. You—what was your name?"

"Kian. Kian Knight."

"That's right: Kian. You ride behind me and hang on to me or the side of the saddle."

It wasn't quite the arrangement Kian had envisioned, but he took Jac's hand and allowed himself to be pulled up on the back of the great horse.

"I've, eh, left something back on the road," Kian said. "It may be worthless, but then again, I can't say."

"You know where you left this, eh, thing?"

"Close. It's where I encountered a bearver."

"A bearver! Near the main road?"

"Not too far. There were appleberry bushes. I'll know the place."

"So will I," Jac said, turning Betts upslope. "There's that one stretch where the berries grow and the bearvers come. Good place for berries; bad place for bearvers."

Kian cocked his head to a now familiar sound. It came, musically, tinkling from the oaple tree he had noticed before.

"Jac, if you want skin—eh, silver—why don't you take the chimes?"

Jac looked back at him, astonished. "You daft?"

"No. I'm a stranger. If you want silver, why not—"

"Because," Jac explained patiently, "the flopears treat the chimes with their curse. You don't take a chime or even a part of one. If you do, you'll die before night."

"Really?" This might be the outlaw's notion of a joke.

"Really."

Kian thought of that as they rode nearer to where he had left the weapon. "Jac, if you don't mind my asking, why the chimes?"

Jac laughed. "You certainly don't know much of the world, do you!"

"N-no. Not this world, at least."

"It's to mark boundaries," Lonny said, turning her sweet face. "At least that's what's always said. Something to do with where the serpents are and where there are ancient secrets much better kept by flopears. No one in his right mind goes near a chime. You must be—you must be from another world."

"I am," Kian said.

"That doesn't surprise me," she said. "Anyone who would come wandering into Serpent Valley on foot has to be from a really distant place."

Considering that he had come into it in order to rescue her, this remark seemed ungracious. "Actually, in my frame, it's—"

"That's it?" Jac demanded, pointing at something that gave off reflections in their path.

"That's it," Kian said, relieved to have the subject changed. He eased himself down from the horse as Betts came to a halt. He was facing the others at close range as he did so. Lonny had nice legs, he thought, looking at the portion that emerged from her gauzy gown. Then he made his mind shut up, and turned to fetch the device.

"Weapon, isn't it?" Jac said as Kian put it in his scabbard. "Any good?"

"No. At least I don't think it is. I tried it on the bearver. First time."

"May I see it?"

Kian drew the weapon and handed it to him butt-first. Jac took it, reversed it, and looked into the bell. "No bow?"

"It's not a crossbow."

"So I see. It's something of Mouvar's, I'll bet."

"It is."

"And it doesn't work?"

"Didn't for me."

"Hold on to it. Could be valuable. You ready to ride? Really ride?"

Kian climbed up and got a good grip on the saddle. "I am now."

Jac dug his heels into Betts' sides. "Get, Betts!"

They rode like the wind through forested, mountainous country that would have been near dragon country had Hud been Rud. They rode past towering cliffs and stunted trees for what seemed miles, then onto a side path that took them through brambles and brush. After numerous slaps from branches and scratches from vines they were in bleak, semi-desert country known in the world of silver serpents as the Barrens. To Kian, contemplating the bleakness, the Sadlands seemed a much better name.

4 /

RELATIVE PAIN

KELVIN WASN'T AT ALL happy about having to leave Heln and Jon and his friends the Crumbs, but he was even less happy about St. Helens' offer to accompany him. He thought around it all day long while they visited and caught up on family matters that neither had learned before. There was just no way out of it, he concluded. Every time he attempted to say that it was his responsibility and his alone, St. Helens was certain to turn it about.

"Yes, yes, I agree, Hackleberry! Very important that we get your father here if he lives. He can train the troops and make the plans better'n me. Not that you're not round-eared, of course. But then remember, so are St. Helens and your old man." It was evident that St. Helens had pretty well assessed Kelvin's incapacity as a leader and was moving to fill the void. That was a significant part of what bothered him.

Kelvin tried to explain it reasonably. "I really don't know about Aratex yet. I feel Rud shouldn't interfere unless we're urged to by Aratex's people. Beside King Rufurt—"

"Rufurt, that old fraud!"

"He's a good man. A good king."

"Hmpth. Good for nothing, if you ask me. Who let the bitch-queen take over? Who sat around while your father—no offense, lad—bedded her and made a son?"

"By then the king was in the dungeon, and—"

"And your old man was weak. He wasn't like that in the old days! Or maybe her old man, Zatanas, cast a few spells. A little tampering with the wine, and any man . . ." He faded out, evidently understanding that kind of temptation all too well.

"It could have been," Kelvin agreed, a bit jealous that he had no basis to understand the temptation. "Zatanas was a powerful magician."

"Destroyed by a boy! No offense, lad, but that's what you were. So now,

236

a few months later, you're a man, or think you are. Doesn't matter. The point is, you're right. That old man of yours was my commander, and from what I hear, he's come to his senses. We need him for Aratex and for what comes after."

"I really don't know yet." If only he had some of that competence and certainty his father must have had!

"Of course you don't! How could you? Roundear of Prophecy or not, you're still the boy."

"Mr. Reilly," Heln put in.

"St. Helens, lass. It's St. Helens or Father."

Heln reddened. "I'd rather not call you Father. To me, my father is—"

"Flambeau. Yes, yes, good man. I know how you feel. I don't insist on it, though it is my due. St. Helens will do just fine."

"St. Helens," Heln said with a spot on either cheek that was now intense. "What do you mean by coming here and insulting my husband and his father? We didn't even know you were alive before you knocked on our door. Why should you—"

"Hey, hey! A chip off the old block, hah, Hackleberry? My own daughter, sure enough!" Reaching out a brawny arm, he gave her an obviously unwanted hug, pressing her soft cheek to his rough beard. "Well, I didn't insult them. I'm not insulting the best commander I ever had in the Normerican Army and his son! No, ma'am, not me. Not the old saint! They didn't call me Truthful Reilly for nothing before I tired of it! When I spout off, I spout the truth. Always have and am always gonna."

She was unmollified. "St. Helens, I really think that's enough!"

"Yes, it is, lass. 'Deed it is. Hackleberry, don't you think those red spots on her cheeks are cute? Her mother used to get those. Once when I came home late with a load—potent stuff, that local brew!—she got 'em real fierce. Gave me the tongue-lashing of my life, and I stood there and took it because I had it coming. She made me sleep in the barn that night, and me a big, randy buck in those days who lived mostly for lovemaking and fights."

"Mr.—eh, St. Helens," Kelvin forced himself to say. "We're grateful for your visit, but my wife and I aren't used to, eh, visitors. We've just gotten back from visiting my mother and her parents—her mother and foster father, I mean—the Flambeaus. We've just gotten this house built and the furniture moved in and then Heln checks up on my missing brother—"

"Yes, you told me. Nothing to do but go there and rescue them, I agree. Fools shouldn't have gotten themselves in a mess, but things happen. Me, I want to see that other frame so bad it's tormenting me, but from what I'm told, it will probably be almost the same as here. I'm not sure of that myself. It just could be that other frame is Earth, where your father and I came from."

"It can't be Earth. Heln and I saw."

"Yes, the vision bit. Guys in my army outfit used to inhale an herbal smoke and claim they had visions where they could see all over the earth. Maybe they did, but me, I doubted it."

"That's very interesting, St. Helens, but with dragonberries you don't just see visions, you move away from your body at the speed of thought. You go anywhere you want to, and—"

"Yes, yes, and I'm ready to take your word for it. My old commander's son doesn't lie."

Kelvin tried to control his reaction. Why did that statement make him feel so defensive? "No, sir. He doesn't."

"So when do we go? We've been wasting time talking here when all the time you say the commander's in trouble—in a jailhouse, no less."

"Dungeon. Apparently the dungeon of the local king."

"Then we'd better get moving, hadn't we? You ready to go now? I'm ready if you're ready."

"Now?" Kelvin couldn't believe this was happening. St. Helens was like a force of nature resembling a great wind. "But you've been traveling by foot and the day's far gone. I thought—"

"An early morning start. Most sensible. The commander would approve. Can't fight if you're exhausted. That reminds me: Heln, you got any more of that appleberry pie? And how about some of the local grog before we sleep —a little wine?"

Kelvin gave Heln a look of helplessness, looking over his father-in-law's shoulder. Possibly he could resolve the matter in the morning. Certainly he did not feel that St. Helens was anyone he would wish to have constantly at his side, but how could he convey this without setting off the man's volcanic temper? Subtlety just didn't seem to exist in St. Helens' universe!

"I'll get the wine, eh, Father," he said. The sarcasm was heavy, but he suspected the man would not detect it.

"Fine! Fine, lad. Nothing too expensive, though from what I hear the king settled on you, you can afford it. Take no heed, son. I know the pride you'll take in serving your daddy-in-law the best."

Kelvin left the house for the local wine shop, hoping his formidable irritation wasn't showing. He wasn't sure whether St. Helens really was Heln's father, and wasn't sure whether he would prefer the man as an impostor. An impostor could in due course be unmasked and kicked out! But those round ears made it all too likely that the man was genuine. What a mill-stone!

He reached the shop and made his selection by the nearness of the bottle. He was counting out the rudnas from his coin-bag when he looked up and saw a large man with the point of one ear missing. Mor Crumb, Lester's father and Jon's father-in-law. This was the day for in-laws, he thought, but was still glad to see his old companion-in-arms.

"Kelvin, you rogue!" Crumb exclaimed. "You and the little girl celebrating a Hackleberry-to-be already?"

"Eh, no. Not yet, I'm afraid. May be just as well. Things keep coming up besides those you know about. We have problems."

"Your marriage?" Mor was concerned.

"No, no. Nothing like that." In a moment he was telling Mor about Heln's visiting relative.

"And you're really going into The Flaw with him?" Mor demanded.

"Not if I can help it. But he's a little hard to discourage."

"Tell you what, Kelvin," Mor said, putting a friendly arm around his shoulders. "Lester and I will just sort of casually drop by in the morning. It's a long way to the old palace and that river chamber. Least we can do is tag along. If you want your St. Helens to stay, we'll see that he does. Call it payment for the times you've saved my life and my boy's life."

"If he doesn't talk you into thinking it's a good idea!"

"Huh," Mor said. "That windbag you describe couldn't talk Mor and Lester Crumb into a free fight!"

Kelvin didn't answer. That "windbag" seemed to be having no trouble talking Kelvin himself into anything.

Heln busied herself in the kitchen while St. Helens ate the pie. As she scrubbed away at a pan that had held the pie and didn't really need that much scrubbing, she tried hard to control the temper she knew she had inherited.

That man my father? I can't stand him! I can't stand him!

The center of the pan became mirror-shiny as she scrubbed it too hard with the grit she was using. She could see her face. At the moment she did not like her face: there was too much of St. Helens in it.

The man was twisting Kelvin around his fingers! He really was! St. Helens obviously wanted to use Kelvin for his own plans. Poor Kelvin wouldn't stand up to him because he thought he was doing her, Heln, a favor. Kelvin thought that just because she derived from the man in name and in blood, she was a devoted daughter. Some father! She wished he had never showed up. She wished he were back in Aratex. She wished he were dead.

She froze, appalled, staring into her reflection in the pan. How could she even think such a thing? Yet she knew she did.

In the Hackleberry dining room St. Helens was savoring the last bites of the pie. Appleberries baked in a pie had the tartness and texture of raspberries combined with the flavor and aroma of a Jonathan apple. How the memories of Earth food and drink lingered! He could still recall the smell and taste of fresh brewed coffee and of at least a thousand foods and beverages. Yet there was nothing wrong with local fruits and vegetables and local cooking. True, both he and John Knight had had to teach the baking of pies, but then the local fruit tarts were quite tasty and satisfying. Still, man did not live by dessert alone.

The little girl was angry with him. He could see why. He'd have to work on that, hide the old basic nature and bring out the winning charm. After all, it would be only for a short time, and then he'd be no more charming than he felt like being. Once he had control he'd be in charge, and they would know it as well as he.

"Heln," he said, raising his voice slightly. "Does Kelvin still have the laser the commander gave him? You know, the Earth weapon he used in the war?"

"He has it, St. Helens. His father said to get rid of it, but he held on to it. As long as he has it he doesn't have to worry about any danger he might face."

"Father, I said." She was coming around, maybe.

"Father." Her tone suggested that she'd like to call him something else. His daughter, all right! Poor Kelvin. Pity him if he ever got to be a bad husband. She'd put him in his place right enough.

"He's taking it with him into the other frame?"

"Of course!"

"And the gauntlets—he's taking them also?"

"Certainly."

"That's fine, just fine," St. Helens said. He smiled, thinking how very fine it would be even if the boy didn't come around for him. Not that he wouldn't; he was a smart enough boy. But if need be, St. Helens could take the laser *and* the gauntlets, and then let old Melbah try to stop him! Just let her try, and he'd fry her and prove to the Aratexians just how vincible the invincible crown actually was. If need be, he knew he could do it all, entirely by himself. If he had the weapons.

Jon finished polishing the last of her throwing stones and dropped it into her ammunition pouch by her sling. She had been fiddling with these preparations since before dawn, and now soon it would be time to go. She turned from the table as Lester strode in, and seeing he was alone, she voiced her thought.

"Les, I think we should talk him out of it."

"What?" Lester was incredulous, as she had known he would be. "Talk Kelvin out of going for his father and his brother?"

"There's also the queen," she said, just as she had planned to. "We can't be certain she's not there alive in that other frame. Would you want her back in Rud?"

"No, but that's ridiculous. The war's over. She ruled only with the help of

Zatanas' sorcery. Even if she were to come back here alive, she'd be power-less."

"She's Zatanas' daughter. That could mean something."

"Very little. Now that Kelvin's fulfilled the line of prophecy."

Jon sighed, knowing that what she most wanted to say would be misunderstood. She knew that Kelvin wasn't brave; he was just—just Kelvin. Without her and her sling, and Lester and his father, and the gauntlets and laser—without those he would be just another man.

But since there was no avoiding it, she forced a smile and said what had to be said, even to her husband. "You're right, dear. He's slain dragons and he's won Rud citizens their freedom, and he's saved my life and yours. He's a hero born and there's never been his equal in all of history. Kelvin, my brother, is the Roundear of Prophecy."

But she knew how much that hero needed proper buttressing. Prophecy was fine, but it took little note of human weakness.

5 /

NEW FAMILIAR FACES

THE OUTLAW'S CAMP WAS nothing more than a small collection of tents, several of them ragged and flapping with great holes. The land was as barren as most desert, but a few prickly plants of assorted sizes grew, and a fence of sorts had been made around the camp by dragging in some of the larger specimens and forming them into a line. There was no material here for proper shacks of the type used in the mountains.

A man with a broad chest came forth to meet them. He was a startling sight. He was the very image of the opposition leader in Rud who had supported Kelvin: Morton Crumb. Except for his whole, round ears.

"This is Matthew Biscuit," Jac said, making the introduction. "Matt, this is Kian Knight from a far and distant land." Jac dropped off the horse and assisted Lonny down; Kian dropped down by himself.

"This'un's Lonny Burk from Fairview. She was going to be the sacrifice. Between us, Kian and I slew a really big serpent. You should have seen him fight!"

"Silver?" Matt asked, interested.

"What else? Of course silver. But far too big. We'd need a dozen good horses just to drag it here. Besides, you know the flopears will be out."

"No doubt." Matt frowned. "What's he doing here?" He jerked his thumb to indicate Kian.

"What are you doing here, lad?" Jac demanded.

Kian took a deep breath. "My father and mother came to this frame from a world almost like it. We haven't any silver serpents, but we have golden dragons there."

"Dragons?" Biscuit sounded offended. "Them's legendary beasts! Storybook stuff."

"So are serpents big enough to swallow war-horses. Back home, I mean. In the frame I come from."

"Frame? What're you talking about?"

Kian swallowed. "If you don't know—you may think I'm making this up. There are worlds made up of tiny specks my father calls atoms, and much space between these atoms, just as there is between stars. Most everything is space, considered this way. So worlds and universes lie side by side, interpenetrating, sometimes overlapping, touching slightly here and there. Each universe, each world connecting in adjoining universes, only a little different from each other. Our world's people have pointed ears, while another world's people have round ears. One world has silver serpents, while another has golden dragons."

"Bosh! Superstitious junk!" Matt declared. He seemed quite angry. "The rulers want us to believe that nonsense so's they can keep us repressed."

"But it's so! I know it is, because my father originated on a world where they have horseless carriages and moving pictures and talking boxes and all sorts of strange things. Then there's the alien Mouvar, who left a chamber from which roundears could travel to other worlds. Mouvar the Magnificent, we called him. He lived long, long before my time, and he left my home frame after a battle with a local sorcerer. The sorcerer was later destroyed by my brother."

"By your brother?" Matt sounded even more skeptical.

"Yes. The roundear Mouvar predicted would, well, he predicted a lot for him in my home frame. He slew dragons in his youth, as the prophecy says, and he rid his country, Rud, of its sore—a tyrannous government." He did not think it necessary to add that for all purposes his own mother had been that government.

"It sounds as if you had very much the same setup as here," Jac said. "We too have a tyranny. Our leader, King Rowforth, has to be overthrown someday. You don't suppose you could give us some tips?"

"I'm afraid not. I was—"Kian hesitated, knowing that he must not say that he had been on the wrong side. "Not really part of it. My brother could help you, or my father, if we can find him."

"You think he's here? In our world?"

"I hope so. I read the instructions carefully, and I know the setting on the machine hasn't been changed for centuries. I feel this is where my parents went. Certainly this must be where Mouvar went. You have legends about him?"

"We have Mouvar," Jac said. "Or at least we had. Strange old man, it's said. He performed some miracles and then sort of vanished. Some say he's still around, but no one knows."

Kian felt a thrill of hope. Mouvar—the original Mouvar?—here? With Mouvar's help anything should be possible. But then according to legend Mouvar had been defeated by Zatanas, and if that was so, Mouvar was less powerful than Kelvin!

"Of course there's our local magician, who claims him as an ally," Matt put in. "He's prattled about him for years. He's shut up about him lately, though—ever since Rowforth took his daughter to wed. If you ask me, all his talk was just a scheme to make that happen. The one opposition leader in the land—and his daughter just happens to have beauty that kings would trade their thrones for. He makes out fine now, old Zotanas does, but he's not conjuring much. Word is that he's a permanent guest at the palace and King Rowforth's main helper."

Zotanas here; Zatanas at home. Zotanas alive; Zatanas destroyed by Kelvin. Kian shook his head; there were just too many angles. It was getting harder and harder not to be confused.

"Well, I certainly don't believe in your almost identical worlds," Lonny Burk said. As comely as he had first thought her, Kian also found her a bit annoying at times. "I heard those stories when I was a child, but until now nothing has ever shown up to confirm them."

"Mouvar. Mouvar showed up," Kian pointed out. Why did pretty women seem to have an innate ability to irritate him?

"Maybe he did, and maybe he's just a story." She looked at him quizzically, and he had the feeling that she knew something, despite being a woman and a recently intended sacrifice. Why did she choose to disbelieve him? He had come to rescue her, after all!

Glancing around the camp, frustrated, he was surprised at the faces he almost recognized. Men whose aspects he had seen around the palace during his youth. Some of them he identified with guardsmen. They had been loyal to his mother the queen, but enemies of his father and Kelvin. Could all of this similarity be mere chance? He shuddered, thinking about it. He wished he were elsewhere—at least until he had figured out more about this situation. He would just have to watch his step.

A very small man running on the short legs of a dwarf came from a nearby tent and up to them. Quickly this person took the reins of the warhorse, and led it to a spot near the fence where he tethered it to a ring set in a large rock. He clambered up on the rock and moved the horse around while he wiped it down with a rag. Then, rushing to the tent, his legs blurring with the speed, he turned quickly and called, "Happy return, Master!" just as he plunged inside. A moment later he returned, carrying a sack of grain for the horse on his bent but adequate back.

"Queeto!" Kian said. Queeto—the dwarf apprentice to the magician Zatanas! Destroyed, along with his evil master, by Kelvin and a great cleansing fire!

"What's that?" Jac asked.

"Queeto. The dwarf."

"Heeto, here," Jac said. "You knew him well?"

"Not very." He did not care to elaborate. Queeto had been a most misshapen creature in both body and mind, as evil and fearsome as his magician master.

Jac called his attention to the way the dwarf was patting the horse's muzzle and feeding it by hand. "That one's a saint. Kindest person I ever saw. Hardest-working person I ever knew. Cheerfulest, best-natured person ever. Was he in your world as well?"

"Not exactly a saint," Kian said, thankful that he did not have to tell the embarrassing truth.

"How do you plan on finding them?" Jac asked.

Kian jerked his attention away from the dwarf and back to his host. "What? Oh, my parents. I have a plan. Unless, of course, you can help me."

"What's your plan?"

Kian told him about the dragonberries and showed them. "You have anything like these in Hud?"

Jac shook his head. "Never heard of 'em. But they sound like something that might eliminate the need for a lot of spy work."

"They did." He proceeded to tell about Heln's spying on the evil queen and magician during the war. Carefully he avoided mentioning that they were his mother and grandfather, and that he himself had fought on their side.

"When you going to take one?"

"I thought—"He swallowed, made uncomfortable by the thought. "Maybe when I had somebody to watch me. My heart will stop beating. My breathing will stop. I'll look as if I'm dead."

"I'll watch," Jac said. "Come along to my tent."

Kian followed him. In a few moments he was stretched out on a bearver hide on the floor of the tent, holding one of the small dark berries up to the lamplight. Nothing much to do now but to go through with it, though he dreaded the prospect. Not giving himself a chance to think, he popped the berry into his mouth.

He tasted a taste that made him want to retch. He fought off the urge, then swallowed.

There was nothing for a moment. Wasn't it working? He felt a guilty relief. But if it didn't work, then how would he search for his father?

Then he noticed that the top of the tent was nearer than it had been. Had a supporting pole broken? He turned his head and looked down.

There was his body below, lying deathly still. The bandit stood peering down at it, frowning. The berry had worked! He was out of his body! He had felt no pain at all! In fact, it had happened so readily that he felt wonderful!

But he had a job to do. He thought of moving outside—and abruptly he floated through the tent wall without making contact, and emerged at the front.

There was the fire—and there was Lonny, looking back at the tent with a scared and anxious expression. Evidently she was concerned about him, and that gratified him. Not that he had any personal interest in her, despite her beauty. Or did he? She had tried to warn him away from the serpent, and that struck him as a pretty selfless attitude. Maybe—

He brought himself back to business. How did Heln do this? Oh, yes: concentrate on a person. On a face.

A face came to mind: a woman's oblong visage, of clear complexion, framed by hair as red as the sheen of a dragon, with eyes the color of green feline magic.

Instantly he was transported, moving past hills and villages as if flying, to a palace high on a river bluff. The palace was almost like the one in which he had grown up, though the Rud structure had been on low ground, with an underground river almost beneath it. Then he was inside, moving from room to room so blurringly swiftly that he was unable to note their details.

He stopped.

There was the face: his mother's beautiful face. She was seated on a divan. Beside her, holding her hand, was a tall, straight, elderly man with dark gray hair. His grandfather!

Both were gone from his home frame, one departed, the other dead—yet here they were alive and unhurt. His mother and his grandfather, oblivious of his presence. He was shaken, despite having no body to shake.

He could hear them speaking. His mother—or was it really she?—had been crying. Zatanas—or was it he?—had evidently been comforting her.

"Please, please, my child. Remember who you are. You are Zotanas' daughter, and the queen."

"But—but he—how can you permit him, Father? How?"

The old man sighed. "I told you, my magic is only for little, good things. I can help keep him controlled, but I'm powerless to destroy him."

"Oh, Father. Father, if only you could stop him!"

"Hush, dearest, you are speaking of your husband the king."

"But he's so—so evil!"

"I know, and he's getting more so all the time. Bringing flopears here was bad enough, but offering to share his rule with them if they would help him conquer is worse. I have nothing, I fear, to combat it."

Hearing the words, Kian was finally able to realize that the woman and man were not his mother and grandfather. Both had round ears, while his relatives had ears as pointed as anyone in Rud. But this was Hud, he had to remember, and here things were different. Yet they did have the faces.

How long would the berry last? He had wanted to find his mother, but he had zeroed in only on her face. Did that mean that she wasn't in this frame? Or did it mean that the berries worked only on natives? He could not decide, and he knew there was little time.

His father. Think of his father.

He visualized John Knight's face as well as he could. The walls of the palace disappeared and he was above hills and rivers and farmlands, moving with that unreal velocity of thought. Then he was back in the valley where he had killed the serpent. He moved along the ground, everything blurring, and then through a rock wall and into an area where flopears abounded. Their ears—but he was already past them. Along and through a rock doorway in a cliffside. He halted.

There, on a bed, pale and unshaven, was John Knight.

"Father!" Kian cried. "Father, you're alive!"

The man's eyes flicked back and forth, but he did not open his mouth. "Who's that? Who spoke?"

Astonished, Kian saw the other person in the room: a young flopear female. Yes, those ears really were flopped over! What a sight!

The woman moved over to the bed. She raised a straw broom in her hands and looked around the room threateningly. "You leave, bad spirit!" she cried. "You leave!"

She had heard him! He had no body, he was present only in spirit form, he could make no physical sound, yet there was no doubt that this odd woman had heard!

Should he speak again? Should he try to let her know that he was visiting his father? She seemed protective. Could she mean John Knight harm?

Kelvin's wife, Heln, had discovered that dragons were sensitive to the astral state and could hear her when she spoke in the astral state. The odd-eared folk here must be similarly sensitive!

"Go away!" the girl insisted. "Leave here! Leave before I get help! Herzig can capture you, you know! He can imprison you, put you in tree or serpent! You want that, spirit?"

"No. No," Kian said. Her manner was so fierce he thought it best to placate her. Yet he still felt he would like to tell her who he was, and that he meant no harm.

"Then go instantly!"

He went. It seemed the politic thing to do. Obviously she could hear him, and so her threat might have substance, too.

Besides, he had the feeling that his astral time was about used up. There was a feeling of waning, of diminishing, that gave him warning.

But he made himself pause to look at the huge cauldron where the flopears were melting down silver. Even as he looked, one came bringing an armload of what seemed like featherlight serpentskin. The flopear mounted the wooden steps of the scaffold and dumped the armload into the silver soup. There was a puff of steam. Another flopear stirred the broth with a huge ladle.

"Boo!" Kian cried impulsively.

The flopear almost dropped the ladle. He teetered for a moment at the edge of the soup, in danger of falling in. He recovered his balance and looked frantically around. "Who spoke? Who said?"

Kian willed himself back, away from the connected valleys. Back to where he had started.

In a moment he was in the camp again. He zoomed from face to face, trying to see how many he almost recognized. There were several that would have been a previous part of his life, with pointed ears.

Then he was back at Jac's tent and inside and lying on the bearver hide. He struggled to sit up, to open his eyes. He managed.

"Gods," Jac said, looking at him somewhat wild-eyed. "I thought you were dead for certain."

"Not dead, just near," Kian said. As rapidly as he could, he told the bandit leader what had happened.

"And you're certain he said Rowforth is making a pact with the flopears?"

"I told you what I heard."

"If that's true, there isn't much time. Zotanas could be mistaken, and I hope he is. But if he makes a pact, Lord, old Rowforth will end up bossing all the Seven Kingdoms with them!"

Kian wondered whether Rowforth could be that bad. Then he considered that this man had been the one ultimately responsible for sending beautiful maidens to the flopears for sacrifice. Could any ruler possibly be worse?

"If we can rescue my father, perhaps he can help. I'm not sure how, or maybe he can go back to Earth and get Earth weapons. Lasers, flying devices—they might help."

"I'm not sure what you're talking about. But if you think your father can help us defeat Rowforth, then we'll rescue him. Only that won't be easy. The serpent people aren't like ordinary mortals. They have magic—the ability to stop a fighting man in his tracks with just a glance. That's only one of their talents."

So Kian had discovered! "But there has to be a way!"

"I'll grant you that. And with your ability to spy, just maybe we'll find it. To start with, we can't actually face flopears. If we try it, they stare at us and we're helpless sticks. That means we'll have to steal your father from them some way, and that won't be easy. From what you say, they can even detect you in the astral state."

"Yes, but only when I spoke, I think. When I was silent they didn't know I was there."

"But you didn't keep your mouth shut! Thanks to that, they may now know what to watch for."

Kian was chagrined. Jac could be right. *Damn!* he thought. *If only my brother Kelvin were here! He's the hero of prophecy, while I'm just an accident!*

It occurred to him that he had never felt less confidence in himself in his life.

6 /

GOING, GOING . . .

KING PHILLIP BLASTMORE OF Aratex chuckled happily with his own cleverness, and moved the black queen across the board. "Check."

Melbah, pudgy and squat and so wrinkled of face that it resembled a badly cured animal pelt, looked up. Her rheumy eyes seemed to focus not on the board but on his artificially darkened little mustache. It was as though she did not even have to glance at the board.

"Well?" Blastmore demanded. He felt like jumping up and down. "You concede?"

"Oh, King," the witch inquired in her creaky, wispy voice, "do you wish to win this game, or do you prefer for Melbah to demonstrate her strategy?"

"Demonstrate your strategy," he said challengingly. But it was a bluff. He had a feeling that he knew what she was going to do, and he didn't like it. Melbah was Melbah, and she had been surprising him for all of his fifteen years.

"Then this is what I will do." Leaning over the board, eyes still focused on him, she puffed up her cheeks so that the wrinkles faded to mere patinas and blew out a stream of breath so foul that it staggered him. He heard a thump, and when he finished blinking his eyes he saw his black queen on the carpet.

"I'm afraid that's not permitted, Melbah," he said. "You can't touch a piece except to move it in the designated way."

"You say this is an ancient game of war. In war all things are fair."

"Well, yes. But—"

"I did not touch your queen. I only sent air to remove her from the battle."

"It's still not permitted." He sighed. Melbah had such a one-track mind. Yet who else was there for him to teach this game to?

"Then perhaps another strategy," Melbah said. She pointed a finger so

249

knobby it most resembled a dead twig from an appleberry tree, and the black queen burst into flame. Within a couple of sharply drawn breaths it was only a charred piece of wood on the carpet.

Blastmore blinked. "Really, Melbah, you should not have done that. Now that the roundear has left, who will duplicate it for me?"

"No problem." Melbah snapped her fingers and the piece on the floor became uncharred painted wood. "This time illusion. In battle to save your kingdom, real."

"That certainly does make an impression," Blastmore said. The old hag had to be insane, but her magic was formidable. It had been a whim to teach her St. Helens' game—a whim whose price turned out to be endless frustration.

"Or," Melbah continued, "if the markers you call men were really men and threatened the kingdom . . ." She picked up a vase of flowers and tossed them on the carpet next to the queen. Just as he was wondering what she was up to, she sloshed water on his side of the board. As he hastily left his chair the water spilled across and dripped on the floor, carrying with it a wash of black pawns.

Blastmore stood over the board and contemplated the prevalence of white chess pieces. He picked at a pimple on his right cheek and pondered what to say.

"I agree," he finally said. "That would win a battle. But this is a game."

"Yes, game." Melbah moved her hands in a circle above the board and the board began to shake. One by one, the black pieces were jolted off while the white pieces remained. When all of his pieces except the king were gone, and he was surrounded by white chessmen, the shaking stopped.

"Game finished now," Melbah said.

"Yes, finished." In fact, he wished it had never started. He should have known how she would act. But he exercised kingly discretion, and complimented her. "You did well. So well that we will not have to play again."

"Good! Game pieces not needed here. Melbah can direct forces without."

"I'm sure you can, and have." Poor Melbah must think chess an aid to magic warfare. Not that her magic was of the sympathetic kind. Or maybe it was. He had seen her cheeks puff out and a great wind rise. He had seen her eyes glow like coals before there was a fire. Perhaps if one understood it correctly, all magic used similar principles.

Melbah stood up. "I go now to my quarters. Your general is coming."

"He is? How do you know that?"

Melbah laughed. It was an awful sound; "cackle" was not adequate to the description. He watched her swirl of dark skirts as she seemed to drift rather than walk across the floor. By the time he had blinked and reblinked she was gone, apparently vanished from the room and possibly the palace. It was the way she always exited. He never had quite pinned down the exact nature of it. Certainly it awed others; he had almost no palace staff, because ordinary servants tended to be too frightened of the witch to function properly. Fortunately he didn't need many, by the same token: Melbah could do almost anything that needed doing.

He sat there for a moment, rearranging the chess pieces as if for a game. The black ones were scattered across the floor, forcing him to reach and collect tediously. He wished that he had not had that falling out with St. Helens. He had really enjoyed the roundear's companionship, especially his wonderful stories about an unlikely world called Earth. He thought again about the way the big man had shown up asking for something called sanctuary, and the way he had paid for it by making himself a friend. In all his life, St. Helens the roundear had been his only friend.

True, when he was a child he had had playmates. But when he became angry with them, as he concluded in retrospect he too frequently did, Melbah had arranged for things to happen to them. By the time he cooled off, it was too late; they were gone. Then there were his parents and his sisters and brothers and all his relatives. Things had happened to them, one by one, and not by his design. The kingdom of Aratex just seemed to be experiencing a wave of misfortune that never became overwhelming. He would have been more inclined to wonder about this, if it had not coincidentally worked to his advantage.

So there had been servants and courtiers and soldiers in diminishing number—and Melbah. Mainly there had been Melbah. She was bad company, but there was something about her; she was always there when he needed someone. As with the attemped chess game just now; he had wanted someone with whom to play, and she had played—in her fashion. At least it hadn't been boring!

But in the past, when he had somehow been unhappiest despite his improving material position, St. Helens had shown up. The big gruff man had seemed to like the young prince for himself, and they had gotten along fine. Sometimes when misunderstanding threatened, Melbah had assisted; nothing had happened to the roundear. Blastmore had suspected that she was responsible for the roundear's existence. Then he had decided that St. Helens was too complex to be her creation, but that she tolerated the friendship for her own reasons. He did not question this, because he valued the man's company too much. St. Helens might be big and rough and crude, but he was real; no need to worry about him being involved in any conspiracy. St. Helens always said exactly what he thought, and his remarks about the, as he put it, "ass-kissing" courtiers were delightfully on target. If Blastmore wanted a candid opinion, St. Helens would give it, not worrying or even caring much about possible offense. Even about Melbah herself—though there the man had had the caution to lower his voice before calling her a "bag of excrement." The actual term had been unfamiliar, but the context had clarified it.

Now St. Helens was gone, and depression had returned. Blastmore's one hope was that soon he would be of an age to marry. He was viewing some of the young ladies of the court with increasing interest. Melbah never let him get really close to any of them alone, but once he got to marry one, it could get really interesting. At least he would have good company again.

The chessboard whirled before him as he sat staring at it, waiting for the general Melbah had promised. Sometimes he got these dizzy spells when he thought of St. Helens and how much the big man had meant to him. They had gotten along so well! If he had asked the man about women, he was sure to have had a crude but pertinent answer—exactly the kind he craved. St. Helens had given so much and asked for so little: just food and sleep and safety. "I know what it is to be lonely, lad. I know," he had said.

But then the roundear had started paying attention to what Blastmore did and what Melbah did and to all who came and went about the palace. He began asking questions. Suddenly, unexpectedly, St. Helens had become angry with him.

"It's not right, the condition of your people, lad. It's all that old bag's influence! You've got to stand up to her! You've got to rule on your own!"

"But how, St. Helens? How?" He had been genuinely baffled, for this was the first time anyone had said anything like this to him.

"I'll tell you how, lad!" St. Helens' big fist had smacked into his own palm. "First of all, you've got to realize that she's just a person. She might know some good conjurer's tricks, but let me tell you, I've seen some pretty clever performances back on Earth. She's got the people scared of her, and for good reason. You've got to undo some of that! Let people bring you gifts because you're their monarch and they love you. Don't force them to bring tribute or face ruin at the hands of your witch! A good king can rule wisely and well and have everything. A wise king doesn't have to worry about enemies. Tell your tax collectors to ease up on people. Sometimes a man can't pay and sometimes he doesn't want to pay. If he really can't pay, you have to try treating him so that he can."

Blastmore shook his head. It hadn't surprised him that when he did nothing about the tax collectors or Melbah, his friend had disappeared. He remembered seemingly unconnected episodes of the past, when there had been murmurings among relatives about policy and taxes, and then those relatives had suffered misfortune. Getting a glimmering of the way of it, he had been smarter with St. Helens. He had had the man followed and watched. He had forbidden Melbah to harm him. "Let him alone and things will be as before," he promised her. "He can't harm us. He doesn't have your power."

"That is true," the witch had replied. "But still, roundears do bear watching."

"I'm having him watched," he reminded her. "If he tries to do harm I will learn of it, and then I will give you instructions."

"You will give *me* instructions?" She seemed amused, and not as displeased as he might have imagined. "Very well, when he causes trouble, you give me instructions."

Blastmore knew he was young, but he was not as young as he once had been, and he had taken the trouble to learn as much of the way of things as he could. He knew that he was the last of the royal line; if anything happened to him, there would be no help for it but revolution, because the people were incapable of selecting a new monarchy without violence. Melbah would be their first target. So it was in her interest to keep him safe. After all, he hadn't countermanded her tax policy; he knew the value of wealth, and the advantage of keeping the peasants poor. He wished St. Helens hadn't chosen that particular case to argue. The man had assumed that Blastmore was ignorant of the ways of the tax collectors, and it would have been awkward to disabuse him. But now it was time to begin asserting himself with Melbah, knowing that they were in agreement anyway. He needed to prepare for the time when they might not be in agreement.

Now, raising his eyes from the chessboard, he found General Ashcroft standing in front of him. A tall man with heavy eyebrows, he had always appeared as if conjured by Melbah's magic. The general was her man, Blastmore knew. He was making it a point to know the identities of all her men, just in case.

"Your Majesty," General Ashcroft said. "Following your specific orders, I have kept track of the roundear known as St. Helens. As you know, he tried to stir up sedition and create rebellion in various parts of the realm. Each time, following orders, Melbah has thrown the fear of magic into those he appointed leaders. A tornado, a fire, a groundquake, a flood—and rebellion dies before it's born. All who foolishly still opposed your policies have died, with the exception of St. Helens, who was allowed each time to escape."

"That is well," Blastmore said. How clever of him to have thought this out! It hadn't even been Melbah's suggestion, though he knew she gladly dealt the punishments. It was like a chess game, leaving an avenue for the opponent to escape a trap—an avenue that led to a worse trap. "And now?"

"Now, Your Majesty, the Roundear has left Aratex's borders."

"What?" Blastmore could hardly believe his ears.

"He has recrossed the river into Rud. He has heard reports that his daughter is now married to the Roundear there. It is believed by my agents that he has gone to this Roundear of Prophecy to get his aid and perhaps also help from the king of Rud."

"Against me? Against Melbah?"

"Do you wish to send assassins?"

Hmm. Assassinate the Roundear of Prophecy, and that would stop St. Helens from seeking his help. But possibly St. Helens wasn't bent on mischief, and besides, Blastmore had so enjoyed his stories and his chess. He had hoped that after some experience with the degenerate rebel elements of the kingdom, St. Helens would recognize the need to keep them down, and would have a change of heart. That might still occur. Suddenly he had an inspiration.

"I want him followed in Rud. When this is practical I want him captured, taken across the river into Aratex, arrested, and brought here in chains."

The general nodded, saluted, and departed.

There, he thought with a satisfied smile. This was going to fix everything.

Kelvin regretted having the Crumbs and his sister along, long before they reached the capital and the site of the old palace. St. Helens was like a lizard that changed its coloration to suit its background. Not only did he soothe them with his rough charms, he also won their respect. When he wasn't talking to Mor about the battles that had been fought on Earth, he was imparting knowledge to Lester of what Earth was like. If he wasn't reciting bits of Earth poetry to Heln—who seemed to like it in spite of herself—he was delighting Jon with accounts of something called Women's Liberation.

"We need that here," Jon said at one point. Trust her to pick up on this! As roughnecked as ever, despite her latefound femininity, she had just demonstrated her prowess by downing a distant game bird. As she put her sling away Lester rode for the bird. Kelvin stayed and listened, trapped here regardless of his preference. "I never did see why men should have all the fun."

"Bite your tongue, Brother Wart!" Kelvin said in the manner of their so-recent youth. "You walked with me into dragon country, you helped fight Rud's war, you reached the palace ahead of the troops, you rescued me from the magician, and you got yourself almost drained of your last drop of blood. What more could a man enjoy!"

"I did all that disguised as a boy," she reminded him. "And when you treat me as an equal you always call me Brother Wart! What kind of equality is that?"

"All right. *Sister* Wart."

St. Helens slapped his meaty thigh where it bulged from the borrowed saddle. He laughed, making it almost a roar. "Brothers and sisters are the same on Earth! Mabel, my sister, and I used to tease each other all the time. She talked Women's Liberation, too, and I always made fun of it. It's not that I don't think women should be equal to men, it's just that most aren't."

"Oh, is that so!" Jon said, clearly enjoying this. "Well, I tell you, St. Volcano, it isn't easy being female!" She had learned that his name derived from that of a volcano back on his home world of Earth, and made much of it. She did not seem to share the dislike Kelvin and Heln had for the man. "I wanted to be a boy until I met Lester! Do you think I would have gone around disguised as a boy if I hadn't had to?"

"Hah, hah," said St. Helens, turning red in the face. "Hah, hah, hah."

"Well, it's the truth!"

Lester was returning with the blue-and-green ducphant swinging from his saddle. "Good news—we eat! Jon, Heln, get the fire started and the bird plucked. Your menfolk want a feast!"

"Chauvinist!" Jon spat, but the edge was gone. She and Heln did as they were bidden, and the bird, even in minute portions, was delicious, as only the food cooked outdoors could be.

The next day of travel St. Helens got on his political horse, lecturing one and all on and on about one world and the necessity of having one. "Now, Aratex just isn't right! It's too much the way Rud was before the revolution. Oh, they don't have slavery or the Boy Mart and Girl Mart, but they've got tax collectors who are just as bad as Rud's used to be, and soldiers as uncouth and discourteous. People aren't satisfied with their boy king, nor should they be. The truth is that it's that old witch Melbah who rules! It's time for a change. Once the witch is out and the country has a good, strong man in charge, Aratex can unite with Rud just as it says in the prophecy."

The astonishing thing to Kelvin was that the others seemed increasingly to buy it. True, he had always known the prophecy would get him into additional trouble sometime, but he had hoped to put it off, just as he had hoped to put off this rescue. Just listening to St. Helens' enthusiasm was getting to the others even if not to him. Thus the sight of the burned-out ruins of the old palace in the morning mist was in every way a relief.

"You say we'll need a boat?" St. Helens asked. "Well, seems to me there's a river above ground and people have boats along it. Why not get one ready-made instead of making one?"

"Those stairs aren't in good repair," Kelvin reminded them. "It might be easier to carry down the material for a raft and then—"

"Nonsense!" St. Helens insisted. "You're the Roundear of Prophecy and I'm your good right-hand man! No raft for us—it wouldn't be fitting."

And so it was that Jon again spoke to the river man who was Tommy Yokes' grandfather. He had been the one to row her across the river and help her with her disguise before she rescued Tommy and went on to the palace to rescue her brother. The old man smiled to see her and they embraced as though they were long-lost kin.

"My, you don't look like a boy any longer!"

"Nor do I want to! But thank you for helping me before, and now in renting us your boat."

"No rental! Glad to lend it to you. You did a mighty good turn for Tommy, and your brother ended slavery permanently. Things are better now for everyone, even old duffers who live by fishing and feeding a few goats. But I know some people who are going to want to see you just to shake your hand. Don't worry about getting the boat down those stairs—there are plenty who will be proud to help."

Thus did they spend an enjoyable day chatting until finally, assisted by a dozen pairs of willing hands, Kelvin and St. Helens were at last properly launched and on their way on the river. The water was aglow with the lichen's eerie luminescence. Kelvin only hoped that this strangeness did not foreshadow the nature of their mission.

7 /

FLOPEAR MAGIC

"I UNDERSTAND," Kian said over lunch with his host and the girl who so resembled the girl he now longed to wed. Funny that it had taken this otherworld twin with round ears to make him realize this!

"You understand flopears," Jac said, chewing thoughtfully on a leg bone of a desert fowl. "But do you really? From what you say, there is nothing like them in your world."

"Only legends," Kian said. "Old legends—stories, really. We heard them as children. The small immortal people who once lived in the mountains and invented gold smelting. They were supposed to have gathered up the scales the dragons shed. No one really believed it, but they were nice stories for children. We all got those tales along with stories of knights and dragons and magicians and castles. Some of those last were true."

"Hmm. But here we have the serpents. Acid flows in their mouths. Their teeth crush rocks. They tunnel constantly, only coming to the surface to shed their skins and collect their yearly sacrifice. Flopears collect the skins, and have from time immemorial. Our government has always traded with them, though they live as a race apart."

"Intermarriages?" Kian mused.

"Unheard of. It may be possible, but then again it may not. The flopears seem much like the serpents in that they're somehow of a different, more magical nature. I can't imagine any normal human wanting to unite with a flopear. But the objects they make from the silver are beautiful. They never do art objects picturing themselves. Another name we have for them is serpent people."

"The ear flaps keep little serpents out," Matt Biscuit said. "If there's one death more horrible than being devoured by a giant serpent, it's having one of those little ones tunneling away, little by little, into your head. A man with one of them in his brain lives for a long time, but he doesn't live sane."

"Little ones? I've never heard of little dragons. I mean, of course when they first hatch they're smaller, but even so they wouldn't tunnel into a head, they would snap the head up entire."

"Well, the serpents may be different. It's believed they take many centuries to grow big and that if the big ones keep growing they will eventually be the size of hills."

Kian shuddered. "Has anyone—"

"In legend, of course. But that one you described is as big as is known. That was gigantic, and I don't see how you survived."

"It was—"Kian hesitated, not wanting to reveal too much about the gauntlets. "Luck."

"More than that, I'd say," Jac said. "You should have seen this man! He ran right up the serpent's back and grabbed the spear and worked it in deep into the eye! Blood and poison spat all over, but he jammed the point right on into the brain before he let go. Then I pulled him out before the dying convulsions crushed him. We outlaws have slain serpents from time to time; we rope them and drive our spears in both eyes. But we never tackled anything even half the size of that one. It was big!"

The others were gazing on Kian with new respect. This embarrassed him. "Will the flopears follow us into the Barrens?" he asked, trying to divert their interest.

"They never have. Probably they can't take the sun. Once we're in the Barrens we're safe."

"Don't the soldiers of the king come after you?"

"Not often. The Barrens, as you may have noticed, isn't a particularly inviting place."

Heeto, the misshapen dwarf, ran to the fire carrying a bright silver vase. Unasked, he carried it to Kian and held it out to him.

Kian looked at his host. "What?"

"Flopear work," said Jac. "But flopear art of a special kind. He wants you to look at the figures."

Kian took the vase and held it to the firelight. Rotating it, he made out the figures of a knight in armor and a woman who might have been a princess. The road and the castle were in the background, and the knight and the lady appeared to have come from there.

"I don't see—"

"Look close," Jac advised. "At the people."

He did, and saw nothing other than perfect execution. Real artists had made this; the figures appeared almost alive.

"Here," Jac said in exasperation. His finger reached out and stroked—and immediately knight and lady turned, arm in arm, and strode back to the castle, disappearing at last through the gate.

Kian blinked.

"Now to make them come out, do this." Jac's finger pressed the gate.

Immediately it opened and the two strolled arm in arm to their former place.

Kian drew up his fallen jaw. "I've never—never—"

"It's flopear art. We don't understand it, so we say it's magic. From what you say, there are few objects in your world as strange."

"Very few," Kian agreed weakly. "But in my father's world—"

"The match of this?"

Kian told of the box his father had described, with the pictures of real people moving and speaking inside. Now he was finding that less unbelievable!

"Amazing," Jac said. "So his world has magic even more wondrous!"

"He always said it was science," Kian said. "He always said science has cause and effect, while magic just happens."

"To me they seem the same."

"And to me also. After all, magic does have cause and effect if you understand it. Flopears caused this vase to have a magic effect. How and why, I have no way of knowing."

"Nor I!" Jac agreed.

"Perhaps," Heeto said suddenly in a piping voice at Kian's elbow, "it's to remind. Flopears can and do command magic."

"Of that," Kian said, turning the vase around in his hands, "there can be no doubt."

Morning, and Jac woke him with a gentle shake.

"Well, Kian, you ready for another trip?"

Kian looked up at Jac looming over him and tried to decide. He could plead that it was too soon, that he might die if he tried another astral trip. But then he thought of his father lying there in that bed, and shame for his hesitancy overwhelmed him. He had, after all, eaten and slept. Heln might not have taken journeys so close together, but that didn't mean he couldn't. He did, however, feel excessively weak.

He got up, dressed, and meekly followed Jac to his own tent. At the flap he looked back and saw Lonny. She was staring after him with achingly blue eyes, fingers to her lips, her face pale. The foolish girl probably didn't even know what was going on, and yet she sensed that he was endangering himself. She had listened to everything Jac had said, to everything Kian had said, and she had made no comment. Possibly she was starting to realize that many of the things she had rejected as nonsense were actually fact.

In the tent he lay down again on the bearver hide. He took out a berry from the pouch, held it between thumb and forefinger, and popped it into his mouth. This time it slid down easily, and though a taste rose to fill his mouth, he did not feel quite the same need to retch. Could he be acquiring a taste for this?

He lay back, looked up at Jac, then focused on the ceiling of the tent. When that grew closer, as it had before, he would be out of his body and into his astral state.

He started counting his heartbeats. One, two . . . three . . . four . . .

That was the sky overhead. He had drifted up through the tent ceiling without realizing it. Definitely the astral state. He felt relaxed to an extent he had never experienced in the body. He really could get to enjoy this! Possibly he should have taken two dragonberries, so as not to be rushed. But his supply was limited, and he didn't know his tolerance for them, so one at a time seemed best.

A bird flew by, and he realized it was far below him, as were the distant objects that must be the tents. He had to will himself down or he'd be leaving the planet and would drift above the moon and around the stars. At another time he might do that, just to satisfy his curiosity, but now was no time to drift.

He concentrated on his father's face and the room he had been in. Then he was down near the Barrens, above the hills, above the mountains, moving across and then into and then through the connected valleys. He watched the bright flashes as the serpents in the serpent valley squirmed about and shed their skins. There were several large serpents, though none as big as the one he had slain. Among them were two boys. Two flopear boys armed only with pink and blue flowers in their hands. These boys ran to the serpents, spoke to them, patted them, and picked up their cast-off skins.

Kian felt distracted. What he was seeing was new and strange, though evidently routine in this frame. He needed to hear what was being said. He willed himself close.

"Hissta, sizzletack," one of the boys was saying. "Nice serpent, nice giver of silver. Thank you for your gifts, revered ancestors. Someday we will join you and be one with you and live forever and be great."

He shouldn't have snooped, Kian thought. But somehow he just had to hear it. This was, after all, something few if any humans had witnessed.

The great serpents, easily of a size to swallow the boys, allowed their snouts to be petted and their nostrils to be touched with the blossoms. They did not purr in the manner of houcats, but he could readily imagine it from their actions. Obviously the boys and serpents had no natural fear or distrust of each other. It was as though the serpents were pets—or actually the boys' ancestors. That was a disturbing notion!

Well, enough of this. He didn't have all day, much as he might like to. He kicked himself, mentally, for swallowing only the one berry. The risk entailed seemed slight, compared with what he might gain by making a full study of the interaction between the flopears and the silver serpents.

He had to think of his father and go to him while there was time. He had to discover something worthwhile on this trip that might enable Jac and his band to rescue John Knight.

He thought of his father, wanting to be where his father was. Without any obvious transition, he was back in the room where he had seen his father stretched out in a bed.

The bed was still there. So was his father. The flopear girl was there, too, now feeding John Knight from a bowl.

The flopear girl dipped a spoon into the bowl and brought out what appeared to be a chunk of well-soaked bread. There were pieces of vegetables and bits of what might be meat in the bowl. This was obviously broth.

"Here, nourishment," the girl said. With tender care she positioned the spoon before John Knight's lax mouth.

Slowly, as though controlled by forces outside himself, John Knight took in the spoon and the broth-soaked bread. He chewed, swallowed, and waited for more. He gave little other indication that he was alive.

"Good, good, Mortal! Soon you be well! Soon your mind and body whole again. Gerta cure. Gerta would like to keep always, but Gerta not boss. Herzig want to trade you to mortal king of Hud. Make Gerta sad, but Gerta not say. Gerta like mortals too much. That why Gerta not really serpent person. Gerta's mother lay with mortal father, and that why Gerta not all good."

Lord, Kian thought. *What I'm overhearing!* But aside from Gerta's belief that she had a mortal father, there was information here. Kian's father was to be made well and traded to the king of Hud. If the king had any sense, he would not simply kill him. The flopears might know he was from another world or they might not. Having magic, they probably would.

Gerta fed John Knight until the bowl was empty, then blotted his mouth with a cloth. Kian watched his father close his now lusterless eyes and ease back onto the pillow. Gerta left the bedside and carried the bowl into another room.

Kian considered. Gerta believed herself to be part mortal and she was as tender a nurse as he had ever witnessed. Perhaps while he was here he might risk speaking to her again. This time not accidentally, and not just to placate her. He'd try to tell her what he had wanted to tell her before. If she knew he was a disembodied spirit and was not evil, then perhaps the mortal strain in her would be required to help. If his father was to be traded, there might not be any problem anyway, but he trusted the king of Hud less than he would care to trust a serpent.

He willed himself into the kitchen, where the flopear girl was washing the bowl. "Gerta, please don't be frightened," he said.

Her eyes widened and she looked frantically around the room. "Spirit! You returned! That not wise! That not good!"

"I mean you no harm, Gerta. I mean none of your people harm. I'm here because of my father—the mortal for whom you are caring."

"He not well!"

"I know. But you are making him well, aren't you, Gerta?"

"Y-yes." A little hesitantly.

"Then listen to me, Gerta, because I may not have much time. I'm here because I swallowed a dragonberry. My body lies back in the Barrens, and I will need to return to it. I'm mortal, like your father and like mine."

"Like my father?"

"Yes, just like your own father. And I've learned something, Gerta. I've learned that the Hud king wants to involve your people in wars with other mortals. Your people must not agree to it, Gerta. It would mean disaster for the mortal people, and for the serpent people as well."

"Spirit," Gerta said craftily, "I can help you."

"You can?" Hope filled him as it hadn't for some time. "How?"

"I show you." Opening a cabinet, she reached in and brought out one of the silver serpentskin chimes. She held it by its top and ran a finger along the inside of the spiral. The spiral vibrated to her touch and gave off a clear, musical note.

Kian listened to the note of the chime. He felt himself moved by it, and he vibrated as it did. He was part of the note. He was the chime!

"Now, spirit, are you there?"

"Yes, Gerta," Kian said, and the words vibrated out of him, out of the silver. The note was silver, purest silver, and he was the chime.

"Now," Gerta said, "you prisoner. You not go back to Barrens. You told me what you are. You evil being, evil mortal, like Gerta's father."

Lord, Kian thought. *What did I say?* "Please," he chimed. "I only want to leave now. I only want to go back."

"No!" Gerta said sternly. "You should not have come where it is forbidden mortals come. Herzig will decide. He may leave you as you are and hang you in a tree to guard against our enemies. Or he may put you in a serpent."

A serpent! Kian thought, and shuddered so hard he chimed.

8 /

GONE

As THE BOAT MOVED slowly around the bend, propelled by the current and St. Helens' expert rowing, Kelvin reflected that he had previously seen all this through Heln's eyes. But did spirits have eyes? Rather, did a disembodied mind have eyes? If a mind could separate from the body, how was that different from the spirit?

Well, perhaps the distinction wasn't essential. He *had* seen, and this remained eerily familiar. But this time he was in his physical body and would not be able to float free of any danger in the manner her astral self could.

He watched the softly glowing walls and continued to muse in a way totally unlike himself.

"Houcat got your tongue?" St. Helens asked.

"Sort of." The man used the same Earth expressions as his father. All his life Kelvin had been familiar with houcats, but had never seen one with anyone's tongue. He had concluded that the expression was intended as alien-frame humor, so naturally it didn't make much sense here.

"You thinking about what I was telling you? About what we'll do about Aratex?"

Kelvin had to reorient his thoughts. He had been mainly watching for the turn into the side passage and the chamber, letting his thoughts muse on about Heln and their out-of-body trips. "You mean the Aratex affair? Their boy king and the witch Melbah and the troops you want to recruit?"

"I mean the Aratex revolution! Haven't you been listening to me? Don't you want to displace that kid dictator, get rid of the witch, and unite Aratex with Rud? Aren't you a little bit enthused?"

"I'm afraid I don't like it, St. Helens."

"Why not? You'll be running things. You with your dad's help, and my help, too."

"I don't like war. The glory of slaughtering people is lost on me. I don't feel that when I fight it's fair. I'm not a natural warrior, but as long as I have the gauntlets there's not a champion anywhere in the Seven Kingdoms who can win against me."

"That's bad?" St. Helens was incredulous. "Seems to me you should be glad the gauntlets exist."

"Sometimes I feel as though everything is an accident. I never wanted a prophecy and I certainly didn't want round ears. My sister, Jon, was always more battle-minded than I."

"Quite the little Viking, isn't she?"

"She always had the spirit," Kelvin admitted. He had heard of Vikings from his father: some sort of warrior who had lived back on Earth. He wondered if St. Helens had been one.

"She and Mor Crumb seemed enthusiastic. Lester sounded as if he'd come around. But it's your choice. It's not for me to talk the Roundear of Prophecy into anything."

Then what was the man trying to do now? Talk him out of it? Ha! "I've never been comfortable with that title."

"It's you. You slew dragons and you rid your country of a sore. Now that the queen isn't oppressing Rud, it's time to move on to another line of that prophecy. Next line: 'Joining Two.' Only two words, but clear enough."

"My mother used to say, 'It's as true as prophecy.' "

"That's it, lad. As true as prophecy. It's your destiny, like it or not. Manifest destiny, I say."

Something was bothering Kelvin, in addition to the man and his attitude. Suddenly he put his finger on it. "I thought you were like my father."

"Lot like him, lad, in what counts," St. Helens agreed. "Different in what doesn't count."

"He never believed in magic."

"And right he was! It's all just sleight of hand and smoke and mirrors and illusion. But the credulous folk believe, and that gives it its power."

"But prophecy is magic. So why do you accept that?"

"I *don't* accept it, lad! Except to the extent that it influences people. What they call self-fulfilling prophecy."

"Then how can I have any manifest destiny?"

"Because the people believe," St. Helens said earnestly. "Because they accept it. So we have to make it come true. You're the one they think will do it, so they'll follow you. It won't just happen on its own—you have to *make* it happen. Otherwise you'll ruin their belief in the prophecy, and the whole thing goes down the tubes, and our one best chance for making things better is gone. That's why you have to do it."

Kelvin was dismayed. He had thought he had caught the man in an inconsistency, and instead St. Helens had made the case stronger yet. He trailed a hand in the water and watched silvery bubbles form off his fingertips. The air smelled damp and green here, probably from the lichen. As damp as his hopes of reprieve!

"You know you'll come to it," St. Helens prodded. "You've got to. It's our, eh, your manifest destiny, just as I said."

"Perhaps." Kelvin felt even further out of sorts than usual. "But really, one step at a time. Once Father and Kian are back in this frame, then—"He paused, took a deep breath, not liking where his father-in-law was leading him.

"Yes, son, yes?" How eager he seemed!

"Then I will think about it."

"You'll *think* about it? Is that all you're going to say? Can't you at least say that I'm right?"

Kelvin shook his head. "Not until I have thought."

St. Helens eased up on the oars. His face got very red as he stared into Kelvin's. Anger pulsed just below the surface.

"Am I to understand, Hackleberry, that you might not go with me into Aratex?"

"I might not," Kelvin agreed. It was only his honesty speaking, not his good sense.

St. Helens' eyes grew hard and his expression harder. When he spoke it was with a threatening lowered tone. "How would you like it, sonny, if I were to abandon *you*? I could row the boat back and leave you to go on to the other frame alone. Leave you to search all by yourself for your relatives. How about that?"

Kelvin's heart leaped. *Oh, thank you, Gods! At last something is going right!*

"St. Helens, that would be wonderful!" *Just what I hoped for! That you would go back!*

St. Helens erupted. He swore fearsome Earth oaths that John Knight had sometimes used, and some he had never used. He banged a fist repeatedly against the air, seemingly trying to hammer a nonexistent spike. He swore on and on for what felt like a very long, uncomfortable time. No wonder he was named after a volcano!

Unfortunately, he did not row back the way they had come. Apparently that threat had been a bluff.

"There's The Flaw!" Kelvin exclaimed. It had appeared just in time. "Bear to the left, St. Helens. We have to keep away from it. That's our passage over there." He pointed to where the water branched from the main channel. The spot was unmistakable.

St. Helens sat at the oars. His lips firmed. He folded his arms on his chest and rested his beard.

The man was stubborn and dangerous, Kelvin thought. St. Helens would try to force a promise from him by waiting as the terrible roaring falls loomed closer and closer. He could see stars shining up from the dark anomaly like cold, hard eyes: the occasional bright spark streaking through the blackness that waited to swallow them.

"Row, St. Helens!"

St. Helens took no heed. His expression was that of a statue carved from ice.

The danger was real. The gauntlets, propelled by his knowing, acted. With a swiftness that startled both St. Helens and himself, his hands grabbed the oars. It was awkward rowing from the bow, but the gauntlets were expert.

"LET GO OF THOSE!" St. Helens roared, grabbing for the oars. He caught them below the gauntlets, but his resistance was like nothing to them; the gauntlets just kept pulling, moving Kelvin's arms and shoulders and torso as required. St. Helens, heaving back with all his strength, was yanked forward to the extreme limit of his arms. He paled noticeably, as though his blood had drained.

Guided by the gloves, the oars bit into the water, turning the boat around, so that now Kelvin was in position to row it effectively. He did so.

"You surprise me," St. Helens gasped. He struggled for a moment, his face reddening again, and then again white. "I—I see now that you're the true, the one, the only Roundear of Prophecy. You, not I."

"Do you, St. Helens?" Kelvin asked, surprising himself with his own level voice. "Considering that you don't believe in magic?"

The boat was now crawling into the passage. Just ahead was Kian's tethered boat on a small ledge. The gauntlets pulled their boat up beside it and tethered it to a waiting ring.

St. Helens seemed to have recovered from his surprise. "Look, lad, you've no call to get smart-mouthed about—"

Quite independent of Kelvin and what he might have done had he been making the decision, the right gauntlet swung wide and whacked his father-in-law on the side of the head, interrupting his statement.

"OW!" St. Helens cried. He held his cheek, looking startled as well as pained. Then a cloud of renewed anger crossed his face. "Why, you young snot!"

As St. Helens started to rise from his seat, the gauntlet slapped the top of his head, crushing his stockelcap flat, and pushed him back down. The boat rocked; water lapped the top of the gunwales.

"You stay here, St. Helens," Kelvin said. He now fully appreciated the enormous advantage the gauntlets gave him. They were making a man of him—a man of prophecy that did not exist without them. "I'll go on alone. You go back and tell the others what happened."

"No, sonny, no!" St. Helens gasped. "I was foolish to have doubted you. I was going by appearances. To me you look and act like a boy."

Kelvin's gauntlets were already exerting the small amount of strength required to move the lever on the round door. With no squeak whatever, the huge metallic thing rotated, revealing, as in a vision, the sphere's interior. Lights of an alien magic lit up the chamber as brightly as day. In the center of a table waited the parchment. Beside it lay the levitation belt Kian had scorned to take. Next to them, the closet with what to Kelvin appeared to be clocks.

Kelvin found that he was actually feeling heroic. Getting the upper hand over his father-in-law accounted for it.

He began reading the parchment. He skipped over the sections concerning the chamber and its other contents as well as the message he had read through Heln's eyes. What he wanted to learn about, and quickly, was the transporter to other worlds.

"Wait, son!" St. Helens cried from beyond. "We're kin—remember?"

Kelvin glanced up from his reading, annoyed. "We're not—"

"I'm Heln's father, at least. If you don't want me along, that's your right. But let me inside with you, please."

"You can stay where you are."

"No, I want to see the chamber. I'm from Earth, remember. I might be able to tell things you can't."

What harm would it do? St. Helens was no worse than many of the men Kelvin had commanded during the fighting for the kingdom of Rud. And St. Helens was his wife's sire. He might hate the thought, but he couldn't deny it.

"All right. Come on in." He took off his laser, perhaps unnecessarily, and placed it on the table next to the parchment. Now just let St. Helens try something as foolish as he had in the boat! One wrong word from that coarse smoothie mouth and he'd point the laser at him and order him home. No way to treat decent kin, perhaps, but this was St. Helens.

Obediently, even meekly, St. Helens climbed from the boat and joined him in the chamber. Possibly, just possibly, he had learned. At least the chamber didn't object to the man's entrance; he was a legitimate roundear. At times Kelvin had wondered; after all, surgery on pointed ears could make them look round.

"You've got your nerve, St. Helens."

St. Helens looked around, wide-eyed, at the chamber's few contents. "Always have had, son. Nerve is why I'm here. Your old man knew."

Kelvin decided to ignore him. His gauntlets were bothering him now by feeling warm. Since there was nothing to fear from his father-in-law, he bared his hands and dropped the hero-savers beside the levitation belt.

He went back to studying the parchment. The instructions were simple in the extreme: "Set the dials, then walk into the transporter. A living presence within the transporter will activate it."

"Hmm, maybe so," Kelvin said, looking at the closet. How long since the dials on the outside of the closet had been moved? He took a step away from the table, thinking to examine them.

A sudden movement by St. Helens startled him. He started to turn, but in that momment St. Helens acted. A ham of a fist struck the side of his face.

Stars exploded. He reached out, took a wobbly step, stumbled, and collapsed forward. Falling, part of him realized, into the waiting transporter.

Into—

Purple flashed inside the closet. It was deep and bright, yet almost black. St. Helens blinked as the color vanished, and with it Kelvin.

"Gods!" St. Helens said, awed more than he had even been before in his life. "Gods!"

He shivered from head to toe. *I shouldn't have done that! I shouldn't have! But dammit, the kid needed a lesson! Better him than me. Better get out!*

He glanced at the parchment, written in those hen-scratchings that he had never bothered to learn to read. Then down at the levitation belt and the gauntlets.

"At least I can take the laser. At least that!" he said.

His hand shook as he picked up the familiar weapon, checking its setting and safety. It would do. Do for old Melbah and, if necessary, for the brat king and an entire army.

He felt a little better now. The weapon put him in command.

He would like the levitation belt. He could work out how to use it, he was certain. Take that with him into Aratex, levitate above Conjurer's Rock, and scorch the old crone's feathers. That would end things fast!

The gauntlets lay like severed hands on the belt. If he was to take one, he might as well take all.

Reaching down, not letting himself think about it, he grabbed up the gauntlets and quickly slipped them on. He stood for a few moments trying to feel something, anything, but his hands felt just like his hands. Interestingly, the gauntlets had stretched over his hands for a perfect fit: hands twice the size of Hackleberry's.

"Damn," he said. "Damn!" He flexed and unflexed his fingers, feeling stronger second by second. They would work for him, these fancy gloves; he knew they'd work for him! He would succeed now; he'd have to. With a levitation belt, a laser, and the gauntlets, he had to be very nearly invincible.

Placing the laser under his shirt and stuffing the levitation belt down beside it, he reflected that he was now as well equipped as he could imagine. Unless the old witch had an atomic rocket hidden, she was finished.

Feeling good about his suddenly improved prospects, St. Helens left the chamber, closed the door, and climbed back into the boat.

9 /

LONNY

T HE MORNING SUN WAS partway up, its warming rays lighting the sparsely spaced rocks and plants of the Barrens. Facing the rays, feeling their warmth, Lonny Burk tried to lose her thoughts in the physical sensations of the sunshine, the very light breeze, and the sand she was trickling between her fingers. None of it worked. She was still thinking about him: about Kian Knight and what he was doing for them. She knew he had consumed one or more of the berries, and she knew why.

A scorpiocrab the size of two of Kian's hands darted from behind a pile of horse droppings, snapped its pincers, moved its eyes in and out on their stalks, and then disappeared behind Jac's tent. They had been in there for an unusual length of time and it worried her. She hated to think of him lying there, his perfect body unmoving and lifeless while his inner self went out to the flopears. It was so much like death, this astral traveling.

Jac wanted her. She had no doubt of that! Why couldn't she desire him instead of the stranger? She knew Jac was a good man, a fine thief, and a true patriot who wanted to overthrow their king. Such a man should be a logical catch for a girl from Fairview. He had even been in the serpent valley to save her, and of course he had done that, with Kian's help. She had seen him looking at her, appraising her, as the tax collector led her out of town on what had been her father's favorite horse. It could have been the horse that interested him, but she knew it wasn't. Thus Jac had gone alone to try to rescue her, to steal her as he stole the skins. Then Kian had come, Jac had rescued Kian, and Kian had behaved madly or heroically or both and rescued them all. Then they had come here, and now things were proceeding much too quickly. She had hoped to love Kian once, just once, before his leaving.

But Kian hardly seemed aware of her. When he had charged down to rescue her, she had assumed, naturally enough, that he was somehow smitten with love for her, for why else would he have taken such a terrible risk?

He was handsome and evidently from a far realm, and that fitted so nicely with her notions of the ideal man that she had responded instantly. Of course she had urged him away, crying to him, "Leave! Oh, leave!" without really meaning it, and of course he had seen right through that and become more determined than ever to rescue her. Somehow she had known that he would be brave and kind and gentle, each when it counted, and then when he had acted with such total mad bravery, actually running up the serpent's neck and ramming in the spear—well, there had been no doubt in her mind or heart.

Then Jac and Kian had talked, each not wanting to rush to free her in the presence of the other. Men were like that; they considered it a weakness to get openly emotional about women, so they pretended they didn't care. Finally Kian had come to chop away her chains, and she had thanked him effusively and told him she was a virgin—that was another thing about men, their interest in this detail—and he had rubbed her wrists while she thrilled to his touch. She had been about to find a pretext to embrace him, perhaps arranging to fall so he would catch her, and then their lips would meet—but Jac had come up too soon. Jac had acted indifferent, and so had Kian, as if neither had had anything to do with saving her life (there was that man syndrome again), but they *had* saved it, and that was what counted. She really had nothing to regret, considering that she had almost been eaten by the serpent, yet somehow she wished that the timing had been just a shade different, so that she could have gotten close enough to Kian to break down his masculine reserve and make her preference known.

She thought back to when she was three years old. Her parents had been working in the field, powerless to avoid this service, and she had been left playing in the yard. In front of her was a stand of trees, screening off their view and hers. Thus she had stumbled while running, the way she had done off and on since as long as she could remember. She fell hard, and was helped to her feet, crying. Her helper, she saw, hovered in midair, and had a very large head and a greenish skin. The fingers of his hands where he held her were webbed.

"I am Mouvar," the being had said, "and you have a destiny." Then he had flown with her secure in his arms above the fields and the farms. From above she had watched her parents toiling, and the wild creatures moving at the edge of the forest. He had taken her over Serpent Valley, and she had looked down to see a flopear approaching a large serpent. "Someday you will be brought here, but that will not be the end. You will meet someone here and you will love him and then he will leave you and return to a distant world. Remember this when you are grown, for that, too, need not be the end if you do what you can."

Then the being, so different from anyone she had known, took her back to her backyard and put her down. He rose into the air and up into the clouds. It was a hot day, and when she told her story her parents had believed she had been sunstruck. For years she had tried to dismiss the memory as a dream, and had stoutly denied the prediction. People spoke of other worlds from time to time, and of Mouvar, and always she pretended she did not believe. If Mouvar did not exist, the man she was to love could not return to another world. (She ignored the corollary that the man might never come at all.) For too long a time she had lived with this persistent memory, and tried to abolish it.

Indeed, it *could* have been a dream! She could have been struck by the sun, or by the shock of her fall, and suffered a vision concocted from wisps of stories she had heard. What little girl didn't dream of becoming the object of distant love? So probably her parents were right, and the persistence of the memory was simply because of her secret longing for just that sort of thing.

But when she had been chained out as sacrifice for the serpent, that memory had blazed forth again, undimmed by time or reason. Now she *had* to believe, because it was her only hope of rescue! She had been brought here, and it must not be the end. It was the place of the vision, and Kian had come, and he could be the man! She remembered now that the vision had not said she would lose him, just that he would leave her but that it need not be the end. Now she had a better notion of what she should do, for she knew herself to be a pretty woman, and men liked that. So if she could just capture Kian's heart before he went far away, then maybe he would change his mind and stay. It certainly seemed worth the try, and even if it wasn't the vision, it was worth doing. Because the dream might not be real, but her love was, however foolishly based. It wouldn't be foolish anymore if she could only—

Jac stuck his head through the tent flap and called for the dwarf. Heeto came running, his short legs blurring in the way they had as they carried him from the horse he had been grooming to his master's tent.

"Heeto, bring a shovel!" Jac said.

"Master, is he—"

"He must be. It's been far too long."

"NO!" It burst from her involuntarily. "No, he can't be dead!"

Jac looked at her with a stricken face. "I don't want him to be, but facts are facts. If he was going to come alive he'd start breathing. It's been too long. He took one berry, same as before, so we know how long it takes."

"Wait! Wait, because he will come around!"

"You seem certain."

"I am!" she said, hoping that her vehemence made up for her uncertainty.

He studied her, perhaps coming to understand the secret of her heart. If Kian died, there would be no one for her but Jac. But not if Kian died because Jac had buried him too soon. "You want me to wait until he deteriorates?"

"Yes! Yes, wait that long!" For that would happen long before her love died.

"The ants will be coming. And the flies."

"I'll watch! I'll keep them off him."

Jac shook his head. "That won't be pleasant. Perhaps Heeto—"

She pushed by him into the tent. Kian lay there on a bearver hide, apparently quite dead. She sat down, crossed her legs and arms, and waited. Jac, accepting the way of it, silently squeezed her shoulder once and then left.

As time passed and no life returned to the body before her, she reached over and took up his pouch. She tipped it up and four of the berries rolled out into her palm.

She gazed at them, appreciating their nature. These were otherworld berries, and they caused a round-eared person to do an astral separation. Apparently roundears were rare in Kian's world. They were common here; did that change things? Would the berries work for a local roundear as well as they did for him?

She had to do something, according to the vision. She had thought it was to make him love her, so he would return, but maybe it was more than that. Maybe she had to *bring him back*. From whatever realm his spirit had gone to. Suppose, just suppose . . .

Quickly, not thinking further about what she did, lest she reconsider, she pushed the berries into her mouth. The taste was strange, though not unpleasant. She hesitated only a moment, then swallowed.

In mere heartbeats she began to feel that she was in fact leaving her body. She saw the top of the tent much too close. Then she was outdoors, and the sky was as blue overhead as her own eyes in a mirror. There were soft, wispy clouds.

If this was another vision, it was a fine one! But she was gambling that it wasn't. "Kian, Kian—I am coming for you," she said voicelessly. "Whether this be death or astral separation, I am doing what you have done. I am coming to where you are, Kian. We'll be together, maybe for always."

The world drifted by, and Serpent Valley. She shuddered, again with no body, knowing what had almost happened in that valley. She had guessed that Jac would come to save her, but had not been sure whether he would come in time, or whether he would choose to free her before the serpent arrived. If the flopears were watching, and saw him do that, they would kill him. Once the serpent came, they would not watch, because they honored the serpent's privacy during special moments such as feeding. So what had been her chances, really? She had had to believe in her private prophecy, because it couldn't happen if she got eaten first. She had had to believe that she would somehow survive—and indeed she had. But she had doubted, too, and now she understood how deeply she had doubted. Jac had not come in time; Kian had. There was the key to her emotion.

Then she passed another, connecting valley and went right through cottages, rock walls, and deep through the ground.

She was in a room. It was an ordinary enough room with a bed. There was a man in the bed, but he was not Kian. Could this be Kian's father, whom Kian had sought? Did this mean that Kian, the man she loved, was after all dead?

There was something in the room that seemed to her not to belong. It was a spiral serpentskin chime such as Kian had asked about. She felt drawn to it, but could not fathom why. It seemed to her that she hovered beside the object, seeing its silver brightness and scaly beauty. Why was she here? Why, when it was Kian she wanted?

She heard footsteps outside. Two flopears entered: a girl and a man. "Here he is, Herzig," the girl said, indicating the chime.

The male flopear stared at the chime, not touching it. "You're certain?"

"Yes. He's in there. He can tell you himself."

"You in there, mortal?" Herzig said to the chime.

"He's sulking," the girl said. "Spirits sulk when trapped. Maybe he think if he be silent you not think he there."

"You would know, Gerta. I wish I did. I can't talk to spirits the way you can."

"That no matter. I do it for both. You take out?"

"Might as well. The ancestor needs a tenant."

A spirit trapped in the chime? Lonny hardly needed to guess whose spirit that might be! But how had it happened, and how could Kian be released?

She followed the male Herzig as he carried the silent chime out of the stone house, with Gerta coming along. They crossed a yard and entered a shed. Here lay the long body of a serpent, its head and one eye covered with a heavy greenish glop.

"Almost healed, not yet activated," Herzig said. "Better a flopear spirit, but mortal spirits also need rest."

"Not get rest," Gerta said with a smile. "Not in ancestor."

"No, perhaps not. Not if they don't like being there. But given time— several hundred or a thousand years—a mortal spirit will be the same as a flopear ancestor. It can take that long to become, though usually much faster."

"Yes. Tunneling, bringing silver, enjoying sacrifice. In time mortal spirit and ancestor be one."

What were they talking about? Lonny had the feeling that the body of the serpent Kian had slain was going to be brought back to life. By—a mortal spirit? Just what was going on?

Herzig climbed some steps to a platform. Here he held the chime over the serpent's head. He looked to Gerta.

"Have you something to say, spirit?" Gerta asked.

The chime spoke, musically chiming each word. "Let me go! Let me go! Let me go!"

"Kian?" Lonny said, excited. "Kian, is that you?"

"Lonny? Lonny, Lonny—go! Go, go, go!"

Just the way she had begged him to go before the serpent came, not meaning it! Now she had to try to rescue him from the same serpent, dead though it was. "Kian, I am here! Let me touch you, bring you back—"

"No, Lonny, no! Get out, get away, before they trap you!"

Gerta looked about. "There's another one!" she said. "He spoke to it."

"Can you get it, too?"

"Maybe. Activate ancestor."

Herzig shook the chime. The chime vibrated with a sweet musical note. Then the serpent raised its massive head.

Lonny knew she had to act. She dived for the chime, reaching out to Kian. She caught hold of him, somehow, astrally, and tried to pull him out, but he was securely anchored.

"Lonny, let go!" he cried. "You'll only trap yourself!"

She let go reluctantly, aware of the truth of his warning. But as she did, she saw something move from the chime to the nose of the serpent. Kian was being drawn to the monster!

Now Gerta took the chime and swung it toward Lonny. "Go in chime!" she ordered.

Lonny jumped away—but in so doing, she came up against the serpent. She felt a strange sensation. Could the serpent that had come to devour her body be ready to devour her spirit? Kian had killed it, but now it seemed that his spirit was being used to reanimate it. If it took in her spirit, too, she would be with him. Alive with the man she loved!

"Go, Lonny!" Kian cried. "She'll capture you as she did me. Go tell the others back at camp!"

It made sense, but she hesitated. To return and give warning, or to be with him? What was the meaning of her vision? To leave him—or join him?

Then she saw Gerta extend the chime again with a crafty expression on her face. Gerta would have her in the chime instead of Kian!

It was not right! She would not stand for it! She would be with Kian! Now!

She was abruptly in the serpent's body, looking through its single eye. With her, she sensed, was Kian.

"Lonny, why, why?"

"To be with you," she said.

"It will be for eternity. Or until we both forget."

"Not eternity, Kian. Mouvar said you'd leave for another world."

"This *is* another world—the astral realm. But—"

"Mouvar said it need not be the end if I did right. So I joined you."

"Lonny, what are you talking about? Mouvar? Have you seen him?"

"Once, long ago. He said what would be. He told me and then I forgot. Or tried to."

"Lonny, are you mad? You're not making sense."

"You have part of an eternity to decide that. During that time all that must be said will be said."

"But you are young and beautiful! You have a good life to live! It is crazy to throw it away like this!"

"It would be an empty life without you, Kian. I want only to be with you. Now I am."

"They're both in the ancestor," Herzig said. "Good work, Gerta. That is as good as having one in the chime. The ancestor has been much weakened, and two spirits will help it recover better than one would." Climbing down from the platform, he put his head out the door and called: "Tripsic, Synplax, Uternaynie—come!"

Three flopears came running from a stone wall they had been constructing. They stood obediently before Herzig, awaiting his instructions.

"Ancestor ready," Herzig said. "Clear way."

Tripsic, Synplax, and Uternaynie ran out, waving their arms and shouting to busily working flopears to clear a path. Gerta stepped outside the door and back inside carrying a freshly picked blue-and-pink blossom. She touched the blossom lightly to the tip of the serpent's snout.

Lonny had the sensation of a lovely perfume in her nostrils, but they weren't really her nostrils or Kian's. They belonged to the serpent, and the smell was rousing it.

The great body began to undulate. It flexed along its length. Then it crawled from the shed, following Gerta, sniffing the blossom she held.

"Kian, are you doing this? Are you moving us?"

"No, I have no control," Kian said. There was no sound from the serpent; it was a mental signal that came across as speech. "I'm here. You're here. I don't think either of us can do more than we can in our spirit bodies. Worse than that, we're trapped. We're in this thing forever."

"No, not forever, I told you."

Neat stone cottages, stone walls, and patches of carefully tended ground slipped by. She was seeing it through the serpent's one good eye. She saw it but could not affect it; she had no control over the serpent's motions.

"Oh, Kian, isn't this fun!"

"FUN!" he responded indignantly.

"Yes, the thrill of being a part of this! Oh, my goodness, I never thought of this, never dreamed of it!"

"Yes, it's a nightmare."

"But look at how beautiful everything is! We're a part of this creature, and we're conscious. We're alive, both of us!"

"I wonder for how long."

"For hundreds of years, they were saying! Much longer than our regular bodies would last!"

"How long as *us*," he clarified darkly.

How depressing, she thought. She wanted to snap him out of it. Just being alive, just being with someone you truly cared about, that was after all what life was mainly about. She did not quite dare express this. Kian didn't know that she loved him. She was able to read this in him now, and it did not cause her grief, because she saw his side of it. He had come to rescue her because he believed it was the right thing to do. He—he did not think that he had any future with a woman of this world, when he was only going to leave it soon. So he—he liked her, he found her beautiful, but he did not think more of it than that. He did not understand that she had loved him the moment he came to her rescue, because of the prophecy. He did not understand how important it was to her, just being alive, just being with the person she truly cared about, fulfilling the prophecy. But there would be time, plenty of time! She would at the proper moment acquaint him with her love, and she was sure that then he would love her back. It would be wonderful. It was already wonderful, for her; then it would be wonderful for him, too.

They followed Gerta through the flopears' valley and on into Serpent Valley. Here there were a few serpents shedding their skins in the bright morning sunshine. They wriggled on, into the higher hills and then into the mountain.

Here Gerta stopped. She stroked the monster's snout with the flower, talking to it, telling it what a beautiful ancestor it was. Then she said, "Return, Ancestor. Return, live, thrive."

Lonny noticed that Gerta was gone from the serpent's sight. Going back home, she suspected. That left the two of them alone in the serpent, as it were.

Light from the eye ceased and all seemed black. The serpent was tunneling, its teeth crushing rock, boring into the mountain. "Oh, Kian!" Lonny cried out. "Isn't this exciting!"

"Isn't it, though." He did not seem pleased with her. She would have to curb her enthusiasm until he understood.

"We're together now!" she continued, though she knew she should wait for him to get better adjusted. But in her spirit form, or her serpent-residency form, she lacked the controls that her natural body had. She tended just to express herself without thinking. "We're together, and—"

She began tasting what the serpent was tasting: a rich, sharp tang that her —its—instincts knew was silver. The serpent was dissolving the metal ore, digesting it with its acid. And she and Kian could taste it!

"Oh, Kian, oh—"

"It won't last forever," Kian said. It was grim the way he saw it; she felt the aura of his concept. "Even this enormous body can only hold so much."

Behind them, the serpent's digestive processes functioned, and wastes squirted. They had killed this creature, and now they had brought it back to life, their spirits replacing the one it had lost when it died. This notion would have horrified her before, but now she was part of the serpent's new life, and it was all quite natural and even grand.

Oh, but she enjoyed the taste of silver! She loved the shivery feel of the scales sliding along the forming tunnel, the mighty body undulating, even the casting of wastes. She knew that Kian didn't. Was it that all men were unappreciative, or was it just him? Yet she loved him just as she had when he had first come to her rescue. Her ignorance was being displaced by knowledge, but her emotion remained intact. Someday, when it was right, he would know and share.

"Gods, I hate that taste!"

Lonny sighed, nonphysically. Being with Kian in the interim might not be quite as much joy as she had imagined. It was said that those who got married soon enough discovered things in each other they didn't like. She did not believe that, but she was beginning to wonder. Still, this was far better than having him leave her for another world.

But suppose, she thought uncomfortably, he somehow left her *here*. All alone in the serpent, shut away from all human contact, becoming daily more and more serpent, less and less human. She had come here to be eternally with him; without him, it might not be fun at all. She shivered, and it seemed to her that her shiver went out through the body they were in.

Unheeding, the great serpent tunneled on in the dark. It seemed that though their spirits might lend it strength for its recovery, it was not aware of their presence. It was an animal, however remarkable it might be.

Heeto stepped into the tent and looked down without surprise at their bodies. The girl had taken the berries, he feared, and now both of them were dead. Unless, of course, through some means he could not know about, they could wake again and live.

A fly buzzed. He swatted at it with his hand. He touched their faces: cold.

How long should he wait? A body would deteriorate if not alive. They would start to spoil and stink and then they would have to be buried. But until then, he'd wait.

Sighing regretfully, Heeto sank down by the bodies and prepared to wait out the entire day.

IO /

TAKEN

J ON HAD BROUGHT DOWN a goouck with what she knew was a
lucky stone but what she pretended was only the skill that had
saved her brother and the king from the evil sorcerer. Lester, shaking his
head admiringly, had ridden across the river and fetched the big bird back.
Mor had stood stroking his chin and pulling at his one-half ear and his full
ear alternately, saying over and over, "I don't believe it! Nobody's that good
with a sling! Nobody! A girl especially!" Now, somewhat later, the bird was
a mouth-watering brown on the spit and the chauvinists and heroine alike
watched as Heln, so unexpectedly expert at culinary skills, turned it, pausing
now and then to savor the aroma.

Mor was there first with the big knife he had carried into war. He cut off
a generous slice of the bread Yokes had brought them. He took a big sniff
through his big nose, tried to bite into his repast, and burned his tongue. He
moved back a way with his meal, and took up the bottle of rasple wine he
had hidden from St. Helens. He took a swig, made a face, and then passed
the bottle on to his son. Lester followed suit, though waiting just a bit on the
bird. Jon sawed off another two hunks of bread from the generous-size loaf
and joined Heln.

"He really should have waited," Heln said, watching the juices trickle
into the fire and make loud spats and tiny curls of steam. "It was bound to
be hot."

"Men!" Jon said, as though not a dedicated liberationist. "All they think
about is their bellies and their—"

"JON!"

"Eh, horses."

"Yes, horses." Heln smiled. Jon was going to be a tomboy until she
became a mother. Considering the way Lester and she doted on each other,
that might not be such a long time. It was hard to think of Jon ever being a
mother to anyone, but then she had proved herself to be an unusually gentle

and caring nurse, a fact that must have gone a long way to winning a grateful Lester.

"Well, I'm going to try a slice."

"Just don't put it in your mouth too fast."

"I won't."

Jon cut a slice of the white leg meat, preferring that to the dark meat of the breast. In that preference, at least, she was typically female.

Heln watched her march away to join the men where they were laughing over some joke and passing the wine back and forth. It was such a warm night that no one actually needed the fire to keep warm.

Heln fixed her own meal, scooped a few ashes onto the fire with the board she had for that purpose, and looked toward the rest of her party. They were laughing it up now, and Mor's heehaw competed with his son's more gentle laughter and Jon's unfeminine thigh-slapping accompanied by giggles. Why couldn't she enjoy this sort of camaraderie? Heln wondered. Somehow she couldn't. Perhaps it had something to do with that Female Liberation her natural father had explained. Too many of the jokes people laughed at seemed to her to be demeaning rather than amusing. Sometimes she thought people laughed out of nervousness and embarrassment. Certainly she could never see humor in a supposed joke that centered on someone's debasement. She suspected that having been brutally raped in the notorious Franklin Girl Mart and almost destroyed as a consequence affected her outlook.

Musing on how Kelvin had saved her in more than just a physical sense, Heln took her sandwich, dripping with hot goouck grease, along to the bank of the river. Such a nice night! So good to get out and just breathe. She appreciated the spicy smell of the pinruse trees and the water roslies growing pink and beautiful in the backwaters. There was the splashing of a raccossum in the shallows searching for crasters and other succulent water creatures. A fish popped out of the water with a splash, and a small wolok splashed eagerly after it. Night birds sang away in the woods, putting the calls and whistles of their daytime cousins to shame with their natural symphonies.

As she walked now, danger was the farthest thing from her mind. The war was over, unless of course her natural father could persuade enough Rudians to start it up with Aratex. In her heart Heln believed he would not prevail; people had had enough of war. Even Kelvin's old comrades-in-arms, the Crumbs included, would not want to go through again what they had suffered for their homeland. Jon possibly, but then Jon seemed to have put all the agony of her torment by the sorcerer and the dwarf out of her mind. Jon, to hear her tell it, had spent the entire war rescuing her clumsy brother and insisting that he be brave and fulfill the prophecy. Jon was really something, and Heln quite understood when Kelvin, sometimes exasperated, would say with the hint of a sour growl, "But so what?"

Perhaps it was thinking about Jon and her boyish ways that made Heln assume that the stealthy footfalls were hers. It would be just like Jon to sneak up on her, she thought, though Jon knew Heln didn't enjoy that sort of thing. Any moment there would be a bloodcurdling screech and Jon would leap out of concealment and grab her.

But there were two sets of footfalls. Two people behind? Something moved in the bushes ahead. Bearver? At night? Possibly, and if so, she should not just walk up to it.

Heln slowed her feet. Should she go back? Should she call out, hoping to scare the animal and alert her stalkers? And how could there be two, anyway? Lester wouldn't participate in his wife's foolishness, and neither would Mor. Besides, Mor was much too big and clumsy to sneak.

A shiver started at the base of Heln's spine and traveled all the way up her back. Bandits? Within hiking distance of the capital?

A sudden hand around her mouth cut off her thought. She twisted half around and saw a face covered with a dark hood. The hood resembled a torturer's in that it covered all but the eyes. Another arm was around her waist. Breath, redolent of onlic, puffed into her face.

"Be quiet and nothing will happen to you!"

She tried to believe this, but all she could think of was the physical and mental agony of rape. She had to scream out, she had to.

But there was no chance.

Back in the bushes, out of sight of the camp, a light appeared in the form of a shaded candle. Another dark figure stared into her face, again breathing onlic.

"Where is he?" the face demanded.

"Where's—who?"

"St. Helens."

"St. Helens? You want my father?" Heln was bewildered. She would not have imagined them after him.

The man looked close at her, moving the candle. "It *is* his daughter! Look at those ears!"

Someone moved nearer, looked, and nodded a hooded head.

"He left with my husband for—"Something warned her. "Some place."

"Ah. And St. Helens will listen to reason if we have you."

"No!" Had she made a mistake? Perhaps she shouldn't have said that.

"Corry! Bemode! We're taking her with us back to Aratex!"

The two men moved near. Both wore the dark hoods and dark clothing. Corry was tall; Bemode, wide. Corry took her by her left arm, Bemode by the right. The other man, the one who gave orders, walked ahead carrying the shaded candle.

They walked through the woods on a path probably pounded out by meer. The night birds still sang, as they did in nearly every forest. The moon and stars shone down through overlaps in the branches. As the trees thinned out along the path, the man walking ahead paused, raised the lantern, lifted its shade, and blew out the candle. Now it was only the natural light that showed their path.

"It's not much farther now," Corry whispered to her. "We'll cross the river and then we'll be in Aratex."

"Shut up, Corry!" Bemode snapped.

They walked on in silence, except for the crunch of their footsteps and the sounds of the birds. They came out of the forest and paused long enough for the men to sweep the moonlighted banks with their eyes. No one was in sight as they stepped down into the water, and it swirled up cold around her ankles. She wished now that she had her boots. There was already a thorn in her right foot, picked up on the path.

The man carrying the dark lantern splashed ahead. Water rose up around his knees and then his waist. Still he splashed on, confident that he knew the river here and that no unseen ledge was about to trap him. Moving just behind him, propelled partially by the hands of the men on either side, Heln was thankful that she wore greenbriar pantaloons instead of skirts.

The man at the head of their procession reached the opposite shore and climbed up on the bank. As Heln started to follow she tripped and almost fell. Corry let go of her left hand, and she planted a knee and hand firmly in the mud before Bemode yanked her back to her feet. Well, at least she had left a sign, she thought, not bothering to comment.

The man with the lantern pushed back his hood, revealing dark hair and eyes in a stern face. Corry and Bemode pushed theirs back as well. Each of them seemed to be just a man. That was a certain relief, though not a great one; men were not as bad as supernatural creatures, but men were more apt to rape a woman. How well she knew!

Still unspeaking, the leader led the way up a bank and to four horses tethered in a small clearing. He made motions, and Corry and Bemode saddled and bridled the mounts while he stood watching her. She thought to run, but knew it would do no good. Even if she could outrun the men, she could never outrun a horse. If they had to chase her down and catch her, they would surely bind her and perhaps do much worse. Her best course for the moment was grudging cooperation.

Corry finished his work and led her to a mare. He helped her up and into the saddle, retaining his hold on the reins. The others joined them. All mounted. All rode.

They followed a road, well lighted by the moonlight, through towering cliffs that loomed up like tall bright sentinels. Past a huge rock with a road winding to its top. On through the night, no one speaking, and then they were approaching a palace with high gates. The gates were opened by guards wearing armor and swords, looking horribly formidable. Heln knew that her chance for escape was gone.

They rode to a stable and stopped while liveried attendants took charge of the horses and led the people inside.

"Well, Major?"

The tall man with the dark eyebrows had appeared so suddenly as to startle her despite her worn, frightened state. He looked her up and down. "This is his daughter?"

"Yes, General Ashcroft." The major saluted; so did Corry and Bemode.

"Very well. At ease. I'll take over now." The general motioned for Heln to walk ahead of him, into the palace. She obeyed him, not certain whether this was normal procedure for the handling of prisoners. The sun was just coming up, lighting the palace and its grounds with the first pearly rays of day. They had traveled all night.

Inside, an aged servant escorted them across carpets and down a hall and into a bedchamber. There, sitting upright, eyes very wide, was the dark young man with the pimply face she knew to be His Royal Majesty King Phillip Blastmore.

"Your Majesty," the general said. "Pardon the intrusion so early in the day. This is the daughter of your former companion, St. Helens of the round ears. She is also the wife of the upstart who destroyed Rud's sorcerer and defeated Rud's queen and ended her reign. He is known as Kelvin, the Roundear of Prophecy."

The young king drew in a long, shaky breath. "Thank you, General Ashcroft. You have done well to bring her to me."

Heln could feel Phillip's eyes on her, and she did not like the feeling or his rosy blush. He was not a man grown, but he was of an age where his glands were telling him things. She distrusted this young monarch's sly, almost timid expression, and the way his hands whitened where they gripped the bedclothing.

"Perhaps you would like me to leave her alone with you?"

"No! No, General Ashcroft." Now the boy's face was as red as a sunrise. "That won't be necessary. Yet."

"But you like her?"

"Yes."

Heln knew herself to be a complete mess. Her legs were steeped in drying mud, her hair was in tangled disorder, and she was sure there was dirt all over her face. But she also knew that any man could see through such superficialities when he wanted to, and recognize her beauty. If the king liked her now, that meant real trouble the moment she got cleaned up—or before.

"Perhaps she would make a nice toy," the general said. "A man your age needs toys, Your Majesty."

"P-perhaps a queen? I need a queen."

"Perhaps, Your Majesty."

Heln jerked. She had been listening to their soft voices, watching their strange eyes, and now there could be no doubt of what they were discussing.

"But I'm married!" she exclaimed. "I have my husband!" Which was one way of reminding them that she was no virgin, though she feared that would not turn off this stripling king. Men cared a lot about virginity when they chose to, and not at all when they chose not.

"Husbands die," Ashcroft purred. "Girls are widowed."

So much for that feeble ploy. She knew already that she would do far better to pretend to forget all about her husband, no matter what that entailed. But she couldn't.

She looked from one face to the other. She took a step back from the bed and then another step. She tried to move a third step, but General Ashcroft fixed her with his deep yellow eyes, and it was as if she were shackled to the floor.

"I suggest putting her in the guest chamber for now, Your Majesty. She can be watched there, and if you wish to visit her and play—"

"No, no. Not until after the royal wedding."

Ashcroft's heavy eyebrows drew down. It was evident that he thought of Heln as a hostage and a potential plaything for the king, not as a potential bride. "As Your Majesty wishes. And, of course, Melbah can prepare her some wine. She can forget the roundear in Rud, and even her father."

Enchanted drink! That would ruin any chance at all for her to escape, assuming any existed. "No! No!" she shrieked, terrified.

"Yes, that will be fine, General. For now, she is my guest."

"I don't want to be your guest! I want to go home! I'm a roundear, can't you understand? A *roundear!*" She yanked back her hair and showed her ears, making her status quite plain. Her ears had made her almost valueless at the Girl Mart.

"His Majesty is not prejudiced," Ashcroft said. "Though perhaps those ears would tend to disqualify you for queenly status."

Heln shut her mouth, as it was just getting her into deeper trouble. A potential queen would be treated better than a potential plaything, and perhaps spared the enchanted drink if she seemed to cooperate. It gagged her to think of it, but she might do best to play up to the stripling king.

"This way, please." The general indicated the hall beyond the king's chamber. The king did not protest, though his eyes were doing their best to strip away her tattered clothing. All too soon his boyish reticence would become fumbling boyish eagerness, and she wanted to postpone that as long as possible.

She found her feet moving, though she hardly knew how. Silently she went down the hall and up some stairs with a long polished banister on either side. Then another landing and some more stairs. A third set of stairs, and then a wearying fourth. Finally, near the roof, General Ashcroft opened an isolated door.

She went in. It was a beautiful room with a window giving a view of the grounds. The window was not barred, but the drop to the cobblestones below would surely kill her. Best she think about that.

The general faced her, blocking the exit. "I must ensure that you do nothing foolish."

She glanced out the window again, and shuddered. "Have no concern, General. I won't jump." Because that would certainly end her chance to escape. She had endured rape before, and tried to kill herself. Having survived both, she concluded that another rape would not be as bad as successful suicide. Then she had had no one else; now she had Kelvin. She had to live, whatever the cost.

"Strip," Ashcroft said.

"Oh, not you, too!" she exclaimed, almost beyond outrage. She had been bracing herself for the king's gropings; this was too much!

"It is necessary that I verify that you carry no weapons, before I leave you alone with King Blastmore. You will strip, and I will take your clothes; then you may clean yourself and don new clothing."

Oh. He had a point. It would surely have occurred to her soon enough to try to kill the king and get away while others assumed he was indulging himself romantically. She knew that if she did not cooperate now, the general would force the search.

She gritted her teeth and stripped. Ashcroft watched impassively. When she stood naked before him, the knife she wore strapped to her thigh was revealed. She removed it and its holster and dropped them on her pile of sodden clothing.

Ashcroft gathered up the bundle and walked toward the door. "You will find appropriate clothing in the closet," he said, nodding toward it. "I will lock you in, but if you ring the bell, a servant will come." He indicated a pull-cord that evidently operated the bell. "I repeat, it is best if you do not do anything foolish."

Dully, she nodded. He had more than made his point.

The general stepped back and started to close the door. He moved so silently, even burdened by her clothing, so almost floatingly, that it was eerie.

"Wait! Wait!" she cried. "What about my husband? What about Kelvin, the prophesied hero of Rud?"

Ashcroft's eyebrows drew down. "He will be remembered there. You may be remembered also. Only you yourself will not remember."

Because they intended to dose her with a potion to make her forget. How was she to avoid that? "You mean he will be—"She swallowed. "Killed?" She hoped that threat had been empty, or only to force her cooperation.

"Of course. The sooner the better. Unfortunately, His Majesty needs a bit of prodding."

Sudden realization washed over her. The general's odd ways, his evident disinterest in her naked body. "You're not—you're not—"

"Yes, my pretty?"

"You're not a man."

"I'm not? Then what am I?"

"A witch. The witch Melbah."

"Very astute of you, my dear." With that the tall figure vanished, and with him his uniform. In his place was a squat, ugly old crone, still with the armful of clothing.

Heln shivered. "You control him! You run the boy king!"

"Obviously, my dear. But I do try to provide him with suitable entertainments."

Heln refused to be distracted by that implication. "And you want Kelvin destroyed so that he can't destroy *you*. And you want my father—"

"The king will decide about your father, once he is in chains as he commanded."

"That's why I was brought here, so that my father and my husband will come to rescue me."

"Why, of course. That's very, very good reasoning. You just may live to make a shrewd queen of Aratex."

"But you don't want me as queen! You only want me as a distraction for the king!"

"Perhaps I have changed my mind. You just might become both. Suitably prepared, you could become a genuine asset to our cause."

"*Your* cause! If the king should—should fall in love with me, you would have an even better lever to control him!"

The witch nodded. "Yes, I believe you will serve very well, my dear. Those round ears will prevent the populace from ever supporting you, so you will have no base for power in your own right. Only I will be able to make the people accept you—so long as the king wishes."

With that the large door swung shut without being touched by the witch. There was a loud click from a lock, and the sound of a heavy bar falling in place across the door.

She had known she was in trouble. Now she realized how much worse that trouble was than she had imagined!

Heln looked at the bed and the dresser and then back at the window. If only she had some dragonberries! How she would like to fly home and see what the others were doing. Then maybe, just maybe, on into that other frame world to Kelvin and St. Helens. And if she could somehow find a way to communicate with her husband, to warn him—

But then reality returned. She had no chance to do any of that. She flung herself on the bed and sobbed.

II /

RESOLUTE

T HE LASER AND THE levitation belt were concealed beneath his brownberry shirt and the gauntlets hidden in a deep pocket of his greenbriar pantaloons when St. Helens reached the top of the flight of steps. It wouldn't do to let them see too soon. Time enough when his plans were made.

They were still camped near the ruins of the old palace. Jon and Lester and Mor, all with worried expressions. St. Helens studied their unsmiling faces in the early morning light. Something was definitely wrong. Where was Heln?

"Where's Kelvin?" Jon asked.

"Why, he, ah, went on alone. We decided it would be best."

"He went and you stayed?"

Was this sharp-eared girl accusing him of something? St. Helens felt an uncomfortable squirming sensation, though it was not fear. They couldn't know what had happened.

"Never mind," Mor said. "The fact is it's morning and your daughter hasn't come in yet. She's been missing all night. We were just about to go in search."

"Missing?" St. Helens chewed on the thought. "You think she wandered off, got lost?"

"No. More likely kidnapped. And by somebody you may know, St. Helens."

"I assure you, if Heln is missing, I don't know what could have happened." An agent from Aratex, trailing him, not finding him, finding instead his daughter? The thought chilled him. St. Helens did not care a lot about these people personally, but his daughter was something else. He had always known that eventually he would be reunited with his baby girl. Her name derived from his, from the time when she had first tried to say his name and garbled it into a single syllable: Hel'n. It had been so cute they had kept it. She was a big girl now, but still his to protect. For sure, he wouldn't let the minions of Aratex get her! If that boy king ever laid eyes on her—

"Well, let's not waste time!" Lester said. "We knew she went along the river. We could see her footprints even in the dark. Kelvin said she liked to wander off by herself sometimes—almost the same as he does. Just to look at the stars, listen to the birds, breathe the clean river air, and think."

"That would be my daughter," St. Helens said. He had done that himself when she was a little girl. Her mother hadn't always been too pleased, either, thinking he would run into one of the queen's agents. Now, over a dozen years later, Heln was following the practice she had learned from him, just as Kelvin must have learned it from John. To be restless seemed to be a roundear's nature. No television or radio or bars here, so what else should be done when the night was around and the need was for solitude?

"St. Helens, come!" Mor ordered, and started with the others in the direction of the river.

They weren't even giving him time to catch his breath! He was resentful of anyone who commanded him, even a man who reminded him of a top sergeant. But he stifled that, and followed; he could not afford to arouse any suspicion.

There was a burned-out fire with bones of a fowl around it, the bones now being chewed by chipoffers and gomunks. The furry little rascals always seemed to be there when food was dropped. He wished he had some of that fowl; it appeared to have been a goouck or an incredibly large ducoose. Good eating birds in this existence, even though he sometimes remembered stuffed turkey and fried chicken. You can take the roundear away from Earth but you can't take Earth away from the roundear, he thought. John Knight had said that to the men he commanded one stormy night when there had been much grousing about unfamiliar foods and unfamiliar ways. He had been right, the commander had, about that and a lot more. Too bad he hadn't thought of those words when the bitch-queen had worked her wiles!

"Here's her footprints," Jon said. She was pointing at the very clear prints in the mud at the river's edge. Heln had been barefoot again. She liked taking off the heavy leather boots they all wore and walking in the mud. But that could be dangerous. She could cut her toe, or get stung by something.

St. Helens shook his head. He was starting, he realized with a shock, to feel like a father. Of course he had always been a father, but it had been mostly memory and dream, something removed in either the past or the future. He had told himself how great it had been or would be. Now it was the present, and it wasn't great, it was nervous. He was really worried about her! If she really had been kidnapped—

"She stubbed her toe on this rock," Lester commented. "See how the ball of her foot came down here and then here, and then she caught her balance and went on walking."

"Good tracking eye," St. Helens observed. That was another thing about the pointed-ear folks—many of them had the sharpshooter's eye and the tracking ability of legendary frontiersmen. He wished he had thought more about that before returning to Rud.

Lester was wasting no time. Like a hound St. Helens had known in the American South, he was dashing along the bank checking for indents in the mud and signs that were far less obvious. Here she had stopped, half turned, obviously listening to something. Here—oh-oh, here were other signs. Boot signs, and not quite the heel marks of the boots made in Rud. They had come from the woods in the dark, stealthily: two men. They had come up behind, and here they had grabbed her, she had struggled, and they had dragged her into the woods. There the two men had been joined by a third.

Now, frantically as the light got better, Lester moved on ahead, checking the grasses and the bushes for signs of passage. His darting eyes found indications aplenty, and he did not pause to explain—if it was possible to explain—what to his eye was as clear as a map.

Over here, over here, and now over here. One of the men had stopped to relieve himself. Heln had stepped on a thorn with her bare foot, leaving a tiny speck of dried blood. They had gone straight through a thicket, thorns pulling threads from their clothes. A candle-lantern had been set on a bare spot of ground, drops of wax spattering on a rock as the candle had been extinguished. A meer trail had intervened and they had followed it, their own feet beating away more of the soil and crossing the hoofprints of the trailmakers. The trail led to a river and a fording spot, and beyond it, a marker on the other side proclaiming the kingdom of Aratex.

There was no doubt now. Agents of King Blastmore had indeed kidnapped St. Helens' daughter and spirited her into the adjoining land.

"Whoa, we can't go crossing borders. This border especially," Mor said.

"They did! And so can we!" Mor's son replied.

To that there could be no argument; they could not rescue Heln if they did not follow her trail. But somewhere ahead, St. Helens knew, there would be an ambush. They wanted him, after all, not his daughter. They wanted him to follow—which was why they had not bothered to obliterate her trail.

But what the agents did not know, what Mor and Les and Jon could not realize, was that St. Helens was prepared. The agents were unwittingly playing right into his hands. With the laser and the gauntlets, he could defeat three or a dozen agents and rescue his daughter. Then he'd be the hero he needed to be, to enlist the aid of the Rudians in the battle for Aratex.

Yes, indeed, the campaign ahead would be triumphant. The very first skirmish, the histories would proclaim, in St. Helens' war of liberation.

Mor rode ahead with Lester at his side and Jon following. St. Helens was bringing up the rear. That was not the place he should occupy, he thought. As the horses splashed across the river, their feet sucking at a mud bottom, he thought hard on how best to deal with the ambush he knew would be ahead. The first thing would be to get the Crumbs out of danger; once that was accomplished, he could deal on his own.

Mor brought his horse to a stop on the opposite bank. "Here's her knee and palm prints," he said. "She must have stumbled, probably deliberately."

"Nice going, Heln!" Jon said.

Lester looked along the shore and the edge of the Aratex forest. "They may have an ambush."

"Exactly what I was thinking," St. Helens said. Now was the time for him to move, if ever. "I think it best if the three of you wait back in Rud, and I'll go on alone. I know this country, and I don't think the rest of you do. If I'm not back with her in a reasonable length of time, say by nightfall, bring help."

"You think you can rescue her all by yourself?" Mor asked.

"I think I should try. If I can't, then I'll call on the rest of you."

"You think you can just sneak in and fetch her out?" The man's incredulity was evident.

"I know people who can help. I know ways to avoid detection and get to the palace. But I'll need to leave the horses and go it on foot."

Lester jockeyed closer. "St. Helens, you really think you can avoid an army patrol?"

"I was a good soldier," St. Helens said.

Jon hefted her sling. "St. Helens, maybe—"

"No! Trust me, all of you. I think I can get Heln back. She's my daughter; I'm the one who should try first. If I can't do it, then I may need you to act."

The Crumbs looked at each other. St. Helens dismounted and handed his reins to Lester. "I'll be back," he promised. Then, before anyone could say another word, he turned his back and walked up the old horse path into a clearing where horses and Heln's captors had recently been. He avoided looking back, and started down a meer path that should take him out of the forest and away from the road. A few steps in, and he left the path for the thicket and let the thorns tear at his clothing until he had gone some way. He paused, looked back, and saw nothing but solid green. Time to prepare for action.

Removing the gauntlets from his pantaloons pockets, he drew them on. Now let a soldier attack him! Let three or a dozen try! He knew a trick or two with the sword, but mainly, he knew the laser. He drew it out and checked its setting. Better set it on wide sweep, just in case he did find an ambush. He set the laser, and aimed it, making a quick test. The beam touched nearby foliage, slicing it away as if by an invisible sword. Yes, it worked!

Next he drew out the levitation belt. Now this might be more difficult, but it was certain to enhance his power enormously. He carefully fastened it around his waist and looked at the controls. They seemed simple enough: a vertical and a horizontal motion lever that should control his flight, and a button that should activate the lift. He moved to a place where there were no tree limbs overhead. Really slow, now, so as not to get out of control and injure himself; unfamiliar equipment was dangerous! This was not only unfamiliar, it was alien. But time was passing, and he needed to test it.

Carefully he placed his thumbs on the large red button in the center of the buckle. He pressed. There was no hum, no flashing light, but he believed it had worked. All right, now slowly vertical up and then horizontal a few yards, and then vertical down on the ground. If it worked as it should, he would consider it to have been an adequate test. He didn't want to waste its power, because he didn't know how much remained.

He placed a forefinger on the lever that had to be for vertical and nudged it in the direction he judged would take him up. Immediately he found himself pulled down by the belt so hard that his pantaloons slipped, baring part of his rear. Oops! Evidently the up position of the lever did not mean that he went up, but that the ground went up relative to him. Alien logic, surely. He made a hasty grab at the control and nudged it in the other direction—too hard. He shot up above the treetops, his pantaloons raised back not only to their proper position but beyond it; he was hanging painfully on the crotch of them.

He nudged the lever to the neutral place. He now hovered above the forest. He worked his body around so that his crotch was more comfortable and looked around. He could see the Crumbs behind, moving across the river with their horses.

If they looked this way they would see him. That was no good. He lowered himself with an exceedingly careful nudge to the lever. He started down slow, then edged the lever back into neutral. He hovered near treetop level, out of sight of the party on the ground.

Now horizontal: another exceedingly delicate testing. Forward, and he moved smoothly forward; at least the alien logic had not reversed this! Backward, and he moved back, not liking the height or the sensation, but loving the feeling of power.

The lever would also move to the sides. He tried that, too, and it worked properly. Left, right, forward, back, up, down. He had it. He was master of the device!

He lowered himself to the ground, landing with barely a bump. He had completed his test, and the power was so sure and strong that there had to be plenty of reserve. Whoever had made this device was some craftsman! After decades or maybe even centuries, it still worked flawlessly. He could use this thing right now, and strike much faster than the enemy would believe possible.

He prepared to travel to his destination as rapidly and effortlessly as possible. He tightened the belt so that it would act on him rather than on his pantaloons—after all, he hoped to have some wenching yet to do in his life! —and turned it on again. Moving the controls with a featherlight touch, he rose to a comfortable height above the ground and maneuvered himself back to just above the meer path, staying clear of the thorns. Then he decided to take a chance and rise up so that he could get better visibility.

He floated just above the forest. Deadman's Pass was back that way, and over there was Conjurer's Rock. He knew his way around. If he could bring himself around to the west side of the palace and escape discovery, his old guest room would be right above him. Heln, he felt reasonably certain, would be there. He should be able to rescue her without great difficulty, providing he went undetected. Travel was so swift and easy with this belt that he could cover in minutes what would have required hours on foot.

He did the necessary maneuvering and was soon concealed in the woods, looking up at the west tower. He waited for someone to show, but no one did. Until, just about the time he was ready to give up hope, Heln's face appeared at the window. Confirmation!

Now was the time to act! But an instinct that had served him well in the past made him wait. The cunning witch Melbah could have set her trap right here.

On the roof he finally spied a soldier, undoubtedly armed with a cross-bow, looking down. The soldier seemed to be making a routine scan of the nearby woods. Yes, that was where St. Helens himself would have stationed a watch, had the situation been reversed. He steeled himself to wait until the man's head had disappeared from his sight. Then he stepped quickly out of the woods, oriented on the window, and activated the belt.

He floated up, clicked the control into neutral, and looked in through the window at the woman he now thought of as his daughter. The cherished little-girl image was fading, and the adult version was taking its place in his heart. She had seemed like a stranger at first, there with her stripling husband, but now he knew she wasn't.

Heln looked back, turning to peer out the window just at that moment. Since the belt made no sound and he made no noise, it was either sheer coincidence or feminine instinct.

"Father!" she said. Not St. Helens, but Father. His heart leaped with pride.

Then pain lanced into his left hip with shocking impact, catching him totally by surprise.

I2 /

FLIGHT

Almost, st. helens hit the control in panic. Almost. He twisted his head, fighting the pain, resisting any urge to cry out. There in his left hip was the bolt. Down on the cobblestones was the crossbowman, taking aim for another shot.

Quickly, almost reflexively, he snatched out the laser, thumbed off the safety, pointed it, and fired. But the bowman loosed his shaft first; it just missed as St. Helens touched his lever and jogged aside.

The bowman, having no inkling of the nature of the weapon he faced, took no evasive action—and indeed, it would have done no good. The laser scored—and the wide red beam made an ugly smoking hole where the crossbowman had been. Not a hole in the man, a hole in the ground. What power in this Earth weapon!

"Father! Father!" It was Heln at the window, all astonishment, all surprise, all anxiety.

"Help me in!" St. Helens ordered. His fingers moved the control infinitesimally and he floated through the frame. In the process he bumped his wounded leg; he winced and almost lost consciousness.

"Oh, Father, you're hurt!"

"Of course I'm hurt! Rip off a sleeve and get a tourniquet on that! Don't get fancy; we haven't time."

Shaking, she did as he bade. Meanwhile he gritted his teeth, grasped the shaft, and wrenched the bolt from his thigh. New pain seared through him, but he was braced for it. The bolt tore out, and he threw it away.

He had to balance on his right leg and watch the blood coursing down the wounded leg and puddling. Heln wasn't squeamish, he noted with peripheral satisfaction. She tugged at a sleeve of her silken dress—she was dressed like a princess, he saw with surprise—and when it wouldn't tear she quickly turned her back and took it off. She wore only panties beneath. Suddenly he realized that they must have taken away her original clothing, to make her dependent on what was at the palace. How could she flee, wearing a royal gown? She would stand out among the peasants like the royal prisoner she was!

"Hurry, lass! Hurry, there's no time!" For the report would be bringing guards clambering up the stairs to this suite; he expected to hear the pounding momentarily. If only he'd kept an eye on the ground as well as on the roof, and spotted that bowman! He had been such a fool to overlook the obvious. He'd been that way in the old days, too, which was why John Knight had been the commander. Old John had his points, good and bad, but he'd been a good leader in the crunch.

Heln turned, holding the bundled dress in front of her. She noted the size of St. Helens' thigh and stretched out the dress, making a kind of rope of it. She hesitated, obviously reluctant to give up the scant concealment the dress offered; then she decided that squeamishness was foolish here. She knelt to pass it around his leg and knot it in front. Having no stick handy, she reached to take his laser.

"Uh-uh. I'll hold it. Just knot it tight as you can and get on my back."

"Your back!" In her amazement she straightened up, showing her bare breasts for the first time. What a looker she had turned out to be!

"Remember when you were tiny? I used to carry you that way. But grab something else from that closet! I'm not going to have the whole frame gawking at the naked body of any daughter of mine! Not that it's a bad body, mind you—"

"Father!" she exclaimed in proper flattered outrage. But she hurried to the closet and grabbed another dress. Had she not been disoriented by his sudden appearance and his wound, she would have thought to grab a new dress as a tourniquet, instead of baring her body. She had missed the obvious—just as he tended to. She dived into the thing and jammed her feet into fancy slippers. Those would fly off the moment she tried to run, effectively hobbling her—but she wouldn't need to run.

He heard the pounding of boots on the stair. "Now get on me!" he ordered. "Arms around my neck. Here, I'll move to the bed." He made two hops, braced himself against the footboard, and motioned with the laser for her to get on.

"Where's Kel—?"

"Later, lass, later! Just get a hold!"

She climbed on, moving carefully. Her left leg barely touched his, but the pain was excruciating. But he'd taken injuries before; he could handle it, because he had to. He had to get her to safety before he passed out from loss of blood. He allowed no more than a gasp to escape as he fought to concentrate on her problem as well as on his own.

"Lock your arms! Get a good hold—I don't want you dropping off."

"I'm ready," she said bravely. "Ready to fly."

"Lock your legs around my middle."

She struggled to obey him, hurting his leg again. "I—I'm afraid I can't—"

"Yeah, too much gut on me. All right, just hold on." He touched the control as he bunched his good leg for a painful but necessary hop. He wanted to nudge the lever just slightly, just the right amount. There was more weight now, so he needed more lift than before.

The pounding reached the door. It was locked; there was a respite while someone fumbled for the key. Time to act!

He nudged the lever, released the headboard, and hopped, jumped, and fell at the window. Behind, the door burst open. Floating almost as if in a dream, he lowered his head and shoulders and felt Heln flatten herself against his back. Then he was out the window and bobbing in the air, trying to keep his balance when his body was off-balanced by hers.

There were soldiers below, and they all had crossbows. There was another at the window behind. He hit the control hard, and they shot off and away at roof height. Turning his head, he saw crossbow bolts cleaving the air behind them at the spot where they had exited.

"Father—you—you're rescuing me!"

"What else?" A bolt flew by his face, far too close. From the roof, or the window. He had to counter that, and fast. He pushed up the lever and they rose at a belly-lurching rate. When they were higher than he judged crossbow range to be, he neutralized the lever and looked down at the toy palace and its miniature grounds.

"Father! Fa—ther!"

"Just hang on! You'll get used to it." What a flying device was this flying device! It sure beat the jetpacks he had trained on. Not only more maneuverable, but no roar. Truly this Mouvar's people had a technology!

"Father, I can't hold on!"

This was the last news he wanted! "Yes, you can!" he replied gruffly.

"I—I can't! I'm going to—going to—"

"You aren't either! You aren't going to faint!" That was all he needed! It was all he could do, trying to hang on to his own consciousness!

But he felt her arms loosening around his neck. Frantically, still holding the laser with his right hand, he grabbed her left-handed. He missed her left hand and his leg protested, and then he was dropping the laser and grabbing her with the right. He caught her right wrist and held on.

They floated while the laser fell butt over muzzle, spinning around. He followed it down, but knew it was hopeless. There would be no getting that back again, and that was the only existing laser and what he considered his irresistible weapon. Down below it bounced from the cobblestones and bounced again. He knew it would be in no fit condition to fire.

"Fa-ther!"

He stood to lose more than the laser! "Here, get hold of me! Arms tight around my neck!"

She did as directed. What a relief! Her problem was evidently just the height; now that they were lower, she could handle it.

But without that laser, just what could he do? Well, he still had the gauntlets, and this belt. Conquering might be harder than intended, but then it always was.

The wind hit them out of nowhere. One moment all was calm, the next they were being pushed by this incredible blast. Hanging on to Heln, thankful that the gauntlets multiplied his strength and influenced his dexterity, St. Helens looked down and saw a small dark figure with arms stretched in their direction. Melbah! If only he still had the laser!

Now they were moving, really moving, and the belt was putting up no resistance. They had to push back against the wind, to resist it with all the power of the belt. He moved a gauntlet to the control and tried to concentrate. The wind took away his stockelcap and streamed out Heln's hair and dress. The gauntlet had to move the control to push them back. It touched the control as he concentrated, hard.

Now they were resisting the wind, and they were moving back. But suddenly they were doing it very fast, as the wind ceased as abruptly as it had begun.

He hit the neutral position. Then, just as suddenly, they were moving again. Independently of what he wanted. They swept above the palace in a curve, the ground and flagstones blurring. They were curving more and more, spiraling. They were in a whirlwind!

Frantically he worked the control. They were moving horizontally but still losing altitude. The forest was below, and a great big tree directly ahead. He grasped Heln tightly to him as the tree limb whipped out in the wind like a scythe and the branches opened and closed like grasping, evil hands.

Something struck. Things whirled, faster, blurring. Then everything went black.

Heln felt the gauntlet holding her slipping on her hand. Then she was falling. She reached out, grabbing and grasping for anything. She caught hold of rough bark. She held on, and looked down to the ground so far away. She felt dizzy, dizzier than when they had been far higher. Her fingers hurt on the bark, and she realized suddenly that there were branches holding her, and that she wasn't about to fall after all.

She looked at St. Helens, held there with his belt. The belt was pushing hard against the trunk. St. Helens himself was out, head down, breathing but unconscious. The blood from his wound was leaking from her crude bandage, running down his leg and dripping through the leaves to land far below.

The first thing she had to do was stop that belt. St. Helens' face was right up against the trunk and it looked squashed, though she thought that was just from the pressure. She had to stop the belt from pushing—but how? He had moved that little lever, but if she moved it wrong, what might happen? St. Helens could shoot up into the sky and then that whirlwind could come and suck him down again. Yet she had to try.

The gauntlets—perhaps if she put them on? They were supposed to know what to do, weren't they? Kelvin had spoken as though they did. And where was Kelvin? Why did her natural father have her husband's gauntlets and why did he have his laser and this belt? There were many things she did not understand, and there was no time to think them out. Perhaps Kelvin needed her—but how could she know?

The blood on St. Helens' leg bothered her. The head of the bolt might not have lodged in the bone, but it had certainly torn up the flesh! The way he had yanked it out—she could never have done that! It might have been better to leave it until there was competent help. At any rate, she hoped it was merely a flesh wound. St. Helens had a lot of flesh, and that was his good fortune, maybe. But she had to stop that blood.

The dress was knotted as it had been, but it had slipped. Consequently it was pressing against the bolt and the wound was being pushed partially open. She wished she were less squeamish, and that she had Jon's touch for this sort of thing. But she had to do what she could.

She pushed the blood-sodden dress a bit higher on his thigh. She took St. Helens' sword from its sheath and cut a stick from a branch, then rested the sword in a crotch. Next she loosened the red-stained knot, pushed the stick through its center, and twisted a proper tourniquet. *There,* she thought, *maybe I'm not as helpless as I sometimes think.*

St. Helens did not thank her. He remained unconscious. He seemed to be breathing adequately, and his heart maintained a steady beat. But his face remained pressed to the trunk.

Well, maybe this will help. She stripped the gauntlets from his hands. The soft leather with the metal plates yielded readily to her touch. She slipped her own fingers into the gloves until her hands were all the way inside. To her amazement the huge gauntlets fitted her perfectly, and now seemed like an extension of her skin. It was apparent that any roundear could wear them, though the prophecy applied only to Kelvin.

Hesitantly she reached with her gauntleted hand for the control on the belt. This little lever must move forward and back. But which way should she move it now?

Use your own judgment, gauntlets, she thought.

Her fingers acted. She was not certain whether she controlled them or the gauntlet did. The lever moved, pressing back all the way. The belt changed its thrust, and St. Helens' body shot through the branches with a speed and motion she had not expected. She watched helplessly as it left their tree and ·was stopped by the trunk of another.

She had to get him down! She knew that—but the neighboring tree couldn't be reached from this one. Even worse, the tree St. Helens was now in was growing straight up and down, with no branches at the lower levels. How was she going to touch him, let alone get him safely to the ground? She had expected the gauntlets to help her, and instead they had only made things worse!

A movement at ground level took her attention. Two horsemen were there, astride their steeds, looking up.

"There he is, Corry. How're we going to get him down?"

"Don't ask me, Bemode. We're going to need some help. Look over there!"

"What?"

"His daughter. How'd she get over there?"

"I dunno. What's that shine?"

"A sword. Must be St. Helens'. You up there, girl, you hurt?"

"N-no," Heln said. "But my father—"

"You climb on down. Bring the sword."

She hesitated. But according to Kelvin, the gauntlets were good at climbing. Besides, she had done some tree climbing in the past. Still, there was the blade. If she tried to carry that down without its sheath, there was every chance she might cut herself. She started down without it.

"Bring the sword, I said!"

There was no helping it. She was largely helpless, with or without the sword, and would only make things worse if she tried to defy these rough men. She reached up with the left gauntlet and it took up the sword as if it belonged in that hand. As she drew it down to her lower level she saw that there was an inscription on the blade that she hadn't observed before. Her eyes read it without conscious effort. "Given in Eternal Friendship, From His Majesty Phillip Blastmore, King of Aratex." Now what did that mean? Had St. Helens stolen the sword, or had he and the king really been friends?

"Come on, hurry it up!"

That Bemode sounded ugly. Probably he was a mean man, given the chance. Better not anger him. She tried to shut off all other thoughts except getting down.

"Look at those legs!" Bemode exclaimed.

She had forgotten what she was wearing! This silken dress exposed everything from below. But what could she do? If she tried to stay up in the tree, they would fire a crossbow bolt into her. She gritted her teeth and continued climbing down, though she felt the gaze of the two men almost physically on her moving legs. It was as if slime were coating them.

Sooner than she had expected, the right gauntlet swung her out on a limb and dropped her the short remaining distance. The men stood as if mesmerized, their eyes round, their mouths open. Because of her legs? In other circumstances she would have taken that as a compliment. As it was, she was disgusted, but didn't dare say so.

"You see that, Corry? She must be part houcat! I thought she'd fall."

"That would've been a waste!" Corry said.

Bemode dismounted. "Bring me that sword, woman!"

Heln transferred the sword from her left gauntlet to her right. The gauntlets did not feel as if they wanted to relinquish it. According to Kelvin, they made the wearer a master swordsman. But could they do that even for a woman?

"Help my father," she said.

"We'll help him when we get help. We've got chains all ready for him. Haven't we, Corry?"

Heln saw that there was a length of heavy chain fastened to Bemode's saddle. As she watched he unfastened it and the chain dropped to the ground.

"You are going to chain my father?"

"Have to. King's orders. But maybe not the same for you, if you cooperate. Your sword."

Cooperate? She hardly needed to guess what that meant. She remembered the first time she had been raped.

Corry dismounted. "Don't be rough, Bemode. The king wouldn't like it. He doesn't want her badly marked. Worse yet, Melbah wouldn't like it."

"Melbah's not going to get it."

"Still—"

"Pity," Bemode said, evidently daunted by the thought of Melbah's ire. "Still, we can make her say it's all right. Then—"

The sword in the gauntlet lifted without Heln quite willing it. A sudden determination came to her. A determination that if she could not be in charge she would at least be on her way to get St. Helens some help. He was, after all, in his predicament because of her. As for what these two planned for her—she wanted no part of it.

Bemode reached out to take the sword. "Give me that!"

Whereupon she would be weaponless, and largely helpless to resist them. "No!" she said. The sword darted at Bemode's face, pulling back before touching it.

"Well, I'll be a cuckold!" Bemode said. He whipped out his own blade and made a swipe with it. As he did, the gauntlet feinted, twisted her wrist, and Bemode's blade rebounded. Not only rebounded, but flew away with great force. The sword lit in some bushes and left Bemode standing with open mouth.

Corry reached for the sword sheathed at his hip. He paused, eyeing the tip of Heln's blade that was suddenly at his throat. Suddenly his mind was no longer on the sight of bare legs, but on bare steel.

"You," Heln said to Bemode. "Get that chain and drag it to this tree!"

Bemode did as instructed, looking worriedly at Corry. His horse neighed: it was almost a laugh.

"All right, stand with your back against the tree!" she snapped. "You, Corry, stand next to him." It was the way she thought a man would have talked.

The men obeyed. Keeping her eyes on them while they eyed her blade, she took the end of the chain and circled the tree several times. Bemode looked as though he wanted to make a sudden move, but always the gauntlet guided the point of the sword to bear on his left eye and he reconsidered. Now what? Oh, yes, there was a lock at one end. She drew the two ends together and locked the chain. Then she stepped out in front of them.

"I'm going for help now. If your help arrives before mine, my father is not to be chained. His wound is to be cared for and he is to be rested and fed. If this is not done, your king and your Melbah will answer to the Roundear of Prophecy himself!" What was she saying? This seemed crazy! It was almost as if the gauntlets were making her speak!

Corry and Bemode looked at each other. Bemode swallowed. They might disagree, but they were not in a position to argue.

"And one other thing." Her gloves stuck the sword point down into the ground. "When my father revives he will want his sword. Take good care of it; it's a gift from your king."

Amazed at what she was doing, Heln mounted Corry's horse and the all-knowing gauntlets took expert charge of the reins. She thought she would remember the way to the border, but she doubted that she would have to. With her wishes firmly in mind, the gauntlets could be relied upon to do the rest.

As she walked her horse past her onetime kidnappers, Corry said to Bemode: "You, you fly-blown idiot, you had to tell her to bring the sword!"

"Well, if you hadn't been so busy looking up her dress, you'd have told me not to!" Bemode retorted.

Heln almost smiled. Maybe that dress had done her some good, after all!

I3 /

PRISONERS

JOHN KNIGHT LAY ON the straw-filled mattress and watched as
Gerta, his flopear attendant, ladled his soup. Miraculously his
injured hand and broken finger had healed perfectly, as though treated by
Earth's best surgeons. It had to be partially magic, he thought ruefully. He
who had always declared that there was no such thing, even in the face of
mounting evidence to the contrary—he owed his recovery to magic!

That reminded him of Charlain, his pointear wife, now his widow of the
other frame. Wonderful Charlain! She had believed in magic, and now he
knew she had been correct. He had a fine son and daughter by her. If only
he hadn't had to leave her! But her life would have been put in peril had he
stayed longer, and he couldn't tolerate that, so he had left. He had done so
with deep and continuing regret, but had never doubted the need for it. He
could not return to her as long as the fate of Queen Zoanna was unknown,
and as long as Charlain's second husband, Hal Hackleberry, lived.
Hackleberry was a good man, and so John meant never to return to that
frame.

Gerta handed him the beautifully wrought silver bowl and exquisitely
designed spoon. He took them, marveling again at how well his hand
worked. He also admired the moving picture on the bowl; when the spoon
approached it, the face on the bowl smiled. This seemed to be an actual
change in the image, not a mere illusion. What phenomenal artisans these
folk were! He sipped at the broth, really appreciating its rich chicurk flavor.

Gerta smiled down at him. Such big ears, covering the sides of her face
like the ears of a puppy. Such gentle eyes, such a sweet face, albeit with a
large slash mouth. About three feet tall and a little bit too wide, she was his
picture of a female gnome.

"You want bread?"

"Thank you, Gerta. Yes. Please."

He watched her cross the room, its walls of unbroken stone, its interior that of a neat, clean cottage. She sawed him a hunk of bread from a loaf, using a large toothed knife. The handle was decorated, he saw.

"Gerta, would you bring the knife?"

She brought it, handing it trustingly to him along with a thick piece of bread. He bit into the crust, enjoying its rough oat texture and caraway-seed taste with a hint of pizza crust. The handle of the knife was in the form of a silver serpent, the tail expanding into the blade. When he touched the end of the handle, the eyes of the serpent moved to follow his motion. He knew this was just the magic of the sculpture, but it was eerie. How did they manage to animate their carved figures?

"You call yourselves the serpent people, Gerta?"

"That is true, John Knight."

But others would call them flopears, inevitably. He considered his outstanding luck. Injured, floating down a river toward the great incredible falls that seemed to drop into blackest, star-filled space. It had been coming closer and closer, that falls, and he had been paddling to save his life. Then the water and the raft and himself falling, then floating, then . . . here. It was a different world, a different existence from either the Earth he had originated on or the world that was inhabited by pointed-ear people who considered roundeared people strange. He had found himself on the raft on a different river, singing birds all around. He had realized that something, some force, had taken him and brought him here. Some atomic force such as had been released by the artillery shell that had transported him and a few of his men into a near fairyland of pointy-eared people and magic. It had somehow, someway, happened. That hole, that flaw in reality, The Flaw, had somehow brought him here.

He thought again of Zoanna, the red-haired queen of Rud who had bewitched him with a magic well known on Earth: the magic of sex appeal. He thought of how evil she had been, how she had killed and destroyed good folk without conscience, and been in almost every way a terrible monster. But he had been slow to appreciate that side of her, being fascinated by the single facet she showed to him alone: her beauty and her desire for him. How foolishly flattered he had been, how possessed by lust for her body—a lust she encouraged and freely obliged. He had willfully blotted out the evidence of her true nature for an unconscionably long period; he was ashamed to remember it now.

He had tried to destroy her in the end, even as his remarkable son Kelvin, by lovely Charlain, was fighting to free the kingdom from her. He felt he had destroyed her, and yet he was not certain. At least he had tried! It did not make up for his long sojourn on the wrong side, but it was better than nothing. He still owed that frame, he felt, though he had no idea how he could ever make it up. It was all far away now, in another existence, and perhaps best forgotten.

He dipped the bread in the soup and sucked at it. "You know, Gerta, I'm nearly well now."

"Yes, your mind and body both healed."

"Mind?" What could she know of his tumultuous inner doubts?

"You were mad."

Had he been? He thought back. Images came to him erratically. As in pictures flickering on a television screen while his mind dozed fitfully, coming awake now and then. Could he make any sense of them? Maybe if he tried to put them into chronological order.

Falling into The Flaw, down, down, eternally. Then, somehow, he wasn't falling, he was floating, in a sea of stars. Drifting without direction, without orientation. That strangeness penetrating his mind, making it—mad? Stray thoughts: how foolish to travel through this maelstrom without a map! So he had conjured a map, or dreamed it up, and scratched a route on it. A route to Mouvar. That made so little sense, even in his madness, that he laughed and laughed—but nevertheless moved along that marked route, which now was a glowing band in the void ahead. The band became a stream of light or of darkness, and a current carried him along. Until it became too swift, and he spun out or fainted or dropped into another level of madness.

Crawling up a slippery bank. Realizing suddenly that it was actually the muddy shell of a turtle as large as the Galápagos kind. Or larger. But not the tortoise on which the world was supported—wrong mythology. Maybe.

Running, falling, again hurting his sickeningly injured right hand. That hand was mangled horribly, dripping blood, sending pain messages in increasing waves. Trees, brush, rocks. Run, run, run.

Falling, falling, falling. Pain.

Something silver, long. A rope? He reached out his left hand, his working hand.

A loud hissing sound and the rope undulating. Jaws of a serpent, opening wide. A drop of clear venom hanging on a fang and then dropping.

Pain, pain pain.

Screaming. His own.

Now a flower gently tapping the head of the serpent. A blue-and-pink blossom resembling a cross between a violet and a wild rose. A stubby-fingered hand, holding the stem.

The serpent's jaws closing. The serpent settling down, sliding away.

Now a face above the hand holding the blossom. Very blue eyes and very large ears like a puppy's. Gerta's. She looking down at him, her mouth making a moue and her eyes squeezing. A tear running down her face.

Flower petals touching his forehead, gently, gently stroking. A flower scent a little like a poppy's, soothing his tired mind, easing the long pain. A puppy with a poppy! Pained laughter. Oblivion, again.

He shook himself mentally. It had been so dreamlike, and yet so real. It was more than a hallucination, or else hallucination could return in memory with entirely too much reality.

This was really Gerta. This room that was lighted by large phosphorescent toadstools placed all about. Walls that were rock, and apparently solid rock. It was like a room in a cave or cavern, but the walls were smooth. Laser construction here? Or magic?

"You wish to eat?" Gerta asked.

"Please." The language was the same, at least. Strangely, it seemed like other things to vary only slightly from frame to frame. Perhaps not so strange, if it indicated that man had spread out from a common origin and colonized the several frames. Obviously there had been travel between them, because Mouvar had sown his legend among the pointears in Hud, and if those legends were to be believed, Mouvar hadn't been the first. How could he have predicted the uniting of kingdoms if there were no kingdoms to unite? Roundear and pointear could interbreed; he had proved that! That meant they were closely related species. But these flopears, now—how close were they?

She brought him a robe. It was white and smooth and shiny, and on Earth he would have known it as satin. There were underdrawers of a less shiny material resembling cotton.

He hesitated, a holdover from his Earth life when the sexes were cautious about naked exposure, then rolled out of bed and quickly donned the garments. Gerta, after all, had been his gentle nurse for a length of time he couldn't begin to estimate. It might have been weeks, though he had only been aware of days. During that time he knew she had aided him in all that was necessary, or else the magic was of a kind that allowed him to heal while suspending all body functions. That seemed unlikely! So though his memories were blurred, he was sure that Gerta had seen all of him, and all his functions.

"I haven't been up before, have I, Gerta?"

"Yes, you have. With me walking you."

"I don't remember."

"No. The healing clouds as it soothes and rebuilds the mind."

He thought about that, and he also thought of how very capable he felt on his feet. Gerta handed him a pair of soft slippers with curled toes. As he sat down to put these on he marveled that both slippers were decorated with large buckles, and that the buckles were silver. The designs on the silver changed as his feet entered the slippers. He had given up wondering what the point of such magic was. Art did not need a point.

He stood up, looked around the room, and spotted a door. He was certain he had looked at it for hours on end, but now it was like seeing it for the first time. It, too, had decorated silver panels that changed in their own fashion in their own time.

"I will take you to the workplace, John. You are now quite well. The magic has finished its work."

He marveled as he followed her. She moved quite fast for someone with such short legs. He felt a kindness toward her, a feeling that he might have had for a younger sister.

They went under stone archways, through some rooms without windows, and finally came out in a large natural amphitheater. Here there were many flop-eared men, wearing pointed caps not unlike Rud stockelcaps, and leather aprons. They were working at individual anvils. The cauldron around which the work centered contained silver in the molten state. The fire burning so brightly beneath the cauldron must, he realized, be of a magical nature to melt silver.

As he watched, one of the flopears walked to the cauldron carrying an armload of silvery, scaly-patterned skin. He turned the skin around in his hands and tossed it into the cauldron. Another flopear on a scaffold stirred the cauldron with a long ladle.

"My God!" John said. He whistled, then could do no better than to repeat his exclamation: "My God!"

The skin was serpentskin, and was purest silver! Shades of dragons with golden scales! Was there nothing that couldn't be in different existences?

His mind went back, scrabbling frantically for a shred of sanity. High school, science teacher getting his attention: "This article tells how shellfish ingest heavy metal and how the metal migrates to their shells. The flesh of these shellfish is unfit to eat, and the coloration metallic. I suggest you read this and report on it for tomorrow's class." John had nodded, sorry that he had thrown the paper wad, and he wanted now to shout back through the years: "Yes, and immortal dragons live on and on for centuries!" Serpents that were as immortal as dragons, ingesting silver instead of gold, the silver migrating through centuries to those brightly shining scales?

A flopear who had been going from anvil to anvil, checking the work, came up to them. He was no taller than Gerta, but his head was larger and he had the facial expression of a harried foreman.

"He healed, Gerta?"

"Yes, healed."

"Good. He will trade well."

Gerta squirmed. "I don't like to think of that, Harlick."

"No matter. You know the way."

"Yes."

John stared at them. "Trade? Me? To others like yourselves?"

"To others like yourself, John."

"Like me? People like me but with pointed ears?"

"Ears, pointed? No, John. Ears like ears on you mortal folk. Tiny ears low on the sides of your head." She tried not to show her distaste for this abnormal configuration.

John thought of this as they left the workplace and ambled back the way they had come. On the return he saw that there were many cottages but that the rooms he had been in were in fact inside a cliff. There were other doorways in the cliff, and some round holes that might have been bored by lasers.

"What will happen to me, Gerta? Will I be a slave?"

"I don't know, John. The roundears have their ways and we have ours. Their king of Hud buys all mortals who are prisoners of flopears if they are healthy. They trade for their own kind. What they do with them, I do not know."

John Knight pondered that, and was not reassured. It was quite possible that he would be better off remaining with the flopears, if he had any choice in the matter.

Kian tried to concentrate on other things than their punishment. He had discovered that he could think for himself without Lonny knowing his thoughts, but if he thought in terms of speaking, she knew them immediately. This was nice to know if they were going to be spending an eternity together. But would they? Would their thoughts and those of the serpent gradually merge, becoming one? Maybe that was what would eventually happen, but maybe it could be slowed, if not stopped. What they had to do, he felt, was concentrate on thinking thoughts that were human. That might enable them to merge while retaining human nature and intellect, instead of descending to serpent level.

John Knight, his father, had talked about were-animals once. He said it was all superstition and invention, but that some people believed in them. On Earth anything might be possible. Wolves and cats and other Earth creatures holding the spirits of humans and changing with them from time to time. Perhaps these stories owed their existence to beings like the flopears. If spirits could exist, and he was inclined now to believe that they might, then why couldn't there be two apparent species that shared the same spirits? If the serpents were truly immortal ancestors of the flopears, then was it strange that the . . .

His thought faded out, distracted by the serpent's feeding. The rock had a peppery taste. Seasoned with silver. The bad aspect of it was that he was beginning to like it. The worst of it was that he thought of the ingesting and could not otherwise concentrate. The serpent nature was taking over!

"Kian?" Lonny asked.

"Yes, Lonny." He had to be careful. He wanted to merge with her, and he doubted that he should. Because their mergence would be but the prelude to mergence with the serpent, and that would be the end of their humanity. Somehow he must get out of this body and into his own and go back to his home frame and Rud and find the girl she resembled. Only—how long had it been?

"Kian, do you think we can ever return? Be in our own bodies again?"

"Of course! What a question." Yet it was only the echo of his own doubt. His belief in that return was diminishing, but he didn't want to discourage her. He thought of the words of a song and tried singing it to her: "Oh, bring back, bring back, bring back my body to meeeee." It was a parody he had sung as a child, but it would do.

"I'm afraid, Kian! I just want to taste the silver and feel our body working."

"Not *our* body, Lonny! Get that out of your head!" Of course she had no head of her own at the moment, but it was no time to quibble about terms. "You're human, not serpent! You're a beautiful girl!"

"Am I, Kian? Do you really think that?"

"Of course it's true! Of course! I'm going to marry someone who looks just like you. I'm going to—"He fought back a surge of doubt. "I'm going to—to return."

"You really think so, Kian?"

"Yes, we're both going to return." How, he had no idea, but he had to cling to the belief.

"I mean, that I'm beautiful?"

"Yes, yes, I told you."

"You really mean it?"

He laughed, the mental version even more natural than the physical one. How could she doubt that? Their possible escape might be hard to believe, but her beauty was certain! "Of course!"

She evidently picked up more of that thought than he had intended. "You find me beautiful," she said, believing. "And you would like to—to hold me and kiss me and—"

"I didn't say that!" he protested.

"But it's true, isn't it?"

He discovered to his surprise that it was. He wanted to do it all with her! "Yes, but—"

"Yet you will marry this other girl?" Now she was angry. He felt the surge of it, and he could not deny the justice of it.

"I have to, Lonny. I can't marry you. I'm from another frame. That just wouldn't be right."

"Not right?"

"My—my father came to our frame from another, and—"He tried to sort out the immense skein of complications that his father's consortion with two women of Rud had generated. Kian himself was one result, and Kelvin another. What mischief! Was he to spread it farther by doing the same thing?

"Kian, Kian, I love you!" she cried, and the emotion washed through him, demolishing his bastion of objectivity as a wave destroys a castle of sand.

"I love you, Lonny," he replied helplessly.

"I want to—to do those things with you. To hold you, and kiss you, and—"

"No!"

"And make love to you," she concluded. "And you feel the same."

It was as though they were blending, melding like silver. He knew he must not allow that. He tried to resist, but simply could not think. "We—we have no bodies," he said desperately. Was that a commitment to do it at such time as they did recover their bodies? Then how could he return to his own frame? He was lost either way.

"Oh, Kian!"

"Oh, Lonny, I did not mean to—"

"I think we can do it now, Kian. Let me try."

"Now? But—"

Then he felt her kiss on his lips. He might not have a mouth, but he had the awareness of his human anatomy, and so did she, and it was certainly a kiss.

He tried once more to resist. "We shouldn't—"

She embraced him. Her spirit within the serpent interacted with his, and the sensation was exactly like a physical embrace, only more so, because there was nothing to get in the way. In physical bodies there could be no complete understanding; people more or less pretended that they understood each other, but it could be deceptive, as it had been with his father and his mother. His father had hardly known his mother at all! But here there were no physical barriers. He knew Lonny was speaking truly, and she knew he was not. The act of sex, physically, was said to be knowledge, but it could be nothing like this!

He gave up the unequal struggle. "Oh, Lonny! Lonny, Lonny, Lonny!" In one sense he was speaking her name, but in another he was speaking her essence, in that repetition possessing her and being possessed by her.

"Kian, Kian, Kian!" And she of him, similarly.

They no longer fought it at all. They came together, more intimately than either had imagined possible, and—

With a slurping, sucking motion daylight broke into their one functioning eye. Jolted out of their incipient mergence, they raised their silver head to the setting sun and breathed in through their nostrils and the air passages covered by their scales. They undulated, crawled, and wriggled out of the rock tunnel they had made.

Boys with big floppy ears were there for them. They shivered all their length, anticipating gentle touches, the soothing strokes, the exhilarating yet calming scent.

The boys held out their blossoms and touched their nostrils with the pink and blue flowers. They sucked in the scent in great waves. It filled their being, taking away all doubt and hope and questions. Taking away, finally, all sense of duality, and of self. They were one with the serpent.

I4 /

THE CLIFFS

JAC HESITATED OUTSIDE THE tent flap, dreading to go inside. Death had always been upsetting, though he had seen enough of it in his time. He thought of Heeto and the girl sitting in there side by side watching the body. He wanted her badly, but there could be no mistaking where her heart was. He would try to comfort her, and then, if the stranger's body had deteriorated the least little bit, he would bury him himself. Steeling himself for an unpleasant sight, he pushed on into the tent.

The sight that met his eyes was shocking, even to him. The lovely, recently intended sacrifice was stretched out by the body of the stranger, and both were apparently dead. She had joined him in suicide!

Heeto sat cross-legged by their heads, a leather fan in his hands. There were no buzzing flies.

"Master, I could not stop her! She took the berries. She followed him."

Trembling, Jac wiped perspiration from his forehead. The bodies were so perfect! All day long and no bloat and no smell. That beautiful face, that perfectly formed body, that had to go into the ground before it began to rot. Burying the bodies was going to be the most unpleasant task he had performed in his life! Yet it had to be done, and quickly.

"When did she—?"

"This morning, Master. Just after you left."

He had had to choose this day to get supplies for the camp! He should have known that Lonny had something like this in mind, and taken those berries away before she got to them! Yet he had also had to get his mind off the problem, and work or activity helped.

"We'd better—"He choked on the word "bury" and simply motioned at them.

"Master, I do not believe that they are dead."

"They're not breathing. Have they any heartbeats?"

Heeto shook his head. "No breathing, no heartbeats, but also no stink and no bugs."

"I'm not sure that means anything, Heeto." Yet maybe, just possibly, it did!

"I've touched them, Master. I have taken their hands. It's strange, Master, but I felt something besides their cold flesh. I was floating, Master, or felt I was floating, though I did not leave this tent. I was somewhere dark. There were rocks about, and dirt, and I could feel them the length of my body. It was not her body and it was not his; it was a serpent's."

"A serpent's!"

"Yes, Master. I waited to tell you. I thought that perhaps—"

"Yes, yes, I want to try!"

"That is not what I mean, Master. I thought that perhaps you would know."

"I know only what the stranger Kian told me. But if a serpent has them—has their spirits—"

"Is that possible, Master?"

"I don't know." He sat down by the dwarf, took a good grip on his feelings, and reached for Lonny's hands.

They were cold, but there was no stiffness. Proof, perhaps, that this was not actually death. He gripped the hands and closed his eyes. "Is this the way you did it, Heeto?"

"Yes, Master, but that was this morning. I had not the courage to try it again. Perhaps it will not work now. Perhaps I only imagined it."

"No, no, something's happening! I sense black and roughness and—a taste."

"A taste, Master?"

"Dirt! Bah, ugh! Now a more peppery taste. Silver! Silver ore! She likes it; he doesn't. They're inside it, inside the serpent!"

"I told you, Master!"

"Now I'm seeing something. Something through an eye. One eye. The serpent's eye!"

"Only one eye, Master?"

"Yes, only one. Now she and he are talking—talking in the serpent. I don't know the words, I don't know what they are saying, but . . . they seem to be—"He swallowed, disliking this, but obliged to recognize the truth of it. "They are attracted to each other. They are kissing, and embracing, and—"He took a deep breath. "And they seem to be merging, mingling as one mind. It's like sex, only so strange, and—"How he wished he were the one experiencing that! "Now—oh! Light! Outside, ground. Boys with flowers, extending them toward the eye. The flowers touch the nostrils, it breathes in and—"

He pulled himself away, dropping her hands. It was an experience he had never imagined. He looked at Heeto and the bodies, and he trembled and shook in every part.

"Are you all right, Master?" Heeto's hands were on him, touching his face.

He continued to shake. "It's—it's—I think it's digesting them!"

"Then they will die?"

He tried to still his shaking hands. "I think they must! I think they must! And, Heeto, this is mad, but—I think the one-eyed serpent is the one he killed!"

"Killed, Master? With your spear? In the eye socket?"

"That's the one! The very one! I'd swear to it!"

"Calm down, Master! Calm down!"

"We can't bury them, Heeto. Not until, until—"

"Until morning?"

"Until we have to! Until we know they are gone for good and there is only the serpent left."

"Master, that's so, so sad."

"Very sad, Heeto," he agreed heavily. "Very, very sad." With difficulty he got his hands to stop shaking. It was such a monstrous thing to think of her there. To imagine her spirit, or "astral self," as Kian Knight had called it, becoming a part of that gigantic serpent.

"We will leave the bodies in the tent for as long as we can. For now, we'd better sleep outside."

"There's nothing we can do, Master? Nothing to save them?"

"Nothing I know of," he said, wishing it were otherwise.

That night there was no way he could sleep. He kept throwing off his blanket, getting up, pacing, and then lying down again. All he could think about was her, she of the beautiful eyes and long, flowing blond hair. If only there were some way to save her, to bring that splendid body of hers back to life.

At dawn he moved quietly about the camp so as not to awaken anyone. He got his best and biggest spear and tiptoed with it to his horse. He saddled and bridled the mare, rubbed her muzzle, and called her "Betts, my pet." He fastened the spear to the saddle with his best rope and walked the mare until they were clear of the camp. He hiked up his sword, mounted, and rode at an easy walk. He had gone only a short distance when he heard the other horse. Turning around, he was quite surprised to see Heeto riding after him. He waited. The dwarf pulled up.

"Master, I want to go with you. I brought this." He held up the weapon Kian Knight had brought with him from another world, lost, and then found again. The "worthless weapon" to its former owner, though he had not relinquished it. A Mouvar weapon was still a Mouvar weapon.

"What good do you think that will be?"

"I don't know, Master. I just brought it."

"Do you know that I do not expect to return?"

"If you do not, I will not."

They rode on for Serpent Valley and its great curve of surrounding cliffs.

There were holes in the cliffside that he had seen before, some large, some small, many in between. The mist was still heavy as they approached. Jac kept glancing back at Heeto, adjusting his spear.

The largest hole in solid rock might have been made by the serpent they were after. But if they rode down it, would they find the serpent? Did the serpents use the same tunnels? It was surprising how little they actually knew about the serpents or about the flopears who guarded them. Yet morning after morning he had slipped into the valley to collect discarded serpentskins before the flop-eared boys arrived to pick them up. Sooner or later he might have been caught, almost certainly would have been, but now he sought a confrontation. The outcome of that would mean his death and Heeto's as well, but it might also mean the extinction of the life force in the serpent.

A slithering sound came from one of the larger holes. He motioned for Heeto to follow him and rode his horse into one of the smaller holes facing the larger one. They waited as the sound grew nearer. Then a stir of darkness within the larger hole, and the serpent's head appeared. As he started and stared at it, he saw that one eye was damaged; he could still see the wounds the spearhead had made.

Not giving himself a chance to think, he spurred his horse and charged with spear poised to stab into that remaining orb.

The serpent's head came up. It hissed, long and low, disturbing the morning mists. The eye, that single strange eye, bored at him. In that dark mirror he saw her face, and on the instant of that seeing he was paralyzed.

The serpent wriggled out of its tunnel. Its great mouth opened. Drops of acid formed on its fangs and dripped to the ground, hissing.

Jac saw but could not comprehend what was happening. He was frozen in place, unwilling to move or to think of moving; his mare, being but mortal, was in similar shape. Together their eyes saw the huge head advancing, lifting back, the mouth opening wide. There was no will or thought left for avoiding the strike; still less for making an attack.

Back in the dark Heeto saw his master ride out with raised spear. He saw the serpent's head rise up, though the mist fogged the details. He saw the horse stop; both horse and rider were motionless. Both were awaiting death.

He saw death emerge from the hole in front of them as the serpent drew the rest of its body out and made ready to strike. They did not move.

It must not happen! He had to help! Hardly thinking what he did, Heeto pulled out the weapon from another world and raised it until it pointed over Master's head at the gigantic head of the serpent. He pressed the trigger on the weapon, as if this would accomplish anything. He knew the weapon didn't work; the stranger had said so.

Bright light filled the tunnel and splashed outside. Heeto was blinded by it; he felt as if that light struck right through his head! There was a WHOOMPTH noise, loud and unexpected and somehow echoing on and on instead of ending. His fingers loosened on the weapon. It slid from his hand and dropped to the floor. Unheeding, he placed his hands over his eyes, and he screamed less from pain than from shock.

Stillness.

He put down his arms. He could see again, his vision clearing by the moment. He took up the horse's reins. In the mists that were rapidly dissipating he could see both Master and horse and the swaying form of the otherwise motionless serpent.

He rode out, hardly thinking, blinking his eyes against the mist.

The serpent remained frozen in striking position; it seemed almost a statue of itself. His master suddenly jerked, and his horse jumped, almost throwing him.

"Master, Master, kill it!"

His master got the mare controlled, raised his spear to the eye, and looked directly into the eye. "She's not there, Heeto! I can't see her now. She's gone back to camp!"

"Master!" Heeto cried, hardly believing.

"I don't know what happened. It's not moving. Maybe it's dead."

A great slithering sound came from the neighboring holes. Serpents coming out to them! Master looked as dazed as Heeto felt, perhaps even more so.

"Let's get out of here, Master! Now, while there's a chance!"

Master's mouth worked, as if his jaws were still partially paralyzed. Finally he nodded, and together they took off at as great a speed as their mounts could carry them.

Kian opened his eyes and stretched. Above him was the familiar roof of the tent; under him, the bearver hide. He turned his head to the right, expecting to see Jac, and instead saw Lonny's lifeless form.

Even as he sat up with a cry of horror, her breathing started and her color returned. She stared at him, then sat up as abruptly as he had.

"Kian!" Spots of red came to her cheeks. "Kian, we—"

He thought rapidly, trying to deny it to himself. Wishing despite himself that it could be true, yet knowing it was not. "It must have been an illusion that we were together," he concluded. "How could we be alive, without bodies, in the serpent? But even if it wasn't a dream, it hardly matters. It wasn't as though we were lying here joined. Astral bodies are like bodies we dream. Whatever they are, they don't count."

"Don't they, Kian?" She sounded faintly disappointed.

"No, not really." But was that the truth? If any part of what he remembered so clearly were true—and it had *felt* so true!—what did it mean? "But what happened? The last I remember we were—"Now he felt himself blushing. "Together in the serpent." More than together! They had been making love! More than love!

"I remember after that," she said almost eagerly. "I remember seeing Jac. He was on his horse and he had a spear and . . . and then there was a light."

"I remember the light." And how sorry he had been to have that serpent break out into the light of day, distracting them from their mergence within it. He knew it meant oblivion, because once they merged with each other they would be ready to merge with the serpent. Yet it had been such a wonderful experience in the making!

He reached out and took her hand. It was as cold as his own. "Jac must have come for us and slain the serpent. Reslain it, I guess."

"Yes." Her eyes widened in internal pain. "Oh, Kian, I hate for it to be dead!"

"So do I," he confessed. For he had seen an entirely different side of the monster, and not an evil side. The serpent, he realized, had been brought back to life by the presence of their spirits, and perhaps could not survive well without them.

The two boys stayed hidden in the mouth of one of the smaller ancestor tunnels as the two mortals rode away from the cliffs. Both remained silent, watching. After the horsemen had vanished in the mists, they crept out and approached the ancestor with their blossoms. The ancestor was aware now, and pulled back at their approach.

"Hissta, sizzletack," a boy said, extending his blossom.

The silver snout came forward. There was a great sucking sniff. The ancestor was already forgetting. But should it be happening this soon?

"Herzig must know," the other boy said.

"Yes," the first agreed. "We must hurry back home and tell Herzig what happened. Mortals must not be allowed to torment our ancestors."

The ancestor snorted loud, enjoying the fragrance of the blossoms. It had seemed bemused, but now was recovering.

* * *

They were almost to the Barrens when Jac felt his head fully clear. Turning to Heeto riding beside him, he addressed the matter he had not quite understood. "That white light—what was it, and how did it happen?"

Heeto yanked his horse's reins so hard he almost tumbled from the saddle. His face was stricken, as was his voice. "Oh, Master, I forgot it! It worked, Master. I'm sure it worked! Only I'm not sure what it did or why! I pointed it, I pressed the trigger, and . . . and then there was the light."

"Lord!" Jac said. He tried to digest this. "The Mouvar weapon—where is it now?"

"Where we were, Master. At the cliffs. Inside the tunnel."

"Lord!" Jac repeated. He shook his head. "It had to have been that! Because after that flash, the serpent changed. Maybe that weapon didn't work on a bearver, but the serpents are different; they carry captive spirits." He shook his head, hardly believing what he was saying. Was he raving? "We're going to have to get it! It could be the answer to everything! If it works, we may have the answer to flopears and Rowforth!"

"We can't go back now, Master. The sun is up."

"Yes, it is, isn't it!" He let the fact infiltrate his consciousness. Day made things so much clearer—usually. But the revelations he was experiencing, assuming they made any sense at all . . . "If we go back now, they'll get us. So we won't do it now. We'll do it as soon as we safely can." Which meant evening or night.

They rode on toward the camp, following their faint trail through the Barrens. That was as familiar to both as though marked with signs, but anyone else would not find it at all.

When they arrived, there was confirmation: Kian and Lonny in front of his tent, standing hand in hand, without question alive.

There went perhaps his last hope to win Lonny. But somehow the pain was less now. He was glad to have her alive—and a new horizon was opening on his activity.

Even as Jac hailed them he was already making plans for the recovery of the weapon that had worked so strangely to rescue them.

15 /

AMBUSH

JAC DREW LINES IN the sand with a stick and motioned everyone
around. It was battle plan time, and all his men—all fifty-six,
including Heeto and of course the newcomers, Kian and Lonny—were
grouped outside his tent.

"We'll have to do it this way." His finger pointed out the spot on his
crude map. "Right here on the main road where you lost your way, Kian.
We'll hide behind the trees and wait. Smith," he said to the man behind him,
"you're the best crossbowman, so we'll station you in a tree where you can
take out the leader. Take the leader out as soon as they offer resistance, and
we may have a chance. If the flopears don't get to us first."

Kian felt constrained to speak. He had been mentally counting their
numbers since they came outside and guessing at the number of troops he
had seen and the number of flopears nearby. "I can't be certain this is the
route they will take. I only know what I heard in the palace. By the way, that
was my last dragonberry. If we don't win and you haven't got dragonberries
growing here, that's the end of astraling."

"Yes, you're right, it's our only chance," Jac agreed. "Then, when the
fighting is heaviest—and there'll be fighting, make up your mind to it!—
maybe Heeto and I can get back to that tunnel and get back your Mouvar
weapon."

"Are you sure it will do any good if we have it?" Kian found it hard to
believe it would. Even though he and Lonny had been rescued by its use, he
didn't know what it had done. Whether it could be effective against the
flopears themselves, let alone the armed soldiery of Rowforth's—that
seemed too good to be true.

"We'll see," Jac said. "And, Lonny—"

"Yes?" She looked up at the leader with her blue eyes.

"We'll station you on high ground overlooking the valley. If you spot any
flopears, you'll warn us."

"Will my voice carry that far?"

"No, you'll have to run back. If you shout from the high rock on this spot above the road, we'll hear."

She nodded. "I won't have a horse?"

"Can't spare one. It all depends on your legs. It's a distance of about twice around this camp."

"My legs are good," she said with unconscious understatement. "I'll look out for flopears."

"It's too bad there's not another good spot for an ambush. But then maybe the soldiers won't think to ride for flopear help, and maybe the flopears wouldn't help. There's a chance."

Kian considered how different Lonny was from Jon back home. Jon would have been protesting that she should have a horse and her sling and a supply of rocks. Jon would want in on the fighting, and Lonny would be conscious that she was female and that fighting was only for males. As for Lenore, whom Lonny so resembled in appearance, he really didn't know. All he could remember of Lenore was looking away with embarrassment whenever she was near. Yet her appearance was almost identical to Lonny's. How blind had he been?

Matt Biscuit moved through the men until he was beside Jac. "You'd better use him," he said, jerking his thumb at Kian. "Him and his gauntlets."

"Right. Kian, you'll be in the forefront of the charge. Assuming there is a charge, and there's sure to be one. Rowforth's men won't give up your father without a fight. So you and I and Biscuit here will be at the head of any charge. Biscuit's good with a sword, I'm good, and from what you say, your gauntlets will make you better."

"I, uh, really haven't had the practice," Kian confessed. Now that he was facing battle, he felt quite ill. Kelvin, the hero, would never feel like this!

"You want *me* to wear your gauntlets?" Biscuit demanded.

"No! I'll wear them, and I'm good! I wore them in one battle back in my home frame, and there was only one other warrior my equal."

"Your brother, Kelvin," Jac supplied.

"Yes, Kelvin." He did not add that Kelvin had worn the left gauntlet, he the right. Nor that they had fought each other to a draw. Some things these local patriot bandits could know, and some he didn't want to reveal even under torture.

"Then it's settled. We know from your last reconnaissance that they'll be coming at dawn. On their way home we'll stop them and take away your father. If we do, we have your word he'll help us against Rowforth and the flopears. That right, Knight?"

"You know it is." Jac seemed just a bit belligerent, but then they all did. It was probably battle nerves and the fact that so far he had been more of a source of problems than a solution to any.

* * *

When he got a look at the soldiers through his physical eyes, Kian marveled at how little he had noticed with his astral vision. They were ordinary men by Jac's reckoning, but they were obviously top fighting men. Sturdy, strong, well disciplined, and their quality showed. His mother's troops had looked nothing like these! They would not release his father without a fight, and studying them from concealment, Kian wondered if Jac's ragtag crew could possibly prevail. Then he remembered the gauntlets he wore, and he knew that they did have a chance. Assuming he could stay astride his horse and get into the fray where it would help.

He sighed. He knew he would soon be taking men's lives and he hated it. But the alternative was to leave his father, and possibly, though he had not seen her, his mother. He willed himself strong for the coming fight.

The few crossbow bolts struck the road directly in front of the marching men as Jac rode out of the trees and raised his hand. "We want your prisoner! Resistance or a refusal to turn him over means death!"

"By the Gods, we'll have none of it!" The ruddy-faced captain turned to his troops and commanded: "Shields ready! Prepare!"

A lucky crossbow bolt from Smith found its target. The captain clutched at the feathered barb piercing his throat above the mail. Gurgling horribly, he pitched over the head of his war-horse, spraying blood on his way to meet the ground.

"Charge!" Jac ordered his bandit army, and Kian hardly had time for it to register before he was charging the foremost men. In a moment more he was crossing swords, cutting down, stabbing and chopping expertly. His gauntlets knew, and did what was necessary. He saw his father through the dust that now covered everything, and after he had dispatched his fifth man, he felt fully that he was effecting a rescue.

"Flopears! Flopears!" It was Lonny calling from the rock. If it weren't for the dust he could have bent back, looked up, and seen her. The battle had hardly started, but she was there, calling down to them.

Obviously the flopears had not been far away. Had they known what would happen, through their magic? Had one of them been astral-spying here? Or was it simply that the valley and its flopear population were far too close to the bandit camp? Whatever the case, it was doubtful that a rider had gotten back to them to beg their assistance.

Flopears, it seemed, were now fully allied to Rowforth and did not necessarily wait to be asked. In the past, Jac had confided, things had been far different, and dealings with mortals had been restricted to the once-a-year sacrifice.

Faster than he would have believed possible, the fighting tide turned. Kian found his gauntlets taking complete control of his hands and arms and almost his mind. Blocking, stabbing, slashing—his sword was busy while his shield hid the faces of dying men. But their horrible screams cut through to his ears. Who had ever fancied that combat was glorious? He could not think now, even to marvel at the speed of his blade and the intricate motions of his arm. He was simply a killing machine.

Then his horse screamed, and he was flying from the saddle over its neck. Somehow the gauntlets flung sword and shield and forced his body into an acrobatic roll. He bounced to his feet, twisted out of the way of a sword slash, saw Biscuit run the man through, and retrieved his weapons almost under the horse's hooves. These gloves played it entirely too close for comfort!

"We have to retreat! Quick, before the flopears arrive!" It was Jac's voice in the dust. Biscuit reached down a hand to Kian, but the gauntlet with the sword in it motioned him away.

Thinking only that he must get Lonny, Kian scrambled up the hillside, out of the lake of dust. How nice to catch a breath of fresh air! Once a sword cut at him, but his shield deflected the blow without even jerking hard. Then he was above the horses and on his way to the high rock and to Lonny. It was much too steep going, but the gauntlets knew no defeat. Without giving him a chance to do more than fight for breath, they grabbed saplings and brush and pulled his errant feet constantly upward on a path that seemed impossible for a mountain goeep. How nice it would be to have enchanted boots that governed his feet the way the magic gauntlets governed his hands!

Now he was at the crest of the hill, coming up by the rock. Lonny was on the rock, her eyes fixed glassily on a flopear advancing on her with raised club. In a moment the flopear would bash in her head and send her lifeless body tumbling down to the battlefield below. No wonder the gauntlets had hauled him up here so rapidly; had he realized the reason for their urgency, he would have strained yet more to make it sooner. As it was—

He could not make it in time; the remaining distance was too great. But even as he realized this, his right glove whipped his sword down, slicing at the ground broadside. The point caught a stone and drove it out and up in what his father called a golf drive. The little stone sailed across and flew at the flopear's face. Then, as if its job were done, the gauntlet sheathed the sword.

The flopear, no slouch, saw the missile coming and ducked, and the stone missed. But this distracted him from the girl. He looked across and saw the new enemy cresting the hill. The flopear reoriented, bracing himself and taking a defensive posture with the club. Then, satisfied that he faced only one new enemy, he lifted the club for a smash. There was no point in bashing the helpless girl if he got his own head lopped off immediately after!

Kian's gauntlets got him to the top and on his feet and his shield up in front of his face before the flopear could fully turn and redirect his blow. But he no longer held his sword! He had foolishly sheathed it, and had no time to draw. Kian lurched on his feet as the club smashed against the shield. Despite the gauntlets, he almost fell. This flopear was a true warrior, balanced and ready despite his surprise, while Kian was a bumbling fool!

Then his right glove jumped forward to catch at the flopear's left knee, and his left glove shoved the shield back hard against the club and the attacker's face. The flopear tried to step back but could not, because of the caught knee. He had been caught by surprise by an unworthy foe. He cried out and flung away his club, trying to recover his balance, but he could not. He fell, and now the gauntlet let go of the knee with a shove, and the flopear stumbled back too violently. He lost his footing at the edge of the steeper slope and fell down, rolling over on the slope, tumbling head over boots. Thump, thump, thump, bash. Then, mercifully, a speck of silence.

Other flopears would be here momentarily. Kian had dealt with one, thanks again to the genius of the gauntlets, but there was no reason to think he could handle three or four. That one had been too apt, too quick and sure; only the surprise hold and push when Kian had seemed to be falling (seemed?) had caught him. Once a flopear eyed him, he would be done for, and the same for Lonny.

He grabbed her hand and yanked. "Come!"

He ran, hauling her along, his gauntlets helping him decide the route. But Lonny tried to hang back.

"Kian, we're going the wrong way! The serpents—"

With shock he realized that his hands were urging them past a pole holding a serpentskin chime. Turning his head, he could just barely see short-legged flopears toiling up the hillside. That way would be suicide or capture. Ahead—ahead was the bigger of the two valleys: the one Lonny's people called Serpent Valley.

Unhesitatingly the powerful gauntlets pulled them on, down the steep hillside where silver serpents lay basking lazily in the morning sun.

John Knight could hardly believe that they had arrived, but they had, and they looked just like the troops back home that Rufurt had maintained. Only here it was Rowforth, and if he didn't misinterpret Gerta's expression when she talked of him, he was not the ideal monarch for this familiar yet strange fairy-tale land.

"I'm sorry you go, John," Gerta said as she led him from her cottage. "You good man. Not like most mortals."

Blinking in the sunlight, John considered the good manly uprightness of the troops, the neatness of their green uniforms, and the shine of their highly polished mail. With troops like these, could Rowforth be bad? Possibly he had a wife such as Rufurt had had—Queen Zoanna, sinister mistress of men, certainly mistress of John Knight. Evil women, he was beginning to think, existed everywhere.

"Good-bye, Gerta," he said, directing a grateful look at her. The flopear girl had been kind to him. She was strange in the way she had talked to that chime as though it contained something living, but he had come to know her as a person rather than as a thing.

"Up on your horse, you!" a captain commanded.

He mounted. The saddle was a bit tight. Riding horses had been but an occasional recreation in his Earthly life. Flying with a jetpack or legging it over mountains was more in his experience. Of course, he had ridden bicycles as a boy and later driven cars and trucks.

The procession rode out. Turning, looking back, John marveled anew at the cottages and the round holes that had been turned into dwellings and buildings in the surrounding cliff. The roundness of the holes made him think of wormholes. Had he imagined the great size of the serpent he encountered? Gerta hadn't said, but he remembered vividly her holding out the pink and blue blossoms to that great, flat head.

He breathed in, savoring the delightful green smells of spring. It was spring here, he'd bet. You could mistake a lot of things, but you couldn't mistake the feel of seasons. Not when you were outside and a part of the natural scene.

They were leaving the valley now by a road he didn't recall but must once have traveled. He could see that it was a valley and that there was another valley connecting it. The hills, the mountains, were much like those in Rud. In a way it was like some areas of the Americas, if they had not been ground down by glaciers. But if there had been no glaciers here, should there be such valleys? Pondering this, he mentally shook his head. He was no geologist, so his conjectures were hardly definitive. Whatever made the valleys in these mountains, they ran big, and whatever made the mountains, they ran rough. Now, as in other things, he wished he were more the expert on the subject.

Ahead were wilds: trees and brush. He supposed he had run, crawled, or somehow moved through these parts. Yet he could hardly remember. The magic medicine Gerta had used on him had dimmed any memories of what otherwise might be coming back. It was plain that he had gotten here from the river, and he must have traveled this road. More he simply could not evoke.

They were stopping. The captain was talking to someone, and oh, how red his face appeared. Then the captain was falling, clutching at his throat. Horses neighed and danced. Swords leaped from scabbards. Shields were raised. In a moment a full-scale battle was on. It was like old times, thus abruptly: swords swishing and shields clanging and men crying out from wounds or giving their death rattles. Wild-looking men without uniforms were everywhere, attacking green uniforms.

A man screamed and fell from his horse, and another man and horse raced after a third. Dust billowed voluminously, like smoke. That was the thing about battles: they were never neat and choreographed; they were always messy and dusty and ugly in both sight and mind.

Briefly he glimpsed the face of a man not wearing a uniform: a young, now very grim face. *Kian!* he thought. *Kian! My son!*

Kian must have followed him to this frame. But who were these men he was with? Who were these rough, ill-clad, undisciplined folk? They looked like bandits from the Sadlands! And was it really Kian, or did it just look like him? With similar-looking people turning up in this frame, it was hard to be sure. He had to find out!

He dug his heels into his horse's sides and crouched low on the neck, trying to make a break. The horse leaped forward as it was supposed to do, and as he took off he shoved the soldiers on either side of him from their mounts—or tried to. His outflung arms did not accomplish much. Then he was past and there were other matters at hand.

The man he had thought to be Kian was in that battle ahead. John didn't have a sword himself, or any kind of weapon. Still—

The blow took him from behind and sent him out of the saddle and down to the dust. He threw up his arms to protect his face. The ground came up very, very fast.

The next thing he knew, someone was pulling him up by his arms. Who had him, and why, he did not know. It was all he could do to hang on to his dwindling consciousness.

16 /

SERPENT'S HOLE

K IAN FELT HER STIFFEN and the gauntlet jerked. He knew she had been pierced by the gaze of a serpent or a flopear. At least he hoped that was it, rather than an arrow! He felt himself swing around, pulled by the left gauntlet, and the jarring thud as shield struck hard against a flopear's face. The flopear went down in a heap, his raised club flying from his hands.

Kian gave Lonny a quick slap and saw her eyes unglaze. He could hear more flopears coming in the distance, uttering hoarse shouts. The only flopear in sight was the one he had knocked unconscious.

They had to hide! There was no fighting these flopears! If they didn't get out of sight, they were going to be killed or captured.

A hole showed there in the rocks. A cave? A den? What did it matter? It was a hiding place!

He jerked Lonny the distance and pushed her ahead of him into the darkness of the hole. If they could just stay here until the flopears were past —until nightfall, perhaps.

Outside, the flopears were calling to one another in hoarse shouts. Yes, they'd have to stay hidden. They hadn't been seen or discovered yet. They had found the club-wielder and were trying to decide what had happened.

"Kian," Lonny whispered, moving close. "Kian—"

"Not now, Lonny." God, how he wanted her arms around him! But he didn't want her to feel his trembling. Heroes, after all, were supposed to be brave.

"Kian—I—I love you."

That was what he had been afraid she would say! He was so attracted to her—and this in the wrong frame!

"Kian, there's something you should know."

He was afraid he already knew it. That mergence in the serpent—that hadn't been just because they were both captive. It had been because they both wanted it. They both wanted it now, in their physical bodies, too.

His arms found her and held her. He could feel her heart beating under her light shirt. The trembling of his limbs now didn't seem to matter. In a moment, except for the danger, he might forget himself. Blessed be the peril, part of him thought. *Damn!* another part retorted.

But if they were in immediate danger of dying, why was he holding back? Why save himself for a woman of the other frame if there was to be no encounter with her? Wouldn't it be better simply to take advantage of that scant time remaining here?

"Kian, we're about to die."

"M-maybe not," he managed to say. Evidently her logic was paralleling his. She was such a precious armful, all sweet and soft and female. "I've still got my sword and my shield and the gauntlets. Even if they find us, they can't make eye contact in the dark. I can defend this cave for a long time." But was that what he really wanted to do? How much easier to abandon thoughts of combat and simply lose himself in her!

"Kian, this isn't a cave. This is the tunnel a big serpent makes."

He shuddered in spite of himself. A part of his mind had known where they were, but he had been suppressing it. Trust Lonny, troublesome as only a comely girl could be, to come out with it.

He moved his back up against the wall of the tunnel. He resheathed his sword and put his gauntleted palm against it. A thought screamed at his consciousness: *If we move back, back, back, maybe they won't come in here after us! Maybe they'll never find us!*

Lonny moved still closer to him, scaring him almost more than the darkness, in quite a different manner. He took her hand firmly in his and whispered low so as not to be overheard by any sharp-eared flopear. "If we retreat far enough back—"

"But, Kian, we can't know what's here! There might be a—a—"

"And there might not. Not all the holes are occupied." He hoped! "Come—"

He led her stumbling and cringing through the blackness, his gauntlet scraping the side of the tunnel. The gauntlets wouldn't lead him into unnecessary danger, would they? In any other place he would have found it easier to believe that.

There was no indication, but he felt that the tunnel was old. If it hadn't been used for a long time, just maybe they might follow it to a spot where the original tunneler had resurfaced. It was a possibility, though remote. After all, the one they had been in had eaten silver, then come to the surface. They did like to sun themselves after a meal.

"Kian, is that a glow?"

He paused. He had thought it wishful thinking, but yes, there was a lightness. Outdoors! They'd survive after all!

But no, he felt no breeze, no hint of fresh air. His nose, in fact, seemed clogged with dust. So if that wasn't daylight, what was it? There were no alternatives but to go on, or stay where they were, or return to the entrance. Even now the flopears could be tracking them down, entering the tunnel; the flopears had no fear of serpents!

His gauntlets were tugging at him, forcing him to move away from the wall and follow their lead, lest he be drawn off balance.

It could be daylight! he thought without any proper conviction. *It could be daylight!* he kept telling his doubting self. But his self knew it was a lie. The light was greenish, and that meant—

At home it would have meant moss of the luminous variety that had enabled him to row out on the underground river and travel through the rock walls to Mouvar's concealed chamber. Here—

Here it meant luminous moss on rock walls. There was a blaze of green light and then he stopped, grabbing Lonny's arm. They were right in the exiting mouth of a serpent tunnel that led from a wide, natural chamber! The chamber's walls were coated with the luminous lichen. Other serpent tunnels, not of this size, also entered it at irregular intervals.

Kian took a great breath. "Maybe we *can* find a way out! By taking another tunnel."

"Yes, Kian! Oh, yes!"

She was so quick, so positive! He liked that, knowing he had no business to react to it. He had aroused her hope, he thought, and now he would have to deliver. The gauntlets, he feared, really did not know more than he did which serpent tunnel might lead them to a reasonably safe exit. How *could* they know? They were not of this frame!

Holding Lonny's hand in his, feeling awed by the size of the chamber, he led her into it. There were outcroppings of rock and stalactites of great size above them, stalagmites rising up like raised spears from the floor. In the green radiance all was clear for a surprising distance. It was as though they had entered some mammoth building. There was little dust, and fresh air was coming in through serpent holes far overhead.

Lonny's face held the same awe Kian felt. The place they were in stretched as far as they could see, and there seemed no end to the radiance. Even if one of the serpent tunnels presented an immediate exit, the impulse to explore was overwhelming.

They walked hand in hand, admiring the beauty. Fear diminished; fear could not flourish in loveliness like this! There were crystal outcroppings, natural shelves and stairs and doorways. There were beads in some outcroppings that seemed bluish and yellowish and even reddish in the light. With some difficulty Kian realized that the beads were actual gems of a size that in his home frame would have been unheard of. Silver ore outcroppings here and there, like rivers and streams of shining mineral flowing frozenly through the rock. A crystal waterfall, greenish and sparkling, as high as any waterfall Kian had ever seen.

"Oh, Kian! Oh!" Lonny exclaimed.

Inadequate, but accurate, he thought. It was almost worth the danger to see this place, to know of its existence.

"It's as pretty as the flopears' silverwork," she continued.

He had to agree. The people of this region drew the beauty of their images from it, along with the horror of their serpent companions. Yet, after being inside a serpent, he realized that horror was mainly how a person saw it. There was beauty within the serpents, too.

They walked between the stalagmites and found themselves in a narrow chamber. Here there were luminous mushrooms such as flopears used for lighting, and beyond the mushrooms was an area that descended as if by means of man-made stairs to a lower level.

Kian took a deep breath, thankful again for the good air here—who would have thought he would appreciate serpent holes like this!—and led Lonny on. There seemed no end of wonder to this place; no physical end in sight.

Ahead, silver. Lots of silver! He stopped, staring. The silver was in long, thin belts and made of overlapping scales. The silver was discarded serpent-skins, many of them from giants!

"Gods, Lonny," he said, "there's a fortune! They must have been coming here for ages!" His eyes swept along the shining carpet. It stretched for as far as he could see and then was closed off by a bend in the cavern.

"If only Jac and his men could get down here! They'd never have to steal silver from the flopears again! They'd be rich as any king! They could go out and buy themselves an army or a kingdom!"

"Kian?" Lonny whispered. Her face was very pale; what was the matter with her, reacting so to such wealth?

"It's all right," he said.

"Kian," she gasped, "remember where we are!"

Yes, she would remind him, he thought. Remind him that they would in all probability never get back to Jac and his bandits. Still it was something, just knowing this was here. If an army needed to be raised, the means of raising it was here.

Listening, he heard a great, dry rustling. It grew louder and louder, and then silver appeared in one of the serpent tunnels. They stood frozen as a great serpent snout—larger even than the one they had been in—protruded from one of the holes. That could be why the tunnel they had entered was empty: it was too small for a serpent this size! It did not see them, and Kian pulled Lonny away, back into a natural alcove.

Other rustlings, other sounds. It was as though the cavern walls had come alive. Serpents of great and simply large size, serpents the size of ordinary snakes, and serpents the size of worms, squirming out of open tunnels and tunneling themselves out of rock. Bits of rock dust fell here and there as serpents broke free of the honeycombed rock. The slithering grew louder and louder and was accompanied by hisses as the serpents broke into the cavern.

"Oh, Kian, Kian, hold me! Hold me before it's too late!"

He did, trembling and shaking. Any moment a head might emerge at their backs. Any moment a serpent might set its freezing eyes on them. Once discovered, they would be gone. There was nothing to prevent their being snapped up, chewed, swallowed, digested, and made physically a part of these monsters. Magic gauntlets, sword, and shield were as little protection as their clothing. There was nothing to do but stay hidden and wait.

Plop! Plop! Plop! The sound of serpent bodies sliding, gliding, falling onto rock. This huge cavern that had seemed so much like salvation from pursuit had turned out to be the most dangerous place of all!

He held her tight, no longer daring to speak any word. It was amazing that the serpents didn't smell them, but perhaps the odor was too diffuse to alert them. But any sound now—

After a time he found her face turned to his. Silently, he kissed her, and it was very sweet. Perhaps they would soon be horribly dead, but at the moment they were wonderfully alive.

Herzig came as fast as his short legs could carry him. The flopear motioned to the body on the ground, and he pulled up by it and looked down. Danzar, he thought, staring into the wide features of the unconscious man. His club lay near his hand, but there was a bruise on his forehead.

"Herzig, do you think they have a way of deflecting the serpent eye?" Kaszar asked. Kaszar was bending over Danzar, his stubby fingers lifting his eyelids to reveal the whites.

Herzig snorted. "With a bruise like that? No, if they could resist the eye, they would have taken him with them. Look here in the dirt; tracks of two mortals."

"Then Danzar got careless?"

"Yes. Never underestimate a mortal. They are stupid, but some are less stupid than others."

"Like Rowforth?"

"Rowforth, their king of Hud, is too cruel to be entirely stupid. Not stupid but not wise, and not what mortals call good!"

Danzar groaned and looked out again through his eyes. "Ohhh," he said, his hand going to his bruise. "Two mortals. A man and a woman. I thought to club the woman dead, but he threw a stone to distract me and then swung without looking at me."

"He swung without looking?" This was very interesting. Suggestive of a power, if not actual magic.

"Yes, his shield. He swung around fast and the shield caught me so fast I didn't see it. And my knee—he grabbed my knee, so that I fell. I never expected such coordination when I thought him done for."

Herzig nodded. He didn't really like fighting mortals. They were so frail, for the most part, and few were worthy of joining in the cycle. It had been an act of kindness to put those two into the ancestor, just as it had been pity for a wretched creature that had driven Gerzah, Gerta's mother, to mate with one and bear it a child. But mortals by and large were untrustworthy, as that one had proved to be. Poor Gerzah had joined an ancestor early, and her daughter, Gerta, was without mate or child. That was what came ultimately of kindness to mortals. Still, as it had turned out, Gerta's mortal heritage enabled her to understand mortals better, and so she was good at helping them recover. That had been most useful in the case of the mortal John Knight.

Kaszar pointed to an opening in the rocks. It was an old ancestor tunnel rather than a natural opening. A pair of footprints were clearly in the dust in the tunnel's opening.

Herzig delivered himself of a long, painful sigh. Such stupidity just wasn't possible! But there it was—they had entered the domain of the ancestors. Deep in the ground the ancestors would find them and devour them, and then, just as food eventually became flesh, they would become part of the cycle.

"Should we go after them, Herzig?" The question, Herzig thought, was really quite rhetorical.

"Why? You know what will happen to them."

"But should it?" Kaszar's face flashed with anger. "These mortals, a part of our ancestors, joining in the cycle?"

"The cycle has seasons," Herzig replied. "We are none of us but ourselves, and yet making up ourselves are all our past ancestors. Mortals are the same way but don't realize it. On the next cycle it won't matter. Do you ever wake to remember tunneling, Kaszar? No, nor do I. The lives of ancient serpents are not a part of our daily existence."

"Uh," Kaszar said. He nodded, seemingly mollified. He reached out, grasping his leader's shoulder. His face smiled, widening his mouth. "I've heard it before, all my life, but I have to be reminded."

"We're none of us dirt, Kaszar, and all of us are dirt. Mortals as well as serpent people."

"Yes. That is true."

"What do you want to do about those mortals? Now that you have been reminded of what they are and what we are and of the endless cycle governing all?"

Kaszar took his hand off his leader's shoulder and walked to the tunnel's opening. He funneled his hands around his mouth and shouted in: "Mortals!

We are coming to get you, Mortals! Run! Hide! Run until your hearts burst!
We are coming, Mortals! We are coming!"

Herzig glanced at Danzar on the ground and found the big club-wielder
smiling broadly in satisfaction. He helped him to his feet. Then all three left
the tunnel to the ancestors and to the very temporary mortals therein.

Heeto watched from concealment in the rocks as the flopears left the vicinity of the tunnel. He had watched as Kian and Lonny ran into the tunnel to
hide, and he had seen the three flopears talking and now leaving. They
would be back, he thought, with help.

Should he go down there and try to get the two strange young people out
of the tunnel? No, he knew he hadn't time. It was sheer chance that he had
remained undiscovered as flopears had raced by his hiding place.

"Heeto!"

He turned to see Jac on his mare. Jac had ridden up behind him, knowing
where he was, coming to him by way of the cutoff route that few actually
knew about.

"Heeto, we're not winning," Jac said. "Too many flopears joined the
soldiers. We can't get John Knight from them. We can't slip into Serpent
Valley and get the weapon. We're beaten, Heeto, beaten!"

Heeto looked at the master with sorrow. He had been against the ambush all along, knowing as he did that flopears were too near and too
numerous and far too magical. Against the soldiers alone Jac and his men
and the magical gauntlets might have a chance, but once the flopears came,
the fight was done.

"Master, Kian and Lonny are in that tunnel. Three flopears have just
left."

"Then they are as good as dead," Jac said. His face showed his sorrow.
The lady, Heeto understood, had been special to him.

"Kian knocked a flopear down with his shield, Master. Then the two
others came. The two who did not see them, but I know they know they are
there."

"Good man, that Kian. Young, but good. It was the gauntlets that did it,
of course. They did the fighting and they struck the flopear."

"I know."

"The flopear was caught because he thought he was fighting a man. Had
he known he was fighting magic, it might have been different."

"That must be," Heeto agreed. "But the serpents—the gauntlets can't
overcome them! Not down in their own realm!"

"Come."

Reluctantly Heeto let his master take his hand and lift him up onto the
front of the horse. He had always found riding uncomfortable. More so this
way, half lying on the neck of the mare.

The horse walked at a slow pace back the way it had come. Soon they came out of the brush, and dead and dying men were everywhere. Some were like statues, frozen in place by some absent flopear's stare.

Jac called to Matt Biscuit, who was helping a man who had been wounded in the arm by an arrow. "Start rounding up the survivors! We're going back to the Barrens."

"We lost, didn't we?" Biscuit demanded. "All because we trusted that foreigner! Him and his magic gauntlets and his hero father and brother! I knew it was a mistake!"

"We had to try," Heeto's master said. "Now at least we know Rowforth *can* enlist flopear help. Knowing that, we know what we're up against and who we fight."

"We! How many do you think you have left? Maybe twenty men, and half of them wounded. You think you'll take over a kingdom with that?"

But the master simply kept riding, acting as if he saw no death and hadn't heard a word of Biscuit's.

17 /

EXITS

KIAN DREW LONNY BACK behind a rock outcropping and dared not peek out at the serpents. As near as he could tell, this was a gathering place where they sometimes shed their skins and where perhaps they mated. It could be that they had other things on their minds than feeding, so weren't alert for prey here. After all, how much thought did he himself have of food when he was guiltily kissing Lonny? So maybe the serpents were attuned to prey when on the surface, where living creatures ran, and to silver when tunneling below, and to shedding when in this cavern, and simply had a one-track-at-a-time mind-set. So they might smell the living intruders here but not be hungry, and would ignore them. If so, it was about as lucky a break for the two people as they could ever have hoped for!

His father had talked about an elephants' graveyard, where the beasts came to die, leaving their valuable ivory tusks. But how could there be a serpents' graveyard if the creatures were immortal? Yet how was it known that they were immortal? That could be just another story. Also, what about the little ones? They would have no business coming to a graveyard—and there should be no young in an immortal society.

The hissing and slithering convinced him at last that he had been correct the first time: serpents of all ages gathered here, shed their skins, and mated. Maybe there was something very sexy, in serpent terms, about shedding, so mating naturally followed. Or maybe not—but certainly the shedding occurred here, and that was enough to account for what he saw. After all, if they died here, there should be skeletons, and there were none.

Lonny was trembling within his embrace. Neither of them dared make a sound. Yet eventually one of those sliding silver bodies would come close and discover them. Then his theory about their safety would be tested—and he had little faith in it. After all, even if a serpent wasn't interested in hunting at the moment, it would hardly pass up a couple of succulent morsels that turned up right under its nose.

If they could only get away! But how?

Feeling behind him in the dark, Kian felt no wall. Maybe a passage was behind them? A way to escape?

Or another serpent tunnel, along which might be coming their doom?

He tugged Lonny in that direction, his gauntlets helping him. He had to trust the gauntlets; their guess was at least as good as his!

The serpents were clicking on rocks, hissing, tumbling. What a dialogue they must be having! Maybe this was an annual or a seasonal thing, during which they could renew acquaintances. Well, the more distraction for the serpents, the better.

There was some chance that the two of them could fade back unseen into this unknown darkness. But there was no telling what the tunnel held. If not an oncoming serpent, perhaps a sheer drop-off to some unfathomable depth. Or possibly a dead end.

If he was hesitant, the gauntlets were not. They tugged at him, pulled him, and he followed their lead. The smoothness of the tunnel floor meant there was little to trip them, and the gauntlets apparently sensed in a way he could not the turnings and bends. There was no doubt now: this was a serpent hole. But evidently the gauntlets believed it was unoccupied.

It was terribly black; there was no phosphorescence here. He felt as if he were walking into a wall of black velvet, almost feeling the physical touch of the darkness. Why was there no dim green glow here? Because the monstrous body of the traveling serpent wiped the passage clean?

Gradually the sounds behind them faded, first to a steady spluttering, then to a softer, muted roar. Finally it seemed hardly audible. But this only let the darkness close in even more tightly, as though it was now so thick that not even sound could penetrate it.

They had been walking for what his father would have called miles. Lonny was gradually developing a whimper that tore at him and added to his own discomfort. Even though they were trying to flee death, he didn't want her hurting.

Then, ahead: greenish radiance!

Was it the cavern they had left? Did this winding tunnel simply double back to where they had been? That did not make much sense to him, but his opinion didn't count; what counted was what made sense to the serpents. The persistent gauntlets seemed to slow, perhaps not quite certain, but they did not stop.

Gradually the radiance grew stronger as they emerged from the total darkness. Suddenly there was a big gap in the floor. It cut off the tunnel, and beyond it the wall was blank; the other side of this fault had slid along, taking the rest of the tunnel with it. That must be why there were no serpents here: even they did not care to navigate a discontinuity of this size! It would be easier to use an unspoiled tunnel. Or perhaps they had redrilled it, only to have the fault slide again. Maybe this was a low-silver region, so they didn't bother to maintain the tunnels. The radiance came from the crack.

They stopped. Kian had no idea how to proceed, and Lonny seemed as if she would not dare even try to think of an idea. Were the gauntlets in similar doubt?

He examined the cleft more carefully. This seemed to be the same type of moss that lined the cavern walls. The rent in the stone was a fracture that might have been caused by a quake, or by the movement of a gigantic body. It had sundered the serpent tunnel, cutting it off, making it useless. Probably there were a number of tunnels spoiled by such cracks. Odd that the moss grew so freely here, and not at all in the tunnel. Perhaps there was a better supply of nutrients in the air that passed through here. For there was air; he felt its slight, cool motion along the crevice.

By the glow he could see Lonny's frightened, drawn face. "Kian, what—"

"Shhh," he said. It was all he trusted himself to say. The serpents might hear, true, but mainly it was that he needed to appear positive, and anything he said would soon dispel that impression.

There might be a use for this luxuriant moss if it could be carried. The radiance was an inferior light source, but it did permit a limited vision, and it was far, far better than nothing! He drew out his sword from its scabbard, thinking to scrape off a handful.

"Kian," Lonny whispered. "Down there, way down, see it?"

He placed his cheek next to hers, an act which would have been delightful in any other circumstance, and perhaps even in this one, and strained to see what she saw. There was something! Way, way down the narrow cleft he could see a softer, lighter glow. It seemed to come from a series of fist-sized knobs.

"Glowrooms," Lonny whispered. "Flopears use them for lighting. They have them in their cottages and carry them like lamps."

Kian remembered seeing them in the cottage where his father was kept. He knew nothing about them except for what Lonny had said. "I'll get one," he said.

"Be careful!"

"I will. You wait." Worming himself down into the cleft, he banged his head and scraped his back.

Slowly, painfully on hands and knees and sometimes on his stomach, he made his way toward the lighter glow. There they were, clustered about another crack from which came more greenish glow.

Kian sucked in his breath as he saw that the crack opened almost directly below him. Creeping slowly so as to avoid a sudden pitch downward, he was able to see moss-lighted water far below. Another underground river, and this one not of his world. But was the other any different? Did this, too, lead to a Flaw that went not only through this entire world but through many? He had used Mouvar's machine to come to this frame, but it might be that the rivers crossed between frames, too. Mouvar might simply have found a mechanical and reliable way to do what the rivers and The Flaw did randomly. He shivered uncontrollably as the mental vision became increasingly real. What a vast and complex thing might this system be!

"Kian, can you get it?"

"Y-yes." Her voice brought him back to sanity of a sort. He dared not think about what could happen if rock and dirt gave way almost beneath his face. The crack here was big enough to fall through, he felt, and might for all he knew to the contrary dramatically open up. The fall past glowing walls to the river so far below would surely kill him, and that would leave lovely Lonny with no further help.

Cautiously he cut off the thick toadstools and impaled three of them on his sword blade. Equipped now with a light, he twisted, turned, bruised himself some more, and got his head pointed the right way.

"Kian, I can see you well now! And, Kian, that hole, it goes way down!"

"I know. There's a river below us. Way below us!"

"Oh, Kian!"

"Better not talk! We can't be certain there's not a serpent about." But after seeing that eerie river, he had a notion why there were no serpents here. They must have the same awe of the environs of The Flaw as he did! The crevice had opened the tunnel to the dark river below, and the serpents did not trust that. Smart serpents!

"Y-yes."

He reached the edge of the moss-coated crack and raised the sword with its light. The tunnel continued ahead of the crack, after its jog to the side, he saw now; they had merely to squeeze through and across.

"We have to try going on, Lonny. This tunnel has to come out somewhere." His sword tip scraped the serpent's old roof. "We have breathable air, at least."

He helped Lonny with a gauntlet. They got into the next section of the tunnel, and soon left the crack behind. He was getting tired, physically, and he wondered about Lonny. He looked at her in the toadstool light and marveled at how very dirty she had become. He must be the same way. It was a dirty business, this scrabbling around inside a serpent hole. He wondered if the serpent who had once used this had been the one they had been part of for a time. This tunnel was evidently very old, but so was the serpent.

Something did not smell bad. He had gotten so used to the all-pervading earth smells of an abandoned serpent tunnel that he had difficulty with this concept at first. He sniffed hard. Then it came to him what the smell was— and he realized at the same time that he was starving. Bread!

Here? How could that be? In the light of the toadstool he saw the hole of a smaller serpent on either side. Apparently the lesser monster had cut through this one at some later date. He wasn't sure whether serpents had proprietary rights to their individual tunnels, so that intersecting one was forbidden, but that surely would not apply to a deserted one. The baking smell was coming from the hole on his left.

Motioning Lonny to silence, he tiptoed to the cross tunnel and sniffed again. Definitely bread! Looking at Lonny, he realized that she recognized it as well.

"A bakery," she whispered. "Down there?"

"Or a cottage. Flopears use old tunnels for rooms or for cottages."

"I know. We were there together."

"I wonder how far down the hole goes. If I go down there, I should at least be able to get us some bread."

"Kian, remember what happened when they had us!"

"But now we have our bodies. Maybe they'd just turn us over to Rowforth."

"Rowforth! He's worse than a serpent!"

"Perhaps." He divested himself of his shield and scabbard and handed her the sword. "You stay here and hold the light. I want to see just where this goes. If we have to just walk away, well, maybe we can."

"Kian, I'm afraid!"

He hesitated a moment and then took off the gauntlets and handed them to her. "You wear these for a while. If I'm not right back, they may have to get you out."

She drew the gauntlets on over her hands. "Why, they—they fit perfectly! How—?"

"Magic. Just think what you want them to do and they'll do it for you. Sometimes they do more than you'd think to do yourself."

"Be careful, Kian."

"I'll try to be."

He started crawling on his hands and knees and soon the light had disappeared and there was total darkness. His knees were soon punishing him, and he wondered whether he'd get to the end and find only a small hole just big enough to let the smell through. Turning around would be impossible if he didn't come out in a room. Of course he could always back out, but the thought was not one that he cared to contemplate. Just moving forward was hard enough.

Suddenly he put his right hand out and brought it down on a point lower than he. The passage was sloping steeply downward. He put his left hand down by his right, and as he did a loud clatter came up and startled him, so that he forgot to brace himself. The next thing he knew, he was sliding, sprawled out at full length, trying desperately to stop. His face scraped and he tasted dust and the clatter got louder and a round light was below, and—

He dropped. There was a white room, and startled flopear faces.

He landed on something solid, and his face went into something soft that filled his nose and mouth before he had time to realize it. He was blind for the moment, his breath was knocked out, and his face, he realized, was down in a lump of dough.

"What's zat?" A flopear turned with a pan of bread just as Kian got dough out of his eyes. He saw four flopears, flour, and loaves of bread. He flung away bread dough that had clung to his face and breathed in the smell of a bakery. He looked around wildly, and then he saw the frying pan coming down at his head. There was no time to duck, no time to think about it.

He sank into oblivion.

When he next opened his eyes, painfully, it was to a familiar face. Gerta's.

Lonny tried to see into the hole, but the light would only reach for a couple of body lengths. The source of the baking was farther than Kian had thought, as she had feared. It seemed to her that he had been gone for a long time. Should she follow? No; if Kian was captured by flopears he'd need help. It seemed unlikely that she could get him help, but she'd have to try. He should have kept the gauntlets; then he'd be all right. But then she wouldn't have them, and without them she couldn't even think of going for help.

From far down the hole there came a clatter. There were crashing, banging, clanging sounds, pounding noises, and yelling. The voices of the flopears were surprisingly loud. "Get Gerta! Get Gerta! Get Gerta!"

They had him! She had feared they might catch him. She hadn't wanted him to go down there. But she was so hungry, and that smell of bread was so good! She should have made more of a protest; it was her fault.

But now that he was in the hands of the flopears, it was up to her. She would do whatever she could do. After all, he had saved her from the serpent when she had been set up as the sacrifice. She loved him, and even if he wasn't going to remain here, she wanted him safe.

"Gauntlets, help me find the way out!" she commanded. "Take me to the outdoors, Gauntlets!" She felt silly saying this, yet the gauntlets had seemed to pull Kian along in total darkness when it had been his wish simply to get away from the entrance. Now she wanted to get back to that entrance with all her heart, or at least to an exit. A *safe* exit! Even if she were captured by the flopears, that would be better than dying here. But she didn't want to get captured; she wanted to escape, and find help, and rescue Kian. Should she try to explain all that to the gauntlets?

The gauntlets tugged at her hands. She followed their direction, carrying the sword-light in her right hand, the shield in the left. The scabbard she had buckled around her waist, pushing it around to the side so it did not get between her legs. How did swordsmen manage these things? She was obviously not much of a warrior!

In a surprisingly short time, she found herself running, despite her fatigue, following the pull of the gauntlets. They seemed to lend strength to her entire body, though perhaps it was only their decisiveness that countered her confusion and made her seem stronger.

Great shadows danced and leaped on the walls, but they were shadows cast by her into the glowrooms' light. The gauntlets were more insistent than she had thought! She tried to make herself slow, knowing the danger of falling on a naked sword. Yet the gauntlets grew warmer, squeezing her hands and pulling her at a pace that terrified her. Kian had never told her of this, but then maybe he had not experienced it.

Her heart was pounding hard, painfully, and her breath was coming in gasps that felt as though they'd tear her lungs. She was no long-distance runner, she was only a poor soft girl! Yet the gauntlets would not let her rest. It was as if her life—or Kian's?—depended on her exerting herself to her limits.

Ahead shadows danced on the walls and the outrageous figure danced in a pool of wet. She tried to stop, at least to slow, but the gauntlets made her plunge on. Icy water grabbed at her ankles, splashed up on her legs, and even touched her face. She sped through the pool as though there could be no danger from it, her feet wanting to slow and the gauntlets pulling relentlessly. She stumbled, slipped—and it was as if the gauntlets gave a great yank on her hands and wrists, sending her head-down through the water and around a sudden bend. She negotiated the curve in the tunnel in a half-sprawling run that gave out at its limit and deposited her facedown on the rock. The sword with its glowrooms was stretched ahead at arm's length, and she did not touch the blade as the roof of the tunnel fell with a great and rumbling roar, dust belching up and over her, dirt and rock cascading just around the bend where she had been. She choked on the dust, gagged, closed her eyes, and felt dirt dropping on top of her. But in a moment the rumbling noise completed its course and the vibration came to a merciful halt.

Now she understood why the gauntlets had urged her on so mercilessly! Without them, she would have been killed!

She was buried, but not for long. The remarkable gloves let loose of the shield and sword and moved dirt away from her head and face. She sat up, fumbled for the glowing glowrooms and sword, and found these and the shield under the dirt.

She stood, shaking, gasping, her eyes tearing, bruised but alive. The broken glowrooms on the sword still gave forth their light, though the gauntlet quickly broke them all the way and put the seven separate pieces on the very tip of the sword. The tunnel behind was full, blocked solid with rock and dirt. Her grave—but for the gauntlets.

Kian, oh, Kian! she thought. *I must get help for you! I must!*

The gauntlet gently squeezed her hand and tugged. Now that the immediate danger was over, it would lead her at a more moderate rate.

She experienced a rush of feeling. *Thank you, Gauntlets!* she thought. *You are the best friends anyone ever had!*

Did the gauntlets give her hands a little squeeze in response? She couldn't be sure. But she felt so much better wearing them, now that she understood the manner in which they helped. She wondered what land they had come from, and whether there were many others of their kind, perhaps a whole society of gauntlets that used people only as mechanisms for moving around. When any two such people shook hands, it would be the gauntlets making contact with each other, not the people!

She smiled—and wondered again whether she felt their response, a trace quivering as of laughter. Maybe she was just imagining it, being alone and tired and frightened. But she lifted her right hand and kissed the back of the glove, just because.

The dust gradually settled as she walked. When she reached a spot where she could actually see the pieces of glowroom on the blade, she began to think it over. Up until this point she had visualized the entire tunnel collapsing. Yet she wasn't out of it yet and she didn't know if she ever would be. Her stomach growled its complaint of not being fed and her mouth protested its lack of moisture.

Bodies, she thought. *What a nuisance they are!* How much better not to have muscles that ached and bruises that hurt. Yet with only an astral form there had been limitations, too. They had been dependent on the life-style of the serpent, and doomed to eventual absorption. Still, there had been rare delight in the prospect of mergence.

Would she and Kian ever join their physical bodies in the way that they had started with their astral selves? She hoped so. After this, Kian had to see. Whatever the qualities of the girl he had known, she was certain that girl would not do more for him than Lonny herself would. Yet if he truly wanted that other . . .

It seemed that she had been walking forever. Her calves ached and her ankles pained. How long ago had it been since Kian had gone down that smaller tunnel? Since that tunnel had collapsed? It felt like many hours, even days. She hadn't eaten, and she was so tired—

The gauntlets abruptly tugged her to the side. She followed their lead without resistance—and in due course came to a chamber that ended in a blank wall. "What?"

But the gauntlets drew her down. She felt along the wall, and found a hole at the base. She put her face down to peer into it, bringing the sword point close—and got a whiff of bread! The odor was wafting through the hole!

One gauntlet reached into the hole. It caught hold of something, and carefully tugged it out. It was a loaf of flopear bread. This must be a hole in the wall behind a flopear kitchen or pantry! She had just raided their food!

She stood, carrying the loaf. Now the gauntlets led her to another dark region, where a stream of fresh water flowed. She was thirsty; she put her lips to it and drank deeply. Then she sat down and gnawed into the loaf. The gauntlets had become quiescent, letting her rest and eat, so she did not worry about being discovered. What relief to eat at last, and to be off her weary feet!

She finished the loaf. She ought to get going, but it was so tempting to rest just a little more. The gauntlets would surely have her rushing forth soon enough.

She lay on the rock and cradled her head with her arms, making herself as comfortable as she could. She wished Kian were with her now; she could snuggle into him, and his arm would be protectively around her, and if there was anything she could do to make him realize what she offered, she would summon the energy for that before sleeping. It would be so nice . . .

She woke. It seemed just a moment, but her bladder was so full that she must have slept for many hours! She got up, found a place, and did what she needed to. But her legs were stiff from all the walking and running, so she lay down again for a little more rest—and in a moment was deeply asleep again.

Two more loaves and several sleeps later, she was rested and feeling much better. The gauntlets must have given her several days to recover. But what about Kian?

Abruptly guilty, she resumed action. "Gauntlets," she said severely, "you shouldn't have let me sleep so much! I've got to help Kian! You know that!"

The gauntlets gave a little squeeze on her hands. They seemed apologetic. Maybe they had needed to rest, too, after their labors! "I'm sorry—I wasn't thinking of your needs," she said contritely. "But maybe now—"

Immediately the gauntlets tugged at her, leading her on, resuming the route they had been following before she ate and slept. They were back in action! She only hoped the delay had not been disastrous for Kian.

There was still a long way to go. She tired more rapidly than she had before; evidently her strength had been more depleted than she had realized. All too soon she was trudging again, but this time she did not plead for any rest.

There was another serpentine bend. No more water seepage, at least. Every time she went around one of these bends she wondered whether there'd be a serpent or a pool of water waiting. Or maybe, incredible thought, a small, irregular opening to the outside.

The gauntlets teased at her hands. *They* knew the answer! They knew where they were going, and she trusted that. They were quite comfortable now, not making her run, letting her walk at a natural if decreasing pace.

She did not want to go slow, but she was so tired! Kian needed her help; that was all that really kept her going.

She walked around the bend and almost fell. Here was a larger tunnel crossing this one as the much smaller tunnel had done. The gauntlets pulled her, not overly roughly or insistently, into the larger serpent tunnel on her left. It was just like a mess of interconnecting roads, she thought. This new tunnel appeared to be no more recently used than the other; this entire region seemed to have fallen into disuse by the serpents. She wondered whether she and Kian could have been through this one before. Probably not; there was too much dust here, and it really hadn't been that long. The serpent's body would certainly have wiped it clean if they had taken this particular route. Actually, she doubted that she had circled around to their starting place; her sense of direction was hopelessly confused, but it made more sense to her that the serpent tunnels should go more or less in lines than in circles. Why tunnel through rock just to return to your starting place? So this was most likely some distant place.

Ahead—could it be?—a round hole of daylight! Was she hallucinating?

And voices—the voices of people!

She stopped, though her gauntlets didn't direct a halt. Those could be flopears, and probably were! Maybe she should just wait until the voices went away?

The gauntlets tugged at her with a come-along-now urgency. She decided to trust them.

Shivering with a renewed fear despite her faith in the gauntlets, she took a step forward, then stopped. The glowrooms would be readily seen! Fearfully, yet with determination, she stripped them from the sword blade and tried to conceal their glow with handfuls of dust. When she had effectively buried them and was standing in the darkness, she turned her attention to the exit.

It was then that she saw the object lying on the floor of the tunnel. The incoming daylight made it shine. She blinked, but it remained. Unless Mouvar had been down in the tunnels, that was the weapon Heeto had left. This had to be that tunnel! Which meant that it could be Jac and Heeto outside! But if it turned out to be flopears—

She had to get that weapon. It could be the means of rescuing Kian and defeating Rowforth! She must not let it fall into the flopears' hands!

She crept closer, closer to the daylight. Now if she could just reach out and snatch it back into the dark—

A man appeared in the daylight. She waited, hoping to see who it was. She dared not approach, though he was right near the weapon. Maybe he wouldn't see it.

The man stooped down to pick up the weapon. As he did, a ray of sunlight lit up his thinnish, tall form, and then his face.

It was a man Lonny had never seen before.

18 /

LATE ARRIVAL

KELVIN BECAME GRADUALLY AWARE of the chamber's soft blue radiance, and the throbbing pain in his temple.

St. Helens! The man had treacherously struck him, and he had fallen into the transporter. Then what had happened? He strained to remember, but it wouldn't come.

He checked what was on him. His laser was gone, left where he had foolishly set it down. The gauntlets were also missing, left by the laser. St. Helens must have possession of both.

He still had his shield and sword, as befitted a hero of Rud. Much good either would do him without the gauntlets! Without the magic gloves to fight for him, he was simply no champion, just an ordinary (and not too bright, it seemed) person. St. Helens had played him for the fool he was.

As he looked around he could detect small differences in this almost identical chamber. This had to be in another world than the one of the golden-scaled dragons. This had to be the world where somewhere a king who looked like King Rufurt held his father and half brother in a dungeon. It could also be a world that held Rud's former queen, just in case she wasn't dead.

His first practical thought was that he should go back. Without his gauntlets and his laser he would be better off home. But if St. Helens anticipated this, and was waiting, did he want to confront him? He was too apt to be a sitting target, and this time he might lose his life as well as his weapons.

On the other hand, if St. Helens had taken the boat and the levitation belt and the weapons, wouldn't he be stuck there in the chamber? Better to give this new world a chance, whatever world it might be.

He rose, stiff, sore, and a little dizzy. There were footprints in the dust that had not been in the other chamber. They led across the chamber to a bluish curtain of light and, not quite to his astonishment, to a large and glowing E X I T sign. Through the curtain he could see a rock ledge. Kian had gone this way, and so must Kelvin.

He stepped through the curtain and found himself outside. Not in a subterranean cavern or by a dark river, but all the way outside. Looking back, he saw no sign of a blue, shimmering curtain of light. There was only the rock wall of a nearly vertical bluff.

A rope ladder led down from the cliff into tree branches. He approached the edge cautiously, feeling weak and dizzy enough to pitch over. The very notion of how high he was made him almost lose his balance and fall.

Have to get hold of myself, he thought. *Have to be the hero.* He knew that he was trying to build his own confidence. Like most do-it-himself chores, it was an amateurish job. After all, there had to be a solid basis to build on.

He turned back to examine his place of emergence. It looked like blank rock, but when he put his hand out, it passed through. In a moment he was back in the station, by the glowing exit sign. From outside, the curtain was an illusion of rock, perfectly concealing its nature.

But what if some native climbed the rope to this spot and blundered into the station? Well, that curtain would probably seem just like real rock to any person or creature who was not a roundear. Certainly there had been no such intrusion in a long time, if ever; the dust proved that.

He stepped out again and went to the ladder. Now he saw that the rope was not hemp, but some metallic material that would surely last millennia longer. It was of a grayish color, of a very fine weave, if that was the appropriate term, and anchored fast to a metal ring set firmly into the rock. That gave him the confidence to use it. Maybe the metal was another form of what the transporter was made of. All this had been Mouvar's doing, of course, or one of Mouvar's race.

He grabbed the ladder, got his feet on the rungs, and did not look down. This descent probably had not bothered Kian, but the very notion of such height made Kelvin's palms sweat—the worst thing they could do at the moment! He rubbed each hand against his shirt between rungs, so that it would be fresh and dry for the next hold. He adjusted his sword belt—some hero, he thought sardonically, letting the scabbard get between his legs!— and trembling at what he was doing, started down.

He had never liked heights. Just climbing that beenut tree in Franklin had been a task. As for scaling and descending cliffs—that was not in this hero's line. Sister Jon might have relished this, but she had the nature to be a hero. He felt a little sick to his stomach, and tried to keep his mind off that as he slowly descended for fear he would become a *lot* sick. He pictured himself trying to explain to some anonymous bystander: "Why did I vomit on the ladder? Well—" That made him feel ashamed, but not better.

The branches reached up like hands, though it was just the breeze that made them seem to clutch. At least he was getting down to that level! His feet found the limb at the end of the final rung and then he held the ladder, trying to look down through branches to the still-distant ground. His head throbbed and the dizziness returned. *Why did I vomit on the tree branches? Well—*

He swayed, hung on, and then lowered himself from one branch to a lower one. After that it was almost like the ladder, except that he could not see as much. He had kept his eyes rigidly fixed on the cliff before his nose, so that hardly made a difference. All he could think of as he descended was how much more confident he would be if he were wearing the gauntlets. His palms never sweated in those! Finally he reached the ground, and stood for a moment, weak with relief.

But he still had no clear route to travel. The huge tree was rooted at the edge of a tangled forest that left no leeway for intruders. He had to scramble just to make progress.

The river purled along beside him as he stumbled along, looking for a path. Where had Kian gone? He saw one faint trail, perhaps made by meer or some other ruminants. He directed his steps that way, wanting to sit down, feeling he might fall, but willing himself to be brave and durable. Here he would be just another roundear, he thought—just another contemptible misfit who happened to have the wrong ears.

Midday and the sound of splashing. Fish jumping in the river. Jon would have been interested, and have wanted to fish. He wished she were here, with her optimism, her unfailing courage, and her sling. But she had pointed ears, so could not get through the transporter—and anyway, would he want her to suffer dangers that frightened him? Her bravery was the very thing that too often got her in trouble.

Bring! Brrring! Brrrringgg! A sweet metallic chiming from a big oaple. Those three silver spirals he had seen through Heln's eyes on their astral trip. The tree was close enough, and his time was not pressed; he could afford an inspection.

He walked over and found the chimes within reach. They did appear to be snakeskins with scale patterns, but the material was of a light metal. Silver in thin belts resembling the skins shed by snakes. Whatever the meaning of this, silver was precious where he came from. If this land was similar, as it should be, silver would buy things such as a horse, food, shelter, and a way to the dungeon, discreetly managed.

Yet the silver was not his, nor did he know its purpose. He pondered the matter until his stomach growled, reminding him it needed feeding. One chime might not be missed, and besides, he might be able to replace it on the way home. So he made up his mind: he would borrow one of these.

He drew his sword, cut through the leather thong holding a chime, and caught the silver trinket as it fell.

Bring! Brringg! BRRRINNGG!

It was as if the two remaining chimes were angry. Well, his need was great, so he would just have to endure their anger. He compressed the spiral flat and found it held its new shape. He slipped it into a back pocket of his pantaloons and walked on.

For a moment or two he felt great. Doing something on his own initiative always had that effect. For what it was worth.

A mountain path was ahead—a real one, not a mere animal trail. It seemed similar to a path he and Jon had once trod in dragon country. No dragons here, he hoped; if there were, it was going to take more than one silent silver chime to save his unheroic self. He noticed that he was growing weaker; he had been growing weaker since taking the chime. Could there be some magic connected with the things? This was a great time to think about it! But it hardly made any sense. Maybe he was having trouble adjusting to this new frame, since he hadn't traveled this way before.

He was only a little way up the path when dizziness and weakness overwhelmed him. At the same time he heard a drumming: horses.

His knees buckled as his legs turned limp and folded. His head buzzed like a nest of hornees.

The horses came around the bend and he got a look at a rough-looking, ill-clad man on a horse, followed by at least two others similarly clad. The horse was black, and the man had black hair; something about the combination bothered him.

Mists of memory rolled through his foggy head. Jon, screaming as she was carried away on horseback. Himself, staggering back from a blow delivered by the horseman. The horseman had been clad all in black, had black hair, and rode a coal-black horse. There had been a scar on that man's face that was probably an old sword wound.

The face looking down at him had a smooth cheek. Otherwise it was the same: exactly the same. Kelvin struggled to deny the thought that came immediately to mind, but could not.

Jack! Cheeky Jack! Outlaw villain of the Sadlands!

Kian felt the bump on his head with his fingers and winced as Gerta reached out a finger covered with ointment and motioned his hand away. Kindly people, these flopears, sometimes. He obeyed with mixed feelings as she touched the bump and made a circling motion. A coolness spread out from her fingertips and the pain and the headache vanished, as had the delicious smells of the bakery.

He sat up, realizing fully for the first time that he was in bed. It was, he guessed, the same bed his father had occupied, and his nurse was now Kian's. It was the room where he had come in astral form.

"Gerta!" he gasped, determined to use her name. "Gerta!"

"You know my name?" She did not sound as astonished as he had expected her to. "Explain."

"I was here before. I am Kian Knight. You put me in a—a serpent."

"That was my cousin Herzig who put you in a serpent ancestor. You may wish you had remained."

"I come from another world, Gerta, as does my father. That's why I'm here. I came to take him home."

"John Knight, your father?"

"Yes. You cared for him, maybe saved his life."

Gerta stared full in his face. He froze as though from the paralyzing stare of a serpent. Not for nothing were they called the serpent people, he remembered.

"Now, Kian Knight, we see if you lie to Gerta. Maybe you think Gerta dumb. Maybe you think all serpent people ignorant."

He wanted to respond, to give her some reassurance, but could not. He was unable to move.

Her hands cupped his face. Her pupilless eyes stared into his and melted into a blue sea. He felt her *coming in,* and knew that he was more truly naked than he had ever been before, even when merging with Lonny in astral form.

She pulled back, startling him. He felt a weakness that had spread all through him. Her gaze had done that, and still he was paralyzed.

Gerta went to the door of the cottage. She called outside, out of his sight. "Get Herzig! Hurry!"

She came back to him and looked again into his eyes, her eyes again melting. His eyes seemed to have become wide-open windows into his brain. "Herzig will have to see this. As leader of our people, he must decide what to do about it."

Do about what? he wanted to ask. But there was no moving his lips. Those deep, deep blue orbs—not like a serpent's, but somehow as powerful. It might be what his father had called hypnosis, and he had said that serpents did it to birds. Was he then just like a bird to Gerta's people? Were all of them mere birds, King Rowforth included?

Herzig came in and walked to the bed, his body rolling in the manner of a flopear. This had once seemed almost comical to Kian; it hardly seemed so now. Herzig stood on his short legs, staring at him. "You must see, Herzig," Gerta said.

The cousin leader held Kian's face. His eyes were black, and they seemed to sizzle as something happened in them. Kian was reminded of the void of The Flaw.

Then Herzig frowned, puzzled, turning to Gerta. "It is as he said. They are from the other place. They have no magic themselves but they use what magic comes: the dragonberries, the gauntlets, the Mouvar weapon that stopped but did no harm."

"The weapon lies in an ancestor tunnel, dropped there by the short-legged one."

"Yes. This one does not know which tunnel."

"You seem hesitant, Herzig."

"I am. I wonder what Rowforth will want to do when he learns of the place from this one's father. Will he want to go there as a conqueror?"

"You know Rowforth better than I."

Herzig looked back at Kian. "Can serpent people know mortals? Even such mortals as this? Perhaps with the gaze we can."

"You would gaze into Rowforth's murky mind?"

"I must. Only then can I learn what he truly intends. Only then can I know if we must break the alliance."

"If he wants to conquer this world and others—"

"Then we must withdraw ourselves. Serpent people cannot long leave these mountains, let alone this world."

"Will Mouvar interfere, Cousin?"

"He will if Rowforth conquers. We must not go against Mouvar. His race has magic even stronger than ours, and unlike ours, his is not bound to one world in one frame."

"Do you think Rowforth can be overthrown by his people? Replaced, as you replaced Dunzig as our leader?"

"Not if we give him all our help. But maybe we do not have to. You and I will take Rowforth a present."

"Kian?"

"Yes. He will have understood little, but it is best that he now forget. He will be our present to Rowforth, and he will remember nothing of what has been said."

Herzig snapped his fingers under Kian's nose. Kian realized on the instant that much had been said. But exactly what had been said he could not recover.

19 /

DEAD

"K IAN'S BROTHER," THE BANDIT face said. The words were directed to a large man whom Kelvin could not see clearly. It was alarming how suddenly weak he had become; before midday he had thought himself recovering from his father-in-law's blow. These bandits, if that was what they were, knew Kian by name. Not only did they know Kian, but they knew who Kelvin was as well.

"You ill?" the bandit asked him. "You appear unwell."

"Hit with fist," Kelvin gasped. "Walked far in sun. Dizzy."

"Hmm, yes. I know the feeling. They call me Smoothy Jac. Your brother told us about you. You don't look much like a hero."

"I'm not. Not here." *Not really anywhere. It was all luck. Luck and maybe a bit of magic, and a lot of belief by others.*

"In your own world you are."

"I had to be."

"Maybe here also." Jac moved his hand to his brow, pushing back a sweep of long hair. Naked ears were revealed as round as Kelvin's own.

"You—you're a—a roundear!"

"Most people are, in this world. Kian told us that in your world it's pointed ears that are the norm."

"Yes." He had known as much, or at least suspected it. His surprise had been a foolish reflex. That scene in the dungeon he had witnessed through Heln's astral eyes: the ruler who appeared to be Rufurt, their own beloved king. The prisoner. Not only faces that might be familiar, on totally different people, but also round ears.

Jac straightened up. "We'll take you to our camp in the Barrens, Kelvin. We have medicine there, and you can rest and recover. Can you ride?"

"I—I can try." He struggled to stand, felt dizzy, and gave up the effort.

"Biscuit," Jac said. "Get him on a horse. Tie him on."

"Ain't you had enough of foreigners?" Biscuit asked. "His brother got most of us killed. I say we leave him here."

What was this? The man addressed as Biscuit was the near image of Morton Crumb. Curse the dizziness, it was making things more and more unclear.

"Matt," Jac said, touching his sword hilt, "you and I have never fought each other. You have accepted me as leader and have done what I said."

"That's not changed," Matt said. "Just want you to know how I feel." He dismounted, picked Kelvin up, and slung him across the saddle. Kelvin felt himself being tied by his arms and legs. Then the big man mounted behind him, barely whispering, "Damned foreigners."

"Ready, Matt?"

"Ready, Chief."

"Friend. Companion. Jac."

"Yes, Chief." Not surly or disobediently, but not humorously. It was clear who was in charge.

"Let's ride." If there was tension, it did not sound in the voice. Jac spoke just as he had spoken at first.

After an infinite number of jolts, Kelvin realized that he was seeing sand passing beneath his eyes and that he had been regularly lapsing in and out of consciousness. Sometime after that he felt himself lifted from the horse. The big man's voice rumbled near his ear: "He does look pretty bad. I wonder why. That little bruise on his face can't account for it."

"Maybe poison."

"Maybe. Hey, fellow, you eat or drink anything since you arrived here?"

Kelvin struggled to think. "Nothing at all." He labored to deny the possibility that he was about to die. "Maybe that's why I'm so weak."

"You bitten or stung anywhere?"

"No. Nothing like that."

"We'll have Heeto check him," Jac said. "He knows more medicine than the rest of us."

"Hopeless," Biscuit said. "Some savior! Worse than the other!"

"Easy, Biscuit. It's not his fault."

Kelvin felt himself carried. Through blurring eyesight he caught the sight of faces: bandits, every one, judging from appearances.

A tent flap brushed his face, and then there was the rough texture of a bearver hide under him. He concentrated on seeing, and what he saw was a small man with a wide mouth. The face was familiar, hideously familiar. He screamed.

"Hey, hey, son!" Jac's tone was kind. "It's just Heeto! He's a dwarf, not a flopear."

Flopear? What was that? Not Queeto, but Heeto? Not the fiendish apprentice sorcerer? In his mind he saw again the crimson drops of Jon's blood falling slowly, drop by drop. He experienced again the tingle in his hands as the gauntlets he had worn then fastened like the jaws of a wild beast on the evil dwarf's neck and crushed it. He had killed the sorcerer's apprentice, or the gauntlets had. Later the body had burned, along with the body of the old sorcerer, and the terrible workplace in the wing of the old palace. It seemed to have happened in another life—actually in another world.

"Ahh, ahh, ahh," he said, his tongue swollen, his vocal cords strained so hard they were refusing to work. He needed to say something, but he didn't know what. The dwarf was staring in his face, making soothing motions.

"I'm Heeto," it piped. "You're Kelvin, Kian's brother."

"Y-yes," Kelvin managed.

"There's something the matter with you. Maybe I can help."

"No! No, no, nooo." He didn't want this creature touching him. Not after what he and Jon had endured by that parallel-dwarf's hands.

"He is hysterical and delirious," Jac said. "Dying, without a doubt."

"Yes," Heeto said. There was sadness in the voice, as though Kelvin's death meant something to him.

"Where's Kian?" Kelvin managed. It came out a croak. "Where's my brother?"

"He's dead," Biscuit said. "Swallowed by a serpent."

"We can't know that for certain," Jac said. "What do you think, Heeto? What's killing him?"

Kian, dead? Himself, dying? It couldn't be, it couldn't be!

"What hurts most, Kelvin? Tell us."

What hurt most? The something digging into his butt on the left side. The silver chime he had compressed into a spring, now trying to resume its former spiral.

"Ohh, ohh," he said, his voice loosened by the sudden pain. "Back pocket. Pantaloons."

"Let's see." Biscuit's big, rough hand lifted him and felt. "Something there, all right! I'll take it out and we'll have a look."

"Ohh," Kelvin groaned again. He felt as if the chime had grown a serpent mouth and sunk its fangs into him. Then he felt the fangs pulled away.

"Gods, look at this!" Biscuit exclaimed. He held the chime, releasing it so that it made its sound, as if celebrating its release. "Talk about your lack of sense! Dumb foreigner!"

"He didn't know," Jac said.

"Poor man," Heeto soothed, stroking Kelvin's forehead. "Poor man, not to beware of magic."

"He'll die with the sun," Biscuit said. "Like a snake's tail at sundown. When the sun goes, so does he."

"Poor, poor man," Heeto mourned. The dwarf made a whispering sound that had the quality of whimpering.

"I've heard of something," Jac said. "I don't know if it's true, but I've heard that if the chime is taken back to its tree and properly hung there before nightfall, the victim lives."

"Old wives' tale," Biscuit offered.

"But maybe true. It does make sense, because the point of a curse is to prevent molestation of the thing it guards. That's no good if people steal chimes and then throw them away or sell them when they get sick. You've heard the legend, Heeto?"

"No, Master. I've never heard of a chime being taken."

"Nor I. But it could be. Since it's our only hope, we'd better try it. Kelvin, where did you get this?" He touched the chime, and it sent out peals that went round and round inside his head.

"I—I—" Kelvin struggled to recall. "I found it in a big oaple. Three together. I took only one. Near the river, before the mountain."

"Hmm, three chimes together. Big oaple. Mountain. I know that place. It's too far."

"Maybe not, Master. Maybe if I ride your horse—"

"You, Heeto? Alone?"

"I'm light, Master. Your horse can carry me faster than anybody."

"But, Heeto, to get there before night you'd have to start now and ride hard all the way."

"I will, Master. And I'll rest and feed the horse before starting back."

"I guess you have to try. I guess we all do. But it may not save him even if you get there in time."

"As you say, Master, we all have to try."

Biscuit snorted. "Huh! If the idea is to save him so he can save Hud from King Rowforth, I say don't ride. Save yourself, Heeto. For something important that can work out."

"You're a skeptic, Matt. But come along and help me get him started. That light saddle you had the other day . . ."

Rolling his eyes toward the tent flap, Kelvin saw that all three had exited. He closed his eyes, alone. It was hot in the tent; globules of sweat formed on his forehead. There was nobody to wipe it off for him, and he no longer had the strength to do it himself. A fly buzzed noisily and lit on his nose. *Heln, Heln!* he thought. *Oh, Heln!*

By and by he heard a horse's hooves pounding sand as it raced by the tent. Then silence as he fought with himself not to sleep—because he feared there would be no waking.

The sun was right at the top of the mountain as Heeto rode Betts down the ridge. He had spotted the two spirals in the big oaple from above, the sun glancing from the twin spirals in bright flashes.

"Please hold back, Sun. Please!" Heeto said. He spoke aloud, not bothered by the thought that it was insane. His thighs hurt from the saddle's chafe and he sympathized with Betts as she wheezed and blew back foam from her lathered mouth. Such a long ride, such a great effort for them both, and almost certainly for naught.

Bring, Brinnng, BRRRRRIIIIINNNNNGG! the chimes sang, urging him on with their companion. But the sun was already hiding, a dark shadow creeping relentlessly down the mountain at his back. "Please let me save him! Please let me save us all," Heeto prayed. He did not think of what he might be praying to, he only prayed.

The young man from another world was a hero. His brother had said that Kelvin had saved his own land, so similar to Hud, and might save Hud as well. But the young man looked like a tall boy almost too slight to wield a sword. Yet he had come here just as his brother had, and if there was a way for him to live and to recover the Mouvar weapon—well, then all might not be in vain.

But first Kelvin had to be saved himself. He had to be saved by Heeto.

The sun was but a crescent at the top of the ridge, letting no more than a fingernail of light escape. The tree was almost shadowed, but stood where it caught the last of the rays. Urging Betts nearer with sharp jabs of his heels, Heeto continued to pray: "Sunlight stay! Sunlight stay!"

He stood up on the saddle, swaying, almost overbalancing, and grabbed the limb. Quickly with his free hand he wrapped the leather thong, tied it, and fell free of the limb and the horse.

Bring, Brinng, BRRRRRIIIINNNG!

Had he succeeded? Had he done right? Had he done anything?

Bring, Brinng, BRRRRRIIIINNNG!

The last glint of sunlight was gone.

20 /

PACT

K IAN WAS SURPRISED WHEN Gerta and Herzig returned to him as soon as he had eaten. Somehow he had thought they intended to keep him in this small room indefinitely. Possibly (and the thought squeezed his guts) they had a hungry serpent.

"Kian, do you wish to be with your father?" Herzig asked.

He nodded. Silly question.

"Then the three of us will leave immediately for Hud's capital. Do you feel you can walk?"

He did. Their food and medicine were wonderfully restorative. The days (this was a sheer guess, falling between hours and months) he had spent in the serpent tunnels were as if they had never been. But what of Lonny? Was she still wandering around with the glowrooms, or, worse still, in the dark?

"You look troubled, Kian," Gerta said.

"There's someone else," he confessed. "Someone who was with me underground."

Gerta and Herzig looked at each other. He wished he could read the significance in that exchange!

"I wouldn't fear for her," Herzig said. "She will survive."

"But—"

"A little magic, Mortal. Magic spells can protect anyone we choose from the ancestors."

"The ancestors. You mean the serpents?"

"That is what we call them among ourselves. We believe that our people descended from serpents, while yours descended from apes."

Kian was startled. It was almost like his father talking! He had conjectured on the different lines of descent for roundears and pointears. But he had also said that the two were closely linked because they could interbreed. When Kian, then very young, had asked what that meant, John Knight had laughed and said, "You're the proof of it, son!"

Kian doubted that there could have been any physical descent from serpent to manlike creature. But his experience as an astral presence in the serpent suggested that there was indeed some kind of compatibility between them. Could the early flopears have taken astral residence in the early serpents, and could the minds of the serpents have come to the bodies of the flopears? Then the present flopears would indeed have serpent ancestry on the astral level, and the serpents would have flopear ancestry. It made a certain sense, especially considering the serpentlike power of the flopears' gaze, and the way the serpents cooperated with the flopears.

"We will go, then," Gerta said. "Walking, as is our way."

Walking to the capital? That, Kian thought, was going to take days! But once there he would be reunited with his father. Then perhaps he could find out about his mother and what kind of alliance the king had with the flopears. He was ready, and he felt quite excited about the prospects.

At the end of the second day they had left the mountains and were paralleling the river. The big oaple with the three silver chimes Kian remembered was somehow a welcome sight. He listened to their music for as long as he could. It was as though the chimes welcomed their approach and then bade them an affectionate farewell.

"You remember being in a chime?" Gerta asked him, seeing his attention.

"Well," he said, "I remember everything until after I was part of a serpent, and then my memories are blurred."

"That is because serpents have simple minds. You were becoming part of the mind you were in."

"But that serpent was dead—or had been! We killed it with the spear! How could it have a mind?"

"It was not dead, only badly hurt. We tended to its body, and healed it to the extent we were able. Then we put your mind in it, and the other, and you revived its mind as a new spark revives an old fire."

"What would have happened to me and—and Lonny?"

"You would have been absorbed. Generations from now you might have been part of a new intelligent serpent, or you might not. We serpent people have much magic, but we do not know all there is to know about the life force. There are mysteries even our wisest members have not penetrated."

"When I was in astral form I was me," Kian mused. "As alive and conscious of being alive as I had ever been. Yet in the serpent—"

"In the serpent you were changing, becoming more like the body you inhabited—but not entirely. This is why we put you there: we knew you would enhance the serpent after it had lost so much of its own mind. Whether you would pull it up beyond its natural level we could not judge, but certainly you would help it."

"Yet I felt as if I had a body when I was astral, and in the serpent, too, in different form. Nothing that hurt or could move objects, but a body. When Lonny and I—" But he did not care to discuss that merging, though probably the flopears already knew.

"That we think is mainly illusion. You are accustomed to a body, so you think of yourself as having a body. But then our spirits simply return to the serpent ancestors voluntarily and are absorbed into them. Your spirits—who can say?"

"Not I," Kian confessed. He plodded on, conscious that his feet hurt, and musing on the nature of things.

The capital, when they arrived, was just as he remembered. So was the palace. He would feel right at home here. But Herzig was speaking to a servitor, and then two palace guards were escorting him away from the flopears and toward—he recognized this route!—toward the dungeon.

For a moment he fought hard not to panic. Then he forced himself to relax, thinking: *Wily serpents! They do after all have a pact with Rowforth. They didn't bring me here just for my own good. Rowforth is a bad man here; I was told as much.*

Their footsteps rang hollowly down the long, twisting stair. Dank, dusty dungeon smells assailed his nostrils. Oh, this was going to be fun! Just as it had been back home, only here it was he and his father, rather than his father and brother imprisoned.

Light coming down from a high barred window revealed the ugly cells. In the first cell, a battered and obviously injured Smith, one of Jac's crossbowmen he recognized but did not know very well. In the second cell was a tall, haggard man who looked at him with wide-eyed recognition.

"Father!"

"Kian!"

The guard unlocked the door and pushed him inside the cell and into his father's arms.

Herzig watched with Gerta, his misgivings rampant, as the soldiers took a dazed Kian to join his father. They stood on the palace grounds, their firm legs supporting them with customary indifference. Soon they'd be ushered into the palace itself and have their audience with King Rowforth. For his part, Herzig was not looking forward to it.

"Cousin Herzig, will they put them together?"

"Almost certainly, Gerta. So they can talk and a guard can spy on them and listen. So that father can be tortured before son or son before father."

"Are they really that cruel, Cousin?"

"Rowforth has been in the past. Dunzig should have known, but Dunzig was cruel himself. If the king knew all our mind abilities, he'd want us to get the information. Only Rowforth is so cruel that he would probably torture them anyway."

"I am glad we are not mortals," Gerta said.

The servitor from the palace was approaching, his manner solemn and purposeful, as befitted his position. He stopped, inclined his head in a short half bow, and said, "You may come. His Majesty will see you now."

They followed the man as he strode off. A couple of guards joined them, one on either side, and a couple more marched in back. Rowforth took no chances with guests. Getting him alone and probing into his murky mind was going to take planning and luck. True, guards could be treated with the serpent-gaze at any time, but it was necessary that Rowforth not suspect.

Herzig stole a look at his cousin. She was looking askance at the inferior sculptures, tapestries, and paintings the palace held. The lowest of the serpent people artisans could greatly improve on the best of mortal work, Herzig thought, eyeing a broken-armed statue as they passed.

The great audience room was empty except for Rowforth on his throne. They approached him slowly, inclined their heads as was the custom, and waited.

"Welcome, friend serpent people," Rowforth said. It was about as sincere a welcome as anyone ever got from his mouth. "I am pleased at your gift of the stranger mortal, and now bid you welcome to Hud's royal palace."

"Thank you, Your Highness," Herzig said. "We are honored to be here in your presence."

The king nodded to Gerta. "And this is your wife?"

"Cousin. She nursed both the stranger mortals and restored them to health." *So that they may be tortured by you,* Herzig thought, thoroughly disgusted by the fact.

"Ah." His Majesty seemed interested. "And can she perhaps reveal things that they have said?"

"Your Majesty," Gerta said, "I spoke to them only as needed. What you would be interested in—military secrets and affairs of state—was not discussed."

"Pity," Rowforth said. His eyes moved back to the leader, seemingly evaluating him as he once must have evaluated his predecessor, Dunzig. "I suspect we shall need to make plans. Errotax, our neighboring kingdom, is becoming quite vexing to me. I plan on taking over that throne, and I believe you might occupy it for me."

"I'm afraid, Your Majesty, that serpent people have no wish to govern mortals. That, Your Majesty, is your responsibility."

"Hmm, yes. But surely you will want something. Dunzig did."

"Dunzig and I were not directly related," Herzig replied. "Nor did we always bask in the same light. He wished power over mortals for himself and for the serpent people. His wish for power drove him to make the alliance. One mortal sacrifice a year, he decreed, given freely by Your Majesty. In return we would freeze with the serpent-stare any enemy who opposed you."

"You are bound by Dunzig's word?"

"I am bound," Herzig agreed.

"But now you do not wish to rule mortals?"

"I never have wished that, nor have most of the serpent people."

"You would have wealth?"

"We have wealth already." *More than you dream of, Mortal!*

"Then, aside from the sacrifice and the goods delivered to your valley, only friendship?"

"That is sufficient," Herzig said. Rowforth hardly looked pleased; he did not trust those who weren't greedy.

"I, ah, see. But perhaps in the future?"

"Possibly. But for now, only friendship."

"Good." Rowforth seemed appeased. "When you want something, you will ask?"

"Yes."

Rowforth nodded sagely, as only a monarch can. "Tomorrow we will talk further of my plans. For now, you and your lovely cousin enjoy the palace grounds, the fruits of its orchards, the shade of its trees. When you get ready to leave, I will bestow on you a scrumptiously outfitted carriage, horse, and driver."

"Thank you, Your Majesty, but my people prefer to use only their own legs. We allow ourselves to be carried but seldom, and then only for pressing reason."

"I, ah, see." The distrust had returned. "Whatever you wish during your stay, simply ask it of a servant. Any special foods, drinks, entertainments, anything at all that you desire. The dungeon where the stranger mortals are now will be locked and guarded, but if you wish you may tour."

"No need, Your Majesty. One dungeon is like another, and the fate of the mortals does not concern the serpent people." He felt unclean, speaking like this!

"Enjoy your stay, then." The monarch made a gesture, and the servant and soldiers escorted them from his presence.

That night Herzig slipped from his bed, dressed, and rapped lightly on the adjoining door. Gerta joined him in a moment, looking to his eyes as though she had never slept.

"Be ready with the serpent-stare," he whispered. Outsiders thought that the stare was merely a function of looking, but this was hardly the case; it required a singular effort of will, and was best if prepared for. "Even this late at night there may be servitors, even guards."

She nodded, and together they left their room and climbed the stairs. They were almost to the king's chambers when, by a shaft of moonlight coming through a window, they saw a tall woman approaching in a filmy white gown. The woman had red hair and green eyes, and neither of them had encountered her before. Yet there could be no doubt who she was: the queen.

Herzig debated the matter only briefly. Then he used his stare to intercept the queen. They could not afford to have her spying on them! It would be a simple matter to cause her to forget that she had seen them.

She froze. Then it occurred to him that the queen could be a source of useful information. Should he take the time and energy to read her? He hesitated but a moment; then, standing on tiptoe, he cupped her chin in his hands, tipped her head forward, and probed deep, deep into her glassy eyes.

It was a shock. He had gotten much more information than expected! He withdrew, shaken. He turned to his cousin, controlling himself as well as he could.

"We will not need to go on to the king's chambers," he said. "He is asleep there with another woman. He taunts his virtuous queen constantly with his infidelities and the evil he does. He is the most evil of all evil mortals. There is no need to awaken him, for I have found what he intends."

"He intends to conquer?"

"Everything. Even our valley. Every land that he and his armies can reach. The stars themselves he would conquer. Only death or displacement will cause him to stop conquering. And the queen has a father—a father we must now go to see."

"The queen—?"

"As good a mortal as the king is bad. She will remember nothing of our meeting. Nightly she prowls these hallways clutching her agony inside. Come." He motioned Gerta back into a doorway and shadow, then snapped his fingers. Immediately the queen stirred, walking on; her mind, he knew, was in a quandary as she contemplated again the evil of her husband.

They walked down the stairs, and then, via another passage, to another set of stairs. They climbed the stairs in the dark, opened a door, and were in the tower chamber of Zotanas, aged sorcerer. A high window let in only a little moonlight and starlight, but a serpent person's eyesight was such that it required little in the way of luminescence.

Herzig walked to the big bed where the old magician lay sleeping. Gently, very gently, he awakened the man.

Zotanas' eyes opened. He saw Herzig bending over him, or at least his form. Not floundering in his thoughts as a normal aged person would be expected to do, he simply said: "Flopear?"

"Correct, Zotanas."

"Why?" Reedy voice, questioning everything with a single word.

"Because you may be able to help. You want to free your daughter of her marriage and your land of its tyrant. I know, I have looked into your daughter's mind, though she and the king must never know of this. There are mortals in the kingdom of Hud who would battle the soldiery and free the land, but they will need help. We serpent people, wily as serpents all, would break our alliance with your king."

"Why?" Zotanas repeated.

"I am the ruler of our people. I know that following your king would mean disaster for us. In other worlds nearly identical with ours, our people did not long coexist with mortals. Only separately can our people survive and prosper."

"What would you have me do?" Zotanas asked. Evidently this news came as no special surprise to him.

"Be ready to help the strangers to this world who will try to help other mortals overthrow your king. We serpent people are bound by an unwise covenant to aid your king, but it is a covenant I wish to have broken."

"But if you give aid, the king wins. Mortals can't fight your kind."

"No, they cannot. But neither must serpent people fight mortals."

"I'm not certain I understand."

"Nor is that necessary. You have been dreaming, but you will think on what you dreamed. When the time comes, you will use your strength and your magic. For now, sleep."

Obediently Zotanas closed his eyes. His shallow chest heaved and he began snoring.

Silently Herzig and Gerta stole down the stairs and tiptoed softly to their own rooms and beds.

For three days Herzig and Gerta remained at the palace, nominally enjoying the hospitality of the king, but actually studying every aspect of his government. They were aware when the king and his trusted brutish guard went to the dungeon to threaten the prisoners John Knight and Kian Knight by torturing their wounded companion, but did not interfere, because that would have revealed both their knowledge and their sentiments. But Gerta was shocked and furious.

"They have a baby ancestor!" she exclaimed. "How did that happen?"

Herzig was similarly angry. "One of the king's men must have found it strayed from its nest, and trapped it in the bottle. To force it to feed on mortal brains—this is shameful abuse of an ancestor! But we must not interfere. The serpent will have to fend for itself. Perhaps when it escapes, we can intercept it and try to ameliorate the bad food before it becomes too negative."

"We must keep alert," she agreed. "What an outrage!"

But the little serpent was slow to emerge, and two days later it was time for them to depart, without having had the chance to help it. Depressed, they departed the grim palace.

On the walk back they were to pass a big oaple with three chimes. But as they approached it Herzig saw that there were but two. *Brung, Brung, Brung!* they sounded angrily, out of tune.

"A mortal has been here and taken a sacred skin," Herzig said to Gerta. "It is another outrage! Whoever that mortal is, he will surely die."

"Yes, Cousin. But if that mortal is one who should live? Perhaps a stranger from another world who would not know of the curse?" For her experiences with the two prior strangers remained fresh in her mind. She knew she was too much influenced by the mortal part of her heritage, but she could not help it. This missing chime—she knew it was no routine matter.

He saw that she had a premonition, so he followed it up. Each member of their species had slightly different abilities, and she was excellent at perceiving and controlling astral spirits, whether within their hosts or separated from them. The magic of the chimes related to this, for it was to the astral portion of a mortal that they fastened, when disturbed. "Uncaution brings death. It has always been so. It would be an insane universe were it otherwise. But perhaps it needn't be."

"How?" By which she meant that this particular case was different, and deserved his attention.

"I will think, project my thought as well as I can. The talisman must be returned by the thief before night."

"But if the thief is already too weak, too far away?" She definitely knew something!

"I will project as well as I can. With the ancestors' help it may be possible. We must conceal ourselves and wait."

"That is good."

He began thinking, projecting outward the tale that no mortal had heard from another mortal for longer than any had lived, with the single exception of Zotanas. The way to avoid dying at sundown was to replace the talisman. He sent the thought out, following the faint astral spoor left by the thief. Out across the rough country and into the Barrens, where only the bandits and the true patriots went. Out too far for a dying man to return to. But a thought could be directed at more than one fading life; it could be directed to anyone near. Herzig projected at the main silver thief who had come time after time to their valley, the leader of the mortals who had attacked Rowforth's men. For a long, long time he projected, but though he knew the thought was received, the bandit leader did not come. The minds of mortals were so frustratingly limited! Still he waited, knowing that leaders sometimes sent others to do their bidding.

As the sun was creeping down below the ridge and out of sight below the far horizon of the Barrens, a rider appeared on horseback. It was the small mortal who in stature resembled the serpent people.

They waited until the talisman had been returned and the small mortal was rubbing down the sweaty horse. Then, and only then, did Herzig stretch out his hand. From his fingers an energy bolt of astral matter traveled as swiftly as only such energy could.

BRING! BRING! BRING! sang the talismans. They were back in tune. The small mortal turned to look, his face surprised by the sound coming without being evoked by a breeze. His broad features broke into a smile, for this was a song sweeter than any heard before.

"Thank you," the mortal mouthed, his eyes on the talismans. "Thank you for helping us. For helping all of us."

Concealed by the shadow on the mountain, Herzig had to wonder what if anything the small mortal had sensed. But more important, why had Gerta attuned to this particular mortal, the absent one who had thieved the chime? She might not be sure herself, but surely it was important.

21 /

STRANGER COMING

HELN RODE CORRY'S HORSE out of the brush and waved at the Crumbs and Jon on the opposite side of the river. They were probably thinking of going for help, she thought, as her hands inside the magic gauntlets urged the horse down the bank and into the stream. But this was the fording place where Corry and Bemode had crossed the stream with her. They had trailed her this far, and her father must have gone on alone. Even Kelvin's sister wasn't in Aratex, a fact that rather surprised her.

Jon was, as Heln had known she would be, the first to greet her on the proper side of the border. "You all right, Heln?"

"Couldn't be better!" That was a considerable overstatement, but it would do in this circumstance. Certainly she could have been worse! Had Jon really thought to use that sling against soldiers? Would Lester and Mor have let her?

"I didn't know you could ride like that!" Jon exclaimed. "And those gauntlets, and that dress!"

"I'll tell you about it on the way to the capital."

"The capital? Why? What for? And where's your old man? Where's St. Helens?"

"That's why we're going to the capital. I'll tell you while we ride." And she did, as they rode back the way they had all come and then on the main road for the capital and Rud's new palace.

"You're certain he's a prisoner?" Lester asked when she had finished her narrative.

"He has to be. I'm worried about him. He was still unconscious. And that Melbah is such a terrible person!"

"Terrible, all right," Mor agreed. "Best thing to do with a witch is to burn her. Once they're burned up they don't come back."

"Yet these gauntlets made me leave him there—and his sword," Heln said, bemused. "They almost seemed to put words in my mouth, making me sound like a warrior-woman!"

Everyone laughed, thinking she was joking. Who could imagine her as a warrior! She had to admit it was ludicrous, especially garbed as she was. She had not told them about the way the men had watched her climb down the tree, but probably they had guessed. Yet as it had turned out, that ugly business had helped her gain the upper hand. The gauntlets really did seem to know what they were doing, and could be quite devious on occasion.

"Why didn't we just ride on in and get him?" Jon demanded. "We're Rud citizens! We might even have gotten there before they got him down from the tree."

"No," Heln said. "Not a chance. We weren't that far from the Aratex palace. I don't think our being Rud citizens would bother Melbah, though Phillip might be a different matter." And there was another detail she had avoided mentioning: exactly how the boy king had considered using her, aside from as a hostage.

"King Rufurt may not want to send soldiers!" Mor protested. "He's cautious about starting a war, and not just because of Melbah."

"Have we any choice?" Heln asked heatedly. "They kidnapped me and now they hold my father! Rud can't allow its citizens to be kidnapped and taken to Aratex and imprisoned! They made the mistake, not we!"

"But could we win against them?" Lester asked. "From what you said about Melbah—"

"Yes, Melbah is powerful!" Heln agreed. "But we've got something Aratex doesn't have: we've got Kelvin!" As soon as she said it, Heln had to wonder. "Where is he, anyway?"

"He's not back."

"But Father's back! And he had that flying belt and the gauntlets and Kelvin's laser!"

"WHOA!" Mor cried, pulling his horse to a halt and signaling the others to do the same. Rud's shining new palace was in sight, complete with observation tower and newly planted orchards, but this was not why he stopped. "Excuse me, lasses and son, but old Mor smells a rodent on the dinner table and he think's it's St. Helens!"

"What? What do you mean?" Heln demanded. She was really angry with herself, because as soon as Mor spoke she had thought the same thing.

"He came back, your husband didn't. He had the weapons Kelvin was going to use to rescue his father and his brother and possibly another person I'm not about to mention. That sound right to you?"

"No," Heln admitted. "But—but he must have had a reason." She hoped! What could it be?

"Who had a reason—St. Helens or your husband?"

Immediately Heln was reminded of how badly her father had wanted a war between Rud and Aratex. Could he—would he have harmed Kelvin?

Just how much did she know about him, anyway? He was brave and he could be charming and fascinating in a way that only a talkative adventurer could be, but he had been such a pain when visiting them. It was as though St. Helens had been struggling to make up for a first unfavorable impression. *Should they have trusted him?*

"Heln, you're losing your color!" Jon cried.

She did feel weak and dizzy. *I am not going to faint! I am not going to faint!* she thought.

"Grab her quick! She's going to fall!" That was Mor's voice.

Things were going gray. She felt herself sliding, and then, with no transition at all that she could detect, she was lying down and looking up into the face of a man she hadn't seen before. He was bearded, and it seemed to her that he was something in a thinking profession. Over his slight shoulder she saw Jon gazing anxiously at her, holding her gauntlets.

"Who—who are you?" Heln asked the beard.

"I'm Dr. Lunox Sterk, personal physician to His Royal Majesty King Rufurt of Rud. You shouldn't have ridden so far so hard, young lady. Not in your condition."

"What do you mean in my condition?" The way he spoke made her feel more than a little trace of alarm. She had not been wounded!

"You are with child."

She absorbed that, stifling a mixed cry of delight and protest. She had thought there might be a child, had hoped there would be, but now—now was hardly the time.

"I'll—I'll be all right. The baby, it wasn't hurt?"

"No, your baby should be fine. But that foolish dress and that collection of bruises on you indicate that you haven't been careful. You'll have to start eating right, and resting."

Resting? At this time? Incredible! "What I need," she said evenly, "is to swallow a couple of dragonberries."

The doctor looked horrified. Hastily she explained about the dragonberries' effect on her. "So you see," she concluded breathlessly, "I have to check on Kelvin! I have to know that he's all right!"

Dr. Sterk pulled at a pointed ear and cocked his head sideways; that made him look almost like a bearded bird. "I'm afraid, young lady, I can't allow that."

"*You* can't, but I can!" *Thank the Gods and my father I've learned of Female Liberation in time!*

"Heln," Jon said unexpectedly, "you'd better think about this. You know what a hero Kelvin is. Only roundears can follow him to where he is now, and that means either you or your father."

"Yes! Yes!" Heln agreed, suddenly reassured. "You're right, Jon, I *can* go *as I am,* without going astral. That's what I need to do! Oh, Jon, thank you! Thank you for telling me the way!"

"That's not what I mean at all!" Jon said. "Tell her, Doctor. Tell her she can't go into another world frame in either form!"

"Well said," the doctor agreed. "Young lady, if you'd keep your baby and want it born strong, you'll do what I say."

"But—but Kelvin—"

"Will have to take care of himself," Jon said. "He has before."

"But Father *left* him! He came back with the gauntlets only roundears can use, and the laser Kelvin had from his father and the war, and—and that belt!"

"We'll have to ask your father," Jon said, looking uncomfortable.

"Father! But he's in Aratex! Maybe in a dungeon!"

"Yes. Lester and Mor are taking steps. They're in audience with King Rufurt."

Heln sat up. On the instant she discovered she was lying in a big four-poster bed in a large bedroom with ornate statuary all around. They had brought her inside the palace!

"Jon, how long was I unconscious?"

"Hardly any time," Jon assured her. "Lester carried you right in the main entrance. I think the gauntlets kept up your strength until you got here, and then they did something to your nerves that made you faint. Heln, you *need* rest!"

"Piffle," Heln said.

"For the baby's sake." Jon looked over at the doctor, who nodded as though it was certainly true and obvious. Pregnant women should not gallop horses and run around interfering with affairs of state.

"Damn!" Heln said. It was an unladylike expression she felt justified in using as she had never felt justified before. Female Liberation at least permitted her that.

Someone knocked on the bedroom door. "Jon," Lester called.

"It's all right. Come in," Jon said.

Lester entered, looked at Heln in the bed, looked at the doctor, and looked at his wife. Evidently he had not received the news.

"With child," the doctor said, taking pity on him.

Lester's face cleared of momentary doubt and he clapped his hands and said, "Congratulations! Kelvin is going to be so happy!"

Heln permitted herself a frown. "Well, I'm not happy about it. Not now. I want to know about Kelvin and Kian and his father and my father in Aratex."

"Well, you certainly can't take any dragonberries now," Lester said. "They bring you too close to death—and what would they do to your child? Especially if your child happens to be a pointear, as it could be."

Heln hadn't thought of that. One of her parents and one of Kelvin's were pointears; it was certainly possible!

"So you can't go near those berries," he repeated. "Can she, Doctor?"

"No." Stern and positive.

"I'd take them for you if I could," Jon said. "But you roundears are the only ones who can take them. If I tried I'd get sick."

"You'd die," Dr. Sterk said. "Any normal point-eared person would. Apologies, Mrs. Hackleberry; it may be otherwise in other universes. All it means in ours is that here you roundears are in this way blessed."

"Blessed by Mouvar, I suspect," Lester said. "But even Heln gets weak after astro-trips. It takes a lot of energy from her."

"Then you won't do it, will you, Heln?"

Heln found herself glaring. But these were her friends, and they wanted to help her, not keep her from Kelvin. She knew that they were right.

"What was King Rufurt's answer?" Jon asked, turning to Les.

"He's sending a delegation to Aratex. My father and I are going along."

"I suppose that means I have to stay?"

"Right. You and Heln. You two hold the palace until we return with St. Helens."

"If, you mean," Jon said, and Heln saw her bite her tongue.

"Right again, Wifey Dear," Lester replied with gentle irony. "There may not be a fight, you know. We just may get to King Phillip without difficulty."

22 /

BORDER CROSSING

Mor and lester rode at the head of the column of hand-picked troops with General Broughtner. It had been determined that a show of force would be best. They were to cross the border, ride on to the capital, and demand St. Helens' return. Since all were properly outfitted in Rud uniforms and the armor and weaponry polished until it shone, they did indeed make a magnificent spectacle to impress the imagination of the boyish king.

"What do you think, Dad?" Lester asked into his father's war-shortened ear. He had pulled his horse up close so that they were almost touching as they rode. The lusty lyrics of "Horsemanure! Horsemanure!" the obscene cavalry song (whose title was actually a bit more direct and less polite than the official representation), were just fading.

"Gods, son," Mor said, sounding almost angered. "How do I know? If that Phillip has the brains of a crawling loustick, he'll keep Melbah on leash. He can't really want war with us. Besides, he can't know that Kelvin isn't along."

Yes, Kelvin, Lester thought. Everyone believed he could do anything now, and the farther one went from Rud, the more exaggerated the stories. Mythic heroes were neither ignored nor challenged with impunity! Phillip might be a boy, but he was a boy king. Melbah might run things, but Phillip had the official final word and had to be aware that his commands were those of a king.

"You think we'll just ride in with no fighting and then out again with St. Helens?"

"Out again, anyway, I'd think. But I don't think it's fighting we need worry about."

"You mean Melbah and magic," Les said.

"Of course."

"What are you two talking about?" General Broughtner inquired, jockeying his horse near. It always made Lester smile to think of him as a general, though indeed he was the best; before Rud's War of Liberation he had been Franklin's ne'er-do-well, drinking himself into a ruddy complexion and a daily stupor.

"Just speculating on Melbah," Lester said. There, he had said it, and now must follow his unsoldierly doubts.

"It's wise to plan," Broughtner said. "If Phillip lets her at us, we'll demand her head."

"That'll stop her?" Lester wasn't quite certain he was joking.

"Gods, yes. She's not that powerful. If she turns on her big blow, we'll just squat down and wait it out. None of us will be flying like St. Helens. I could have advised him against that! Magic is bad enough, but when you pretend to understand it and call it science, it's worse."

"It is untrustworthy?"

"Right! Look at all the trouble it caused at the Rud palace."

"We don't know it was John Knight's laser that caused that destruction. But it probably helped."

"I just hope he burned up Rud's former queen with it. Personally, I doubt that she or the consort she was using survived."

"Kelvin thinks she fled," Lester said, not telling all that he knew: if Broughtner hadn't heard of Kian's trip and Kelvin's following after, he needn't enlighten him.

"Kelvin could be wrong. Remember, I rode with him, and you and I were there when you were downed and he got himself captured. That almost cost us the war."

"Only because no one but his little sister thought we could win against magic! We did win, eventually, though it took John's lasers and Kelvin's gauntlets. It was both magic and science that won."

"And the prophecy. Don't forget the prophecy!"

"Yes, maybe that helped most of all." They were approaching the side road that led to the river and Aratex. The general held up his hand, and the column that had been formed of four riders abreast now formed itself into a column of twos. They rode on, the general ahead on his big white horse, Mor on his black horse behind him, and Lester on his roan at the side of his father. They approached the stream and started to ford it. Lester raised his eyes and looked at the sky; clear, with only a few soft clouds. There was no wind, no breeze rippling the low waters.

The war-horses' hooves made a monotonous splashing. Now and then a few drops of muddy water lit on Lester's face. A glob of mud hit him in the eye: he knuckled it out, and again looked at the sky. The sky appeared darker now. Clouds were scudding overhead, possibly propelled by magic. A ray of sunlight fell full on the flat top of Conjurer's Rock, looming like a dark sentinel beyond Deadman's Pass. Was old Melbah up there? Or had she turned herself into a eagawk or more likely a buzvul? He could imagine that one of the dark birds circling was her. With such power as she was reputed to command, could the boy king possibly control her? Would Phillip the Weak even have the will to try? One did not start anywhere on just a whim. A delegation from one kingdom to the next, even if it was composed of armed cavalry in full armor, would hardly justify their attack.

Wind howled suddenly. Whitecapped waves formed on the water ahead of them and beneath their horses' bellies. Huge drops of rain began spattering them. Lightning cracked ominously in the sky.

General Broughtner raised high the standard of Rud: a flag displaying a large appear fruit crossed with a corbean stalk on a field of alternating brown and green stripes. Such a symbol raised in such a way at the head of a column meant peace, or at least nonhostile intent. It was the plan that they be accepted as a diplomatic mission from one sovereign to another, from one kingdom to another. Later, if this mission failed, as well it might, they could decide just what the show had accomplished. Back in Rud, King Rufurt had already cautiously dispatched a mission to Throod to arrange for mercenaries in case of war.

The wind blew stronger, stronger, much stronger. Head lowered against the blast, half suffocating in the water splashing from above and below, Lester wondered why General Broughtner did not order them back. Was it because it would not look right? Was it because if they succumbed to a bluff, he and his troops and all of Rud would be disgraced? But supposing it wasn't a bluff? Suppose old Melbah meant to attack and finish them?

The wind calmed, though the water continued to rise. Overhead flew a large dark bird. Was it the witch? Melbah?

"Ack! Ack! Go back! Go back!" the bird screamed.

So much for any doubt! Lester looked at Broughtner, then urged his horse up by the general's. "We'd better—"

"NO!" Broughtner said. He had made up his mind. He was not to be bluffed and turned away.

Mor rode closer. "I wish your Jon were here to clunk the witch with a rock, Les."

"Don't say that, Father! Jon would be sure to try!"

The general turned his face. "Archers, shoot down that detestable bird!"

Instantly a dozen arrows snickered from a dozen quivers, bows were lifted, strings drawn, and the arrows loosed. In the meantime the bird was climbing, seeing their intent. "You'll be sorry," it squawked.

Then the arrows caught up with it: four above, three below, two to each side, and one into its dark body. Blood and black feathers flew as an arrowhead lanced through the creature's heart. The bird plummeted, falling farther downstream. The current took it for a way and then bobbed it under. Blood stained the water where it had been.

The men gave a cheer. Lester found he was cheering as well. Good old Broughtner, he'd done exactly right! Thus would end the witch and her hold on the boy king of Aratex: end it forever and restore the kingdom to what it should be, a near duplicate of Rud.

As abruptly as a thunderclap, the sky was dark. The rain renewed itself, and the river seemed to rise all by itself to above its banks and above normal flood level. A hideous cackling laughter filled the air.

Their horses were now swimming, battling for their lives against a torrential current that had abruptly grown deadly. Large tree branches were swirling in it, and lesser debris.

"Don't leave your horse!" Mor advised. "Don't try, or your armor will sink you like a stone!"

Lester tried to answer, but a huge wave of muddy water splashed in his face, nearly drowning him upright. He was all but torn from the saddle, but hung on. Other horses, other men, were washing downstream, some free of their mounts. The river was bigger and uglier than any Lester had ever seen in what he thought fleetingly might be his short life. Banks went by and leaves and now the debris of whole trees. His roan swam for her life, as other horses were doing. There was no thought of reaching the other shore now, only of escaping.

If there were time. If only there were still time. They had really fallen into the witch's trap!

St. Helens opened his eyes and found himself looking down from a height. His face was pressed up against a tree trunk, his belt holding him there. His gauntlets were not on his hands and his sword was missing. Down below, two men were chained to trees—soldiers of Aratex, one of whom he was certain he recognized. Where was Heln? If they had her—but maybe she had fallen.

"Hey, up there!" the man called Bemode cried. "You, St. Helens, you awake?"

"What's it to you, child abuser?" This man St. Helens did not like. He had made up his mind definitely about Aratex and its need for Kelvin-style revolution after seeing what this man considered fun and within the rights of soldiery. St. Helens had ridden up on him one day when he was entertaining himself and a couple of friends with the small, sloe-eyed daughter of a peasant. The father had been begging him to desist, but the man had only laughed. Until St. Helens and the sword gifted to him by the boy king had put a stop to it. Had St. Helens had his way that day, Phillip would have hanged Bemode or at least demoted him and thrown him in the dungeon after a whipping.

"What's it to me? I'll tell you what. When our friends get here, we're going to chop you down. Then, after we break your arms and legs so you can't fly, and kick in your teeth so you can't sass us back, we'll turn you over to old Melbah for some real fun. Meanwhile, my friend Corry and I will ride after that girl of yours. We'll let her ride all the way to the border and then we'll grab her and use her in a way she's never been used before, and if she still lives we'll bring her on back so you can watch us do it some more."

"So that smart girl went to the border, did she?" St. Helens remarked. "Thanks. That's all I wanted from you; now you can shut up before all that dirt in your mouth poisons you."

"Big mouth!" Corry said to Bemode.

St. Helens pushed the lever on the belt, pushed himself back from the trunk, and let himself drift slowly down. There, stuck in the ground, was his sword! Apparently Heln had been so confident that he would wake before the soldiers got help that she had left his weapon for him to pick up.

He lifted the sword, eyeing the abruptly silent men chained to the tree. It would be so easy to run them both through right now! But much as he was tempted, he could not do it; they were helpless, and it would be no more than murder.

Instead he sheathed the sword, touched the belt, elevated, and locked himself on flight. He stayed low to the ground so as not to attract Melbah's attention. If another whirlwind came, he'd land.

"Get him! Get him!" Bemode cried.

Arrows zipped by, but they had been loosed from too far back. He twisted his head enough to see the soldiers riding hard through the forest, and then he zigzagged between trunks, finding a meer path and following it. He should have killed those chained soldiers when he had the chance! Then they would not have been able to give the alarm before he got clear.

If he could stay out of Melbah's sight and not catch an arrow, if he could catch up with Heln and get her across the border, all might yet be saved. But he did regret the loss of the laser; with that he'd have had few problems. Had Heln taken the gauntlets? Little, fainting Heln? It seemed doubtful, and yet he knew she must have. The gauntlets would have given her the courage and skill, and that Female Liberation crap he had spouted might have helped. She was one fainthearted little lady, and even with a warrior sister-in-law she hardly seemed his daughter. But now, if he was right, she was on the way to getting herself rescued. And maybe, just possibly, to bring her old daddy reinforcements. That gesture with the sword—the gauntlets might have thought of that, to let him know.

The thought of what he had just considered struck him: the war he had wanted could now get under way. But without the laser, what could be done? Well, if he could get the gauntlets back, and if Kelvin somehow survived . . . but he wasn't certain he wanted to think about Kelvin.

Conjurer's Rock was looming up there to his right, far above the tree-tops, like a giant guardian for the old witch of Aratex. He'd bypass that and Deadman's Pass again and just hope Heln was far ahead. His wound hurt abominably, now that the immediate threat had eased, and his head ached from its collision with the tree. He might have a cracked rib or three, too.

But he looked on the bright side: he really hadn't lost much blood, thanks to Heln's tourniquet.

What he needed to do was get back, get healed, and then it would be St. Helens' wartime. He'd fix that old crone and he'd give young Phillip the long-delayed hiding of his life! Yes, sir, once St. Helens got into action the fight should be as good as won!

But what about the witch? Old Melbah could do a lot of damage with that wind of hers. What damage might she do with her other tricks?

He contemplated the situation as the ground slid on below. Grass, brush, rocks, meer, deese, squirbets, rabells, flowers, and weeds. Brown and green and gray. His head throbbed, but not nearly as much as his leg, and he wished he could make better time. Damn that crossbowman! If only the rest of him were as hard as his head!

Well, what about Melbah? He'd get her if he had to run her down. Sooner or later he'd catch up to her despite her tricks, and if he had the gauntlets on he'd grab her scrawny throat with them and they'd squeeze out her foul life the way another pair had strangled the dwarf for Kelvin. Yes, that's what he'd do eventually, just give him the chance!

Ahead the river flowed and sparkled through the trees. So peaceful, so pretty. For the sake of safety and in hope of spotting Heln, he'd have to stop. He aimed himself at a tall maysh tree and maneuvered himself carefully into its upper branches. Poised there, he could look down at the river from on high. There, starting from the opposite bank, were Rud cavalrymen. And at the head of the column, Kelvin's friends the Crumbs. There was no mistaking Mor on that big horse with that big girth. That was them all right, so Heln must have made it back.

Should he go out to meet them? No, he decided; that would mean a stop. If he stayed hidden and waited, the war would get started. Then he could come out, get a little medical help, get those gauntlets from Heln, and he'd be back on his way to victory. Yes, that was what he'd do.

Four very black buzvuls flew by his perch. One looked at him and seemed to wink. Funny, he didn't know they could do that! "Croak, croak," the bird said.

"No, *you* croak," St. Helens said, and almost lost his grip on the limb. The bird flew on by.

He watched the buzvul fly over the advancing party. It yelled something. Soldiers shot at it with arrows, and it was falling.

St. Helens mentally echoed the cheer given by the soldiers. One ugly bird down. Might it be Melbah!

But now something else was happening. The sky was in disorder. The clouds were gathering, the sky darkening. Big drops of rain were falling, and lightning flashed. Yet just a moment ago the sky had been clear!

"Damn!" St. Helens said, holding on to the limb for dear life. Could this be natural? No, it could not be natural! Nor could that bird have been!

Down below on the river, the soldiers were having problems. The river was rising with completely unnatural speed, making for unsteady going. Wind was lashing cold water and flinging it on the men.

Now the sky was darkening worse than it had before. Only momentarily did it clear. The rain was really coming, and the river rising yet more, and the wind whipping the tree, shaking it so hard that St. Helens thought his teeth must rattle.

Have to get down, he thought; *have to get down.* But there was no getting down with the levitation belt. With the wind blowing the way it was, he'd be smashed into one of the other trees. Melbah must be one of those birds, or have the eyes of one of them. He had heard that witches could do that—project their eyesight into the heads of birds and animals. He hadn't believed it before. Now he suspected that he had greatly underestimated the witch.

That first passing buzvul had been mocking him! The witch had seen him, and known he was about to be dashed down by the storm! The bird must have taunted the soldiers, too. They had gained nothing by shooting it down; in fact, they had allowed themselves to be distracted for precious seconds when they should have been scrambling quickly out of the water. The witch had tricked them all into deep trouble.

Now the tree shook so hard that it began to bend. Branches cracked off. Leaves sailed by. He hung on, unable even to see the river anymore, able to think only of himself and his predicament.

There was a roaring sound, not that of the wind. A roaring as of water. Of flood. He heard a horse neigh, a sound of pure horror. Men yelling, screaming. He began to fall.

He hit the button on the levitation belt just before he alighted. It cushioned his fall slightly and perhaps saved him from a broken back. Even so, the jolt was good and hard, and his wounded leg flared with pain.

He rolled over, gasping, choking, screaming inwardly from the agony. He hadn't broken anything, he was alive, but God, he'd landed with a smack!

It was calm now. The light was better. Looking below, he could see a river in flood and horses and men far downstream, struggling. Some mailed vests and other bits of armor seemed bright in the sun as the soldiers wearing them were tumbled over and over in the current.

Mor? he thought. *Lester?* Had they escaped? Was this pitiful handful of drowning men what was supposed to rescue Aratex?

"Curse you, old woman!" St. Helens screamed. Maybe she was around to hear!

"Yes?" a dark bird croaked. It had lighted on a branch over his head. It looked down at him with a scavenger's bright, merciless eye.

He got to his feet, staggering as the pain in his leg stabbed him. He wanted to grab that bird and choke the life out of it.

"Yes?" the bird asked again mockingly.

"Yes!" he said, throwing himself forward. Promptly his leg collapsed, the ground rose up, and try as he would, he could not protect his face.

"Come back, St. Helens," the bird advised as he spat out dirt. "Come back to the palace and your friend."

"Go to hell, witch!" he snapped.

The bird flapped its wings, issued a hoarse croak, and took off. It loosed a smelly dropping at him as it passed above him.

St. Helens was alone, looking out on a river and the destruction of his hopes. Far below, men struggled hard to save their lives.

Was it she? Or just her eyes and voice?

A chilling, cackling laughter sounded overhead. It went on and on while St. Helens lay on the ground and tried to think of something more sensible and productive than just cursing.

23 /

RECOVERY

K ELVIN OPENED HIS EYES and blinked. The interior of the bandit's tent had not changed, and the faces looking down at him were the same, with the exception of the dwarf's. Yet something *had* changed, and it took him a moment to figure it out: *he was no longer dying!*

"Well, Heeto made it," the bandit Jac said.

"He may still die," Biscuit said skeptically. It was almost as if he preferred that possibility.

"Look at those eyes. They're clear! He's about halfway recovered already. About all he's going to need to get his strength back are rest and food."

"The—dwarf?" Kelvin asked. He couldn't get out of his memory the way he had choked Heeto's counterpart to death. "I owe him my life?"

"You do unless you go ahead and die," Biscuit joked.

Kelvin considered that, not finding it funny. In his home frame, Heeto's counterpart in appearance had been the most evil being imaginable, but here in this frame Heeto had undergone hardship and risked danger to save a stranger's life. What remarkable differences in such similar-seeming folk!

True, Heeto had round ears, as did Kelvin, while the evil Queeto had had pointed ears like those of the evil sorcerer Zatanas; indeed, like all who were not from Earth or descended from Earth immigrants. Here everything was similar and yet twisted around.

"Better get some sleep, Kelvin," Jac advised. "You can thank Heeto when he gets back, and then when you're strong we'll make plans."

When I'm strong, Kelvin thought. *Have I ever been strong?* He drifted into a dream in which Queeto awakened him to show him the pale corpse of Jon drained of her last drop of blood. There was blood on the dwarf's lips—surely hers. The dwarf gestured, and Jon was replaced by Heln, fastened to the table as Jon had been. Zatanas bent over her, preparing to take her blood.

"NOOOO!" He sat up, his hands reaching for the dwarf's throat. The throat was there, and he fastened on it and squeezed, hard.

"Stop him!" Jac ordered, and Biscuit grabbed Kelvin's wrists. He was back in the tent, and the throat he was attacking was that of Heeto, his benefactor.

"I—I—" Kelvin said. The enormity of what he had been trying to do was a shock.

"You dreamed," Jac said. "You dreamed Heeto was someone else."

"Y-yes." Kelvin looked into Heeto's wide-mouthed face, saw the finger marks on his throat, and the tears that had started in the dwarf's soft eyes. He was overwhelmed. "I'm sorry, Heeto. I didn't mean—"

"I know."

Suddenly he had his hands on Heeto's shoulders and was pulling him near. His hands, almost of their own accord, reached around and patted the dwarf's hump. "Thank you, Heeto! Thank you for saving my life."

"It is a favor you may live to repay," Heeto said. "As your brother would repay."

"I'd like to try," Kelvin said, with no real idea of what he was saying. "You knew—know—Kian?"

"Yes," the dwarf said. "And with great good fortune he may still be alive. But it may take you to rescue him."

"That's why I'm here," Kelvin said. He stood up, astonished at how well and strong he felt, and looked down at his now foreshortened benefactor.

"We'll have to fill you in," Jac said. "About Kian and Lonny and the serpents, and—"

"Serpents? Did you say serpents?" Kelvin found himself shuddering. After his experience with what seemed to be a silver snake hide, he hadn't any desire to hear more of reptiles! But that might be what he most needed to learn about.

"We've got some big ones in our world, and they have silver scales on their hides. The flopears are an ancient people and wise, but once a year they make a sacrifice to what they feel are their living serpent ancestors, and—"

On and on, and at the end of Jac's explanation Kelvin felt he knew all that had happened to Kian since coming here. It sounded as though Kian and Lonny must have perished, but no one could be certain. Possibly they had been taken prisoner by the flopears. More likely they had been eaten by the monstrous serpents. But assuming the first, they might have been taken to Rowforth's palace. In fact—

Hastily he told Jac and the others about Heln's astral visit to this frame, and how they had found John Knight and Kian in what must be Hud's royal dungeon. There was the confirmation!

Biscuit swore. "That fiend! Putting a serpent in Smith's ear!"

"He was a good man," Heeto agreed. "A rough man, but good. No one deserves that treatment! Kelvin, you must help us free Hud from Rowforth!"

"I—I want to," Kelvin said. *But I'm not really a hero! I'm just a man who feels like a boy! The only thing that made me seem like a hero was the pair of magic gauntlets—and I don't have them now!*

"What's the matter, Kelvin? You look pale again." Jac looked really concerned, exactly the opposite of the way his unfeeling counterpart, Cheeky Jack, would be.

"I'm not sure that I can help. If I had the Mouvar weapon you had and that Heeto somehow used to rescue Kian's and Lonny's astral selves . . ."

"That's why we're so glad to see you now," Biscuit said with a grimace that belied his words. "You're going to recover the Mouvar weapon you had and show us what it is and how to use it to rescue our land."

Kelvin sighed. Now there was no help for it. They really thought he could do it, or wanted to believe that he could. He would just have to act as they wanted him to, and maybe, somewhere along the line, he'd find that he was able. It was a faintly comforting thought, and he tried recalling it frequently as the next few days passed, for what little it happened to be worth.

Then, one fine misty morning, they rode out: Kelvin, Jac, Biscuit, and Heeto. After crossing the Barrens they followed a road through mountain wilderness that reminded Kelvin of dragon country. That did not encourage him. Finally they reached the rim of one of two connected valleys.

"This is the one," Heeto said, pointing to the tunnel below them. "I dropped the Mouvar weapon after I triggered it. The shock was so great I never even thought of retrieving it until we were nearly back. And that tunnel way over to the far side of the valley is where Kian and Lonny entered."

Straining his eyes to see in the mist, Kelvin took the dwarf's word. But if he had been told correctly, and he felt certain he had been, they would face flopears or serpents down there. Was he really better off than he would have been facing golden dragons?

The mists thickened as they descended into the oblong valley, becoming what was very nearly rain. At least there would be no serpents sunning themselves today! But if they chose instead to let the rain wash the dirt off their scales . . .

Kelvin wanted to forget the Mouvar weapon and ride directly to the tunnel where sharp-eyed Heeto had last seen Kian and his friend (girl-friend?), but knew that would not be prudent. Once the Mouvar weapon was in his hands, he would feel a shade more capable.

While they were still trekking down, less than halfway to the valley's floor, a rumbling started. The vibrations seemed underground, and felt like a drumroll beneath their feet. Dust belched from three separate serpent tunnels to the left of their destination.

Kelvin swallowed and turned to Jac. "A serpent?"

Jac shrugged. This was evidently new to him.

"It could have been the Mouvar weapon," Biscuit remarked. "A serpent could have swallowed it, and the digestive acids destroyed the weapon and the serpent."

"I doubt it," Jac said, worried. "Let's wait for that dust to settle."

They waited, continuing their march. By the time it had settled, they were at the tunnel's mouth. There was no avoiding the matter of the weapon.

"I—I think I should go in alone," Kelvin said. He had decided on that far in advance. It was really only a gesture. If a human life had to be sacrificed, it should be his own life, on behalf of his rescuers. At least that might make him look like a hero!

"Suit yourself," Jac said.

"I'm agreeable," Biscuit remarked. Indeed, he looked quite agreeable, this time.

"The weapon should lie just beyond the entrance," Heeto said in his ear. The dwarf had stood up on his saddle and ridden up close in order to be at Kelvin's height.

Kelvin nodded, watching in wonder as Heeto resumed his saddle seat with a decided smack. The little man couldn't even use stirrups, he thought —at least not any made for an adult.

There was no stopping it now. Kelvin dismounted, handed the reins up to Heeto, and nerved himself to enter the tunnel of the serpent. By the size of the aperture, the reptile that used this hole must be big enough to swallow a war-horse!

The mist had vanished almost entirely during their short pause. The sun felt hot on his back. Did that mean that the serpents would be stirring momentarily? Delightful thought!

He stepped in. It was dark inside, but then his eyes adjusted. And there, lying just beyond the entrance, just as Heeto had said, was the Mouvar weapon. He could fetch it and get out of here with no trouble at all! What a relief!

He took another step, bent down, and picked it up. It hefted almost the same as the laser he had used to destroy so many golden dragons during Rud's war. Yet this weapon had been made by Mouvar's people, he knew, not by his father's people on Earth. That meant that this device was alien, and might not work in any familiar manner.

"Kelvin?"

He jumped. The voice had come from deeper inside the tunnel! But it was definitely human. "Huh?"

He saw her then as she stepped into the pool of incoming sunlight. She was covered with dirt and grime, and her hair was a tangled mess, and she looked hungry and tired—yet she was as pretty a girl as he could have imagined. But she looked like a girl he remembered hearing about in Rud.

He hoped that if Kian loved this one, she was as different from her counterpart as Heeto was from Queeto.

"Lonny?" he asked, remembering the name they had told him.

She rushed toward him, dropping a sword. Suddenly, somehow, to his amazement, she was in his arms. "Oh, Kelvin, Kelvin, how I hoped you would come!"

"Where is Kian?" He felt embarrassed holding her like this, because though she obviously needed comfort, she was such a lovely creature that anyone who saw them would be bound to misunderstand. What would Heln think?

"The flopears have him!"

She was wearing gauntlets that looked exactly like those Kian had taken from the Mouvar chamber. Magic gauntlets, he hoped! He touched the one on her right hand. "These are Kian's?"

"Yes." She withdrew from his embrace, to his relief, and slipped them off and handed them to him. "Yours now. Yours to use to rescue us. To rescue Kian."

And with these gauntlets he just might be able to do it! He could try to be the hero he was supposed to be! What a break!

He put down the weapon and drew on the gauntlets, saying nothing. The gloves felt right, adjusting immediately to his hands. But they tingled as soon as they were on.

That tingle meant danger. He had ignored that magical warning for the first and last time with St. Helens. He snatched up the weapon from the floor. He wondered as he did so whether he should instead have drawn his sword.

The ground rumbled. Outside, the horses whinnied and jumped and bucked with their riders. Kelvin whirled to look, Lonny clutching his elbow.

Very near, just outside the tunnel, a great silver head broke the ground. Huge serpent eyes bored at those who were out there, freezing them all: Jac, Heeto, Biscuit, and the four horses. All of them became as motionless as statues.

The stare penetrated past the group outside, and in to where Kelvin and Lonny stood. Something tingled in him and ran all the way from his brain stem down his spine.

This is it! he thought. *It's no wild story. I'm frozen! Just the way it happened to Kian!* But now the ones who had rescued Kian from the stare were frozen as well. Kelvin was helpless, and no help was possible. He could not shift his eyes to look at Lonny; he could not change any part of his position at all. What awful power in that serpent's gaze!

The silver body undulated and the great head passed under the high entrance. The stench was something he had never smelled before. Standing there, paralyzed, as helpless as he had ever been in his life, he was reminded of the dragons.

The serpent reared its head. Behind it, its body undulated and coiled in a way no home-frame serpent could. Then it was in striking position, and the head was directly in line with Kelvin's face. The serpent had bypassed the men and horses and come directly for him. Somehow it knew! It could swallow him whole, and that might be preferable to being cut up by those fangs.

The gigantic serpent mouth opened.

For the second time since coming to this frame, Kelvin tried to accept the knowledge that he was about to die.

24 /

DUNGEON DAZE

SMITH STIRRED ON THE straw, rolled over, groaned, and peered through the bars and into their adjoining cell. His face twisted with pain, and beads of sweat hung on his face. He lifted his filthy water jug from the even filthier floor and put it to his cracked lips. He rinsed his mouth and spat out the water he did not swallow. He fixed his yellow eyes on them, and a hint of recognition crossed his face.

"Kian? I thought I was alone. They catch you afterward? After the battle?"

"After the fight, yes." It was hardly a battle, Kian thought. He had been in battles, and the attack on his father's captors hardly qualified. "Lonny Burk and I ended up in Serpent Valley. She's still alive and free, I hope."

"Gutsy little girl. Make you a good wife. Ohh." He clutched his side where blood soaked his brownberry shirt.

Kian turned to his father. "Why separate cells? Why isn't he in with us?"

His father shrugged. Then he said what Kian had been waiting for. "Son, we've got a lot of catching up to do. You'll have to tell me everything right from the start. You came to this frame by a slightly different means than I did, didn't you? I blundered in on a raft. Went right into The Flaw on it, and then I was here."

"Mother?" Kian asked. He feared to know and yet he had to know.

His father's face looked strange, and he seemed to take the longest time with his answer. "She's gone, Kian. Lost from the raft. Drowned, almost certainly."

Kian hung his head and for the first time in years allowed himself to weep. Only after he felt partially recovered did he resume talking, and then there was no end to it. He went on and on, recalling every single detail of what he had witnessed and the adventures he had had. Now and then his father interrupted him, but only to ask questions. In the neighboring cell

Smith seemed to be listening intently, but then the man's eyes closed and he slept.

The big guardsman with the craggy face brought them a tray. He motioned them to the rear of the cell and then pushed it through a slot in the door. There was moldy bread and a jug of dirty water and some unappetizing cheese. Smith received the same fare.

"Can't he have his wounds treated?" Kian asked, indicating Smith.

The guard shrugged indifferently. "What's the point?"

Kian shuddered as the guard left. What an attitude!

But Smith was wiser than he. "They may use me to try to get your agreement to cooperate," he said. "Torture's a game for Rowforth, isn't it, Guard?"

The guard took his keys and the empty tray and went back up the stairs. He had made no attempt to answer Smith's question. Smith made an obscene gesture in the guard's direction and lay back down.

But Kian was shaken more than Smith seemed to be. What were they in for? What would he do, in the face of torture? He had never anticipated having to face this!

Zanaan, queen of Hud, climbed the winding stairs to her father's quarters. She had been thinking about the two prisoners. Something needed to be done, but she was uncertain what she could do.

The big crested door at the top of the stairs was closed, so she opened it. Zotanas was up, as he normally was with the first morning light, and feeding his bird. "Eat your seeds, Precious," he was saying to the dovgen, and the bird was cooing and rubbing its head against his hand.

"Ah, daughter, what brings you to my quarters so early in the day?"

"You call yourself a magician, Father—don't you know what brings me?" she teased him.

"As it seems I never cease explaining, my precognitive abilities are, if anything, negative. I know nothing about what is going to happen at any one time."

She sighed. "The prisoners, Father. I think we should help them."

"I agree, my child." Zotanas fed his bird another seed. "Unfortunately, there is little that can be done at this time."

"We could release them. Save them from my husband's torturing."

"We could, perhaps, but would that be wise?"

"You're the one with wisdom!" She was becoming annoyed with him, as often happened.

"Age. I have not wisdom but age, and a little of the art."

She glared, wanting his help but recognizing the signs. When his back was turned and he was clucking to the fat bird, she edged across the room to his collection of powders and elixirs that were positioned handily but seldom used. It was but a moment's work to fill a tiny vial with a greenish liquid from a retort. Often he had given her the liquid when her cares became too great and burdensome. But this time the substance was not to help her sleep. This time she had a far different purpose in mind.

Thus it was that a bit later in the day she paused outside the royal dungeon and offered the king's man there, one Sergeant Broughtmar, a refreshing sip of wine. She pretended to have imbibed freely herself, thus making her unusual action a bit plausible.

"Come on, Broughtmar, old sourpuss, have a little drinkee on your one and only queen."

"*On* her, Your Highness?" Broughtmar asked with a straight face.

"Oh, you men!" She dug him familiarly in the ribs as she thought one of her husband's trollops might have done. It was difficult indeed to act this way, but she considered it to be a necessary evil. "You know what I mean. Just a little drink to beat the heat."

"I assure Your Highness, I meant no disrespect." Because even the hint of disrespect could cause a head to be loosened from the shoulders.

"None taken. Drink?" She sloshed the bottle around, waving it just within his reach.

"Your Highness, I am not permitted to drink while I am on duty." He did not even look tempted; he looked distinctly nervous.

"Oh, I know that! But the king isn't permitted to bed other women, is he? Yet we know . . ." She shrugged, not caring to speak what all knew. "Besides, I order you to drink."

"You order me, Your Highness?" He was having trouble assimilating this.

"Yes."

"In that case, I have no choice." He leaned his heavy pike against the wall, took the bottle in both hands, and lifted it to his lips. She watched as his throat worked and blue liquid streaked from his lips and got on his uniform. When he handed the bottle back, there was definitely some gone.

"Sergeant Broughtmar, aren't you sleepy?"

"I am, Your Highness." For of course there was more than wine in the bottle.

"Then sit down, for goodness' sake! Take a load off. Lean against the wall here. I won't tell."

"Your Majesty, it is forbidden to—"

"I order you."

Abruptly he leaned against the wall and slid down until he was sitting on the floor by his pike. A moment elapsed while he did eye tricks, opening and closing and then rolling them, and finally rolling them up. He snored.

She set the bottle down beside him, took his key-ring, and tiptoed past him and down the dungeon stairs.

* * *

No sooner had the queen vanished in the dark of the stairs than Broughtmar lifted his head, spat, and looked about for the king. The king, as he had anticipated, was only a few steps away. When he came around the corner of the castle, His Majesty had his finger to his lips and was winking conspiratorially.

"Did she guess you were faking it, Sergeant?"

"No, Your Majesty."

"You did just what I said? You swallowed none of the wine?"

"None, Your Highness. I did just what you said. I hate wine."

"Good. I myself prefer Hud's bleer. But you did right, Sergeant. You always follow my orders to the letter. That's why you're so efficient both as a dungeon guard and as a torturer. Come, now, we'll follow very softly and see what she's about."

Together they tiptoed after the queen.

John found himself looking into Kian's face and wondering again how such an incredibly evil person could have borne him. Kian was everything he wished he was: even-tempered and thoughtful to a degree that positively shamed Kelvin and Jon. Of all people to share a dungeon cell with, his son had to be among the best.

Kian had now gotten through all his story and answered all his father's questions and was now starting to grieve for his mother. John wondered again if she was really dead—that beautiful, sensual creature who had bewitched him and reduced him to the depths. Thinking back now, he was convinced she had really enjoyed tormenting him. One by one, she had ordered the deaths of his men from Earth, not because they had done wrong but because they opposed her will. He remembered the way she had tossed back her red hair, smoldered his soul with her greenish stare, and said: "What, Dear Lover, you will not teach my loyal servants how to use the war toys of Earth? Then another roundear must die. And another tomorrow, and another the next day. Each and every day one must die, until there is only you left."

"What will you do then?" he had asked. "Will you kill me as well? Will you kill Kian, your own roundear baby son?"

Her eyes had grown if anything smokier, swirling greenly and catlike in their inner depths. "You wish to try me, Lover? To push my will that far?"

He did not, for he knew there was no bluffing her down. If he did not do her bidding, she might actually destroy all of them, himself and the infant Kian as well. After all, hadn't the sorceress Medea of Earthly lore brutally sacrificed her own children when the hero Jason left her? Queen Zoanna seemed to be cast from a similar mold.

"And so, Father," Kian was saying, startling him back to current awareness, "I really know now that I want to marry her. I hadn't realized it when it was what Mother wanted, but now, now that it can never be, I do. Mother was right all along. If I live to get back, I will marry her."

"If it is to be, it is to be," John said, wondering what he had missed. Charlain used to say that all the time, meaning it more literally than he did. Another saying of hers was "It's as true as prophecy." By that she meant that it was absolutely true, despite his considerable skepticism. After all, Charlain had married him, a ragged stranger, because of her confidence in prophecy. What a woman! Would he ever see her again? Would he ever hold her as he had so long ago? No, of course not, for she had remarried, believing him dead. Kelvin had told him that. It was as true as prophecy! Gods, how he wished for a prophecy that he would have her back!

"Father, do you think she's still alive?"

"Charlain?" Damn, why had he said that!

"My mother."

Again that Medea image! "You know it's unlikely, son. I was too weak to have helped her." If he would have helped her, he thought. Yet he had been bewitched by her, again, despite his break from her. He had tried to kill her, and had helped her escape instead, hating himself. "I'm sure I saw her drown. She was badly injured, hardly able to walk. She went in the water and bubbles came up and she never appeared again."

"She couldn't have swum away?"

"Not in that fast current." But it hadn't been that fast at that particular point. Yet if she had somehow gotten out, where could she have gone? No, it was most unlikely that she had done anything other than drown.

Better her than me, he thought. *Better her than me or you a thousand times over! Medea has to be dead!*

Kian nodded, his face solemn and wet with newly shed tears. "I guess you're right, Father. Only it's maddening, not knowing."

Yes, it was; how well John Knight knew! It was extremely frustrating. Now that he thought about it, he wondered: could she somehow have escaped? She had known about the river and the raft, as he had not; she had guided him there. He had come to kill her, and she had tried to kill him, yet somehow they had gone together to that underground river and set off. Could there have been some good in her, manifesting once the evil situation was destroyed? Could she have wanted to save him at the end? Or had she merely been using him to save herself, because she couldn't make it alone with her injury? Had she drowned—or had she known of some other route out, beneath the dark waters, and taken that, taking care to provide a witness to her "death" so that there would be no further search for her? In that case, could there be something yet to find, in that place that only he could locate precisely? Maybe, maybe . . . Oh, Lord!

Kian rose from the straw and looked toward the stairs. "Father, I think I hear someone coming."

Smith chose that moment to groan. He had rolled over suddenly, returning to what now passed for life. "If they torture me, don't agree to anything," he gasped. "I'm about to die anyway. They can't kill me more than once. Promise me you won't do anything Rowforth wants."

"I'll try," John said. But he was listening for the sound Kian had heard. It wasn't surprising that Kian now had the better hearing, but as always, it bothered him to remember that he had aged. What had he accomplished in his life, in his travels through the frames? Could the good outweigh the evil?

After a while he heard it: very faint footsteps on the stone steps. Light tread, cautious footsteps. Someone coming to rescue them? Who? Some of the bandit Jac's men? Perhaps Kelvin? Kelvin, his son by Charlain? No, how could Kelvin be here! Anyway, the tread was too light, almost childlike, or female. That made it baffling. No child or woman should be here!

He counted the steps. Three, four, five, six—how many had gone before? Now the person, whoever it might be, was at the very bottom of the stairs. It was dark there, even compared with the overall gloom of the dungeon, and he could not see.

Then the person stepped out into the single long ray of sunlight that was coming bravely down from high above them. The light from the barred window that was all the prisoners here ever saw of daylight. It was indeed a woman, in a gauzy night dress, finely formed. Almost like—

Her face turned toward him. Her hair was as red as the sheen of a fiery dragon. Her eyes were the color of feline magic.

"ZOANNA!" he cried, unable to restrain himself.

For to all appearances it was Zoanna. Zoanna, his lost illicit love and enemy, Rud's terrible, evil queen! Zoanna, the mother Kian mourned.

25 /

ROYAL PAIN

Yet how was it possible? Even if Zoanna had survived, how could she be here in this frame?

She tossed back a lock of red hair. Her ears were revealed: round, not pointed. So it was Zanaan, the queen of Hud, and not Zoanna resurrected from the river and death. Kian had been talking about Zoanna, and suddenly there was her face! But it was the face of her double, the local queen —who would be good instead of evil, if the usual inversion held.

She carried a set of keys. She was coming to free them! There was the proof of the inversion!

To look so much like the woman he had foolishly loved, and to be good instead of evil—there was a dream he had not before dreamed! He had tried in his mind to resurrect the evil Zoanna, knowing it was futile, because even if she lived, she was not the type of person he could respect or even tolerate. But a good version of that woman—that was a person he could love. Indeed, already in this instant—

She extended a key. But as she did so, two figures materialized behind her. "One moment, Your Highness," one said. It was the sergeant, the guardsman who had brought them their fare.

Zanaan jumped, startled. She turned slightly toward the stairs. She seemed stunned. The sergeant reached forward and took the ring of keys from her unresisting hand. There was no further chance for her to use them to free the prisoners. Even if she had thrown the keys into the cell, it would have been hopeless, for the guardsman was armed and strong and could have killed them all before they managed to open the gate.

"Your Highness, that was dumb," the guard said. It was hardly the tone or the words one should use on a queen.

But the graybeard behind him, in the blue-black robe, turned out to be the king himself, His Majesty King Rowforth of Hud. There was the authority behind the sergeant's insolence!

Now the queen's eyes blazed at the guard, as she realized how she had been tricked. They had known of her effort all along!

To John Knight, it was as though Queen Zoanna of Rud had been affronted. Lights seemed to explode in the greenish depths, and her mouth firmed. Did she resemble Zoanna in other ways? Only Zanaan's face was somehow softer than that of her double. Zoanna's complexion had been nearly white marble, while Zanaan's was that of very rich milk. The milk of human kindness? A foolish notion, yet perhaps true.

John looked at Kian to see whether he was seeing the difference. Kian was standing, staring, as if mesmerized. Yes, he appreciated the irony of this situation!

John looked back at the king. Rowforth certainly possessed Rufurt's big nose and tannish complexion. But this face was cruel in a way that Rufurt's had never been.

"So you sought to betray me," Rowforth said grimly.

"You talk to me of betrayal!" Zanaan snapped. "You, with strumpets in your bed every—"

The king struck the queen hard across the face. John winced, feeling as if the blow had struck his own face, and behind him Kian gasped. In the neighboring cell Smith emitted a groan, as though he too had felt that terrible hit.

The queen touched her right cheek. The king had struck carefully, calculatingly, John felt sure, with the back of his hand. A large gem on each finger of his hand had torn the lovely cheek, so that it dripped blood. The queen gave no other sign of the pain she must have felt.

"Yes, Zanaan, that was very dumb," the king said, echoing the insolence of the guard. "To think you could put something over on your lord and master. Was it your father who put you up to this?"

The queen did not speak.

"I should have you stripped and publicly whipped," he continued. "That would give the peasants something to enjoy! And your dear daddy I should have burned!"

The queen flipped drops of scarlet from her fingers, so that they lit on the front of Rowforth's robe. A single drop found his large nose. It was an oddly insulting gesture whose import was not lost on the king.

"You wish, then, to have me make good on my threats?"

"No." She was unrepentant, sad.

"I thought not." The king did not wipe away the single drop of his wife's blood. He turned to John and said: "You have had time to think over my proposition. What is it? Are we allies? Will you or this other one lead me to your crossing place?"

John had to think of what the king wanted: for them to agree to serve him and just incidentally show him how to cross frames. What mischief that would bring! "No, we won't," he said. "Never!" Actually, he hardly knew how he had crossed; the best he could do would be to lead the king to The Flaw, where the king might only get himself lost without return. But Kian had come here by design, using Mouvar's device, so it was best to keep the whole matter secret from the king.

"Never? That's a long time. Broughtmar, you may proceed with the demonstration."

Demonstration? For a moment John thought the king referred to his threat to strip the queen and have her whipped. But the guardsman went to the neighboring cell door, unlocking it. Then he was inside the cell, bending over Smith. The injured man groaned as the guard moved him, then spat carefully in Broughtmar's left eye.

"Last chance to reconsider," the king said. He spoke as if he didn't really care. In fact, as if he preferred to make the demonstration.

"You have my answer," John said. So it had already come to the test they had anticipated: the torture of their companion. He hated this, but knew he had to stand firm.

"Mine, too," Kian said.

The king signaled Broughtmar with a wave of his hand. The guard took a silver tube from under his shirt, held it close to Smith's face, and grinned.

Smith's sick eyes widened. "No! No, don't! Let me die clean, please! For the love of humanity, don't!"

"Very last chance, John," the king said. "Otherwise we demonstrate what will happen to your young companion, and you as well, if that should prove necessary."

"No!" the queen breathed, horrified.

What was so horrible about the vial? If it contained poison, then Smith's agony would soon be over. He felt the impulse to speak, even so, but knew that had to be overruled. If he could help Smith he would, but he would not sacrifice his adopted world for him. He would not ally himself with a king who might be as wicked as the queen of Rud had been. Nothing that could be done would ever force him to follow another Zoanna.

The portly king reached up and adjusted the silver crown on his head. "You two are wrong to defy me. Very wrong," he said with wicked satisfaction. "You have so much to lose. You'll see. Watch, now, what can happen to you."

At the king's gesture, Broughtmar pushed Smith's head down, twisted it sideways, and held the silver tube above Smith's left ear. He unstoppered it. Something silver oozed from the tube and flowed, undulating, into Smith's ear.

Smith's eyeballs rolled back until only the whites showed. He screamed.

The king formed a ghastly smile that was all the more horrible for being on King Rufurt's face. "Silver's not so nice, now, is it, Smith? Now that the little beastie's chewing in you?"

John Knight experienced a new and uglier chill. *Something alive had been put in Smith's ear!*

Smith shook from head to toe. His arms and legs spasmed. He screamed again and again while John shuddered.

"He's going to scream like that until his vocal cords quit," King Rowforth said. "Then for days and nights he'll feel that tickling, chewing sensation in his head. Into his brain, chew, chew, chew, tunnel, tunnel, tunnel. Not much pain, there in the brain. Just his mind. And he'll go mad."

"You put a—" John was too overcome by the horror to speak.

"Broughtmar put a tiny serpent in this man's ear. It's just like the big serpents but hasn't lived yet for centuries. It'll eat its way out, all the way out, and emerge from the farther ear. By then you'll be half mad yourselves, just watching your friend. Before then you'd better declare yourself my ally. We can begin making plans and you can move upstairs and be my honored guests. You will have anything you desire. Indeed, my lovely wife here will be directed to cater to your every whim, of any nature. That should be easy for her, since she evidently likes you."

John felt horror of another nature. Did the king know of his affair with the king's wife in the other frame? Did he know how phenomenally appealing John found the queen? That Kian saw in her a better edition of his lost mother? Surely he suspected—and had abused the queen in John's presence deliberately. The queen herself was hostage to John's cooperation!

"As a symbol of your appreciation, you will lead me to your crossing place from the other world," Rowforth continued blithely. "I could ask the flopears, my allies, but they are conservative and reticent on ancient matters."

"I am, too," John said, though fundamentally shaken. How could he even think of unleashing this monster in another frame—any frame? He could see the king going back the way Kian had come, leading an army. He could see King Rufurt of Rud and Kelvin and the Crumbs fighting for their freedom all over again. He could see terrible carnage and misery for those he had tried to help.

No, he would not slacken! No way, ever, would he tell that monster anything. No way, ever, would he allow him to win!

But if the silver serpent was next to go into Kian's ear? He looked at Kian's shocked expression and felt himself shake. The king didn't know that Kian was the only one who truly knew the route between the frames. If he killed Kian, Rowforth would throw away his chance to cross the frames. But could that irony make up for the horror of Kian's demise? Could he, John Knight, stand by and allow that to happen? Or would the mere threat cause him to capitulate? He dreaded the answer.

"Suit yourself," Rowforth said. He faced the queen. "Move it, bitch. Your turn will come."

Yet again, John felt a surge of horror. What did the king mean by that?

That there would be a serpent in the queen's ear, too, if John did not cooperate? He was very much afraid that this was exactly what the king meant.

Smith's screams continued without pause as Rowforth and Broughtmar ascended the stairs. Ahead of them walked the weeping, now hideously pale queen. Kian stood as if dead and cold on his feet, staring blankly.

The screaming went on and on and on.

Gods, as Mor Crumb would say in his own frame, would it ever truly end?

"Cousin Gerta," Herzig said to his companion. Both were in astral form at the moment. "It would seem that our appointed hero has found the weapon."

"Yes, Cousin. But can he use it?"

"He must, Cousin, if disaster is not to strike and the frames to fall."

"Disaster now?" Gerta referred to Kelvin, who was holding the weapon but remained frozen by the stare. The ancestor, unfrozen and unreasoning, was about to incorporate the man's substance. Nearby the girl was also motionless, as were the two mortals outside.

"Observe the gauntlets, Cousin Gerta. They helped make this mortal a hero in his home frame." He paused, then addressed the gloves:

Gauntlets, danger threatens! Use the weapon!

Who speaks? Not a mortal?

Correct. An immortal.

What weapon? The sword?

The weapon you hold. A Mouvar weapon.

The gauntlets were confused. *Mouvar programmed us to fight with swords and spears. This is of a different order. We can enable the mortal to aim it as he would a bow; the principle is the same. But we cannot use it ourselves. We only guide our wearer; that is our limit.*

Yes, the weapon is of a different order. But you can still act. You can stimulate the nerve of the finger resting on its trigger mechanism, causing that finger to convulse. Act now, Gauntlets, to save your host.

Still there was doubt. *We cannot fight immortals. We cannot fight magic. We cannot take the initiative in such a case. It is not in our program. We must have the directive of a mortal.*

The Mouvar weapon will fight magic. The Mouvar weapon will resist even immortals. You need not take the initiative; you need do only what you know the mortal must do to survive. To fail in this is to betray the trust Mouvar put in you.

Click-click, clack-clack. The gauntlets struggled with the concept. *We cannot. We cannot. We cannot.*

You must, you must, you must! Herzig directed them. *Now and henceforth. You must reinterpret your program to enable you to do this.*

A drop of digestive juice fell from the ancestor's open jaw as the reptilian head was poised ready for engulfing. The drop lit on a gauntlet, and the gauntlet screamed as its substance burned. The cousins shook from the force of the scream that permeated all the ether around them. He could almost feel the agony, but Herzig ignored the pain in his desperation.

You must, Gauntlets! You must! The destinies of not one but two frames depend on it!

The corrosive fluid ate through the gauntlet, adding urgency to the decision. The gauntlets had to decide: suffer destruction, or do what the immortal directed. To revise their program in a way they had never done before.

Click-click, clack-clack . . .

26 /

HERO'S PROGRESS

S NAP!
Bright light filled the tunnel as Kelvin's gauntlet activated the weapon. WHOOMPTH! echoed and reechoed inside his head. His hand was hurting, and he was screaming, and above his face and head was an enormous open reptilian maw bordered by gaping reptilian jaws. The weapon was almost in the monster's throat, and the sword-length fangs were dripping acid drops all the way around.

He wasn't certain how it happened, but he was out from under the frozen reptile, and feeling the terrible burns on his arms and legs and shoulders where corrosive drops had hit. The girl, standing so close in the now darkened tunnel, was screaming, while outside in the sickly morning sunlight there was renewed activity. Heeto and Jac and Biscuit and the horses danced and jockeyed and moved with the unfreezing that coincided with the abrupt immobility of the serpent. *It* was frozen now, while *they* were free.

He grabbed Lonny's hand and pulled her outside. There, still screaming inside himself and starting to echo those screams with his voice, he pointed at his acid burns with the weapon, and waved at Jac's prancing horse.

Jac was down in a moment, applying the ointment that immediately soothed the skin and ameliorated the burn. There were four burns on his body, and the burn on the gauntlet, but all of them ceased to hurt the instant the balm was applied, and commenced rapid healing.

"Thank you, Gods, and thank you, Jac!" What a relief, what a relief! No longer to burn!

"We've got to get away," Jac said. "Before you-know-what happens."

"Right!"

In a moment he was in a saddle, the weapon stuck under his belt, Lonny in front of him on the war-horse. Then they were riding back the way they had come, out of Serpent Valley and its horror.

"You did it!" Biscuit exclaimed as they were clear of the tunnels. "You've gotten the weapon and you've rescued Lonny Burk! Now we can challenge Rowforth properly, and—"

"I didn't—" Kelvin started. But what could he say? That he had been frozen like the rest of them, but that the gauntlet had seemingly made his finger pull the trigger? That hardly made sense; the gauntlets had never done anything of themselves, they had only implemented the desire of their wearer. Sometimes they had been pretty devious about it, but that was what they had done.

Well, he had wanted to stop the serpent! So maybe he had done it. Maybe he had been physically frozen, but had willed the gauntlets to pull the trigger. Yes, that must have been it. So maybe he was a bit of the hero others thought him to be. He only wished he could be more certain of it.

"We'll need an army," Jac said. "Don't think that with one great hero and one great weapon—whatever it is—we've got the means! No matter how good Kelvin is, and I admit he's tremendous, we still need an army to pit against Rowforth's."

"You can have one." Lonny spoke up, surprising all of them. "Kian and I found treasure back there. With enough silver scales to buy all the weapons and men it will take! The only problems are that I'm not sure I can find the place again, and it's guarded by serpents in such numbers that there's no chance of getting in there, getting the treasure, and getting out alive."

"You did it," Kelvin said. "You got in there and out. You and Kian."

"Yes," she said. "But not with treasure. The silver skins were all over, piled head-deep. But the serpents—no way can I ever return there!"

"Not even to save Kian's life?" Kelvin asked.

She swallowed, looking into his face. "For that. Only for that."

The next day was spent in going over every detail of the time Lonny and Kian had spent in the tunnels. Lonny's memory wasn't perfect, but she recalled all the main events and the order in which they had occurred. Then they talked of going back, entering the tunnel she and Kian had found, and making their way to the treasure. With the treasure they could buy an army that was composed of hired soldiers. Here there was Shrood, a kingdom that dealt in mercenaries. All that was needed to buy an army was wealth: exactly as was the case back in the other frame.

"But the weakest part of all this is the weapon," Kelvin said amidst plans. "We don't know that it will always work. I have no idea what it does or how."

"You understand magic, Kelvin?" Biscuit growled.

Kelvin shook his head in negation.

"But you use it, right?"

"I—guess."

"Well, just say it's magic. Somehow it stops the critters. That's enough, isn't it?"

"I—I suppose." But would it *always* work? Would he always have time to point the weapon and activate it? He still could not remember pulling the trigger, or telling the gauntlets to. He must have done it, but . . .

"Your gauntlets know what to do," Lonny said. She seemed to be one of the nicest girls he had encountered, next to his wife, but like his sister, Jon, she was always speaking up.

"That seems true enough," Jac said, and Biscuit and Heeto both nodded enthusiastically.

"If only Kian had brought more dragonberries," Kelvin moaned.

"Well, he didn't," Biscuit said gruffly. "And I never heard of them before he appeared. I don't think they grow in our world at all."

"Maybe not," Kelvin said. "If you don't have dragons." What a crazy mixed-up world, that didn't have dragons!

"Who cares about dragons?" Biscuit demanded impatiently. "Or their berries? It's serpents we have to deal with!"

"Exactly," Kelvin said. "The dragonberries enable us to spy out the terrain before we go there. Without them—well, if we go in and let the gauntlets lead us to the chamber, and I carry the Mouvar weapon in my hand, what's to prevent a serpent coming up behind and—"

"Whatever that weapon is, it didn't seem to hurt us," Jac said. "It somehow released us from the motionless spell just as it froze the serpent."

"It's as if the spell is returned," Kelvin mused.

"Returned?" Biscuit asked.

"As if it bounces back. As if it returns somehow to affect the serpent instead of its prey."

"Good an explanation as any," Biscuit admitted.

Was it? Somehow Kelvin didn't think so, now that he had voiced it. Certainly his father would have wanted more of an explanation. But what after all was the difference? He couldn't come to any clear answer on that, either.

"You have how many men to carry out treasure, assuming we get there?" he asked Jac.

"There's eighteen of us," the bandit said.

Eighteen to carry out treasure. Eighteen to raise an army and fight a war. But at home it had been that way as well. He always seemed to be on the side that had to scramble just to make a decent showing, while the enemy always seemed to be dominant.

"What about the horses?"

"Heeto and Lonny can have them ready at the valley's rim. When they see us come out loaded with skins, they'll come."

"If they're not discovered!"

"They won't be. Heeto's very alert, and no flopear can run as fast as a horse."

"I want to come, too!" Lonny said, surprising all of them. She really looked determined.

"You said you wouldn't go back," Kelvin reminded her.

"I said I would, to save Kian."

"But you said Kian's a captive of the flopears, so he's not at the silver hoard."

"I changed my mind. I can help him best by helping you."

No one cared to argue with that.

"We'll need someone to handle the horses, and Heeto shouldn't have the burden alone." Jac spoke like a real leader then. "If you want to help Kian and your kingdom, you do what you're told."

"I—" Her face flushed. "I—will," she finally said.

"Good. Then it's settled. We'll leave the desert now, and camp in the mountains. First drizzly morning we get, we ride down into Serpent Valley as planned."

Thus it was much sooner than he had expected that Kelvin was leading a small army of bandits on foot down the winding road through a drippy morning mist that was nearly rain. No one spoke on the walk down, and Kelvin felt the knot in his stomach hurting him as he walked. He was reminded of the trip he and Jon had made so long ago into dragon territory. The dragon's gold had financed an army for them and made a revolution possible. Was serpent's silver going to do the same? All he could do was go along with events and hope; somehow it always came down to that when things were happening and a great deal was dependent on him.

But I never wanted to be a hero! he protested in his own mind. *Only the prophecy and a pair of gauntlets like these ever made me one! Only these, and in a different world than this!*

The mist was rising as they crossed the valley to the serpent hole that Kian and Lonny had originally entered. They would not be quite in the dark, because every third man would carry a large glowroom impaled on a sword blade. Coming back, if they came back, the blades with the fungus might reduce the amount of treasure they would carry, but light would be essential. Each man had a large basket strapped on his back, sufficient, it was thought, to carry a load of skins that would buy the mercenary services of a thousand good men. Even Kelvin had a basket, though he would rather have had his arms and shoulders entirely free. The thought of meeting even one gigantic serpent was chilling, but if Lonny had spoken true, and he feared she had, they might encounter a hundred. Would the gauntlets be able to move fast enough? Would the Mouvar weapon somehow magically cause all the serpents to freeze?

They reached the tunnel and entered it without mishap. They encountered not a single serpent or flopear. Somehow, that did not make Kelvin feel easy. The gauntlet on his right hand holding the Mouvar weapon led them on and on, and finally, just as he was beginning to lose hope, to the natural chamber with its eerily glowing moss.

Kelvin kept waiting for his gauntlets to grow warm and start tingling with the danger signal, but nothing happened. The party walked past the natural doorways and openings of serpent tunnels, seeing no serpents. They passed under stalactites hanging like gigantic teeth above them, and between stalagmites rising like gigantic teeth from below. They passed the crystal outcroppings, and there indeed were the gems Lonny had mentioned. They came to the crystal waterfall, and Kelvin had to catch his breath in wonder.

Then the narrow chamber, which they entered single file between two stalagmites, where the glowing mushrooms grew, similar to those they carried. Now the natural stairs to the deeper level, the good air coming in, the high-up serpent holes, and the piles and piles of discarded serpentskins.

Yet still no serpents. None at all. The others were gratified, but Kelvin was increasingly nervous. Where were those monsters? How much better he would feel if he only knew!

Thankfully, they gathered up the skins and stuffed their baskets. Then, loaded with several fortunes, they made their way back. The serpents never made an appearance.

Lonny and Heeto brought the horses as soon as they were outside. They loaded the baskets on the animals, and still disaster did not strike. How strange!

The sun was out now, and it was a very bright day. There should have been serpents sunning themselves, but there were none. No serpents, no flopears.

They walked up the road, out of Serpent Valley, leading the horses. Everyone was watchful, but no one dared to speak. When they had at last reached the tree with the silver chimes, Jac spoke to Kelvin: "I think that the Mouvar weapon scared them so that they kept out of sight."

"That must be it," Kelvin said, but inside he very much doubted it. There had to be more, some sound reason why they had not been attacked and devoured by the serpents, or killed or captured by their guardians. Somehow they had been allowed to get away with it, and that bothered him even more than if they had been attacked.

Kelvin had little time to contemplate the oddity of their successful foray into the serpents' realm. Almost immediately they were buying pack animals and replacement horses. Two days later, slicked up and disguised as successful merchants, they were on their way to Shrood.

For Kelvin, it was almost like a return trip to Throod. The territory they passed through seemed almost the same. They ate the same fruits, saw nearly the same people and wildlife. Only one incident on the way seemed remarkably different. A large purple-and-cream-colored bird flew overhead, calling from its long beak: "Ca-thar-sis! Ca-thar-sis!"

Kelvin watched the bird fly over, and then asked Jac, who was riding next to him, "Primary bird?"

"Purgative bird," Jac said.

"Purgative? I thought it was excretory," said Biscuit, overhearing.

"It's called both," Jac said. "But primary? Where'd you get that, Kelvin?"

"From home," Kelvin said. "Another bird." He did not add that the bird was blue and white and called what sounded like "Cau-sal-i-ty! Cau-sal-ity!" Both frames, it seemed, had birds in this kingdom afflicted with philosophy. Somehow this seemed part of the natural order.

As on the first trip, or rather his almost identical journey back home, Kelvin noted that the bird had chosen to fly over just where the road ran downhill past a stone cairn. When he reached the cairn he was not at all surprised to be told that it was dedicated to the memory of Shrood's soldiers who had perished in the two-hundred-year-old war with Hud. Histories had paralleled closely, even to the length of apparent time that had elapsed.

"Recruitment House ahead," said Biscuit, wiping orange fruit juice from his mouth and pointing. Except that he was Biscuit instead of Crumb, and the fruit juice was of a different shade, it was the same as previously, when they had brought dragon scales for wealth.

"I suppose you have a Flaw?" Kelvin asked. It wasn't really a question. He knew they had to have one, because that was what linked the frames. What he really meant was whether they had a place where it showed at the surface, where they could go and look at it without boating a long way in the dark on some subterranean river. No matter where or how it showed, The Flaw was the primary mystery of the age.

"Of course!" Jac said. "You'll have to see it while we're in Shrood."

"I suppose I must," Kelvin agreed, though he felt he had already seen more than enough of the anomaly.

They dismounted in front of Recruitment House. Jac, Biscuit, and Kelvin entered to meet with Captain McFay. For Kelvin, it was almost like entering a familiar room. The furnishings were as sparse as they had been in Throod, and the soldiers hanging around drinking, playing card games, and swapping stories might have been what his father would have called a rerun. About the only difference he could see was that here the soldiers had round ears instead of pointed. Then he spotted the big, slightly balding man with one peg leg; except for his ears and his peg leg, he could have been Captain Mackay's twin. Captain Mackay had been gray-haired; Captain McFay was slightly balding but still had dark hair. Captain Mackay had been missing one arm; Captain McFay was missing one leg.

"You've received my letter?" Jac asked the captain.

McFay nodded. "If you've got the skins, we'll do business."

"Outside on the pack animals, and there's more that may be possible. Revolutions come high, I understand."

"They do," Captain McFay said. He was eyeing Kelvin with a puzzled expression, as though searching to recall.

"Oh, this is Kelvin Knight Hackleberry. He's the hero from the other world. The one they called the Roundear."

"His ears don't appear overly round."

"Here they aren't," Kelvin said. "In my own frame they were freakish."

"Hmm, really unusual, huh? But they're just like mine, only mine are bigger and redder." And his eyes were hazel, not gray, as were the home captain's eyes.

"That's because in my home frame most people have pointed ears."

"Pointed? I've never heard of that! I'd like to hear a little about your world, Kelvin." He motioned for them to sit down at a table, and then motioned for two grizzled officers to come join them.

And so, as at another time in another place, Kelvin was launched on his long, familiar story.

"Sorcerer's Spell!" cried a clean-shaven man with both ears intact and no scar on his cheek. "That was some story!"

Kelvin sighed. If only he could be certain that this one would come out as well. Different frame, different experiences, with possibly entirely different outcomes.

"Well, we've got to negotiate," Jac said. "We'll need an army of probably five thousand, and I'm afraid there won't be much help from the populace of Hud."

"There may be help," Kelvin corrected. "We may be able to get people to join us, if we ask them." He explained about the posters he had put up in the other kingdom before its revolution. "Some did join, but they were largely untrained farmers and villagers."

"We'll train them!" McFay promised. "If they respond to your posters."

"People did at home. Some."

"And you'll send a message to the king of Hud, Rowforth, giving him a chance to surrender?"

"Of course, once we're prepared to fight."

The talk went on and on, and for Kelvin, it really did seem to be a replay. Would the fighting also seem to be just a redone past experience? Possibly, he thought, but he couldn't escape the thought that at home there had not been flopears who had allied themselves to the enemy. Nor had the slovenly troops of the queen been comparable to the well-disciplined, fully trained troops of Rowforth. Would five thousand men be enough? How many would be killed or mangled under his leadership? How many would he personally kill before he was done?

"You look as though the heat's affecting you," McFay observed. "How about a mug of bleer?"

Kelvin nodded. Wine at home, bleer here. Whatever bleer was.

One of the company brought him a mug topped by foam. He took it, sipped bitterness, and wanted to spit it out.

"Your first bleer, Kelvin?"

Kelvin nodded again, miserable. Manly drinking seemed to him to be such a foolish means of escape. He downed more of the liquid and got an idea. "The Flaw—is it far?"

"No. It's very near, in fact. One of my men can show you. Why don't you go gaze at it while Jac and I conclude our business?"

Kelvin nodded and stood up. "I think I can find the way."

And thus it was that Kelvin again found himself gazing through a wooden barrier into the star-filled depths of the anomaly. Was it, as he had heard said, a crack through space-time that ran through countless worlds and countless nearly identical and some highly strange existences? His recent experience certainly seemed to confirm that!

On his first trip to The Flaw his sister, Jon, had tried to hit a star with a stone from her sling; it had been one of the few times he had seen her fail to hit anything. He smiled, thinking how annoyed and determined she had been. He wished that somehow then was now and that Jon and good friend Lester were there at his side looking into what felt like eternity.

Deep, deep in the blackest black something flashed brightly, streaked across an area where there were no stars, and vanished. Would they themselves vanish? Everyone at once in this foreign and yet so familiar world?

Kelvin decided he didn't need to drink bleer or wine in order to make his head swim. All he needed to do was gaze into this depth and let his thoughts dwell on its nature and the nature of all things.

Ahead, in only a few days' time, there would be a message sent to King Rowforth. After that, should history repeat itself, the killing and dying were as certain as prophecy to begin.

27 /

EARTH

S T. HELENS STEPPED OUT from behind some bushes and hailed the Rud army. General Broughtner and both Crumbs, Mor and Lester, were in the lead, as they had been before. St. Helens vented a sigh. He had assumed they would have survived, but as he had seen, many a brave man hadn't.

"Whoa! Halt!" the general addressed the troops.

The column obediently came to a stop. St. Helens spoke directly to the general: "They didn't release me, I escaped. There's bad business over there. You going to cross?"

"My orders—" Broughtner began.

"Hang your orders, man!" His leg gave a twinge of pain, but it was worth it. "Is Rud going to let Aratex get away with yesterday? How many men drowned? How many war-horses? How much good equipment washed away?"

Broughtner glared. "St. Helens, my orders are to cross the river, march on the capital, and demand an apology and reparations."

"Well, why didn't you say so!" St. Helens nodded at the Crumbs, glad they were alive. A thought hit him. "My girl, did she—"

"Why'd you think we came yesterday?"

"She wasn't hurt? She seemed to be getting weak—"

"Not hurt. Pregnant," Lester said.

"Pregnant? You mean—?" He started to smile then, in spite of himself. "You mean the Roundear—"

"Who else?" Mor thundered. "What'd you think, witchcraft? Don't you know your own daughter? She is with child."

Lord, and all that activity! The incredible flight he had taken her on! No wonder she had had trouble hanging on! It hadn't been weakness of spirit, but of body—because of her condition.

"That's, eh, good news." He got hold of himself, swiftly putting back the thoughts of being a grandfather and focused on the present.

"You look pretty beat," Broughtner remarked, eyeing him.

"My leg can use some attention. Maybe Heln told you; it got in the way of a crossbow bolt. A flesh wound, and she bound it up pretty well, but I am a bit worse for wear."

The general nodded and gave appropriate orders. A wagon pulled up; a young medic got out, took St. Helens aside, and worked on him. St. Helens gritted his teeth and went along with the disinfecting and bandaging without comment. When the medic was done, he had to admit to himself that the job was perfect.

"You had better rest now," the medic said. "You've lost blood."

"No time for that! There's a war to be fought!"

"But any other man with a wound like that—"

"I'm too old and tough to let a pinprick like that stop me," St. Helens said, proud of the effect he was making. The wound did hurt, and he did feel weak from loss of blood, and he'd like nothing better than to flop down on a soft bunk and sleep for a day or two, but he wouldn't let any of that show. He thanked the man and went back to the general, who was staring at the stream.

"General, how do you expect to get across? You don't want a repeat of yesterday."

"There won't be," General Broughtner said. "We'll make rafts and build a bridge. It's high time there was a bridge across this river."

"That's a good idea, General. But bridges wash out and rafts can be washed away. I say let me fly a couple of ropes across and then you make a suspension bridge: well above the water, see?"

The general scowled. "Strong enough to take the war-horses and the armor?"

"It can be."

Broughtner shook his head. "And if Melbah decides to blow up a wind?"

"She will. You can be certain of that. But with extra guy ropes holding the sides, the chances are better than in the water."

"I don't like it."

"The alternative, General?"

The former heavy drinker's frown intensified. "I didn't say you weren't right, St. Helens, just that I don't like it. If we construct the bridge so that it hangs just above where the highest waves might reach, then take a few men and a single war-horse across at a time, it'll work."

St. Helens found himself staring. He hadn't really expected Broughtner not to argue. But it seemed the man was competent after all. If they did things right, old Melbah might delay them but she wasn't going to stop them —he hoped.

"Right, General Broughtner, sir." He touched the control on his levitation belt and rose until he was a couple of feet off the ground. "Now if you'll just get me some rope, we'll get started."

The general turned and issued orders. An equipment wagon pulled forward and rolled almost to where uprooted trees and flood debris marked the limits of yesterday's water rise. Looking inside the wagon, St. Helens was surprised to see cut lumber and piles of heavy netting. General Broughtner had let him talk, but he had planned this all the time! Well, at least he could suggest a spot on a bend between two facing hills where the wind couldn't strike suddenly.

But Broughtner and the men in charge of the detail seemed to have planned well ahead of him. Quicker than he had thought possible, he was flying the end of a rope across and securing it to a tree. Then another rope for the other side of the bridge, then the netting sides, the guy ropes, and the plank floor. By noon they were finished and a secure bridge swayed in place.

Lester Crumb was the first across, and then his father, and then the general. The war-horses and pack horses were led across a few at a time, and then the wagons, and finally the men who had remained on Rud's side crossed by threes and fours. When the last man reached their side, the general looked across the bridge and beamed with obvious pride. "Good job, St. Helens."

"Very." What foolishness: the general was complimenting him for suggesting what the general had planned on all along. St. Helens knew this was merely an attempt to gain his favor and keep him in line—but it was working. He wasn't going to give Broughtner any trouble. A leader was a leader, and this was turning out to be a good one.

A black bird flew overhead. St. Helens half expected the bridge to burst into flames, or the river to rise. He had the unhappy feeling that they were doing just what Melbah intended.

"General, if we follow the road through Deadman's Pass, there may be an ambush."

"What's the alternative?"

St. Helens pondered. He didn't like having them pass under the eyes of Conjurer's Rock, but to try slipping through the forest might be even worse. Possibly if he were to scout on ahead, he could find any traps and save the day. But then he didn't like the thought of either flying low and getting hit with another crossbow bolt or flying high and encountering another whirlwind. At least he could check the cliffs of Deadman's Pass for archers and then come in behind Conjurer's Rock and check for old Melbah. He twisted his mouth at the thought of flying in behind her, unseen. Of Melbah watching the troops in the pass, preparing some magical attack, and his dropping on her suddenly like a hawk. With luck, it just might work.

"I, eh, believe the road in is the only way, General. But I'd like your permission to scout ahead. If you can agree to delay your departure from here and reach the pass at about sunset . . . ?"

"I can agree to that, St. Helens. But why?"

"The light will be less then." *And old eyes may have to strain.*

"You have something in mind?"

"I have a witch in mind."

"You will need help. Some of the men to accompany you?"

"Better alone, General. Better just me and my levitation belt and my sword, the personal gift of Aratex's King Phillip."

"You have something definitely in mind. Some strategy I should know about?"

"Only that it involves Conjurer's Rock. Buzvuls roost there by the thousands. I just want to make certain there's not a particular buzvul there. If she is there . . ." St. Helens touched his sword hilt.

"I understand, St. Helens. But a party of archers, perhaps?"

"Alone," St. Helens said firmly. "It's the only chance I have of reaching her undetected. If I pluck her magic, your archers will no doubt have adequate targets between the pass and the capital." Was that true? Would the Aratex army even be out? It was *she,* not King Phillip, who ruled. "If she's first with her magic, it's going to be at least a hard fight."

General Broughtner nodded. "Good luck, St. Helens. We'll time our march to be in the pass at twilight."

But as usual, his simple plan was complicated by random events. Thus it was that St. Helens, forced to walk partway because of flying buzvuls that could have been scouts, reached the edge of the forest under the surly lip of Conjurer's Rock later than he liked. He swore under his breath, but plowed on as his leg jabbed him with new pain. He paused in despair, because the shadow now lay like a great black blanket across the pass, and there, just within range of his sight, were the men and horses and wagons that he had hoped would be far back.

Then, even as he despaired, something happened that astounded him. The ground just beyond the rock's shadow shook as if from the tread of a giant. Ground that was occupied by horses and men and wagons cracked, gaped open, and swallowed troops and horses and wagons in huge, ugly closings. Rock from above cascaded downward, loosened by the trembling of the cliffs themselves. The rumbling sounds of an earthquake and of falling rock went on and on. With it were mingled the frightened screams of horses and the cries of dying men.

Just like that, the tide of battle had turned—before the battle even started. His worst fear had been not only confirmed but multiplied. He had assumed that all they had to handle were wind and water. What a misjudgment!

Melbah was up there, all right, and she was destroying them.

* * *

Heln sat up in her bed with a shrill cry. "Kelvin! Kelvin, oh, Kelvin!"

"Hush, it was only a dream," Jon told her. Heln's eyes were glassy; this was the worst nightmare she had had in the palace.

"Oh, Jon!" Heln's arms tightened around her neck. Jon found this both flattering and embarrassing, though she couldn't have said why. Heln had been so magnificently brave when she was wearing those gauntlets of Kelvin's, and now the gauntlets waited here for his return. Sometimes she wondered whether making Heln wear them would stop her nightmares.

"He was fighting again, in an army. And, and the faces—one of them looked like the guard in the Girl Mart who—who—"

"Hush. It's only a dream. That man is dead, slain by a brother of another of the girls. Lester saw it, and I know he wouldn't lie."

"But not in the dream, Jon. Not in the dream! He was alive. Alive and fighting."

"It's natural that you dream of Kelvin fighting him. After all, that evil man was the one who violated you."

"Not fighting against!" Heln's eyes were wide. "Fighting *with!* The two of them in identical uniforms fighting side by side. Fighting monsters, Jon, and about to die!"

28 /

BATTLE

ROWFORTH, KING OF HUD, stood at the edge of the training field and unhappily inspected the twelve flopears in bright red uniforms. So squat, so broad, so ugly, and yet possibly of great value to him. They did not look like soldiers, and he hadn't anticipated that they would. What they did look like were flopears in especially made Hud uniforms.

"And now, oh, King," Herzig was saying, "you must see that they learn to ride."

Rowforth permitted himself a sigh. Herzig had proved unexpectedly difficult in insisting that his handpicked dozen fighters wear the Hud uniform. That had entailed special orders and individual tailoring to fit the odd contours of the flopear bodies. What needless delay! Now they had to learn to ride—these squat, seemingly awkward creatures! It would mean special saddles with special stirrups and a long, painful instructing time. He hoped that his cavalry master could do the job before the abominable green-clad troops swept all the way to the capital. This had originally not been his plan, but there was sense in it: a uniformed flopear cavalry should prove to be even more efficient than a few stationary flopears waiting for eye contact. On horseback these unlikely troops could ride up to the rebel leaders themselves, paralyze them with a stare, and strike them dead. There would be little need for executions after the war. The flopears could execute the entire armed force right from their saddles. When they went into action, no matter what occurred before, victory was assured.

Brownleaf, the cavalry master, stepped smartly forth from the stables, leading a mare. The mare bore a special small saddle on her broad back and towered well over the heads of her potential riders. As she was led near she began to whinny and skitter and jerk in the manner of an untrained horse.

King Rowforth eyed the cavalry master and the horse and the untrained troops, and wondered. Beside him, Herzig spoke: "Danzar, eye!"

One of the uniformed flopears stepped out of line, displaying all the soldierly style of his short-legged race, devoid of grace. The flopear eyed the mare, who was now trying for all she was worth to break free of her handler.

The horse froze. Danzar waddled close, climbed the rope ladder depending from the saddle, settled into the cupped depression, and took the reins.

"Danzar, release!" Herzig commanded.

Instantly the mare reared, came down on her forelegs, and bucked. Danzar flew clear of the saddle, letting go of the reins on his way up. In awe Rowforth watched the tiny body sail up to a height that bordered on the magical. Then down, down, like a stone. SPLAT!

To the king's astonishment, the dust had scarcely settled around the small body when it stood. The flopear was unhurt! It focused its large eyes on the mare—and the mare, turning her head, rolling her eyes, was caught as before.

Danzar waddled up again, climbed the short rope ladder, and resumed the saddle. And went flying.

"How long will this go on?" Rowforth asked Herzig rather than his cavalry master.

"Until Danzar controls."

"That will be—?"

"As long as it will take. Horses can be stubborn. That is why none of the serpent people now ride."

"So these will be the first? The first in history?"

"Yes, the first in history, for this species of animal. The first of the serpent people ever to conquer the equine." But Herzig's tone indicated that he did not consider this remarkable. Evidently he expected the flopears to succeed; it was just a matter of time. Herzig did not seem concerned about the rapidly diminishing time the king had left. Who would have thought those ragtag revolutionaries would be able to hire such a well-equipped and trained army! Where had they gotten the money?

Only twelve, King Rowforth thought. Only twelve, but a sufficient number considering their power. Yes, indeed, the flopears, even more than his fine army, would hold and expand his realm. Once the revolution was dispatched, he would torture its surviving leaders until they revealed the source of their mysterious wealth. Then he would make that source his own.

Out on the practice field Danzar was again clawing wildly with both hands as he climbed above their heads into the blue, cloud-flecked sky. It would have been comical, if not so serious.

As Kelvin had feared, it was one obscenity of a battle. Oh, his men fought hard enough and his gauntlets knew what to do, and there were volunteers aplenty, even in the midst of a fight. But war was war, and after he had spilled the blood of perhaps his twentieth man, Kelvin would have liked to give up the fray. Was it worth it? he wondered, watching the guts spill from his last opponent. Were even the lives of his father and his brother, and the freedom of this country, worth it? He saw the man topple with a stricken face and land under the hooves of the war-horses. Maybe that enemy soldier was somebody's father or somebody's brother; maybe he was just earning money to support his family! At what awful price was anything being accomplished? Yet really, what choice did he have? What choice did any of them have, other than to fight?

Day followed day, and the Shrood mercenaries fought for Hud as if it were their own land. Nobody liked a dictator bent on world conquest; even Rowforth's closest people seemed secretly to hate him. But people followed dictators, intent on the spoils that conquest brought. Whether such plunder was logical, considering that the opposing armies were apt to do the same to the families of the plunderers, Kelvin could not say; he just knew that he wished he were no part of it.

The soldiers of Hud's royal army were at least as good fighters as Hud's Freedom Army; in fact, the two sides were astonishingly well matched. Kelvin was glad that in this fight the Shrood-trained officers were in charge, not he. Yet they did ask his advice, and looked on him as a champion, as did all the troops. With luck and his magic gauntlets, he thought wearily, he could win against the toughest fighters.

Only one thing bothered him, and that was that the flopears did not appear. If they did show up as Rowforth's allies, he hoped that the weapon he carried sheathed on his hip would come to his aid as it had back in serpent territory. But until they did appear, if they did, the Mouvar weapon was only so much extra drag on his sword belt.

"When are they going to use them?" Biscuit demanded one evening, as if he knew.

Kelvin shook his head. "It bothers me as much as it does the rest of you. Maybe he's holding them in reserve."

"And maybe just knowing we have the weapon keeps them out," Smoothy Jac said. These days, in his green officer's uniform, he looked nothing at all like a bandit chief. Neither did he sound like a man whose main interest had been in stealing silver serpentskins from the magical flopears. All of them seemed to be changing, Kelvin thought. Considering what bandits were, that was for the best.

Shagmore came and went, and it was almost as big and potentially as disastrous a battle as the one for Skagmore had been in the home frame. Possibly Kelvin's recounting of the battle of Skagmore helped, as his recollections, suitably modified, of other battles had helped. He was watched carefully by Jac and his compatriots and did not get himself captured as he confessed he had at Skagmore. He had thought that here, surely, the flopears would appear, because this spot had been such a turning point in Rud's history and could be the same in Hud's history. Shagmore, like

Skagmore in the home frame, was within a day's ride of the country's capital.

Thus it was that they were fighting a pitched battle outside the capital itself and winning, little by little, without having yet seen Rowforth's magical allies. It began to seem that the flopears were not going to appear, and that the palace itself would be taken by the Freedom Army. Kelvin fought on, trusting the gauntlets, and gradually as men died all around him he ceased to think of the flopears and of the Mouvar weapon he carried. In the back of his consciousness there was a cry of alarm, but that was hard to hear when the immediacies of battle preempted his attention.

Men with pitchforks and staves were in their midst, some riding plow horses and others traveling on foot. Peasants from neighboring farms were coming to help the Freedom Army take the palace. Kelvin winced to see those unarmored men and boys who had never before stood up now standing up. As a consequence too many of them were dying, often horribly. Better late than never, some had said, but as he watched them being mutilated and killed, he wondered. Yet peasant hands did pull the proud, red-uniformed Royalists from their saddles; knives, axes, and clubs did bring the Royalists death, as did the flashing swords and twanging bows of the Freedom Army. On and on they battled, the day becoming bloodier as it wore on.

At noon, when the sun was beating down most cruelly, and fatigue was a smothering blanket weighing down the muscles that guided the horses and swung the swords, they arrived at the very gates of the palace. Still no flopears, Kelvin thought, that alarm sounding again in his mind. Victory almost in their grasp—

Suddenly the gates fell, crashing thunderously. They fell *outward,* pushed by men in red uniforms. A dozen war-horses charged from the palace grounds. Each horse carried a rider: squat and ugly, with great flopears. Flopears in uniform! Flopears on horses!

There was no time to react. Men in green uniforms froze before the flopears' stares. Men in red uniforms froze as well, but these were not the targets of the ferocious young flopears with swords. Those swords cut down only the men in green uniforms, and these toppled and died without resistance.

At the side of the action Kelvin fought to move close. Oddly, the gauntlets did not cooperate. They were warm on his hands, and he was reminded again that this meant danger. Well, danger there certainly was, but with luck he and the gauntlets would stop it. He reached for the Mouvar weapon holstered to his waist.

His gauntleted fingers encountered nothing where the weapon should have been. The holster had been cut away. He was without the critical weapon!

A flopear was standing up on a saddle, right in front of Kelvin, his oversized sword raised, his eyes glowing. Those eyes held Kelvin *and* his warhorse!

The flopear was going to split him all the way through, and he had no way to stop it!

On his hands his gauntlets were very, very warm. As if he couldn't see the danger for himself!

29 /

VICTORY

Zotanas turned away from the high window where he had been watching the ongoing carnage. The king had mismanaged the war so badly that every last soldier and guard had had to be marshaled to defend the palace. The servants had fled—or, perhaps more likely, sneaked away to join the Freedom Fighters. The palace was virtually empty. If the flopears turned the tide, as the king believed they would, everyone would quickly return to serve as before; otherwise . . .

Something was happening that he should know about; his magic told him that much. Zotanas tiptoed down the winding stairs to the palace proper and slipped by slow degrees through the glittering array of objets d'art that took up so much space. If only the quality of the king were up to that of the artifacts he collected! He came to the statue of a former (and better) king and paused behind it, hidden for the moment. Just on the other side of the statue, King Rowforth was berating Zotanas' daughter, the queen.

"Trying to release the prisoners once was bad enough, but twice! And with those idiot soldiers losing the battle and the flopears refusing to help until the last moment! What was in your mind, woman?"

"You must not do what you swore to do, Husband!" she responded. "You must not destroy them! Your enemies are already at the palace gates!"

"Yes, Wifey, yes, but they will not destroy me, I will destroy them! The flopears have delayed participating, and I can't push them, but once they eye the enemy, it will be over. You know that; you always have. So why?"

Zanaan began sobbing like a little girl. "Oh, Husband, they are good and you are evil. If the Freedom Army loses, you will know no restraint. You will war on other kingdoms and take them with the help of your magic allies. You will conquer this world and you will attempt to conquer others. If the strangers live, you will make them take you to their own world, or show you the way to get there."

"Yes." The word was spoken grimly, through obviously gritted teeth. The king lived for power! "And you will be instrumental in making them cooperate, because the young one sees you as very much like his mother, and the older one sees you as very much like his mistress. When you promise them both fulfillment in return for their loyalty to me, they will capitulate."

"No!" she cried, appalled. "That cannot be true!"

"It *is* true! I had my minions listen from hiding as they conversed. I suspected something of the sort, and now it has been confirmed, thanks to your visit there. After they saw you, it all came out. So you have power to work my will, woman, and you shall work it."

"No!" she repeated despairingly, belief overcoming her.

"Yes!" Zotanas winced as that word was immediately followed by the sound of a blow and a falling body.

"Oh!" There was shock and pain and fear in the queen's voice. It was obvious that she had never imagined such depravity, even in the King.

Hastily Zotanas stepped around the statue. Zanaan sat sprawled on the throne room rug, her red hair all about her beautiful face, her green eyes seeming to spark in their depths. Rowforth stood over her, fists clenched. He had one foot raised, ready to kick her. The king, for all his expressed confidence in his victory, was evidently badly frightened; he was reverting to childish force and cruelty.

"Because if you don't," the king was saying, "you will persuade them by suffering in a way they cannot abide. You will bring them great pleasure or great pain; I will settle for either. But my will shall be done!"

His head swiveled as Zotanas came into view. The king's eyes blazed almost as brightly as the queen's. "What do you want, Zotanas? To use your magic for me?"

"Yes." It was what he had long planned.

"Yes? It's a bit late, isn't it? With the enemy at the very palace gates?"

"It is, Your Majesty. But now that you have lost—"

"Lost? What are you talking about, you doddering old idiot?" Rowforth put his foot down without kicking. "Lost? I've won!"

"Have you, Your Majesty? I suggest you go out on the balcony, or up in my tower, where I have a view of the fighting."

Rowforth went pale to the edge of his grayish hairs. "My flopears, have they—"

"The strangers from another world have with them a weapon. A Mouvar weapon. Against that, the serpent's stare rebounds as a sword rebounds from a shield. Against that, the serpent people are helpless."

"No! No, you're lying! You're making that up!"

"Am I, Your Majesty? I suggest you go see for yourself."

"Yes, yes, I have to see. I—" Rowforth ran as hard as he could for the stairs.

"Father." His daughter spoke softly from the floor. "You said you'd help him? Use your magic for him?"

"Yes, my magic. I will use it to give him the help he needs—to surrender."

"Then—then you actually have magic?"

"For little things, daughter. For little things, as I have often said."

Smiling his most careful smile, Zotanas raised his palms to his eyes and brought them up close until all light was blocked out. Concentrating hard, he mumbled the words he had learned so long ago that aided in the transference. Unbidden and not completely welcome, a face intruded into his concentration: the face of Polzamp, who had saved him from a terrible fate as an infant and had bestowed immortality on him. Polzamp the Restless. Polzamp the Kindly and Just. Polzamp, the onetime ruler of his people before his change. Polzamp, born from the mating of a mortal sorcerer and a serpent person not unlike Gerta. Polzamp, his own most extraordinary father.

Concentrate: black, black, blank. *Cannot see, cannot see, cannot see. Blank, blank, black. As in deepest outer space, nothingness.*

He couldn't see. His eyes were shut tight. Now he could visualize Rowforth looking out from the familiar tower window. Staring down at the grounds, the swirling men and horses, the clouds of dust, the carnage at the gates and beyond.

From above their heads came a scream. "I can't see! I can't see!" The screaming was Rowforth's. In a moment it gave way to crashing sounds and a continuing series of thumps. "Oh, oh, oh!" screamed His Majesty, his pain-racked body at last reaching the foot of the unseen winding stairs. "I can't see, Zotanas! You are the official sorcerer of the realm—help!"

"Hud must surrender to the victor," Zotanas said, using the tone of wisdom. "Afterward your sight will be restored."

"NO!" Indignation supreme. "Never! Rowforth will battle forever! Rowforth will fight though he's blind!"

"Are you certain, Your Majesty? The magic here is very strong. It will be displeasing never again to see pain in a face or torment in a soul. Strike the flag now and you will see, even though it may be joy instead of suffering."

"It's you! You're doing this! I will never surrender! Never! GUARDS!"

Listening to running feet, Zotanas kept his eyes firmly closed and his hands in place. For as long as he could not see, neither could the king. He knew this; the king did not.

"Help! Help!" the king cried. "Broughtmar, is that you? I can't see, Broughtmar, old friend. It's magic—magic used against me."

Broughtmar? Naturally that thug had managed to escape being assigned to the hard battle outside! But Zotanas suspected that the man would not be much comfort to the king at this moment. Broughtmar was a bully who seemed to exist only to torment the helpless—and now the king was helpless.

"You can't see?" Broughtmar's voice came. "What a pity when there's so much for you to revel in. Outside a man looks at his own steaming innards and a flopear swings a great sword at another man and creates a fountain of blood. You'd enjoy those scenes, Your Highness." Obviously Broughtmar had not checked recently, but that hardly mattered.

"Ouch! You stepped on my hand! Find that doddering old fool who shares the palace! Make him stop whatever he's doing! Make him stop! Kill him *and* the queen!"

Oops—that would break up the magic fast enough, if the guard obeyed. "Hide us, daughter," Zotanas murmured. "This must be complete, before—"

He felt the queen's hands guiding him to a safer place. He kept his own hands locked in place, maintaining his blindness—and the king's. How quickly it was degenerating into a comedy of malice, as the king's empire fell apart before it could form. Now was the falling out of thieves. But he had to keep the king blind while it proceeded.

"You fool, you lost!" Broughtmar's voice came again. "Those Freedom Fighters won the war. The mercenaries did it—the ones they bought with silver."

"No! No! No! Ouch! That hurt, Broughtmar! You're stepping on me deliberately!"

"How perceptive of you, blubber belly. Maybe a heavy tromp here—?" Broughtmar was certainly acting true to form!

"AHHHH! Stop, stop, stop! This is your king, Broughtmar! Your king! I thought you loved me! I thought we were friends!"

"You were wrong, Your Arrogance."

"NO! NO! NO! AHHHHH!"

It was exactly such sounds that had given the queen nightmares. Only now it was not some unfortunate prisoner or fancied enemy of the realm Broughtmar was methodically beating, it was the king himself. Zotanas recognized a bit of evil in himself as he hesitated to stop the torture. But perhaps it had proceeded far enough. Reluctantly he took his hands down and opened his eyes.

"I CAN SEE!" the king cried. "I can see, Broughtmar, I can see! Don't you realize what this means? I'm back in control, no thanks to that sorcerer! Find him, stop him!"

"Stop whom from doing what?" Broughtmar inquired nastily. He was evidently too far gone in his sadism to reverse course now. "Stop me from doing a little more of this to you?"

"AHHHHH! STOP!!"

Zotanas crossed the throne room and the dining hall and came to where Broughtmar was brutally beating the monarch. It was obvious that the moment it appeared the king lacked power, the guard's loyalty was forfeit.

Very softly Zotanas said: "It wouldn't be wise to kill him, Broughtmar. He needs to surrender us."

Rowforth raised a bruised and bloody face. He pointed a shaky finger. "KILL HIM! Kill him, Broughtmar! I order you. Kill!"

Broughtmar grinned, ignoring His Majesty. "You say he should surrender? By lowering the flag from the tower?"

"Yes. That is the way surrendering is customarily done. Can you carry him back up the stairs? Place the flag-rope in his hand so that he can lower the flag himself?"

Broughtmar looked confused. "Why?"

"To live. Or at least not to be tortured. One who does this thing is certain to be rewarded."

"Rewarded?" Broughtmar sounded both suspicious and eager at the same time. He liked the notion of a reward, but wasn't quite getting Zotanas' drift.

"With life. Instead of execution."

"Oh." Now at last it dawned: his own life could be at stake.

"Well?"

Broughtmar leaned over the king to pick him up. The king promptly kicked him expertly in the mouth, sending blood and broken teeth spraying.

Zotanas sighed. He should have foreseen that, though Broughtmar hadn't. The king was like a wounded animal, dangerous even when seemingly helpless.

Broughtmar spat out more teeth and blood, looking surprised. In a moment the light of kill would be in his eyes. He was not the smartest man, but he made up for that in viciousness.

"This isn't going to do," Zotanas said aloud. He closed his own eyes again, cupped them with his hands, and concentrated. It was easier this time. Blackness, blackness, black blank. *Transfer.*

"I can't see! I can't see!" Rowforth cried. "Broughtmar, you must help me! You—what are you doing!"

"Take him up the stairs, Broughtmar, and see that he surrenders," Zotanas said. "For a man with your strength, it shouldn't be difficult."

"P-please," the queen added, sick at heart.

Even though concentrating heavily on the black, Zotanas heard Rowforth gasp as Broughtmar picked him up. Then Broughtmar tromped heavily as he carried the king to the tower and beyond it to the roof.

Blars Blarsner, amateur wrestler and boxer in better times, was fighting with the confounded sword that seemed forever out of his control, and putting all his energies into staying alive. He finished off the Royalist with a sudden lucky stab and looked for an opening between thrashing horses and battling men. The back of the otherworlder known as Kelvin was toward him. As usual, the hero of another place was battling three Royalists with his shield and his sword, handling both brilliantly. He chopped off the hand of the

Royalist in front of him, swung the sword back, and slashed the eyes of the man to his left. He seemed hardly to look; it was as if he knew exactly where his opponents were without having to use his eyes. In the meantime the swordsman on his right had stabbed him, not quite touching him but severing the leather thong that held the Mouvar weapon secure against Kelvin's leg.

The Mouvar weapon! It had fallen! It was down there in the dust!

While Blars was wiping sweat and dust from his eyes, Kelvin finished off the third of his three attackers with an expert stab. But ahead the way was clearing before the gates. There was a clanging noise and a billow of dust that hid even Kelvin from him. Something was happening!

There was no time to speculate. He had to get the Mouvar weapon while he could, and get it to Kelvin. Without it Kelvin couldn't continue to win, and none of them could win.

Unless, he suddenly thought, he could manage to use the weapon himself.

With sheer brute strength Blars reined his huge war-horse over to where Kelvin had been. One of the Royalists was still there, horrified as he stared at the spouting end of his arm. Reluctantly, Blars finished off the man and turned his attention to what was under the horse's hooves.

At first he didn't see it, and then he did, next to a dead Royalist and a riderless horse that was whinnying pitifully with its guts pouring out. He reached, grabbed, and had it.

He stared dazedly at what he held. He pulled his horse to one side of the fighting and examined the weapon closely for the first time. He had heard so much about it, yet had never seen it in action. It was a strange-looking device that resembled a crossbow only in the most superficial manner. It had a bell-shaped muzzle that would be pointed at whatever was to be attacked. The part that fitted the hand was like the handgrip on the smallest of crossbows—the kind used mainly for games, for children to train with. There was a strange dial set in it, with two odd marks and a little fin-shape pointed at the higher of the marks. Without thinking, Blars turned the fin-shape to the lower mark.

"Flopears! Flopears! Flop—" came the cry.

Realizing that things were happening and that he was wasting time, he urged his horse out into the dust. Now he could make out the figure of Kelvin sitting oddly still astride his war-horse. Riding hard down on him, standing upright in a small saddle on the back of a gigantic war-horse, was a small figure with upraised sword. A flopear! About to kill Kelvin!

Blars hardly knew that he pulled the trigger while pointing the weapon. All he knew was that it hissed and jumped slightly in his hand. Nothing seemed to come from the bell of the weapon except for a few too-bright sparks.

Had it failed? Yet it had seemed to do something. He had felt the slight recoil, seen the spark. But was that all?

But as he watched the flopear swing down, he saw Kelvin save himself and his horse with some amazing maneuvering. Freedom Fighters who had been stationary in the dust resumed their motions. All kinds of action were occurring where a moment ago there had been none except that of the flopears.

Blars looked at the weapon in his hand. It must have worked! He felt that he had accomplished something. He said a prayer of thanks to Mouvar. He had no idea how the weapon had worked, but it seemed to have brought the Freedom Army to life again.

The flopears were still fighting, but no longer against frozen opponents. How a weapon could bring folk back to life instead of making them dead, he hesitated to guess. Certainly this was nothing for him to gamble with. Concentrating hard on the deed at hand, he maneuvered his horse, bypassing fights when he could and working steadily closer to Kelvin. When he reached the hero, he would place the weapon in his hands, where it belonged.

The movement of the gauntlet surprised Kelvin as it had never done before. It shot up, grabbed the swiftly descending blade, and wrested it from the flopear. The flopear lost his balance, toppled from the saddle, and fell under the war-horse's pounding hooves. There was a scream of agony from below which should add spectacularly to Kelvin's future nightmares.

He pulled his eyes away from the gory sight of the small ruined face. In so doing, he turned his head.

He could move! The stasis spell was gone! He could move hands, arms, feet, and legs. The horse was moving, too. Everyone was moving—every man and every horse. All the Freedom Fighters and the Royalists and their horses—unparalyzed! All moving as they were supposed to, naturally and right. What had happened? What magic had come to his rescue and stopped the flopears' spell?

"Here, Captain, you lost this."

It was a large, swarthy Freedom Fighter who was holding out the Mouvar weapon to him, using the rank Kelvin had been given. Something about the man's face instantly bothered him. With supreme shock he realized that this was the near duplicate of the pointy-eared guard at the notorious Franklin Girl Mart who had forced himself on Heln. Kelvin had seen the ravisher dead after one of his Knights, a brother to one of the other girls there, had finished him. At the time Kelvin had both thanked the gods that he hadn't been the one to strike the fatal blow, and regretted deeply that he had *not* been the one. Now here the man was, or his counterpart in the frame, unbloodied and alive and round-eared. Holding out to him their one small hope of winning this fight. This man, nearly identical in appearance with the one who had raped Kelvin's wife.

"I . . . lost it, and you . . . used it?"

"I saw one of those three last men you fought cut your belt with his sword. Your horse did some jerking after that, and the gates fell and the flopears appeared. I got the weapon for you because I knew you'd want it, and had it in my hand and—you were frozen then, so I tried it—and now you're unfrozen, and I brought it to you. I don't know what I did with it, but I guess the thing worked, somehow. You're the hero, not me; you know how to use it. I—"

Kelvin took the weapon from the big man's hand. He had to say something, and he fought to get it right.

"You're the hero. You, not me. Thank you for saving me and for returning the weapon I should have guarded with my life." *You are the hero,* Kelvin repeated to himself. *You, who in another world, another time, raped my beloved. You, who in that other world, were a person who ruined and harmed without conscience. Only it was not you, but another who resembled you in all things but character. What a universe this is, that two who look so much alike could both so touch my life in opposite ways!*

"Captain," the man said, "the war's not over until they lower the flag on the palace."

"I know."

After a startled intermission the fighting continued. Nobody was frozen that Kelvin could see, either Freedom Fighter or Royalist. Mortal Freedom Fighters now fought immortal flopears hand to hand.

Yet the battle had seemed to be turning, just before the flopears appeared. Now, looking around, he could see more green-clad soldiers on their mounts than red-uniformed Royalists.

The battle was not over. The war was not over, until the flag was lowered. Would it come down? Kelvin did not yet know.

Zanaan looked up from the floor at her father as he covered his eyes. She listened to her husband screaming. Then, assuming a philosophical poise befitting a queen, she got to her feet, wiped her face, put her robe in order, picked up the ring of keys she had been carrying, and resumed her journey to the dungeon.

John and Kian were at the bars as she descended into their gloom. Both were thinner than they had been, worn by the days and the nights of harsh confinement. Dark half-moons were under their eyes, reminders of more than sleeplessness.

The neighboring cell was empty. After Smith had finally died, the result of his desperate banging of his head against the wall with all the strength of a madman, there had been a lingering and sullen silence. Broughtmar had complained about having to carry out the corpse; in the old days he would have let it ripen. But the king had remembered that prisoners subjected to bad air sometimes died. Rowforth had wanted the prisoners alive and helping him. How well she knew!

That reminded her of what the king had said: that John regarded her as resembling his mistress, and Kian, as resembling his mother. In the frame from which they came—

She shrugged that off. Certainly she had not misbehaved like that in this world! Nor would she. She was simply doing what was proper.

She also wondered whether her father had done something to deflect the king. She had never seen him use actual magic before this day, only minor illusions for show.

The young man looked at her with widened eyes, swallowed, and said, "You look so much like—"

"Hush, now," she chided him, oddly flattered. Her husband had sought to use her to corrupt these men; it would not have been an unpleasant task, were it not so reprehensible morally.

She inserted the big key in the lock and turned it, knowing that they watched. "Your ordeal is over and your victory all but won. The Freedom Fighters are at the gates and winning back the land. Your brother, Kelvin, is in their very midst—a hero to base legends on. Soon, very soon, it will be over."

"Thank the Gods!" John Knight said, and his son echoed him.

Looking at the Mouvar weapon he held, Kelvin saw that the knob on the butt had been turned. Possibly when it fell, he thought. Could a different setting account for the fact that the flopears were not themselves the victims of their own stares? He had wanted to see them frozen into statues, as the serpent in the valley had been. If he moved the knob to its former place, would that cause it to happen?

It was worth a try. He twisted the knob, heard a click, and raised the weapon just as another flopear rode at them with suicidal fury. He pulled the trigger, wondering whether he should be raising his sword instead.

Bright light dazzled him. There was a WHOOMPTH noise that echoed on and on. Then silence.

The horse and the flopear were stopped, frozen as if by the staring paralysis. The mortals and their horses were not affected; the fight could continue with the flopears out of it. But would it?

Just then there was a shout. He saw the big man pointing. There was the silver-and-gold flag creeping down the pole on the palace roof. This meant that the king was surrendering—finally, totally, unconditionally.

As he looked toward the palace, past the gates, two men and a woman awaited him.

"Father! Kian!" he shouted. "We've won! We've won! We're going home again to those who love us. Home, home, at last!"

But Kian, though released from a dungeon, looked as if balanced on a precipice. His face, already pale from imprisonment, paled perceptibly more. When he spoke it was in a hoarse croak that seemed devoid of the joy it should have held.

"Home. That's very good. Really wonderful," he said without enthusiasm.

"Well, Cousin, it's over," Herzig said. "The good mortals won."

"Yes, won well," Gerta agreed. "As planned, though the Mouvar weapon cost us."

"Did it, Cousin? Good members of our band?"

"Your enemies, Herzig, though not acknowledged as such. Those who wanted to go with Rowforth and share his triumphs. Those who wanted to be rulers of mortals in this and other lands. Was it fair, Herzig, giving them what they wanted?"

"Fair is a mortal concept. Call it just. They wanted to fight for Rowforth, and they fought for Rowforth. Now, slain or not, they will never again be involved in a mortal's fight."

"True," Gerta said. "You are very old, Herzig, and very wise. You prove the wisdom of a saying mortals have."

"Yes, Cousin, and that is—?"

"Wily as a serpent," Gerta concluded.

Kian could not understand why he felt as he did. He was going home. Home to the girl he wanted and always had wanted. Why, then, did he feel that his execution was at hand?

"I'm going to miss you, Kian," said Lonny Burk. That made him realize why he felt so inappropriately bad. "We will all miss you, but I know that I will miss you most."

"I—" He swallowed a lump. "Know." And how he wished she was the girl who would be his bride. But the right girl had pointy ears and always had had. Not too long ago Lonny wouldn't even have looked desirable to him. No, the right girl had to be the one at home. It hurt, but somehow it had to be right. His mother had known what was right—hadn't she?

"Good-bye, Lonny, good-bye." Saying it, he felt his insides tormenting him as if from a sword wound. Dungeon food did not account for it. "If—if things were different—"

"I know." He felt her hand delicately touch his, and then, incredibly, her kiss. It was almost—in fact it was—too much for one weak man to bear. Tears filled his eyes.

They were waiting for him. He forced himself to turn away from her and to begin, step by step, what had to be his successful return.

But Kelvin and John Knight were with Queen Zanaan, and the older man looked just as uncomfortable as Kian felt. The queen turned, her great green eyes bearing on him, so familiar yet strange in their gentleness.

"I understand that in your frame my analogue was your mother," she said. "I have had no children, but had I done so, I would have been pleased to have one like you."

Kian found himself hugging her, just as if she were indeed his mother. If only things were different!

30 /

VICTORY HOME FRONT

T HEY EMERGED FROM THE chamber to discover Jon and Heln waiting. Without a moment's delay all embraced.

"Oh, Kelvin," Heln said against his chest. "I had this dream! I think the dragonberries have caused me to dream what is actually happening! I saw all of you back here, so I persuaded Jon—"

"There was only the one boat here, and that too small for the four of you," Jon explained. "Mr. Yokes was kind enough to lend us another, particularly after I explained about the baby coming."

"Baby! Baby—you?"

"No, you idiot!" Jon managed to sound offended. "Your wife."

"Heln! Heln?" Kelvin's face paled, as though real danger was upon him. "You?"

She nodded, smiling prettily in the manner only a pregnant wife could. "You're going to be a daddy, Hero, like it or not."

Kelvin's whoop echoed and reechoed from the surrounding rock for a distance up and down the underground river. Kian pounded his back and shook his hand enthusiastically. But even so, there was a certain half-hidden reticence to his congratulations that registered with each of them.

St. Helens took a deep breath, trying to shut out of his consciousness the sounds of screaming men and terrified, suffering horses. She might take all their lives, he thought, but by the Gods, he'd get this witch! Burn a witch alive, he'd been told. By the heavens, if that was what it took, he'd do it!

Back in the pass, the avalanches went on and on, boulders dislodged by the quake bounding and rebounding and often striking flesh. Great cracks were opening like hungry mouths, swallowing men and horses unfortunate enough to be under.

Was she laughing, up there? If so, he'd stop it! He'd stop it for all time, whatever it took!

St. Helens drew the polished, razor-sharp sword the young king had given him and pressed its cool metal to his lips briefly. Now, he thought, and activated the levitation belt.

He floated soundless as a rising balloon. He cleared the overhang and the three ledges of Conjurer's Rock and disturbed some buzvuls brooding on their nests. In a moment they were after him, circling, crying out hoarsely, snapping their beaks, trying each and every one of them to snap out an eye. He swished the sword, downed two of them, and then another. The remaining buzvuls circled, coming in more cautiously. He wished that Melbah could have been one of those killed.

Stunted trees, twisted and gnarled, grew on the sides of Conjurer's Rock as he approached the top. At the crest the trees seemed all occupied by buzvuls—hundreds if not thousands of them. His sword made a continuous flash, but few of the ugly birds risked the blade. Silently he drifted above the trees and the buzvuls, ignoring the squawks. If she was preoccupied with her magic, maybe then he had a chance.

There she was! At the very edge of the rock. Her black cloak flapping, her arms stretched out toward the pass, her lips making sounds that were lost in the rumbling of the earth and the cries of brave and good men. She couldn't hear the buzvuls, he thought, and she couldn't hear him either. Now, now was his chance!

He drifted at slow speed toward her back. Not quite sporting, he thought, but then how sporting was she? Just end her life and he would end that of a killing germ. He visualized her head bouncing down the rock with her hair flowing. He raised the sword, prepared to sever her neck.

A buzvul screamed above him, and the witch vanished. "Fool!" the bird cried. "Fool, to seek to destroy me with nothing more potent than an ordinary sword!" She had fooled him again, the cunning crone!

He raised the blade but could not reach her with it. "Come! Come!" he cried.

Suddenly the air thickened between them. It was a wall of heavy air, pushing down like a wedge of water, forcing him down with his belt.

"Two can play at that game," he said, though he knew he was in trouble. He pushed the control to Accelerate, Maximum, Up. His body shook and he felt as though being pressed flat. Then the trees of Conjurer's Rock were nearer and he was in them. Buzvuls flew up in a cloud. Sharp branches like oversized thorns reached and grasped. Wind shook him. Tips of ugly gnarled branches entered his arms, his legs, his back. He screamed, loudly, and he thought finally. The wind took away his scream and left him impaled and mute: a crucified prisoner. He was stuck, probably forever. The penetrating branches burned with the fire of thistles deep in his flesh.

Finally, it seemed a year or two later, he gained some control. His flesh was tormented, but there appeared to be no vital injuries. He could still fight his way free, and—

A buzvul lit at the edge of the rock. Abruptly it was an old woman with a wrinkled face and a squat body wrapped in a cloak that flew like dark wings on either side. Her naked form was grossly distorted. Ugly? There were no words!

Her hands reached, claws extended, as if seeking to grasp the men and horses down in the broken and trembling pass. St. Helens had to see, and for once cursed the fact that he had eyes. Men and horses were fighting to get free of rocks heaped upon them; men and horses and parts of men and parts of horses, squashed, broken, ruined. Equipment sticking up through jagged wounds in the earth. It was a victory that would have seemed complete to any general, but the creature on the rock's edge was no human general. There was, he realized at last, little that was human about her.

Melbah, the witch triumphant, raised her hands, palms facing each other. Was that a chant? St. Helens shivered, despite the heat and the pain.

A small spark formed between Melbah's stubby fingers. It grew to the size of a grape, an apple, a watermelon. Suddenly there was a great roaring ball of fire floating just off the rock in front of her stark and disturbingly ugly form. The heat blasted back at him, suffocatingly. *Gods,* he thought, *she intends to hurl that at them! To burn them, each and every one! Gods!*

A loud, cackling laugh chilled him even through the heat. "Now, St. Helens, you pitiful excuse for an opponent, see what becomes of my enemies! See the folly of defying me! See the destruction you have wrought!"

St. Helens wanted desperately to stop her. He could not. Failing that, he wanted only to close his eyes—and could not. She had him captive, as audience as well as enemy.

Mor crouched beside a fallen boulder next to a horse's sightless head, the body of the animal buried in the solid earth. "Lester," he said, feeling the bump on his own forehead and the gash made by the rock. "Lester, where are you?"

Then he saw his son, half buried under his own dead horse. Lester's head and shoulders were visible, the rest of him under the horse's throat. It was hard to know whether he was crushed, or unconscious, or even dead.

Mor crawled to him, swearing softly, angrily, helplessly. So many dead around. So many hurt. So many screaming and moaning. Brave men in the prime of health but a short breath ago. Now—

A figure staggered over to him through the dust. With shock he recognized General Broughtner.

"Mor, we're done. We need to retreat, if we can scrape up the strength even for that. There's no going into Aratex. The witch beat us! I thought her magic was fake . . ."

Mor had to agree. Only something like the laser John Knight had used with his son Kelvin to slay dragons could accomplish anything now. But they didn't have any such weapon, and as far as he knew, none now existed.

"They were right about her," he gasped, hating the taste of his own bitter words. "She's more powerful than any army! Deadlier, even, than the sorcerer the Roundear destroyed."

"Stronger than the Roundear," the general said.

Mor winced to hear it, but he had to agree. Zatanas' deadliest magic never equaled an earthquake, and for all the prophecy, Kelvin would be as helpless as they were. How could anyone fight a witch who could make the very earth open up and swallow an army?

"He's alive," General Broughtner said, bending over Lester and looking under his eyelids. "Unconscious." With his strong hands the general lifted the dead horse's head. Despite his dizziness, Mor managed to pull his son free. He could see that Lester was alive, and might recover with proper care if they could get him home to Jon in time.

But that brought up another question. "Do we have the men and strength to get the wounded out?"

The general shook his head. "It will be tough. We'll need help just to retreat. If we surrender now, maybe she'll let us go."

"You think so?"

"No, but we have to hope. I'll get the surrender flag out of the supply wagon. If I can find it."

The general moved off, head down. Mor was alone with his son. He smoothed Lester's brow, wiping away some blood and sweat and dirt. He cursed for a while, then swore for a while, and finally prayed a little. They would never get away from here, he thought. None of them. The witch meant to destroy every vestige of their army. This, barring a miracle, was total defeat.

He tried looking at Conjurer's Rock and wishing St. Helens had gotten there. Yet he knew that even if the man had, Melbah would have smashed him as readily as a man swatted a fly. There was no defeating Melbah; the witch was just too strong.

As he looked toward the distant stubby shape, trying to discern her form, a great brightness like a rising sun formed between him and the rock. There was a fireball there—a great mass of flame. It was streaking toward them, like a monstrous flaming arrow. It was witch's fire, the stuff Mor had heard about. Coming to burn them all, to destroy every one of them.

Mor tried to grasp it. Not defeat; this was beyond that. Annihilation.

On the way out of the underground river to the remains of the old palace, Heln and Jon filled them in on St. Helens and the affairs of Aratex. Kelvin listened carefully, not revealing too much of what had happened after he had started out with St. Helens. His anger at his father-in-law had been burning like a white-hot coal ever since he stepped back into his home frame. Now, hearing what trouble the man was in, he could almost rejoice. *Let him stay there! Let old Melbah have him for a plaything! Good riddance to bad in-law!*

His father surprised him. "I think the three of us had best get to Aratex fast!"

Kelvin gave him as cold a stare as he could manage. There was just no way that his father was making sense.

"He saved your Heln, Kelvin. Surely that must move you, if the insult to your country and your countrymen does not."

"Not to mention the prophecy," Jon said.

But can we help? Kelvin wondered. *Can we do anything at all against a genuine witch?*

"You're right, Father," he said. "We have to try."

They deposited Heln back at her room in the Rud palace. King Rufurt was there to greet them and shake their hands. He made no objection to their leaving immediately for Aratex. Lines etched in his face told more deeply than words how seriously he was taking this.

"I'm coming, too!" Jon proclaimed.

"No, Brother Wart, definitely not this time."

She stuck her tongue out at him. "I've got better eyes than any of you! I can spot danger before you think about it! Who hit Zatanas with a rock?"

"Who nearly had all her blood drained?" Kelvin retorted. "You have to stay, Jon. It's not right that you—"

"Chauvinist! Whose man do you think may be in trouble? My man Lester, that's who!"

"Certainly you can come, Jon," Kelvin's father said, to Kelvin's disgust. "Glad to have you along. I don't think we could leave without you."

Thus were things settled as they usually were where Kelvin's point-eared sister was concerned. The four of them rode to the river without incident, found the new bridge, and crossed it into Aratex territory. The ride to Deadman's Pass was marked by numerous horse droppings and wagon ruts. Just as they reached the entrance to the pass, there was a roar ahead, and the ground shook under the hooves of their borrowed war-horses. The shaking continued, and clouds of dust billowed from the pass. A terrible roar developed, making it worse.

"Earthquake and avalanche!" John Knight proclaimed. "Lord, if they're caught in that—"

"It's her!" Jon shrieked. "It's Melbah, up on Conjurer's Rock! She's doing it! She's causing the ground to shake!"

"You're crazy, Brother Wart!" Kelvin said, in his usual patient way with her. He was trying to control his mount's nervous jerking.

"Crazy, am I? Look, just look! On top of Conjurer's Rock! Up above the dust cloud, up above the pass! Look!"

Kelvin strained his eyes, and so did his brother and his father. From here Conjurer's Rock looked like a foreshortened tree stump rising above the dust and the pass. Could there be a little ant on the top of that stump, with outstretched arms? Jon seemed to think so. He had known that his sister possessed almost unnaturally clear eyesight, but seeing Melbah on top of Conjurer's Rock from this distance seemed impossible.

"You've got to *do* something!" Jon insisted. "You've got to, Kel! She'll kill all of them! She'll kill Lester!"

Do? What could he do? From this distance he couldn't even see Melbah, let alone stop her if she was indeed there.

"The Mouvar weapon," his father said. "Use it, Kelvin! Try shooting it at her!"

"It won't do any good," Kelvin said. Then, recognizing the desperation in his father's voice and his sister's face, he reached for it. Immediately he was jolted, almost lost his balance, and had to grab suddenly for the horse's mane. Jon, in an unlikely maneuver, joined him on the back of his war-horse. She had almost dislodged him!

"Hurry! Hurry!" she said urgently.

He got out the weapon. What should he do, just point it at the rock and pretend he could see something there? Should the weapon be elevated, as an impossibly powerful crossbow would have to be? Just what should he—

A tiny spark shone brightly against the top of the stump. It did not dim and go out, but immediately started swelling, moving like a flaming arrow.

"It's a fireball!" Jon shouted in his ear. "Stop it! Stop it now!"

As if he could! Yet all he could do was try.

The Mouvar weapon was pointed in the right direction. *Do your stuff, Gauntlets!*

Jon's hand was over his and the gauntlet. Her finger was over the gauntlet finger. The trigger squeezed in a quick, sure motion.

Bright light flashed, filling his eyes and head. WHOOMPTH! echoed and reechoed as before. The horse reared, and Kelvin and Jon slid together down the sloping back and ignominiously off the rump.

Thump! Oof! And the world spun around and about for what seemed far too long a time.

St. Helens watched the fireball as it receded from the face of the cliff. It grew larger as it flew, streaked with terrible brightness and destructive potential. The men at the pass would be cooked along with their horses, and only their charred bones would remain. This was a victory for Melbah so complete, so overwhelming, that never again would Aratex be invaded.

"Damn you, witch!" St. Helens muttered. It was an insignificant thing to do, hardly even a decent oath. Yet a bit of defiance, however futile, was better than silence. His flesh hurt where the tree branches pierced it, but the pain of his crucified form was as nothing compared with the agony of witnessing this total defeat of his side. This was, of course, why Melbah had let him live: so he could suffer more.

Suddenly, almost as if the fireball were responding to his curse, the fireball slowed. In fact, it hesitated. Melbah, on the cliff's edge, screamed at it. She leveled her arms, fingers extended, but to no avail. *The fireball was reversing course!*

Now it came roaring back in all its fury. It loomed monstrously large, throwing off sparks, hissing loudly, its heat blistering even as far as St. Helens. The foliage of the trees shriveled and twisted, and the sky seemed ablaze.

Melbah did not wait to embrace her creation. She raised her arms and flapped them wildly. The arms became wings, and her body had feathers, and she was climbing desperately skyward as only a frightened buzvul could.

The fireball changed direction. *It was following her!*

Melbah climbed higher. She zigged and zagged in the evasive action of a bird. But the fireball caught her, engulfed her, and devoured her in its flames. There wasn't any shriek, only a loud pop as the fireball and its contents disappeared.

Then, seemingly from the open sky, came a fall of feathers, burning as they fell. As they landed where the witch had been, they became bits of flesh and bone. The fragments continued to burn, steaming and blackening, losing all semblance of human or animal nature. Not even a skeleton, not even bones remained, only simple ash, spread across the edge of the rock.

St. Helens found that the tree branches had loosened. They were only misshapen trees now, no longer the magical henchmen they had been while the witch lived. Wincing from the pain, he pulled himself out of his trap. He activated his belt and flew over to the rock edge.

Still it was only ash. Had his curse done this? Was there something magical in his makeup? He did not believe that for a moment! After all, he cursed all the time, and it didn't even generate a haze, let alone incinerating fire. But certainly the witch was dead; that he had to believe.

He lowered himself to the rock's edge. He scattered Melbah's ashes and watched them fly away in the wind. She wasn't coming back! There were no buzvuls bothering him. He had won, or someone had won, though he couldn't figure out how.

He had to get down there in the pass and see if there was a magician among them. Somehow this thing had happened, catching him completely by surprise, not to mention Melbah! Someone there had to know.

He reactivated his belt, flew from the rock, and lowered himself down into the pass, where the carnage appeared even worse than it had from above. The witch had just about finished this army before sending the fire-ball!

He spotted Mor, bent over his son, and suffered a stab of remorse. Was the boy dead? He paused and called out to Mor, getting his attention.

Mor's face lighted as he looked up. "You did it, St. Helens! You stopped her! You destroyed her for all of us!"

St. Helens decided against enlightening the man at the moment. "Lester —is he—?"

"Unconscious. Not hurt bad, I think. He's a Crumb. We Crumbs have hard heads."

"General Broughtner—is he alive?"

"He's checking the damage done back there," Mor said, indicating the way with a wave. "There's a lot of it. At least up this way."

"Thanks, Mor. I'll be back." He flew up the pass, seeing more and worse destruction the farther he went. Men were squashed by great rocks, and horses were half buried.

Finally he spotted the general straining with other men to lift the huge supply wagon off the shattered leg of a mercifully unconscious man. When the job was accomplished, St. Helens landed silently beside them. The general had the aspect of a thoroughly defeated man.

"The witch is dead, General," St. Helens said. "She was the main obstacle."

"Dead?" The man seemed reluctant to believe this.

"She sent a fireball, and it turned on her and destroyed her. It burned her to ashes. She is gone, dead by her own magic. Didn't any of you see it happen?"

"I saw the fireball," a man agreed. "I saw it turn—and then it winked out."

"When it burned up its creator," St. Helens said. "What are your plans, General?"

"Plans?" Broughtner looked around at the dead and dying. "You think I've got plans?"

No, St. Helens thought. Of course he didn't. His army was in sad straits, even without further molestation by the witch. It was a shame, because with Melbah gone, King Phillip should be vulnerable. There was that prophecy for a Roundear that was supposed to apply to Kelvin: uniting two.

Yes, damn it, if Phillip would just abdicate! That would complete the job.

St. Helens made up his mind in that moment. His hands played at the controls on the levitation belt.

"Don't give up hope, General. I have a plan." With that he rose vertically with the belt, angled his body and flight path past Conjurer's Rock, and took himself down the darkening sky to the palace of the boy king of Aratex. Once there, he entered the window he had left with Heln a lifetime ago.

The room appeared much as it had before, and with his careful surveillance and good luck, he believed he had not been spotted. As he looked around the room a horrible apparition was suddenly facing him. He grabbed for his sword, and the other did likewise in perfect synchronization. With a shock he realized that it was he himself, reflected in a mirror: battered and bruised, hair and beard unkempt, blood and dirt on his clothing and hands and face, and bits of leaf and bark from the trees he had been in.

He shuddered, wishing he could clean up. He had never been a really handsome man, and he wasn't young anymore, but this was ridiculous!

He tried the door and found it unlocked. The guards had not bothered to lock it after the prisoner had escaped. He started down the stairs. If the king was inside today, as he was nearly every other day . . .

He had made up his mind that what young Phillip needed was a hiding. That was what his own daddy had administered to him on occasion, and eventually it must have worked. Today he was what he was, and if he hadn't had the hidings, there was little question that he could have been worse. Yes, indeed, young King Phillip was going to get the hiding he had long promised himself to deliver.

"Where do you think you're going?"

It was Bemode, standing at the foot of the stairs, sword drawn.

Well, I've done it before, St. Helens thought, and drew his sword. Only this time he was weaker, more tired, and older in all respects. So it would be more difficult. He started down the stairs cautiously, hoping he could last.

"Bemode!" a shrill voice called out. His Majesty Himself strode from the playroom and stopped, standing there with red, swollen eyes, but with more than a hint of command in his voice.

"But, Your Majesty—"

"Please go outside, Bemode. Leave us alone. There are things we have to discuss."

Bemode looked from St. Helens to his nominal boss and back again. His piggish eyes drifted in confusion and he seemed to be trying to decide.

"That's a command, Bemode!"

The man sheathed his sword. St. Helens sheathed his. The man left. St. Helens was disgusted. John Knight, back in the old days of their unit, had never given a command twice, knowing it would be obeyed with alacrity the first time, whatever it might be. John Knight had been a real leader then. These undisciplined palace guards nauseated him.

"Now, St. Helens, friend, come with me."

St. Helens followed, wondering why. The king was acting as if this return were routine. Inside the toy room was much as it had been; toys were on the shelves, and there was a table set with a chessboard and chessmen St. Helens himself had made.

"One last game, friend," Phillip said, gesturing at the board. "One last, and I won't throw a tantrum if I don't win."

St. Helens brushed some sweat out of his eyes, trying hard to understand what was in the young king's head. "You kept it set up, just as when we played every night!"

"Yes. Melbah was no good as a player. So please, one last game, and then you can kill me as you plan."

"Kill you!" St. Helens exclaimed, genuinely astonished. "Kill you? Why?"

The boy's stricken face rose from its contemplation of the chessboard and the chairs. "She's dead, isn't she, St. Helens? Isn't that why you came here? You couldn't have, otherwise. Not alone. She was watching for you; she had magic telltales set. She would have captured you, tormented you, and then brought you back."

"You really think that I—with this sword you gave me—?"

The king lowered his eyes. "It is all I deserve or ever have deserved."

"Gods!" St. Helens said. There was just no beating the kid after this. He had been in effect checkmated—by a pupil who had learned his lessons better than the teacher.

Mor blinked in astonishment, and Lester gaped, as St. Helens dropped from the air with the young king on his back. He started to reach for his sword, but then stayed his hand. This was the king, after all, and St. Helens obviously had brought him in for a purpose.

"Lester, Mor, the fighting's over and there's no more Aratex. My son-in-law's prophecy is going to be fulfilled, with him or without him." *And how I wish he were here, alive and in good health! How I wish I had not tricked him, betrayed him, with all the arrogance and forethought of a Phillip. Maybe I was bewitched at the time, or at least out of my head. But no, I know St. Helens better than any man, and I know the responsibility is mine. What would I say to him now if I had the chance? What would I say?*

"Hello, St. Helens. I'm glad you managed to redeem yourself."

It was St. Helens' turn to blink. Four horsemen were there behind the fallen rocks. He was certain they hadn't been there when he had left.

They were: Jon Crumb, Lester's wife. John Knight, his old commander and Kelvin's father. Kian Knight, Kelvin's half brother. And the fourth was none other than Kelvin Knight Hackleberry, who had just spoken.

"Kelvin, can you—can you forgive me for what I have done to you?"

"Maybe, Father-in-law. Maybe when your grandchild is old enough to ask. Maybe then I'll forgive you for helping me fulfill the two words of prophecy."

"Grandchild? Heln?" He had been told before, but it was almost as if he were hearing the words for the first time. Recent events had almost banished the matter from his mind. The world whirled, and somehow it seemed quite natural that he crash-landed on his face with the young king on top of him. He lay there, quite moved but unmoving, as King Blastmore proclaimed the words they had agreed he should:

"As the sovereign ruler of the kingdom of Aratex, I solemnly proclaim Aratex's complete and unconditional surrender to the kingdom of Rud. With this I abdicate Aratex's throne, relinquish all claims, and beg the mercy and forgiveness of King Rufurt of Rud!"

Sweeter words, St. Helens thought happily, he would never live to hear.

Heln dreamed, and knew that she dreamed.

In her dream a beautiful young woman with long blond hair and deep blue eyes was undressing. With her was a man, a former queen's guardsman she had seen at the palace petitioning for a pension. The man, too, was undressing, his every motion evincing eagerness. In back of them stood a waiting bed.

Must I see this! Oh, must I! Heln thought.

Instantly she was outdoors, outside the cottage her dreamself had been in. There, coming toward the cottage door, a smile on his face that she somehow recognized as forced, was Kian, her husband's brother.

Oh, poor Kian! Poor Kian! she thought. Then she was awake, a sob choking her and taking her breath.

"Oh, poor Kian!" she said aloud to the empty room. "Poor man! I feel so sorry for you, Kian! But there isn't anything I can do." For though she had seen it in a dream, she knew it was not; it was another aftereffect of the astral separations she had done before. She had seen the ugly truth.

Her life was happy now, but that wasn't enough. Sadder than she had been for a long time, Heln broke down and wept.

Epilogue

T HEY WERE FINALLY GATHERED together again in Kelvin's house. The wars were over for the time being, and they could relax and be family and friends.

"Apparently it's antimagic," Mor was saying, looking at the Mouvar weapon Kelvin was showing them. "The way it took the fire back to the witch, and the way you say it stopped the flopears and the serpents in that other world."

"Yes," John Knight said. "I figured out that it turns the magic energy back, whatever it is, on the sender. Thus in the other frame the hypnotic freezing stare was returned, while here it was the witch's fireball. When the control knob got moved, it merely blocked the magic without returning it in kind. Thus the flopears remained a danger but could not paralyze with a glance. But once the knob was at its original setting, it returned the magic and the flopears paralyzed themselves."

"Hooray for here!" Jon said, lifting her second glass of razzlefruit wine with bright enthusiasm. "Hooray for making Kel use that weapon!"

Kelvin glared at her, deciding that his little sister should never, ever be allowed to touch wine. It was obvious to him that all she had done was interfere in what he and the gauntlet would have handled.

"Well, at least you were saved," Lester said, coming to Kelvin's rescue and taking the glass from her hand.

"Except that you did fall on your butt," Kelvin added, referring to the time she slid off the rear of the horse and he fell on top of her.

Jon glared at all of them until Heln rescued her in turn.

Heln, now rapidly approaching parturition and all that it implied, began reciting without the help of wine:

"A Roundear there Shall Surely be
Born to be Strong, Raised to be Free

Fighting Dragons in his Youth
Leading Armies, Nothing Loth
Ridding his Country of a Sore
Joining Two, then uniting Four . . .

"You've joined two, Kelvin," she pointed out. "Now that the citizenry of Aratex has voted to unite its country with that of Rud!"

"That means," said St. Helens, now permanently reunited with the group, "that the next task you face is uniting four. I suggest—"

Kelvin gave him a hostile look and St. Helens subsided, doubtlessly remembering. They had almost been to blows after Kelvin's timely arrival in Aratex. The tongue-lashing Kelvin had delivered on the spot in front of Aratex's young king was more than St. Helens had stood for since his basic training. Now the two were friends, or at least relatives. But Kelvin suspected, and St. Helens knew, that St. Helens felt he should have been given a governing position. Kelvin didn't believe in nepotism, particularly extended to in-laws, and the voices of the people were now being heard in the first of the infant country's elections. The new name for Aratex annexed to Rud was going to be Kelvinia, not Helenland, as St. Helens had unblushingly suggested.

Kian still looked sad, an entire month after their triumph in Aratex. Everyone noticed it, particularly Heln.

"Why so sad, Kian?" she finally asked.

Kian was not long in answering. "Lenore. Lenore Barley. I don't want to marry her. I want Lonny back in the other frame."

"I could have told you that, son," John Knight said gently.

"You could? Why didn't you?"

"I felt you'd need to find out yourself. Didn't you notice that almost all the look-alikes had characters opposite to their counterparts? King Rufurt, for instance, is mostly kind and gentle, but his counterpart was cruel and delighted in inflicting pain. Cheeky Jack was a contemptible bandit who sold mere boys and girls into slavery. Jack's counterpart is a heroic person, a genuine patriot, and one of the finest men I've met. What does that say to your inherited intelligence, son?"

Kian thought for a moment. Then his expression lightened as he faced the notion that he had somehow resisted before. "Lonny—she's opposite!"

"Right!"

"When I called on Lenore she was—" He choked, his face now red. "With someone. A man. An ugly man who had served the queen. It wasn't like Heln imprisoned in the Girl Mart and unable to help herself. She—she wanted him. He challenged me to a fight. She laughed, clapping her hands as if delighted. I walked away, the first time I ever walked away from such a challenge. I didn't want to give her the satisfaction. I—"

"And what does this say about the nature of your mother?" John Knight spoke with dignity and sadness. "Think back. Her counterpart was as different from her as Lonny is from Lenore."

Kian's face clouded. This was the source of his reluctance to accept the situation. "She's my mother. She's—"

"Probably dead," John said. He said it matter-of-factly, having come to terms with this in his own time. "Remember, I thought her everything the queen in the other frame is, and she wasn't."

Kian wiped at a tear. "I guess I have to accept."

"You'd better, Kian. There is no real choice. You loved what you felt should be there, just as I did."

"Lonny—"

"People have some choice whether to be good or bad," St. Helens said, breaking in. "Phillip had no choice, but if I had had his upbringing, I might have been as bad. Now he's got a chance to be good, and he's going to be, making chessmen and chessboards with me and having tournaments. You know, the boy has a real talent for chess. Right now, except for me, I'd say he's this world's champion."

"But only two of you play that silly game in this world!" Jon retorted. Everyone laughed.

"No, I know how to play, too," John Knight said, ignoring St. Helens. "You'll have to go back to get her or to stay with her. You haven't any choice. It's like Kelvin and the prophecy: no choice for either of you."

"No choice," Kian agreed. He stood up from the table, a determined and happy look on his face. "I'm going back! To live there or to bring her back!"

"And I'm going with you," John said, also rising. "There's no way I'll miss attending my older son's wedding."

Kian paused, looking at him. "You know, Queen Zanaan's a widow now, technically, and—"

"And it remains awkward for me in Rud, where I'm supposed to be dead. Charlain—"

"Is married to a good man," Kian agreed. "I don't think she'd mind if you—"

"That was my thought," John Knight agreed. "I think I need a wife as much as you do, and you need a mother again."

The two exchanged glances, understanding perfectly.

St. Helens, wineglass in hand, flush on nose, lurched to his feet and, unasked, led everyone in a rousing cheer. "And don't come back!" he bawled as the two departed. There had been a time when that would have been an insult.

Kelvin looked at Heln, and then at Lester and Jon. They nodded. It was the best way to lose a father or a brother.

It was a great, fine time in Kelvinia.

Chimaera's Copper

Contents

Introduction

THIS IS THE THIRD novel in a fantasy series in which the inhabitants of alternate worlds are distinguished by the shape of their ears. In the first novel, *Dragon's Gold,* young round-eared Kelvin and his point-eared little tomboy sister Jon managed to kill a golden-scaled dragon and later save the kingdom of Rud and their father John Knight from the clutches of evil Queen Zoanna. In the process, Kelvin found love with round-eared Heln, and Jon with Lester Crumb.

In the sequel, *Serpent's Silver,* Kelvin's half brother Kian discovered an alternate world where most folk were round-eared, but it wasn't John Knight's world of origin, Earth. Some folk had flop-ears, and many folk were similar to those of the point-eared world, except that their characters were reversed. Here good King Rufurt was evil King Rowforth, and evil Queen Zoanna was good Queen Zanaan. Instead of golden-scaled dragons there were silver-skinned serpents. Again the forces of evil were finally thwarted—but the mysterious Prophecy of Mouvar had not yet run its full course.

The third novel, *Chimaera's Copper,* covers another stage of that prophecy. But that does not mean the outcome is certain; for one thing, there are those who doubt that the prophecy has any validity. There are many characters, and versions of characters, so it may be best to refer to the following descriptions of characters when there is confusion. They are listed approximately in the order of their appearance or relevance to the story, and of course there is much about them that is not told here. Things are often not quite what they seem, when magic is involved.

Characters

Mouvar—fabled roundear who made the prophecy and set up a chain of scientific transporters linking the frames

Queen Zoanna—beautiful, evil former queen of Rud in the pointear frame; lost in dark nether waters near the Flaw

Professor Devale—demon sorcerer and educator

King Rowforth—evil king of Hud, deposed. Analogue of good King Rufurt in the pointear frame.

Queen Zanaan—the good version of Zoanna, in the roundear frame

Broughtmar—former aide and torture-master to King Rowforth; a mean man

Zotannas—good magician, but little real magic; Queen Zanaan's father. Analogue of *Zatanas,* evil magician of the point-eared frame.

Kelvin Knight Hackleberry—the unlikely hero of the prophecy, and thus of all the novels of this series

King Rufurt—good king of Kelvinia, a gentle and somewhat ineffective man

Charley Lomax—one of the king's guards

John Knight—traveler from Earth, stranded in the magic realm; father of Kelvin and Kian

Slatterly—another guard

Kian Knight—Kelvin's half brother, the son of John Knight and Queen Zoanna

Lonny Burk—girl of Hud whom Kian loves

Heln—Kelvin's roundeared and pregnant wife

Jon—Kelvin's younger sister. His ears are round, hers pointed. He sometimes calls her "Brother Wart" because she once posed as a boy

St. Helens—familiar name for Sean Reilly, Heln's father from Earth; once a soldier in John Knight's platoon

Lester "Les" Crumb—Jon's husband, son of Mor Crumb

Charlain—Kelvin and Jon's mother; wife first of John Knight, then of Hal Hackleberry

Hal Hackleberry—Charlain's second husband; a good but simple man, whose name Kelvin and Jon took

Easter Brownberry—Hal's girlfriend

Old Man Zed Yokes—river man who ferries others across

Phillip Blastmore—former boy-king of the kingdom of Aratex before it became part of Kelvinia

Morton "Mor" Crumb—former leader of a band that helped Kelvin overthrow the evil Queen Zoanna of Rud; now a general

King Bitler—king of Hermandy, one of the seven kingdoms

Chimaera—with three heads: Mervania, Mertin, and Grumpus

Dr. Lunox Sterk—Royal Physician of Kelvinia

Stapular—prisoner of the chimaera

King Kildom—boy-king of Klingland

King Kildee—boy-king of Kance

Helbah—old sorceress of Klingland and Kance, good version of *Melbah* of Aratex

Katbah—Helbah's houcat familiar

Bloorg—Keeper of the Chimaera and official greeter of travelers

Captain Abileey—officer in Mor Crumb's army

Captain Plink—officer in Mor Crumb's army

Captain Barnes—Lester Crumb's second-in-command

Grool—Bloorg's second-in-command

Squirtmuck—a froogear leader

General De Gaulic—Commander of the Army of Kance

Lieutenant Karl Klumpecker—mercenary officer from Throod

King Hoofourth—monarch of the kingdom of Scud

Bert—a guard at the transporter cave

Scarface Jac—outlaw of Scud, analogue of *Cheeky Jac* in another frame, and of *Smoothy Jac*

Queeto—evil dwarf companion to Zatanas

Heeto—saintly dwarf companion to Zotannas

Smith—or a man by a similar name, member of Jac's band

Marvin Loaf—analogue of Morton Crumb

Hester—Marvin's son = *Lester*

Jillip—member of Marvin's band, analogue of *Phillip*

Corporal Hinzer—soldier in Lomax's camp

Redleaf—member of Marvin's band

Bilger—member of Marvin's band

Commander Mac—in charge of the Recruitment House; similar to *Captain MacKay* and *Captain McF*

Trom—guard
Mabel Crumb—Mor Crumb's wife
Charles Knight—Kelvin's son
Merlain Knight—Kelvin's daughter

Prologue

NIGHT

S HE KNEW WHERE SHE was going, if only she could get there.
She had prevailed on the foolish John Knight to bring her this
far; now she had to go on alone.

She stepped off the raft and sank into the dark water. One arm was
useless, but she could still move the other, and her legs. She swam as well as
she was able, down, down toward the bottom, not even trying to hold her
breath, for it would only buoy her body. The air in her tired chest squeezed
out of her nose and mouth and bubbled up in a silvery stream toward the
raft and the confused man. Let him go; his usefulness to her was done. The
current would carry him into the dread Flaw.

She found the lock, and managed to drag herself into it. In a moment she
came up in air, gasping. She sprawled onto a platform, and finally let her
consciousness fade.

Sometime later, in the dead of the eternal night that ruled here, a figure
came. It was gross and masculine. "You have returned, Zoanna," it rasped.

She roused herself. "I need your help, Professor," she said weakly.

"I see you have broken bones. I can heal them. What will you pay?"

She struggled, and managed to turn over, so that she lay on her back. She
spread her good arm, and her good legs, and smiled despite the pain.

The figure stared down, interested. It reached out to squeeze a breast, as
if checking its freshness. "For how long?"

"I want—I want to go to school, this time," she said. "To learn sorcery.
For as long as it takes."

"That is long enough." The figure heaved her up and carried her away.

MORNING

T HE WIDE MAN had once worn a crown. Now he wore only a torn robe and many bruises as he stepped from the transporter into the empty chamber. This was the world they had come from, he was sure. He had watched from concealment as they climbed the ladder to the ledge. Then he had followed, certain of what he would find: their gateway between worlds.

In the otherwise empty chamber on his home world he had not hesitated before using the transporter to follow. What was there for him at home, now, as a usurped king? Nothing but death at the hands of Broughtmar, his former aide, or some other disgruntled soldier. Or possibly at the hands of Zotannas, his queen's treacherous old father. If not death, certainly imprisonment, or life as an outcast. No, there was nothing there for him! Better to plunge boldly into something new, where his chances might be better and could hardly be worse.

Besides, there was something else. It was as if some mysterious impulse drew him along, as if someone were calling him. Someone he wanted very much to meet.

There was a subtle difference between this chamber and the one he had entered. The one on this world had no exit sign. It was cleaner and there were no dusty footprints on the floor. But the smooth sphere-shaped walls were similar, and there was the same magical radiance, that lit the machine and the table holding the parchment.

He hacked, coughed, and rubbed the bruises on his arms, legs, and face. What treachery Broughtmar had shown him! How he would like to go back and destroy the man. Well, someday he might. Meanwhile, he could relax at night by dreaming up torments for his former torture-master. He had thought the man worshiped his master above all men and gods. It showed that no underling could be trusted.

He read the parchment:

To whom it may concern: if you have found this cell, you are a roundear, because only a roundear could penetrate to it without setting off the self-destruct mechanism.

I am Mouvar—and I am a roundear.

But because the natives look with disfavor on aliens, I masked my ears so that I could work among them without hindrance. I used the technology of

*my home frame to set things straight, then retired, for it was lonely. I set up
the prophecy of my return, or the appearance of any roundear, to facilitate
better acceptance in future centuries. The tools of my frame are here, and you
may use them as you find necessary.*

*If you wish to contact me directly, seek me in my home frame, where I will
be in suspended animation. Directions for using the Flaw to travel to the
frame of your choice are in the book of instructions beside this letter. Please
return any artifacts you borrow. Justice be with you.*

The man who had been king looked around and saw no artifacts. There
was only the closetlike transporter, the table, the parchment, and the in-
struction book. He read the book. Phew! There was extraordinary power
here! He could change the settings, and—

No, it was better not to tempt fate further. He wanted to leave no evidence of his presence at this time. Later, when he had a better notion of the
situation outside the chambers, he might return and do something. All in
good time. He was amazed at what he had learned already.

Smiling with satisfaction at the change in his fortune, he crossed the
chamber to the big, round metal door. He pushed the lever. The door
opened onto a ledge above an underground river—a complete change from
the high cliff at the entrance to the chamber on his own world. The surface
of the water was eerily lit by luminous lichen on the rock walls. And there,
as if specifically placed for him, was waiting one small boat.

Former King Rowforth of Hud, the kingdom in the other frame, smiled
his cruelest smile and clapped his big, powerful hands. Again he felt that
mysterious influence, as if this had been prearranged. Ordinarily he would
be suspicious of such a thing, but in this case he was thankful, because he
suspected that it had saved his life and freedom. Maybe it was destined: he
was fated to survive and dominate. If that smooth-skinned boy, Kelvin
Knight Hackleberry, could claim a prophecy applied to him, why could not
he, a legitimate king, have a preordained destiny? All his life he had believed himself destined to conquer, so why not here first, instead of his home
world? Might he not eventually conquer all kingdoms in all worlds? The
notion was intoxicating!

There came a kind of laughter in his head. Rowforth jumped. It was like
his wife's voice, his queen, yet also quite unlike hers. This was the sound of
victory and cruelty, while his wife was a submissive and kind creature, fool
that she was. Insanity? No, surely not, for he was a king, and a king could
not be insane. It had to be some kind of magic.

With rising excitement, the king launched the boat on the somber river,
got into it, and applied himself to the oars. The wood handles, though
splintery, fit his hands as well as those he had used at home. He put his back
into it, eager to see what destiny had in store for him.

Ahead was a black, roaring falls with deep, deep darkness and stars and
moving points of light. This was no ordinary night, he knew; it was the dread

Flaw! He bypassed it, fighting the current. He knew he didn't want to get swept into that horrendous abyss.

He guided the boat away from the walls and out into the middle of the water as he rounded the bend. He was getting near to something now, and he was feeling it. He believed it would be his aid to destiny. His aid to conquest.

Suddenly he stopped rowing. He seemed to have no choice. What was guiding him?

He gazed down into the water, seeing nothing but his own bruised features. In this world there was a king who looked like him in a country not unlike Hud. That king, unlike himself, had pointed ears. He knew this without knowing how he knew it, or questioning its validity. Here in this world existed a king whose place he might take, if only he hid his ears.

He stood up in the boat, not knowing what he was doing, and peered deep, deep into the murky water. Nothing, not even fish. Only the dim reflections of himself and the boat, and the rock walls gliding by, illuminated by the lichen.

Yet again he felt that mysterious impulse. He took a deep breath and dived. Swimming competently, conserving his breath and energy, he stroked down. Truly he was in the hands of destiny, now.

He dived deeper, deeper, though his body was growing hungry for air. His arms and legs worked steadily, refusing to be halted by fatigue. Silvery bubbles floated from the corners of his mouth. Into a tunnel, its smooth walls coated with more glowing lichen. He had better be going somewhere, because no way could he turn, let alone reach the boat again before drowning.

Then up, up, and suddenly the water parted. Air! He gasped, his chest working like a bellows, pumping in the air. That had been close! Yet he had been guided, somehow.

As his panting eased and his vision cleared, he realized that he was in a chamber not dissimilar from the one he had recently left. There was a woman here, holding a crystal ball. She had very red hair, and eyes incredibly green. Zanaan, his docile queen!

But there were two things distinctly different about her. This woman had no bruises, and her expression was not at all submissive. Also, her ears were pointed.

Pointed ears? Zanaan?

AFTERNOON

RUFURT, KING OF ALL KELVINIA, rode his favorite mare to the ruins of his old palace. With him were two guards with whom he joked in what was his unkingly yet customary fashion.

Leaving the road, he pulled up by the pile of crumbled, fire-blackened masonry. He dismounted just as if he knew what he was doing. Actually King Rufurt, though a hefty enough man, was the soul of innocuousness, and lacked any real force of decision. That, he realized with a certain mild reflection, might be why they considered him to be a good king. He seldom knew exactly what he was doing, but he depended on good subordinates, and they enabled him to govern the kingdom well.

"Stay here," he ordered his guards, and walked casually away. The whim that had taken him was unusual, but perhaps he wanted to urinate behind a tree in privacy.

Around him were piles of ashes, blackened timbers, and the broken statues of former kings of Rud. Many a piece of once-valued art was buried here, though no one cared to recover it, remembering the history of this place. His evil Queen Zoanna had wrought horrendous evil here, and it would be a long time before that was forgotten.

Almost of their own accord, his feet carried him through the ruins. He went down the three flights of crumbling stairs. There, just as he knew it would be, was the underground river.

Standing there on the final landing, he remembered the words of an ancient prophecy:

> *A Roundear there shall surely be*
> *Born to be Strong, Raised to be Free*
> *Fighting Dragons in his Youth*
> *Leading Armies, Nothing Loth*
> *Ridding his Country of a Sore*
> *Joining Two, then uniting Four*
> *Until from Seven there be One*
> *Only then will his Task be Done*
> *Honored by Many, Cursed by Few*
> *All will know what Roundear can do*

To think the Roundear had come in his reign, and then in the unlikely form of someone who seemed to be but a boy: Kelvin Knight Hackleberry! Kelvin had saved the kingdom, and then saved it again. As the prophecy had foretold, he had joined two kingdoms. Rufurt still ruled, thanks to Kelvin, whose nature was almost as benign as Rufurt's own, but now he ruled more than twice Rud's former territory. The merged kingdom was called Kelvinia, after the boy, and Rufurt begrudged him none of that credit. But for Kelvin, Rufurt himself would probably be ignominiously dead now.

Why was he thinking of this, and just why had he climbed down all those awful stairs? His legs ached abominably. He needed to rest, but something screamed at him that he must go back or rue the consequence. At the same time he realized that he hadn't really wanted to climb down these stairs. So why had he done it?

Something went "Click." Something that had no business being here.

He half turned. As he did, a sudden chill formed somewhere in the region of his heart. It was uncanny what was happening to him. It was something he was sure had never happened before.

She stood there behind him, holding a crystal ball. Her hair was as red as dragon sheen, and her eyes the green of feline magic with sparks like tiny stars. Her pointed ears identified her with a horrifying certainty.

"Zoanna," he said. "Zoanna, I thought you dead."

"Yes, one-time king, once my feeble husband. I have returned to reclaim all that I once had and all that has since been gained for me. I am back to rule, Sweet Husband. Back to punish the likes of you, and to destroy the likes of that Hackleberry brat."

"No! No! You drowned! I know you drowned, and—"

She made a pass over the crystal ball with her hand. A repellent shade of red immediately suffused the crystal.

King Rufurt clutched his chest in sudden agony.

"Yes, yes," she murmured, her white teeth glistening as she smiled. "Did I ever tell you how pretty your ears are, my erstwhile liege?"

He fell forward, trying vainly to talk. The dock, when he struck it, seemed to be and not to be, while he—

EVENING

WHEN THE KING finally emerged from the ruins the sun was setting. His face had somehow gotten bruised, though the bruises had the appearance of those acquired days before. His clothes were now soiled, and he wore a stockelcap pulled all the way down over his ears despite the warmth of the day. He wore an expression that was not at all typical for Rufurt: malevolent.

"Your mare, Your Majesty," said Lomax, the tall guard. Though his voice was controlled, he was upset. *This is not right, not right at all.* What had happened to the king, this past hour?

The king went to place his foot in the stirrup that was being held for him. A hoof came for him, grazing his hip. The king stumbled and fell. When he rose a moment later there was no mistaking his expression: mean, extremely mean. Lomax had thought he might be mistaken before, but now there was no doubt. How could this be?

"What's the matter with you, idiot?" the king demanded. "Can't you control a stupid horse?"

The young guardsman swallowed. "Your Majesty—"

The king drew a riding whip from its harness scabbard and lashed the mare across her face. The horse reared, and Lomax was so startled he let go of the reins. The mare took off, running as though for her life.

The king swore, using an oath Lomax had never even heard. "I can't abide an unruly animal! Catch it and slay it!"

"But Your Majesty—" Lomax started, horrified.

"Do it, idiot!" The whistling lash just missed taking his eye out. Lomax swallowed and ran after the horse. She had stopped some distance away, her white-rimmed eyes as frightened as he himself felt. *What is going on here?*

"Here, girl, here," he said, holding out his hand.

The mare let him take the reins. But as he turned to lead her back he saw that the king had drawn a sword. The king intended to kill this beautiful horse! Unbelievable!

Sensing what the man sensed, the mare yanked hard on the reins. This time Lomax deliberately let them slip. The horse ran off.

The king glowered at him. "Never mind, Your Majesty," Lomax said quickly. "I'll catch her again. She caught me by surprise; she isn't usually like this. It may take a little time. Perhaps—" He strove desperately to think of something. "Perhaps you would prefer not to wait. It's a long ride to the palace. Another horse—"

"Yes," the king said grimly. "Another horse, in any event." He spoke roughly to Slatterly, the other guard. "Bring me that roan!"

"Yes, Your Majesty," Slatterly said, and obeyed with alacrity.

Slatterly held the reins and the king mounted. The guard handed up the reins.

The king raised his whip and brought it down first on Slatterly and then on the horse. "Get on your own horse. You ride ahead of me!" he ordered. "Fast! I want to reach the palace by nightfall!"

"Yes, Your Majesty." Lomax had never seen Slatterly move so fast before. But Lomax himself was moving fast, pretending he was going to catch and possibly slay the king's favorite horse.

Hoofbeats, and the king all but rode him down. The roan whirled, raising dust, and the king turned a terrible face down at him. "You, I want you to get that horse!"

"Yes, Your Majesty. Yes, of course."

"And I want you to ride her."

Hope leaped suddenly in Lomax's boyish chest. "Ride her, Your Majesty?"

"Until she drops! Ride her to her death!"

"Majesty, no—"

The whip caught him across the face, stingingly, telling him more plainly than words that this was not the same man who had entered the ruins. "You will do as I order! If you don't, I'll see you in the torture chamber!"

"But Your Majesty, you haven't—haven't got—" He swallowed, knowing that what he most needed to do was shut up.

"Haven't what?" the king demanded ominously.

"Haven't a torture chamber," Lomax said reluctantly.

"That," the king replied, "will be remedied. Now find that horse, ride her until she drops, then beat her to death. Failure in this will cost you your life in much the same manner!"

Lomax watched the bay whirl as the king rode away after Slatterly. He felt tears welling in his eyes, and knew they weren't entirely from the sting of the whip.

"What's gotten into him? What's gotten into him?" he asked the trees and rocks. He didn't know and wasn't certain he wanted to know. Witchcraft? Magic? Something old and evil and ugly? That ruined palace—who knew what evil spirits lurked in there!

But he was only a guardsman. These were, alas, questions his kind was not authorized to ask. But he knew that this was not his king—not the real king, whatever the body was.

There were tears on his face as he went after the mare. It was as though all the good that the roundear had done were now undone, and the bad was returning with a vengeance. How could this happen, so soon after the great victory of the forces of right?

When he caught up to the horse he discovered without surprise that he simply did not have the heart to hurt her, let alone kill her. She was not at fault; she had reacted to the alien nature of the king, being more forthright than the guardsmen dared be. She was too fine an animal to destroy.

He approached the proprietor of a farm where there were a number of horses. "I will trade you this mare for your worst mare of this color and size," he said. "Provided you keep the transaction secret."

"For how much gold?" the sharp farmer demanded.

"No gold. An even trade."

The man studied the mare. He could see that she was as fine a horse as existed in the kingdom. "You stole her?"

This was getting complicated. The truth was better. "She inadvertently offended the king. He ordered me to kill her. I can't do it. Give me a mare I can kill, and never speak of this."

The farmer nodded. "Now I understand." He brought out a scruffy-looking mare. "This one's ill, and due for slaughter anyway."

"She'll do." Lomax rode off on the new mare. When he reached a suitable place, he dismounted, drew his sword, and stabbed her carefully in the heart, so that she died quickly, without extended suffering. Then he took a whip and lashed the body, leaving stripes all over it. He paid special attention to the head, so that it became unrecognizable. This horse now looked as if it had been cruelly beaten to death. The original scruffiness of the animal only enhanced the effect.

He left the corpse there for others to find, knowing that the news would reach the king soon enough. He walked away, not looking back, thinking that if it were not for a certain lady, and not for his love for his homeland, he would desert for another kingdom. He had no pride in what he had done. He knew he had only reduced the evil somewhat, at great risk to himself. If the living mare were ever recognized—

Late in the day he slunk silently into the royal stable. There he found the groom cursing ceaselessly as he treated the deep welts on the roan.

"Rufurt," Lomax whispered softly to himself. "Rufurt, good king, where are you and who is this impostor who so boldly wears your face?"

I /

TRAVEL

ELVIN WAS NOT AT all happy about returning to the world of
silver serpents, but Kian had asked him to please come and be
his best man, and their father was after all going to attend. It was, he vowed,
going to be the last time he'd travel there. If Kian and Lonny wanted to
visit, let them come here, or better yet, let them move here and live here.
This world was the way a world should be, without monstrous silver serpents that could swallow a person or capture his soul. Of course in this
world there were golden dragons, who had been known to gulp people
down, but that was natural.

He was seeing things more clearly as the five of them rode along. His wife
Heln was accompanying them as far as the palace ruins, as was his sister Jon.
Heln was getting into the later stages of her pregnancy, but she had insisted,
to his mixed pleasure and dismay.

"I still say," Jon said in her argumentative way as her horse pulled up
alongside his, "that a pointy-eared person could use the transporter."

"Yes, Jon, once," he replied patiently. "Then there'd be no point-eared
person and no transporter."

"You can't know that!"

"I know it certainly enough. Look, Brother Wart, has Mouvar ever lied to
us? You know what that parchment says."

"Well, it just doesn't seem right," Jon fumed. "And I've asked you not to
call me that. It makes people think there's a big mole on my nose or something. It might have been cute when I was little and dressed up like a boy,
but now—"

"Right, Sister Wart."

Jon, as was her custom, raised a hand as if to strike him. Kelvin pulled
back on his reins so that she rode ahead and he now rode beside his growing
wife.

"Teasing Jon again?" Heln asked, flashing him a grin.

454

"She started it."

"She always does, doesn't she? Why is it you two can't act like adults?"

"Because we're brother and irritant," Kelvin said, proud of having thought of it.

Predictably, Jon turned in her saddle and stuck her tongue out.

"Now that's *really* adult behavior. Ladylike, too."

Jon said some naughty words that drew an immediate frown from Heln and a bit of amused head-shaking on the part of Kelvin's father. "Who's a lady, you—you—" Jon demanded.

"She's got you now, Kel," John Knight interjected. "Ever since St. Helens showed up and talked about Female Liberation she hasn't wanted to be one."

"She never did, Father. You didn't grow up with her as I did. If she could have grown a penis she'd have done it."

"Darn tootin'," Jon said, affecting one of St. Helens' cleaner expressions

"Somehow I don't think Les would have approved," Kelvin remarked, referring to Jon's absent husband and his own good friend. "But she would have interests appropriate to her anatomy."

"Kelvin, that's enough!" Heln scolded. Jon, seemingly taken aback, merely rode on ahead.

"I'd think she'd get over that," Kelvin said.

"Kelvin, you really have to grow up a little! You and your sister both."

"Yes, Mama," Kelvin said.

For a moment, just a moment, Heln looked as if she'd stick her tongue out. Little crinkles formed at the corners of her mouth but she managed not to laugh.

Kelvin got her message. She really was annoyed with him and she wanted him to appreciate it. Well, he appreciated. So maybe he'd try not to tease his sister as constantly. He just hoped she was resolving the same about him.

John and Kian had been all but dozing on their horses. Kelvin could imagine that both were thinking of their return to the land of silver serpents and of Lonny. Kian hadn't any doubt he could wed Lonny, and John really seemed smitten with the former queen who so resembled Kian's own mother in outward aspect. But why was he, Kelvin, returning? he had to ask himself. Why when Heln was carrying their baby and might need him, and couldn't use dragonberries to separate her astral self at this time? Why? Because he was John Knight's son and Kian was his half brother. Because each of them had saved the other's life. Because they were roundears on a world where roundears were uncommon, and kin. As his mother Charlain had said repeatedly, claiming it was a saying from John Knight's Earth: "Blood is thicker, Kelvin. Blood is thicker than air, earth, fire, or water. It's stronger than any magic, any witchcraft." So what did that mean? he'd asked, and she had talked about kinship.

John suddenly spoke. "I never knew the ruins were so far away."

"It's the riding," Kian said. "You're not used to it."

"That's for certain," John said. "To ease my backside I'm tempted to use the belt." He referred, of course, to the levitation belt that had been in the Mouvar chamber and was now around Kelvin's waist.

"That wouldn't look right, Father. You know how nervous people get when they see magic." Kian himself had once been nervous about such things.

"Science! Confound it, *science!* Magic is—magic is what that witch had and that the Mouvar weapon put a stop to."

"But then it has to be magic, doesn't it, Father?"

"No! At least I don't think so. It's antimagic, so it can't *be* magic. It has to be science."

"You know," Kelvin said thoughtfully, speaking up and surprising himself, "it just could be we're in some sort of war. Not a war between armies, exactly, but between science and magic."

"Horse droppings!" Jon said. As happened more and more frequently these days it was a slightly more acceptable version of an expression used by Heln's father.

"Now I don't know there, Jon," John said, easing himself up in the stirrups. "Kelvin just might have something. Back on Earth there was sometimes talk about a war between faith and technology. That was not the same as here, in this frame, or in that frame with the silver serpents, but it's close. Mouvar seems to have science, albeit advanced. The citizens of this world, and the one we're going to, don't. Here or there a sorcerer might fly with a spell, but on Mouvar's world or mine it would be with a mechanical apparatus or belt."

"That's different?" Jon inquired. For once there was no sarcasm. She must really be curious, Kelvin realized.

"Well, I'd say so. But then you have to remember that I'm from a world and a culture where magic wasn't. As a boy I often wished there was magic, but then there were cars and radios and TV sets and airplanes. Unfortunately there were also scientific horrors that I don't like to think about."

"Horseless carriages, talking boxes, glass with moving pictures of sometimes living and sometimes dead people in them," Jon enumerated with satisfaction. "Though why anyone should want to listen to corpses talking I sure don't know! Machines that fly and what you called atomic explosions. Gee, Father, what would life have been for you if you had just called it magic?"

"Only Mouvar knows," John said. Then, fast, as if correcting a blunder, "I mean Mouvar's people, of course. And possibly others who have lived with both."

"Both magic and science? You think that possible?"

"That's what I was asking, Sister Wart," Kelvin said. So much for resolutions, he thought. But the seriousness of the subject seemed to nullify the previous conversation. "I mean, you take these gauntlets, for instance." He raised them high, as if for inspection. "Are they one or are they the other or are they both?"

John gave a sigh that seemed to owe nothing to the chafing on his backside. "You know I wish I could decide. The gauntlets *seem* magic, but then so do many things that are science."

"I personally don't see what it matters," Jon said. "If something works, why not just accept it? Why did people on Earth have to deny magic anyway?"

"There you've got me," John said. "Magic doesn't follow natural laws, we are told. Magic doesn't follow our logic, so we say it *has* no logic. Magic, simply, unequivocally, can never, ever exist. Why? Because magic is impossible, that's why."

"That sounds stupid," Jon said.

"I agree. Magic does exist here, now. But on Earth where I grew up things were entirely different. To say you believed in magic was to be laughed at, or worse."

"Well I for one don't believe in science!" Jon said stoutly. She was so emphatic that each of them were forced to laugh. When the laughter died down, and her face was flaming, John gave her a most serious look.

"You have to believe in cause and effect, Jon. That's what science basically is. If something happens it has a cause. I still believe that, only today I often don't know the cause and so I accept with other people that the cause is magic. I admit it took me some time to get this far. Beliefs are hard to change."

"Like the transporter," Jon said. "And the spell on it that will destroy it and me if I try to use it."

"If you say so, Jon. To me it's science, but the results are certain to be the same. You and Heln rest overnight and then go home, once we reach the ruins. I know you'd like to follow, but I know too, as you must, that your trying to follow would be disastrous."

"I . . . know," Jon said. Then in a very small, slightly defiant voice: "Magic."

Late that day Jon repeated her now legendary feat of downing a game bird with her sling. They all enjoyed a hearty meal and a good night's sleep. At least Kelvin slept well, he reflected as they approached the site of the old palace, its blackened stones and burned timbers looking ghostly in the morning mist. He wasn't sure about the others.

"I suppose we'll need to get a boat from Old Man Yokes," Kelvin said.

"Where else, dummy?" his sister demanded, as politely as he felt she was capable.

"Of course," John agreed.

So again they met the old river man who had once indirectly saved Jon's life, and through that action the lives of John and Kelvin and possibly even Kian. Yokes was as before pleased at the company and after he and Jon had embraced like fond grandfather and gentle granddaughter, they had to tell everything that had occurred in the interim. This meant that Kelvin had to relive in his memory the experience of almost being killed by a curse and almost swallowed by a serpent. For Jon and Kian it meant telling of days in a dungeon, among other things. Jon sat fidgeting through the recitals until they got to the part about the witch at home and her own very small part in defeating her. Somehow Jon's part became larger than Kelvin remembered it, but the old man's eyes sparkled so that he forbore interrupting and telling it right.

After the stories were all told over steaming mugs of cofea and a plate of mufakes generously spread with aplear jelam, Yokes leaned back in his old rocker and sighed.

"Makes me feel I was right along with you," he said. "And now you're going back?"

"The girl I met," Kian explained. "We're going to be married. At least we are if I have any say."

"Ah, the only one in either frame for you, eh?"

Kian nodded, face flushed but obviously content.

"It was that way for me once," the old man said, and launched into the tale of an improbably courtship with an improbable young woman who later became an improbable wife. The tale took a long time, and Kelvin was surprised to find his emotions stirring as the gentle, aged voice cracked on the sad parts. He hadn't thought of worn old men as having been young and romantic once; he had pictured Old Man Yokes as being old from the moment he was born. It seemed it wasn't so, if the tale was to be believed.

Much later than they had intended, the men of the party said goodbye to the women of the party and staggered down the long flights of stone stairs with a boat. Before they'd had help, but this was a working day and Yokes had neglected to call in the distant neighbors. By the time they reached the bottom landing and the old dock, Kelvin was sweating. The gauntlets made the lifting easier, but hardly the carrying. The legs that supported the boat's weight were entirely his own, however light it seemed to his arms.

"Look at this!" Kian was pointing. At the dock was an old, worn boat.

"Why that was on the ledge!" Kelvin said, remembering. "The ledge outside Mouvar's chamber!"

"One of those old men probably towed it in," John said. "Now that everyone knows the river is here, there are bound to be people exploring it."

"I hope nobody enters the chamber," Kelvin said. Would any pointy-eared person really be destroyed along with the chamber as the old parchment claimed?

"Anyone who gets down here will have heard about it," John said. "The story's widespread. I wonder that Yokes stood for all our retelling of what even he must have heard."

"He was being polite," Kian said. "Anyway, that's what Jon would have said."

Kelvin smiled, but then he wiped it. Time to think of his sister's annoying ways at another time. Now there was work.

Thus it was that they launched the boat, got into it, and rowed by natural rock walls covered by eerily glowing moss. They bypassed the terrible falls that emptied into a darkness filled with stars, negotiated the bend without difficulty, and were at the ledge. To Kelvin it looked different without that boat there.

He was still thinking about the missing boat as they entered the smooth chamber. He almost expected things to be different here, but things were as before. There was the parchment and the book on the table, and the closet with knobs on its outside that was the transporter.

Something struck Kelvin as the three of them prepared to step together into the adjoining world. Those knobs on the outside of the transporter appeared to him to have slightly changed positions. If the knobs had been moved, that might mean that they would not go to their proper destination and might, for all he knew to the contrary, be unable to return.

His gauntlets began to tingle. That meant danger. In fact—

But even as that thought occurred, he was in motion into the transporter, his body not responding in time.

There was a flash of white that covered all existences. The three of them stood in a transporter in a Mouvar chamber, but not the one they had entered. Nor was it the chamber in the world of silver serpents. This one was rounded like the others, lighted by strange ovoids on the chamber's walls. It was definitely not the same. The open door was the giveaway. That and the orangish daylight filtering in, revealing a grouping of large prickly plants and an assortment of rocks and heaps of red sand just outside.

"This is wrong!" Kian said. "We're not where we should be!"

"Someone changed the settings!" Kelvin said. "I thought those knobs were set differently, but I didn't realize it for sure until—"

"Don't panic," John said. "We'll just step out, step back in, and we should be back where we started."

Kelvin felt a great doubt stirring as the gauntlets tingled on his hands. Could the air here be poisoned? No, Mouvar's people wouldn't have built a transporter on a world like that. Still, there was something. Trembling in spite of himself, he stepped out with the others.

"I wonder," John said, walking to the doorway.

"Father! Don't!" Kelvin cried. He felt ridiculous the moment he said it. But his father was pushing his head out around the rounded edge of the metal door. Curiosity ruling his actions, he was about to see where they were.

Suddenly John gasped. His shoulders slumped, and he dropped there in the doorway.

"Father!" Kian echoed Kelvin's earlier cry. With a quick leap he was beside John, grabbing his shoulders, seeking to turn his face. Then, with a similar gasp he collapsed on top of his father.

Kelvin stared for one horrified moment. Then he snatched out his Mouvar weapon from the hip-scabbard and leveled it at the doorway. If there was hostile magic being used, this would stop it and send it back to the source.

He squeezed the weapon's trigger. Sparks and a low hissing came from the bell-shaped muzzle. No magic, then. He replaced the weapon in its sheath and drew his sword. He took a step for the doorway and the unmoving bodies of his kin. Too late he saw the small purple fruit lying there. Too late he realized that he could have stepped back into the transporter and been gone.

He breathed a spicy fragrance. He noticed that the sword was slipping from his fingers and that the gauntlet wasn't even trying to hold on. He noticed the floor and the sand and the dust near the doorway. Then he noticed that the fruit was near his face, and—

What a spicy, spicy smell!

2 /

SUMMONED

S EAN REILLY, BETTER KNOWN as St. Helens, was elated. As the king's own messengers left the cottage's yard he leaped up into the air, waving his arms like a boy. He came down, oof!, on the soles of his aching feet, put his head back until his short black beard pointed skyward, and whooped.

"Did you hear that, Phil?" he asked the pimply faced youth at his side. "Did you hear that?"

"I think all Kelvinia heard it," the former king of Aratex said. He had been staying temporarily with St. Helens while his hereditary palace was reconditioned, to better accommodate the newly appointed government. His position had been reduced to that of figurehead, but that was what he had been all along anyway. Kelvin and King Rufurt had if anything been too generous with him.

"We're going to the palace, boy! To the Kelvinia palace that used to be just Rud's. King Rufurt is finally getting around to honoring me proper! And he wants Kelvin and his brother Kian and John Knight and Les and Mor Crumb there as well! I tell you, there's going to be a place in the new administration for us, just as I always thought there should be! There may be medals for those of us who fought! Maybe a complete pardon for you!"

"I'm not going," Phillip said. He picked at a pimple. "I wasn't included in the royal command."

"Who cares! I'm certain you'll be welcome. You don't know the king! He's the most friendly man in the kingdom!"

"I was pretty friendly," Phillip said. "With you, I mean. I gave you sanctuary, protected you from Melbah, and allowed you to beat me at chess."

"Allowed me! Why you young pupten!" St. Helens bellowed, outraged. Then he got hold of his notoriously volcanic temper as he realized that he had again been had. Phillip was not even trying to hide his smirk.

"All right, all right. So you were a good friend and you resisted that old witch Melbah some, and after I rescued you from defeat—"

"You rescued *me!*" Phillip cried. Then, more calmly. "Oh, I see what you're doing. What you call tit for tat."

"Tat's correct," St. Helens said, in the manner of a long-ago other-world quiz master. "Now we're even." Which of course they were, and had been for some time.

"Another game?" Phillip asked, asking for another game of chess.

"No, no, I've got preparations to make. You've got preparations to make. We've got to get to the Crumbs. We've got to get to Kelvin and the others before they get to the Flaw! What a time for them to take off for a wedding, now that there's something important happening."

"The messengers will get to them," Phillip said. "St. Helens, don't you realize anything about how things are done?"

St. Helens glowered back at him. That was a snottish thing to say, and another time he might have exploded mildly, but now it hardly mattered. The fact was he had never been in the officer class, let alone the governing class. He had always been a common soldier, and proud of it. "I, uh, guess they will. The old man's just a little excited."

"A *little* excited?" Phillip rolled his eyes upward, looking less like the ex-king and more like the young scamp. Looking at him, St. Helens was forced to think that if his wife had borne him a son instead of a daughter, his kid would have been just that impudent.

"I guess we'll all ride together, Phil. I just hope they head off Kelvin and his party in time. I wonder if the girls will ride along. Cursed if I don't think Kelvin's wife, my daughter, should share her husband's and her father's triumph."

Lester and his father were working on a wall when the king's messenger appeared. Les hopped down from the scaffolding, mortar on his hands and the trowel he held, and gazed at them openmouthed.

"Don't get excited, Son," his father said from the top of the ladder. "It may not be anything bad. Maybe something good."

"I knew I shouldn't have let her go," Les said, meaning his wife. As he had found out repeatedly since their marriage, cute little tomboyish Jon had a mind and will that was hers alone.

"You know you couldn't have stopped her," Mor said. "Short of chaining her. And then you'd probably have gotten a lump on your head."

Les unconsciously raised a hand to his sweaty forehead and immediately felt the mortar on it. He would have cursed if the messenger had not been dismounted and there at the gate.

"Lester Crumb. Morton Crumb. You are both summoned to appear before His Majesty King Rufurt, acting king of Kelvinia. You have three days to comply."

Les frowned. "That sounds more like an order than a request."

"I just deliver 'em," the messenger said. "My orders say I'm to tell you three days."

Les looked up to where his father was straddling the wall and glaring down. They had never been summoned in quite this fashion before. Not by King Rufurt. What did this mean?

Mor held his peace until the messenger had left, then spat. "Danged king! Double his territory, and he treats you like dirt!"

"I wouldn't have thought it," Les said. "But maybe it's an honor, a place in the government or something."

"Maybe," Mor said, scowling.

Jon was the first to see the riders approaching. Instantly her hand was on her sling, rock in place, ready just in case history should repeat. But these were no kidnappers from a foreign nation, she saw with relief. They were two of King Rufurt's finest, their Guardsman Messenger uniforms bearing the winged insignias. Now they were slowing their horses and coming up to them at walking speed.

The messengers pulled up. They glanced down at those in the temporary camp. "Mrs. Hackleberry? Mrs. Crumb?"

Jon found herself nodding, as she saw Heln doing. She'd never been approached by a King's Messenger before, and she knew that Heln had not. She waited, wondering.

"Your husband, Mrs. Hackleberry—has he gone to the Flaw?"

Heln nodded. "He, his brother, and their father."

"Then we're too late. We were to give them a message. They are supposed to be at the palace in three days."

"Why?" Heln asked. "Is there trouble, or—?"

"We're only messengers. You ladies are also summoned. The Crumbs, Lester and Morton, will be there as well. So will the roundear Sean Reilly, alias St. Helens."

"Alias?" Heln asked sharply, not liking this reference to her father.

"All of us at the palace!" Jon exclaimed. "Something must have happened!"

"The messages have been delivered. The king ordered us to stress that you have but three days."

"You know Mrs. Hackleberry is pregnant?" Jon demanded. "Does Rufurt still expect—"

The messengers rode slowly away without answering.

Jon swore.

"Now really, Jon, you shouldn't!" Heln reproved her. "You know—"

"I know those goldbuttoned monkpes weren't polite! What's gotten into Rufurt, sending out creiots like those! Why they're not fit to wear their uniforms! Just wait till Kelvin hears! He'll tell them how to talk to his wife and sister!"

"Hush, Jon. Hush. It doesn't matter."

"Yeah? Then what *did* they mean by 'alias' St. Helens?"

Heln frowned. Her name derived from that of her father, so there was a certain personal as well a familial interest. "I'm sure it was just a misspeaking."

"Sure." Jon whirled her sling and let a rock fly to the rump of the horse bearing the sauciest messenger. Stung, the steed jumped, bucked, and almost threw its rider. Then the big war-horse leaped forward, and the other horse speeded up as well. Horses and riders disappeared in a whirl of dust.

"Jon! You shouldn't have!" Heln exclaimed. But her protest lacked force, and there might even have been the merest trace of a hidden smile.

"Maybe I shouldn't have," Jon said. "But I did." It felt good, she thought, secretly pleased with herself. "Well, come on. We might as well get loaded up and meet the others at the palace."

"But Jon, we haven't good clothes! All we have is our riding togs, and they've been slept in."

"Who cares?" Jon demanded. "If we're invited to a ball, Rufurt neglected to advise us."

Angrier than even she thought she should be, Jon began packing their cooking gear and gathering up their blankets. She knew herself to be a liberated woman. No mere king, let alone king's messenger, had the right to treat her as less.

Charlain laid down a card. "Yes, they need help, Hal," she said. "They are too proud to ask for it, but they need it."

"I'd better go, then," Hal Hackleberry said. "The Brownberry folk have helped us when we needed it."

"Yes. I can manage here well enough for a few days."

He got his things ready, then kissed her goodbye. He set out on foot, walking the two hours' distance to their neighbor's farm. It would have been faster on the horse, but Charlain would need the horse here.

As he walked, he pondered. He had been trying to suppress the awareness, but it was becoming difficult. Charlain's kiss had been perfunctory, without passion. Once she had been more attentive, but never enough actually to bear his children. Well, attentive, maybe, but she was a woman who bore children only when she chose, and she had not so chosen with him.

He knew what it was. He was her second husband, and she had never stopped loving her first husband, the roundeared John Knight. She had thought John dead, and needed a man to support the farm, and he had been there. She was such a lovely, competent woman that he had been thrilled to join her on any basis. Hal knew himself to be a good but simple man, the kind seldom destined for greatness or success with women. He had done his best, and treated Charlain's two children as his own, and indeed, he had come to like both Kelvin and Jon very well. There had been no stepfather problems with them. Now both were married and on their own, but they always welcomed his occasional visits and made him feel at home.

But then John Knight had returned. He had not been dead after all, only imprisoned. John had been scrupulous about staying clear of Charlain, letting their divorce stand. But Charlain—any passion she might have had for Hal had evaporated with the knowledge of John's survival. Oh, she hadn't said so, but he had felt it. Their marriage had become a shadow.

But what could he do? He loved her, and could not bring himself to leave her, selfish as he knew that to be. Also, there was no certainty that John Knight wanted to return to her. Kelvin had been mostly silent on what had gone on in the other frame, but it seemed that there was a beautiful and good queen there who looked like John's first wife, the nefarious Zoanna, and who was in want of a man. If Charlain still carried a torch for her first husband, John might carry one for his first wife. So there was no point in Hal's doing anything; it might only hurt the woman he least wanted to hurt.

If only she loved him *back!*

They gathered together in the second audience room. Wine was brought, and all sipped it except Jon. Of the five, only St. Helens was smiling. Jon had to wonder why. Knowing Heln's natural father, she would have thought he'd arrive still smoldering, ready to blow his top on any pretext. But maybe the messengers had treated him with a little more politeness. Maybe they hadn't called him "alias" to his face. Yes, that was probably it; men like those messengers treated women and absent men with habitual disrespect.

"I'd guess we're about to get our due," St. Helens whispered. "Even you, Jon, for riding with the Roundear."

Jon glared at him. Though he had told her about Female Liberation, she sometimes considered him a chauvinist. No one had helped him more than she. Why if she hadn't grabbed Kelvin's hand and aimed the Mouvar weapon for him, the witch would have won! Maybe she should tell him about the alias bit and see how snug his infamous top was then.

But was this really about that? St. Helens seemed to think they were here for some sort of reward or recognition, but he could be, and usually was, mistaken.

Curtains were pulled open by two lackeys in royal livery. There sat King Rufurt on his throne. Instead of his crown he wore an absurd, tight-fitting stockelcap. He also wore a deep frown, which was even more unusual for him.

"Hackleberry, Crumbs, and Sean Reilly, alias St. Helens, you have been summoned to my presence without explanation. You are wondering why."

This was not, Jon thought, the king's customary way of speaking. But she couldn't ponder that right now; she was too busy trying to look covertly at St. Helens to see how he liked that "alias"!

But the fool hadn't even picked up on it. "Your Majesty," he said, "I suspect the recent conflict with Aratex and its annexing has a little something to do with it."

"Roundear, I did not give you permission to speak," the king said sharply. "My patience has been severely strained lately. Do not strain it further."

St. Helens looked surprised. In a heartbeat or less he'd realize he'd been insulted and get angry. But even as Jon thought this, the king was standing, glaring at them. Judging from his expression, he was about to order their executions.

Jon found that she was doing what everyone else was doing. All five were trying hard to close unsightly gaping mouths.

"You know of course about Klingland and Kance," Rufurt continued. "Those two related kingdoms ruled by brats Kildom and Kildee. Long have they been a thorn in your kingdom's side."

"But—but Your Majesty!" Mor exclaimed, unable to hold his peace. "There has *never* been trouble between our kingdoms! Never, in all of history!"

"You're a historian, Crumb?"

"N-no, Your Majesty. But it's common knowledge. With other of the seven kingdoms, such as Aratex before we annexed it, there might have been trouble, but never—"

"Silence!" the king shouted. "You will not interrupt again! Not on pain of torture!"

Mor looked as if he were about to choke. After having been treated as an equal by King Rufurt, this was embarrassing in the extreme to him.

"As I was saying," Rufurt continued grimly, "there have always been difficulties. Only recently it has come to my attention that these two kingdoms plan aggressive war. We must take action before they invade our territory. The roundear should have known this. 'Uniting four,' the prophecy says, but just when the 'hero' is needed, he's gone. Probably dallying with wenches in a far foreign land."

"Your Majesty, I protest!" Heln exclaimed, for once not philosophical about a slight.

"Silence!" the king roared. "Do not presume that because you are mated to the roundear and carry his brat that you are above punishment!"

Heln gasped, started to open her mouth, then closed it. Jon, though furious herself, was glad that the woman managed to stifle her reaction. This had gone beyond error or thoughtless affront. This was deliberate insult, by the last person expected to do it.

Something was not right, here. This wasn't the king who had spent all those years in his own dungeon with her father. It couldn't be!

"So they plan aggression, and we must move fast," the king said, as if satisfied with his logic. "Fortunately there is another kingdom willing to be our ally: Hermandy."

"Hermandy!" Les cried. "But Hermandy has always been—"

Again the king's eyes glared around, as if with a hatred of all present and, indeed, of all mankind. It was a look that had never been seen on Rufurt's face, even during imprisonment and humiliation. There was more than hatred there; there was madness.

Jon swallowed. That didn't help, so she swallowed again. Something was starting to form in her mind, something she dared not consider directly right now. But it pushed forward relentlessly.

In the other frame there had been such a king. She had not seen him, and none present had, but Kelvin had, and John Knight, and so had Kian. *Oh, if only they are all right! If only they are safe in that other frame with nothing more serious than flopeared persons and overgrown snakes to worry about!*

Les hung his head. "I'm sorry, Your Majesty. I did not mean to interrupt."

"Do not do so again. As I was saying, the situation is critical. Obviously I will have no help from the Roundear, so I am ordering you male Crumbs to lead troops into Klingland and Kance. And you, Reilly, do you have that belt that allowed you to fly?

"No, Your Majesty. Kelvin has that, as well as the gauntlets and the Mouvar weapon."

"Typical," the king said sourly. "Irresponsible in an agent of prophecy. But never mind that. You are ordered to proceed forthwith to Hermandy, as my personal messenger to King Bitler."

St. Helens looked startled. "Your Majesty, I've never been—"

"Those are your orders. Are you refusing to obey?"

What an attitude! The king seemed to be trying to provoke dissent, so he could claim treason. "No, Your Majesty," St. Helens said. "It's just that I haven't been to Hermandy and I haven't dealt with kings."

"You dealt with Phillip of Aratex."

"Yes, Your Majesty. But—" Then, seeing the way the king was looking at him, St. Helens reverted to his charm, which was a considerable asset because it was normally well hidden. "Though I haven't had the honor to serve you in such a capacity before, I certainly will now."

If the king was charmed, he did a remarkable job of concealing it. He turned brusquely to Mor and Les, as if he had never even spoken to St. Helens. "And you, Crumbs?"

Mor shrugged, perhaps not trusting himself to speak. There was something about the way the king had pronounced their name that made it seem derogatory. Les answered for both of them. "We certainly will follow your orders, Your Majesty. Though neither of us have been in uniform since the recent war, we'll endeavor to serve you as we must."

Again this graciousness was wasted on the king. "You will do that." His dour attention now turned to Heln. "Since your errant husband is not here, you will stay at the palace until he returns or the royal physician delivers you of child. Whichever event occurs first."

Heln had the wit not to show by her expression that this was the last place she preferred to be. The king had not called her a guest, and it might be more like imprisonment.

Jon straightened her shoulders. She was next, she knew.

"And you, Jon Hackleberry, sister to the hero and mate to Lester Crumb—" The way he spoke those words made it sound like a disparagement. He was suddenly very good at sounding bad! "You will stay with her as her companion. Is that acceptable?"

"Very acceptable," Jon said tersely. *As it has to be. But at least I'll have the chance to watch over Heln. She'll need an ally. Until Kelvin's return. Until he's back here, and knocks your lying carcass off the throne you usurped, you impostor!*

"Then this audience is at an end." Uncharacteristically, the king clapped his hands, and retainers who had assuredly not been here during their recent visit took them in charge and led them from his presence.

When they were alone, getting their breath, getting their color back, Jon said what she had been thinking. "He's not."

"Lass, I've thought that myself!" Mor said. "But if he isn't who he looks like, then—"

"That other king, I think. The one Kelvin talked about."

"King—" He paused, his brow furrowing. "Rowforth. Of Hud? King Rowforth of the torture chamber and the serpents?"

"Who else?" she asked, and saw no disagreement in the others.

"But how—?"

"I don't know. I thought they were going to execute him," Jon said.

"Kelvin wouldn't execute anybody in cold blood," Heln said.

Jon nodded. "A pity, maybe. He must have escaped. It has to be. How else?"

Mor nodded. "Uh, I don't know. But it just doesn't make sense. Even if his own people didn't kill him, and he got here, there's Rufurt."

"Which is why we have to play along, Father," Les said. "For the sake of the real king."

"You really think he's not?" St. Helens asked.

"Don't you?" Mor returned.

St. Helens said some volcanic words. Heln turned away, but did not seem to take strong exception. "But kings will be kings, as the saying goes. It could be he's had a lot on his mind. Maybe his imprisonment is catching up with him, a gear loose somewhere. A bad situation coming up, a bad time for it, and—"

"You don't believe that," Jon said.

"No," St. Helens admitted. "We'd better do just as this one says. If he's not the Rufurt we fought for, then it will be out with him."

"And if there's a war started as a result?" Les asked.

"Hm, there is the prophecy."

"St. Helens!" his pregnant daughter said. "You really want to be fighting again? I thought you'd had enough. After your crossbow wound and after old Melbah—"

"Yes, yes, it was a close thing. But Kelvin did come back in time, didn't he? Just in time. Right, Jon?"

Jon found herself nodding. "We stopped her," she said. In her mind she saw again the moment of the Mouvar's weapon finally going off and sending its antimagic to turn the evil back on its sender. But that seemed almost a lifetime ago. The situation now was not that desperate. But would it become so? She was very much afraid it would.

St. Helens was smiling. He liked the idea of a war that would fulfill that prophecy line. He liked it, though the last two words, "uniting two," had almost cost his life and the lives of Les and Mor.

You'd better not give me any trouble, St. Helens, she thought viciously. *I'm a liberated woman, and I'm on to you. You're an opportunist, but you won't opportune your way with tyrants. Try, and I won't wait for Kelvin. Succeed, and I'll rock your charming head off!* And she made a tiny motion with her hand, as if using her sling to hurl a rock at someone's head.

3 /

TRIBUTE

KELVIN OPENED HIS EYES to see a squat, ugly being with a head growing out of its shoulders and no neck at all. The being was crouched down, turning the Mouvar weapon over and over in webbed, long-fingered hands. The creature's arms and legs and webbed toes matched its fingers. On either side of the blunt head were round, flat spots resembling those on the head of a froog. More than anything it seemed like a giant froog with human additions.

As he turned, he could see the others of his party, also conscious. His father looked as bewildered and helpless as he felt. Kian looked, if anything, worse, as though all his buoyancy and confidence were now replaced with despair. Froog men and women were all about them in this steamy swamp. All their weapons were being inspected and chatted over. Kelvin and his companions themselves were bound hand and foot.

"Ohhh, we're not where we should be," John Knight said. "I'm sorry, Kelvin, you were right. The controls on the transporter were tampered with."

But by whom? Kelvin dared not speak the question. There were more immediate matters. One of these squatted directly in front of him and thrust a large, flat thumb of a greenish webbed hand into his face.

"You godhunters go to god," the creature said. Its voice was liquid and bubbling, as if breathed out under water. Throat sacks just beneath its head vibrated as it spoke, obviously with difficulty.

"We're not godhunters," Kelvin said. *Whatever they are.*

"We see," said the being. "We see. God see. God see all."

What god? A god to creatures who looked like these could be evil and multieyed. He imagined a serpent with eyes all along its back and belly and sides: gigantic, looking down at them from concealment in those prickly tree branches, or invisibly from the orangish sky.

"There won't be any wedding," Kian moaned. "I'm sorry, Kelvin, Father."

"You didn't bring us, Son. We came of our own accord." Trust John Knight to try to make them feel better. "We'll get this straightened out and then we'll go to the right place and get you and Lonny married as planned."

"You go to god," the froog-eared creature said reprovingly. "Strangers, tribute. Tribute, strangers."

As it spoke, another of the creatures was poking a stick with sticky needles on it into the Mouvar weapon's bell-shaped muzzle. Its webbed fingers touched and squeezed the trigger. Pretty sparks and a low hissing amused and possibly delighted the meddler, doing no harm. There was no hostile magic so the display was entirely meaningless.

"I'd say these are real primitives," John Knight said. "Not sophisticates like the flopears."

Kelvin knew what he meant. The flopears of the other frame had been extremely savvy and tough creatures. It might be nice if these were their analogues in this strange frame. The beings here seemed to have no inkling. If John had insulted them by calling them primitives, they did not realize it.

The froog-face in front of him repeated, "You go to god. You go to god. All of you together to god."

"Persistent devil," John remarked. "You lads have any idea how to define a godhunter?"

"One who hunts a god," Kelvin said. Stupid talk, but it was necessary to keep their courage up. Where was the levitation belt? He had worn it around his middle and now it was gone. His father-in-law St. Helens had become quite expert with it during the late unpleasantness, and afterward Kelvin had practiced with it and gotten quite good himself.

Where *was* that belt? With it, he could extricate them all from this predicament.

A great cry went up. One of the froogears was strutting about wearing it over its naked loins.

"Oh, boy," John said. "If—but maybe it won't."

Just then it did. Webbed fingers found and pressed the pretty red button. The froogear went sailing up. Froog-faces turned upward, greatly excited or indifferent as suited the individual. Some of the faces made croaking sounds. The biggest of the creatures stretched out an arm and croaked advice.

The fumbler fumbled some more. Off he went, first to the east and then to the west, and finally smack into a prickly tree. While hanging there, not seriously hurt or alarmed, the aeronaut moved the lever at the side of the belt forward and back. The result was that the creature worked itself deeper into the prickly branches.

The big froogear stepped over to John and nudged him with a webbed toe. "Get him down!"

"I'm tied," John said, reasonably.

"Tell how. Get down."

John considered briefly. "Press red button. Move lever to middle position. Climb down tree."

The big froogear turned his face treeward and croaked an evident translation. Almost immediately the adventurer was visible sliding and scrambling among the branches. He fell partway, landed in greenish mud, and got up laughing. A quick roll in a pile of red sand and he approached the leader and held out the soiled but unharmed belt.

"Did we win one, Father?" Kelvin asked. "Are they going to think twice before croaking us in some form of sacrifice?"

"I'd like to think so, Son. These aren't flopears. Maybe they've got something like our dragons, and maybe something like the serpents the flopears sacrificed to. But if they've got the brains of a fleouse they'll be impressed."

The impression seemed to relate only to John Knight. The leader and his followers acted almost as if levitation belts weren't really strange. What was with these creatures, anyway?

After a suitable interval, during which all their gear was examined and reexamined, the leader gave orders. The prisoners were lifted and carried on slippery smooth froogear shoulders. The creatures might look clumsy, but they were quite strong. Behind them, Kelvin managed to discern, other green shoulders carried everything they had brought that was not presently attached to them, including all weapons.

Well, now. If they had any chance to escape, they could grab one of the weapons and make it good. Evidently the froogears didn't really understand the nature of those devices.

Then most of the stuff, including the weapons, was deposited in a hollow tree, and left behind. Kelvin's hope sank; so much for having their things handy!

They were carried an interminable distance. Through vast expanses of swamp. Between prickly tree trunks that looked like something that ought to be growing in a desert. Past huge piles of reddish sand sometimes shading to an orange the color of the sky of this world. Through brush growing in greenish water and up from patches of semiliquid land. Swamp creatures like allidiles splashed out of their way, snapping great toothy snouts, slapping broad tails that made muddy waves.

"Father, do you think one of those?" Kelvin asked, nodding his head at one of the toothy horrors. "Their god?" The thought was revolting, but had to be considered. Allidiles fed most nastily, and these scaled reptilians were the same except bigger.

"Let's just try to wait and be surprised," John said. "And be alert, both of you! Don't give up hope. There just may be—" He broke off to curse as a froogear snatched a wriggling orange serpent from his chest. The snake hissed, bared dripping fangs, and snapped at the face of the froogear—but immediately lost its head in the crunching jaws of the froogear. John's rescuer chewed, spat, then raised the still squirming body and directed the squirting blood into its wide, open mouth.

"Gross!" Kian said, using one of the expressions his father had taught him. "That's worse than anything I've seen on two worlds."

"Or three worlds, for me," John agreed. "Ugh! What must their god be like?"

Kelvin didn't say anything. He was trying not to vomit on himself and his carrier. *Some hero,* he thought again. *Some legendary hero to upchuck just at the sight of blood.*

The froogear squeezed its very fresh lunch. Now other juices escaped through ruptured tissues and mixed with the blood. Yellow, brown, black, and mixtures.

Kelvin lost his battle of the gorge. With no transition at all he was vomiting. The contents of his stomach splashed out across the froogear in front. He was afraid the creature would turn and kill him, or at least drop him in the swamp, but it took no notice at all.

Much later, a year or two by the feel, Kelvin's retching abated. Feeling horribly weak and nauseous, he hardly noticed the slowing of the party. When he did manage to notice, they had come to a complete halt in greenish mud before a flat, still, scum-topped lake. Great prickly trees grew in the water, seemingly out of the scum. An island of some size soaked up orange sunrays and seemed to wait, curiously idle and foreboding. A rock battlement fronted the island and disappeared around the sides.

The froogears repositioned their loads, startling Kelvin and causing his father to give a groan of apprehension. Then the froogears were in the lake itself, wading, and finally swimming with their powerful hind legs. Somehow the froogears kept them above the surface.

This is where it is, Kelvin thought. *Now we'll meet their god, or what they think of as a god.* He shivered and felt cold, though the orange sun beat down with fiery waves reminding him of an overheated stove in his mother's kitchen.

They splashed up a ramp. There, concealed until now by the black thorny tree branches, was a huge gate. The froogears put their prisoners down on a dry surface and backed off. Kelvin saw some of them as they dipped back below the scum; bubbles traced their route away from the island.

Tribute, he thought. *They've brought their tribute.* It was almost like the time the flopears had tried to sacrifice Lonny. Kian had rescued her, then, and started what turned out to be a significant interaction. He hoped Kian would have the chance to marry her! At the moment that seemed doubtful. He wondered whether Kian appreciated the parallel, and debated breaking the silence to tell him. No, it probably wouldn't be kind.

In an aperture high in the wall there was suddenly a woman's comforting face. She wore a coppery crown on coppery tresses, with coppery rings dangling from two definitely rounded, not pointed ears. She was, Kelvin had to notice, a beauty. But what could such a woman be doing here in this ironically godforsaken place? Or was she another captive, brought here for tribute?

The woman looked down at them from disturbingly coppery eyes. She spoke one word: "Tribute."

Gods, Kelvin thought, *she read my mind! But who is she? Is she the froogears' god? If so, she can't be the monster I've expected. She's absolutely lovely!*

"Thank you so much, Kelvin Hackleberry." Her voice tinkled almost in the manner of a bell. She was looking right at him, reading his mind!

Kelvin felt himself blushing. What would Heln think?

But now the beautiful face was gazing at his father. "Oh, and you, John Knight, trying so hard to get that knot untied! What a great pleasure to meet someone whose original home is far down the Flaw! With your son, Kelvin, a hero! And your other son, Kian, wanting to wed his truelove in still another frame!"

What was this? Were they supposed to respond? Should he be the one to break their silence? What should he say? Should he ask this queenly woman for their release and her help? For obviously she was a queen, which the froogears took as a goddess.

"Oh, but you mustn't judge by appearances," the woman told him in her musical voice. There was just a hint of reproval. "I am more—very much more—than you imagine."

But human, he thought carefully. *A human being who thinks and speaks and has the power of life and death. That is correct, isn't it? You do have the power either to save us or destroy us?*

"Why of course I have those powers, Kelvin!" she agreed brightly. "What do you think I am?"

A compassionate queen, he thought with hope.

"Physically," she prompted him.

Kelvin tried not to picture the phenomenal contours he was sure her body had, hidden by the wall.

"Ah, you are married, so you hesitate to conjecture," she said, smiling. "Yet suppose I were to offer you your freedom, in return for that conjecture?"

She was toying with him, he knew. Yet try as he might, he could not stop his mind from picturing that gorgeous body. Was she naked? Was that why she kept all except her face concealed?

She laughed. "Oh, it would be delightful to make you do with me what you so dread! Perhaps I should indeed free you, instead of saving you for a late-night snack."

Kelvin felt the hair prickle at his nape. Her face and tone were beautiful, but the words were teasing to the point of discomfort. A late-night snack? Was that figurative, or—?

"Go on, Kelvin," she said encouragingly. "It is such a pleasure, following your thoughts."

There seemed to be an admixture of cruelty. Beauty and cruelty were not incompatible, he knew. He remembered Queen Zoanna, Kian's lovely but evil mother. But there could be another reason for her to hide her body. Was she something other than she appeared to be, physically, as she had hinted? Perhaps old, as the witch Melbah had been, yet able to assume the semblance of youth and beauty?

The coppery tresses tossed. The laughter was that of a cheerful hostess. "A witch! Me? Shame on you, Kelvin! A hero of your stripe should know better. You have heard of me, or of something like me. Certainly your father has. He told you, too, though you thought he was speaking nonsense. And you as well, Kian. Indeed, I am not like your mother!"

Insane, Kelvin thought with a chill. But even as he thought it, there came another voice. This one was gruff and masculine, reminiscent of the toughest of working men:

"Mervania, do you always have to play with our food?"

"Of course I do, Mertin," said the pretty tresses. "And why not? Aren't human females and felines that way? Here I have almost coaxed this innocent young man into lusting after my luscious torso! It can be fun, accomplishing that!"

"GWROOOWOOF!" growled a decidedly unhuman voice. Certainly that dragonlike roar had come from no human throat! The vibrations hurt Kelvin's ears.

"Oh now, Grumpus," Mervania said, "you know it's not really feeding time yet."

"GROOOOWOOF!"

"Yes, yes, I agree. We will have to show ourself. But it's going to be a surprise. Particularly for Kelvin, who is resolutely focusing on my forbidden sex appeal. Kian is thinking of his Lonny, and John of his Charlain and of another named Zanaan. Naughty, naughty John! Only one can be your wife. But you, Kelvin, you are thinking of me, and that is the naughtiest of all."

"That's not entirely true," Kelvin said, embarrassed by the amount that *was* true. "I'm thinking also of Heln."

"Yes, that night you got her pregnant. But now she is gravid, and doesn't look quite like that, whereas I may—"

Mervania's face moved away from the wall opening as if shoved aside. Replacing it was a man's face: coppery eyebrows and copper warrior helmet emphasizing high cheekbones and a bulging forehead. He scowled, and snorted through his nose in the manner of a bull. "Mervania, these aren't even fat!"

"But it will be fun fattening them up," Mervania's voice said. "If I could somehow pose as Kelvin pictures me, voluptuous, almost naked, plying him with succulent grapes—''

Damn that mind-reading! And damn his errant mind! She was so infernally good at tuning in on what he most wanted to suppress!

The man's face disappeared. There was a clumping sound, as of something huge and unseen. Then in the opening appeared the snout of a dragon. Its scales were copper rather than a more normal gold, and the eyes it turned down on them were as coppery as its scales. A forked tongue emerged from its terrible mouth, vibrated, then shot down at them. The tip of it dripped coppery saliva and was much too close for comfort.

"Father! Kian!" Kelvin cried. It was quite involuntary. He had been this close to dragons of the golden-scaled variety, but never while bound. The dragon's head drew back. A loud female laughter filled his ears. It was not pretty; rather it was taunting.

It had to be illusion, Kelvin thought. It had to be magic—witchcraft. There couldn't be a dragon here! Not that close to human beings! It would have gobbled them up. Even the sorcerer Zatanas had not been able to control dragons that well. True, Zatanas had ridden one, but that was a treacherous business. No magic could safely handle a magical creature for long.

"I think I know what it is," his father said. "Remember when I was telling you stories about Greek myth? Remem—"

He broke off. With horror, Kelvin realized that his father was helplessly rolling his eyes as if stricken. Magic used against him by Mervania? Magic used so that he would not talk?

The coppery tresses reappeared at the aperture. The coppery eyes that no longer seemed entirely human looked down on him. "You are quite right, Kelvin. I did stop your father from speaking. A simple paralysis hold on his vocal cords. It's wrong for him to want to spoil your surprise. I'd much rather share your naughty vision of me leaning forward to feed you a delicacy, my breasts becoming more visible as my gown falls away, their delightful contours—exactly how does that go, after that?"

Kelvin thought desperately of what his father had been saying. Greek myth, all mixed up with history and therefore partially true. His father had told of such things as the Hydra, a great serpent with nine heads, or was it seven heads; cut off one head and two others grew magically in its place. Then there had been Medusa, a monstrous woman with hair filled with living, hissing snakes. Why did everything he thought of have to involve snakes?

"Keep thinking, Kelvin," Mervania teased. "Keep thinking. There was also Circe, with whom Odysseus dallied for twenty years before returning to his wife. Now *there* was an example for you! Will poor little Heln weave a tapestry by day and unravel it by night, waiting for your return?"

"I think I know!" Kian said. "It's—"

Coppery eyes glanced at his brother. Kian choked and went silent. A spell like a serpent's gaze? Why, oh why couldn't he think!

"You can, Kelvin," Mervania said encouragingly. "You just have to try. You are getting warm, as you used to say in that children's game. Multiple heads. Yes, that's close. But do you recall the particular mythical being that caused you the most terror? I'll give you a clue: it wasn't your wife's namesake, Helen of Troy." She paused, tilting her head prettily. "Oh, excuse me! She was named after her father, a figure of quite another nature!"

He thought hard. Multiple heads. The trinity? Something like that? But something Greek. Something legend. Something that had worked on his boyish imagination and given rise to a nightmare.

"A great hero fought this one, Kelvin. But then they always did, in your father's frame. One of us visited that world back in its infancy, and that's the source."

Kelvin felt as though he were failing a test. All he could think about was the face at the aperture, and whether there was any clothing on what was below it, and his bonds, his father and his brother.

"Dunce!" she snapped at last. "I tire of this. I'll *show* you my fascinating body. I'm coming out."

The gate clicked, then swung wide on creaky hinges. Back of the opening Kelvin saw a walk, a garden, and a building. Then the face, the beautiful woman's face, was peeking around the gatepost.

"Mervania," he started.

The face kept coming. It was on a long, coppery-scaled neck.

A serpent woman! I knew it! Gods, she's a snake!

"Oh, fiddle," Mervania said, and stepped all the way out.

Kelvin drew in a disbelieving breath as he took in the sight.

On clawed feet, a coppery scaled body of immense size. Beside her head, a dragon's head, and beside the dragon's, Mertin's. All three heads were on the front of a body that was all coppery scales, but was otherwise that of a scorpiocrab in all but size. Great pincers reached and clicked in front while at either of the monster's two sides were two human arms: scaly feminine ones on Mervania's, scaly muscle-bulging ones on Mertin's. On the farthest end of the body, coming up last, the tapering crustacean posterior and the long sting, this one of copper.

Kelvin was forced to think, now. The one creature he had been suppressing because of a nightmare. Modified greatly, but recognizable. Instead of a goat's body, the body of a scorpiocrab. Instead of one lion head, one goat head, and one dragon head, two human heads and the dragon. Instead of a serpent's tail, a scorpiocrab's sting. The realization overwhelmed him. To think that he had imagined peeking at the luscious feminine body of *that!*

"Chimera," he whispered.

"Chimaera," she said. "Or Chimæra, if you can fathom it. Get it right, Kelvin."

Chimaera. A monster that had to be far smarter and even more dangerous than the one the ancient Greeks had known.

4 /

AMB-ASSADOR

S T. HELENS RODE THE big gray war-horse down the country road, musing to himself as he shooed a buzzing insect away from his black beard. It was a sunny, nice day for a ride, but this was to be a long one.

Damn! Special messenger to King Bitler of Hermandy! Sounds great, but I don't like it. What skills do I have for dealing with kings? Charm, right? But from what I hear, Bitler is about as nice as old Adolf! Sometimes I wish I were back on Earth, I really do. I don't feel like an ambassador for anyone, particularly that guy at the palace. That just can't be Rufurt, it can't! I feel like an ass. Ambassador. Ass. Amb-assador.

"St. Helens! St. Helens!"

He turned in his saddle to see the former boy-king Phillip Blastmore riding down on him. The boy had evidently been awake after all. Naturally the lad would have followed him, waiting until he was well started on his journey before showing himself.

"Damn!" He pulled up and waited until Phillip's brindled gelding was alongside his mare. "I thought I told you to stay! This is official. Damn it, I don't need a kid along!"

"I'm coming to keep you out of trouble." His mouth smiled, but St. Helens suspected that truth resided in that statement.

"YOU! Keep ME out of trouble?! You, young pupten, have been trouble since you were hatched!"

"I wasn't hatched. I was found under a rock, same as you."

"Probably you were. And old Melbah then took complete charge of you."

The boy's face fell. Immediately St. Helens regretted saying it. Bantering insults were one thing, but real ones were another. There was too much truth in Melbah's early influence over the lad.

"I'm sorry, St. Helens." Phillip's voice trembled. "If you really don't want me along—"

"Now where'd you get a dumb idea like that! Of course I want you along! Glad to have your company. What would I do for trouble without you?"

"But you said—"

"I say a lot of things. Curse of the Irish—one of the curses, anyhow. Haven't I taught you about jokes?"

"Eh, yes. Like when you said 'That girl has nice jugs!' when anyone could see she carried wine bottles."

Ouch! Under Melbah's evil care the young king hadn't gotten out much. A trip or two with the old man might add immeasurably to the lad's education. "You happen to notice anything else about her, lad?"

"She had an excellent figure. I'm surprised you didn't realize that."

Well, maybe there was hope; he was beginning to catch on to the basics. "Maybe next time."

"I can really be a lot of help, you know. I was king once, if only in name. I can tell you the protocol that's expected, and then you won't embarrass us."

"Tell you what, Phil. If you catch the old saint crapping on the carpet, you speak right up."

"Oh I will, St. Helens, I will. Only you didn't do that, even in Aratex. I'd have smelled it if you had."

St. Helens rolled his eyes upward. Smart kid, but sometimes he was a smarty pants. A little dusting of the britches cured that, but royal posteriors presented problems.

"Just let's say that I'll appreciate your help. Whenever and however." *And* if *ever.*

But Phillip was now looking back the way they had come. A horse was approaching with a rider. As the horse drew closer the uniform of a palace guard was evident.

"Now why would one of those fellows be riding after me?" St. Helens asked. "Something new come up?"

The rider was a young guardsman St. Helens had seen at the palace but not spoken to. He could have sworn the fellow rode the king's favorite horse.

"Messenger Reilly," the guardsman gasped. "I'm from the palace detail, but I'm on my own. I've heard a lot about you, how you fought the witch and all. Sir, I'm Charley Lomax."

"I recognize you, close enough. What's the urgency?"

Lomax eyed the boy. "It's for your ears alone, St. Helens."

"You can speak in front of Phil. I trust him."

Charley Lomax, Royal Guardsman, breathed rapidly in and out. His brows knitted as if he were forcing a difficult thought. "Sir, I beg permission to accompany you on your mission to Hermandy."

"The king send you?" This was indeed strange.

"No, sir. As I said, I'm doing this on my own."

St. Helens had heard, but hadn't assimilated it. "You mean you're deserting your post?" He didn't like this. Deserters always had his sympathy, but helping one was trouble.

"I mean I wish to serve the true interest of my king and country. I know that you do too, Messenger Reilly, so—"

"You serve your king by deserting him?" St. Helens asked sharply.

"I don't believe the man at the palace *is* the king."

There it was. "You did right. Very right. Certainly you can accompany me." Then, after a pause: "And call me St. Helens."

"Thank you sir!" Lomax exclaimed, breaking into a grin. "St. Helens, sir!"

The man was in trouble with the man who wore the crown, he thought. If his guess was correct, all of them were about to be in similar trouble. If they couldn't head off that trouble, they would have to prepare to meet it head-on.

They rode on together, the three of them, on Messenger Reilly's mission to Hermandy.

Lester, sweating under the new bronzed helmet with its ostark feather marking him as officer, reviewed the assembled troops. Up and down the columns he rode. From the back of the fine gelding he had been given he looked down into the disciplined faces. Now and then he inspected a sword or crossbow. Briefly he examined the mobile catapults. He felt, he had to admit to himself, and only to himself, like a total fool. Here he was pretending to be an officer when he had never before been one. Serving a king who was probably an impostor, he couldn't have said why. It was one bad, bad situation.

He pulled the reins on his horse's bridle and steered around the huge wheels on the last catapult in line toward his father. Mor, though having been born to fight, looked as uncomfortable in a general's uniform as he felt.

"General Father," Les said in a low voice, "you see anything wrong with these?"

"Top-notch," Mor replied. "The finest mercenaries and equipment Throod had."

Yes, Lester thought, the finest bought fighters. Each trained to kill or die for the cause that pays and never once to question the rightness or the wrongness. Each trained to believe soldiering the highest calling. Good soldiers all, damn it, and not the sort to doubt.

"You want to make the speech, Father? You've got the wind for it."

Mor gave him an almost invisible frown, then stepped his horse around the catapult. He was a big man, on a big war-horse.

"Men," Mor boomed, "we are about to march into Klingland and Kance, the twin kingdoms ruled by twin brothers. Half of you will go to Klingland. Half will go with my son, General Lester Crumb, into Kance. While we are marching, Sean Reilly, whom you know as St. Helens, hero of the war with Aratex, will be on a secret mission to secure Hermandy as an ally. Our armies will meet after victory in the twin capital of Lonris on the Thamesein River. Any questions?"

As Les had expected, there were none. Military commanders normally did not speak that way to troops, and certainly did not ask for questions. The troops might be bemused by this approach. But Mor and Les were not militarily trained except in the fires of revolution. In the war for Rud and then again in the war with Aratex they had served interests they had entirely believed in. It was too bad the same could not be said in this case.

"Then we march. And may the gods smile and bring us united to an easy victory."

Yes, but what victory? To Les, victory was holding Jon lovingly in his arms. That little tomboy could be extremely feminine when she chose! Sticking a sword in a stranger wasn't in the same league. *Oh, if only Kelvin comes to our rescue again! Oh if only, for I fear we are making a mistake.*

Unbidden, a thought came to him. If their king was really an impostor from the frame Kelvin and his brother Kian had visited, then could Kelvin be safe? If the impostor had done something evil to their rightful king, what of the roundear who had bested him? Wouldn't that evil man want revenge?

He was afraid to come too close to an answer. Anyway, it was time to march.

The Brownberries had been in need, all right! The man was struggling to bring in the harvest before the season turned, and the woman was ill with the ten-day fugue. The daughter was just fifteen, and willing and able to work, but could not do enough.

The crux of the problem was this: one man could cut and haul the brownberry plants if he had to, with the help of his good horse. But immediately after cutting they had to be brought inside and the long fibers separated before they hardened. That was a two-person job. If the man took the time to work with his daughter on the separation, he would not have time to complete the arduous cutting and hauling, and much of the crop would be spoiled. But if he did not, the separation could not be done.

Hal's unexpected arrival had been welcomed with something almost like tears. He was not skilled in brownberry farming, but that didn't matter; the girl was.

So now he was seated opposite her in the curing shed, holding the root-end of each plant while she deftly separated each long fiber at the blossom-end, and stretched it out until it came neatly away from the main body of the stem. A good stem could have as many as a dozen of the tough fibers, each of which could in due course be woven into the developing fabric of a new brownberry shirt. Then the squeezed juice of the berries would dye that shirt the traditional brown. Those shirts were the best and cheapest staple of local apparel; almost every rustic wore one.

This also meant that Hal had spent the day doing little except gaze at the young woman opposite him, Easter Brownberry. She had seemed like a plain girl, but now that he saw her in her area of expertise, her hands moving quickly and cleverly, he realized that it was only her shyness. Her hair fell down around her shoulders, the exact color of brownberry, the tresses moving like snakes as her head turned. Easter was well-endowed for her age, and her face was attractive as she concentrated. Her breasts shifted slightly within her own brownberry shirt as her arms drew out the fibers. Every so often she glanced at him and smiled, letting him know that she appreciated his help, even though he was only holding. She became even more attractive when she did that.

Then he took a turn, because Easter was tiring. She had to take him through it in pantomime first, standing behind him and reaching around to guide his arms in the necessary motions. The fibers did not just let go; they had to be tweaked just so.

Hal felt her bosom pressed against his back. It was almost as if she were embracing him.

He went a little crazy then. He turned within her arms, coming to face her. He kissed her.

Easter was so surprised she almost fell. "Mr. Hackleberry!" she exclaimed.

Damn! Why had he done that? He was not a man to take advantage of a girl young enough to be his daughter!

"I'm sorry," he said immediately. "I'll leave."

"But—but the job isn't done!" she protested.

True. "Then I will do it. I promise not to touch you again. I don't know what happened."

They resumed the work. But now when Easter glanced at him, she did not smile. Hal felt terrible.

Finally, shyly, she asked, "Mr. Hackleberry, did you mean it?"

"Of course I did! I had no business touching you, and I won't—"

"I mean," she murmured, blushing as she averted her gaze, "when you kissed me?"

"I said I had no business—"

"But did you?" she persisted, still blushing.

"Yes," he said. "You are a most attractive girl. But—"

"You really think so?"

"Of course I do! But that's no excuse to—"

"I guess you want a quiet affair."

"I never intended to—" he began.

"Mr. Hackleberry, I think you're great, the way you came to help us out. Nobody ever thought I was pretty, before. So if you want to go to the loft—"

"No!" he protested.

"I've never done it," she said. "But I'd sure like to do it with you, Mr. Hackleberry."

Hal stared at her, realizing that she was serious. He was helping her, he found her attractive, and she was flattered, so she was ready to jump into the hay with him. The worst of it was, he was so strongly tempted.

Heln was worried and she let Dr. Sterk know it. It wasn't that she had any great faith in the physician as anything other than a doctor, but talk she must.

"Hmmm, young lady," the royal physician said, his eyebrows rising like a crest and making his sharp features even more birdlike. "You say the king is not the king, and—"

"Yes! Yes! He must be that look-alike Kelvin told us about. If he is, he's got round ears like mine and Kelvin's. He can't have pointed ears like you and King Rufurt."

Dr. Lunox Sterk did a little hop from one foot to another, a characteristic that heightened his bird impression. "I think, young lady, that you're imagining. Many women think strange things when they're with child."

"Damn it, Doctor," Heln said, feeling herself getting angry. It was awful to be treated like an unreasonable person, especially when one felt that way already. "You can at least look, can't you? King Rufurt never wore a stockelcap in his life. This king always wears one pulled down around his ears. Isn't that strange?"

"Young Lady, the king is the king. What he wants he does. It is not for you or me or any other subject to question."

"Horse droppings!" Heln said, adopting one of her natural father's crude expressions, slightly edited for decency. "We have to find out if it's the king with the round ears. *You* have to find out!"

"Young lady, you are being most difficult."

"Darned right," Heln said, now trying a pose of Kelvin's sister, again suitably edited. "And I intend to be more difficult. Either you get a look at his ears and tell me that they are pointed, or—or—I'll leave the palace!"

"Leave the palace!" Dr. Sterk was alarmed. "Really, that would never be allowed. I have my orders. Your husband wouldn't want—"

"Wouldn't want me here if the king is the evil impostor!" she retorted smartly.

The doctor held up bony hands. "Calm yourself! It's not good for you to get excited. For the sake of the child, be calm."

"I'll be calm if you'll check his ears. Will you?"

He sighed. She had him over a barrel. If she miscarried or left the palace, he would get much of the blame. "Yes. Yes, I will try to. But the king isn't acting irrationally, for a king. Kings are different. He may be losing his hair, or it may be turning gray, so he's covering it up. Kings can be even more vain than women."

Heln realized that the good doctor thought he was exaggerating for effect. She managed to disregard the insult to women, and fixed him with her eyes. "Forget the hair. Check the ears."

"I—will try. If it's the hair that is disturbing him, I can prescribe a magic ointment."

Victory, maybe! "Now, Doctor," she said in her steeliest tone. She wasn't good at this, preferring normally to be soft and feminine, but she was desperate.

He went to the chamber door as if dismissed by royalty. Without another word, he exited.

Heln lay back on her pillow in the big four-poster bed and sighed. How totally unlike her! But it was necessary. Why have a sister-in-law like Jon if not to learn from her?

Yes, she thought dreamily. *Yes, now we'll all know the truth of this matter.*

But then a dark thought came, unbidden and bothersome. "Suppose it *is* Rowforth?" she whispered to the bust of Rufurt's grandfather. "Suppose it is that evil king Kelvin encountered? What of Kelvin? What of your grandson? What of all Kelvin's gains?"

The bust made no reply. Try as she might, Heln could not make it wink.

"How's she doing, Doctor?" Jon stood outside the chamber and caught the royal physician exiting. She had been standing there throughout his examination, knowing how embarrassed Heln was about her swollen abdomen.

"Delusional, I'm afraid. She has this fear that other-frame folk are coming here. She thinks our king is the one your brother helped defeat in the other frame."

"I think she's right," Jon said. "As a matter of fact, I know it."

Dr. Sterk shivered the full length of his skinny body. Disappointment was on his face. He had wanted agreement. "She wants me to look at the king's ears."

"So do I." Jon felt there was no sense in denying it. If she was to be thrown into a dungeon, too bad. In the meantime, she would hold the sling she had, with the rock that was just the right size for a false king. "There's risk?"

"With royalty, Mrs. Crumb, there's always risk."

"Not with the real King Rufurt. Remember how he laughed? Remember how he enjoyed a joke? This king seems never to enjoy anything."

"I remember his manner. Perhaps some sorcery has brought about a change."

"You will find out?"

"If he'll let me. Yes, yes, I will try."

"When, Doctor?" They had to pin him down. Otherwise he'd be stalling forever. Men were like that, and doctors especially.

"I suppose I must request that he have an examination. If he refuses—"

"Tell him it's his regular examination. He won't know."

"I . . . sup . . . pose." He seemed to speak ineffective volumes in the pauses.

"Now, Doctor."

"Oh, very well." With as much dignity as a man with birdlike beak and ungainly gait could command, he left her for the royal quarters.

Jon sighed. *For worse or much worse. I hope for all our sakes I'm wrong. But if I'm right . . . gods help all of us!*

Dr. Sterk entered the royal bedchamber and stopped. The king stood there wearing his stockelcap and nothing else.

"Well, Doctor? I haven't all day!"

Knowing the king's usual routines, Dr. Sterk doubted that. Nevertheless that was his signal to go to work. He tested the king's muscle tone (excellent), listened to his heart (beating strongly), and tested his breathing (powerful, like that of an athlete). He checked everything that he was supposed to. Except for the ears.

"Well?"

"Your ears, Your Majesty."

"What about my ears?"

"You're wearing a stockelcap. I need to look in your ears for bugs, and—"

"You think I've got bugs in my ears!"

"Check your hearing. It's just the regular checkup, Your Majesty."

"Oh, very well!" The king whipped off the covering.

Dr. Sterk blinked. Those women had been so convincing! But here were two ears as pointed as he had ever seen. A little bit cleaner than he expected, and not quite so hairy, but—

"What are you doing there?"

"Nothing, Your Majesty." He swallowed, trying to remember that he was the doctor. He really had to ask it. "Why, Your Majesty, wear the stockelcap?" Certainly it wasn't because of developing baldness or gray hair.

"Why? Because I want to!"

"Oh." So he wouldn't find out!

"I caught a little head cold in the ruins. Started giving me the sniffles. But they're gone now."

"Y-yes." Now just what was a head cold, and what was sniffles? Some sort of curse? But the king was right about one thing: he was healthy now.

Dr. Sterk was quite relieved when he finally left the royal presence.

5 /

CHIMAERA

IT WAS STRANGE BEING picked up and carried by two left scaly human female arms and two right scaly male arms. Kelvin watched the bulge in the male pectoral muscles where they joined the side of the creature. He hardly dared look at the female side where he imagined there was a bit of breast beneath the coppery sheen.

"I hate to disillusion your fond conjectures, but my kind don't have breasts," Mervania told him. There was a slight reproach in her tone, as though he had insulted her, or perhaps disappointed her. "Perhaps if my body was of the goatish nature envisioned by Earth's Greeks, I'd have an udder or two on my chest. But as you can see," she clicked the huge claws that were helping to support his weight, "my main body is of the crustacea."

Yes, he had noticed. Oh, did those pincers feel hard! He was almost disappointed that her body had turned out so unlike his guilty expectation.

"Why thank you, Kelvin!"

He tried to stifle his further thoughts. Now they were descending a ramp. At the bottom a door was ajar and his father and brother lay still bound hand and foot with the froogears' vines.

There was a third individual, unbound, rather plump, wearing a suit of transparent body-covering armor. Through the armor he could see a body-length undergarment that showed neither seams nor fasteners. The stranger had dark red, wirelike hair, a stern slash of a mouth, and ears that were not quite round as his own, but pear-shaped.

"Why didn't you run out?" Kelvin demanded of the stranger. At that moment the chimaera dumped him on the floor. The scorpiocrab pincers reached past his face, sending a thrill of alarm through him, and neatly snipped the vines. His bonds fell away, and he scrambled to his feet as the monster released the others.

"Because, stupid, it's a chimaera!" the stranger snapped.

Kelvin noted the iron rings set in the stone wall. This place was evidently a dungeon beneath a castle. There were piles of straw for beds. The only other furniture was a trough that stood chest-high and held an assortment of chopped fruits in some sort of gruel. Kelvin could not believe the mouthwatering smell coming from that trough, and he realized that his stomach was really empty. In the far corner he could see an open drain. There was a small stream of water running through a narrow stone depression that entered one side of the cell and exited the opposite. The water looked as inviting as the food, and cool.

"Go ahead, eat, all of you, make yourselves fat!" the stranger said. "If the monster eats you first, that's longer for me!"

"Goodbye for now," the Mervania head said dulcetly.

"Hearty appetites," the Mertin head added.

"GWROOWOOTH!" spat-snarled the dragon head. Huge jaws opened. A forked tongue reached out and just missed licking Kelvin's flinching face.

"Grumpus, no tasting!" Mervania chided.

With astonishing ease the huge mixed-up beast turned, its long copper sting scraping first the wall and then the ceiling as the tail elevated and curled over the back. With a fast scuttling motion the chimaera exited. It turned around its massive copper crustacean body and its human arms grasped the door's edge. The heads looked in at them as the door swung shut. From outside came the sound of a heavy bar dropped firmly in place.

The cell was not really dark. Light filtered down to them from narrow slits spaced at intervals near the ceiling. By that light, Kelvin could see his father and brother rubbing their arms and legs to restore circulation. The chimaera had not bothered to take the vines. Contemptuous of any plans they might form, it had left their bonds where they had fallen.

"I would have thought there was nothing worse than a golden dragon or a silver serpent," John said, rubbing his feet. "But a chimaera, for god's sake! And copper!"

"Huh," said the stranger. "Where you stupids been? A chimaera could eat your golden dragons and silver serpents for breakfast! Most probably have!"

John Knight gazed at the stranger. "You've encountered them? Other frames?"

"Certainly. You think other worlds don't have transporters?" There was something mechanical and metallic about the stranger's voice. Maybe it was merely its arrogance.

Kelvin watched his father's face. For someone who imagined his own world as far more advanced than others, it was a shock. Kelvin felt a little of the shock himself, and he hadn't his father's illusions.

Kian tiptoed to the door. He listened for a moment, then walked back. "It's gone. I don't think it's listening."

"So we can speak freely now, huh?" The redhead laughed as contemptuously and falsely as could be imagined.

Kelvin found himself looking from stranger to father to half brother. This was a totally incredible situation, even by adventuring standards. Trapped in a chimaera's dungeon with a know-it-all stranger from a different world! That armor had the appearance of glass or plastic, though Kelvin knew of these invisible substances only from his father's description.

"We've never been here before," Kelvin said. "In our frame the chimaera is thought to be only legend."

"You're here by accident?" the man inquired sneeringly.

"Why else?" John Knight demanded, stung by the stranger's manner. "Why else would anyone come here?"

"For the chimaera, of course. Just for the sting of it." Again that incredible, irritating metallic laugh, as though deep inside himself the stranger pushed a button. He seemed at times to be almost as inhuman as the monster.

John's mouth tightened. If the stranger kept irritating him, there would be trouble. No one made fun of John Knight.

"We're all on the same horse," Kelvin said quickly. It was an expression he'd learned from his mother, his father having a similar expression about boats. "We might as well get to know one another. I'm Kelvin Knight Hackleberry. This is my father, John Knight. This is my half brother, Kian Knight. Father came to our frame by accident, and together we came to this frame by accident. We were hoping to arrive in a world like ours but with silver serpents instead of golden dragons."

"Real novices, huh? Call me Stapular. I'm a hunter. I'm here by design. I'm the last of my party that's left."

"The others in your party, they were—"

"Destroyed, of course. Damned locals' fault. They interfered, or we'd have gotten it."

Kelvin felt more and more helpless. Just how had he gotten to be the mouth for his party? Yet of the three of them he felt he was best qualified. Stapular was the most irritating person he had encountered, next to his father-in-law, and he wasn't certain his father or half brother could endure that long.

"You mean a superior, frame-jumping party came here to find a chimaera, and was captured by lowly froogears?" Kian voiced the question before Kelvin thought of it. Kelvin had to suppress a smirk; his half brother did have a certain talent for implied sneering, when he chose to exercise it. It was a legacy from his heartless mother, Zoanna.

Stapular responded to the rudeness as rude people often do. "You want your nose flattened, roundear?"

"He just wants information," Kelvin said quickly. "We all do."

"Do, huh?" Stapular's mouth snapped shut as if he intended to keep all the information he had.

"And exchange. Though there's little we can tell you that will help."

"Nothing I can tell you that will help either." Stapular seemed satisfied.

"We were captured by froogears. That fruit they rolled into our chamber—"

"You fell for that, huh? Hah!"

"Yes," Kelvin said evenly. Was this oaf trying to bait them? "We are, I guess you'd have to say, unseasoned in frame travel. We didn't know this world existed, and as I've mentioned, we thought chimaeras a myth."

"Mythstake, wasn't it?"

Kelvin tried not to grind his teeth. Whether Stapular's superior attitude, his repeated use of "huh" or his grating laugh were the most irritating qualities he couldn't have said.

"Well, I'll tell you, Calvin. Unlike your roundear trash, some of us travel freely to any world not proscribed."

"Proscribed?" Ignore the messed-up name and the insult, he told himself. Go for the information. Keep the oaf talking.

"By the green dwarves. You've heard of them?"

"No. Unless Mouvar is one."

"Mouvar is. He visits the Minors. My world is Major."

Kelvin's head whirled. Major, Minor. Minor, Major. How little he knew about things Stapular took for granted.

"The Major worlds—they have more magic?"

Again that irritating laugh, indicating no humor. "Magic! Does this," he tapped his transparent armor so that it gave out a crystalline ring, "look like magic?"

"To us it does. But then we're ignorant."

"Yours must be a science world, then," John Knight said. "Like Earth."

"You claim to be from a science world?"

"More science than magic. As a matter of fact, magic isn't supposed to exist, though some in my frame do believe in it," John said.

"Huh, then you are science."

"Sort of. We were just getting around to discovering frame worlds, perhaps, and—"

"Horseless carriages, flying machines, moving and talking pictures, boxes with little living people imaged inside," Kian offered. It was as though he were intent on reporting all the wonders of his father's birthworld in one breath.

"That's primitive science," Stapular said. "You say you were discovering frame worlds?"

"Not me personally," John said. "My people."

"Then you went from a primitive Major to an even more primitive Minor?"

"If that means science world and magic world, yes. It was all an accident with us. Can't you tell us how you came here?"

Stapular nodded. "It wasn't froogears. It was the squarears. They live here but separate from froogears. They're brighter than froogears, but Minors. They tried to keep us hunters out. When we ignored their ludicrous laws they used magic. They're protecting this last of the chimaera, even bringing it copper. Damn fools! If they realized what that sting is worth on other worlds—"

Stapular broke off. It was as though his flow of speech had been silenced with a switch.

"You're merchants! Traders!" John exclaimed. "Not only hunters but dealers. In fact, from what you say, you're poachers!"

"Hah, you think we'd risk chimaera for the fun of it?"

"No," John said grimly. "I doubt that you'd risk chimaera except for some great profit."

"The squarears don't know the sting's value. No way they can use the transporter and find out. Only roundears and those like us can use the transporter here. The dwarves have the transporters booby-trapped to keep Minors from mixing too much with Majors and vice versa."

"These squarears who live here," Kelvin broke in. "How'd they stop you?"

"Magic, of course. Huh, they used a spell before we could act. We didn't know they were around, and then we were paralyzed, our weapons useless. One of those timelock spells you probably know about."

John interrupted the pregnant silence that developed. "Paralysis we understand, but timelock?"

"Time stoppage in a small area. Gives 'em time. Very unscientific."

"Magic, then," Kelvin said.

"Magic."

"These squarears," John prodded, "they just left you for the chimaera?"

"They left us for the froogears. The froogears delivered us and all our equipment."

"Then it was just the same as for us. Only we didn't encounter squarears."

"Right."

"And the others in your party?"

"Eaten one by one."

"By the chimaera. That doesn't seem possible."

"Huh, a lot you know about it."

"I didn't say it didn't happen. Only it does seem strange. On any world I've ever been on eating something as intelligent as your species is unheard of."

"You're not as intelligent, stupid. Not even I am."

"I, ah, see." John mentally shrugged as he realized that Stapular regarded the chimaera as more intelligent than all of them. Maybe it was true, but the notion took some adjusting to. Was it that those two human heads counted double?

"Could the squarears stop the chimaera?" Kelvin asked. "With their timelock?"

"Magic is magic. Why'd they want to try?"

Kelvin couldn't have answered. It was just a long shot, that they might get help. Long shots seemed to be their best shots, now.

A sudden unbarring of the door drew all of their attention. The door opened enough to admit Mervania's head. She peered in at them, seeming so much the coppery-tressed woman as almost to fool them. She evidently liked doing that! Then the door swung wide and there was Mertin-head and Grumpus-head beside Mervania-head. The scorpiocrab body scuttled inside.

Mervania looked down on them while Mertin added more food to their trough from a large bucket. Deliberately, teasingly, she lifted something large and green to her mouth and sank her pretty white teeth into it.

Kelvin felt his stomach twist. That thing she was eating. Like a giant pickle, but—

It was a forearm. Green, with little seeds stuck to it. Fingers, a thumb. A pickled arm.

Kelvin's stomach heaved, but it was already empty. He was able only to retch without substance.

"Really, Kelvin!" she said reprovingly, licking off her petite lips. "It is as you thought, a pickle. Pickled arm. Very tasty with added copper." She took another bite, her teeth now showing points.

Kelvin retched again.

"And you, Stapular," she continued between bites. "I'm thinking of a new recipe. First I'll dip you in lye while you're alive, and then—"

"Mervania!" Mertin snapped. "Don't give away your recipes!"

"Oh, all right! I'll just leave that for a surprise." She sucked on some now-fleshless fingerbones, then bit them off with a crunch. Those dainty jaws were stronger than they looked!

"This is boring," Mertin complained. "We've slopped the stock; let's go."

Mervania's mouth curved into a frown. "Spoilsport!" she muttered.

Tail raised over its back, the chimaera departed.

"Whew," Kelvin said. "Whew!" Cold sweat beaded his brow in large drops. He felt even sicker than his stomach did.

6 /

DUPES BY DEFAULT

S T. HELENS WASN'T HAPPY about having Charley Lomax and
Phillip Blastmore along. Young bloods were hot bloods and
youthful self-control was not ideal. He himself had never had self-control at
their ages, and look at all the trouble he'd seen! Yet the young fellows
remained as good companions and took his few orders in soldierly fashion.
He had been afraid that when they reached the palace in Herlin, capital city
of Hermandy, there would be questions. But no guardsman of the dictator
bothered the official messenger, and neither did the boys.

King Bitler looked mean. Ornery lock of black hair over his eyes, aggressive black mustache under sharp nose, he was just plain ugly. St. Helens
mused on it as he watched the king unseal and read the official letter.

"Sean Reilly," the dictator's slightly mad voice said as his moderately
mad eyes gazed down at him. "Kelvinia and Hermandy are now allies."

"Yes, Your Majesty." *And how I wish it wasn't so!*

"Our mutual enemies are the twin kingdoms of Klingland and Kance. By
order of Kelvinia's King Rufurt and myself you are to be put in full command of Hermandy's armed forces. Your rank is to be commanding general.
Do you accept the commission?"

I'd better, St. Helens thought, *or I'll never live to accept or decline another.
You'd like that, wouldn't you, pigface!*

"I do, Your Majesty."

"In that case you will proceed against the enemy as soon as you are
issued the proper uniform." The tyrant leaned back, a palace flunky bowed
to him, and then with a peremptory, sweeping gesture he motioned St.
Helens out of the Royal Presence.

The audience with the Hermandy king was at an end. None too soon, by
his reckoning! St. Helens knew that like it or not he would be fulfilling the
wishes of both Bitner and the king he suspected was Rowforth. He felt his
stomach do an experimental turn.

494

*   *   *

Mor Crumb rode the big horse at the head of the column of the finest troops money could buy, and silently and bitterly chastised himself.

We're on the way to Klingland, on the way to fight! To destroy boys like my Lester! Lester to destroy other boys in Kance. Damn my weakness! Damn my not standing up to that impostor! Damn, damn, damn!

Ahead was the border, its location marked by guardhouses on either side of the road. The guardhouses were empty. Though King Kildom must have received the declaration of war, the border here was wide open.

Now what, Mor the old soldier had to ask himself as they crossed, *can that possibly mean?*

Lester did not like generaling. Here he was in fancy uniform approaching the border between Kelvinia and Kance. His father would be at the Klingland border now. St. Helens would be getting fitted for a new black uniform. One way or another they were all going to war. This was not as it should be, kings and prophecies be damned.

Ahead were the wide river and the waiting ferry. An old man with bleary eyes took the pass and poled him and a couple of lieutenants across.

"Something's happening in Kance," the oldster said.

"Yes, what's that?" Les was watching the straining horses pulling the cable as the ferry crossed. He had never ridden a ferry before. The water was high and muddy, so the horses were working hard.

"No one here all morning. Unusual."

"There are usually soldiers on the Kance side?"

The oldster slapped his thigh and cackled. "That's a good one, that is!" he said with a mouth full of rotted teeth. "And you wearing the uniform of a general! With Hermandy for a neighbor and the caps so near the river who'd—" He stopped, aware that his mouth might betray him.

Yes, with the capital city for both Klingland and Kance so near to the river, who would leave the border here unguarded? He knew that there was a witch running things, but he had never heard she was stupid. Witch Melbah had guarded Aratex from Conjurer's Rock, but here there was no high rock overlooking a pass leading to the capital. Why leave the border open? Why not raise the river and a storm such as Melbah would have done?

The log raft dipped and rose with a wave, and the men at the Kance side prepared for its landing. Stolid working types, they had their poles ready.

No problem, but no guards. The raft landed in its berth and Les and the lieutenant disembarked. They watched the barge go back, the old man bending to his task with the sweeps. No one made comment.

So here they were starting an invasion. So far it was a picnic. Les had imagined there might be rows of archers on their shore. But there were no troops and no one to stop them and demand that they surrender. In a way Lester felt disappointed. He'd almost rather be made a prisoner at the outset than have to lead a fight he didn't believe in. He should have spoken up, but somehow he hadn't.

No soldiers waiting. No resistance mobilized. What did it all mean?

Hal gazed at Easter as they lay in the loft. "You know this is wrong," he said. "I'm married and you're too young."

"I've loved it every time!" she said. "I'm only sorry you have to go now."

So it seemed. He had lost count of the number of times they had done it, these past three days. It seemed she was a lonely girl who had never had this sort of attention before. He could understand her attitude—but what of his own? He was long since old enough to know better! "So have I, Easter," he said. "I think I love you. But—"

"And I love you, Hal! But I know how it is. You're married. You never told me wrong. But will you come again?"

"I shouldn't."

"But you will. I promise, I'll never tell! I just want to be with you, Hal."

Gods help him, he wanted to be with her too. She gave him the love and passion that Charlain lacked. But how could he leave Charlain? She needed someone to run the farm.

"I'll try," he said. And knew that neither storm nor drought could keep him away, wrong as it was.

Jon confronted Dr. Sterk in the hallway. "Well?" she asked with raised eyebrows.

The doctor sighed. "He does indeed have pointed ears."

"So then it is Rufurt, our proper king!" Jon had been so certain!

But the doctor did not look as if he believed what he himself had said.

Kildom faced Kildee in the throne room. Both were lying on the carpet on their bellies. Between them was the playing area for their cards.

"Now you take this one," Kildom said, slapping down a queen. The queen, like all playing-card queens, wore a smirk, as though she and the knave were up to naughtiness.

"No problem," Kildee said. Slap, down went the laughing sorcerer.

"Damn," said Kildom. "I forgot about that."

"You always do. This is the fourth game in which you forgot the sorcerer."

"Better to lose to magic than to might," said Kildee. He studied the face of his twin, so similar to himself that both had identical moles on their cheeks: Kildom on the right cheek, Kildee on the left. That made sense, as Kildom was right-handed, Kildee left-handed. Both faces were quite handsome in childish ways. Today was special because it was the day both rulers turned six.

"Why is it," Kildom inquired, "that we count a birthday only every four years?" Every birthday he had the same question.

"Because," his baby-faced brother replied, "it's Leaping Day, also Monarch Day, a day that comes up on the royal calendar once every four years. If we'd been born on Zebudarry twenty-eighth instead of Zebudarry twenty-ninth we'd be twenty-four."

"True. Quite true." Kildom rolled over and stood up on little pudgy legs. He looked down at his twin, his hands toying with his lace collar. "If only our bodies were grown! Some days I don't think I can wait until I'm a hundred before taking a queen."

"What would you know about *that!*" Kildee retorted. "We're only six and what you have in your royal pants I have in mine."

"Do not! Mine's bigger."

"Bigger butt, maybe."

They tangled, arms and legs and heads. Kildee was on top and blacked his brother's right eye with his left fist. Then Kildom rolled over and blacked Kildee's left eye with his right fist. It was always thus.

"Boys, boys, boys!" Helbah said reprovingly. She was very old, far older than they had reason to think about. She bent over now and picked them up by their lace collars, shook them hard, and sat them down.

Kildom, king of Klingland, looked up at her wrinkled face and tried not to cry. His eye hurt, as it always did when his brother blacked it. "He hit me, Helbah!"

"And you hit him back. You both got what you deserved."

Kildom sighed. So true, so very true.

"You boys are going to have to exercise a little restraint. Your kingdoms have problems."

"They have?" This was news to them both.

"They do. Some people think you are babies. They don't realize that you have the intelligence of grown men."

Kildom wished that his emotions were not those of a six-year-old. He could convince his intellect of almost anything, but his emotions were another matter.

"Now we know," Helbah said, "that Kelvinia has made a pact with your hereditary enemy in Hermandy. We know because old Helbah has her ways."

"Magical," said Kildee.

"Witchy," said Kildom, not to be outdone.

"Yes, yes. Now we mustn't negate the craft by putting false names to it.

Helbah has a power that is good and for your protection. She knows you are threatened and by whom."

"We understand, Helbah," Kildom said. He knew his brother would not have to withdraw his suggestion of magic. Magical or witchy, the powers were hers.

Helbah squeezed the boy's tiny hand. She looked into his face as if he were indeed all man.

"Kildom, your kingdom is now being invaded by forces led by Mor Crumb, the former opposition leader in Rud. Kildee, you have his son's invasion on your hands."

"Your magic can stop them, Helbah," Kildee said confidently. "It's more powerful than armies."

"Perhaps. You know that Helbah will try."

Kildom felt more alarm and saw alarm on his brother's face. If Helbah expressed caution, the matter was serious!

"You see," Helbah explained, "Hermandy would not attack you without magical assistance. Bitler wanted help from Zatanas, the sorcerer slain by Kelvin. Now Bitler has found the help he lacked."

"You are certain?" Kildee asked.

"I am certain that there is a power in the newly formed kingdom of Kelvinia. How well controlled and how powerful I can only guess."

"Then you do not know everything," Kildom suggested, disappointed.

"No. My clairvoyance is limited and my precognition all but absent. I know that Melbah, my duplicate from another frame, was killed by Kelvin. I did not know she would be killed or see it happening. There are limits to all abilities, including mine."

"Never mind, Helbah," Kildom said, impulsively grabbing her around the neck. "My brother and I will protect you."

"That's nice," she said, managing to look reassured.

Rowforth, formerly king of Hud in another world, now the imitation king of Kelvinia, looked into the mirror and laughed. His ears looked so preposterous to him. Newly pointed and with no more hair on them than on a baby's rump, they were the proper size and shape for this frame. They had to be, considering where he had obtained them.

Zoanna, his fully pointeared consort here, tweaked his left ear as she massaged it and pulled its point. "They are quite ready to show now, dear Rufurt. The magical ointment has worked its wonders."

"Don't call me Rufurt."

"It's your name now. You have to get used to it. You are after all taking the man's place."

"King's place," he corrected her. Though very bright for a female, she didn't quite seem to recognize the qualitative difference between mere man and godlike king.

"Yes, stoneheart," she said affectionately. She nuzzled the ear, as if liking her handiwork almost as much as him.

Rowforth rubbed his cheek against hers and wished that for all her beauty and her magic she were not so much the local. He had enjoyed punching her counterpart, Zanaan. He couldn't imagine punching Zoanna, since the queen had magic and would retaliate. Too bad, but eventually he would find other women he could beat and pummel and kick and bite with impunity.

"What are you thinking, my lusty king? About destroying those who thwarted me before? About tormenting those who robbed you of your kingdom in that other place?"

"Not exactly," he confessed. In the mirror reflection he did look like the rightful king. It was both reassuring and angering. Round ears, after all, were natural. "I've been thinking of revenge."

"The Roundear of Prophecy? Kelvin, spawn of the roundear John Knight?"

"Sort of. That woman in the palace is his wife. She carries our worst enemy's brat."

"Yes, yes." She seemed delighted with his dialogue.

"I plan on torturing her. Before his eyes."

"Yes, yes, yes." Her eyes were bright, her lips parted and wet. Her queenly robe was falling open, showing more of her intriguing figure. One would hardly have guessed her true age, looking at her body. Magic was wonderful stuff!

"And perhaps a bit of magic. Make pointed ears on them both."

"That would take time. It's not like something you do to extract a confession. Yours was a very special case. They don't have convenient doubles to borrow from."

"You could start now. Get Sterk to ointment her ears. Maybe give her something to affect the cub in her. If she could give birth to something misshapen and revolting before they all are allowed to die . . ."

"Oh yes, yes, yes! Brilliant! You are the greatest, most magnificent consort ever!" She put her hands to his head and turned his face to hers with a ferocity and eagerness that almost scared him. Zanaan had never been like this! She kissed his lips, pressing them hard with hers. Her passions were aroused by what he accidentally said. It seemed that the same sort of thinking aroused them both. He took her in his arms and then to the bed. She looked just like his consort in the other frame, but she was a world different! That malice and savagery lent her phenomenal sex appeal, while Zanaan's disgusting niceness made her appealing only when she was screaming with pain and humiliation.

"It's so early in the day!" she exclaimed. There were golden lights in her greenish eyes. Zanaan had had those too, but they hadn't ever lit up for him.

He enjoyed kingly privileges all morning in a manner he had seldom if ever done before. Thanks, he felt certain, to some magic substance added to his wine that gave him a seemingly indefatigable potency. The queen had done it, surely, but he didn't mind at all. What a lithe and joyfully vicious creature she was! Her rapture was almost like that of pain, which really turned him on.

During and after his exertions he thought not so much of Zoanna, or even of Zanaan. What he most thought about were delightful new means of extending torment in helpless folk, especially in attractive women. How similar the reactions of sex-making seemed to those of agony. Once he got into the real thing . . .

7 /

SQUAREARS

IT HAPPENED SO SUDDENLY that Kelvin hadn't time to think. One moment he was trying fruitlessly to sleep on the straw bed the chimaera provided, and the next it was broad daylight and he was looking up at an orange sky with whippy yellow clouds.

His back felt as though a stick was poking in it. He felt around with his hands and recognized the prickle of grass. He was on the ground, outside. But how?

"Greetings, visitors."

Kelvin sat up. The person who had spoken stood beside him: blocky of build, with straw-colored hair and ears that stuck out and were square. There were several similar folk beyond.

Kian and John were sitting beside him. Stapular was nowhere in sight.

"You—you—what?" Kelvin inquired intelligently. He wasn't yet sure whether this or the chimaera's den was reality.

"The squarears," his father supplied. "Remember Stapular telling us?"

Kian was looking past all of them. "We're back at the cave!"

"Very true," the squared individual said. He held a huge copper needle that seemed a duplicate of the chimaera's sting. "You are now free to leave here and continue your journey."

"But—" Kelvin said. Could it all have been a dream? But no, dreams never remained this clear. Besides, he could still taste the mash he had eaten from the chimaera's trough.

"I am Bloorg," said their apparent rescuer. "Official Greeter and Sender, Keeper of the Transporter to Other Worlds, Keeper of the Last Known Existing Chimaera. I'm sorry that we did not check on you in time. We were preoccupied with more deliberate visitors."

"Stapular's people?" Kelvin asked.

"Yes."

"He's still there? In the chimaera's cellar?"

"Yes. He deserves to be, though I doubt the chimaera will find him tasty eating."

Kelvin shivered. Poor Stapular! But why had they been rescued, and that man not?

"That magic Stapular spoke about," John said, almost answering Kelvin's thoughts. "Timelock?"

"Yes," Bloorg said. "We simply took you away without the chimaera's awareness, or yours, or the other captive's."

"But why?" Kelvin demanded. It surprised him that he demanded anything, but the hero's role was gradually growing on him. "Why were we rescued, and not him?"

"Stapular's people were here deliberately. They came to do harm. You, in contrast, arrived by chance."

"You—you know?" *Telepathic?*

"Limited telepathy," Bloorg agreed. "Enough to know your thoughts, though unable to communicate that way."

"And the chimaera is telepathic," Kelvin said. "I know, because—"

"Because it exchanged thoughts with you. Yes, it is a complete telepath, able to receive and send, which is part of what makes it unique. But we have kept it confined for some time. We know how to keep it from our thoughts."

"You're like zookeepers!" John said. "You're a chimaerakeeper!"

"Correct."

"But why?" Now John looked as bewildered as Kelvin felt.

"Uniqueness. In all the frames we know of, this is the last of the chimaera's kind. Should it be destroyed, the victim of genocide, to satisfy an alien's greed?"

"No. No it shouldn't, but—"

"You think of your fellow prisoner and his claim to be from a Major world. Major and Minor are in the eyes of the beholder, as your people say. It was no love of knowledge that brought them here."

"But you did let them be slaughtered, eaten by the chimaera?"

"Of course."

Kelvin looked at his father and brother, and wondered. Were they as appalled by this as he was?

"Your property was also rescued," Bloorg said. He gestured with squared-off fingers. Other squarears stepped forward carrying the levitation belt, the Mouvar weapon, the gauntlets, and the swords.

"So we really are free, then?" Kian asked, seeming hardly to believe it.

"Yes. Go now to your wedding."

Something was not right. Kelvin almost knew, but could not quite pin it down. He buckled on his sword, the Mouvar weapon, and drew on the gauntlets.

"Well I for one am ready to go!" Kian said. "I've had enough of chimaera and poacher. I'm ready to go any time."

Kelvin looked at his father. John was frowning, maybe disturbed about the same thing that was bothering Kelvin. They had after all been confined in the same place. Driven by hunger, they had eaten from the trough Stapular must have eaten from. Kelvin had felt like a piog, gulping slops, but the stuff had been amazingly tasty.

"Do not waste your sympathies on the hunter," Bloorg said. "He is not quite as he seems, and he knew what he risked."

But dipped in lye? Cooked alive? Pickled? Eaten? It seemed all too much. Even the sorcerer Zatanas and the witch Melbah had received kinder fates, and they, more than gruff Stapular, had seemed to be of a different species.

"I repeat, your sympathies are wasted," Bloorg said. "Once you have considered the enormity of what they planned, you will agree that their fate was deserved."

Sympathy then for the chimaera? A creature that mocked them from a feminine face? A monster that munched human limbs with enjoyment? Was that where his sympathy should lie?

"No," Bloorg answered patiently. "You should not feel sympathy for either. They are what they are, and nothing you or we could do would make any difference."

Evil beings deserving nothing more? But Stapular had seemed human. Not likable, certainly, but human. And advanced.

"Advanced by what cosmic standard?"

Yes. Yes, that made sense. A person might think himself advanced, but that was as likely to be vanity as fact. Greed was after all greed, and cruelty was cruelty. But could a monster be said to be cruel? Wasn't its taunting ways simply part of its nature?

"You are remarkably philosophical for one so recently rescued." The squarear was looking at him from blocky pupils in blocky eyes set in a blocky head. Looking, seemingly, into the roundeared, roundeyed, round-headed depths of him.

"It's my nature," Kelvin said. "I have to question."

"Of course you do."

Kian looked toward the cave. "Any time you're ready, Kelvin, Father."

"All right." John Knight stood. He held out his hand to Bloorg. "In my frame it is the custom to clasp the hand of someone who has saved your life, and say thanks."

"You are most welcome," Bloorg said. They shook, John wincing as he felt the other's hand.

Kian was already on his feet, extending his hand similarly. Kelvin, uneasy for no reason he could quite define, followed their example. When he took Bloorg's six-fingered hand he knew why his father and his brother had acted surprised. It was chilly, like a froogear extremity, but dry rather than clammy. The fingers wrapped around his wrist, showing that they were many-jointed, like little tails. The alien feel of the appendage drove all other thoughts away.

"Come," John said, and Kelvin followed with Kian. It was farther than it had appeared to be, and it seemed to get no closer as they walked. Then suddenly it was much closer, and each step was taking them rapidly forward.

Kelvin looked back. The squarears were gone, vanished.

"Magic!" Kian said, also looking back. "I knew there was something funny about it. We weren't where we seemed to be."

Kelvin had to agree, though he was not elated. Somehow magic and the evident extent of the squarears' powers was depressing. True, the magic of the gauntlets had saved him many times, but it had always seemed to him that having magic was an unfair advantage. What chance did a master swordsman have, for instance, against a bungle-foot like himself, when his sword was clasped by a hand in a magic gauntlet? Kelvin knew himself to be no hero, merely a person whose ordinary abilities were amplified by magic. Now he had encountered creatures who seemed to be far beyond that magic. It was disconcerting.

"Hey, Son, you look glum!" his father said lightly. It was almost a doggerel rhyme, the kind he had done to cheer Kelvin as a child.

"I can't get it out of my head, Father."

"What, that you were rescued? That none of us will be eaten?"

Finally the thing that had been bothering him focused. "No, Father. That Stapular will be eaten." He let that sink, then plunged ahead. "Is that right, Father? Is it?"

"I wondered how long it would take for your conscience to catch up," John said. "You can't let anything be. You always have to work it out to the last degree, so that it makes sense on every level. You are unusual in that, perhaps unique."

"I'm sorry," Kelvin said.

"Sorry! Son, that's what makes you a hero!" His father's friendly hand came around his shoulders. "But look, Son, it's not right by our standards, but this isn't our frame. We shouldn't be here. We're here only by chance. It isn't our business."

"I'm going ahead!" Kian said, and ran on to the cave. He looked inside, looked back, and called, "This is it, all right! Hurry up!"

"He doesn't care," Kelvin said.

"It's his upbringing. It was different from yours. Remember who his mother was."

Kelvin remembered. Evil Queen Zoanna, who had used magic to fascinate John Knight and seduce him and bear his child. Zoanna had evidently liked to play with men in much the way Mervania did, only Zoanna, being human, had been able to take it farther. "Yes, he's seen more cruelty casually applied."

"In the palace he did. His grandfather and his mother were not noticeably kind. Give him credit for turning out as well as he did, given that environment. He did not have Charlain as his mother."

That certainly accounted for the difference! Kelvin's mother was the finest woman he knew, though perhaps Heln approached her.

"Hurry it up, won't you!" Kian called.

"And you can't blame him for wanting to get on with his wedding," John said.

Kelvin abruptly stopped. "Father, I'm going back."

"Of course you are, Son. We all are. First to Kian's wedding, as we planned before getting diverted here, and then—"

"No, Father. I mean back to the island in the lake. Back to rescue Stapular."

"Son, you can't!" But something in John's expression suggested that he wasn't surprised.

"I can. I have the gauntlets now, and the levitation belt, and the Mouvar weapon. I can do it."

"No, wait! The chimaera can stun your mind! Think—"

Kelvin knew better than to think. A man of action he must be, though his nature was far more sedentary. Magic and a prophecy made him heroic despite himself.

He touched the control for "up" on the belt, and suddenly he was floating above his father's head, looking back at Kian's astonished form waving at the cave. It was exactly as it was when he practiced with the belt.

"Goodbye, Father. Wait for me if you will. If not, I'll follow you."

"No, wait, you idiot! What kind of a fool are you!"

"I'm a hero, remember?" And he knew his father understood, despite trying to restrain him. Heroes would be heroes, just as kings would be kings, to the wonder and dismay of others.

Sadly yet determinedly he nudged the control and floated smoothly swampward. A bit of acceleration and the swamp breezed by. Now and then he caught a froogear's surprised face in the greenness below, or sight of one of the swamp monsters. He had no doubt of the proper direction, partly because there was a treeless area that was almost like a road, but mostly because the gauntlets tingled ever so slightly when he started going wrong. Soon the lake and island with its imposing wall were in sight.

Have to think now. Have to think. Face the chimaera's power? Think to Mervania? Demand that it release the prisoner?

Down below was the gate where they had waited for the god of the froogears. He drifted over, slowing. Now there was that peculiar walkway bordered by the more peculiar fence. Even while carried by the chimaera he had noticed it. Greenish, tapering, almost thorn-shaped posts. Then there was the ruined castle with openings like vacant eyes. The chimaera, aware of him or not, was nowhere in sight.

He lowered himself cautiously, with a nudge of the belt control. Past moss-grown walls to a spot directly in front of the doorway to the dungeon. Still no chimaera. Was it going to be this easy? Was the monster going to let him get away with this, knowing that he was now magically armed? Or was the chimaera simply asleep?

He approached the barred door. He lifted the bar, grunting from the weight of it, glancing nervously back over his shoulder. The gauntlets felt warm, but the very existence of the chimaera could account for that.

He hesitated, then forced himself to proceed. He swung the door open.

The chimaera waited inside, sting raised on backward-bending abdomen. All three heads had coppery eyes focused on him.

"Welcome back, Kelvin!" Mervania said brightly. A lightning bolt speared from the tip of the sting and sizzled past his head. A warning shot, surely.

He was prepared as he had not been before. The Mouvar weapon was in his hand and properly set to contain any hostile magic. He pressed the trigger and the antimagic weapon emitted a few colorful sparks.

What was this? It wasn't supposed to do that! It was supposed to make a barrier to hostile magic.

The tip of the chimaera's sting moved, almost imperceptibly. Lightning leaped from it to one of the greenish posts. Sizzling, the bolt leaped from post to post. Now Kelvin realized, belatedly, that the posts were copper stings stuck in the ground. The chimaera was emitting lightning, and the stings in the ground received the lightning and made the spectacular display. A stench hit his nostrils that was partly ozone and partly something he had not known before.

"Stupid roundear!" Stapular cried from the cell. He wasn't even trying to attack, but was instead flattened at the very back of the enclosure.

Time to think about Stapular later. Kelvin's hands burned in the gauntlets and he didn't like ignoring their warning. Quickly he adjusted the weapon's control. Now it would not only block hostile magic from reaching him, but perhaps it had just done, but would turn it back on the sender. If it worked as he hoped, the magic lightning would double back on the chimaera itself.

"If you insist," Mervania said.

"Real dumb one, isn't he!" Mertin remarked.

"Groomth," growled Grumpus.

Kelvin pressed the trigger and held it down. Lightning shot from the tip of the chimaera's tail and sizzled right at his feet. He felt it, shockingly, through the soles of his feet and all through his body. His hair seemed to be sparking. The Mouvar weapon, amazingly, did nothing but emit a few colored sparks and get very hot in his hand.

"Really, you must go back inside," Mervania scolded. The chimaera crawled outside as the Mouvar weapon sagged in his tingling fingers. The monster confronted him at close range, and another blue bolt sizzled at his feet.

About this time Kelvin realized one or two things. One was that a species that was near extinction was not necessarily a sweet thing to be near. The other was that he was in real trouble.

Slowly, unsteadily, hardly knowing what he did, he backed away. The chimaera moved after, clicking its pincers before it. He backed into the cell, past the trough, and to the wall beside Stapular.

The lightning stopped. He slid to the floor, as did Stapular. The chimaera closed the door, dropping the bar with what seemed a final crash.

Thank you for coming back, Kelvin! I know you'll be delicious!

Oh, the pain! The incredible shaking, tingling all over him. He felt it everywhere, even in the gauntlets. None of his weapons had been any use! Instead of rescuing Stapular, he had made himself prisoner again.

He rolled up his eyes, trying to adjust to the enormity of what had happened. He had tried to play the hero's part, and had only succeeded in playing the fool's part.

"Satisfied, stupid?" Stapular asked.

"It—it should have worked! Mouvar's weapon is antimagic."

"Antimagic!" Stapular laughed his annoying laugh, as nastily as ever. "Dumb, stupid, Minor World creature! The chimaera wasn't using magic."

"The lightning!"

"Electricity. The monster generates it in its body. Copper conducts. Nothing magical about it. Science."

"Science?" Kelvin's morale and hopes plummeted. "Not magic?"

"Now you've got it, Minor World idiot! You've come back to be eaten! Doesn't that make you feel just great?"

"The squarears—"

"They won't help you twice. They have no more tolerance for fools than I do, fool."

"But I have my levitation belt. Once outside, I can—"

"The chimaera can shoot a bolt straight up and cook you in midflight. I've seen it fry passing birds that way. Any that are so stupid as to come within range. Most stay well clear."

"My gauntlets!"

"Won't help a bit. Didn't out there, did they?"

"No, but—"

"But you're back. And you're going to be eaten. Why did you come back anyway?"

"To get you released."

"Me? To rescue me?" The red-haired alien looked astonished. The expression was not typical of the way the good citizens of Kelvinia did it; his eyes widened and his facial lines seemed to click out starkly and then recede in place.

"Yes," Kelvin agreed dully.

"Foolish. Incredibly foolish. Worst possible motive I've ever heard."

"You'd do the same for me."

"I would, huh?" The man emitted his nasty laugh. The laughter boomed louder and bounced around the dungeon, striking one wall and then another. Kelvin had never heard of a building being tumbled by laughter, but it almost seemed possible, now. "Me rescue a dummy like you from a Minor frame? Why should I care whether you're eaten?"

"It's only human," Kelvin said defensively. What was so funny?

Stapular laughed all the harder. With precise control he switched from mocking to insulting to humiliating. He seemed a laugh machine similar to one Kelvin's father had told him about, perhaps jokingly.

"Well gee," Kelvin said wistfully, reverting to a childhood expression, "it sounded right to me."

8 /

BATTLES STRANGE

GENERAL MOR CRUMB AWOKE, dressed, exited his tent and stretched. It was a fine morning; in fact a glorious morning. The sun was shining over Klingland and Klingland was waiting.

He hailed Captains Abileey and Plink, nodded to a second lieutenant, and exchanged perfunctory salutes with a passing private. The horses awaited, as did the mess. As was not customary in any army, he simply got in line. The privates, mostly from Throod, made room for him with haste, while officers tightened their lips at this display of what Mor felt proper. Since when did an officer act like a common man?

"Jerked spameef!" exclaimed one young soldier holding up a twist of reddish meat. His expression and tone suggested anticipation of a bad taste.

"Field rations, soldier!" Captain Abileey said. "What'd you expect, goouck and fish eggs? Be thankful it's not horse manure on a shingle."

The private blanched. Obviously he had not been long in uniform. "Sorry, sir, I guess I was hoping for something else."

"Probably," Captain Abileey said. "But we'll eat well enough later. After victory."

"Yes, sir." The boy brightened at the thought. Klingland was known for its fine shepton and poreef as well as less common cuisine.

"If we don't delay we'll reach Bliston by noon. There's supposed to be only a small garrison, so there shouldn't be much of a fight. Then Gamish and Shucksort and finally the double cap itself. I make it three days."

"I know that, sir. But thank you anyway."

One way or another, they all filled up on dry rations washed down with steaming mugs of cofte from the army pot. In no time at all they were assembled and on their way, riding single file. The officer in official charge rode at the head.

I don't know why we're doing this, Mor thought, looking ahead at the blur of green. *Klingland never did anything to us that I know about. Why didn't we just give old Rufurt the thumb in the nose? Maybe it was that wine. Yes, that was probably it. I've never been this complaisant about soldiering before in my life. But he did make me a general. Not that I asked for rank or even wanted to volunteer to fight.*

Prod, prod, prod.

Someone, probably one of the officers, began the "Horse Manure, Horse Manure" song. It felt good to belt out the familiar lyrics, and Mor found himself bellowing jubilantly with the rest: "Makes the giries scream. Horse—" And so it went. All morning went, little by little, unnoticed by man or horse, undisturbed by sniper's arrows or any appearance of armed locals. It was, he had to admit to himself, a dream march. Absolutely nothing was going wrong. Ahead and to the sides the green blurred steadily.

At noon they stopped and rested, ate field rations and drank spring water from canteens while the horses chomped grass. In due course they remounted and proceeded as before.

Prod, prod, prod.

Mor was bothered, perversely, by the ease of this. He didn't trust an easy campaign. Only in dreams was everything perfect—until the dreams turned bad.

"Horse—"

A horse whinnied. It was Mor's own. Then, as though urged by the song, it defecated. Mor, for no particular reason, turned in his saddle and looked at the steaming dung as the horse's hooves pounded the ground.

Prod, prod, prod.

Something was not right. Something definitely was not right. The horse should have outdistanced its dung in its first stride. Yet the horse walked and the dung remained directly behind. The horse walked but the ground kept pace. So did the smell.

Mor frowned, trying to understand, and to shake the unnatural euphoric mood he was in. All morning it had been this way. Almost as if he had drunk heavily of wine and experienced nothing but its exhilarating effect. He could hardly damp down the feeling, though he knew it was unnatural. He was after all on the way to a fight. Fear was a better emotion than contentment!

There it was, horse dung, steaming and fragrant, gathering flies.

Finally it registered. "Damn!" he swore, appreciating the subtle beauty of it. He knew what was wrong.

"Captain Abileey, Captain Plink," Mor said. "We are in deep manure."

"Why is that, sir?" Captain Abileey's boyish face just missed being ecstatic. Mor knew that this was going to be difficult for him, because he was entirely taken in by the illusion.

"We're making good time, General," Captain Plink said. "No opposition all morning. We must have come a good twenty—"

"Bliston's not that far," Mor pointed out.

"Well, sir?" Captain Abileey inquired. His cheeks were as ruddy as if he'd just stepped from a tavern. Unquestionably this was one of the most contented moments of his life. But Mor, nominal leader, had no choice but to end it.

"Look there," Mor said, pointing.

"Yes sir." The young captain's nose wrinkled. "Horse droppings."

"Watch."

Prod, prod, prod.

"We're not moving, sir!" Captain Abileey was astonished. "We're—something's wrong! What can possibly be wrong?"

"Magic!" Captain Plink said, appreciatively. He was older, and had seen more oddities; he was thus more ready to grasp this insight.

Mor sighed, and said with equal appropriateness, "Horse droppings!"

After that there was nothing to do but call a halt. There was horse manure all around; they could not get away from it. The joy of the advance diminished.

Lester Crumb saw them first: the Kance soldiers riding down on them, poised, swords drawn, in an all-out charge.

"Archers! Crossbowmen! Pick off the leaders first!" It was what his father would have ordered. Sensible and right: officers, after all, had ordered the charge.

Lester's men formed a line, ready to fire at Lester's signal. Les dropped his hand, readying himself for the sight of death. Why was this army charging his own army so suicidally? Like a lot of things lately, it didn't seem to make much sense.

Arrow strings twanged. Crossbows fired. The missiles flew straight for their targets. But the enemy cavalry neither swerved nor slowed in its charge. The arrows and crossbow bolts fell well beyond them. The charge continued, unaffected.

"What? What?" Les couldn't believe it. Not one of the enemy had fallen, or even taken a hit. Every shaft had missed!

The distance between the two forces became smaller. Les imagined that he could see the angered eyes, the set lips, even the sweat on the attackers' foreheads. How could they be immune to arrows?

"Cease firing! Form a phalanx!"

The troops formed the square, spears pointing out protectively on all sides. The enemy riders came closer, closer, while all Les' men waited. There was muted grumbling; they didn't like taking a defensive posture when they plainly outnumbered the opposition.

Damn, he thought, what was there to do?

"Sir," said Captain Barnes, his second in command. "It's magic!"

"I can see that, Captain."

"We need the Mouvar weapon, sir. To turn the magic back on them."

"Agreed, Captain," Les said tightly. "Unfortunately we don't have it." Kelvin had the weapon, and why, oh why wasn't he here, when so much depended on him?

Lester stared gloomily at the ever-charging cavalry. He had to wonder whether they were going to have to squat here and wait indefinitely until Kelvin returned from his brother's wedding.

Then he had a new thought, an alarming one. If King Rufurt had been replaced by the king from another frame, what then had been the rightful king's fate? And if Rufurt had been destroyed or somehow magicked, what then of Kelvin? *What was going on, in that other frame?*

St. Helens should have felt great. Leading troops again—not that he ever had before, exactly. But campaigning was something he knew from the ground up. So why wasn't he happy, now that he was at the head end of it instead of the tail end?

Charley Lomax rode by his left and young Phillip at his right, and behind them stretched the Hermandy army. All seemed to be in order. So what was his problem?

"Sir," the young guardsman whispered, bending near in his saddle. "Have you noticed our well-wishers?"

St. Helens saw what the lad meant. A few sullen faces were staring at them from passing yards and doorways. There were no flowers strewn in their path, no cheers or patriotic cries of well-wishing. The faces were mostly glum and the bodies often ill-fed. The populace of Hermandy reminded him of another. Would the former king of Aratex be reminded? St. Helens turned in his saddle and glanced.

Phillip's face was wreathed in boyish smiles. Taking no notice of anything around them, he appeared as happy as when he was beating St. Helens in chess. After viewing all the death and destruction in Aratex, he still was thinking of glory. St. Helens knew how it was for him because he had once been that way himself.

"I don't think the military is popular in this land," he whispered to Guardsman Lomax. "Considering that the Hermandy government is highly repressive, that's normal. It was that way in Aratex, and, not long ago, before the roundear, in Rud."

"And after this war it will be different here also?"

St. Helens had had a top sergeant once who answered each and every question a private could muster with irrefutable logic. The answer was always the same in St. Helens' experience. He used that sergeant's answer now.

"Shut," he said reasonably, "the hell up!"

They rode on through deeper and deeper gloom brought on by the fact that nothing was as either of them would have wished.

Helbah had to smile as she gazed into the twin crystals. One showed Mor's difficulty, the other his son's.

"Yes," she said aloud, perhaps to Katbah, her houcat friend. "Yes, old Helbah knows a thing or two! Never could defeat my evil frame-sister, but I kept her from invading us long enough! Glad she's gone! She's my malevolent mirror image, you can bet!"

"Meoww," Katbah remarked, arching his slick back. He would rather be battling a leaf or climbing a tree. Instead he was here in her defense headquarters giving her support.

"Now, then," Helbah continued, checking her brewkettle in the fireplace and giving it a stir with its ladle, "here's our plan. Once we've got them stopped we wait until they go back discouraged or until their decent leaders come and surrender to us. No killing. You like that?"

Katbah rubbed his head against her gnarled hand and purred. It was a gentle soothing sound that befitted a feline creature that never, ever killed birds. From the same gentle frame and mold as Helbah, he preferred finding and returning baby birds that had tumbled from their nests. Yet feline was feline, and Katbah, her familiar, responded as only a familiar could.

Helbah looked down at the touch of the velvety smooth tongue on her hand. She ruffled the black fur, tweaked the triangular whiskers, and stared into the oval eyes.

"Katbah, I think we've won. But—" She frowned as she thought of this. "I wonder why? Not just that we've won, but why the invasion. This is utterly unlike pleasant, ineffective King Rufurt of Rud. Or whatever they call that kingdom now. Kelvinia—that's it, after that good lad."

Katbah rubbed against the third crystal on the table. This one was a smoothed square. His paw reached out and tapped it. The crystal was opaque.

"Yes, yes, I'd better. I hate spying, Katbah, but now and then I have to. There is too much of a mystery about this matter."

She drew the square crystal across the rough wooden table to her. She held her clawed fingers above the smooth surface, closed her eyes, and concentrated. In a moment she felt the quiver in her arms and the lightning sparks from her fingertips.

She opened her eyes, staring into a universe of tiny bubbles. Now where? Where? To Kelvinia to find out the cause of the attack. She visualized a man with a big nose, wearing a crown. Yes, there he was, reflected in the crystal as though in a glass box. Rufurt.

Why, she wondered, why? Under her prodding thoughts the view widened. The king was in his bedchamber and he was not alone. Helbah frowned, not wanting to intrude on a private moment between king and—

The woman in the bedchamber turned. As she did, Katbah raised his fur and spat.

Red-as-dragon-sheen hair. Eyes the color of green feline magic with little cometing lights in them. The eyes might have been directed right at her!

Zoanna! Zoanna, the evil queen all thought dead. Hadn't she drowned? Yet here she was with the king, whom she had despised in life. Could this be Rufurt, the real Rufurt?

She peered close, moving in on the man with her thoughts. There was a mean look to him, an insane light in his eyes. His ears were tipped, but with a tipping that was new.

This was not good King Rufurt.

So, then, it was another paired set, like Melbah and Helbah, from other frames. Similar appearance, dissimilar nature. Only the ears gave such folk away, physically.

And the queen?

Helbah moved in on the queen. The face, just as haughty, just as inhumanly cold and devoid of genuine feeling. The original Zoanna, without a doubt.

So the queen had not died. She had hidden, and now returned with a look-alike to replace Rufurt. Rufurt had been easygoing and appreciative of life, but Zoanna had manipulated and misled him. When he and John Knight were released from the Rud dungeon, having sprung themselves during the battle, Rufurt had been just the same. She had checked up on him from time to time, not to interfere but to assuage her curiosity and make sure that no mischief was afoot. This, she was now sure, was not he.

Zoanna had been taking something from a wooden stand. She held up a round crystal. Her face a study in suspicion, she closed her eyes.

Now what? The couple had evidently been about to make love, but now seemed to be up to something else. Had Zoanna learned magic? Her father, Zatanas, had known little, though he had faked much. But Zoanna had been absent for some time. Perhaps she had learned. Maybe she had developed a dormant witch-sense.

In the crystal Zoanna held, Helbah's own face appeared. Zoanna's eyes opened as she peered at it.

"Helbah, I thought that was you! Are you so hard up for thrills that you have to spy on the pleasures of your betters?"

Horrors! She *had* learned magic! She had felt Helbah's questing, and challenged it. Only a few selected people, male or female, were able to master sorcery, and even fewer ever made the attempt. Zoanna had evidently discovered that she had the ability, and now had developed it. Here was real mischief!

The king bent forward, also looking. "She the witch?"

Zoanna ignored him. To Helbah she said: "Your time has come, old woman. You won't exist much longer. We're taking over the brat kingdoms. When we complete that chore, you will die. We shall throw you away like the garbage you are."

Katbah leaped at the crystal in sudden fury. Sparkling sharp claws raked the crystal, producing a screech that hurt Helbah's ears. It was the way she herself felt.

"I have stopped the armies," Helbah said. "Just as in years of yore."

"Yes, witchy bonebag, but not for long. I now have means of countering you."

"You can nullify my spells?" Helbah asked skeptically.

"Watch." Zoanna gestured. In the crystal she held was Mor and his army in Klingland. They were paused, looking at a pile of horse droppings. Zoanna took a small vial from a drawer in the stand and sprinkled an orange powder. The crystal flared bright. Zoanna held a finger pointed, and the horse manure lifted from the ground and hovered in midair. A sudden cutting gesture, and the dung fell.

A horse leaped. Mor assumed a startled expression, as did his officers. Then they were riding on, into the target territory.

"No you don't!" Helbah snapped. She made a gesture of her own, and the advance, though it seemed to be going forward, stayed even with a tree.

"That is the last time that will be tolerated," Zoanna said grimly. She made a new gesture, and the movement resumed.

Angered by this insolence, Helbah raised a hand. At that moment Zoanna raised her own hand. There was a loud snapping sound, the smell of ozone, and all three of Helbah's crystals vibrated.

"I can keep this up, bag," Zoanna said. "I can keep this up until they crack."

Helbah reluctantly directed a thought, and all three crystals abruptly turned opaque.

She looked at her familiar, who was now glancing all around, as if fearful that the queen were hiding right in this room.

"Yes, Katbah, she's going to be trouble," Helbah said. "Far more than ever before, I fear."

Katbah spat, angrily and knowingly. Meanwhile, Helbah felt drained.

"Yes, I greatly fear, Katbah, that it is going to be a long, wearying fight. Who could have guessed that that evil queen would return, worse than before?"

The question was rhetorical, but the situation was grim. Helbah wished she wasn't quite so old and tired.

Rowforth looked from the now-opaque crystal to his consort's face. He didn't like what he had just heard. This witch sounded like trouble. "Can you keep her from stopping us?"

Zoanna came as near to smiling as she ever did. The expression she normally used was an artifice that affected only her lips, unlike her tepid analogue in the other frame who smiled with her whole face, on those few occasions she had reason to smile at all. This was one of the things he really liked about Zoanna. "Stop us? You must be mad, lover mine. She'll never stop us. Nothing can."

He wanted to believe her. Then, as he looked into her eyes, he very nearly did.

Torture, torment, pain. With her help, all would be inflicted on their enemies, and especially those treasonous ones who had defeated him in his own frame. That Kelvin, how he would enjoy strapping him up in each newly created torture device! But would the iron maiden, the strappado, and the rack be enough? For that soft young man who yet had caused so much mischief he would devise some special pain.

He began dreaming of the child the roundear's wife was to bear. With Zoanna's help it might come out so hideous as to cause both parents unremitting anguish. Yes, that would be fitting—and fun!

"Zoanna, have you heard of a beast called a chimera?"

"Chimera?" she asked blankly.

"With three heads and a scorpiocrab tail."

She smiled. "Oh, you mean the chimaera! Of course, though it is almost extinct. What a lovely beasti!"

"Could the—could the child of Kelvin be made to resemble that?"

Her artificial smile slowly became genuine. "My dear, you are a genius! Why not?"

So confident, so certain. Surely he would have had to look through all the frames before finding so ideal a consort!

9 /

FOOL'S RETURN

"WHAT'S THIS ARMOR YOU'RE wearing?" Kelvin asked his cellmate.

Stapular, as usual, managed to look as if he were sneering. In a tone just to the right of insulting he said, "What's it to you, Minor World dolt?"

Kelvin sighed. He tried so hard to be polite and Stapular always ruined it. He took another big handful of fruity mash from the trough and munched it, eying the redhead speculatively.

"That's right, go ahead and stuff! Put on some fat so you'll be just what old triple-head wants! You don't see *me* gulping that stuff! But you do what you want. Maybe it'll fry you. Sauté you with a little onlic. Yes, that should be good."

Kelvin shuddered. He had never liked onlic. The other man was obviously trying to nettle him; what made it worse was that he was succeeding. If the chimaera was going to eat him, he almost preferred that it eat him raw.

Still, he was hungry, and he wanted to keep up his health and strength, so as to be ready to escape if any opportunity presented itself. He finished chewing the mixed nuts, fruit, and grain mixture, reflecting that it wasn't bad, in fact it was delicious. He then lay down at the edge of the little stream and sucked up water. Good, crystal-clear spring water, the best. He had to admit that the monster had excellent taste in food and water.

At last he stood and faced Stapular deliberately. *Have to control the body language now,* he thought. *Don't want to appear hostile.*

"I asked, cellmate, about your armor."

"Why should I tell you?"

"I told you about the Mouvar weapon."

"I didn't ask you to. Does that mean I'm obligated?"

"You want to get out. You want to save yourself. Surely you don't want to be eaten."

Stapular hesitated. He was doubtless trying to think of a reason to refuse

Kelvin's reasonable request. Even the most unreasonable people liked to appear reasonable, oddly.

Kelvin reached out and touched the transparent plating. It covered all of the hunter except the head and the hands. Just like the armor worn by his Knights of the Roundear and the royalists fighting for the queen. Only this armor was not metal. His father had labeled it "Some sort of glass or plastic." It looked very light, but felt hard.

"The chimaera lets you keep this on. Surely it will take it off you before it dines on you."

"That it will, pale hair. How'd you guess?"

"Seems sensible. I don't think Grumpus could dent this."

"It won't have to. The armor's stout but that's not its value."

"Then—"

"It insulates against the electric bursts. The bolts can climb all over it but not get inside. Particularly when—" He touched something inside his collar with a nudge of his chin. Instantly a transparent hood that covered his entire head sprang up from in back and snapped securely down in front. Similar hoods in the shape of gloves snapped over his hands, and others protected his feet. Stapular was now fully encased.

Kelvin was amazed. "You mean the chimaera couldn't have hurt you at all if you'd done that?"

"Where's your brain? Of course it could. It just couldn't have electrocuted me."

"But—"

"The sting could have pried me right out. Likely Mervania will get me out with lye."

Kelvin shivered. Lye! But he had known that was in the monster's plans, and indeed that had figured largely in his return. Still, it angered him to think that Stapular had remained back in the cell and not attacked the creature's elevated sting from behind, when Kelvin was distracting it. That jointed abdomen must have a weak spot, and if the lightning couldn't strike him . . .

"You think I should have jumped on the tail, right?"

Kelvin nodded, and refrained from saying something nasty like "How'd you ever guess, idiot?"

"Dumb, Minor World imbecile! It would have whacked me against the roof! Maybe flung me over its heads and against you!"

Surely a fate worse than death! But Kelvin refrained from making that sarcastic comment too. "I could have dodged, or even caught you and helped you get your feet."

The man merely glowered at him.

Kelvin tried again. "I once saw a dragon attacked in almost that manner. Of course the heroic knight paid for his bravery with his life, but at least he'd made the gesture, and perhaps saved the lives of his companions."

"You think I should have, don't you?"

Idiot! "You were wearing the armor," Kelvin pointed out. "You might have survived. It might have given me a chance to—"

"To what? Attack with your sword and magic gauntlets?" The tone made this seem ludicrous.

"Better than nothing." He didn't like the disparagement and contempt at all, but realized that this was just Stapular's way. Did the man have any love-life? That thought almost made Kelvin laugh.

"You think so, do you? You know how quickly one of the bolts would have shriveled you? If the chimaera hadn't been playing with you, you'd have been charred."

Undoubtedly true! But Kelvin pressed on. "I will be charred later anyway, according to you. Why not in a fight?"

"Because there would *be* no fight! The chimaera controls great quantities of electricity it makes in its body. You'd be no threat at all."

Kelvin tried to consider that, mindful that Stapular was repeating his prior argument. Yet the redhead was after all from a world he called Major.

"Nothing to be done, then?" He remained perplexed by the man's seeming reluctance even to oppose his fate.

"No."

"But you were going to attack it. You and your companions. How?"

"With lasers, of course. Some of us would have been destroyed, but we'd have lopped off the heads and tail."

"That tail means something to you, doesn't it?"

"Yes, profit."

Kelvin wondered about that. Could copper be so valuable where Stapular came from? It didn't seem possible.

"You're confused, aren't you, dolt? Huh, let me tell you those stings are no minor matter. Conductors of electricity while they're growing and attached, and afterward—"

"Yes?" Stapular had shut up, as if catching himself revealing too much. What could be so secret that it couldn't be told even to a companion in death?

"Other," Stapular said. "On Minor Worlds, at least."

Conductors of other on Minor Worlds? Minor Worlds were magic-using worlds. That suggested that the stings were conductors of magic! The revelation made his knees sag.

"What's the matter with you?"

"There's a fence made of those old stings outside. You saw the lightning leap."

"So? A fortune, but not for us. For the next hunters perhaps."

"Magic, Stapular. Magic."

"What are you getting at, Minor brain?"

"Conductors of magic. Magic to fight the chimaera with."

"You're crazy!"

"So you have remarked. I have my levitation belt and my gauntlets now, and I come from a world where magic exists. If I can get outside again, get one of the spikes uprooted, hold it with the gauntlets and channel magic through it—"

"You've got magic?" Stapular seemed less skeptical.

"Y—" Kelvin had never been so tempted to lie before. But deep-grained habits were hard to break. He converted what he had been about to say to the exact truth. "—es. My gauntlets are magic. They often know what to do when I don't."

"Seriously?"

"Yes." But a pang of conscience forced him to add, "Swords, shields, crossbows—they even used a laser."

"But do they know how to *use* magic?"

"M-maybe. Perhaps."

"And perhaps not?"

Kelvin shrugged. "Any chance, it seems to me, is better than none."

"Right, Minor brain. Right. So what are your plans?"

"To get a sting. To confront the chimaera with it."

"While I distract it, I suppose?"

"You'll have to."

"And if it knows your thought? I can keep it out of my head. Can you?"

"I'll have to."

"Easily said. But when it's around, your mind is open to it. You know you can't conceal your plan. Whatever plan."

"Then that is why we must do it now," Kelvin said. In that moment he realized that the only plan he had was for him to get the sting while Stapular interfered with the chimaera. That would be difficult, even if Stapular was effective.

"You could grab hold of the chimaera's sting. Hold on to it. Keep it from directing its bolts."

"I could put my entire weight on it and I don't think I could hold it."

"But you will try?"

"I will try," Stapular said.

Kelvin dared hope. He had finally gotten the man to cooperate. That meant they had a chance, maybe, however small.

Kian looked at his father in astonishment. "What will we do, Father? We can't leave him!"

"No. Of course not. But it's a long way back. We were carried before, remember?"

Kian nodded, looking at the transporter and thinking secret thoughts. Darkly secret thoughts.

Kelvin was his brother. Half brother, anyway. He should not, would not abandon him, especially since Kelvin had followed them to the serpent world. Kelvin had saved them all, several times. He had first saved their homeland of Rud from Kian's own mother. Following the Rud revolution which Kelvin had led, Kian had gone through the transporter searching for his missing father and mother. In the frame-world that was so similar and yet so different from his own, Kian had found his missing father, and the girl he now wanted so desperately to return to. Kelvin had arrived late, defeated the royalists, and gotten Kian and John Knight out of King Rowforth's dungeon. Now Kian had a chance to repay all that.

But damn it all, damn it, Kelvin had been stupid! Going back to that monster-lair to save that—that poacher! No one with any sense would have done that! No one but an idiotic hero!

"Maybe," John said, "we can get help from the squarears. They do want us out of this frame."

"If they'll let a hunter be destroyed, they'll let a fool be destroyed." Immediately he regretted the application. Kelvin *was* at times a fool, but he was also his brother.

"I'm afraid I agree with you," John said. "But if we just start back through the swamp, we'll be caught by the froogears. Then it will be the same as before."

"Will it, Father?" Kian wished there were some other way.

"It will have to be."

Kian scuffed at the floor of the chamber with his toe. "Father, do you think they'd rescue us all over again?"

"I don't think we can count on it."

"Neither do I. Why should they have patience with fools?"

"Why indeed!" John exclaimed with an ironic laugh.

"If only Kelvin had left us with something. He took the levitation belt and the Mouvar weapon. What have we got to fight with?"

"One pair of magic gauntlets and our swords. Plus our wits," John said.

"Lot of good they'll do."

"I'm not so certain. That fruit the froogears rolled in here—do you suppose that grows nearby?"

"Suppose it does? It'd knock us out if we breathed the scent from it."

"Yet the froogears handled it."

"Maybe they're immune. Maybe it just doesn't affect them, Father."

"Hmmm. Possibly. I'm not saying we could use it, just thinking of possibilities."

"The gauntlets, do you suppose they can lead us through the swamp to the island?"

"Possibly. Just barely possibly. They have a wonderful sense of direction, you remember."

"But only the one pair."

"I'll tell you what." John Knight stripped off the right gauntlet and handed it to him. "I'll wear the left and you the right. That way we'll both be protected to some extent."

"Thank you, Father." Kian put on the gauntlet. Though his father's hand was larger than his, the soft dragonskin contracted and made a perfect fit. Had his hand been larger, it would have stretched, magically.

John shrugged. "Why should I let my son be in avoidable danger?"

That was rhetorical, but it made Kian feel warm. He knew that Kelvin was the hero, the son borne of the woman John truly loved, and sometimes he doubted John's feelings for the son of the evil queen. Kian flexed and unflexed his right hand with the gauntlet. He drew his sword, made some experimental slashes at the air, and returned it smoothly to his scabbard. How, he wondered, would his right-handed father handle *his* sword?

John Knight was already adjusting his scabbard on his right side. He drew the sword left-handed, swished it expertly, twirled it, and resheathed it. The glove made *any* hand dextrous!

Kian nodded appreciatively. "That's better than I believe Kelvin could do."

"I'm not so certain. He fought most of the war in Rud with just the left gauntlet. Remember?"

Kian remembered. Lying on the ground in the swirling dust kicked up by the war-horses. His right gauntleted hand locked with Kelvin's left. The two gauntlets wrestling for their wearers, moving their fingers and wrists, pulling their arms and bodies along. It had been a draw. It had been the first indication he had had of the full extent of the power of the gauntlets.

"I'm ready, Father."

"Yes, I thought you would be."

With that they turned their backs on the chamber, and its transporter and all of Kian's waiting dreams. Together they left the cave and walked step by step, never faltering, to the greenish swamp and its incalculable dangers.

There were many, many steps, and many, many wearying days ahead.

Bloorg, the squarear chieftain, scratched his straw-colored hair on his blocky pate and indicated to Grool, his second in command, the crystal. In the crystal were two tired, hungry, insect-bitten roundears, slogging their way through hip-deep greenish water. The roundear known as John Knight suddenly grabbed a serpent in its left hand and flung it far. Kian, the younger roundear, congratulated him.

"Should we let the chimaera have them?" Grool asked. "They are innocent, and intended no harm."

Bloorg shrugged. "Innocent is as innocent does. They are also stupid."

"Stupid. Yes, by our standards. Still—"

"Still they have chosen. They could have gone their way."

"But the other one chose first. If he had not gone back—"

"Yes, as the hunter says, he was very stupid."

"But can we just leave them? Let our cousins the froogears take them again for tribute?"

"It is our ethics not to destroy or allow to be destroyed the purely innocent. Yet once made wise—"

"No longer innocent!" Grool sighed, fluttering her triangular eyelashes above her blue and squarish eyes. "It is an old, old truth, as old as our civilization. They should have learned."

"But it bothers you?"

"Yes, I don't think they intend other than a rescue."

"Unaided? Hardly that."

"Then they are doomed."

"Assuredly. As certainly as the other and the hunter in the chimaera's larder."

"A shame."

"Isn't it."

Bloorg made a magical gesture with entwined fingers and the crystal flickered and went blank.

The chimaera was digging in Mervania's garden. It had a nice assortment of herbs growing for use as condiments. Onlics tossed their purple heads in the breeze blowing over the island, their bulbs waiting below ground.

"I don't know why you bother with this!" Mertin grumbled. What he really meant was that he was not all that enamored with the flavor of onlics, chilards, and musills.

Grumpus' head suddenly snapped upward, and its mouth opened. At the same time the chimaera sting elevated. A bolt of blue sparked from the tip and into the sky above. Sizzling, smoking, still on fire, a foolish swampbird fell into Grumpus' waiting maw. Grumpus crunched, chewed, and swallowed. The chimaera's abdomen unbent and its sting lowered.

"Now, Mertie, you know you like the stew I make," Mervania chided her headmate. "None of us refuses it. Even Grumpus likes it."

"Ain't fittin'," Mertin said. "We, a superior species, eating like our foodstuffs!"

"Nonsense." She patted the dirt lovingly over the bones she had brought from the pantry. Good fungus would grow up out of those eyesockets. It always seemed appropriate that they be buried here. "You know you're just saying that. Fitting and not-fitting has nothing to do with it."

"Groowth," Grumpus agreed, licking singed feathers from his mouth.

"Our kind always used to eat 'em raw, Grumpus. But Mervania had to take up with baking and frying and stewing and pickling."

"Oh, I'm so glad you reminded me!" she exclaimed. "I need some dilber seed. I've decided on pickling that young hero. His arms and legs are so nice and slim."

"Bah!" said Mertin. "Me and Grumpus would just as soon—"

"Yes, yes, I know," she said impatiently. "You've made your point dozens of times."

"Well, it's still true. We would rather eat them au naturel."

"Speaking of the heroic roundear, I wonder what he and his lardermate are up to." Having decided, instantly she reached out with her thoughts. The thoughts she encountered surprised and excited her. "Oh my! Oh, my!"

"What is it?" Mertin asked. "Sneakiness?"

"I'm afraid so. They actually conspire to fight. At least the roundear thinks they do. The pearear's thoughts are impervious, as a pearear's always are."

"Shame to disappoint them," Mertin said.

"Oh, we won't, we won't, Mertin."

"Roast it, Mervania, must you always play with our food!"

"Yes, Mertie. After I do, its taste is delectable!"

IO /

STICKY, STICKY

T HIS WAR WAS GETTING to be what St. Helens had once called a bummer, and it hadn't even started. He was just now leaving the border between Hermandy and Kance. Behind him was a file of Hermandy troops. Ahead were forests and lakes and streams almost to the twin capitals. Why didn't he feel great, being a general?

Because this was not a war he liked. Hermandy reminded him too vividly of a country and dictator that had made history on Earth. King Rowforth, if that thing in the palace of Kelvinia were truly he, had really put him in a bind.

"Gee, this is exciting!" Phillip said. Practically in the important general's ear.

"Excitement doesn't start until the arrows fly," remarked young Lomax. "That's what they told me, at least."

"You're right, Charles, only this time it'll be terror. The first time in battle always is. And the tenth time, only you learn not to show it."

St. Helens thought he'd put it right, but the boy was frowning, first at the young man, and then at St. Helens. "Oh, I know it's not a chess game, St. Helens. Real blood will get shed. But gee, just to be leading an army at last!"

"You're not leading it, I am."

"Yes, you're the witch this time."

"Don't say that!" *Brat!* he thought. "I've seen all the witches I ever want to see. Your Melbah was enough witch to last me for a greatly extended lifetime!"

For a moment there was silence from the boy. *Good!*

Then he popped up again. "St. Helens, you do know that we'll be fighting against a witch?"

"WHAT?" He was momentarily dumbfounded. The dictator had spoken of troops and of two brat rulers, but not a witch. He might have known. And here he was without gauntlets or levitation belt!

"Helbah. A Melbah look-alike."

St. Helens allowed himself a groan. "I suppose she creates floods and fires and earthquakes. Probably throws fireballs as well."

"I haven't heard that she does. But she might. It's what witches do. Melbah didn't like her."

"That's something," St. Helens conceded. Any witch that Melbah hadn't liked couldn't be all bad. Or could she? Maybe one more powerful than Melbah? Melbah, after all, hadn't invaded this other witch's territory.

"I've heard she stops troops cold," Lomax spoke up. "Confuses them with illusions. What's called benign magic."

"Why haven't I heard about it? I'm supposed to be leading this outfit! Even it Bitner didn't tell me, you'd have thought I'd have heard!"

"You never asked," Phillip explained. "And you wouldn't have talked to Melbah even when she was in her guise as General Ashcroft."

St. Helens bit his lip. "This one a general, too?"

"She might be. Melbah never talked about her enemy, and as you know I had few friends."

"I can believe anyone cared for by a witch and manipulated the way you were had few friends," Lomax said. It was a camaraderie he had developed. "St. Helens was your friend, wasn't he?"

"Yes. He was my first real friend."

St. Helens felt uncomfortable. The boy had had playmates, he knew, and as he had grown tired of them the witch had disposed of them like outworn toys. Was the lad still subject to such tantrums? He doubted it, and yet Phillip remained a puzzle. He'd better hope that he didn't attach himself to Melbah's rival.

"I was wondering about those brats," Phillip mused. "Hermandy's king mentioned them and I've heard them mentioned before. Young, aren't they?"

"They are," Lomax said. "Rumor is that the witch keeps them that way."

So she was more powerful! Great! Just what the commanding general needed to hear!

Glumly, General Sean "St. Helens" Reilly resumed his tight lips. He rode on with all the silence he could muster, importantly leading a dictator's brutally trained and brutal troops plus the best mercenary soldiers money could buy.

This was certainly getting to be tiring, General Morton Crumb thought. They were now outdistancing trees and horse droppings, but moving far slower than was natural. Every horse-stride forward carried them only half a stride's distance. It was like moving underwater. Yet the trees and the hills and the silent farm buildings moved slowly, slowly by as they rode the deserted road. They were after all making progress.

"Her magic may be weakening," Captain Abileey said. "Witches too get tired."

"I've heard that," Mor said. Unhappily he was recalling the unequal battle in Deadman's Pass in what was formerly Aratex. That old witch hadn't gotten tired until she'd raised flood, wind, earthquake, and fire. Could this one tire from doing far less?

Captain Plink drew abreast of them. Turning his head, watching the captain's horse, Mor had the impression that the swiftly moving hooves were, though a blur of motion, moving slowly. Something about time-slowing, a trick that was said to be in some witches' repertoire.

"I think we'll get there in a month, General," Captain Plink observed. "We're slow but not stopped."

"Right." Nor would a complete stoppage have bothered him more. If the witch was just playing with them, what would she do when she got mad?

"General Crumb, sir, this may be a little out of place, but why don't we stop and forage the farms? At the rate we're going we will be out of rations long before we're done."

Mor sighed. True enough. This was after all an invasion. It wasn't stealing, though that was what it felt like.

He called a halt. Watching the horses' legs he saw them drift down to the ground. All were halted in what seemed a normal amount of time, though just how much time he was taking to think he could not actually say. His stomach growled as he gave orders to pillage the closer farms.

"Six men to a farm. Eggs, milk, a chicuck or two. Take nothing but food, no more than necessary, and no liberties with the women. Be quick!"

The soldiers ran off at top speed, drifting on their mounts, as Mor saw it. He shook his head, knowing that even this was taking longer than normal. A roasted chicuck would put a smile in his belly. There had to be something that would help him feel decent. An end to the war might, though he would have had to have been a mercenary to feel that it was right.

How had he gotten into this in the first place? It must have been magic tampering at the Kelvinia audience. Something in the wine that made him receptive to orders he couldn't justify, and made him even a bit eager to fight. King Rufurt using magic? But it was not Rufurt, he felt certain. Rufurt, the rightful king, must have been slain or had something else happen to him. He had known, he did know, but he felt helpless.

"General! General Crumb, sir."

"Yes?" Mor didn't stand on ceremonies with enlisted men.

"We can't get near the buildings, sir. The air holds us back. Neither we nor our horses can enter the driveways."

"Magic again," Abileey observed. "If we run out of rations before she runs out of magic, we'll have to return home."

"I'm certain that's what she's counting on," Mor said. Since he really wanted to return he should have felt elated.

Why did he feel certain that this time the witch's tactics were not sufficient to stop them?

The charging cavalry had long vanished. Lester, searching in vain for some evidence that an enemy had really been there, was forced to consider implications. Arrows, crossbow bolts, and spears were lying spent, beyond an area where there never had been an enemy force.

He gave orders that the various projectiles be recovered. His men fetched them. Thus went the day that could hardly be termed a fighting day.

That night Captain Barnes walked over to him at the camp fire. He saluted smartly as a Throod-trained mercenary naturally would. Les had to think what he was supposed to do, and finally remembered and returned the salute.

"At ease, Captain. What's on your mind?"

"Magic, sir."

"Mine too."

"If every time we encounter the enemy, the enemy turns out to be unreal—"

"We'll end up with no weapons other than swords."

"Yes, sir. But suppose we encounter the enemy and the enemy *is* real? Suppose they have real arrows and crossbow bolts and spears; suppose ours have been lost to the phantoms? I mean, if real ones come right after the phantoms, and we don't know the difference?"

"Good point, Captain. Pass the order, no one to fire as much as one arrow until we determine that our attackers are real."

"Yes, sir. Immediately, sir."

Later that night Lester was trying to sleep and was thinking that one of the mercenaries really should be in charge. The long, mournful howls of wolotes came from all around, chilling human blood with their canine songs. He drew his sword and stepped from his tent, intent on nothing. Outside he blinked in the firelight and breathed a deep breath of cool night air. The wolotes must be in the woods just past the fire.

Suddenly there was a great, gray shadow, with glowing red eyes, leaping at his throat!

He raised the sword and struck, all in one motion.

The animal was gone. In its place, completely in uniform, was a large Kance soldier. Before Lester could recover, the enemy had a sword to his throat and a shield protecting his vitals from a dying commander's retaliation.

Les thought of Jon. His eyes saw starlight and drops of oil on the sword blade. The enemy had only to shove the sword. Les' blood would gush out over the blade and arm and against the armor of the man. His breath would go WHOOSH, and he would fall and everything would turn black.

The soldier smiled, wickedly. A light of triumph sprang up in his eyes, and then—

As suddenly as he had come, he vanished.

Les stood alone in his tent opening. He swallowed, and swallowed again.

This sort of thing could get quite discouraging to an invading army. In the past it must have worked effectively many times.

Why was it, Les wondered, as his knees weakened under him, that this time it wasn't going to?

Zoanna watched as Rowforth, looking so much like the king she had married, rowed the boat with strong pulls of the oars. The eerily luminous lichen on the walls gave a feeling of late in the day. Yet it was early, just before sunup.

She smiled her coldest smile as the swirl of water marked the installation. Such a little thing, so easily missed. No roundear had ever discovered it, and none would if she and others like her had their way. Rowforth was enormously privileged.

Moving carefully so as not to rock the boat, she stripped her soft, velvet robe from her creamy shoulders, and fluffed back her beautiful red-as-dragon-sheen hair. She felt Rowforth studying her naked body, appreciating her soft, round breasts with their firm, rosy nipples. His eyes were traveling down her flat stomach, lingering, enjoying in his lecherously honed way. She was no longer young, but discipline and magic had preserved much of her physical youth, and this was always useful when it came to handling men.

"Now," she said, and slipped over the side. She swam skillfully, like a slick-skinned ottrat, diving deeper, deeper. Carefully she expelled her breath. Above, she knew, her consort would be waiting, leaning on his oars, anticipating the moment when she would again break the surface.

Her eyes saw a fish or two, and then the airlock. Grabbing its edge she pulled up her legs, ducked her head, and somersaulted over and inside.

She gulped air. The interior always had air because of the membrane material that removed it from the water. Here one could breathe and rest and hide a century if need be. Here one could take a transporter and go to a world where magic and witchcraft reigned supreme.

She had been here first as a child, and then later as a young woman. Then there had been a long time when she had not been to this place, or used the transporter. During her last trip, after the defeat of her father's weak magic and her tame guardsmen at the hand of Kelvin's Knights, she had done it right. She had gone back to school and learned what she should have learned as a child. Because of what she had learned, she now had power, more than her pathetic old father and his bloodthirsty dwarf ever dreamed.

And what had been the price of this knowledge? Only what she had in infinite store.

She lowered herself onto the waiting platform, rested a moment, smiled contentedly to herself, and then entered the room. The transporter awaited her, and it would be but an easy step, and she would be back at her school. The horned and horny teacher would get her her supplies. How surprised Devale was going to be! Even while they embraced, he had not realized the extent of her ambitions.

She was prepared to offer him a thousand children from defeated kingdoms. In return she was certain he would give her what she needed to defeat Helbah, and the chimaera powder as well. She twisted her mouth as she thought of it: the Roundear of Prophecy's deformed and monstrous child.

She checked the controls on the transporter and then stepped into it. Space-time flashed through her being. Then she was being lifted up in a man's strong arms.

"Professor Devale! Damn your shiny horns, you sensed me!"

Professor Devale did something quite improper for a decent man, that was quite customary for him. "Zoanna," he said, squeezing her close and intensifying his actions. "Of course!"

Heln woke with a startled cry.

"What was it, Heln?" Jon asked. In the days that they had been here, she had become used to Heln's nightmares.

"The monster!" Terror made her voice shrill. "A terrible thing! Three heads! Two of the heads were human, and the other was a dragon!"

Jon took her hand. "That's pretty wild, Heln. I've never heard of such a monster. This one must have been imagination."

"No, Jon, it wasn't!" Heln shook from head to toe under the bedclothes. "Kelvin was with it, and, and—Jon, I think it was going to *eat* him!"

"The dragon head?" Jon was curious, despite the dream's evident horror for Heln.

"No, all of them! It was all one beast!"

"Impossible."

"But it was! And, and that female human head! It had copper tresses, and eyes just the color of copper. It wore a copper tiara and had copper rings in her ears."

"Pretty detailed," Jon said. "I never dream like that."

"Neither do I! That's why I know it wasn't just a dream! It's like the time they were in that frame with the serpents."

"Yes, you did dream accurately then."

"Jon, I'm afraid for Kelvin! I'm afraid for his life!"

"He has to come back," Jon said. "He has a prophecy to fulfill."

"Yes! He must return!" Not really reassured, Heln lay back and closed her eyes.

*   *   *

Kildom pulled Kildee's nose, arousing him from sleep. "You big dunderhead!" Kildee protested.

"Don't hit me, stupid! We need to talk."

"What about, dumbbutt?"

"Helbah. I think she's really worried."

"So?"

"So we should help. Be kings like we're supposed to be."

"Lead an army?"

"Why not? We've lived twenty-four years each. We're as smart as any twenty-four-year-olds."

Kildee scratched his thin red hair and climbed from the bed. He stood in front of the mirror, looking at himself and his brother, both apparent six-year-olds.

"Well, I admit we don't exactly look our age," Kildom said.

"So?" The reflection didn't change.

"Let's ask her to make us big."

"If she could, she'd have done it long ago."

"You think?"

"Yeh. Uh, I don't know."

"Come on, then."

Kildee followed as his brother led him to the witch's private quarters, where they were strictly forbidden ever to go. Naturally they went there all the time, kings being kings and boys boys, and them more than both.

Helbah, her back to them, was talking to her familiar. "Katbah, I don't know if I can. I just don't! If her powers are now greater than mine, and I can't stop her . . ."

Kildom let the door swing back into place. Finger to his cherubic lips he pulled Kildee away from her possible hearing.

"See? It's just like I said. We're going to have to do something!"

"But what?" Kildee was now genuinely and maturely concerned, as indeed he should have been.

Kildom screwed up his face. He pondered the matter, trying hard. "I'm sorry," he said finally. "You and I are just going to have to watch for our chance."

II /

THE BERRIES

K IAN AND HIS FATHER were lost. Kian had to admit it to himself the second day when they awoke in their tree-perch beds and saw nothing but swamp below them all around.

"Father," he said, grasping a crawling spider the size of a small bird with his right-gauntleted hand and crushing it, "I do believe it's time."

"I hate to have you do that, Son. It never seems to me to be safe."

"I've done it before, Father. Besides, if we want to save Kelvin—"

"Yes. All right." John climbed down from the tree next to his and stood in ankle-deep slime. "You'd better position yourself there in the bough, because it's too wet here."

"Right, Father." Stoically, but not without apprehension, Kian took the dragonberry from its associates in the armpouch and gulped it down. He could have used a sip of water, he thought, grimacing at the taste. Unfortunately, fresh, safe water was scarce in the swamp, and the hollow gourd they had filled was rapidly emptying.

As usual, he imagined that there would be no effect, that this time it would not work. This business of astral separation was difficult to believe anyway. Then he noticed that his father was noticeably lower than he had been, and that in the next tree there was a body. The body, he realized with his usual surprise, was his own.

The berries had performed as usual, separating his awareness from his body so gently that it seemed it wasn't happening, until it was done. They would kill pointears, but Heln had discovered that roundears suffered only partial death. This had turned out to be an extremely useful thing.

But he had business. There was nothing to do but find their route. To think of Kelvin, and be drawn to him like a needle to a magnetstone. Of course he'd far rather think of Lonny, but Lonny was in another frame and reaching her right now posed difficulties.

He discovered he was going toward the transporter. His thought of

Lonny had started him that way! That was the danger in letting one's thoughts wander, when one's mind was in a condition most resembling thought.

He formed a mental picture of his brother's face. Instantly he was going back the other way, over the swamp. The greenery below blurred. Now and then a bird winged past or through his astral form. There was a special exhilaration to this kind of travel; there was no freedom like astral freedom!

Then, abruptly, the blurring stopped. He was over the island. He saw the ancient castle where they had been confined, and the chimaera itself was there, doing something in what seemed to be a garden. Willing himself to join Kelvin, he drifted cautiously down the path that was bordered by the pointed posts. Those posts had green patinas, intriguingly. He floated straight through the barred wooden door.

Kelvin and Stapular were there, both alive and—miracle of miracles— talking to each other. They were hunched side by side at the trough, whispering. Should he eavesdrop, or get out? One berry would not last long, and he needed to return slowly enough to memorize the way.

Another thing: he didn't want to risk getting trapped. He had been snared by a flopear once while in astral form. He had been lucky to survive, and he had vowed never to risk that happening again. The chimaera might be sensitive to the astral form as were dragons and flopears. The fact that the monster had one dragon head meant he could be at risk, for dragons were the original users of dragonberries.

"There's this mental block," Stapular was whispering. "Huh, I can do it but you can't. With my help you can."

Kelvin nodded. "It's what my father would call hypnotism."

"Right. Posthypnotic. You forget until it's time. I don't even show a thought."

"I don't know, Stapular. If I trust you—"

"You have to, if you want to make your play."

"All right. All right." Kelvin seemed determined. "You hypnotize. You make the block."

"Huh. I'll hold up a finger and you focus both eyes on its tip. I'll move the finger back and forth in front of your eyes. All you do is keep your eyes on the fingertip."

"You're certain it will work?"

"It will unless you're an idiot! Now, stupid—"

So they were planning something! Kian thought. Hard on the heels of that surprise came another: a startled thought that was not his.

Another! Another! There shouldn't be! Mertin! Grumpus! HELP!

Kian wasn't staying around to find out. Instantly he visualized himself going to his father. He envisioned his father's face as he had Kelvin's.

Blurring greenery. He didn't try to slow it. He had to get back, back to his physical body before he was trapped. Once he was in his body he didn't think he'd ever leave it again! He was so panicky that he noticed no details until he saw the froogear staring into his face.

Mervania was shaken. Physically she was standing there in her garden, sting upraised in fright. Never, ever had she thought to—ever!

"What is it, Mervania?" her companion head asked. "You catch a thought you didn't like?"

"Another. Another," Mervania said, awed.

"You said that. Also 'HELP!' Help with what? You losing your wits? Don't do that. I don't want to have to talk with just Grumpus."

"Shut up!" she exclaimed irritably. "I'd thought it legendary. Mythical. But it isn't. It's *real!* What a discovery!"

"What are you blathering about?"

"Grwoom," Grumpus said in turn.

"Shut up, both of you! Can't you see how distracted I am? There was a disembodied human in there!"

"Disembodied food? Doesn't sound appetizing."

She turned on her masculine side and snarled. "Soul-stuff, imbecile! AS-TRAL!"

"Ghostly, huh? I thought only humans believed in that."

"It's true. Dragonberries."

"Dragonberries?"

"I should have known! But I thought it was just a myth. Anything that fantastic isn't logical."

"What's logical?"

"Shut up. They take the berries, and then they separate, astral from corporeal. They just move around and they hear and see everything. I should have known when I learned that the young hero was from a world with dragons. That's where dragonberries are supposed to be!"

"How come I don't remember that story?" Mertin demanded.

"Because you're obtuse!"

"Grooomth!"

"That goes double for you, big teeth! Both of you put together haven't the brains of a pickled human!"

"Now see here, Mervania, I resent—"

"Oh shut up! I'm too thrilled to argue with you." Her head darted forward, and she kissed him quickly on the mouth. That startled him into silence. "Listen. With those berries we wouldn't be confined. We could swallow them and go anywhere we wanted. To—"

"Gwroowl!"

"Oh very well!" she said impatiently, and kissed Grumpus too, on the nose.

"Food?" Mertin asked.

"No, not food! We wouldn't eat in that form. But we could see and hear everything!"

"Why would we want to do that?"

"Entertainment, moron! Discovery! Adventure! We could visit distant lands, other worlds, other frames. Astrally we could go and see and hear anything there is!"

"Who cares?"

"I do! And you would too, if you had half the brain of a froogear! I want dragonberries! Listen, Mertin, we might find more of our kind the squarears don't know about! We could visit them astrally, and maybe even—"

"Go to them and mate?"

"Maybe. If the squarears cooperate."

"Would they?"

"I don't know. But think of it. We could be a whole colony. A whole world, perhaps."

"Sounds stupid to me. Why should there be more than two? Two's enough to mate. I could take care of that while you sleep."

"Several would be better. Because that's the way it is. The companionship. The communication."

"One more like you would talk me to death."

"Grwoompth!" Grumpus agreed.

But Mervania refused to be dampened. She wanted those dragonberries, no matter what the cost!

Squirtmuck stared into the roundear's face with puzzlement. He had thought this one dead, but now it was awake and looking back at him. Could it be something like the deep sleep in the mud? He could not be certain, and he did not think more about it now that the surprise was gone. But this roundear was reaching for something under its armpit. A weapon? Quickly he grabbed the ugly creature's pale, knobby wrist. The roundear resisted him and struck at him with its other hand. The gauntlet that had been on that hand had slipped off and dropped into the slime while the creature was unconscious.

Firmly, Squirtmuck placed a webbed hand against the creature's loathsome face and held it while he explored under the disgusting smelly arm. What he found was a bag with a drawstring. He pulled it loose, stood back, opened the sack, and peered inside.

The roundear cried out. "No! No! Father, it's got the—"

"Shut up!" the other roundear said. "You're not helping things."

The creature in the tree bole subsided. But his eyes were big and round as Squirtmuck smelled, prodded with a fingertip, and finally tasted one of the dried berries.

"That will kill you!" the roundear cried. "It's poison! To anyone but roundears. It's magic! Big magic!"

Squirtmuck spat out the bitten berry. His tongue burned and he stuck it out and scrubbed its forked tip with his well-slimed hand. He was not too sensitive to tastes, but this was revolting. He retched and spat. Then, to his great distress, he choked out a perfectly good leech. He took in several deep breaths of good swamp air before recapturing the leech with a quick grab and reswallowing it. Good food was not to be wasted!

The roundear for some peculiar reason was vomiting itself. Squirtmuck looked at the mess in the water but saw nothing wriggling. Roundears probably had peculiar tastes like other eared races; it might be that they ate food not even alive. No wonder it made them sick! The roundear quit heaving and wiped its mouth. Any self-respecting froogear would have licked his own mouth, not used his hand.

"Father," the roundear said, "I think they've got us. Again."

"Tell me something I don't know, Son."

Squirtmuck ignored them. He furrowed his head hard, trying to decide what to do with the dried berries. He wouldn't eat them or give them to another froogear even if it was someone he disliked. Possibly they were magic, as the roundear said; in that case the squarears would be interested. He decided to put the berries with the rest of the loot, and not hide any of it except in the great tree hollow where such forbidden objects were placed. Yes, he'd do that, and the god or the squarears might reward him in this or some other life.

Clearing his throat he looked around at the members of his band busily examining the objects they had taken. One, a brother to one of his wives, had the belt and sword that had been on the big roundear. Another froogear had gathered up the two gauntlets and was sniffing them. Others had the younger roundear's sword and several knives.

"Come!" he said, motioning. Under his watchful eyes certain objects were placed in the bole of the collecting tree and others held out as tribute to the god.

That night, while the foragers feasted and splash-danced, Squirtmuck tried to feed and talk with the captives. He was unsuccessful in both attempts. For some reason the roundears tightened their mouths at the sight of fresh, squirming provender. When all reasonable questions were asked, they answered with foolishness about having great magic and powerful friends.

Long before daylight Squirtmuck considered burying them deep in the mud and forgetting that they had ever been. Alas, the god had to be served, and the squarears placated.

In the morning they commenced the trek.

* * *

Bloorg left his dinner and activated the crystal with a thought. His thought was of the roundears in the swamp. He concentrated on the area between the transporter cavern and the chimaera's island, made a sweep, and found them.

The older man and the younger were both captives of froogears, again. Both on their way back to the chimaera, to be eaten.

He sighed. There was no help for it. They were just too troublesome to save twice.

He scanned back to the collecting tree. Yes, all their things were there, waiting. They would not need them now, but the objects would be re-collected. Sometimes he could wish to give such artifacts to the froogears, but that he knew could be dangerous.

There was no help for it. No help at all. Sighing with regret, he blanked out the crystal. Then, exerting great effort, he strove to erase all memory of the roundears' existence.

Grool asked what he was doing.

"I don't know," he said. "But I think I was successful at it."

Satisfied with himself, now, he sat back down at his table and resumed eating the fire-blackened swampfish and chilled lettuage salad he had interrupted.

The chimaera was really in a troubled state. Mervania kept remembering what she had glimpsed with her mind in the larder room. Mertin, maybe just to be mean, kept pooh-poohing the experience.

"We have to make them show us!" Mervania said. "Even if we don't eat them."

"GRRROOOMTH! WAHH!"

"Oh shut up! You'll get raw meat enough! But this is something we can't ignore! All our life I thought it couldn't be, and now I know it is. We just have to get those berries! Why, with those, Grumpus, we could go see dragons!"

"GWROOMTH?"

"Yes! That's what I've been telling you! And Mertin, try to think at least as well as Grumpus! All the sights we can see. The chance of finding us a mate!"

That did strike some interest. Mertin had had time to ponder the pleasures of mating, and was working up some urge for them. "If we can get the berries."

"Yes. That's why we have to get these creatures to bring them. We can't get out, but they can if we let them."

"But they won't come back. With or without berries."

"True, but if we can offer them something in exchange, they might."

"What?"

"Our old copper stings. You know how they value those."

"But they're dangerous! Even to us!"

"But if we make a deal—?"

"We'd be risking all our heads. No thanks, Mervania. To toy with food is one thing; to deal with it another."

"GWROOMTH!" Grumpus agreed.

Mervania felt despair. She knew the lesser heads were right, yet she hated to give up. There were so many places she would like to see again and never could in a physical way. There was that beautiful flower world, for instance, where big-headed wizards with greenish skins grew strange crops. How she had relished the meatloaf plants and the maiden's-blood flowers! Grumpus had had his fill of juicy torso trees and gut vines, while Mertin had gone into ecstatic burps after his first feast of rumpkins and chucquash. Those had been great meals and great times, and the wizards had not begrudged them but let them revel. Why had they ever left? Some mischief on the part of the wizards, or just plain wanderlust? She could not recall.

"Mervania, what are you doing, daydreaming again?"

"I thought you said I talked too much," she said curtly.

"You do. You also daydream too much. But they're coming now. They're outside."

"What are you talking about?"

"Use your mind, Mervania. Your supposedly smart mind."

What was she doing, letting Mertin tell her things? She searched past the wall of their island. There she encountered thoughts.

If I hadn't taken that berry, we wouldn't have gotten caught! That was stupid of me! Stupid as Kelvin!

Kian Knight, one of the escapees! And—

I got the boy into this! I should have watched better! Now he'll never see his bride!

Kian's father! John Knight.

Mervania started their body walking daintily for the big gate. The tribute had been fetched across the swamp and the escapees were back in their power. All was as it should be. Except—

She still wanted those berries. Oh, yes, indeed, she wanted them.

She did not bother with her head-over-the-wall trick. She knew who was there and how they'd be waiting. Such teasing only worked once, unfortunately.

Pushing open the gate she looked after the disappearing row of bubbles and then at the thoroughly bound and helpless Knights.

"Welcome home," she said. "This time it's really no surprise."

"W-what do you mean?" Kian gasped.

"Why, that you were here before, visiting. Did you think I would not know?"

"I deny that! Whoever was here, it wasn't me!"

Poor human foodstuff. So very slow to grasp.

12 /

HELBAH

"**H**ERE THEY COME!**" Phillip was so excited he couldn't contain himself. He was pointing at the Kance cavalry charging down on them. They kept coming faster and faster in overwhelming numbers and still General Reilly, alias St. Helens, did not give the order. At their backs was the open Kance plain and the Hermandy forest they had left.

"Those horse and riders could be phantoms. Illusions," Lomax said. His voice squeaked boyishly, causing Phillip to look surprised. A very few years older than Phillip, so he might have seemed to the former boy-king to be above fear.

"Back into the forest!" St. Helens ordered. "Take refuge behind trees. Don't fire a shot until you see that these are real!"

The men obeyed, as good soldiers should. St. Helens wasn't certain that these Hermans were good, but he knew they were disciplined. They waited behind the trees, arrows nocked, crossbows cocked, swords, shields, and spears ready should these soldiers turn out to be genuine.

The Kance cavalry halted just out of bowshot. A tall Kance general stood high in his stirrups and waved the Kance flag of blue and white. "Truce!" he called out loudly. "Talk between commanders!"

St. Helens relaxed. His caution in taking cover had been justified; this was a real force, not a phantom one. He was glad to have a truce. Better talk than battle, though battle was probably inevitable.

"Agreed!" he called back. "We meet midway." Then to his men he shouted, "Anyone who breaks the truce dies! Second in Command Lomax, you see that that order is carried out!"

"Yes, sir," Lomax squeaked. If necessary he would die for his general, and St. Helens knew it.

"Phillip—keep the faith."

"What faith is that, General St. Helens?"

Would the kid never learn? "Earth expression. Just do right. Be alert for any truce violation on the part of these regulars."

"Yes, sir, St. Helens. I'll do that." The boy seemed eager, and his old chess-playing self.

"Fine. Then—" St. Helens walked out to meet the Kance officer. The ground was a little wet from yesterday's rain and the smell of damp ground and grass would have been a treat to his nostrils if they had not come through the forest. How did the Kancian know if they'd emerge right here at this particular spot on the border? Reconnaissance, of course. Surveillance by an ancient craft that he'd come fully to believe in. To fight an army was one thing, but a witch? He put the thought out of his mind and walked resolutely ahead.

"General Reilly, Army of Hermandy," he said, approaching the other.

"General De Gaulic, Army of Kance," the other said. The man was big and ugly and had a large nose; the nose was his most impressive feature.

Now there was nothing to do but talk. The Kance general had called the truce, so he would speak first. St. Helens waited.

"General Reilly, also known as St. Helens, you serve a madman. Your people have no quarrel with mine and never have. You should go back."

Direct. Also depressingly accurate.

"I serve the interests of he known as the Roundear of Prophecy, Kelvin Knight Hackleberry. It is for the newly formed Republic of Kelvinia that I lead this invasion force."

De Gaulic's dark eyes speared him. "You lie, General Reilly. You serve she who the Roundear fought."

Damn, this man was sharp! "Zoanna?"

"None other."

I might have known! That temptress wouldn't just have drowned! But why didn't Kian and Kelvin find her? Has she been in a different frame?

"You are surprised, and yet not surprised, General Reilly."

"Yes, I—"

"Do you want to serve her? Her interests?"

"No. No, of course not. But—" He hesitated, unsure what he should say.

"You do not wish to serve her? You do not want to attack in her name?"

"Not in her name," St. Helens said. He felt more confused about this than he dared admit. "I'm a soldier and I serve a king."

"A false king."

Damn! De Gaulic must know everything! The witch must have spied it out. Does he know, then, that we can't help ourselves? "It is not the place of the servant to question the master."

De Gaulic smiled. "Yet you hesitate, General Reilly. Do you ask yourself why?"

St. Helens pulled himself together. It was most uncomfortable, standing here like this, having the truth rammed repeatedly into his unwilling mind. "I serve an ideal. A purpose. A good purpose. I have to invade.

"There will be dying. Much slaughter."

"I know. I'm sorry about that. Surrender to me now. Then when the roundear comes he'll make everything right."

"Will he?"

I hope. "He made things right for the people of Aratex."

"Will he with Kance? With Klingland?"

"Both. There shouldn't be fighting."

"And where is the Roundear of Prophecy now?"

"Otherwise occupied at the moment."

The general's expression showed that he knew that there was no certainty of Kelvin's ever returning, but he did not challenge the statement directly. "And yet there will be an evil man in control."

"The Roundear isn't evil!"

"Kelvin Knight isn't in control of Kelvinia. Another person is. He whom the Roundear once defeated in another place. That king and Zoanna, the queen you thought gone forever. Zoanna with more magic at her command than that possessed by her father."

St. Helens felt as if he had been punched. The big-nosed general had better information than he did, and was using it as he might a superior deployment of troops. De Gaulic had just informed him that the worst two people were in control. St. Helens had known it without daring to acknowledge it. Now the truth was undeniable, and pain was in his gut. "Damn!" he muttered.

"I see you will not turn back, General Reilly. You have made up your mind."

St. Helens wanted to say something different. He wanted to explain that he was just a tool, a pawn. The prophecy might compel his son-in-law, with a little help. Yes, it was like a chess game. Kelvin had the power, but others had to make the moves and the sacrifices. Others like St. Helens. He was locked into his slot, unable to escape it.

"I wish there were some other way." He started to turn away, knowing that he was on the wrong side, hating it, but stuck.

A feathered projectile whistled through the air and struck the Kancian general. It made an ugly whacking sound and spun him half around. He cried out, an aged woman's cry, and grasped the crossbow bolt stuck high in his chest.

His chest? No, for on the instant the general was an aged woman. *Melbah!* his mind told him, but he knew that though she had the features, it could not be that one. Melbah was dead.

So the general was the witch! Someone on St. Helens' side had disobeyed his order and the disobedience might mean a victory. Might.

Horses and soldiery raced across the plain. Bowstrings snapped. Shields caught projectiles and bounced them away. The Kance cavalry was charging his force of Hermans.

The woman wavered, then resumed the appearance of General De Gaulic in blood-spattered uniform. His voice was hers, aged and whispery. "Is this how you keep your word, Reilly? Is this the truce of an honorable man?"

"I had nothing to do with it! I swear!" But how could she believe that? He was the man in charge; he was responsible. His side had committed the treachery.

But it was also smart. It was smart of someone back there to realize. Anything against a witch was justified. Take her out and they had a chance!

A chance to win a campaign he might do better to lose. What a mess this was!

Rough hands grabbed him on either side. He did not try to resist, though for him that was difficult. He expected to be slain immediately, but instead his hands were bound and he was put on a horse. Two Kancian soldiers rode on either side of him. Two others rode with the general. The witch-general.

Looking back he heard cries of wounded and dying men and boys, and the screams of horses. Dying because he had led them here. How quickly it had dissolved into carnage! He hoped Phillip and young Lomax would survive. The Hermans hardly had his sympathy, but those two boys were enough like him to be his sons.

They arrived at the caps and the joint palace in what seemed like a remarkably short time. The witch was being helped by a soldier to stay on her horse. Then they were at the palace itself: half blue, half white, the color division running right through the big gate and the drive.

They dismounted, and as they did the general turned completely witch and collapsed. She did not move, lying across equally divided blue and white flagstones. She could be dead. St. Helens watched with the Kancians for any sign of life.

Two very young boys ran from the palace. One was dressed in blue, the other in white. Both had large lace collars. Both ran to the witch and dropped down by her, grasping her, holding her, crying.

Poor kids! St. Helens thought. *She was all they had.*

Suddenly the boy in blue was on his feet, pointing, face twisted and red. A golden crown on his head pronounced him ruler.

"Kill him!" the child shrieked. "Slay us that man!"

The childish finger pointed at St. Helens.

Charlain looked up from her cards. "She's pregnant," she said.

Hal froze in his tracks. "What?"

"Easter Brownberry. I think you had better marry her, Hal."

"But—"

"The cards told me. I know I haven't been what I should to you, Hal. It was only natural that you find someone else. We had better divorce, so you can marry her before her condition shows."

"But you—the farm here—"

Charlain nodded. "It is true. The farm won't run itself. But I can handle it for a time. Perhaps we can work something out. But first things first. We shall divorce, and you shall marry her. She's young, so really needs your support."

"You are a generous woman, Charlain," he said, amazed.

"You are a good man, Hal, and I haven't treated you fairly. I hope this makes it up for you."

Soon he was gone. Charlain knew she had done the right thing. But even so it had come as a shock. She had put on a businesslike front, but now that she was alone the pain overwhelmed her. She put her face down on her arms and wept.

Lomax drew back a bloody sword from the chest of a Kancian soldier. He hadn't time to question it now or to feel shock at what was happening. With blood on him and fighting going on every side, all he could do was act continually to save his own life.

He ducked around the tree, narrowly missing getting chopped. An arrow from a Herman took the new attacker in the throat and toppled him from his mount, the sword burying its point in the ground. He looked at the young Kance soldier's terror-filled eyes and he wanted to feel sorry for him and he wanted to be thankful that his own life had been spared.

A voice screamed pain. A young voice. Phillip's? He hoped not, but there was no chance to look. He battled another soldier and just when he should be feeling the blade in his innards the handsome young Kancian folded over as though made of rags. Not his doing; another's blade had darted in to take the Kancian's life.

"Lomax!"

"Phillip!" The former boy-king had blood on his face and clothing and on the sword he had just used on Lomax's attacker. The boy looked happy, as if he were having the time of his life.

"Lomax, we've got to retreat! We're outnumbered!"

Yes they were, obviously. What had happened, anyway? He hadn't seen who fired the crossbow. St. Helens had warned them, had trusted him. He was in charge, like it or not.

"We've got to get!" Phillip insisted. "Give the order, Lomax! Now!"

Lomax, lacking a signaling horn, shouted *"RETREAT!"* He charged through the brush, hoping others would take the hint. Around him he saw Hermans backing, retreating little by little into their home territory.

After a long, long time—probably several whole minutes, subjectively distorted by the pressure of the situation—he determined that the Kancians were not following. Around them was the supposed safety of Hermandy trees and bushes. Through the bushes he could see the road down which they had marched. Defeated and driven back, but not all killed.

St. Helens had trusted him and left him in charge. He would have to find out who had fired the crossbow bolt at the Kancian general. If the man was still alive, he'd have him executed. After that, taste for it or not, he'd order the Hermans back into Kance by a roundabout way.

St. Helens, Lomax thought savagely, *you will be avenged!*

General Mor Crumb was eating a handful of bright yellow, exceedingly tart appleberries when Klinglanders descended on their camp. Phantoms, he thought. Wasn't the witch going to learn?

A Throod mercenary screamed and fell back, a short-shafted arrow protruding from his throat. Blood stained the ground and the arrow shaft.

Damn! Real this time!

Mor shouted orders, climbing upon his horse, drawing his sword. In a moment they were battling for their lives. A Klinglander raced for him on a big bay mare, spear leveled at his chest. It was like a dragon spear, Mor thought, positioning his shield to take the point. He braced himself for impact, knowing it would be the last thing he ever felt. The point was at the shield, ready to shatter it and take his life.

Then spear, spearsman, and charger vanished, leaving him alive and shaken.

Damn! Another phantom! Mixed right in with the real combatants! Thank the gods, this time.

"Watch out, General!"

He moved his head aside and caught a sword low on his mailed sleeve that almost dislocated his arm. This one *was* real! Damn!

"Fight for victory, men! Fight!" He hoped his words would do some good.

Swords and shields clanged steadily. Bowstrings twanged. Men and horses screamed and both died. Blood bubbled in crimson puddles from torn throats and pierced chests.

On and on into an increasingly weary day. Whoever had thought that war was glorious should be here now!

General Lester Crumb positioned his army for the big charge at the oncoming cavalry. He did not know why he felt so certain about it, but he knew the Kancians were real this time. Real with death and the means to deliver it.

An arrow narrowly missed him and thunked into a rock. That one was real, at least.

Then they were met on the plain behind the row of hills. Ignorant armies, as John Knight would have said. Ignorant armies clashing just before the fall of night.

He had his sword out and was clanging it with a Kancian. The enemy soldier was very good, and he did his best not to lose to him. A second Kancian came in fast and cut him on the arm above the left elbow. He winced, sickened and weakened all in a heartbeat. He opened his mouth to shout, and then the first Kancian lunged hard.

He barely managed a grunt as the blade skidded off good mail and then penetrated, going deep into his chest. He fell, and his thought, strangely enough, was of his father and what he must be experiencing in the adjoining kingdom.

"Commander! Commander!" a voice shouted in his ear.

But by then he was hearing everything as though it were far, far away. Horses' hooves, poundings, screams, swords clanging against sword, shouts —all changed for him, as if to a babbling of a crowd or a murmuring of a brook.

Faint, fainter, faintest.

Jon could hardly give the war a thought. She was too concerned with Heln and what was happening to her. What *was* happening to her? Jon wished she knew. Every single morning Kelvin's wife was sick and vomiting, and it was no innocent morning sickness. It was so violent that sometimes there was blood speckling it, and that didn't seem to her to be right.

Jon, watching Heln's pale face as she picked at her tray of fancy palace food, wished that she had been a girl. She hadn't been, really, until she got together with Les. Growing up she'd avoided girl things. Climbing trees, slinging rocks at targets she moved farther and farther away, angling for fish in a way her foster father enjoyed—these had been her things. Soft girlish interests and especially those having to do with a girl's interest in boys she had dismissed with contempt. She had never worn dresses if she could help it, and her interest in infants had been nil. Now as an adult, as a woman, she had to feel a lack.

Was there a difference between roundears and pointears when it came to birthing? Jon had no way of knowing. How many roundear women had there been in this frame? Heln was the only one she had known, though there had been two females in John Knight's small band of roundears. Two females with round ears somewhere in this frame, maybe having babies in the natural way. Jon wished she had known one.

Heln gave a gasp, rose from her chair, and ran for the bathroom. Sick again, and not gently so. If this was natural pregnancy, Jon wanted no part of it for herself!

Jon picked up the orangmon fruit from Heln's plate and sniffed it. The fruit smelled fine. She didn't believe it was this that was making Heln sick. But just in case it might be—she ate the fruit, finding it good and taut and satisfying. She was wiping the yellow juice from her mouth when Heln returned, looking pale and worn.

"Heln, I'm worried about you," Jon said as her brother's wife resumed her chair. "You've been sick every morning lately. I don't think it's the food; I just tried some."

"It will pass," Heln said almost disinterestedly.

"Yes, but when? You have to think of the baby, Heln. This may not be good for it."

Heln looked impassively out the window at the gardener working on the tulppies and poplics. The flowers were really beautiful this time of year, their red and white, and blue and white blossoms a solace for their eyes. She didn't answer Jon.

That does it! I'm going to get Dr. Sterk to prescribe for her vomiting.

But then a troubling thought: did she trust Dr. Sterk and his medicine! Considering the way he was acting she wasn't sure.

She wondered about it as the sunlight crept over the flower beds and brightened the windows as the birds began to sing. She worried all that morning, and worrying was not like her. Then before she knew it, it was the next day. The oddest thing was that Heln herself did not seem to be worrying; in fact she seemed to have very little interest in anything. What was the matter with her?

There was of course no answer.

Heln was in the royal bathroom, vomiting.

13 /

STAPULAR

"FATHER! KIAN!"

They all embraced there in the chimaera's larder while the alien hunter looked on. As Kelvin had gradually come to accept, looking on was what Stapular did best.

"You've got your belt, Son! And the Mouvar weapon! And your gauntlets! Even your sword!"

"I have, Father." *And a lot of good they've done me so far!* "I've tried the Mouvar weapon but it had no effect. The chimaera could have taken everything from me, but it seems contemptuous and didn't bother."

John Knight heaved a big sigh. "It's something, being prisoners of a creature that doesn't fear our weapons, apparently with reason."

Kian jerked a thumb at Stapular. "The chimaera must fear his kind. They came here to kill it."

"Did, perhaps." *And probably never will again.* "How'd you get caught?"

"Coming back for you," Kian said, seeming annoyed. "We guessed you'd run into difficulties." Politely he did not mention that it had been Kelvin's own choice.

"You were right," Kelvin acknowledged. "The chimaera's too much for me."

"Too much for anyone," Kian said. He did not quite say that that should have been obvious.

"Too much for anyone from an inferior frame," Stapular sneered. The alien had moved away from the wall. One of his hands reached into the trough, picked up a luscious nectorfruit and squeezed it. Pulp and juice squirted from between Stapular's fingers. His hands had to be quite as strong as the gauntlets, yet he had launched no attacks on the chimaera. Kelvin hadn't seen him actually eat, either, though probably he sneaked that in when Kelvin was asleep. Didn't want an inferior observing a superior taking nourishment like any other person, no doubt.

Distracted by Stapular's actions and his own thoughts, Kelvin tried to think of something the two of them had talked about. But had they ever really talked? He remembered trying to interest Stapular in doing something to save their lives, but the hunter had been as adamant then as now.

His father slapped him across the back in a friendly fashion he knew was calculated to build his courage. "Well, Son, we're in trouble!"

"Father, when were we not?" The awkwardness of the situation, and his father's attempt to make light of it were hardly lost on him.

"Say, Stapular, you old phony," Kian said, turning to their cellmate. "You ready to break out of here?" It was a return dig for the hunter's taunt about inferior life-forms.

"Stupid inferior being!" Stapular snapped. As usual his thinking seemed centered on that. Maybe it was because he feared that he himself was mentally deficient?

"Well, we have to do something, don't we, Father?" Kelvin asked. Desperation made his voice squeak. He hadn't felt so unsure of himself since Mor Crumb had propelled him into his first sword fight. The single gauntlet he had then worn had saved him then and many times afterward. Would that it and its mate would do so again!

"I could wish for a laser," his father said. "Unfortunately your father-in-law lost the last one before we fought the final battle for Aratex."

Kelvin remembered. According to St. Helens it was either drop the laser over the Aratex courtyard or let Heln tumble to her death. Although his father-in-law had done many things of which Kelvin didn't approve—in fact, the man had been downright aggravating at times—he had to feel that this was one time he had made the right decision. Now Heln was back home, quietly preparing to have their baby. How glad he was that she wasn't in any of this horror with the chimaera!

Kian spoke up. "A pair of magic gauntlets once propelled me to the top of a huge silver serpent. Once I was up there they knew how to keep me there and how to fight. Kelvin, do you suppose that if you got on top of the chimaera behind the sting—"

Stapular laughed bitterly. "Dumb, inferior life-form!"

"The sting can send out blue lightning bolts," Kelvin said, cutting through his brother's annoyance. "It shot them at me, and—" He launched into his tale.

"Electricity!" John said when he had finished. "It has to be! Like the electric eels we had back on Earth! That's why an antimagic weapon had no effect! Electricity is science!"

"Brilliant!" Stapular said. "For a dumb inferior life-form."

"Listen, Stapular, I'm getting tired of that!" John said, whirling on him. "If you're so brilliant and superior, why don't you tell us how to save ourselves?"

"Because there isn't any way," Stapular said. "You either kill the chimaera with laser bursts or you get caught by squarears and eaten by it. After you're caught you're finished. All you can do is enjoy the food, until you become food."

"You were planning something," Kian said. "You and Kelvin."

"When was that?" Kelvin asked. Never before had he been so puzzled by anything his brother had said. With the puzzle came a lancing pain through his head. This business must be wearing him down more than he thought!

"When I was here before. Not physically. I mean when I returned in my astral form."

"You were here? Astrally?" Now Kelvin understood it, or almost did. His head continued to hurt, as though protesting something. Why was Stapular making that mechanical frown and motioning as if for silence?

"I was. I had those dragonberries we brought, and—"

"Shut up, all of you!" Stapular said.

"Why?" Kian glared at the red-haired, glass-armored cellmate. His expression suggested that he didn't want Stapular ordering them to do anything.

"Because the chimaera reads minds that don't know how to block and compensate."

Oh. They all fell silent.

It was the nearest Stapular had come to admitting that there might actually be a plan.

Mervania tugged at her copper earrings and considered the matter carefully. They had been planning something, Stapular and Kelvin. Probably they intended some ruse, some trick. Stapular, being a hunter, would have controlled his thoughts. But Kelvin—impossible. She considered what she needed to do.

What she wanted was those dragonberries. They would work on her kind, if the legend was correct. They worked for roundears and dragons; thus she, Mertin, and Grumpus all qualified. Together or singly they could search this frame for interesting sights.

What a release that would be! Their body might remain prisoner here on the isle, but their minds would range everywhere! They could spy on squarears who were their keepers. They could watch the froogears at their yearly secret rituals. It would be such a relief to the boredom they suffered here.

Then, too, there was the possibility of visiting other frames, of seeing even more entertaining sights, of listening in on the talk and thoughts of strangers, humans and their superiors. Oh what fun, what incredible fun they could have! As well as, just maybe, finding a potential mate, somewhere.

All of it dependent on dragonberries. There was the treasure beyond reckoning!

"You thinking of that trade plan again?" Mertin grumbled.

"Yes, Mertin, I am." She felt pleased that Mertin was actually asking her thoughts. Maybe she had succeeded in interesting him in something other than food or sex. Of course he would probably just want to use the astral travel to spy on the matings of assorted creatures. Still, if that made him cooperate with her effort, it would be worth it.

"Offer them freedom," Mertin advised. "Let the older roundear go with the one who had the berries. Tell them to find the berries for us, get them back, and bring them here. Then when they don't come back, we eat those who are left."

"Mertin, that's perfect!" she exclaimed, thrilled as much by his support as the notion itself.

"That's logical, Mervania, as you should be."

"Grrrromph," Grumpus added, clicking his mouth as if sampling the tender flesh of a captive.

Mervania sighed. Neither of them had much use for feeling; that was her department. Nothing to do now but go to the larder. She could take along some of the fruit they liked so much, and then she could ask. She did hope they would be open to reason. They should be, but human foodstuffs were notorious for being less than smart about certain matters. Suppose they said no? She tried not to think about that. Maybe if they said no and she butchered one and she and her companion heads ate it while the others watched, that would help them see reason. Yes, if they said no, that indeed might be necessary. Just so long as at least one survived to fetch the berries.

She touched the companion minds and they flipped up their tail and scuttled across the ground to the orchard. She and Mertin filled their joined arms with nectarfruit, and Grumpus pinched a cantemellon from a vine with their pincers and stuffed it inelegantly into his own mouth.

Properly loaded with fruit and plans, they scuttled for the larder.

Squirtmuck could not get the collecting tree out of his mind. The objects taken from strangers had never interested him greatly, but those berries were tempting. The one he had sampled had made him embarrassingly sick, but if a roundear's stomach could handle them, then so should his. It was so intriguing, the thought of dying as the young roundear had done, then coming back to life. Squirtmuck had never thought much about it before, but now that he did, the thought of what existed after dying was intriguing.

Irresistibly, bit by bit, he toyed with the notion. Late during the day, while searching for squiggle worms, he managed to get back to the area of the tree. He looked around, saw none of his mates, and made a splashing run for it. Soon he was there, looking into the cavity and its collection of visitor artifacts.

If he took just one of the berries, would anyone know? Suppose it killed him, and he did not return to life. He wasn't quite old enough to want to die. True, he was tired of a lot of what made life, but not tired enough to give it up yet.

He thought about it for a moment more, while the sun started setting and dappling the trees and the greenish water with orange. Why not, he thought, why not indeed? He might not have another chance.

Reaching into the tree's cavity, he drew forth the bag.

Bloorg scratched a square ear and remembered that he had not used his viewing crystal yesterday. As leader of his people and official greeter of visitors he should check the transporter. As usual there would be nothing, but then again there might. There was always that hope.

Sighing, he picked up the squarish crystal from its stand, held it before his eyes, and concentrated.

At first, as was usual, he saw nothing but his own square pupils in his own square eyes. Then he could see into the pupils that expanded and expanded, and then he was seeing back at the transporter cave. It was as he had last seen it, with a drying narcofruit left by the froogears near the exit.

Why was he here? Oh, yes, to check for possible visitors. There were none, as he had expected.

So he would direct his thoughts elsewhere. He should check briefly on the froogears, and then maybe the chimaera's island. It was a chore, but his job. Work, work, work, always the same boring necessities.

He drifted his sight across the swamp, finding the froogears at a camp on a platform of floater weeds. They were doing froogear things. Here one froogear dived off the platform and crawled along the bottom, finally surfacing with a wriggling stinkfish firm in his jaws. There a female covered her breasts and stomach with greenish muck, the better to attract a lover. There child froogears splashed joyfully at the edge of the platform and took turns diving under. The male with the stinkfish in its jaw swam up to the platform and the female. The female took the fish from his jaws, bit its head, and oogled his form. The male climbed up beside her. In a moment the two would be joining. At such moments Bloorg, bored, moved his viewing elsewhere.

He had almost brought his sight back to the crystal when he remembered the froogear leader. Where was Squirtmuck, anyway? Efficiently he moved his sight in circles, checking froogears. Squirtmuck was not there.

What an irritation! He had to search until he located the missing creature, or was assured that it was dead. Wider and wider he viewed, until finally he thought to check the collecting tree.

Squirtmuck was there. He held a bag in his webbed fingers and from it he took a berry. He held it poised in front of his mouth.

Berry? What berry? As from a great distance—which of course it was—it leaped at him: *dragonberry!*

"No, Squirtmuck, no!"

But it was already too late. Squirtmuck, propelled by some incomprehensible flight of froogear fancy, had suddenly and forcefully thrown away the entire bag.

The bar dropped outside the door. All stood back as the chimaera entered, carrying fruit. Kelvin felt strange, watching it. The head called Mervania still seemed to him to be that of a beautiful coppery-haired woman, a roundear at that.

Thank you, Kelvin.

The male head, Mertin, could have been on the shoulders of any of the soldiers he had directed against Rowforth in the silver-serpent frame.

Forget it, foodstuff!

The dragon head reminded him all too clearly of the dragons with golden scales that he himself had slaughtered.

GWROOOOF!!

While the beast as a whole reminded him of nothing so much as a—

The chimaera had entered, while he was thinking. Now it elevated its deadly tail. Kelvin hastily suppressed his thoughts. The monster dumped its load of nectarfruit into the trough. It smelled lusciously good. Even though he knew it was fattening, he could hardly wait to start eating!

He edged away from the wall, his feet seeming to have a mind of their own. Suddenly he was running, right past the chimaera to the open doorway.

Mervania's pretty head dipped toward his as he passed. "Going somewhere, little toothsome?" she inquired sweetly.

He put on the skids, without knowing why. Now he was standing right beside the monster, with the female human face almost near enough to kiss.

"Well, if you feel that way, Kelvin—" she started, amused.

Kelvin, astonished, realized that she *would* kiss him, even though she intended to eat his flesh later. Because she liked to play with her food.

Suddenly Stapular acted. "Go!" he shouted, and grabbed the tip of the sting, which was now pointed at the ceiling.

There was a flash, as from a close lightning bolt. Kelvin found himself weak and gasping and tingling all over, just outside the door. His feet must have carried him here! Inside the cellar his brother and father lay sprawled, unconscious or dead.

Amazingly, the chimaera too was down. Only Stapular was alive and moving. "Quickly, before it comes to!"

"What?" Kelvin struggled with the thought. His feet wanted to carry him, but he could hardly stand.

"The electricity in this confined space took them all out. But I'm not certain how long before they wake! Hurry!"

Abruptly he was remembering. Stapular waving his fingers at him, implanting a course of action deep within his head.

Kelvin ran to the fence and grabbed a post. The post, slippery and solid, resisted his strength, but he was determined. Then the gauntlets took over and wrenched it from the ground.

"Come on! Get your posterior in motion!" Stapular cried.

He was to run with it back to the chimaera. He was to raise it like a great dragonspear and drive it deep into every living eyesocket the monster possessed! He—

He stood there, his weapon poised before Mervania's fallen face. She looked almost angelic, her eyes closed, her features relaxed. She had been about to kiss him. Drive the point into one of those lovely eyes?

How could he? The chimaera was helpless. It might be a monster, but Mervania was as womanly as any woman he had known, with the possible exception of his own mother. And his wife. Yet here he stood, feet wide apart, tip of the greenish-tinged sting raised above her face, his eyes and muscles concentrating hard on her coppery—

"Now, stupid, now!" Stapular ordered.

Something snapped. Kelvin trembled and pointed the sting away from the lovely face.

"Ineffective Minor World fool!" Stapular screamed. He charged across and took hold of the shaft. "I'll do it myself! I should have known better than to trust a lesser creature to do something important!" He pulled.

Kelvin resisted, pulling back with the strength of the gauntlets.

"You fool, you idiot, you brainless nothing!" Stapular yelled. "Can't you see that it's about to wake?"

True, surely. Yet Kelvin did not yield. "No, Stapular! I can't do it this way! We only want to escape."

"That's all *you* want, maybe, you imbecile! I want more!" Stapular exerted considerable strength, and it was as if he wore magic gauntlets of his own. Kelvin was pulled off balance, but his gauntlets maintained their grip.

"Let go! Let go! Let go!" They fell together, struggling over possession of the copper sting. They rolled over and over on the floor, with Stapular's unexpectedly heavy weight and the armor pressing hard against his simple rustic body coverings.

Then they were up against the trough, and Stapular was bending him back. The edge of the trough struck his head and he saw stars. Then—

Stapular had the sting! He held it poised above the Grumpus head, searching out the dragon's eyeball and its path to the brain. Kelvin had killed dragons that way, and Stapular had learned from his telling, if he hadn't known it before.

"Die, beast!" Stapular said. His body tensed.

Without realizing how he did it, Kelvin was upon him. One incredible leap propelled somehow by his gauntlets; then he and the hunter were going over on the floor. Again they were rolling, fighting for control.

"You fool! You moron! You Minor World trash!"

Kelvin paid no attention to the words. He saved his breath for the combat. It was almost as though the gauntlets had taken weird control over the whole of him. To destroy the monster should be his greatest desire, yet now it was as if his greatest wish were to save the chimaera.

The great beast stirred. An arm with a man's hand on it reached out and grabbed the shaft of the sting where Kelvin and Stapular held it.

"Let go that!" Mertin said. The scorpiocrab claws clicked warningly.

Stapular did not let go. Thus he remained in place as the huge claws reached out, took him around the middle, and lifted him into the air.

"Now see what you've done!" Stapular cried. "Minor World idiot!"

Kelvin released the sting. With a quick motion he brought out his sword. He swished it at the pincer and then struck. Copper gleamed brightly where his blade bit. The pincer would have a scar, but that was as deeply as his blade penetrated. At the same time he felt the shock of impact from wrist to shoulder. Ouch! His arm felt numb!

"You really must not fight!" Mervania said. "You really must not." Her head was awake now, staring at him.

Suddenly the hunter had hold of his own left wrist. He pulled at the transparent gauntlet. It came off—*along with the entire hand.*

Kelvin blinked, but the sight remained. Where the man's wrist should have been was a metallic something that could hardly be bone.

From the foreshortened arm a ruby laser flashed out. It cut through one of the pincers. The pincer and Stapular hit the floor simultaneously.

"Now you'll see!" Stapular said, rising and pointing the stump. "I came prepared! It was planned that I be the last, and hide this until the last moment! I didn't want to have to reveal my nature, but this Minor World scum forced my hand." He glanced briefly at the hand he had removed. "Now, Chimaera—"

Mervania screamed. Mertin made an exclamation of dismay. Grumpus growled. If a monster could tremble, this one was doing so.

Casually Stapular lanced off the second pincer. With his back against the wall, immune from being grabbed, he could proceed to cut off every arm and head.

"Listen, Minor World being," Stapular said. "You wouldn't have it the conventional way! You had to make me ruin my cover! Now listen to the death cries of the last known surviving chimaera in all the frames!"

"No, no!" Mervania cried. It sounded very much like a woman's pleading, and indeed there were tears in her eyes.

Kelvin could not have said how it happened. Suddenly he raised, reversed, and flung his sword forward. It was the gauntlets' doing. For the moment the gauntlets appeared to have chosen a strange side.

The sword turned in the air, the point coming to the fore. The blade penetrated Stapular's throat precisely in the middle. Stapular looked surprised. Then he raised his intact hand and yanked the sword partway out.

Something black gushed forth. Alien blood? No, not blood at all, Kelvin realized. Oil! Stapular was what his father called a robot!

Whatever it was, the fluid was necessary for the thing's functioning. As it poured out, Stapular collapsed. He could not function without oil pressure any better than a living creature could function without blood pressure.

"You have saved us! You have saved us!" Mervania exclaimed, and even Grumpus growled something that sounded appreciative. Monsters valued their lives as much as other folk did.

Now John Knight and Kian were opening their eyes, returning to bewildered consciousness.

"It was all a trick!" Mervania babbled indignantly. "A trick of the hunters!"

"That thing never would have tasted right!" Mertin said with disgust. "It would have given Grumpus indigestion."

"GROOOOMTH!" the dragon head agreed with a disgusted expression.

Kelvin looked quickly to his father and brother, and back to the faces of their captor. Now they were in for it, he thought. Now they were all going to be rewarded in the worst possible way for his colossal stupidity and for the gauntlets' interference. Now they had no way to escape being eaten by the chimaera.

Grumpus snapped his big jaws and darted forth his forked tongue as if hungry already.

14 /

TURNINGS

S T. HELENS PREPARED HIMSELF for death, as well as he was
able. He expected a spear to be rammed through him or a knife
slitting his throat. Yet even as this child-king who was not a child screamed
"Kill him!" the witch opened her eyes and stared piercingly at the men
holding him.

"No, precious," she said, her eyes flicking back to the child. "He must be
a prisoner."

"He killed you!" the child shrilled.

"Not yet, precious. Not yet. Please, darlings, humor me. My kind are
hard to kill." With those words the old woman ceased speaking and closed
her eyes as though for death.

St. Helens heard a sword snick out of a scabbard. She had spoken too
late, or died too early, he thought. Now the brat-king would have his understandable revenge.

"No!" the little guy ordered. "Don't kill him! Put him in the dungeon! As
for Helbah, take her in!"

"But—"

At that moment a large houcat, very black, ferocious of eye, leaped from
behind the second young king and ran to Helbah's apparent corpse. For one
moment St. Helens felt the sharp yellow eyes, and heard the wickedest,
deepest, longest-drawn hiss he'd ever heard from anything feline. Then the
houcat was on the corpse, breathing in and out against Helbah's worn
mouth.

Suddenly the houcat stiffened all over. Then it collapsed like a black,
empty bag. The blackness stayed there and seemed even to be melting as a
soldier jerked St. Helens' arm.

Now there were two corpses, he thought. *Witch's and witch's familiar.* But whatever else he might think of her, he knew that the witch had saved his life.

The soldiers rushed him away.

Lomax steadied his young resolve as he looked up and down the line of survivors of the recent fight. They had lost only about a dozen men in addition to St. Helens, but twenty more were wounded seriously enough to be sent home. The remainder, Lomax determined, were going to cross that border again. But first there was this other matter.

"All right! Who did it! Who fired that crossbow bolt! Who violated the truce?"

No one spoke. All the Hermans remained impassive, while the mercenaries were interested rather than apprehensive. Judging from appearances, none here were guilty.

"You, Phillip, did you—"

He was going to say "see someone do it?" but the boy interrupted him.

"Yes, I did it! I did it! I'm the one!"

"YOU! But why?" His head swam even as he asked it.

"St. Helens plays chess! He knows you have to take out the dark queen!"

"You've killed him! You're responsible for his death!"

"He's my greatest friend! Oh, Lomax, please, please hang me as he asked!"

Lomax shivered. "You really—"

"Please. I did it for him. I did it for all of us. So that we could win. The same as when Kelvin destroyed Melbah in Aratex."

"Damn!" Lomax said, pained and unenthusiastic. The kid really did think it a game! Doubtless he thought that afterward the dead simply woke up and resumed living, ready to play the game again. Kids!

"Please," Phillip repeated. "It was my dearest friend's last request. He was not only my dearest friend, he was my *only* friend!"

Lomax shook all over, unable to stop himself. "You really want me to give that order? You really want to hang by your neck and choke, your eyeballs bugging out? You want to die?"

"Yes."

He considered it. He liked Phillip in spite of himself. Would St. Helens really want him dead? St. Helens had saved the former figurehead king of Aratex from death, and had treated him as a friend. Should he, could he now follow what had been St. Helens' command?

"NO!" he said forcefully. "That'd be too easy on you! You have to go back with us into Kance! You have to fight the enemy and make up for what you've done!"

"Oh, thank you, thank you, kind, gentle friend!"

Was that for refusing to hang him, or for visiting on him presumably worse punishment? There were tears in the boy's eyes, but his voice was not devoid of sneaky triumph. What game was he really playing?

Well, the reality of battle would sweat that out of him, if it didn't kill him first.

St. Helens, Lomax thought in what was almost a prayer, *I promise you will be avenged even if it costs every one of our lives!*

The phantoms were not coming now, Mor thought. They'd quit appearing and disappearing in midbattle. Yet his men were losing, losing badly, and not to witchcraft.

He finished off the Klinglander he was fighting and then wheeled his horse. Dead and dying men lay everywhere, and yes, the tide of battle had definitely turned.

It galled him to do it, but there was no alternative. He lifted the horn to his lips and blew the signal for retreat.

Their only consolation, he thought, was that in the forests grew blood-fruit for the treatment of the wounded. Before this war was over, the magical fruit would save a lot of lives.

Thinking grimly of the surgery that would have to be set up, Mor turned his horse. A forest with bloodfruit was reasonably close behind.

Zoanna stared into her crystal and laughed a most unbeautiful laugh that Rowforth found deliciously chilling.

"Look! Look!" she ordered.

He was looking. He saw the witch who controlled the kingdoms of Klingland and Kance lying motionless without a visible sign of life. There was that black houcat lying on her face, melting into it. There were the Kancian soldiers dragging a bewildered St. Helens away.

"Does this mean we've won?" he asked. He felt stupid asking a woman about anything, even Zoanna. He felt particularly stupid now, knowing that he had done nothing to direct the battles or secure the triumph.

"We will have won if she never recovers," Zoanna said. "We must see that she doesn't."

"You will use more magic?"

"Magic won't be needed in the war. Of course my not helping our side will mean many more casualties. Some of those will be our former enemies."

"A shame," he said smugly. "They'll fight their hearts out and never know why."

"Yes, they'll die for us, one way or another. Those who survive the battles may have to die later."

"Slowly, with our help, and with much pain."

"Of course. That is what we both want."

They embraced, the battles revealed by the crystals fading from their minds. Soon, he thought, there was going to commence the fulfillment of all his dreams. It would be brutally, bloodily, ghastlily glorious.

Lester Crumb imagined that he was back fighting the Queen's Guardsmen, with Kelvin's Knights of the Roundear. Then he opened his eyes and found that the man bending over him wore a different uniform. He strove to think, to reorient, and then it came, the pain of the wound high in his chest. Where was Jon? Jon had saved his life and then gone on to become his wife. What had happened?

Different war. Different battle. Different circumstances. Jon was far away. Safe. Oh, he hoped she was safe!

A gnarled hand mopped at his brow. He felt the sweat that was all over his face, soaking his undergarments, the blanket he lay upon. Overhead was the roof of a tent. The tent was flapping dismally in a wind that howled like disembodied souls slain in battle.

"We were fighting Kance soldiers," he said. "I fell. Someone saved me. It was almost like another battle when I was unhorsed."

"Save your strength, Commander."

Commander? Him? He could hardly remember. His head hurt and pounded like a drum beaten to announce someone's death. Oh, if only Jon were here to hold him! He tried remembering the officer's name. Klumpecker, that was it! Lieutenant Karl Klumpecker from Throod.

He looked into the deep blue eyes, noting the blond hair and the smile so typical of Throod mercenaries. Big shoulders, too, and a strong frame, though not quite as great in these departments as his father.

"Did we win the battle?"

"No, Commander, we lost."

Somehow he thought he'd say that. "Many casualties?"

"I'm afraid so, Commander. On both sides."

"Can we win the war?"

"Eventually, Commander. When Commander Reilly and the Hermans and your father and his troops and ours all reach the caps."

"Yes, the caps." Insane business, two capitals in one. Governed, theoretically, by two very slowly maturing boys. Governed in fact by a witch identical in appearance to the one Kelvin had destroyed in Aratex. Would Kelvin soon return? Would he return as in Aratex to put everything right? When he had started this adventure he had been certain. Now wounded, now defeated in battle, he was no longer certain of anything.

"Commander, your wound is so serious that—" The lieutenant paused, seemingly searching for words.

"If I cannot command, you must, Lieutenant. We must not surrender! We must fight on! My father and St. Helens are depending on us!"

"Yes, Commander Crumb. We will fight our way into the caps and into glory."

With me or without me, Les added in his own troubled thoughts. He wanted to pass out, even to die, but thoughts of Jon would not allow it. Then it seemed that he was but a little boy, that he was lost, and that all others were gone.

Charlain moved her copper locks out of her violet eyes with a quick sweep of her slender hand. The cards she was laying out on the kitchen table had come out the same as before. Every time the Blind Fool headed Kelvin's file, designating great danger and uncertainty for him.

"Does the prophecy still apply?" she whispered to herself. "Can it still?"

She tweaked her right pointed ear to keep herself awake. John Knight had been intrigued by that habit of hers. Strange man, John. She had once thought of him only as a way of fulfilling the prophecy. He, a roundear, would mate with her, a pointed-ear person, and their son would be the one mentioned in the Book of Prophecy. It had all seemed so simple when she was young. John had come straight from the queen's dungeon, torn, lonely, and confess it now, handsome. She had wanted him from the start, and they had married quickly and without attracting attention. They had had their son, and then a daughter. Only roundeared Kelvin could relate to the prophecy, but pointeared Jon had supported him loyally.

In time Kelvin had indeed slain dragons, and freed their kingdom of Rud from the tyrannous Queen Zoanna. The prophecy was being fulfilled, as she had foreseen.

Then things had changed, and nothing was as she had expected. Perhaps her action in implementing the prophecy had caused the fabric of the situation to change. Kelvin had left this frame and returned to it just in time to save Rud and Aratex by uniting them, just as in the prophecy—but that had been by the skin of his fingernails! Now "joining four" were the next words in the verse that applied to him. He was supposed to join four kingdoms. But how could he? Kelvin wasn't even here! He was in another frame, and the prophecy that he would rid his homeland of a sore was rapidly being nullified. Sometimes she almost thought that John Knight had been right.

"Nonsense, this prophecy business! Nonsense!" John had said, sometimes sitting at this very table. She had soothed him, calmed him, knowing even then that he would not always be hers. He had suffered himself to be soothed, not because he accepted magic, but because she was beautiful in his eyes (and perhaps in others' eyes too), and he liked to be close to her. So his contempt of magic had been muted at times, until finally he began to believe. Then she had lost him, through no choice of either of theirs, in the necessary tragedy of the times.

Now things were changing again, becoming even less settled than before, and the cards reflected it. "John," she whispered, pretending that he was there. Oh, how she loved him! Her second husband was a good man, taken as the law allowed on the extended disappearance and assumed death of her first. But John, John had been the stuff of story. Round ears, for sorcery's sake! And from another frame, a world too strange for comprehension. Moving pictures, talking boxes, horseless carriages, and more, much more. Strangest of all was John's insistence that none of those were magic.

"Well, John, I know you are alive now," she murmured through her tears. "I never would have remarried had I known. I know now that somehow the cards lied, or I misread them, and that you survived what seemed a certain death. I know that I was not your first woman, or your last, and you were not my last man, but I love you and want you, and hope that you will still want me." But there had been others to consider, including the man she had married. Hal Hackleberry—she hated to admit it, but she was relieved that things had fallen out with Hal as they had. Perhaps she had suspected what would happen; the cards might have informed her, but she had resolutely avoided reading them with respect to the Brownberry family, after that first crisis. Even so, she had known that they had a buxom and lonely daughter . . .

Hal was good but fallible. Most men were. She had wept when she lost him, as much for her own complicity as for the loss. She had never been able to love him properly. "But you, John . . ."

She found herself weeping, and this annoyed her. Witchy people who read cards and tried to foretell events were not supposed to be soft and blubbery. She had to remember that.

She forced herself to face the truth. She was dissembling when she told herself she had not loved Hal completely. She knew now that she had never loved Hal at all. She had told him she did, and tried to believe it herself, but it had always been John. So she was as much at fault as Hal for what had happened. Maybe he had known, and so had suffered, and been vulnerable. Certainly she hardly blamed him. She had said that before; now she believed it.

When in doubt, deal some cards.

She dealt them out, asking in her mind, *Where is John? Where is John Knight who was my husband?*

John was with Kelvin. Both in another frame. Both separated from her as though by death's gates. The Blind Fool leered and danced, promising naught. They might or might not return.

She turned a card. There it was again: the Coupling card. Kelvin was already married, to a nice girl named Heln, a roundear like himself. The

Coupling card was an unmistakable reference. She placed it on file and turned the following card.

The Birthing card. So they were going to have a baby, a fact she had already learned. But then a third card, to follow the Birthing card—and it came up, yet again:

The Twister card. Meaning grave danger and an uncertainty of outcome.

Poor Heln! Poor frightened little mother-to-be. You are in for great difficulties.

But would it be just the birth, or something happening to the child during the birth? Afterward? Stubbornly the cards would not say. Actually, it was wrong to blame the cards for being perverse; they were perverse only when the situation made them helpless. For example, when something they might reveal would be changed when they revealed it. If they told her she would stub her toe when she left the table, she would be careful to avoid that, making the cards wrong. Paradox incapacitated them. So they compromised by presenting the Twister. They weren't willfully difficult.

Maybe she should be with her daughter-in-law for the delivery? Usually that was not a mother-in-law's place, but under the circumstance . . .

Yes, she would go to Heln and try to help her. With the Blind Fool dominating Kelvin's fate and the Twister twirling in to link hers more closely with his, there was no alternative.

"I don't like to interfere," she said aloud, "but what else is a mother to do? Heln, I'm going to come visiting!"

Jon did not like the way Heln looked! It seemed less like a healthy pregnancy every day. Not only was Heln disgustingly sick at frequent intervals, she was now having bad dreams.

"Jon, oh Jon!" Heln sat up in bed, her face pasty, her eyes wild and glassy. "I saw it again, the thing with three heads! Two of them baby heads and the other a dragon's. The baby heads were crying, and—"

That settles it! Jon thought. *I'm going to get something for her from the doctor. Dr. Sterk has to know something! He was royal physician before I was born!*

"Where are you going, Jon?"

"I'll be back."

She met Dr. Sterk in the hallway. He looked straight ahead with his birdlike eyes and pressed a small decanter into her hands. "Three drops twice a day in her tefee," he said, and passed on.

Well, she thought, at least she hadn't had to press him. Evidently he'd noticed it too. But did she dare trust his medicine, considering his evident toadyism?

She reentered their room. Heln gazed at her with eyes seemingly reflecting horror. That was not the way a young mother-to-be should look!

That settles it! Jon thought again. *Enough torment is enough! I just have to trust. Who after all would want to harm an infant?* Aside from certain royal figures . . .

"Heln, it's time for your tefee." She pulled on the cord to signal the servant. In a moment the servant was there with a big steaming pot of the beverage and a plate with a selection of bite-sized cooakes.

Jon poured the tefee into the cups and carefully added three greenish thick drops to Heln's. She stirred it with a spoon and the syrupy medicine blended into the dark greenish hue of the beverage.

"Here you are, Heln."

She watched as Kelvin's pretty dark-haired wife took the cup listlessly, and slowly sipped.

Heln's eyes widened. She raised the cup again, in both hands. Eagerly she sucked down every drop.

That was good, Jon hoped.

15 /

DISAPPEARANCE

MERVANIA'S HEAD MOVED CLOSE to Kelvin's and spoke in that disturbingly seductive tone she affected: "Kelvin, since you saved us by destroying the cruel hunter, we will not eat you or your companions."

"You are letting us go?" Was she toying with him again? Playing with her food, as her fellow head put it? Kelvin did not in the least trust her.

"Yes, yes, but there is a price." It was prettily said, her face almost touching his. Even her breath was sweet as she said it.

"What price?" They were already in its power. Anything Kelvin or his companions had, the chimaera could take away, for reason or whim. Surely she wasn't bargaining for a kiss!

"Those dragonberries Kian used—I want some." Very plainly spoken, no artifice showing.

Kelvin looked unhappily to Kian. He hated speaking for him and he hated not to.

"Lost," Kian said, helping John to his feet. "Froogears."

"Unfortunate," Mervania said. This time there was just a touch of sadness. If the dragonberries were lost, then they were lost, and there was nothing to be done about it. Which meant that the human party had nothing with which to bargain.

"Groompth," remarked Grumpus. He opened his dragon's mouth wide enough to display his swordlike teeth.

"Now we eat!" Mertin said, making a superfluous translation. He didn't sound at all sorry. If dragonberries were of great importance to Mervania, they were less so to him.

"Wait! Wait!" Kelvin cried. He had never felt so panicky in his life. To fail to say the right thing now would be to condemn himself and his companions to being eaten. "Suppose—suppose we get you some? Maybe we can bring you some seed so you can grow them here on your island. Then you'll always have a supply."

Mervania's head tipped coyly to one side. "That would be nice, Kelvin."

Yes, Kelvin thought. *If we can get the seeds back home, and if the squarears will let us.*

"I read your thoughts, Kelvin," Mervania said reprovingly. "the squarears will let you. But you must tell them first."

"We will," Kelvin said. Unconsciously he picked up the old copper sting with its green patina scratched from being dropped on the floor. Then he looked over at Stapular, now silent and unarrogant, the oil no longer flowing from his pierced throat.

"You may take back your weapon," Mervania said, "but you must not touch the hunter's."

"Fair enough," Kelvin said. He crossed the cell to Stapular's pinned body, and without his willing it his right gauntlet reached for the sword haft. Fascinated he watched his arm lift the sword from the oil. The blade was covered with a thick dark grease that probably would help preserve its metal. The gauntlet wiped off most of the stuff on a clean section of the body, then sheathed the sword in its scabbard. Kelvin's arm was his own again.

"You must tell the squarears about this," Mervania cautioned. "They must know what was planned. They will come to get this robot and its weapon and guard against this ever happening again."

"I'm glad to have been of service," Kelvin said. He looked into the open blue eyes of the robot he had believed to be a person and was forced to think *Junk, nothing but junk. Not flesh and blood at all.*

"Yes," Mervania said. "An excellent imitation."

Yet he had felt that Stapular was living. Had he been, or was that magic?

"It is what your father calls science," Mervania said. "You are now free to go. Do not forget, though, what you have agreed to do."

"We'll talk to the squarears," Kelvin said. "If they will permit us, we'll get your dragonberry seeds." Unconsciously he hefted the sting in his left hand.

"You may take that with you," Mervania said. "To me it is of no more importance than your hair and nail clippings are to you."

"Thank you," Kelvin said. "Thank you for—"

"Come!" his father said. "Before it changes its mind!"

"Minds," Kian corrected.

Kelvin had only one objection: they didn't have a boat, and he doubted that they could swim all the way back to the swamp.

"You will be met," Mervania said, knowing his thought. "Froogears will come."

"They—know?"

"Some are quite near. Their minds, like yours, are always open."

"Oh." That was all he could manage. He looked at his father and brother, but they were already on their way out of the larder and into the gloriously warm and mild sunshine beyond.

Kelvin looked once more at the dead robot. Why did he persist in thinking of it as a once-living man, though now he knew better?

"You have a quaint human way of anthropomorphizing," Mervania said. "You want to believe that thing was human because it seemed so, even though all it did was insult you in order to keep you from getting too well acquainted and perhaps fathoming its secret prematurely."

That must be it. He looked at the Mervania head. "I—"

"Just as you persist in thinking of me as a pretty woman, though you know even better that I am nothing of the kind. Your human capacity for willful self-delusion is amazing."

Just so. Kelvin turned and walked after John and Kian.

"I like you too, Kelvin, perhaps as foolishly," she murmured almost inaudibly. "I would have missed you, after we ate you."

Bloorg withdrew his mind from his viewing crystal and considered the implications. He had just seen and overheard the conversation of Mervania Chimaera and the visitors. So they had agreed to return with dragonberry seeds for the chimaera. That should be fine, so long as they thereafter stayed away. If those berries kept the chimaera entertained, better yet, and should it actually manage to fulfill its dream and discover some other creature of its kind, making a mating unit, that would be wonderful. How interesting that the man's magic gauntlets had fathomed all that, and acted correctly despite temptation to do otherwise.

Yes, he thought, rubbing his square ears with his usual afterviewing massage, that should work out very well. They would meet the human party at the transporter cave and make certain the visitors got their correct transporter setting. After that there would be an end to commerce. Who would ever have suspected that the foolish visitors would not only survive, but benefit the situation!

Think-whistling an inspiring song, Bloorg stepped outside his dwelling and prepared to summon his underlings for the start of a new day.

The trip away from the island and back through the swamp was one Kelvin had not expected to make. He looked over at his father and Kian as the froogears carried them, wondering whether they were as amazed as he at the turn of events. If they survived this journey in good order, he planned to give up this life of involuntary adventure. Nothing was going to pry him away from Heln and his home again! Froogears, squarears, chimaera . . . just too much! Back home things were sensible with only a bit of magic and sorcery and golden-scaled dragons to break the monotony of everyday life. It was so much better to be among normal things, instead of out among exotic and unnatural things like robots and laser weapons!

"I can't believe it," Kian said. "I'm actually going to see Lonny again!"

That was right! All this had started when they headed out to attend Kian's wedding! But Kelvin was ready to skip that event at this point, not wanting to risk another journey through the transporter. He just wanted to stay with safe, normal Heln and their safe, normal baby on the way.

John Knight said nothing, and the froogears splashed away, transferring them from the lake to the swamp and then, by infinitely slow progress, to the edge of the swamp and finally the transporter cave.

Squarears were waiting there. The big squarear with the chimaera's sting greeted them. "I am Bloorg, the Official Greeter and Sender, Keeper of the Transporter to Other Worlds, Keeper of the Last Known Existing Chimaera, Chief."

That had been his ritual greeting before. Kelvin wondered if Bloorg wondered why they had not left.

"I know," Bloorg said, "where you have been. I know you were to have been eaten but I would not have interfered, after freeing you the first time. You are forbidden to go to the chimaera's island again."

"Mervania wants—" Kelvin gulped and started over. "Dragonberries. They are the price of our release."

"I know." Bloorg lifted a squarecut crystal of smoky color in his hand. "The Chief of the squarears tries to know all. Watch!"

With a wave of his boneless fingers Bloorg changed the flat smoky surface into a living picture. In the picture was a chimaera, a now-animate Stapular, and Kian, John, and Kelvin.

Kelvin gulped. "That's in the larder. Where we were kept. And—is this television?" That was another unnatural wonder he could live without!

"Watch!" Bloorg commanded.

In the crystal a tiny chimaera was attacked by an even tinier Stapular. As Stapular hung on the sting there was a flash of blue light. The chimaera, John, and Kian fell unconscious. The tiny Kelvin staggered outside, struggling to tear up the sting from the ground. He pulled the sting out of its row and ran back with it. Stapular mouthed at him, and he was over the Mervania head with the sting positioned above a very feminine eye.

"No! No!" Kelvin cried, reaching for the crystal. He would not do it! He would not, though it happened over and over in a countless number of crystals a countless number of times. No crystal was going to make him do what he refused to do!

"Watch!" Bloorg said for the third time.

Kelvin controlled himself as well as he could. The miniature Kelvin did not destroy the chimaera with the sting. Instead it happened the way it had in life. Now he and Stapular were fighting, rolling over and over. Now

Stapular was pulling off his own left hand, and the ruby light declawed the chimaera. Now the creature was at the mercy of Stapular.

"No! No!" Kelvin protested again, but the crystal merely showed what had happened. Gradually he realized that the image was not a separate thing, but an actual rendering of what had occurred, and could not change the outcome. The miniature Kelvin had out his sword, threw it, and Stapular appeared to die. Now the Mervania head and Kelvin were talking.

At the wave of a strange hand the picture vanished and there was only a smoky crystal in which the tendrils of smoke gradually stopped swirling. There was nothing there anymore except stone.

Kelvin's heart had been beating hard. He felt breathless, as though he had been running. The picture-show was over and he was back, though he had never left. Again he wished he were back in his old familiar, normal world with Heln and his mother Charlain and even his irritating sister Jon, who were surely leading a dull and safe existence.

"What will happen to the oil-blooded man?" he asked.

"The robot will be returned to its makers," Bloorg said. "They may or may not repair it."

"So Stapular may live again?" Did robots actually live? What was living? Stapular had spoken of them as though the living folk were inferior to it in every way.

"It may again be activated, but such a construct will never again deceive us, and none will get close to the chimaera. We owe you our thanks for discovering and nullifying that threat, which would surely otherwise have destroyed the last member of a unique species. We had been aware that Stapular was artificial, but not that he had a built-in laser. As for those doubts of yours about the nature of living, who is to say? There are scientists and sorcerers who hold that there is only thought and that all else is thought's product."

"I—I don't think I can absorb—"

"Never mind. It is only philosophical and abstract. What is important to us is what we perceive. What we accept as real, is real, and what we know to be illusion is generally illusion."

"I . . . see," Kelvin said, not seeing. Ask a simple question, get a lecture in metaphysics with particular emphasis on epistemology. From near infancy he had thought he had more sense.

"That is correct," Bloorg said. "He survives best who does not question too vigorously."

"Stapular won't be back to bother the chimaera again?" He wanted to be quite sure he had understood that correctly.

"Never."

Good enough. He was more than ready to go home.

"But you will return with the seeds," Bloorg reminded him.

"But you said—"

"Correct. You will not go to the island. You will bring the seeds here. They will be carried there by a froogear I designate."

Oh. "You will be waiting? I won't have to—"

Bloorg tapped the crystal. "I will keep watch."

"We will find the same setting? On the transporter?"

Bloorg seemed to have infinite patience. "You will if you look. Come."

They followed Bloorg to the transporter cave and inside. Bloorg showed them the dial on the transporter and where it was set. "Remember this mark. Turn the arrow until it points here exactly. This is where you will need to set the control in order to return. Remember this, all of you."

John nodded. "I don't think I could possibly forget."

"Now you wish to return home. Here is your home marking. Place the dial exactly, or you may go to a world that is not the one you left, such as the serpent world, here." He indicated another setting.

Kelvin reached out and twisted the dial until it clicked at the &, a symbol that reminded him of a coiling dragon but might stand for something else. He had seen his father make a symbol like that while writing. The other setting Bloorg had indicated had a ˜ symbol, obviously a serpent.

"You will return now," Bloorg said, and disappeared with a definite pop and a slight scent of ozone.

"Well, Father, Kian—" Kelvin hated to do this, but had to ask. "We had been about to go to the serpent world—"

"I want to see Lonny first," Kian said. "Maybe we can get married right away, and then—"

Kelvin had been afraid he would say that. "Bloorg wanted us to return to our own world now. Maybe we should go there first, and then—" Then Kelvin could make an excuse to stay in his own frame.

"Bloorg doesn't know Lonny."

"Boys," their father interposed. "Can't we compromise? We brought dragonberries with us, but the jar of seeds labeled 'Astral Berries' was left in the installation by Mouvar. I suspect the seeds are still there. Kelvin, you could go back and get them while Kian and I wait here."

Kelvin frowned. Were "astral berries" and "dragonberries" really the same, as his father assumed? Was the jar still there? It seemed to him now that he hadn't noticed it. Someone had changed the setting on the transporter or the three of them would not have ended up here. Whoever had used the transporter could have taken the seeds. Could it, he wondered, have been Mouvar? If so, what did it mean?

"Well, Kelvin?"

But if the jar remained there, this would be the easiest way to settle things. He could bring it back, give it to Bloorg, then explain that he was worried about Heln, and beg off the trip to the serpent world. "All right."

He took a firm grip on his resolve and stepped into the closet with all the clocks on the outside.

The usual things happened. He stepped out of the closet into the familiar chamber. Things looked the same. Nothing had changed a bit since he and his father and brother had left. Still, he was nervous. Any slight oversight could land him in serious trouble, as the recent adventure had shown.

He checked the table. As he had feared, the jar of seeds was missing.

Well, then, he would have to check to see if the boat was still on its ledge. He crossed the chamber, ducked his head out, saw the boat, and sniffed at the underground river. Time to return.

He checked to make certain the setting was for the chimaera's world—the # mark, surely for squarears—and stepped back into the closet. When he stepped out, nothing had changed in the chimaera's world except one thing:

His father and brother were gone.

Kian had no difficulty in persuading his father. "We'll just hop over and make certain we remember this setting. If we're wrong, we'll hop right back. Bloorg can almost certainly set the control right if I misremember." Kelvin had been standing before the control when Bloorg discussed it, so they hadn't seen the actual settings he had indicated to Kelvin.

"I think it was just before this mark." His father pointed at the & mark.

"I think, Father, that it was just one of the five intervening clicks short." He set it on the % mark.

"You want to try it that way?"

"Yes." Kian was so eager to reach Lonny that he was sure it was right.

"All right. Just be prepared to step out and then back if it's not the right world. That's what we should have done last time." John wasn't worried, because he knew they could check several settings if they had to, until they got the right one. Just so long as they didn't smell any spice!

"Yes, Father." Together they stepped into the closet.

They did not see the same display they had a moment ago when Kelvin exited, but then they were in a slightly more familiar chamber with a soft bluish curtain of light at its far end and a large glowing EXIT sign.

"Come on, Father!" Kian said eagerly, starting across the smooth floor.

"Wait, Kian! You agreed we'd go right back."

"We will. I just want to step outside and make certain!"

There was no stopping him! Talk about your anxious bridegrooms! John started after him—and noticed something.

"There was dust on the floor before. We left our footprints in it. This chamber is clean! Either this is a different chamber, or someone's been here." John wasn't easy with either explanation; both meant trouble.

But Kian was already ducking through the shimmering curtain. He was as unconcerned as though it were sunshine. Not for the first time John had to marvel at how quickly they all adjusted to the unfamiliar and utterly strange. Still, the boy needed to learn proper caution.

"It's here, Father! The ledge, the ladder, and the tree! This *has* to be right!"

But John had doubts. "Come back inside!"

"All right. Just let me get a breath of—"

John waited for him to finish. When he did not, he grew alarmed. Fearful now, yet determined, he crossed to the glowing curtain and stepped through.

Outside. Fresh air. Beautiful day. High on a cliffside. He looked back. The illusion of a solid rock wall just behind was perfect. If this was technology, and he felt it was, the scientists responsible deserved congratulations.

But where was Kian? He advanced to the edge of the cliff. The ladder was there, made of something unfamiliar on Earth, a woven metallic substance he suspected would never age.

"Kian? Kian?" He was really worried now.

There was no answer. Had the lad climbed down into the tree below? Then why wasn't the ladder over the edge of the cliff and dangling down into the branches?

Fear prickled at him, raising the hairs on the back of his neck. He didn't want to leave Kian but his every instinct told him to return. Better to fetch Kelvin and come back for an organized search than to risk getting caught by whatever had happened to Kian.

He started around, ready to duck through the curtain. At that moment human hands reached from apparently solid rock and laid hold of his arms.

For an instant he thought the hands were Kian's. Then he saw that they were larger, and had dark hairs on their backs. This was someone else!

He had only time to grasp this before he was pulled forward, against a rock face that vanished to become a blue curtain of shimmering light at a spot he knew he had not left.

16. /

CHARLAIN

CHARLAIN ARRIVED AT THE palace at noon. In her bag on the dappled gray plowhorse were only her fortune cards and the remains of the lunch she had prepared. She had thought about bringing herbs in case Heln had nausea or other child-carrying complaints. Then she had realized that the doctor here was the best and that she wasn't versed in anything other than amateur prophecy.

How grateful she should be for that one lone skill, she thought, dismounting from her horse and turning the reins over to the stable groom. True, it had deceived her at times. She had known she would lose Hal after a time and she had feared it would be by death. Better to another woman, she had tried to believe. Better to have him happy than to have him destroyed. But what would John think of it? What would his decision be, should he ever return? The cards so far had revealed nothing.

"Mama! Mama! I'm so glad to see you!"

A sudden tattoo of feet and the shock of collision. A slim boyish figure was suddenly in her arms, hugging her as though life had trickled to its inevitable end.

"Not so hard, Jon, not so hard! Goodness, I can hardly breathe! Only boys are supposed to hug this hard, you rough-neck!" She held her daughter back at arm's length. Long yellow hair, greenish eyes, properly filled bosom —she had produced a beauty! She and John. To think that when the children had left on their great adventure with the dragon, really not that long ago, Jon had more resembled the tow-haired skinny boy than the rapidly maturing girl she had actually been. Now Jon was satisfied to be all girl, and that was just as well.

Without knowing why she did so, Charlain reached out and tweaked her daughter's pointy ears. She had done that years ago, mostly from affection. Jon had always resented it because her big brother hadn't ear tips that could be tweaked as effectively.

"How's Heln?" *No sense in delaying it. Get right to the problem.*

"She's . . . doing well." Jon's tone nullified her words, just as they had when as a child she'd tried to conceal the full truth.

"You're hiding something." Just sharp enough to make her answer.

"Mother, why would I do that? You're the one who reads cards. You know everything."

Yes, Jon would still think that. Charlain permitted herself a smile. She walked meekly with her daughter into the royal palace holding her hand. Not long ago it had been she who had led her daughter.

Into the guest wing and down the hall, through a door, and they were there. Heln was sitting up in bed. Brown eyes gleaming, black hair shining as she brushed. She appeared well. Considering what the cards had shown, Charlain wondered.

"Heln." Simple, careful greeting to a daughter-in-law.

"Mother-in-law!" Heln put down the hairbrush on the comforter. Her tone was right but her action seemed mechanical.

They embraced. Heln seemed rigid, not at all the warm girl Charlain had met when she and Kelvin and his bride visited. Something was definitely wrong. She wished that she had been a little less mortal and had studied witchcraft. The cards actually told her very little, however much they suggested.

"You are feeling well, Heln?" A direct question seemed indicated.

"Yes." Almost mechanical, as had been her careful setting down of the hairbrush. Not at all as Charlain would have expected Kelvin's expectant wife to answer.

"She had sickness in the mornings," Jon said. As usual, she was volunteering information when she had the chance. "Dr. Sterk gave me something for her. I put it in her tefee."

"It helped?" Morning sickness was not unusual. She had experienced it while carrying both Kelvin and Jon.

"Cleaned it right up. She hasn't heaved since."

No smile from Heln. Yet Jon's words should have evoked one. Her daughter was a lady, but she did not always use a lady's words.

"We've got a lot of catching up to do," Charlain said, taking the chair Jon brought. "All the news, family and general."

"But Mother, you know everything!" Jon said, and laughed. Still no smile from Heln. She seemed as humorless now as when Jon had found her in Franklin's notorious Girl Market, where she had been raped. Indeed, her attempted suicide by eating dragonberries, then, had opened up the whole new world of astral separation, and given her reason to live after all.

"I'm really not too clear on this war situation. How'd we get into it? My cards won't tell."

"Well, Mother," Jon said, heaving a sigh. She was being quite formal, now, for her, in contrast to her private greeting. That was another signal of trouble. "The situation is complicated."

"Many situations are. Are you implying, Daughter, that your mother can't understand?"

"I can't understand it myself, Mother. Why Kelvin's away or why Lester's fighting. In many ways it doesn't make sense."

"Start from the beginning." Charlain took Jon's hand in hers, in much the way she had when she had wanted her to tell about some school fight.

"All right, Mother. We were all of us summoned to the palace and briefed by . . . by the king."

"King Rufurt?"

"Y-yes."

A lie. The tremble in Jon's hands said it clearly. Jon was not a trembler by nature except when she lied. For some reason Jon wished to conceal something about their king. Could it be that their king was not who he seemed? If this was true it explained the uncertainty card. Charlain felt a prickle on the back of her neck.

Later, when she was alone, Charlain laid out the cards again, checking on the things that had disturbed her most about her daughter's narration. Rather than ease her concern, this made the prickling much worse. Heln was in terrible trouble, about which Charlain could do nothing. But Lester, Jon's husband, was also in dire straits, and about this she could do something.

In the morning Charlain surprised Jon if not Heln by saying goodbye. "I have to get back to the farm. Hal's a dear, taking care of the livestock, and I know Easter will keep the garden weeded, but I don't want to impose on them."

"Mother," Jon said, taking her arm and leading her aside, "how can you—?"

"Because I'm not angry with them. Either of them."

"But—"

"I always knew I'd lose Hal, but the cards didn't explain. When the romance card came up, I knew. It was a relief! Better that he live a happy life than that he die. He was a good father to you and Kelvin and he worked hard. He never intended to do what he did; it was fated."

"But Mother, if Lester ever did such a thing, I'd—"

"Yes, of course you would, dear. But your foster father isn't Lester. It was in the cards. He really couldn't help it."

"But to start a child with that woman! That wasn't right!"

"No, of course it wasn't. But then your natural father succumbed to the queen of Rud and had a son named Kian. The marriage wasn't dissolved when he met me."

"But Mother, Zoanna betrayed her vows! You—"

"It's not the same, Jon. Easter is a good woman. Simple, young, but good. Hal loves her and she him. I declared us divorced for their sakes. My marriage to Hal is now over. His marriage to her is valid. They have a difficult enough course, setting up a homestead, without my making it worse."

"So you let them use *your* homestead!" Jon said bitterly. "How nice for them!" Her tone said that she would never have been that generous. "You're helping them get set up, by giving them free board, and even paying them for taking care of your farm!"

"Hush, hush. You mustn't sound that way. He was a good husband to me, and a good father to you, when we thought your real father dead."

Jon's eyes lighted with a sudden fathoming. "So you think you and my real father might—"

"I don't know, dear. We'll see. The cards don't show me quite enough."

"It seems to me they never did. Until afterward."

"Your father would say that. Well—" She hugged Jon one final time. "Take good care of Heln and the babe. We'll have a much longer visit another time."

"I'll take care of her," Jon said. "But I'm scared for her! Mother, can't you stay?"

"No. I told you why. Now don't pester." With that small lie she was off to the stable and her horse. She did not look back to Jon, who was not following. Jon pretended not to have sentiment, but her mother knew that her outrageous daughter would be secretly wiping at her eyes. Reunions had a way of bringing pain, and this one did especially. Since Jon had turned fourteen and gone off adventuring with Kelvin, they had seen one another only on brief visits.

She rode away from the palace to the crossroads. There she turned resolutely toward Kance. Her son-in-law was in grave peril. The cards had revealed as much, though she had not revealed this to Jon. Had she told her daughter, she knew Jon would be with her, carrying her sling. Charlain couldn't have that. Jon had to stay with Heln. Because it was obvious that something was seriously amiss with Heln, and she suspected hostile magic. Until she could get the cards to be more specific, she had to pretend ignorance, so as not to tip her hand. She could not help Heln directly, the cards said, but might be able to help indirectly, if she found out exactly what was wrong, and if she could find Kelvin and tell him privately. Since she had no idea where Kelvin was, she had to follow up on another course in the interim.

If she could save Lester, maybe then she could find the good witch Helbah, or let the witch find her. It would take a witch to save Heln and the baby, she felt certain. She just hoped that she could do something to benefit both Jon and Heln, and that she would be able to do it in time.

"Cursed cards!" Charlain muttered. "Why is it you can never really tell me anything?" But she knew she was blaming them falsely. The cards could do only what they could do, no more.

She rode on, past the road marker, and into the forbidden territory of Kance.

St. Helens rolled over on the prickly straw and looked up through the bars of his dungeon cell. He rubbed dust from his eyes. The two boyish faces were still there. Two child heads, each wearing a crown of gold.

"Stupid-looking, ain't he, Kildee?"

"Yah. What you think we should do with him, Kildom?"

"Torture. Bend back his thumbs. Tweak his big nose. Put cream on his feet and get Katbah to lick it off. Shove a washcloth in his ears the way Helbah does to us!"

"That's good! That's very good! Let's!"

"Boys," St. Helens managed to say, "the witch, is she—"

"Wouldn't you like to know, blowtop!" Kildee said, and both kings chortled at his cleverness. He dropped a pebble down that bounced off St. Helens' face, and they chortled again.

St. Helens permitted himself a glare. *Damn Katzenjammer kids! Those two need a good hiding! Best thing for bad behavior ever invented. Royal brats or not!*

"Look, he's maaaad!"

"Yah, let's get some more stones!"

"Stones? How about darts?"

The boys rushed away, giggling. St. Helens lay on the dank straw, anticipating more mischief.

Then there was a dark, furry face where the boys' faces had been. Dark yellow eyes and a tail forming a question mark. The witch's familiar! He had thought it dead. According to lore, a witch's familiar was a part of her in a real sense, so that when one died the other died soon after. This probably meant that Helbah was alive.

But why was the houcat here? It did not look healthy. Why should it waste its energy spying on him?

The day wore on. The boys did not return. St. Helens, turning the matter over and over in his mind, saw no reason to regret their absence.

Lomax drew back his sword from yet another unfortunate Kance soldier and watched him topple from the saddle. They were winning the battle, mainly because they had come upon a small force. Then he saw the real reason. Coming down the hill behind the Kance forces were other fighters dressed in the Kelvinian uniform. He strained his eyes to see through the dust. It was Lester's troops, it had to be! But where was Lester?

A scream took his attention. Turning round in the saddle he saw one of his men finishing off a Kance swordsman as young Phillip's horse shied and the boy pulled the reins.

The Kance soldiery retreated, pursued by the Kelvinian troops. Lomax rode over to check on Aratex's one-time king.

Phillip had an ugly open sword wound on his left arm. Blood stained the boy's clothing and dripped onto the shield he had dropped. Phillip stared wild-eyed at him, as if he couldn't have imagined that he might get wounded.

"It—it hurts!" Phillip said.

"That is the nature of a battle wound," Lomax said. He felt some sympathy, but dared not show it. *After all,* he thought, hardening his heart, *he's responsible for what happened to St. Helens.*

"I'm not ready to die!" Phillip wailed. "I'm not ready!"

With that the boy who had been a king and more recently had shed blood and even more recently bled his own, shuddered as if he had plunged into snow. His face turned white as flour and then, like a sack of that substance, he swayed and toppled from the saddle.

Lomax drew in a sharp breath. Phillip had said he wanted to be hanged, but hadn't meant it. Now he might have died after all.

Mor was worried. The fighting was going just too well lately. What had happened to the phantoms that had plagued them? What about the magical slowing of time? Was the witch running out of magic? Was she dead?

Ahead, a great shout. "General! General! General Crumb!"

"Yes?" He waited for the excited scout to reach him and get his breath.

"General! General, sir! Ahead—"

"Yes, yes, out with it!"

"The caps, General! The caps are just over that rise! We've arrived, General! Arrived at last at the seat of our enemies!"

Mor, though he felt he should do otherwise, heaved a great sigh.

Zoanna looked into her crystal and smiled. The war was going so much better than she had anticipated. Here the Mor forces were already at the caps and the Hermans and the Lester forces less than half a day from joining them. It would soon be all up for the witch and the brats. The brats would look nice in a cage, while Helbah might even teach her a few things before Rowforth stopped torturing her. It had been a stroke of lucky genius to prod that foolish boy into breaking the truce and wounding the witch! The St. Helens commander had seemed about to back away from battle, but that had precipitated immediate combat.

She frowned. Would it be wise to keep the witch alive at all? Witches, while they lived, could always be dangerous. How well she knew, from her own experience! The traditional fate of the defeated witch was burning, because that usually killed her thoroughly enough to make her stay dead.

She studied Helbah through the crystal. The old woman didn't look as though she had power. Lying in bed, turning, tossing, covered in sweat. Her gaunt familiar sitting by her on a chair, staring at her from wild yellow eyes. Only the intercession of that familiar had saved her life on the battlefield; the houcat had lent her enough of its life force to sustain her until she was brought back to the palace doctor.

"I could destroy you right now, Helbah! I know enough now, and if need be I can always return to college." She smiled reminiscently at the thought of her horned instructor. She had but one coin with which to pay that horny one, but he was always ready for more of that. "But I don't think I have to, now. I don't think you're a menace."

Contentedly Zoanna blanked the crystal with a directed thought. The tiny bubbles swirled like a confined section of the creamy way in the night sky.

"Helbah, I'll keep you alive until I defeat you. And maybe for a short time after. I need to learn, and Rowforth needs his amusements. Maybe I can make you seem young and pretty, so that he'll enjoy your screams even more. Sadism is always better with an attractive and innocent-seeming subject."

Seldom had Zoanna felt so thoroughly content and so superbly confident.

Lester gasped as he stood holding on to the slim tree trunk and watched his men ride over the rise. A scout rode back accompanied by his second in command, Lieutenant Klumpecker.

"We've driven them off, Commander," Lieutenant Klumpecker said. "And St. Helens' Hermans are meeting our own men."

"The caps?"

"Less than a day's march away."

"St. Helens?"

"I haven't seen him. But the boy who is his friend—the former king of Aratex—is wounded."

"Bad?"

"I can't say. I wasn't that near."

Probably bad. Lester couldn't imagine St. Helens deserting his troops, so probably he too was dead. That left his father Mor and himself in charge of Kelvinia's forces. He wondered how far away his father was. Had he come all the way through Klingland? Was he still alive?

"We can take the caps in two days?"

"Probably, Commander."

"Good." There was a chance, just a chance, he thought, that he might live to see it accomplished.

Holding that thought he gradually loosened his grip on the sapling and let his knees buckle with him all the way down to the sweet, green grass.

"Commander! Commander Crumb!" he heard, but the voice was uninteresting and far, far away.

17 /

NEW OLD ENEMIES

JOHN FOUND HIMSELF IN a lighted chamber surrounded by men in uniforms. The uniforms were familiar because they had the same cut if not the color of the uniforms worn by the soldiers of Hud. But was this really the same world? Or was it an almost-the-same world? Would he face gigantic silver serpents again? Was there an evil King Rowforth here, or a duplicate king almost the same?

He looked at Kian, held by two of the soldiers, disarmed. His own arms were similarly taken. With regret he watched the soldiers go through his pack.

"King Hoofourth will be interested," said the craggy-faced Lieutenant.

"King Hoofourth of what country?" John asked.

"Silence, prisoner!" The slap stung his face, as he knew the lieutenant intended. "You will speak when spoken to!"

Exactly as it had been in Hud! Only of course this could not be the frame where there was a kingdom named Hud or a kingdom named Rud. It would have a name that would be similar and much else would be similar, but not identical. Obviously the bad guys were in control here; there had been no hero of prophecy to set things right. It was almost like a movie that kept subtly changing every time it was watched. Only this was no movie, and like it or not he was a participant.

Movie—now there was one of the few things he missed in his home world. How nice it would be to go into a theater and have a vicarious experience! There was a lot to be said for vicarious experience; it didn't lock a person in a cell for months or years, it didn't threaten the person with death. He could break it off at any point and go home to the familiar. That would be nice, right now! If he got out of this, maybe he would see about finding his way to his true home. It wasn't as if there were a lot to hold him in the magic worlds, now that his children were grown, and he had lost the one woman he really cared for. The last thing he intended to do was interfere with Charlain's second marriage, and his mere presence in her frame would do that. So it behooved him to go elsewhere and find his own woman, and try to forget.

"We'll take them to the capital. King Hoofourth will put them in a dungeon, torture them a little, and get answers from them before throwing them away."

"Answers?" the fellow officer asked.

"Like why are they here? What are they doing at the secret cave? Are they planning on invading us?"

"Oh, you mean routine stuff." The officer pulled his right earlobe. It was a round ear, similar to the others here. Once it had seemed that round ears were a sign of special qualities, but now it was apparent that their shape was all that distinguished them. There were truly special pointeared folk—he thought of Charlain again—and ignoble roundeared folk, such as evil King Rowforth of Hud. Unfortunately, King Hoofourth sounded similar.

"Now, out!" Pushing Kian and himself ahead of them the soldiers emerged from the wall of rock. John had to shake himself mentally. That chamber they'd been in was identical to the other except that it had no transporter. Did the bad guys in this frame know about the network of transporters? If they did, why didn't they use theirs? If they didn't, why did they stay here, watching?

"You and you stay. Watch," the main officer commanded, using the celebrated army volunteer system to select two men. "You, down the tree. You, you guide the prisoners."

Without hesitation Kian moved ahead to the cliff and the ladder and descended after the two soldiers. John followed, feeling the unnecessary prod the man behind gave to his buttocks. The descent into the tree was one he had not actually made before, though he had climbed an identical tree and ladder in the frame of the silver serpents.

He wondered, as he carefully made his way down, branch by branch, if this time there would be a rescue. Maybe, just maybe, it was foreordained that he and his son were to die here. That would certainly simplify Kelvin's life, allowing him to complete the prophecy without interference.

Now I'm thinking like Charlain, he thought. *Next I'll be reading her Book of Prophecy and studying her predicting cards!*

But will there ever be a chance? Will I ever see Kelvin's mother again? Will I ever even see her duplicate?

He sighed soundlessly. Obviously his heart wasn't in his resolution to stay out of Charlain's life. But if he should encounter one of her alternates in another frame, and not an evil one, what then? Actually there had been another woman in his life, evil Queen Zoanna. In the serpent frame he had encountered her good version, Queen Zanaan. Now there was a prospect to conjure with! If Kian could marry in that frame, why not John himself?

His feet touched the ground, bringing his mind to reality. What use were dreams, when he wasn't free to do anything about them? There were more troops and horses waiting here. There was no chance for escape.

At the commander's orders they mounted horses and rode what seemed a very familiar path. Would they meet flopears, he wondered? Maybe Smoothy Jac's duplicate? What about Lonny? Would her duplicate appear? And Zanaan—suppose she was here, too? That could really complicate things!

They rode on, through what became a very tiring day.

Kelvin stepped out of the transporter closet into an empty chamber. Kian and his father were nowhere in sight. Yet they must have come here. Should he stay and search? Or go back and ask the squarear's advice?

He decided to have a look outside. This seemed to be the frame of the silver serpents, but wasn't quite right. There wasn't the dust he remembered. Of course that could mean that this was the right frame and that others had since been here.

He crossed the chamber and walked through the shimmering golden curtain under the glowing EXIT sign. Outside, the cliff behind his back, he saw the tree and the ladder he expected. Only the ladder was down into the tree now, and it had been pulled up. He frowned, wondering, and then his gauntlets began to tingle.

If there was one thing he would never do again, he had promised himself, it was to ignore the gauntlets' warning. Obeying them as much as his own thoughts, he drew his sword and whirled.

A uniformed man, half in and half out of what appeared to be solid rock, was about to strike him on the head with a short club. His sword confronted the man, and at the same time he found his voice, letting the gauntlets somehow choose his words and rap it out as a command.

"Freeze! How many of you in there?" he demanded.

The man was evidently startled to have the tables so abruptly turned. "J-just two. Me and Bert."

"Tell him to come out. Slowly, without a weapon."

"You hear that, Bert? He's got a sword against my gullet. Don't be a hero, Bert. I'm your friend and the commanding officer isn't."

Bert came through the rock, unarmed.

Kelvin sighed with relief. He had been afraid the hidden man would fire an arrow from cover. Give the gauntlets a chance and they took control!

"Where are my friends? Do you have them?"

Bert spoke, looking scared. "Those two men? On the way to the king's dungeon."

"King? What king?"

"King Hoofourth, of course!"

So it was a different frame! He had thought so, when he saw the setting at %, but was taking nothing for granted now. "King of what country?"

"King of the Kingdom of Scud," the crafty-faced roundear said.

So it was a frame not too different from the silver serpent one, but not identical. "Tell me, is there an outlaw somewhere in the desert by the name of Jac?"

"Jac? You mean Scarface Jac?"

Why not? "Enemy to the king?"

"What else? An outlaw has to be, no matter what else."

"Skin thief?"

The soldiers looked puzzled. "Skin? I don't know what—"

"Silver!" Kelvin said impatiently. Not that it mattered, but the silver skins of serpents had proven to be of great importance.

Both men shrugged. Bert said, "I know he's robbed, but—"

"Doesn't matter." Kelvin decided he'd pay the local Jac a visit before planning his rescue of his father and brother. Even with his gauntlets and the Mouvar weapon and the levitation belt he was just one person. This frame, like every frame he had visited, probably contained some surprises.

"Tell me, can anyone in this frame levitate?"

"You mean fly? Mouvar is said to have flown."

"Good enough," Kelvin said briskly. "Turn your backs."

The two men obeyed him and he wasted no time in activating the levitation belt. Silently he rose above their heads and above the cliffs that towered higher than he remembered, then moved out over the tree and the river. The river was much broader than the rivers in the other frames. He looked back and saw the two soldiers still standing with their backs turned. Good, no arrows would be following him!

He settled down to the business of flying. It wasn't nearly as hard as he had once imagined. His father said he had a natural ability, as he did himself. He gathered that some people couldn't get used to the ground sliding away beneath their feet, the clouds rolling in front of their faces. It wasn't anything to do with bravery, for he certainly wasn't brave. Nor could he credit the gauntlets for his acceptance of flying. It was just a case of being lucky in one thing and unlucky in others.

As he drifted dreamlike over the rolling hills of the kingdom of Scud, he found himself thinking about luck. He had been lucky. Time after time he had been saved from impossible situations by what seemed chance. The silver serpents that could have swallowed him, for instance. The chimaera that could have cooked him with tail-lightning and eaten him steaming hot. Was that the effect of the prophecy, as his mother would say? Was that what was protecting him? To him it felt like mere fortune, that could reverse at any time. He really didn't have a lot of confidence in the accuracy of the prophecy, at least not as it might relate to him. It might be talking about some other roundear entirely.

But that line of thinking led only to mischief. It was better to believe that his mother was right. That the prophecy applied to him, and that he would prevail. So he would do his best to believe that, so that he could rescue his father and brother.

Down below was the first of the connected valleys. Serpent's Valley, home of great silver serpents and their spiritual brothers the dwarf flopears. He looked close but saw no serpents. No holes in cliffs that could be serpent tunnels. Sad to think that they were not here. What would Hud have been without its serpents and flopears? What would Scud be like? Whatever dangers he faced here he hoped—no, *knew* now that he could handle them. With his levitation belt and his gauntlets and his antimagic weapon there just couldn't be anything against which he couldn't triumph. Unless there was another chimaera here, which seemed highly unlikely. Like it or not he was a hero, uncertain nature and weak stomach aside.

He left the valley, passing over the cliff where Kian had once fought a flopear and, almost miraculously, survived. The flopear had also survived, he remembered, falling with his club off the cliff and down, down, to land with a probable splatting sound. As Kian had told it the tough little warrior had not only survived the fall, but had a short time later intercepted him and Lonny at the base of the cliff! Obviously Kian too had lived through great dangers, but so too had that murderous flopear. If it was really the same one.

How familiar the country looked! How very familiar. He flew at near minimum speed into the desert. At home they called this land the Sadlands, while in Hud it was the Barrens. In Scud it would be called something equally appropriate. Strange, though near duplication in people and geography prevailed in related frames the names always changed. Fortunately, perhaps, otherwise the confusion for a frame-hopper would be even worse. Suppose he were to meet his mother's duplicate in this frame, and she not only looked like his mother and acted like her, but had his mother's name? Or suppose his wife? If he met Heln here and she looked the same as the Heln he had left at home, and had the same name, he'd think of her as the same person. That could be very bad, and he was thankful that duplicate individuals bore separate identification. For one thing, the only way a local Heln could have the same name was if she had married a local Kelvin. Was he ready to meet himself?

He shook his head, trying to free it of burgeoning concepts that threatened to make it explode. Flying along at a little over a good running speed he began some unaccustomed philosophizing. It was what he had warned himself against. The squarear had said it was bad to think about such things, but now he did. The thought was, which was real? Was it home or was it the silver-serpent world, or the chimaera world, or his father's Earth? Bad question, and quite senseless, maybe. For of course all realities were real in equal proportion. It depended where a person was, and when. Thus the warriors of the past, and ancestors he had never seen or known existed—they seemed unreal, yet were the very substance of reality, for who would exist without that ancestry? Likewise every possibility, every slight change with infinite variations was, by the very nature of things, real and leading to real realities somewhere else. When such realities mixed, as when folk used the Mouvar network to travel between them, or when John Knight and his band accidentally crossed over—

And there was an answer to one riddle! There would be no Kelvin here, no Heln, because they were the children of the members of that group. They would exist only in the particular world to which that band had come. There might be a Charlain here, but she could never have married John Knight. Maybe Hal Hackleberry, or his equivalent, but not—

Head buzzing, as it always did when he tried to think about such things, Kelvin looked down and spied what had to be Scud's outlaw camp. He would land boldly, and—

But suppose it was the bad Jac who had stolen the dragon scale and kidnapped Jon? That was in his home frame, but couldn't a Jac of that nature exist here instead of the Jac he had more recently known? He hoped the answer was no, but he couldn't be certain. An evil Jac and an evil king in the same frame was more than he thought he could manage. Would Lonny be here? And another dwarf either as evil as Queeto or as saintly as Heeto? These thoughts were making his head more than just swim. The height did not make him dizzy, but the thinking it engendered did. He had to get down and put an end to this.

Since he did not want to be pierced with crossbow bolts or arrows, he would land a short distance away and walk in to the camp. Probably he should have been thinking about that instead of those other things.

Moving his fingers carefully on the control levers on the belt's buckle he came to a stop in midair and descended until his feet touched sand. Nothing moving now, as it had been while he was aloft. He was once more on solid earth, and so his thoughts were grounded too.

Ahead was the camp. Horses, men moving. If they had not seen him in the air, they would spy him now.

Even as he thought this, two horses approached. As they came nearer he recognized the riders and men he had known, though of course these were not the same.

"Stranger, who be you? Quick, or die!"

That was poor unfortunate Smith, who had died such a ghastly death! Kelvin strove to get his thoughts in order, knowing that the threat was real and so were their weapons.

"I have business with your leader."

"My leader?" The man was incredulous.

"Scarface Jac. He is your leader, isn't he?"

This Smith seemed to hesitate as if trying to decide whether to use the crossbow he had leveled at Kelvin, or merely cut him down with a sword. Then, deciding it could do no harm, he circled his horse behind the stranger and said, "Walk into camp. I'll be watching you."

Kelvin wished he had landed closer. By the time he was among the tents he was sweating from exertion under the desert sun. A scorpiocrab scuttled out of his way, reminding him of the chimaera. Other than that and a couple of thorny plants he saw no sign of desert life.

They emerged from tents almost as though by magic, Jac among them. He really was a scarface, with a scar that was twice the size and ugliness of Cheeky Jac's, the onetime bandit of the Sadlands. He waited for Kelvin to speak.

"I'm Kelvin Knight Hackleberry," Kelvin said. "I need your help to rescue some friends of mine."

"Why?" Jac asked. It was a challenge as much as a question.

"Their captors are the king's men. My friends and I can help you defeat the king's men. You see, we're from a different frame."

"From a different frame and you want to help us defeat King Hoofourth, Scud's good and proper king? Just why do you want to do that and why do you think I'd be interested?"

Oh-oh, Kelvin thought. This wasn't quite as he had anticipated.

"In the other frame your king was a tyrant and had to be replaced. Isn't he a tyrant here as well?"

At that moment the first woman Kelvin had seen came from a tent and walked straight to Jac. She put her face against the bandit's brawny arm and looked up adoringly. It was Lonny, or at least her duplicate. The girl Kian wanted to marry.

But this wasn't the same frame! Here Lonny could marry the bandit, who had indeed been attracted to her in the serpent frame. There, she could marry Kian. There was no conflict. Just so long as Kelvin managed to rescue Kian and get him there.

"You call our king a tyrant?" the outlaw demanded. "You want him overthrown?"

Kelvin tried to tell himself that it wasn't genuine anger in the bandit's voice. Carefully he said, "It may be that I do not understand. In a world nearly like this one there was a king who was very bad. In that world an outlaw named Jac fought and conquered him."

"You would have me commit treason?" Jac's face was very red, and the scar tissue in the star-shaped mark on his cheek stood out ghastly white.

"I'm not here to start trouble," Kelvin said. "But if your sovereign resembles this other, you must want to be rid of him."

"I must, must I?" This was spoken very aggressively.

This had to be a mistake, Kelvin thought. Time to rectify it. He fingered the controls on his belt and instantly was high above the bandits' heads.

"You come down here!" Jac the bandit ordered.

Kelvin ignored the order. He climbed to a suitable elevation, then moved the lever forward for full speed. He was just in time. Even at this rate of motion, he saw the arrows and crossbow bolts come perilously close.

He heard shouted orders and looked back to see men mounting horses. Fortunately the belt could outrun any horse, even the oversized battle steeds.

He sped away across blank desert, then swung to the east. He would catch up with the king's party himself. Even if the gauntlets and the Mouvar weapon couldn't handle the situation, he'd still have to try. If the prophecy his mother believed were true, he'd have to survive this frame and get back home to fulfill it at what he hoped would be some far future time.

But then, as the green hills appeared, a disturbing thought intruded itself. Just maybe the prophecy had no effect in other frames. He always had believed himself capable of getting killed, prophecy or no prophecy, and in a different frame death might be likely. He remembered unpleasantly almost dying when he first arrived in the frame so much like this one. If it hadn't been for Heeto, the heroic dwarf in that frame, he knew he *would* have died. No, no, the prophecy might or might not be real, but it was nothing to stake one's life on.

Down below the road that led, if the geography of this frame did not diverge too far from the frames he remembered, to the royal palace, there was a big cloud of dust. He slowed, hovered, and tried to make out what was happening.

There were horses prancing. Swords were flashing. Men were dying. Gods, he realized belatedly, it was a battle!

He lowered himself silently, trusting that the combatants would be too involved to look up. In the swirling dust he saw his father and brother kept back by guards wearing the Scud uniform. More uniformed soldiers were battling men who wore no uniforms at all but were clad much as were the bandits in the desert. Those who fought the soldiers must be the good guys. But were they? Uncomfortably, he thought of the encounter he had just had. Similar frames were deceptive in their dissimilarities.

I can't take anything for granted, he thought. *Just because they are taking Father and Kian to the palace doesn't necessarily mean harm to them.*

But he was almost sure it did. Something about the way the soldiers had acted at the cliffs convinced him that the royal side just couldn't be the right side.

Having convinced himself, he acted. Skillfully he moved the lever. When he was at precisely the right spot he cut off the belt power completely.

He dropped, sword in gauntleted hand, like a heavy stone. He was about to join the fray.

18 /

HEALINGS

CHARLAIN SAW THE DUST clouds ahead and heard the drumming of horses' hooves, the clang of swords, and the screams of men. Battle. Men seemed to take such foolish joy in combat! It seemed to her that the very knowledge lent wings to her horse's feet. Not away from danger, but toward it. Toward Lester and whatever danger threatened his life, that the cards had shown her.

Why, she wondered, bouncing uphill on horseback, *am I doing this? I haven't any magical witch's fire! I haven't any laser weapon! I haven't even a sword! What's to prevent some mighty thewed swordsman from swinging down on me?*

A moment later she was at the crest of the hill, and saw just such a swordsman as she had feared. His sword blade was raised high and caught the bright rays of the sun here above the dust clouds. In a moment he would reach her and that blade would lop off her head.

She sat on her horse. She stopped it with a gentle "Whoa, Nellie," and waited with hands on reins. The Kance soldier could see her plainly, could see that she was a woman and unarmed.

Of course there were other things soldiers did besides killing, as Heln had found out . . .

The soldier's horse slowed. The young man, hardly older than Kelvin but more heroically formed, stared at her, mouth agape. The sword hesitated. His blue eyes, cold but still youthful, studied her. Then, as abruptly as he had appeared, he lowered the sword, sheathed it, and rode away. She watched him disappear over the rise and then down into the cloud of battle, and she hoped that he too would be a survivor this day.

What had done it? Certainly not her looks, though she believed she was still attractive. Was it because he saw his own mother in her eyes? She could not be certain, but she knew that an ancient witchery had served her well this day. Soldiers commonly killed soldiers in the heat of battle, but not unarmed, unresisting, and thoroughly helpless innocents. A warrior the young Kance soldier might be, but not a mindless, consciousless slaughterer.

She took a deep breath, and then she simply waited until the battle sound diminished and the dust settled in the valley. Soldiers in Kance uniform sped past her on lathered horses. Below, the color of the uniforms resolved themselves into Hermandy's muddy clay and Kelvinia's forest-green. The side that she had expected to win this battle had in fact won.

She was still waiting when the Hermandy soldier approached on horse-back. Following after fleeing Kance warriors he had spotted her and turned. Now he rode forward deliberately. He was a big man with hair on his face and a cruel set to his mouth. When he stared into her eyes she knew instinctively that he would not be dissuaded as easily as the first had been.

Should she scream? Who would hear her? Should she wheel her horse and try to run? That charger he rode could readily overtake her mare. Should she look seductive and try to buy a little time? The Herman might not be interested. Judging from appearances, his lust might be mainly for causing pain.

She was not certain what she should do, so she merely waited. What would happen would happen. It might be a quick end, or a lingering one.

"Wait, Private!"

The young man wore mail over his uniform of a Kelvinian guardsman. He was covered head to toe with battle dust. The quarter-moon painted on his helmet proclaimed him officer, though she did not know the rank.

"Lomax! You want her first?" The toothy grin on the Herman was at least as disturbing as his drawn sword.

"I don't like your tone, Private! I know this woman."

"Do, huh." The Herman's horse came closer to Lomax's. "I suppose that means you want her all for yourself."

Without warning the Herman's sword swung at the guardsman. But Lomax ducked aside and sustained a bright coppery slash on his left shoulder. The mail he wore protected him, but barely. His own sword snaked out, and with more luck than science he speared the Herman through the throat.

The Herman toppled and crashed to the ground. He lay there on the grass, just another casualty.

Lomax cleaned his sword, then inspected his injury and the damage to his mail. Finally he turned his eyes to her. He studied her face for several long heartbeats. Then he said: "Mrs. Hackleberry? Kelvin's mother?"

"Why yes." She was astonished at being recognized. "But how do you know? We've never met, have we?"

"We have met, but a long time ago. Remember when you read cards for people? You told me I'd be a soldier and do many brave deeds. I thought you were wrong and my mother thought you wrong. But then we had our war for freedom and afterward I became a guardsman for King Rufurt. Today, as you see, I'm a soldier, wearing Hermandy mail."

She shook her head, amazed. Sometimes even she didn't believe in the power of prophecy. "You and your mother. She wanted to know if you'd finish school and I said yes. Then I saw the other, the battle card, and I had to say."

"And you told her my father would die and she'd remarry. You were right."

"The cards were right. The cards that unfortunately can only indicate. They could not have told me how your father was to die or when, or if there was a way of saving him."

"Nothing's perfect. The cards indicated, and they were correct."

"It is always thus. There's nothing truer than prophecy."

There was silence between them, as pregnant as thought. Soldiers came up and dragged away the body of the private; they had seen what had happened. Then Lomax broke it with the logical question: "Why are you here, Mrs. Hackleberry?"

"It isn't Mrs. Hackleberry any longer," she said. "Hal and I are divorced."

"Oh." His face turned grave. "I'm sorry to hear it."

"Don't be. It was in the cards. I feared that he would meet an early death, and I'm happy he didn't. It was only his love for another woman that ended our marriage. It could have been much worse. But as to why I am here—"

"That too was in the cards?"

She smiled. She had been about to say something about Lester, but Lomax had put it correctly. Without the cards' suggestion that she might affect things here, she would not have come. She had no experience in war, but well understood the risk she took coming here.

"We have many wounded," Lomax said, wiping blood. "Our only doctor was killed. Would you—could you possibly help?"

"I'm not skilled," she said. But Lester might be among the wounded. Besides, there would be others like this young guardsman. "I'll do what I can." She would have to trust the cards to guide her correctly.

She followed him, detouring around a horse and a man that were beyond help. She knew a little herbal lore, she knew how to suture and bind up wounds. If nothing else, she could do as her daughter had done at another place, and mop fevered brows and hold chilly hands.

They reached the bottom of the hill as the daylight faded and the sun eased down. The signs of battle were all around: dead men, dead horses, dropped weapons, and the groans and moans of injured and dying.

"This way, Mrs.—eh, Knight."

"Charlain will do." She followed him meekly to an isolated tent. He pulled back the tent flap and there, lying on a blood-soaked blanket, was what appeared to be a schoolboy. The lad's eyes were glassy and filled with terror and suffering.

"A witch! A witch!" the youth cried, pointing feebly at her.

"Not a witch, Phillip," Lomax said. "This is Charlain, Kelvin's mother."

"Don't let her touch me! Don't let her!" He struggled to sit up, blood spurting through knotted bandages. He shrieked at the top of a weakened voice: "Go Way! Burn her, Lomax! Burn—" His eyes rolled up until only the whites showed. He stiffened and fell back.

Hurriedly Charlain grabbed his wrist. There was still a heartbeat, but it was faint. A lot of his blood was missing.

"Why is he here?" she asked. She couldn't help but rage that such a young boy had been allowed to fight. It was her motherly instinct.

"He's St. Helens' friend. Former king of Aratex."

"Ah." Formerly the enemy, though it had really been Melbah who governed that country. Kings did get their way, ex or current. "Is there bloodfruit around?"

"There is, back a way in the forest."

"I'm not sure he can swallow the juice, but—"

"We'll make him. St. Helens wouldn't like it if he died."

"St. Helens is—" She wanted to avoid the word, but found no way. "Captured?"

"Yes. Or dead. He could be in the same state as this." His eyes flicked down to the boy. "Phillip here killed the witch."

"Helbah? Killed?" she asked, appalled.

"Yes. He wasn't supposed to."

"But Helbah is a good witch!"

"But on the other side. That's how the enemy got St. Helens. We broke the truce, and they seized him."

She thought: *Helbah's still alive. I know, I've read her cards. But she may not remain so long.*

"Can you get the bloodfruit?" she asked, turning to the immediate business. "A lot of it? If you have other wounded who have lost blood it could save their lives."

"I'll send some men back. It's a big grove, but a long ride. They might not be able to get the fruit back until daybreak."

"That will have to do." She gave the former boy-king a final check. Unconscious, colorless, he appeared dead. "Are there wounded to whom I can give immediate help?"

"Many. Some not this bad."

"I'll need help setting bones and severing limbs. Get me your doctor's supplies."

Lomax nodded, went outside, and began issuing orders. She joined him, and he took her to more wounded and dying than she had seen before in her life.

Men sought their foolish glory, she thought, but for too many this was the reality. It was a shame, but they never seemed to learn.

* * *

It was nearing dawn when the riders Lomax had dispatched arrived back with the bloodfruit. At her direction the fruit was boiled and the red syrup cooled and administered. First young Phillip, then man after man weakly swallowed a spoonful or a cupful depending on his need. In a surprisingly short time pale faces flushed and men were restored to full vigor.

It was magic fruit, the bloodfruit. The doctor had had the foresight to see it gathered, but in the fighting the wagon with the fruit was set ablaze and destroyed. The doctor had died trying to put out the fire. So until this new supply arrived, wounded men had continually died.

At first she did not recognize him. She had only met him twice, and that under better circumstances. But then the pale, big man she was working on gasped a word, and the word caused her astonishment and joy.

"Jon!" the pale lips gasped.

Lester! This was Lester, her daughter's husband! He had lost a lot of blood but he should be all right once the syrup took effect. Revived by the prospect, she held the brimful cup to his lips and massaged his throat to force him to drink.

"You'll be all right, Lester," she murmured. "You will be, for Jon's sake."

He did not respond verbally. His pulse jumped. From his mouth a trickle of blood issued, thicker and darker than the syrup.

Gods, he was dying! Jon's husband was dying, and she didn't know how she could save him. Yet there had to be a way of restoring him. There had to be!

Desperately she checked through the doctor's bag. Containers of herbs, properly labeled, but often a mystery to her. She wished she had absorbed more herbal lore. Which herb, properly administered, would seal his internal wound and allow the bloodfruit to do its work? There had to be an herb that would do this, but was it the sealant root or the stitching flower? Desperately she tried to remember. She had never anticipated being in a position like this! Her arms and legs felt weighted down. Fog filled her head. Invisible bees hummed in it. She was in need of reviving herself.

She took out the jar of sealant root. Should she try this? Suppose it was wrong? It just might be that sealant root was for some other use. Yet to do nothing, or to delay doing something, might mean Lester's doom. She had come to help him! If only she knew how!

When in doubt, ask the cards. It had been the one thing she had always believed in. Without hesitation she took the deck from her pack, shuffled it, and thought of Lester. Then, head swimming, body protesting more than the disapproving glances of assistants, she dealt out the column.

A single pawn card, representing Lester. A new card representing Lester's fate if she did nothing. It was the death card, skull and crossbones. Tell her something she did not already know!

She dealt again. She laid out the card, there on the bloody canvas. The Lester pawn. Now, administer the sealant root, and his fate would be—the death card.

Her hands shook as she riffled the cards and started the third layout. This time it was the Lester pawn card and the thought of the stitching flower. She held a jar of pink blossoms in her left hand, concentrating. She turned up a card: death card.

No, no, no! There had to be a restorative! Back in the palace she had read uncertainty. Here she read death, only death. Was she too late?

She checked the labels on the jars. Here was a jar filled with white flower blossoms, well dried. But this couldn't be the stitching flower! Yet it was! What then were the pink blossoms in the jar she had held as she turned the card? She read the label, her tired eyes squinting hard: "Stretching flower." She had had the wrong jar!

Quickly she tried a fourth layout, holding the jar of white blossoms. Pawn card representing Lester Crumb, her daughter's husband. *Now I will administer the blossoms in this jar, and—*

The sun with a smiling face: recovery card! Lester would recover if she got the herbal medicine inside him in time.

How to administer it? She didn't know, but she had to be swift. Hastily she unscrewed the jar, shook dried blossoms into a cup, added water and a few drops of raspberry wine, stirred it, and held it to Lester's lips.

She massaged his throat, edging up the cup. Slowly, lest he choke, she poured.

He sighed. His color deepened. His eyes blinked. "Jon? Jon? I love you, Jon! I want you close. Please, Jon, come to bed."

"Hush, Son," she said, stroking his forehead. "It's only your old biddy mother-in-law."

His eyes unglazed and focused on her. His color deepened until it was a bright red. "Thank you, Mrs. Hackleberry," he said. Then, exhausted, he closed his eyes.

She had won this one, she thought, and with the thought she realized how tired she actually was. She had worked through the night and into the day, seeing nothing but wounds and blood. She closed her eyes, sank back against the doctor bag, and thoroughly relaxed.

Sleep, sleep, sleep, the natural restorative.

Helbah remained weak, but revived enough to take some of her own medicines, and they restored her greatly. But her hours of injury had put her dangerously out of touch. She fetched her crystal and oriented on the enemy battle camp. Soon she ferreted out the woman with the violet eyes doctoring the Kelvinian and Hermandy wounded.

A witch, that young man had called her. She looked the part, but Helbah had never heard of another practiced in these arts. She frowned, watching the healings, wishing that she were herself well enough to do more. Magic restoratives were wonderful, but at her age they could do only so much.

Later the woman in the crystal was reading cards beside a dying man and an open doctor case. She watched as the woman laid out a file three times and three times took up the cards. So that was how she was doing it! She was not trained in witchcraft or healing magic, only in the cards—but they were guiding her well. On the fourth try she found her answer.

Helbah watched as the woman gave the medication and restored the young man to life. Then, exhausted as only someone practicing the art could be, for it drew from the soul as well as the body, the woman sank to the floor of the tent, closed her eyes, and went instantly to sleep.

Interesting. She has the talent. Largely untrained, but there. Another enemy? Or could she—dare I think it?—become a colleague? An apprentice, someone to help me fight?

Without quite willing it, she fell asleep herself, dreaming a witch's dreams.

Sometime next morning Katbah entered the room with tail held straight up above his shiny back. He was lean from his ordeal of lending her his life force, but he had taken restoratives and was strengthening. He walked straight to her and stared into her face.

"Those two in trouble again?" She sighed. "Think what we'd have to put up with if they hadn't the minds of grown men!" Actually she was often in doubt about the maturity of their minds; sometimes they were just so confoundedly juvenile that she wished she could take a switch to their little posteriors.

With difficulty she got to her feet, using her cane, and followed her familiar.

St. Helens kept his eyes barely slitted and pretended to sleep. He had successfully ignored the pebbles and the lumps of dried dirt. Now a feather danced before his nose and threatened to make him sneeze. He considered grabbing the string and breaking it, and would have done so in another moment. But then the feather wafted out of his sight, mercifully.

From above he heard them whispering. Little dickens, what would they try next?

Suddenly moisture trickled down on the back of his neck, the side of his face, and on his beard. Horrified, he rolled over and roared. "You brats! You filthy brats!"

At the window, two young faces with golden crowns above peered down, grinning.

"That got him, Kildom."

"You're right, Kildee. Guess this is where we should come next time we have to pee."

"We can fill up with appleberry juice. Come with a big load. Make him smell sweet."

St. Helens mopped at the back of his neck. If there had been anything in the cell to throw, he would have thrown it. He sniffed at his hand, shook some yellow drops from it, and swore an oath so villainous it threatened to char the walls.

"Oh listen to the bad words, Kildom!"

"He's a bad man, Kildee; what do you expect?"

The two dissolved into giggling. St. Helens felt like showing them just how bad he could be. Instead he fought to control himself. This was most difficult because his inner nature urged him to rave and rant and make a spectacular scene. It wasn't through having a saintly disposition that he was called St. Helens, but because his temper had once been as explosive as a famous Earth volcano.

"You brats are going to be in trouble!" he shouted. "You can't do this to a general! You're going to be punished! When I get out I'll warm your butts!"

"Listen to him, Kildom. He thinks he's getting out."

"Never, Kildee. He'll be here forever! Every day we'll come water him like an ugly weed."

"Until the whole cell fills up with appleberry pee!"

"And him swimming in it like a big fat froog!"

"He's already got a big fat froog-face!"

They dissolved into more giggling, unable to maintain their clever repartee.

"YOU BRATS! YOU FILTHY BRATS!" St. Helens exploded. He was repeating himself, but he couldn't help it. They were supposed to have the minds of men, so a little manly profanity couldn't warp them. Just maybe he'd remember that they were men in boys' bodies when he got hold of them, and then—then it would be more than a spanking he'd deliver!

"Do you think, Kildom, that there's another form of elimination! Plants need fertilizer as well as water, don't they?"

"Shit, yes! Let's!"

St. Helens felt his face going purple. He could imagine smoke curling from his ears and his head and body erupting in a geyser of fire. Never had he been more uncontrollably furious in his entire life!

Up in the window he saw that he was being mooned by a plump posterior. Only it wasn't going to stop at that. Oh, for anything to throw, such as a rotten tomato!

"What's going on here?" That sounded like the old witch herself! Unbelievable! Was she going to direct his torment herself? Was her aging anatomy going to replace that of the boys beyond the bars?

Abruptly the bare posterior got covered, but the brat remained standing before the window as if trying to conceal it. "Nothing, Helbah," one of them said with attempted innocence.

"Boys! Boys! You know better than to act like hooligans! You're going to have to apologize." It was evident that she wasn't even slightly fooled.

"We were just having fun, Helbah!"

"I'm sure it wasn't fun for General Reilly. Now come away from there this instant!"

The young faces looked down at his sullenly, then disappeared. He waited, but the witch did not take their place. Apparently she hadn't come here to torment him further, difficult as that was to believe.

The witch's familiar appeared, however. The houcat stared unblinkingly at him and at the interior of the cell, then flicked his tail and left without any sign of mischief.

"Witches!" St. Helens cursed. "How I hate the lot of them!"

Later, though not by much, the guard opened the dungeon door and motioned him out. Meekly, mindful of the drawn sword and the fact that he had virtually no chance to fight his way out of here even if he should manage to overcome this guard and take his sword, he climbed the stairs. On the way up, to his astonishment, the two young kings sped past him on their way down. Both boys carried a big bucket of sudsy water, a scrubbing brush, and a broom.

Outside, warmed by the sun and inviting, was a large tub of soapy water.

"Strip! Bathe! Deflea! Delouse!" the guard ordered.

For once in his life St. Helens was only too happy to obey. There was louse grease and soap and a brush and even a washcloth. With near joy for the relief he made use of all of them.

After a thorough cleansing and soak, he saw the guard motioning him out. The man even tossed him a towel. While he was toweling, the guard brought him loose prisoner clothes to replace the lousy uniform.

He felt remarkably good, he thought while dressing. He turned and there were the two kings, both red in the face. Their heightened color went well with their brickish hair and the plans he was making.

"We apologize, General Reilly, sir," the king on the left said.

"We'll never come to your window again," the king on the right promised.

St. Helens grunted, nodding his head in a curt gesture of acknowledgment. He was alert for a trap that was about to be sprung, but in the meantime he'd gotten what he'd wanted for days: a clean hide and the summary execution of the tenants of that hide. He hated lice almost as much as he hated brats!

The brats disappeared. St. Helens was returned to his cell. He stood and gaped at the door.

The cell had been scrubbed spotless. Fresh straw had been provided.

What magic might have done readily, the young kings had evidently done laboriously.

"Good gods," he said. He sank down on the straw, physically more comfortable than he had been since capture. "Good gods, she really *is* a good witch!"

19 /

REVOLUTIONARIES

THE GREAT WAR-HORSE GAVE a grunt of surprise as Kelvin landed on its broad rump. With his left hand, hardly thinking of what he did but just going with the gauntlet, he pushed the rider from the saddle. Grabbing the horse's mane he took the soldier's place. The reins were loose, but that was no problem to the gauntlet which snatched them up without his thinking. Immediately he was confronted by a burly royalist swinging down at him, and the right gauntlet countered for him and quickly ended the man's life.

Kelvin caught a squirt of blood as the royalist corpse toppled. He felt his stomach heave, but somehow he was learning to ignore it. Assuredly he and the others here were in the midst of a tremendous fight. It was as if he were in a different plane of reality, something that had nothing to do with home and family and human values.

"Kelvin, watch out!" his father shouted. So much for being apart from his family! But already the gauntlets were blurring as they moved, transferring sword to left hand and reins to right. The new attacker ended his life on the point of Kelvin's sword, blood spraying from his throat, his own wild swing breezing Kelvin's right cheek. No time to think! Just swift positions, as the gauntlets acted, and the effort to fight with everything he and the gauntlets had, just to preserve his life. How he hated this!

Now one of the royalists' attackers was before him, his ally. It was a big man dressed in the plainest of clothes. Morton Crumb! No, not his friend and Jon's father-in-law, but this frame's very close look-alike. He focused on the man's round pink ears, neither bearing as much as a scar, and that alone kept him from shouting the name.

"You," the Morton Crumb look-alike rumbled, "fight against the king?"

The last time he had tried to answer that question, he had gotten into trouble. "I fight to save my friends," he said, nodding back at Kian and his father.

"Come!" As abrupt as Crumb would have been.

He maneuvered the horse with sure gauntleted hand and fought his way at the big man's side until they were directly opposite the prisoners. Kian and his father had their hands tied behind their backs, and that could complicate the problem of getting them away. The royalist guards might have been ordered to slay them rather than give them up.

"Father, I think we'd better retreat!"

It was the Lester look-alike who had just pushed in. With him was a younger fighter, the exact look-alike of Phillip, former boy-king of Aratex, except for his round ears. There were two riderless war-horses behind them. On the ground were two more dead royalists. On the Lester's sword was fresh blood.

Kelvin tried to think. *This is not really Lester and Phillip, and this other man is not really my brother-in-law's father.* It was hard to think of anything under the circumstances. He was likely to get himself or them killed if he did anything but concentrate on his business.

He looked around. Indeed they were outnumbered, these revolutionaries. "Help me release them first," Kelvin urged.

"We're losing too many men," the big man protested.

"You help us now, we'll help you later. We have things you may not have. We're from another frame."

"I thought as much! I saw you flying down! But we can't help you if you're dead. If you've got power, use it!"

Kelvin realized he had a point. He nudged the control on his belt and kicked himself free of the saddle. He rose to just over the heads of the combatants. The fighting stopped.

It was only a temporary halt, he knew. In a moment the novelty would be absorbed and the slaughter would resume. He nudged the control forward.

The guards' faces came nearer, and so did those they guarded. They stared openmouthed, amazed at what they had been too busy to see when he arrived. In a moment more someone would think of a crossbow or other projectile weapon that could spell his end. But with surprise to his advantage and the gauntlets on his hands, he had his chance.

Quickly he disarmed the guard who raised his sword at him, then descended and stabbed the remaining guard through the throat. A moment later he was slicing through first his father's and then his brother's bonds, while renewed fighting raged ahead of them.

Now then, how to get out? The gauntlets knew how. Without his quite willing it, the magical grippers captured the reins of a war-horse. At their urging he vaulted into the saddle.

"Father! Kian! Up!"

They extended their hands to him, and the gauntlets pulled them up on the horse. The three of them made a crowded horseback.

"This is going to be difficult!" John said. "We're surrounded."

Kelvin's gauntlets snatched a passing sword and handed it to his father. "Uh, thanks, but do you think—?"

"I'll clear a path. You follow. Close."

With that Kelvin lifted free of the saddle and just over their heads. The horse eyed him suspiciously, but didn't argue; after all, it was a load off its back. Then he pushed the forward lever and flew to meet a royalist riding down on them.

The attacking royalist died, and so did several others as Kelvin fought horselessly and airborne, to open his side of the crowd. The remaining revolutionaries fought inward, led by the Crumb look-alikes. The Phillip look-alike shouted encouragement.

The royalists, caught between enemies, fought hard, but still perished. The sword in Kelvin's hand never ceased its darting and its hacking, ignoring, as Kelvin could not, the cries of slain and wounded men.

Finally the last of the royalists melted from in front of his wild flying attack. There was the big fellow and the big fellow's son and the boy and half a dozen others whose faces had a familiar look. They looked up at Kelvin.

"Now you can retreat," Kelvin said, "and take us with you."

"Thank the gods that's over!" the Morton Crumb look-alike said. "Follow us!"

They raced out of what would have been the pass between the twin valleys in the world of the silver serpents. Up the roads and into the hills, and finally, their pursuit lost, to a familiar-seeming region of farms and villages. Here the big leader of the far-smaller band raised his hand and drew up. "Whoa. Time for a talk."

Kelvin descended until his feet once more touched the ground. He shut off the belt. He waited.

"Marvin Loaf," the big man said. "You strangers have any trouble with that name?"

"Not a bit," Kelvin said. So this was not Morton Crumb as at home, or Matthew Biscuit as in the world of the silver serpents, but Marvin Loaf. It made perfect sense.

"Good. Some think Marvin a peculiar name."

"No more so than mine," Kelvin said, keeping a straight face. "Kelvin Hackleberry. And this is my father John Knight, and my brother Kian Knight."

Marvin nodded. "This is my son Hester. And this young fellow we call Jillip."

As in Lester and Phillip. Good enough. Kelvin held out his hand politely. The custom of handshaking existed here, fortunately, as it had in every world he had visited with the possible exception of the chimaera's. His father and brother dismounted, along with the others of the band. Everyone shook hands.

"We call ourselves Loaf's Hopes," Marvin said. "Sometimes Loafers. We haven't been doing much raiding lately." He paused again, but no one found any humor in the nickname. "After two years of trying to force a change, this is all we have."

Kelvin saw what he meant. Eight men in all, two of them with slight wounds. The rest who had been in the fight were dead or had been captured by the royalists.

"Your king is bad?" Again, Kelvin wasn't taking anything for granted.

"The worst. He has to be overthrown. How I can't now imagine."

"With our help," Kelvin said confidently.

Marvin looked doubtful. "That flying harness of yours should help, but I'm not sure it's enough. There's really only us eight."

"There will be more," Kelvin said. "All you have to do is get the word out once you've got your army."

"Army? What army? I tell you we're only eight."

Kelvin sighed. How elementary it all was. It really pained him to have to explain it. His father was looking at him warningly, but he went right on.

"If you haven't got huge serpents here that shed skins of purest silver, you have dragons that have scales of purest gold." *Simple. Logical.*

Marvin Loaf was looking at him with eyes that now bulged. His expression suggested that Kelvin was a lunatic.

"Serpents with silver scales? Dragons with golden skins?"

Kelvin abruptly realized why his father had sent the warning look. His morale plummeted. He had walked into another subtle but critical difference between the frames. Yet he owed these look-alikes something. There was a debt and he could not leave with it unpaid.

"My mistake. I told you we're from another frame."

"It must be a distant one. Silver serpents! Golden dragons! These are legend! Nothing like them can possibly exist!"

Nor should chimaeras with three heads, Kelvin thought. Oh, well, these good folk still had to have some advantage, and he had to provide it.

"Look," he said, unsheathing the Mouvar weapon. "This is something very special. It will nullify hostile magic and even turn the magic back on its sender."

"Magic? Magic is myth!"

Kelvin suppressed a groan. Another disappointment! This world seemed so similar to his own, yet it lacked dragons, serpents, and even magic? How could that last possibly be the case? But the robot Stapular had spoken of Major and Minor frames. Maybe this world was like his father's, where magic didn't exist but where magical results were achieved by something called science.

"All three of us can fly with this," he said, touching the belt. "We can hover still in the air as you saw, or move at the speed of a fast horse. That should be some help. It was back there in the battle we just fought."

"Back there I lost over half my men!" Marvin exclaimed, looking suspicious. "Is that belt all you've got?"

"Father!" Hester said, and it was impossible not to think of him as Lester. "Father, he wants to help."

"Good intentions don't defeat tyrants. Armies defeat tyrants."

Kelvin swallowed a lump. He still hadn't answered the big man's question. He glanced at Kian and he saw that his half brother's face was as pale as though he faced instant death. Then he looked at his father and saw that he could expect little help there. Yet his big mouth had gotten him into this, the same as it had with the chimaera. Somehow his big mouth was going to have to get him out.

"We have experience. We overthrew tyrants in two worlds nearly identical to this. And—" Inspiration finally hit him. "If we need to, we can travel back to those worlds, and get what we need there, to deal with this tyrant."

"You think so, do you?" Marvin looked dangerous.

"If we have to. Bring you weapons you don't have. Maybe an army."

"Listen to him, Father. Listen!" Loaf's son urged.

But the big man was drawing his sword. "You've come here without our asking and now you'd leave and we'd never see you again."

"That's not true!" Why was this version of Morton Crumb so belligerent? But he realized that the question was pointless. Characters were similar in each frame, but also different, and the differences showed up most strongly in their personalities, rather than their bodies. So this Crumb was more aggressive than the others, and probably more dangerous to rile. He also seemed clumsier.

"Listen, Sonny," Marvin said, testing the edge of his sword with a callused thumb. "We have been this route before. We have had visits from other frames so often that the king has men watching the transporter! One thing we've learned: visitors are trouble!"

"But Father," Hester protested. "He can't know!" He was protesting, but there was a certain whine in his voice. He seemed to be more dominated by his father than Lester was.

"No, I don't know," Kelvin said. "I don't know about your prior visitors." He felt much as he had when Stapular pulled off his hand and revealed the laser weapon. His gauntlets tingled, but only moderately.

Well, he would use the gauntlets for guidance. He would keep talking, and change the subject if the gloves got bothered. "You have a kingdom where you can hire mercenaries, haven't you?"

Marvin's glower hardly eased. "We have that, Sonny, but we certainly haven't got golden dragons, silver serpents, or magic. Neither do we have riches!"

"But you do have round ears. You can use the transporter."

"Not for a mountain of gold!"

"I don't mean you personally, but at least one of you. Maybe Hester here?"

"The king's men guard the transporter," Hester protested. "And even if we got there, I couldn't use it."

"With my help?"

"No."

"Why not?" The gauntlets were not getting any warmer, which was not a bad sign, but neither was it necessarily good. He might just not be getting anywhere, good or bad. "Round ears means you can use the transporter." *I hope.*

"No way, Sonny. There's more than the shape of ears involved."

"But—" This was getting confusing! According to the Mouvar parchment, round ears were the tickets to use and other-shaped ears a sentence to destruction. Or was that only in his home frame? Were there other rules elsewhere?

"Let me explain it, Sonny. Whenever any of us natives enter the transporter chamber we feel as if our fool heads will burst. So will you, if you attempt to go back."

"You mean—" He strove desperately to make sense of this, his head already feeling swollen. "Magic?"

"Technology. What's the difference, as far as we're concerned? What it means is that it's a one-way transporter. No one can leave by it."

"No one?" Kelvin's knees began to feel like cooked macaroodles.

"No one. That's why the king's men don't use it."

Kelvin tried to think. To be confined to this dull frame forever. Never to see Heln again. To be, furthermore, in a world where there was no way to raise an army and defeat a tyrant? And what about the chimaera? The chimaera would be waiting for the dragonberries he had promised. He had every intention of fulfilling that promise, and would be mortified to renege on it.

"Perhaps there's a little hope," his father said unexpectedly.

All looked at him, the big stranger who had been mainly silent. Marvin looked hardest.

"Look," John Knight said, spreading his hands. "We're as much victims here as you are. But if the transporter is technology, or even if it's not, there may be a way."

"How?" Marvin demanded, showing some interest. "You going to kill off those headbees?"

"Maybe. The chamber beside the transporter chamber—I'm certain it didn't exist in any of the other frames. Maybe there's something that will make the transporter two-way. Possibly a control."

"The king's men would have found it," one of the men said.

"Maybe not," John said. "Not if they didn't know what to look for. I remember how difficult it was to make a computer work, when you didn't know the codes; you could make random guesses all week and never get anywhere, and the damn machine wouldn't tell you."

"You think you know what to look for?" Marvin demanded.

"I might. If it's technology."

Kelvin's gauntlets twitched. What did that mean?

Marvin put away his sword. His grim face showed acceptance but no real belief in John's words. "There'd better be an army in this," he said. "There'd better be, or that's the end of all of us."

But the gauntlets were cooling. That gave Kelvin hope.

20 /

A MEETING OF KINDS

CHARLAIN WOKE UP RESTED. The camp was quiet now, the wounded up and around. It was—good heavens, it was late in the day!

She met Lomax as she was scrambling out of the tent. He was grinning as he came with arms wide for a hug. She let him embrace her and then tell her how many lives she had saved and how grateful they all were. "But now," he finished, "we'll be making our big drive and it's not fair to you—"

"You want me to leave."

"Before we reengage the enemy. Yes, ma'am. There will be more casualties, but we have a good supply of bloodfruit and you have discovered the mysteries of the doctor bag. We can manage, although—"

"Yes," she said. He wanted her to stay with them, she knew, and she didn't want to. She had after all come here for just one purpose, and that was to save Lester's fading life. She had done that, and now wanted very much to get well away from this mindless carnage.

"Then you—"

"I mean I will return home now, where I will be safe. That is what you were saying?"

He looked astonished, then crestfallen. He had asked from a sense of duty. She knew that the last thing he had expected was that she would comply. She felt guilty for disappointing him, but she did have to go.

"I'm not really a nurse or a magician," she said. "I'm sure you will manage with those who assisted me. My daughter may need me, and then there's my son and his wife. Heln is having my grandson."

"I—see." He was doing his unsuccessful best to mask his disappointment. If he were a very few years younger, he'd have to cry. It was nice that she was going to be missed.

"Keep the bandages changed, administer bloodfruit syrup as needed, and keep that boy out of the fighting."

"You mean Phillip?"

"That's the boy. He's reckless as my Jon was at his age. I read his cards and he's at continued high risk with the uncertainty card. Keep him safe."

"I'll try. But Phillip was a king. He's hard to control."

"No harder, I suspect, than Jon. And Phillip of Aratex doesn't have a big brother with magic gauntlets and a prophecy. If Jon was here you'd know what unmanageable is."

Lomax tried a grin, albeit weak. He motioned to a passing soldier. "Corporal Hinzer, saddle Mrs. Hack—eh, Charlain's horse and bring it to her. Have two unwounded men escort her to the border."

"That won't be necessary," Charlain assured him. "I know the way and there shouldn't be any danger for one old woman."

"Not old!" Lomax protested in a manner that had to be automatic. "But if you're sure—"

"You need *all* your men. The war isn't over."

"Yes. Yes, thank you, Charlain. Thank you for your help. You saved many lives."

You may not thank me always, she thought with regret. *When things go against you and I'm not there. Then you may want to curse me for abandoning you.*

With some justice, unfortunately.

She waited patiently while her mount was brought, then climbed up and into the saddle. She was a little stiff from all that kneeling. She was about to ride out when Lomax came running to her, his face flaming red. He handed her up a packet and a jug.

"I forgot you hadn't eaten! Here's traveling biscuit, dried meat, and tuber fruit. Wine's in the jug. You must be famished!"

"Not really," she said. "We witches seldom eat."

"Witches?" His face paled perceptibly. For a moment he looked as though he believed her.

"It's what Phillip said when I got to him. And who knows, if I had had a good teacher he just might have been correct!"

She nudged Nelly with her knee, rode through the camp, and out to the road that led to the border.

It was half a day later at leisurely horse-walking speed that she met the cat. It came from the bushes, tail raised, yellow eyes fixed on her, and she knew instantly that this was why she had left the camp.

She said, "Whoa, Nelly," though the horse was already stopped. The cat came nearer. It was very black, blacker than mortal hide ought to be. It sat down, washed itself carefully, pawed down its whiskers, and then did what Charlain had somehow expected. It turned its back, looked over its shoulder once, flicked its tail, and proceeded up a path.

"Follow that cat, Nelly!" Charlain said to her mount. It was silly and impossible that she do so, but Nelly obeyed. That, she thought, had to be the result of magic!

She held the reins loosely in her hands and let the horse plod on at the cat's pace. She sighed and closed her eyes, resting. Not once did she question herself about why she was here or where they were going. She did not even wonder whether it would be a long or a short trip. Somehow she had known that something like this would happen. That had been part of her urgency to get away from the camp. It was as if she had laid down another card, and it had told her to leave the place where she was needed, to find one where she was needed more.

Eventually the path reached its end and they stopped. Here, in an otherwise empty glade, was a huge gnarled tree. Under the tree, waiting, was an old, bent woman, leaning on a stick. Now who would that be, except—

"Helbah? Helbah the witch?"

"Who else, Charlain?"

She felt a cloud lift from her. "I am here," she said without thinking. "Here, as I know you directed."

"You have done well," Helbah said. "Now you will do even better."

Charlain knew that Helbah spoke only the witching truth.

Heln watched behind half-hooded eyes as Jon added seeds and crumbs to the tray on the windowsill. Her task done, Jon glanced at her, saw her apparently asleep, and tiptoed out.

No sooner was the door closed than Heln was out of bed and scuttling, a way she found natural of late, across the room to the window. She stood stealthily waiting until the dark-headed sparren lit on the tray's rim. Bright-eyed, the little bird regarded her carefully. Heln remained frozen, unblinking.

The bird picked up a corbean from the tray, cracked it, and proceeded to eat. Pleased with the fare, it put its little head back and warbled cheerily.

Instantly Heln's hand shot out like a snake. Her fingers snapped closed like jaws on the tiny bird before it could flutter. She raised it to her mouth, her stomach growling for sustenance. The bird raised its beak desperately.

Heln opened her mouth. Easily, without seeming volition, her head snapped forward. Her teeth closed on the bird and crushed it.

She was just swallowing, and brushing crimson stains from her lips, when Jon entered. Jon stared at her and the tray. There were feathers on the tray. There was blood on Heln's mouth.

"Why, Heln, what—" Jon was too surprised and confused to finish the sentence.

"An eagawk dropped on a sparren. I tried to get here and chase it away, but—"

Jon's eyes were large. She was suspecting if not actually aware that Heln lied. Disbelief fought with another suspicion. The kinder, more logical thought survived.

"Oh, Heln, how terrible for you! I know how you love songbirds, how you enjoy seeing them! To have an eagawk drop on one right on the tray!"

"It was only following its nature," Heln said. Stealthily she wiped blood from her mouth and lips, sweeping her hand as if brushing away a crumb.

"Yes, I know, but—Heln, did you hurt yourself?"

"Bit my tongue when I tried to shout at the preybird." She turned all the way from the window. She forced herself to move slowly, as a pregnant woman should. Without another glance at Jon she got back into bed.

"Don't you want to go for a walk this morning?"

"No!"

"But it's so nice out!"

Heln merely closed her eyes as if bored with Jon's presence, which was hardly an exaggeration.

Jon moved to her side and felt her forehead. "You have no temperature, Heln. You seem cool—cooler than I'd think natural."

"You ever been with child?"

"You know I haven't!"

"That's the way it is. For roundears, at least."

"Oh." Jon never seemed to accept that her ears were different from her brother's and Heln's. It was as if the girl thought they were all of the same species. Little did she know!

"I might take another cup of tefee," Heln said, making another attempt to get rid of her.

"I'll pull the cord for the servant. Would you like something to eat, too, Heln? You hardly touched your groats this morning. You aren't sick again?"

"No. I told you I'm all right." When would this nuisance of a girl go away?

Two of Jon's fingers reached out to the corner of Heln's mouth. They picked out a tiny feather. Jon eyed it, and her.

"I was too close to the kill," Heln said. "Blood and feathers sprayed on me."

"That must have been it," Jon said, sounding unconvinced. She held the feather, then carried it as though to dispose of it. But she walked not to the pullcord but to the door. She hesitated, giving Heln a peculiar look, then exited.

Heln delivered herself of a long, low hiss. So good to be rid of that one, if only momentarily. She'd like to be out in the sun, soaking up its rays, warming herself and the other through and through. But Jon, she knew, would think it strange, and the doctor would find it unacceptable. Later, after the other was born, she might go with it into the sunny desert and bask in the warming light and practice—what? She had lost the thought, frustratingly.

A mosqfly buzzed near her mouth, attracted by the stains. It lit on her upper lip, the foolish thing. Instantly her tongue darted out and rolled it into her mouth. The insect buzzed as she swallowed it.

At the same moment she felt the scuttling inside. Reaching down she patted her bulging stomach. *Don't fret, Little Three Heads! Mama will feed you well.*

There was no coherent answer, just a mental growl. It was too soon for the human minds to manifest. But soon that would change. All she had to do was find proper food.

Another mosqfly buzzed through the open window. She waited, rock-still, ready to capture it.

Dr. Sterk listened quietly as Jon described Heln's recent behavior. It was unfortunately evident what was happening to her. "And you're certain she ate it?" he asked.

"She must have! Blood all over her mouth, and this feather." She held up the tiny feather to show him.

"The mind comports itself strangely in pregnant women. Her behavior may seem abnormal, even bizarre, but I assure you it's all part of the process."

"Really, Doctor?" The girl had understandable skepticism.

"Really. Just keep watch and report anything that seems different. If necessary, I can always administer a stronger medicine."

"Oh, Doctor, you've made me feel so much better! You don't know how concerned I've been!"

"I can imagine. But even pointeared women develop strange appetites and behave oddly while carrying. Just go on as you have been, and everything should be all right."

He ushered her to the door and out. Then he allowed himself the grimace he had been suppressing.

Everything would *not* be all right, he thought dismally. Everything pointed to the chimaera syndrome. If that was what it was, and he was sickly certain this was the case, nothing would save that girl and her child except a certain powder.

And for that, he thought bitterly, *I'd have to go to a dealer in such powders.* Alas, he knew full well that any dealers who existed had to operate in some far-removed universe.

* * *

St. Helens heard them talking through the thick door. Then their jailer had the door open, and they were coming inside. He stood, reminding himself that they were royalty and that, as the saying went, brats would be brats.

They stood there with their golden crowns on their heads, two identical and apparent young boys.

"I'm Kildee, General Reilly," said the one on the right. "I'm Klingland's monarch."

"I'm Kildom," said the other boy. "I'm king of Kance."

St. Helens permitted himself a slight bow. *In name only,* he thought. *In name only are you the rulers.* And in his home world of Earth, any royalty that still existed in England and France was purely nominal. No two frames were quite the same, but certain trends did seem to carry through.

"It is our hope," said Kildee, "that you will agree to come over to us."

"You mean—" St. Helens could hardly believe this, "switch sides?"

"That would be appropriate, General Reilly," said Kildom. The boy reached up and took off his crown; he held it down at his side as though respectfully. His twin brother duplicated his actions.

"In what way would it be appropriate? I'm a soldier and I do what's required of me." Strange little tykes. Did they really think as men did?

"General Reilly, you are not a bad man," Kildee said.

"Thank you. I try not to be, though with imperfect success." If this was a game, it was better than their pee game, so he was willing to play along.

"But your side is bad."

I've suspected that. But you can't know about the prophecy.

"There is a prophecy," Kildee said. "We know of it from Helbah."

He should have known! Witches had their infernal sources. "You know about a prophecy? The one concerning a roundear?"

"Yes. Concerning Kelvin of Kelvinia."

"Then you know," he said, sighing, "that there is little to be done to alter it."

"Perhaps in reality but not in truth."

This was puzzling. He hardly expected obscure philosophy from these kids.

" 'Uniting four,' " said Kildom, "may not mean uniting through warfare the kingdom of Kelvinia with those of Klingland, Kance, and Hermandy."

"No? Well, what then does it mean?"

The boy frowned. "Prophecies can be devious, Helbah says, and subject to interpretation."

"You don't think it would mean uniting Kelvinia with the remaining three kingdoms? Throod is where every warring kingdom goes for mercenaries and weapons, while Ophal and Rotternik haven't even been penetrated since before Mouvar's visit! As far as latecomers like me are concerned those kingdoms might not even exist!"

"Nevertheless," the boy said pedantically, "Kelvinia may not have to conquer us."

"Don't tell me you want to surrender!" St. Helens found himself hard put to conceal his mirth. These two were really just what they seemed to be: children.

Kildom looked at Kildee and shrugged. Kildee returned the shrug. They both looked back at him. They waited.

"Well, is that what you want?" St. Helens demanded rhetorically. The punch line of their joke was about due.

"It is, General Reilly," Kildom said.

St. Helens started to laugh, but his mouth froze partway into it. Could it be that they were serious?

"We have discussed the matter out of Helbah's hearing and we are prepared to raise the surrender flags," Kildee said.

St. Helens felt floored. In his wildest dreams he had never anticipated this! They were playacting. They had to be. But suppose they weren't?

Better to play it serious, at least until one of them burst out laughing. "You really want to surrender? Why?"

"To save us," said Kildee. "To end the fighting."

"And to save our Helbah," Kildom added.

Whoa! This was more than just interesting. "Those would be your terms? Your only terms?"

The two boys looked at each other again. "Yes, General Reilly," they said together.

St. Helens let out a breath. This was incredible. It seemed he had won the war single-handed! This was even better than he could have imagined!

If it was true.

But if it was true, then for whom had he won it? For what? For the usurper in Kelvinia?

"Will you take our surrenders, General Reilly?" Kildom asked.

Would he? Could he? He didn't want the winner to be those two back in Kelvinia's capital. And would the prophecy be said to hold if Kelvin himself were absent? Kelvin, off in some other frame, doing the gods knew what, and unaware of what was happening here?

"I'll have to think about it, Your Majesties. I'll have to think things over."

Now they were gaping. It seemed that they had never imagined that he would demur!

He swallowed, wanting nothing quite so much as to sink down on the pile of straw. "Please close the door tightly as you leave. I don't want to escape, and I don't want anyone rescuing me."

The two exchanged another glance. Maybe they did understand. Certainly they knew that he was on the wrong side.

They left, leaving him with his chaotic thoughts.

21 /

RETURN JOURNEY

KELVIN HUNG SUSPENDED ABOVE the ledge, watching for the king's guardsmen. The updraft from the cliff was shockingly strong, much more than there had been in the other frame. He trusted his levitation belt, but this was a balancing act that made him a bit nervous.

He had left just two living men at this site, but more might have come while he was rescuing his father and brother. His gauntlets were tingling a mild warning, and that could mean that he should act while acting was still possible. The others in his party had already begun ascending the tree, certainly a more difficult task than in the world of serpents and flopears. It was time that he and the gauntlets act.

The chamber was to the left of the transporter chamber. No sign of it either from here or the ledge. He would have to just step through the rock face at the right spot, and find himself in either the transporter or up against guardsmen with swords. There was really no choice except to trust the gauntlets.

He landed on the ledge, facing the cliff face. Was he following the guidance of the gauntlets properly?

He drew his sword. *All right, I'm a hero!*

As though annoyed, the gauntlets yanked him forward, into rock that vanished.

He was in a chamber lit by the glow. It was otherwise unoccupied, and sparsely furnished for the comfort of vigil-keeping guardsmen. A couple of blankets, discarded crusts and rinds from lunch, and one broken wine bottle. Some vigilance!

He put his head out the shimmering blue curtain in time to see his father pulling himself up the ladder at the cliff's edge. Below him was Kian and below Kian were the others.

"Guardsmen back there! Six of them!" his father called. The updraft really pulled at him as he struggled the rest of the way up. "Redleaf got 'em with his crossbow! Good man, that! He picked them off so fast and at such a distance that they never knew what happened!"

Kelvin sighed. More dead. That was one reason he knew he was a fraud as a hero: he hated killing. Well, it couldn't be helped. At least his kin and Loaf's Hopes were intact.

Kian came up, followed by Hester. His gauntlets gave them a hand as each arrived at the ledge. Below, Marvin Loaf was having trouble with branches and updraft. Jillip climbed past their leader, grinning broadly and devilishly as only a young rascal could. There was something insulting about the way he hung by one hand and pretended, only pretended, to give Marvin a leg up. Was it a joke, or insolence, or was the kid merely a slacker?

"Sort of slow, ain't he?" Redleaf remarked.

"Comes from too much bleer," Bilger cracked. He had to be the thinnest, with the possible exception of Jillip.

"Bleer, you must mean Cross-eyed Jenny at the tavern!"

"Hey, I thought it was the girls who got fat!"

The Hopers chuckled and laughed at their own great wit, and generally acted like fools while Marvin wheezed along, never slowing and never wasting breath. Before he'd quite reached the top and Kelvin's reaching hand he looked up, very red in the face. "How many you get?" he inquired.

"No guardsmen," Kelvin said, giving him the hand. "The two live ones and the dead are both missing. The men you stopped must have been replacements."

"Very likely."

Kelvin heaved on Marvin's arm and he came the rest of the way. As big around in girth as his look-alike, and with all the muscle, he was not built for trees and ladders. He breathed deeply for a moment, then looked down at his ascending men.

"What's the matter?" called Redleaf. "You a little winded, old man?"

"Redleaf, if you weren't the best crossbowman in existence I'd jump down there and kick your butt!"

Jillip tittered, then corked it. The big man's scowl suggested that he showed good sense.

Still grinning until the top rung, Redleaf, Bilger, and the others battled the updraft until all were together on the wide ledge.

"All right, there's no going near that transporter," Marvin said. "But that anteroom where the guardsmen go is another matter. Have you been there, Sonny?"

"It's empty," Kelvin said. "As I told you, no guardsmen. I made certain, just as we agreed."

"Well, let's have a look." John felt about until he located the entrance. He disappeared into the rock face, and Kelvin followed. One by one the others joined them. Jillip picked up the empty wine bottle and stood examining that while everyone else felt the walls.

Every wall felt solid, with the exception of one spot at the far end where there was a flat area with a transparent section at eye level. Looking through this "window" as his father would have called it, Kelvin saw the transporter.

"I don't see any button or lever in here or in there!" John complained. "Give your gauntlets an order, Kelvin. Let them search!"

Kelvin was quick to comply. The gauntlets did search, just as he mentally told them to, but they did not find anything on the flat area or its window. He wanted to go, but the gauntlets were reluctant, and kept his hands and fingers moving and pressing in various patterns.

Well, Kelvin thought sadly as he let the gauntlets play, *I suppose I can get used to living here. But I'm going to miss my wife and the chimaera is going to think ill of me. I wanted to get the seeds for it. I'd promised, and I always keep my word.*

Stupid mortal, relax and let the gauntlets do your work!

Kelvin jumped. *Mervania—is that you?*

What other head would it be, stupid? You must have known I'd keep track of you!

But you don't have the dragonberries!

No, but I do have a mind! The mind is not limited in intelligent species.

But if you've found me, and—

I have stayed with you. If I had let go I would have lost you for good. I must admit I am growing tired of it. You are most boring. You don't like bloodletting at all. You wouldn't even have had the ferocity to attack those guardsmen if the gauntlets and I hadn't urged you on.

Kelvin glanced around at the others. It seemed impossible to him that they did not know what was going on in his head.

What do you want me to do, Mervania? He hated to admit it, but he felt better having her along. His mind did feel inferior at times.

Why thank you, Kelvin. You are quite correct: your mind requires buttressing. Very well, I will tell you what to do. Bring the entire crew here to my frame. I can help them.

You could eat them! He shuddered, just thinking of it. Then he saw Kian looking at him as if he were crazy. He had been showing his emotions!

Stupid mortal! Mervania thought with something almost like affection. *Of course I could! But I won't. I want those seeds you're going to get. Then I won't need to cling to your frail mind in order to travel across the frames.*

But why help these others?

Because I'm a good creature, that's why! You assume I'm evil merely because my dietary habits differ slightly from yours. That is a narrow view. Besides, I don't like tyrants. I've eaten a lot of them, and believe me, every time their minds gave my stomach trouble.

You've eaten tyrants?

Of course! You don't think I was always confined, do you? All humans are devourable, but some are tastier than others.

She likes to play with our food, her brother head interrupted. *Actually it was only a couple of tyrants. One proclaimed itself a god, and the other built pyramids of human skulls. Delicious thought!*

Mertin, don't mess with my concentration! It's tedious enough keeping such a tiny mind on line! Grumpus, what is that you're chomping? Spit it out! Do you want to make us sick?

Gag, gag, gag. Urp, urp.

Kelvin felt his own innards twisting and fluttering with the monster's retching. This was a disadvantage of telepathy he hadn't thought of!

Then the gauntlets pressed his fingers against either side of the window. There was a pop, and the flat area slid away, taking the window with it. There was now an open doorway between them and the transporter.

"What did I tell you!" John Knight said. "Holy—YOW!" He clutched first his temples and then the front and back of his head.

Everyone else in the chamber was reacting similarly. Someone screamed. Two of the men dropped to the floor and writhed.

Kelvin knew why. There was a buzzing sound so loud and painful that it seemed to fill every crevice in his head. This was the head-splitting effect they had been warned about!

Well, I'm certainly not going to put up with this! Get yourself out of it, stupid mortal! I'm leaving!

No, no, Mervania, wait!

Abruptly he felt her absence, but not an end to the pain. She had made good on her threat. The gauntlets, unperturbed, were feeling carefully above the doorway.

"You want to use that transporter? Go ahead!" Marvin charged clumsily toward the front of the chamber. His men quickly followed.

Kelvin was growing faint. But the gauntlets suddenly pressed hard on a round area above his head. It was a flat, dark spot where the top of the door had been.

CLICK!

Silence. Sheepish faces turned. There was an end to panic.

"You've done it!" his father exclaimed. "Now we can go!"

"Not without us!" Marvin said. He had stopped just short of the shimmering curtain. "You're going to help us, remember?"

"Of course we'll go together," John said, while Kelvin just stood there for a moment, supremely gratified by his success. "You'll get your help, Marvin, just as my son promised. My son always comes through."

Marvin nodded, coming back to them. "Got to admit he's doing that! First two of you transport, then my men, and you and I last. Agreed?"

Spoken like a leader, Kelvin thought. *A cautious one.*

"It will be a bit startling to see," Kelvin told Hester. "We'll step in, there will be a purple flash, and then we'll be gone."

"What's it like to experience?" Hester asked.

"Uh—"

"Does it hurt?" Jillip interjected.

"No. No, it doesn't hurt," Kelvin assured them. "You'll find out what it's like soon enough. Just—follow me!"

As boldly as though it were just an everyday occurrence, he stepped into the adjoining chamber. His gauntlets didn't tingle, so he walked over to the transporter. There he found the chimaera's sting that he had apparently dropped and left. Oddly, he hadn't thought about it. Could that have been Mervania's doing? She had evidently been in his mind all along, until the awful sound drove her out. She might have made him forget about something like that.

"What's that? Copper?" Marvin seemed more than just curious.

"Yes. There's a lot of it where we're going."

"Copper? Lots of copper?"

"Yes." The revolutionary leader's manner was puzzling. Why should he be concerned about copper, when he could go after gold?

"It's rare here. It's our most valuable metal. One copper coin is worth three gold or two silver."

"We'll get you copper," Kelvin said, a mental dawn breaking. So copper was the most valuable metal, here! "Enough to buy your army. You do want that army?"

"Want it? I'd kill for it!"

Expressions had a way of carrying across the frames, Kelvin thought. His father had spoken that way at least once or twice about matters of lesser importance.

Taking a deep breath and a firm hold on the sting, he stepped with faked confidence into the transporter. He was confident that it would work, but not about the rest of this misadventure.

Bloorg was waiting. In his hand was his copper sting, point on the metal floor. Kelvin nodded to him and waited also, feeling that it was the thing to do. The squarear could pick up from his mind what was going on.

Soon they were all there, with the exception of his father and Marvin. Then John Knight stepped from the transporter, and the group leader.

Marvin's eyes widened as he looked at Bloorg. His hand went to his sword.

Kelvin's right gauntlet grabbed the big revolutionary's wrist. "Don't! The squarears are in control!"

"Copper!" Marvin gasped, straining at the gauntlet.

"Friend." *Maybe. In authority, anyway.*

Bloorg spoke. "You were to bring the chimaera its seeds."

"We reached the wrong frame," John said, pretending not to notice the struggle going on.

"My fault," Kian explained. "I'm sorry. Even after you told us the setting—"

"I told you the setting for your own world. You disobeyed."

"I was there," Kelvin said. "I went to our home world for the seeds. They were not where Mouvar left them. I'm certain we can get the seeds, but it will take time to find the berries and harvest them."

"So you came back empty-handed."

"Yes." Kelvin felt uncomfortably like a schoolboy being scolded. It wasn't as if he hadn't run into difficulties.

"Who," Bloorg suddenly demanded, "are these others?"

Kelvin was sure the squarear already knew. But he answered hastily: "From the world we reached by error. They have a purpose in being here. The chimaera was in touch with me mentally. The chimaera approved their coming."

"The chimaera does not make policy. The chimaera does not make law."

"But—"

"You have disobeyed by returning here without the seeds. You have broken law by bringing others."

"I'm sorry," Kelvin said. He had known of no such law, but realized that ignorance was no excuse. Bloorg was like a teacher about to mete out punishment. But perhaps if he explained—

"The cost of our returning was that we help these people," he said. "You see, they have a tyrant, and—"

"Keep your mind still!"

Kelvin tried to relax. He knew that Bloorg was getting the story from him, and he hoped he was getting it right. There were so many things that he himself did not understand. For instance, why had the transporter been one-way until the gauntlets made it functional?

"Mouvar has his reasons," Bloorg said. "The people of that frame were not and are not ready. The transporter was for others."

"Mouvar watches over us all, doesn't he?" The thought slipped out into speech before he realized it.

Bloorg's eyes glowed. "You too are not ready."

Kelvin did a mental shrug. In time maybe his kind would be considered adults by the like of Bloorg and the chimaera. For now they were children or animals who weren't ready yet to learn.

"Precisely. Animals. Mentally inferior life-forms."

Now Kelvin groaned mentally. He wondered how much of this conversation was being followed by Marvin and his men. It probably didn't matter, but they would be affected by the outcome.

Snick, snick, snick! Marvin and his fellows had their swords drawn. Kelvin had stopped watching them and had released Marvin's wrist as soon as Marvin seemed accepting. Now he realized that either he or the gauntlets had made a mistake.

"No squareheaded foreigner calls me an inferior life-form!" the revolutionary leader boomed.

Bloorg waved a hand. The blades glowed red. The men cursed mightily as their swords clanged to the floor.

"They have powers," Kelvin explained belatedly. "In many ways they are more advanced than we are. They have magic here, while in worlds like yours and my father's there's only technology."

"Do you know what you're talking about?" Marvin snarled. He shook his hand, his eyes narrowed with the lingering pain.

"Not really," Kelvin confessed. "Only that it's well to do what Bloorg says."

Marvin wrung his hand. "It's burned!" he said, looking at the palm. "It's burned bad!"

"Is it, Marvin Loaf?" Bloorg asked. His hands did marvelously strange tricks, the fingers twining and untwining like snakes. One finger snapped out at Marvin and made a circle of all his men.

Marvin looked astonished. "It's stopped! It's not burned anymore!"

"Mine neither," Hester said, amazed.

"Or mine!" Redleaf exclaimed, holding out his hands and staring at them.

Awe held the strangers from the wrong frame transfixed, silencing them.

"Now that that little demonstration is over," Bloorg said, "we can proceed with business. The chimaera had no authority from me to do what it did. The chimaera deserves to be punished."

"More than it has been?" Kelvin demanded. "More than being confined to one little island?" Kelvin was astonished by his own words. He must have had some help from the chimaera in forming them.

"Quite right. The chimaera shaped your thoughts and you spoke them as your own."

The chimaera was getting him and all of them into more trouble!

"Wrong. I am quite aware of the chimaera's reasoning in this matter. But I do not understand why it wants to give up its supply of copper to these simple beings."

"Because," Kelvin said, knowing that this was the chimaera's thought and that Bloorg would recognize it as such, "I am tired of being a target. Every inferior life-form with access to a transporter comes after my shed stings. I don't need them now, especially if I can locate others like myself. All I need is enough copper in my diet to keep from growing pale and weak and unmetallic. These roundears had a one-way transporter and can have it again. Let them take the copper to their own world and keep it there, confined. Whenever I shed an old sting they can have that as well. Then let the inferior life-form poachers go to that world to steal the copper. They will discover that they are as much prisoner as I am!"

Hoo! Kelvin thought. *That would serve the poachers right! It would also rid the other frames of them. They would have to settle down to honest work in their primitive prison frame, hating every minute of it. The chimaera had a beautiful notion!*

Thank you, Kelvin, Mervania's direct thought came. *I am rather pleased with it myself.*

"That's very commendable, Mervania," Bloorg said. Now Marvin Loaf's face changed, as he caught on to what was happening. Perhaps the chimaera had touched his mind, too, with a bit of explanation. "But what about the sting you now have? Your kind have been slain through the centuries for single stings. Indeed, the robot Stapular would have slain you earlier, had he not been waiting for your latest sting to mature. That was why he was able to deceive me; I assumed that since he allowed his living companions to be slain, he had no weapon sufficient to harm you. Surely there will be other poachers."

"That," Kelvin/Chimaera said with asperity, "is why I am confined to an island and why you guard the transporter! I expect you to do a better job in the future."

Bloorg's eyes closed and opened, their lids making an audible click. It seemed the chimaera had scored tellingly. "That might reduce the number and strength of expeditions, Mervania, once it is widely known."

"It will be," Mervania/Kelvin said. "And if the transporter is kept locked, at Marvin Loaf's outlet, and these inferior life-forms do not use the sting in magic—"

"We won't!" Marvin exclaimed, evidently willing to ignore the remark about inferior life-forms. "We don't even believe in that stuff! Much. All we want is the copper. Any horserear poachers come for it, we'll know what to do with 'em!"

"Agreed," Mervania/Kelvin said.

"Agreed," Bloorg echoed.

Kelvin was surprised and relieved. He had been afraid that all of them, the chimaera included, would be punished. Evidently the chimaera had understood the situation better than he.

Naturally, Kelvin, Mervania's thought came.

22 /

APPRENTICE

"GRIP MY HANDS TIGHTER," Helbah ordered. "Let your essence and mine mingle."

Charlain tried to do as directed. The glade, the trees, the animals peering on, even the aged face, all blurred. It was the dizzying twirl Helbah had made her do, and that bitter wine. Now her arms and legs felt numb. Her fingers tingled. She was, was . . .

Helbah's hands. Helbah's arms. Helbah. Where did Charlain end and Helbah begin? She could feel her heart beating in Helbah's chest, feel the pain of Helbah's reopened wound, feel the blood seeping, seeping through her black satiny wrapper.

"Helbah! Helbah! I'm you!"

"We're we. Notice which mouth you're speaking from."

Charlain noticed. She had spoken from a nearly toothless mouth with sagging cheeks—Helbah's. But when Helbah spoke it was from a mouth that had all its teeth and was perfect except for a bitter aftertaste.

"We can do it now!" one of the mouths said. "Concentrate!"

Charlain tried to remember. Her legs and arms jerked her. Over to the huge tree. Over to the big crystal sealed in its hollow. Her eyes fixed on its surface, then below. Murky smoke swirled and twirled. Then—

Soldiers fighting. Klingland uniforms against Kelvinian uniforms. In the background, through clouds of dust, the huge dome of the Klingland capital.

Swords clashed. Crossbow bolts flew. Men died. More dead lay in the red uniforms of the Klinglanders than the green uniforms of the attackers. Even as she realized this, more died.

"Hurry! Hurry!"

They had to be helped. They had to be given new strength. She could almost feel the weakness in those red-uniformed arms. She wanted them stronger, stronger, stronger, their minds and bodies refreshed.

It was like a great wind blowing through her, out of her, into the crystal, into the bodies and minds of the defending soldiers. A green-uniformed soldier was knocked from his saddle with a broad sweep of a defender's sword. Now another, and another! The green-uniformed men were going down like harvested stalks of grain! Now they were panicking, turning, running. Their horse's hooves raised dust as they rode into their dust, pursuing them, chasing them, forcing them to keep retreating and not turn back.

"Now! Now! Now!"

Dust rose, twirled, and—

Blurring twin capital domes, city, hills, forest, big hills, bigger hills.

Another army. Green uniforms with a few black uniforms. Bigger than the force driven from Klingland's capital. Fighting soldiers wearing the bright orange uniforms of Kance. The green uniforms and the black uniforms were winning. Orange uniforms lay with dead or dying bodies in them in the valleys and across the hills. There was no doubt the orange-clads were being driven back, closer and closer to the twin capitals.

This must not happen!

Strength, strength, strength surging through her arms. Out of her arms, to the bodies and minds of the defending warriors.

A green-uniformed soldier dropped his sword and died. A second was cut down in similar manner. Here a black uniform screamed its agony until a great war-horse's hoof crushed the unfortunate Herman's head. More and more, the green- and black-clad died or were unhorsed. More and more the orange-clad struck down their opponents and fought with renewed force.

Now the orange had stopped retreating. Now the armies were facing each other in unyielding lines. Now the spears flew and the swords clanged and the spectacle was increasingly ghastly.

The Kance army was fighting well now, but remained outnumbered. No matter how hard the orange fought, they were certain to be cut down in the end. They had to have help. Magic help. Witch's help.

With an intensity she had not imagined she had, Charlain felt the buildup, the great ballooning of rage. In her body, in her soul. Growing, growing, growing. She believed the mechanism to be good and just, yet the force was so strong she could not begin to control it.

In the crystal, above the armies, there developed a great roaring ball of flame. All fighting stopped. The soldiers of both armies looked up. The blacks and the greens trembled. The orange-clads waved and cheered. For the ball was orange. Orange was on top.

With a sudden swoop the ball shot over the invading army. It descended. Men threw up their arms, trying vainly to ward off its heat. It glowed, and the horses danced, spilling their riders and stampeding in terror. Little tendrils of flame grew out of its sides, reaching down, touching, burning, crisping as it sped. Men cowered and threw away their fire-hot weapons. The horses bolted for elsewhere. There was chaos.

The ball imploded with an earthshaking report. Sparks showered down on the Kelvinian army.

The Kancians charged. Encouraged by the panic in the enemy resulting from the witch's fire, they met little fighting resistance. Their swords swung freely. Their spears darted. Men, good, bad, and indifferent, choked and died.

"Oh Lester," Charlain whimpered, remembering how it had been with him, knowing that similar horror was now being visited on so many more on his side. But there was no stopping it. The invading army was retreating, racing headlong for safety.

Charlain felt herself falling. She felt her face against the ground. She felt blades of grass in her nose and tickling her ears. She felt that she herself was dying.

"Oh what have I done?" she moaned. "What have I done?"

"You did what had to be done," said her other mouth there above her. "What I had to do and you had to help me do."

"But all that killing! All that death!"

"This is the idiocy of men. We cannot redefine their nature. We can only intercede to enable the right side to prevail."

"Meow!" said Katbah, her other body's familiar. Gently, soothingly, the creature rubbed against her head and sounded a comforting purr.

Zoanna stared at the crystal with disbelief. The Kelvinian fighting men and the pick of Hermandy's fighting men were being routed! They shouldn't be. She had endowed them with special strength through her newly acquired powers and had weakened the enemy with others. Now they were losing, and this was contrary to reason. What had happened?

Then she knew. "Helbah!" she cried aloud. It didn't seem possible, for she had seen the old witch almost dead. She should have known that the only good witch was a dead witch, not an almost dead witch.

In the crystal a burst of witch fire formed above the Kelvinian army. Men fell from their horses, grass browned in places, and the mud from a recent rain dried.

That settled it. It was definitely the witch.

"Damn her! Damn!" Zoanna swore. She would do that literally, as effectively as her powers allowed. First she would have to get the witch's image in the crystal, and then by all the evil in existence she would crisp her to a cinder!

The crystal's image swirled and opaqued without her willing it. The opacity vanished, leaving a clear crystal with Helbah's grimly wrinkled face inside.

"Helbah, I'll get you! I'll finish you!"

The face smiled grimly. "Will you, Zoanna? Try!"

The challenge was too much! Zoanna raised her hands, spoke the words of power, and sent forth a ball of fire.

It backfired. She was thrown across the room, flat on her back amid a pile of smoking furniture and room furnishings. Behind her there was a large crack in the palace's wall.

She sat up, gasping, feeling her ribs, blinking her eyes. She focused on the crystal. There was Helbah's image, with a pleased expression.

"Helbah," she gasped, amazed. "You're strong!"

"Stronger than you, Zoanna."

"We can become allies. We—"

"You are going to leave this frame forever. You and your imposter of a monarch are to vanish. Leave on your own, or be destroyed."

"You can't threaten me, you old bag of bones!"

"Zoanna, I do not threaten. I, far more than you, have the power to destroy."

"Prove it!" Zoanna screamed, losing all control. "Prove it, you old hag!"

"Certainly, Zoanna."

In the crystal the aged face was replaced by a gnarled hand. The fingers separated, spreading to their maximum. Behind the hand, on a level with it, were two deeply burning feline eyes.

"No! NO! *NO!*" Zoanna cried, panicking.

"Yes, YES, *YES!*" mocked Helbah's voice.

The crystal grew pink, then rosy. Belatedly Zoanna tried to put up some mindscreen to abate what was happening. She had become so enraged that she had neglected to ready her defense.

Suddenly there was a loud splintering sound. The crystal turned black and cindery. Then it imploded with a great whoosh of air. Zoanna, who had climbed to her feet intent on retaliation, was back on the floor. Bits of broken and powdered crystal covered her from head to foot.

"Damn you, Helbah! Damn you!" she cried. The gritty stuff was in her mouth and eyes. She had never felt more frustrated or angry.

"What's the matter, dear?" Rowforth had chosen this moment to come casually strolling into this wing of the palace. He appeared unperturbed by the disorder, and in fact he seemed hardly to have noticed it.

She glared at his pudgy form, seething. How dare he act as if nothing had happened!

"YOU!" she screamed at him. "It's your fault!"

"That it is, dearie," Rowforth said in Helbah's voice.

Zoanna stared at him, appalled.

"Goodbye, wicked woman," Helbah said. Then her projection faded, leaving only Rowforth, standing there with a bewildered expression.

Zoanna gazed for some time at the vacant spot where the crystal had been. This was once, she realized, that she had been outmagicked and bested. She had underestimated Helbah, and thought her dying and finished, and so ignored her. That had been a colossal mistake. The witch had survived and recovered, and gathered her magic for an effective retaliation.

Well, Zoanna could do that too! One more visit to Professor Devale, and she would be ready. But first she had to see what she could do to shore up the crumbling attack forces she had launched. Otherwise the war would be lost before she was ready to finish Helbah.

Needing something to occupy her mind, she rehearsed the brutal tongue-lashing she would give Rowforth the next time he gave her the slightest pretext.

St. Helens listened hard. The sounds that had been growing nearer were now receding like an outgoing wave. Why?

"I wonder, I wonder," he said aloud. There was nobody to hear him except an apparently deaf raouse that went right on nibbling his hunk of bread. Halfheartedly he threw his left boot at the rodent. The boot missed by the length of its tail. He drew off his right boot and threw that with as little effect. He went back to pacing his clean cell.

"Those boys, they said surrender, and I thought it was because they were losing. But now it sounds as if our side has been driven off. More witchcraft?"

A commotion at the dungeon door did not quite startle him. He stood back and waited as another prisoner was brought down the stairs. His cell door opened, and a big Kelvinian was pushed inside.

"Mor!" St. Helens exclaimed incredulously. "Mor Crumb!"

Mor rubbed at a spot of blood on his right cheek. He shook his head as though trying to clear it of cobwebs. "Yah, they got me, big mouth. Me and a hundred or so more they stuck in a stockade. Gods know how many died!"

St. Helens' mouth went slack. "You're blaming me? You're calling me big mouth?"

"That's what you are! You were all for this war. You could hardly wait to get your commission!"

"Mor, I never wanted to fight! But there's the prophecy, and the king—"

"The king you knew is not our beloved Rufurt! He's a nasty imitation from another world! You knew, and yet you approved everything he wanted!"

St. Helens felt his face flushing. At another time he would have exploded like his namesake, but this was a friend. Moreover he knew the man to be right. "We were all of us witched or magicked. It's Zoanna, I'm certain."

"Zoanna?" Mor repeated, with disbelief. "She's dead!"

"I wish she were. We all wish. But she must have escaped John's wrath. She must have gotten away and brought back King Rufurt's impostor from that frame Kelvin visited. It's the only answer."

Mor glared at him, then took his fists out of his ribs and crossed to the straw. He sank down, wearily, as though all his air was out.

"St. Helens, what are we going to do?"

"I fear we are going to lose."

"Can we lose? With the prophecy working?"

"I never believed as completely in that as you pointy-ears do," St. Helens said. "Kelvin isn't in this frame. He might not even be alive."

"That would cancel the prophecy, I suppose." Mor sighed noisily. Clearly he was as much at sea as was St. Helens.

"There may be a way," St. Helens said.

"What way? My men were running as if they'd never stop."

"The boy-kings. They're sort of friends of mine, maybe. Nice little chaps. They even cleaned this cell. They offered me their two countries' surrender."

"WHAT?"

"That's right. Only I'm not sure the witch would let them. Only she's a good witch, not the Zoanna kind."

"Witch's tits! You mean actually surrender?"

"That's what they said. They're afraid for themselves and for Helbah and I think for Helbah's cat. They're only kids, younger than Phillip."

"They're twenty-four," Mor said. "They age one year for each of our four. They only look like six years old."

"So it is said. But they want to surrender, that's the important thing. What should I tell them?"

Mor looked down at the clean floor and scratched a flea he'd brought. "You could tell them yes. Zoanna and her consort we can get rid of once the fighting's over."

"We hope. It was tough going before, wasn't it?"

"Yes. I'd hate to fight a revolution all over again, and this time without a roundear."

"I have round ears," St. Helens reminded him.

"Yah. Yah, you have. But St. Helens, you're no Kelvin."

"It don't look like he and his father and his half brother are coming back. Be nice if they did."

"I don't like to say it, but I figure their disappearing and the evil one appearing may not be coincidence."

They sat in gloomy silence for several long moments. Then Mor spoke his thought: "If they're winning, they won't surrender."

"Probably not. But they're just kids."

"The witch would prevent them."

"I don't know. She bosses them and spanks their butts, but maybe they have the governing decisions."

"You think?"

"Naw. I think they're only kids."

"Difficult situation."

"Yah." Halfheartedly he picked up a boot and threw it at the raouse, missing completely again. The rodent looked up in annoyance, grabbed another bite of bread, and streaked for its hole. St. Helens wished he could do that himself.

"All right. All right. If they'll give the surrender I'll take it. If it's legal it should end the fighting."

The raouse came back out of its hole.

Heln held her tummy and cocked her head to one side as she listened to a conversation in a distant part of the palace. Her hearing was getting more acute than it had been. And something else. Something she hardly dared think about.

"And you really want me, Your Majesty?"

"Of course. Who wouldn't? You're lovely."

"But the queen. Your Mrs., Your Majesty!"

"What Zoanna doesn't know won't hurt her, will it? Now just turn over and I'll unbutton—"

Heln pulled her round ears flat down over her head, pinning them and making them hurt. It didn't drown out the giggly scream of the wench. Yet she wasn't really offended by what she had heard. Once, she knew, she would have been.

Heh, heh, heh, like old times! Doing a maid while the queen naps. This one's a bit fat, but I'll bet she's got bounce!

Oh gods, I wanted to be a good girl! But he's the king! Who can deny the king? Besides, his wife's gone, poor man, and she was bad and threw him in the dungeon. Will he know I've done this before? Ah gods, he's biting me! What is he doing down there? OH! OH! OH! OH!

Heln knew what her thoughts should be, and these weren't her own. She screamed.

Jon woke up with a start.

"Jon! Jon! I'm hearing voices! And I'm thinking other people's thoughts! I know what other people are thinking!"

Poor girl, she's demented! "It's all right. It's all right, Heln. You've just had another bad dream."

"You hypocrite!" Heln exclaimed with sudden helpless fury. "You think I'm crazy!"

"Just a bad dream." *I'm going to have to talk to Dr. Sterk. She's not right! She's all mixed up, and paranoid! But can he help her? Can anyone help? Gods, I wish Kelvin were here!*

Knowing that all was really hopeless now, Heln permitted herself a scream that threatened to collapse the walls of the palace.

23 /

SCAREBIRD

THEY STOOD AT THE edge of the swamp watching the froogears come laden with copper stings. The Crumb look-alikes and their brethren watched with disbelief as the pile grew higher and higher before the transporter. Finally, late in the day, it was all there and the second stage of the operation was about to begin.

"Will this be enough?" Kelvin asked the big Loaf. "Is this enough copper to buy an army sufficient to overthrow your tyrant?"

"Son," Marvin said, very red in the face, "if we lose with this much copper, we deserve it! I didn't know there was so much anywhere. At home I know there's not. Can we start sending now?"

Kelvin nodded. The Loafers began working in a way that belied their name. Bundle by bundle they reduced the pile, tossing each into the transporter. There was a purple flash as the stings traveled alone to their destination. At the other end the men who had gone back were presumably unloading as fast as the stings arrived.

Suddenly Kelvin had an uncomfortable thought: Could they be certain that the people who were to get the copper were in fact getting it? The guardsmen might have come in force and overwhelmed those they had sent back. Consequently the tyrant king could have the copper, and would remain entrenched in a land that was identical to Kelvin's homeland but with a broader river and higher cliff.

Kelvin, you're worrying again!

I am, Mervania. I can't help myself.

Suppose you go back and I stay with you as I did before?

If the guardsmen are there they will kill me or capture me. You wouldn't be able to stop that.

Yes. Mervania managed to make the thought disinterested.

Or can you come to the rescue? If there was something he had overlooked . . .

No, I'm confined.

I mean, mind-stunning anyone who attacked me, as you did with my father when he—

Not at such distant range, Kelvin. I'm only in contact with you, there. It would be like you trying to score on an enemy soldier out of your sight beyond the horizon.

Kelvin thought that over. He didn't like it. *The squarears will help?*

They would not interfere with another world's affairs. That might annoy Mouvar.

But the copper's an interference!

Not to them. Copper's a mineral. Besides, there's no way they can use this transporter.

"No use—? Oh, I forgot! Wrong ears, right?

Your mental deficiencies never cease to amaze me.

Yes, really stupid, ain't he? the chimaera's other human head broke in.

Then I'm really on my own? Kelvin asked despairingly.

You're the hero, Kelvin.

Kelvin looked at his father and brother and his newfound friends. Was he just scaring himself needlessly? No, the chimaera had as much as assured him that his worries were justified.

"I'm going back," he said abruptly. He drew his sword and flexed his left gauntlet. "If all is not going as it should, I'll return." *I hope.*

"And if it is, you'll stay?" his father asked, catching on.

"Until you join me. The chimaera will warn you if I get there and the king's guardsmen are in control and I get caught and can't return." For Mervania could touch other minds more freely, here in her own frame.

"Why can't we all go?" Marvin asked. "One after the other?"

"Because one after the other we could all be killed or captured. The squarears can't help and neither can the chimaera. So I have to find out."

They were still discussing it as Kelvin forced his feet to carry him into the transporter. His heart skipped—

It seemed to be all right. The four Loafers he had seen into the transporter were there with a big pile of sting bundles behind them. All four of the men were covered with sweat from the work of lifting bundles the froogears had carried with ease. The labor of getting copper to this frame was more than any of them had anticipated.

Kelvin heaved a sigh of relief and exchanged greetings. Redleaf, Bilger, Hester, and of course Jillip. The boy, unlike the three grown men, was sweatless and resting. Why did they let him get away with such laziness?

"King's guardsmen been around?" Considering the mountain of sting bundles, the question seemed unnecessary.

"Uh-uh," Redleaf said. "Just us and the copper. Jillip's supposed to be watching. He's too weak for anything else."

"Says you!" Jillip said.

Redleaf grinned and bent to pick up the just-arrived bundle. It was almost like a farm operation John had once told Kelvin about. A machine transporting bundles of grain or grass that had then to be carried by hand. He doubted that the grain bundles had ever weighed as much as copper.

"When the royalists learn what we've got, they'll want it," Hester said. "We may need an army just to get this to where we can buy one."

"Blrood, you said." *Not Throod, as at home, or Shrood as in the silver-serpent place.*

"Yah." Hester grunted as he helped Redleaf swing the latest bundle onto the stack.

"I guess I'll check outside." *Jillip isn't doing it. He must think he's royalty. The kid's a slacker, all right.*

He stepped outside and discovered that it was now an overcast day. Dark clouds in the sky rather than the white pillows that had been there when he left. A day like this seemed made for worry.

To dispel worry he activated his belt. He lifted slowly, slowly by the rock face. Another ledge, narrower than the one he had left, was between him and the top of the bluff. He settled there.

The gauntlets began to tingle their warning.

Now hypersensitive to their messages, he looked quickly down at the great tree and the broad slash of river. He saw nothing unusual. Why then the warning?

Suddenly it was dark. Not the shadow of a thickening vapor, but a deep darkness that covered the cliffside and the ledge while leaving the more distant landscape unscathed.

He looked up, expecting to see a dense cloud or wind-tossed mass of dust. What he actually saw astonished and terrified him. It was a great dark something hung there on outstretched wings, supported by the cliff's up-draft. It blinked great yellow eyes and snapped an improbably large beak. It swooped overhead, darkening the landscape.

What by a god's god was that? It was the size of what his father had described as an airplane. But this was nothing to carry passengers! This—this dragon-sized *thing* was alive!

He stood there trying to shut his mouth. He shivered from head to toe. Birds he knew about, bats he had heard about, but he had never seen or heard of *that!*

The gauntlets had quit tingling as soon as the shadow had passed. They knew the monster hadn't seen him. What if it had? He shivered again, thinking about it. He searched the skies anxiously for some time, actually fearing to move from the cliff face. He looked down at where he had exited from the transporter chamber.

Jillip stood alone on the ledge. He was fumbling with his clothing, intent on relieving himself into the treetop. Fool kid! Didn't he realize that they'd be climbing down that? He could just as well have stood over against the cliff.

The gauntlets resumed tingling, and grew warm. In a heartbeat it got dark again. The great something slid silently down, swooping like an eagawk.

Jillip seemed to sense it. He turned. He screamed. He tried to jump back. But he was too late, too slow. Huge talons plucked him from the ledge.

Men appeared from the rock face. "Scarebird!" Hester exclaimed. "Everybody back!"

They quickly crowded back into the chamber. Everyone except Kelvin and—

"HELLLPPP MEEEEEE!"

Gods, he was still alive! Because the scarebird had gone after Jillip instead of Kelvin. He had to help the boy! He had at least to try.

The gauntlets were ahead of him, activating the belt. He shot up at an angle like a stone from his sister's sling. Before he could draw breath he was up against a leathery neck the size of a tree trunk, breathing the stench of reptile and more terrified than he could remember ever being before.

But the gauntlets, his best friends, knew what to do. They put the belt in neutral. He looked at the unmoving wings carrying him and the creature, at the great beak and strangely shaped, gigantic head. Was this a bird? Even apart from the sheer size of it, it seemed alien. He was here to help Jillip, but maybe it was he, Kelvin, who needed help.

"SCCCRRRREEEEEE!" The creature let out a great scream or cry. It turned its beak, blinked its eyes, stretched its neck out farther, and—

Suddenly there was a slipping sideways. Kelvin saw the cliffs and the rockspears thrusting up. He hadn't time to think of Jillip or anything else.

He was tumbling, over and over and over. Quickly he slapped the control. The rocks loomed closer, and he hastily adjusted his course. Now he was flying just above the treetops.

SNAP! SNAP! SNAP!

Kelvin winced in pain and accelerated with a push of the lever. He leaped ahead and was immediately out of the thing's reach. Looking back he saw a great head with a pointed top, dark yellow eyes the size of ponds, and a pointed, saw-toothed bill with something flapping from its hooked tip.

His back smarted. That was where the tip of the bill had scraped. The brown material in the beak was the exact center section of his best brownberry shirt. Kelvin considered that he now wore two arm coverings and that the fastenings in front had popped off as the flying thing's beak ripped away the back.

"SCCCRRRREEEE!"

"HELLLLLLPPPP!"

Oh shut up! he wanted to say, but didn't. There was no help for Jillip. Unless, unless—

Kelvin climbed to a higher altitude, leaving the monster's air current. He circled above it, keeping the distance. *Even when I fought dragons and serpents I had at least a spear!* No spear now, and no way of getting one. Besides, if he could somehow kill this—this scarebird—Jillip would surely be killed in the fall. That might be inevitable anyway, but Kelvin didn't want to hasten it.

He shrugged out of the remains of his shirt and let the wind take away the ragged strips. *Poor Heln, she sewed on that for a week.* With normal use such a garment would last for years. There was a brownberry farm not far from the Hackleberry residence; he remembered that a little girl lived there. What was her name? Easter. Not that that related to him in any way, other than as a source for the material for another shirt. He hated to think of how upset gentle Heln would be with him when she learned about the shirt. Her life must be pretty quiet now, while she waited on the arrival of the baby.

Now shirtless, he must resemble those bigger-than-life cinema heroes his father had once described. Except that his chest was skinny and not bronzed and muscled the way a fictional hero's would have been. Had it been his place to pick a hero, Kelvin would have been at the bottom of the list!

He eased the speed of his flying and fell back, keeping the scarebird in sight. Oh, if it would only land! Then he might be able to swoop in and rescue Jillip. But it showed no sign of doing so.

Below, the terrain looked less and less like that of home. It was rougher and becoming more so. It was hilly, irregular, and forested, a lot like the way the fabled kingdoms of Ophal and Rotternik were said to be. Faint hope for any rescue here!

A tang filled his nose, erasing the memory of the reptile smell. Salt. The ocean was nearby, just as it would be at home in this region. Maybe that was good news, and maybe not.

He flew on, marveling at how fast they were traveling. The wind, that was what was making the scarebird soar and sail so effortlessly and so fast. The ocean updrafts, the air currents like sea currents, carrying this great, great winged ship. Sky ship—his father had used that term once in telling a story. That was what the scarebird was, only living. A living sky ship.

Now he saw the ocean, and still the great black kite sailed on. An estuary with great mountains of foam and towering rocks. Up the estuary, following the wild, great river that broadened until it was almost as wide as a sea itself. Then trees, gigantic trees! Trees such as Kelvin at his most imaginative had never dreamed of. The tree they had climbed was big, but compared to these it was scarcely a sapling. These were growing up from the water, reaching to the sky, and into the sky, each huger than its neighbors.

And circling, dipping in and out of enormous branches, were dozens of scarebirds! There was a whole colony of them here!

Poor Jillip! The kid's done! There's no rescue from this. I can't—

But somehow he couldn't leave. He circled in the air, like the scarebirds themselves, waiting, watching for the monster carrying Jillip to land. He saw that there were many of the monsters hanging upside down in the trees. Like bats, but big. Bigger than any bats or birds imaginable.

The scarebird flew to the top of a great tree. There, deep in the branches and foliage was a monstrous nest. Beaks the length of swords reached up from the nest, opening wide, waiting. *Mama's coming. Mama's coming with your dinner.*

"KEL . . . VIN! SAVE ME!"

So Jillip was still conscious, and in good voice. That suggested that he had not been seriously hurt, yet. He was looking back, and had spied Kelvin, urging him to do the impossible. Poor kid!

Kelvin accelerated, flew past the nest, curved, and came in low above the trees and just below some clouds. That gave him some cover. He saw ruddy throats, open. Those young were hungry!

The chimaera was telepathic. Could this other monster also communicate mentally? It seemed unlikely, but maybe worth a try. It wasn't as if he had a wide range of promising options. *BIRD! Put down that man! Put him down unharmed!*

"SCRRRREEEEE!"

There was no indication that the scarebird knew his thoughts, or cared if it did. In its talons Jillip was now limp, having fainted or been killed. Those talons could have squeezed him lifeless at any time, unless the monster wanted to feed its nestlings live and squirming food. Kelvin hoped it was death, because to be alive when those ravenous chicks fed—he couldn't bear that thought!

"SCCCRRRREEEE!"

SNAP! SNAP! SNAP! The little rascals were impatient. Would one skinny boy divide enough?

"Bird! Bird!" he called, feeling stupid. "I want to talk! As one rational creature to another!"

Did the monster hesitate? It was probably just deciding how to portion out the morsel. He doubted that the thing could talk. His father had told him of a talking bird in his frame of Earth called a polly, so maybe some did talk, however. What else did he have to try?

Jillip's head lifted. His arms and legs straightened. So he had only been unconscious, not injured. Now the very worst was incipient, and Kelvin saw no good way out.

"SCRRRREEEE! SCRRRREEEE!"

"You already said that," Kelvin muttered with gallows humor. He nudged the acceleration lever and got far closer than he wanted. It wouldn't help Jillip if Kelvin also became a meal for the chicks!

The bird spied him. The saw-toothed beak was more formidable than any sword. It darted at him now, the bird intent on grabbing him. It seemed to be well aware of the value of doubling its investment.

The gauntlets jerked him down. He ducked his head, snapped his feet together, and dived under the incoming head. Below the bird, Jillip's drained face looked at him in startled comprehension as he grabbed a leg the size of a normal tree trunk.

"Kelvin! KELVIN!"

"Shut up!" he said. It was a terrible thing to say to a desperate boy on the edge of losing his life, but necessary. He needed a moment to think, if the confounded bird gave him a chance.

As he might have expected, the bird turned, swooped, slipped, and dived. They were still well up in the air. Kelvin's position changed as quickly and bewilderingly as it might in a whirlwind. Sometimes he was right side up, sometimes upside down. The belt kept him flattened hard against the scaly surface with more than human strength.

He knew the bird would soon tire of this, and soar up and then in to the nest. He saw water below, and Jillip almost skimming it. Then they were rising again, rising with the air current. Now it would be climb, climb, circle, circle, circle, and in for a landing. What had he gained? He remained as clumsy a hero as ever.

As the bird straightened in flight he let go of its leg, and made a grab for the talons. He got hold, nearly upside down, and tried to will his gauntlets to pull up the great, powerful toes. The gauntlets tried; he felt his shoulders and arms take up the strain. But it was not enough. He tried kicking himself back from the foot with all his strength, but still the talon would not budge from the boy.

"Save yourself, Kelvin!" Jillip gasped. "My life is finished. My life's not worth your life!"

Sensible talk, but unfortunately late. Suddenly they were bouncing. Up and down, up and down. Branches the girth of a man's legs were slapping on either side of his face. They had come to a landing at last, on the rim of the scarebird's nest.

"CREEEE! EEEEEE! EEEE!" SNAP, SNAP, SNAP!

The chicks were eager for dinner. Their hungry cries were deafening. In a moment they would have their desire.

Kelvin slapped a branch out of his face and drew his sword.

A great beaked head with huge yellow eyes was looking at him under the gray belly. It was mama's beak and mama's eyes. She would snatch him from her foot like a scared rodent, and some lucky chick would be the recipient. As for Jillip, who was costing Kelvin his life—

"NO!" Kelvin shouted, and jabbed his sword into the fleshy part of her left foot.

The bird's head shot back out of sight, her talons opened suddenly, and she let out a screech which made the prior ones seem faint. Kelvin wasn't waiting, nor were his gauntlets. With one clumsy lunge he grabbed Jillip and tumbled with him into space.

Wind whistled by their ears and brush slapped by their faces. Bits of bone and rotting animal carcasses were strewn on branches they passed. Somehow the gauntlets managed to hold the boy, yet also activate the belt. Upside down scarebirds hung from branches bigger than normal tree trunks. He glimpsed these briefly, peripherally, hoping they got even lesser glimpses of him, and then he was flying.

Below them were hard rocks in deep water. Past them, so close she almost touched, passed the angrily screaming big mama.

Kelvin adjusted their acceleration as the bird caught the air again, ending her dive. They were soon speeding up the river, back the way they had come. When he knew the bird was far outdistanced, he took a more comfortable grip on Jillip, who was now returning again to consciousness. He had fainted somewhere during that mind-numbing scream, which was perhaps just as well.

"Jillip, your leader assured me that there were no dragons, no giant silver serpents, no magic in this frame! What by all the gods is that creature back there?"

"Scarebird," Jillip said, puzzled. "Don't you have scarebirds in your frame?"

"Never heard of them! Never want to see one of them again!"

"Must be a placid existence you have," the boy remarked.

24 /

ARMY

THE JOURNEY TO BLROOD was surprisingly uneventful. For a full day Kelvin labored with the belt transporting the copper from atop the cliff to the ground. Constantly he broke off in his labors to reconnaissance for guardsmen or scarebirds. The guardsmen never came, nor did the wings of the great bird again darken the cliff.

Getting packhorses for the copper proved to be easy. The Loafers knew the farmers they could count on, most of whom had suffered at the hands of guardsmen. Help for them now was not in short supply.

Disguised as merchants, they made their journey and met the Blrood soldiers who had been dispatched to see them on their way. The territory, the fruit they ate along the way, even the people they saw all seemed a rerun. Once a large violet and light-rose bird flew over calling from a long beak "Pry-Mary! Pry-Mary!"

"Primary bird!" Kelvin guessed. He was certain it couldn't be the purgatory bird, though except for plumage they did seem much the same.

"Political bird," Hester explained. "Also termed beginning bird."

Kelvin nodded and let his eyes wander on to the expected monument. The cairn appeared almost identical to those he had seen on similar missions in two related frames. About the only difference was the inscription which here dedicated the cairn to the memory of Blrood's soldiers, rather than Shrood's or Throod's. Again it seemed they had perished in a two-hundred-year-old war, but not against Hud or Rud. Though he had forgotten to inquire, the kingdom he was now attempting to free was the kingdom of Fud.

"Recruitment House!" Bilger called. This time the fruit juice dripping from the revolutionary's mouth was definitely red rather than orange or yellow. More packhorses more heavily laden, more local armed men accompanying them.

This time it was not a Captain MacKay with pointed ears or a Captain

McFay with round, but a Commander Mac. The commander had round ears as did the last such individual, and his facial and body conformations had similar outlines. But in Throod the big gray-haired, gray-eyed man had lost an arm. His equivalent in Shrood had been slightly balding, had had two good arms and one peg leg. Commander Mac had all his hair but was missing half his teeth, a fact that became evident as soon as he spoke. He had all his extremities, but his back was bent more than the others and his right shoulder sloped. In addition to all the other differences, Mac wore a patch over his left eye.

The commander held out his hand. Talk and drinking and card playing ceased. Veterans and recruits alike turned their attentions. "Marvin Loaf. You've got the copper?"

"Some. More back in Fud. Safe, I hope."

Mac and two veterans went out and checked the packs. The stings had worn through their coverings in places and the copper was drawing attention from those who dared not touch. A path cleared for the commander. He cut open a couple of bundles, scratched the copper with a knife, smiled, and felt the other bundles with his hands.

"With what you have here you can buy our finest and best fighting men, all equipment, horses, and catapults. Gods, I didn't know there was that much copper! You've got your army."

"Actually there is a catch to our generosity," John said quickly.

They all looked at him inquiringly. Particularly Marvin Loaf.

"Let's go back in and discuss it," Commander Mac suggested.

They did. On the way in John explained: "The catch is that when all of this is over my boys and I leave this frame forever. We're here by mistake. Marvin's help makes us indebted to him, and we pay our debts. Besides, we had much the same situation back home until we did what Marvin's doing. Only our land is called Rud and its tyrant was a woman."

"Either sex, an army's an investment!" Mac said. "A tyrant is a tyrant is a tyrant until it's dead."

"I like that," Marvin Loaf said.

They found a table, mugs of bleer, and soon had a large assemblage of onlookers. As in similar situations two times before in two different frames, Kelvin was pressed to talk. He did so now with pleasure. But long before he had recited their adventures skepticism reared its monster head.

"Do you really expect," one grizzled oldster demanded, "that we believe that? Dragons are impossible enough, but dragons with golden scales?"

Annoyed, Kelvin broke off his narrative to explain. "They swallow golden nuggets from the streams. Since dragons live until they are slain and many have lived for centuries and possibly for thousands of years, the gold migrates to the scales."

A young man there for recruitment shook his head, studying Kelvin with a skeptical expression. "I've heard of migrating metals in the bodies and shells of shellfish. That's science. But dragons aren't. Dragons are myth."

"Different worlds, different rules," John broke in. "Go on, Kelvin."

He wanted to, but to his astonishment he was losing his audience. None of these tough fighting men wanted to believe this junk. He was hardly into his tale of how they'd had a people's revolution in Rud and the prophecy had made him important, particularly after the dragons.

"And these posters you put up, they really did get you men?"

Kelvin stared at the commander with disbelief. He sounded as skeptical as the recruit.

"Untrained ones. Volunteers. Farmers and others who had had enough of oppression."

"Go on."

He did, but it wasn't fun. Everything he said convinced them that he lied. The painful thing was that lying was one skill he had never cultivated, and one talent that he lacked. He could no more have exaggerated his own part than Jon's.

"That's blood transfusion!" the young warrior snapped. Kelvin had been giving a graphic description of what befell Jon and himself at the hands of the sorcerer.

"Uh, if you say so. Now the dwarf Queeto was catching her blood, and—"

"Science."

"Magic where I come from. Zatanas was using sympathetic magic, the only magic he was skilled in. Rather than using a doll with my fingernail parings or hairs in it, he used my sister. Same blood, so as she weakened, I weakened."

"That's bunk! I don't believe that one."

Kelvin felt exasperated. How could he get through to this clod?

"You have scarebirds here. I'd say they are sometimes as big as dragons, and fully as dangerous."

"Scarebirds are natural! They have been a part of the natural world since before men! What you're talking about is unnatural."

"Here, maybe. Not at home. At home scarebirds would be unnatural." He did not mention the chimaera; he saw no need to stretch their incredulity that far.

"I can vouch for everything he says," Kian offered. "You see, Zatanas was my grandpa, and Zoanna my mother."

There was instant silence. Someone slurped bleer. Then a big veteran with a craggy face and bulging muscles laughed. In a moment all the Blroodians were laughing. Kian's apparently ridiculous statement had convinced them that it was all a joke.

Kelvin felt alarm at the look on his brother's face. In a moment, if he did not act, Kian would. That would mean trouble—big trouble—and he had

had more than enough of that! Kian might have better self-control than his father-in-law, but barely.

Though it pained him to do it, he started to get up. If he challenged the big man right there and the gauntlets helped him in the fight, that would at least end the laughter.

His father came to their rescue. "It's something to laugh at here," he said calmly, addressing the bleer, "but back then it wasn't. Remember I originated in a world where it would all have sounded ridiculous. We didn't believe in magic there. But let me tell you what we did believe in: we believed in the scarebird."

Silence. Every eye turned to John, diverted from the promise of immediate action.

"Father," Kelvin broke in, "you never said you had scarebirds!" Immediately he wished he had kept his mouth shut. Now everyone was looking at him.

"I didn't mean they were there when I left! But Earth had them before I was born. Way, way back in my planet's history. They were around before any humans were. Every now and then some of their bones were found, sometimes a complete skeleton. They weren't as big as the ones here, but they were similar. The scientists in my time called them pterodactyls. They existed, let's see, approximately one hundred and twenty million of our years before my birth."

"How did you know that, Father?" Kelvin had to ask. When his father started talking about Earth stuff Kelvin almost reverted to child stage. He'd been a question box, his father had said, and Kelvin wasn't certain he'd changed.

"Well, Kelvin, it wasn't magic. My people mostly didn't believe in magic, you see, and certainly the scientists didn't. There were scientific ways of determining the ages of bones and other things. The pterodactyls, what you call the scarebirds, flew Earth's skies long, long before there were men, but their bones proved their existence."

"No humans to see them at all, Father?"

"Not on Earth. In other frames, perhaps. Earth didn't have humans and pterodactyls living at the same time. In other existences, such as this one— yes. These are a lot larger than those we had, however; they've had more time to evolve."

The faces had all grown serious. Now Marvin, looking so much as Morton Crumb would have looked back home, spoke:

"I don't know about what these fellows say, but there are mighty strange things in other frames. Tell them, Hester. Tell them what we saw."

Lester's look-alike said: "Short fellows made all of squares. Crystals that they saw things in—things at a great distance. Some big creature we don't even have legends about that ingests copper and produces the copper stings we brought. People that seem descended from froogs, with the ear patches of froogs and a froog's habits."

"All that's true," Marvin said. "We were all of us there. So do you want our copper or don't you?"

Commander Mac swallowed. "Those stings were produced by some monster? Grown on it?"

"You calling us liars?" There was danger in the big man's voice, as though he would risk his beloved revolution on it.

Commander Mac took a swig of bleer, lifted his eyepatch, and rubbed a nasty scar where an eye had been. He contemplated, as a soldier had to, then spoke in a very reasonable voice. "I believe copper's copper." He looked around at his friends and associates. No-nonsense types, all of them more concerned with their skills and their work of killing than with the wild fantasies of others.

"Maybe that's all we need to know," the grizzled old fellow said. "The rest, that's none of our concern. Copper, after all, is copper."

Having pronounced a verdict, the unofficial judge retreated to a distant chair. Others joined him, and someone dealt cards. Left was only the young mercenary.

"Well, I think we really need to proceed on that assumption," said Commander Mac.

Kelvin looked at his father and brother and felt his own mouth gaping. It was all over then—all his story telling. It didn't seem to him to be right.

"Yes, I quite agree," Marvin said. "Why don't you visitors go out and see the Flaw. Quite a sight! You've probably never heard of it."

They had of course heard of it, but didn't say so. "Come along," John Knight said. So they trooped out together, one collection of male kin. Left behind were the locals, who had an important matter pertaining to the revolution to decide.

"Why, Father?" Kelvin wanted to know. "Why leave, when there's so much that's so fascinating to tell?"

John checked to make certain no one else was following. "We have to give them a chance to hash things out alone. As for their incredulity—well, people were that way on Earth, too, Kelvin. Not all folk, but some. If they don't want to believe, they don't want to know. Something like magic."

Kelvin wondered, and thought he understood. His father hadn't wanted to believe in magic for the longest time. He had denied that there was magic until it was impossible to doubt it anymore. He still tended to think in a nonmagical way.

"I want to see that Flaw, boys," John said. "You know I've heard about it, and I've been through it, but I've never actually seen it. Not when I had my wits with me."

Kelvin remembered the first time he had seen the Flaw. That had been at the beginning of his warring experience. He and the Crumbs had been buying an army to use against Kian's evil mom. Jon had tried to shoot a star with her sling, and she had been frustrated. Like people who refused to believe in magic even while experiencing it, Jon hadn't believed in the inefficiency of her sling or the distance of stars.

When they reached the wooden barrier it looked just the same as it had in the other two frames, except that some of the graffiti were different. His father stood, openmouthed, staring through the observation hole and into the velvety-black, star-filled depths.

"It's—it's the womb of creation!" His voice carried awe. "Gods, it's a crack through Earth, Earth's worlds! An opening through all worlds, all possible worlds, all alternatives!"

"You had it on Earth, Father?"

"I . . . don't know. I don't think we did. But maybe another part? Maybe in the Arctic—or maybe another time."

The afternoon passed while John gradually built acceptance for something he hadn't quite believed in. Another day passed while a message was sent to the Fud palace. Another day drinking bleer, playing cards, and waiting for an unanticipated reply to the ultimatum. Still another day while Kelvin worried. Then finally they set out.

At the border a delegation of uniformed guardsmen met them with the Fud flag and a surrender flag. An enormous cheer went up and down the ranks of mercenaries, though many might have experienced regrets. An adventure too soon over. A war not fought. Bonus pay but not fighting pay. No spoils, no captive wenches. Back home to the Recruitment House to wait unemployed for possibly many more months.

"And so," the guardsman spokesman was saying, "His Majesty surrenders unconditionally to overwhelming numbers. In anticipation of a change in government he has abdicated his throne."

Amazing! Evidently the despot of this frame was relatively cowardly. They would have to make sure he didn't have some treachery in store.

"Well, now that that little matter is settled—" Kian said, looking happy.

Kelvin knew that this entire adventure had been just a little matter delaying a wedding, in Kian's view. Well, maybe so.

25 /

TRUE LOVE RUNNETH

HEETO THE DWARF MET them first. They had been traveling their weary way from the transporter by foot, Kelvin now and then soaring overhead to see if he could spot someone. They bypassed Serpent's Valley, not wanting to get involved with the flopears and their reptile ancestors this trip. The gauntlets had been very faintly tingling, not really signaling danger but suggesting that he should move right along to avoid it. In fact, they had been tingling that way for the past day or so, as if they, too, wanted to get this matter over and done with. Finally when their party was on a good road with maybe half a day's hiking ahead, there was the dwarf.

"Heeto! What are you doing here?" Kelvin asked, dropping down out of the sky and landing right in front of him. Was this another wrong frame? He had set the indicator carefully, but there had been so many nasty surprises! Would they never get back to the frame of good Queen Zanaan and lovely good girl Lonny Burk?

The dwarf jumped, startled, then stared at Kelvin incredulously. "You can *fly!*"

"Yes, I can fly, but only with this belt. It's nothing to get worried about. I'm Kelvin, the same Kelvin whose life you saved."

"You saved us all," Heeto said. "From an evil king and his attempted alliance with flopears. Now, thanks to you, we live in a decent kingdom."

"My father and brother and I have come back. But we won't all stay. Kian wants badly to see his Lonny."

"Yes, Lonny Burk. She is to marry Jac."

"WHAT?" Kelvin felt nearly as devastated as he knew Kian would be. To have gone through so much and to have got here finally at long last and to find her marrying Jac! Not that Jac wasn't a fine fellow, a good skin-thief as his fellows had proclaimed, and a capable revolutionary when helped as required. No, Jac was fine, *but not marrying Lonny!*

"Your brother has returned to her?"

"Yes."

"She did not think he would, ever."

Kelvin looked at the sky. It was early morning now; only a short time since they had risen. But how long had they actually been gone from this reality? He could feel the sun warming his skin, and he knew that this reality felt like the only one, and certainly it was now for him. But they had been weeks away by their reckoning. Suppose time here was different, and instead of weeks it had been months, possibly even years?

"She missed your brother, but she thought him gone," the dwarf explained. "She faced the prospect of life as an old maid. Jac believed this too, and asked her to marry him."

"Right, I understand." *I just hope Kian does.*

"Jac would not have asked if he had known Kian would be back. Jac is an honorable man."

"He is." *Here,* he thought. *In other frames he's a villain. But here, yes, as honorable a person as ever comes.*

"You will attend the wedding? You and your brother and father?"

"It's today?"

"Yes. The Grand Ballroom is in the official Hud palace. The ceremony is to take place at noon."

"We'll be there," Kelvin said, knowing now that they were in the right frame and much nearer the palace than he had thought. Now he understood the quiet urgency of the gauntlets: it wasn't a physical danger, but an emotional one. They must have known what was about to happen here, and urged him to get here before it was too late. "Where's your horse?"

"Being shod," the dwarf replied. "I was going to get a silver ring."

"Silver ring? Why?"

"For the wedding. For Jac to slip on his bride's finger."

Kelvin felt stunned. But then he remembered his father telling him of a similar custom on Earth. When his mother and father had wed they had simply declared before witnesses that they were married, and after that they were. People wishing to end a marriage divorced in similar fashion.

"May I come with you?"

"Of course. Can you fly with two?"

"You want to fly? Yes, my belt should support your weight too. But you will have to hold on tightly, because—"

"Don't worry! I don't know how to fly, but I know what a fall can do!"

Thus it was that Kelvin went with the dwarf to the jeweler. The jeweler was an elderly, wizened man who seemingly dwelt in his shop. In addition to accessories to his daily life, there was a fine display of clocks, rings, silver plate, and assorted jewelry. He reached under a counter to a secret place and brought out a polished, highly decorated silver band.

Heeto took the ring and examined it. He held it up for inspection in the morning sunbeam coming through the shop's window, then handed it to Kelvin.

Kelvin looked at the workmanship. Flopear without a doubt. In the narrow silver band, just the right size for Lonny's finger, were incised tiny figures. Held to the light the figures seemed to be those of children, and as Kelvin squinted it seemed that the children were running and tossing a ball.

"I never get over what the flopears can do with silver," the oldster wheezed, leaning over the counter. "Those old folk, strolling hand in hand through flowers. How do they do that?"

"Magic," Kelvin answered, remembering his problem with the skeptical men of the other frame who refused to believe in magic. He did not tell the old man that his eyes saw something entirely different. That artistry was twice as special as it seemed! The old man needed all the comforting illusions he could get. Did the picture change for every viewer? Kelvin had more than a suspicion that it did, and that each would find pleasure in what he or she saw. Heeto did not have to worry whether Lonny would like the ring; it would make her like it!

They left the shop, Heeto carefully putting the ring in a small bag he hung over his shoulder. As they emerged into the bright glare of early day Kelvin had an idea. It was a foolish one, but maybe he was ready to be foolish for a change.

"Heeto, would you like to fly yourself?"

"With you hanging on to me, Kelvin? I don't think that would work very well."

"Well, by yourself, then, if you don't go far or fast. Just to feel what it's like." The gauntlets gave no warning, so this seemed safe.

The dwarf's eyes lighted. "Not far or fast!" he agreed.

So Kelvin squatted and put the belt on Heeto and instructed him in the handling of the lever. When he was certain Heeto understood, he stood back and let the dwarf try it.

Heeto nudged the lever ever so gently. Suddenly he shot up high. "Slow!" Kelvin cried, alarmed.

"I did it slow!" Heeto cried.

"Then even slower on the reverse!"

The dwarf's progress slowed, then he hovered, and finally he came slowly down. "I know what happened," he said, breathless. "I was too light for it."

That made sense. Kelvin caught him as he came within range, so that there could be no further misjudgment. They both agreed that they had had enough experimentation. Yet despite his scare, Heeto was flushed and happy. He had had an experience he would never forget. So it had been the right thing to do, risk and all.

Kelvin donned the belt again. Then he held Heeto, and they flew at a comfortable walking speed the short distance down the road to where John and Kian Knight were still plodding.

"Kelvin, what's that you've got?" Kian demanded.

"Come see for yourself," he replied as he landed.

Kian came forward, squinting his eyes against the far too bright sunlight. He paused, and his eyes widened. He held out his arms. "Heeto! Heeto, my friend! What are you doing here?"

"I was on a mission," Heeto explained, and rushed forward on short little legs that nevertheless were quite swift. He grabbed Kian around the waist as a child might. Kian hugged the dwarf with just as much affection.

Kelvin stood back, eying them and his father speculatively. Kian was the happiest he had ever seen him, so how would he react to the news Heeto brought?

"Lonny—she's all right?" Kian wondered.

"She's . . . in health," Heeto said.

"But—?" Kian obviously sensed something.

"She thought you were never coming back. She thought you didn't want her."

"I want her! Gods, I want her!"

"She's marrying Jac."

Kian clutched his heart region. His face slackened. His mouth gaped. It was exactly as though he had received a sword thrust.

Kelvin watched his brother settle down into the dust of the road, place his head in his hands, and shake. He wasn't crying, exactly, but his reactions were those of a man on the verge of dying. Kelvin knew he had to do something for his brother.

"The wedding's today, Kian. At noon. We have time to get there. My gauntlets have been tingling; they know it's not too late."

Kian looked up, brightening. "Yes, yes! We must go! We must be there!"

"Kian," said their father, "Jac was good to us, and saved all our lives more than once. Hers too. If they want each other, you won't interfere?"

"No, Father," Kian said bravely. "No, of course not."

But Kelvin wondered. His brother, unlike himself, had been brought up and spoiled rotten by a ruthless and evil woman. Kelvin had seen far more of his father and himself in Kian than Zoanna and her evil father Zatanas, yet there was a heritage. When Kian was frustrated beyond sanity, would his mother's side come out? Would he pull his sword against Jac? That, Kelvin decided, must not happen.

"The bride and groom won't arrive until the wedding," Heeto said. "You can take time to clean up from your travels, and Queen Zanaan will get you better attire. I see, Kelvin, that you have lost your shirt."

"Zanaan, she's still queen?" John Knight asked.

"Yes, still queen. The people all love her."

"The people have great sense." John Knight spoke with conviction, as though this were a sentiment he had long needed to express.

"What of Rowforth, her husband?" Kelvin asked.

"Rowforth hasn't been found," Heeto said. "He managed to get a knife into Sergeant Broughtmar, his former lackey. We found the sergeant dying on the roof. The king somehow got away, and hasn't been seen since."

"He's still alive, then?" This was bad news!

"Until he's caught. Everyone wants him taken alive so he can be publicly executed."

"The poor queen," Kelvin said.

"No, no. Not poor queen at all," Heeto protested. "She was a prisoner, a hostage to him. She suffered more than any of us. If she could have, she would have divorced him long ago."

"Yes, I suppose that's true." Kelvin looked at his father's face and thought he saw something there that he did not entirely like. He remembered how evil Zoanna had bewitched him, using her magic to keep him enthralled so that she was able to have a child by him. Was it possible that there had been more to it than that? Perhaps a really good copy of Queen Zoanna without her evil ways was what his father really wanted, and certainly Zanaan was that. Certainly she was beautiful. But did he want his father with that woman? Childhood memories of seeing John so content with his own mother Charlain cried a loud if irrational protest.

His father, for his part, had a look of positive eagerness on his face.

They were almost to the gates, the same gates that had once gone down to permit a charge of flopears on war-horses directed against the Freedom Fighters' troops. Kelvin was recalling that war in all its hideousness and the glory of their triumph, as they approached.

Suddenly a horseman wearing a worn uniform of the Freedom Fighters clattered around the corner. "They got him! They got the king!"

"Alive? Alive?" someone shouted.

"Alive! They found him hiding out near serpent territory! Just barely surviving! They're bringing him now!"

Kelvin and his party waited. Kian and John, a bit more anxious to enter the palace than Kelvin was, were partway up the walk. Kelvin turned back to the street.

Soon horsemen came trundling a cart. Looking out of a cage on the cart, ragged, dirty, sunken-eyed, big nose sunburned and peeled, was the figure of the king. What a relief to have captured him!

But as the cart drew even with him, the face behind the bars spotted them, and the wretched creature called out: "Kelvin! John! Kian! Thank the gods!"

Kelvin blinked. The supposed King Rowforth had filthy, round ears. But if this was not Rowforth—if the ears were not the positive identification they seemed—then it had to be good King Rufurt of his homeland!

Unless the evil king was trying to fool him. Rowforth was capable of anything, to save his evil hide.

"John, remember those days in the royal dungeon? You and I together— remember?"

The cart trundled past. The shouts of angry, enraged, and rejoicing people who had served under the Rowforth yoke followed and drowned out whatever else the prisoner was saying. The face looked back at them, pitifully, and Kelvin wondered. Could it be, was it possible that this was King Rufurt?

He hurried to catch up. "Father, do you think—?"

But his father was looking eagerly toward the palace. Kelvin wasn't sure that he had ever heard the prisoner. He wasn't quite certain he had heard correctly himself.

Was it King Rufurt? Impossible, but also impossible to ignore. Rufurt was pointeared, and so could not use the transporter. But that reference to the dungeon—had Rowforth known about that? How could he be sure?

Things moved so rapidly the rest of the morning that Kelvin hardly thought again about the man in the cage. All he could think about as they entered the great ballroom at noon was his brother and what his brother's reactions to immediate events might be. They had been briefed about how the bride and groom would enter by opposite doors, and how the queen herself would conduct a little ceremony. At the end of some ritualized questioning Jac was to slip the ring on Lonny's finger and the queen would pronounce them wed. Was it Kelvin's imagination, or did she sound a little sad when she explained about her part in it? Was he missing something?

All three of them—Kelvin, Kian, and John—were there to witness but not to make their presence known to others until the ceremony's end. All were dressed in stiff, heavily laced clothing that Kelvin, for his part, would be only too happy to shed. Later they would get new traveling clothes, the queen had promised. She was solicitous and helpful in forming their plans. Kelvin had to hope that his father was not going to stay here and marry her, though he knew this was a bad attitude on his part. John's marriage to Kelvin's mother had been sundered long ago, and Hal Hackleberry was a good man. The past was over and done with.

Someone was playing music. It sounded loud and had the effect of drowning thought. A beautiful woman sat at a piangan and stroked its red and yellow keys. The music changed as soon as everyone was in place, and from an oceanic swelling of sound it went to triumphant march. It was time for the bride and groom to enter by the opposite doors and stand before the queen.

The facing doors opened. Kelvin immediately focused all his attention on his brother's face. Kian did not look angry or enraged, he looked sad, even heartbroken. It was pitiful to see anyone, especially a brother, in such condition.

Lonny and Jac came forward until they met, joined hands, and turned to face the queen. Their audience had a side view of bride and groom while bride and groom were unable to see their unanticipated guests from another frame. No matter, as local custom decreed, bride and groom simply gazed each into the other's face.

Jac, dressed up and clean, was handsome despite his scar, and older than Kelvin had realized, really of John's generation. He looked somehow grim rather than happy, though that was probably because of the gravity of the occasion. Kelvin remembered how he had suffered buttersects in the stomach when he married Heln, even though it was exactly what he wanted to do.

Lonny was beautiful, with her hair garlanded with flowers and her bridal outfit enhancing a body that had at the worst of times been quite attractive. She too was unsmiling, perhaps maintaining her composure by sheer willpower, for she was normally a cheerful girl. Kelvin remembered that she had at one time used the gauntlets, and evidently gotten along with them well. The gauntlets served whoever wore them, but he liked to think that they liked some wearers better than others.

"Lonny Burk," the queen intoned, as serious as the two of them, "do you wish to marry Jac Smite, also known as Smoothy Jac, also known as Savior of our Land?"

"I do," Lonny murmured faintly.

"And you, Jac Smite, also known as Smoothy Jac and Savior of our Land, do you wish to marry Lonny Burk?"

Jac seemed to hesitate. His eyes darted in the direction of the properly attired roughnecks who had been with him in a skin-stealing operation and then a revolution. Possibly, though not certainly, he was having second thoughts. He looked at the queen as if appealing for some recourse, but found none.

"I do," Jac said at last, clearly and unmistakably.

Kelvin's pity for his brother intensified. It seemed that the girl he loved really did mean to marry his friend. Had it been a mistake to keep quiet? Yet what kind of a situation would it have made, if Kian had dashed up and told her of his presence and his love just before she was to be married to another man?

But the ceremony was not finished. The queen now addressed the guests, asking simply, "Is there anyone here who objects?"

Kelvin looked at his brother, hoping he would speak. He had been afraid Kian would lose control, but now was sorry he hadn't. Lonny just didn't look that eager for the union. Neither, surprisingly, did Jac. Was it just a marriage of convenience? In that case—

The queen turned back to the couple. "Since there are no objections, I therefore declare—"

The gauntlets gave Kelvin a sharp jolt. "Wait!" It was out of his mouth before he realized it.

The queen seemed almost relieved for the distraction. "You? You object, Kelvin Knight Hackleberry. Why?"

Kelvin hesitated. The gauntlets jolted him again. "My brother wants to wed her!" he blurted. He was conscious of a roomful of eyes orienting on him. "He's come back from his native frame for that purpose. We were delayed, we couldn't help it, but all the time he intended—" He stalled.

There were murmurings and whispers and some outright exclamations. But it wasn't Kelvin's words that raised the most excitement, it was Lonny Burk's reactions.

Lonny stared at them, focusing on Kian. Her normal rosy complexion turned white, and with one little cry of "Kian!" she sank to the floor, unconscious.

Kelvin had to move fast to keep up with his brother. Already the former princeling was at his truelove's side. Kian knelt by her, taking her hand. "Lonny, Lonny, don't die!"

Her eyes opened, blue and achingly beautiful. "Kian, Kian, I thought you gone forever! That girl in your own world . . . I—I—"

"Hush, sweet Lonny," Kian said. "She—wasn't right for me. You were. It just took me a while to get my mind straight. It will be all right." Then he looked up to see Jac staring down at them. "That is—"

Jac's big hand came down and clasped Kian's shoulder so hard he winced. "Friend, Companion Closer Than Kin, Kian Who Made Me What I Am, if Lonny chooses you, I will not object."

Kelvin sighed relief. But in a moment Kian, who seemed to have been rocked by a fist, was saying, "No, no, my friend, I lost my head. Right is right. You deserve her."

"Why do you say that, old friend? We fought the serpents together. We fought the king's minions and warriors. We dared greatly and we won. You deserve everything, including Lonny. I should never have interfered!"

"Well, actually—" Kelvin started, trying to alleviate the colossal awkwardness of the situation.

"I felt I should marry her because it wasn't right to let her grieve any longer," Jac said. "But now you have returned. That changes everything."

"But I left her for Lenore Barley. I—"

"Who," Lonny asked with sudden strength, "is Lenore Barley?"

"The girl in the other frame who looks like you," Kian explained. "But there is more of a difference between you than just her pointed ears. She made love physically with different men, while you and I—"

"Shared a more intimate joining," Lonny said.

"Yes, yes, that's true, but—"

"But it didn't mean anything to you."

"No, no, that's not true! It meant everything!"

"Did it, Kian?" Lonny's face had found its blood supply. Her eyes flared warningly.

"Yes. Yes. And that is why, Lonny, you must marry Jac! He deserves you, while I do not."

"What he means, is—" Kelvin started, realizing that things had gotten completely turned around.

"That's not true!" Jac insisted. "You deserve her while I do not! I have been with many women in a physical sense, while you—"

"Enough!" Lonny exclaimed. "I'm not the least bit interested in marrying either of you! You—you philanderers!"

Kian and Jac displayed openmouthed astonishment, then fell into each other's arms and shook uncontrollably. Lonny stared at them in near incomprehension, then rose to her feet, picked up the train of her wedding dress, and disdainfully swept past everyone to her door and out the way she had come.

Kelvin looked at his father as the door closed behind the intended bride. John Knight shrugged, obviously as bewildered as Kelvin felt. Had those two jackasses learned their lessons?

"Go after her, Kian, she's yours!"

"No, no, my friend, *you* go after her!"

"Pitiful, isn't it," John Knight remarked. He was looking at the queen, and it was uncertain exactly what he meant.

"It certainly is," she said. "And after all my plans, all the flowers and festivities!" Yet, oddly, she did not seem completely displeased.

The heartbreaking sounds of the prospective grooms' sobbing filled the ballroom and drowned out the sympathetic murmurings of the guests turned spectators.

26 /

OVER

"I TELL YOU, FATHER, it was him!" Kelvin insisted.

"Nonsense," John replied. "King Rufurt here? With his pointed ears? He couldn't even use the transporter! It's impossible for Rufurt to be here!"

"Maybe his ears were changed, Dad. Or maybe Jon is right and the warning is just to keep pointed-ear persons in their place. Maybe he came some other way, not using the transporter. You did, the first time, and Kian did. Maybe it's dangerous and uncertain and painful, but the Flaw makes it possible. They're going to execute him, so I think we should see. I swear it sounded like Rufurt."

"With all that noise the crowd was making, you thought you heard words you didn't. That's happened to me a number of times. Or maybe Rufurt's using magic."

"Maybe somebody's using magic! Bad magic! Dad, we owe it to Rud's king. We haven't been back there since this business started; something might have happened. If Rufurt somehow got sent here—"

John Knight frowned in a way that meant he was considering. Obviously he had something of a different nature on his mind. "I suppose I can stand one more trip to a dungeon. I hate them, though."

"Just to make certain, Dad. That's all. It would be a terrible thing if that really was King Rufurt and we let him be killed in Rowforth's place."

"Terrible, but unlikely. All right, we'll go get permission from the queen."

How glad he sounded, saying that. But Kelvin doubted that his father's joy was at the prospect of seeing their king.

In her throne room Zanaan looked every bit the queen, John thought admiringly. Her very beauty and regality made him a bit tongue-tied. But in due course, trying unsuccessfully to ignore the fact that he had once made love to a body almost exactly like hers, he got out the story.

"And you say this Rufurt of your homeland is a good man?" Zanaan asked. Obviously it was his story and not him she was most interested in. That could, of course, change. She did not know how intimately he had been involved with her evil look-alike.

"As good as Rowforth is bad!" Kelvin said. He had been standing silently all the time his father talked.

That annoyed John, and he wondered why it should. What was wrong with the hero of the prophecy taking the initiative? Was it because Zanaan so enchanted him?

He pondered, and realized that the aspect of Zoanna, without the evil, really did not fascinate him in the same manner. There had been magic and a cutting edge to Zoanna that compelled him; both were lacking in Zanaan. Unfortunately that made her like bleer without the hops: not of great interest for long. He was surprised to discover this, but had to recognize its truth.

"Then we certainly must leave no doubt in any of our minds," the queen said. "My husband deserves execution while his look-alike deserves only the best."

She did not believe them, John realized. He couldn't blame her. He himself had thought Kelvin mistaken, but where kings and executions were concerned, there was slight margin for error.

They followed the queen outside the palace and around the palace wall to the dreadfully familiar stairs. It smelled no better than when he and Kian had been prisoners here. Again he remembered far too vividly Sergeant Broughtmar putting the tiny wriggling serpent into that unfortunate revolutionary's ear. What horror!

"You're shuddering, Dad!" Kelvin said. He had not been a prisoner here, so could not understand exactly how terrible it had been.

"Memories, Son, memories." Was there really anything that could be worse? Even the onset of an illness had never hit him this hard.

"I can go down and check, Father. Just so we find out who's here."

"No, I won't shirk my duty. If it is King Rufurt, I'll know him. We became as close as brothers in our imprisonment in Rud. Thank the gods Zoanna kept a more decent dungeon!"

"He'll have pointed ears. Every guard we talked to said he didn't, but he must!"

"If it is Rufurt. But you were right, ears can be changed. The difference between a pointed ear and a round ear is just a slight extension of cartilage."

They reached the landing and the guards who had preceded them and the guards who were already there parted and permitted them to approach the one cell that was occupied. In that cell, sprawled on a pile of straw which had not been changed since their own imprisonment, a short, squat man with a big nose lay with closed eyes. The sunbeam from the high barred window did not quite reach his face but fell short of it, settling on his water dish. As Rowforth had done with others, the prisoner was fed and watered as if he belonged on all fours.

John stared long and hard. His senses said "Rufurt," but he knew how unreliable senses were. They would have to get him out into the light.

"Rufurt!" he said.

The prisoner sat up. Then he scrambled to his feet and rushed to the bars. He stood there panting, his eyes wild. Truly he now resembled animal more than human being.

"John! Kelvin! Kelvin the Roundear! I knew you would come! When I called to you I knew you would come and rescue me!"

John stared at the ears. They were round. This could not be the man he had spent years with in Rud's dungeon! It could not be, and yet he felt that it was.

The prisoner focused sunken eyes on Zanaan. They widened, reflecting an inner surprise that seemed to border on terror. "Zoanna!"

That did it! This had to be Rufurt. But how?

"I am Zanaan," the queen said. "I am said to look much like Zoanna, but I do not share her personality. But you—you look much like my husband Rowforth."

"I am Rufurt! Rowforth is in my world!"

"Your ears," John said, feeling foolish. "Round."

The prisoner touched those appendages with dirty fingers and scrubbed at caked brown material at their tips. Scars were revealed, healing but visible.

"He cut off my tips! The one who looks like me did it! And Zoanna watched! Then they took me in the boat and they threw me in the water and I went into the Flaw. I came up sputtering by the waterfall, exactly as you did, John! Then I climbed out, and I recognized things from your description and I wandered all around. I found appleberries and other fruits and—and then I reached these valleys, just as you did. I didn't know whether to climb down and meet your flopears or keep going, but then three men came and roped me and tied me up! They called me Rowforth and I knew then what had happened. I knew that I was in trouble and all I could hope for was that you would come back here and get me out. Just as Kelvin got us out before."

"That clinches it," John said. "Your Majesty, let King Rufurt out. He's not the vile man you were married to."

But Zanaan, who also knew her husband well enough to tell him from another of similar appearance, had already instructed the guard to use the key. The key was in the lock and the tumblers falling. With a loud squeak the barred door was opened and good King Rufurt was free at long last.

* * *

If this was Rufurt, then what was happening back home? *Oh, Heln!* Kelvin thought with sudden alarm. *Jon! Lester! Mother! What is happening there?*

John woke, unable to sleep, and lay tossing on the bed. Finally he rose, dressed, and left the bedchamber where his two sons, each in a different bed, were sleeping. He walked the halls, uncertain as to why he was being tormented. The statuary and furniture loomed up in the darkened palace, just as it had when he had paced the hallways at night in Rud's palace.

So this is Hud, and Hud is all. Everything I need to think about. Kian will probably stay here after he and his girl make up their differences. Will I? Zoanna was everything I wanted, I thought, when besotted by her sex appeal. Zanaan has her beauty and not her nature. She has everything good that Zoanna didn't. But Zoanna had something too. The evil creature had an art! She used enchantment on me, or at least doped my wine. I believed her to be my ideal, but I was wrong. Others had been just as wrong. But now here is Zanaan, the good, perfect woman that I longed for. So why this hesitancy? Why is it that I'm still thinking of Charlain?

And there was the other aspect of it! He *had* been smitten with the queen, but then he had escaped her and found Charlain, and now the aspect of the queen lacked power over him. Charlain was married elsewhere now, so that was over—but his heart refused to admit it. His heart still wanted only that one woman. He never would have left her, had he not expected to die. He had not wanted her to be associated with him then, lest she also be killed. He had stayed with her because he loved her, and he had left her for the same reason. So it really didn't matter whether Zanaan was evil or good; he had lost his fascination for her likeness.

The irony was that Zanaan, freed from her evil husband, was now available, while Charlain was not. He would do better staying here, and away from there. Only mischief could come of his return to that other frame.

His feet had unconsciously taken him to a door. He paused, uncertain. He knew whose door this was—but no longer wished to knock on it.

Then he heard voices beyond it.

Zanaan's voice: "Oh, darling, I know you've given her your word and you don't want to hurt her, but—"

A man's voice: "It is true. I did that. I owed her, and once I thought I loved her, but that changed after I met you. But now that Kian is back, if she wants him—"

"Oh, yes! I know she does! I could see it in her eyes. I thought she loved you, but when she saw him, I knew! But the idiot kept denying her, and it is true that Hades has no fury like that of—"

"And we can marry too. You and I. Mr. and Mrs.—"

"King and queen. I see no reason why I should abdicate. And you'll make a good king, a fair and just king! Do you think you can bear being called 'Your Majesty'?"

"I can stand it, if that's the price of you."

"I rather think it is, Jac."

There was the sound of a kiss.

"Oh Jac, Jac! We'll be so happy, you and I! Not like the usual royal marriage."

"Yes. Happy. The former royalty-hating bandit—"

"Revolutionary!"

"If you prefer. The former revolutionary and the queen!"

"Darling!"

"I thought I came to the palace to conquer, but I was conquered."

"You were everything the king wasn't. It seemed so promising! And then Kian didn't come back, and Lonny was near suicide, so you had to—"

"And you know, I lied about having known many women."

"Liar! Hold me! Hold me tight!"

"Oh Zanaan! Zanaan!"

"Oh Jac! Oh Jac!"

John tiptoed away from the door. They were going to be happy, he thought, and so was the land.

He didn't feel envious. He felt relieved that this was happening. So he let his feet take him away from the door to the royal pantry and back to his bedchamber on the second floor. He was happy for Jac and the queen. He only wished that he had some similar prospect for himself.

When he woke in the morning John thought he had dreamed the episode of the preceding night. Kelvin was getting dressed in his conventional clothes: new brownberry shirt, greenbriar pantaloons, cushiony cotilk stockings, and heavy walking boots.

"Where's Kian?" John asked.

"I don't know, Dad. He woke me up and started talking about Lonny and how he couldn't live without her. About how he was going to go to her and somehow make her understand. I must have drifted off again because I've just now awakened and he's gone."

"What time was that? Early or late?"

"Much too early or much too late. Do you think he'll marry her? We really need to get home. At least I do."

"He will, and I do too. There's something strange about King Rufurt being here. If Zoanna is alive and Rowforth is impersonating Rufurt . . ."

"Kelvinia may be in more trouble than Rud ever was with Aratex!"

"I'm afraid you're right, Son. What in the world can that woman be up to! It seems obvious she's alive. I was so sure she was dead, but maybe that was wishful thinking."

"Can we even be sure of that?" Kelvin wondered aloud. "I mean with so much magic and science around—"

"We can be very certain she's not dead. If zombies exist I don't think they snatch look-alikes from other frames. At least I hope they don't."

"Father, do you think she's really planning a war? Maybe has already started one?"

"That's why we must get back. If Rowforth has taken Rufurt's place, the two of them will be ruling the country without bloodshed. Unless they are causing it as rulers. And that is an ugly possibility."

"She could be up to anything. Maybe she's trying for revenge?"

"Could be. Son, don't say anything to Kian about this. I really think he'll want to stay here now, and really, considering that Zoanna is his mother, here is the best place for him."

"You don't think he'll fight for Zoanna again?" Kelvin was incredulous.

"No, he wouldn't do that. But if he's here with his bride he won't have the temptation. If Zoanna's alive, I think you know what we shall have to do. We don't want him there for that."

Kelvin shuddered. "No, not for that!"

"I think we'll attend his wedding this day. Maybe he will come to appreciate Zanaan as the mother he should have had. If he doesn't wed Lonny today, you and I and King Rufurt had better go home anyway. I don't think we dare wait longer."

"All right, Father. But will he—"

"He'd better!" John said.

Later in the day they did indeed attend the wedding. With them, cleaned up and fancily dressed as the others, was King Rufurt. In fact, they were the ones conducting the ceremony of the double wedding of Kian to Lonny, and Jac to Zanaan. If the king had any private sentiments about marrying the woman who so resembled his evil wife to another man, he concealed them well, just as John Knight concealed his sentiments well. Kelvin was privately glad it had worked out this way, because of sentiments he too was glad to conceal.

"Kian Knight from our frame," King Rufurt said, "do you wish to marry Lonny Burk of this frame?"

"You know I do," Kian said, gazing into Lonny's eyes. It was more than evident that any misunderstandings the two had had yesterday had been resolved in the intervening night.

"And you, Lonny Burk, do you wish to marry Kian Knight?"

"I do, oh I do!" Lonny agreed, her good nature restored.

"You, Jac Smite, et cetera, do you—"

"I do!" Jac said.

"And you, Queen Zanaan, lovely and good widow or divorcee of absent abdicated discredited reprehensible former King Rowforth of Hud, do you wish to marry Jac?"

"I do indeed want to marry Jac!" She and he exchanged secret smiles. It was evident that the marriage of compassion and convenience between Jac and Lonny would never have worked out; neither of their hearts had been in it.

Now John Knight took the floor. "Does anyone here have objection to either joining?" he asked the onlookers.

There was a stillness in the ballroom reminiscent of what might have existed at the dawn of time in a primeval frame.

Kian and Jac produced silver rings and slipped them on the fingers of the brides.

It was Kelvin's turn. "Then," he said as forcefully as his threatening-to-quaver voice could manage, "you are married. For as long as you wish it, or until time bites its end." The last words were John Knight's contribution to the service, and perhaps to other minds than Kelvin's they made sense.

"Kiss, kiss," Heeto urged, as if fearful they would forget that detail, and the grooms and brides did.

Someone started the applause, and then the music played, as the group that had been organized for yesterday's festivities acted for today's. The piangan and silver pipes sounded beautifully.

"Goodbye, Kian, good luck, long life," Kelvin said, shaking his brother's hand, feeling that it might be for the last time.

"Goodbye? What are you talking about?"

"There may be trouble at home," John said. "We have to find out."

"But—"

"If I'm here, maybe he's there," Rufurt said.

"Rowforth? You mean—I'm coming too!"

"No you're not!" John Knight said. "You're going to stay here with this delightful, beautiful girl and have a proper honeymoon. If there is trouble and we need help, one of us will be back."

"But really, you can't leave like this!"

"We have to," Kelvin said. "You see to your wife; I'll see to mine."

Lonny squeezed Kian's hand. "I think that's a great idea, Husband."

"I have my gauntlets, the Mouvar weapon, the levitation belt, and the chimaera's sting," Kelvin explained. That one sting he had not included in the shipment to the other frame. "I doubt there's any trouble I can't handle with those! Probably Rowforth is in the palace, and—"

"Rowforth! My husband!" the queen exclaimed, overhearing.

"I'm your husband now, dear," Jac reminded her. "You divorced him, if he didn't die first."

"Yes, of course, but—"

"We don't know that he's there," John said. "But there's a chance that he might be."

"You'll bring him back?" Heeto asked. "For punishment?"

"If we can. If we don't have to destroy him ourselves," Rowforth's look-alike said.

"We'll be back in any case," John Knight said. "Not to stay, you understand, but just to visit and let you know what happened."

"When?"

"As soon as our problem is cleared."

"I still think I should come."

"No!"

Kian looked relieved in spite of himself. Jac, who had been fidgeting throughout the exchange, now said: "If need be, we will both go to their rescue, Kian."

"And if need be you can have all of Hud's armed forces and all the fighting men our treasury will buy," Queen Zanaan added.

It seemed a satisfactory solution. Once again, and then several more times, everyone said goodbye.

Then it was time to travel fast, and without mistake in the transporter.

27 /

RETURN

K ELVIN SAT IN THE middle of the boat, rowing with the help of
the gauntlets while King Rufurt filled the stern seat and John
Knight sat at the bow. It was just as well that his brother hadn't returned
with them, he thought, or they'd have been overloaded.

They passed the roaring falls into star-filled spaces, the Flaw. The gauntlets rowed through the turbulent water without difficulty. Then around the
bend, past eerily glowing walls, their boat and themselves lit by the lichen's
radiance. A swirl in the water that Kelvin had noticed on previous trips—a
sort of dimple, actually—and then finally the boat landing.

"I think we'd better be cautious," John Knight said. "There could be
enemies waiting for us here."

"I'm very cautious," Kelvin agreed, drawing the Mouvar weapon. That
would handle magic, and the gauntlets and his sword were ready to tackle
anything else. After the adventures he had just undergone, a possible scrap
with armed men or even an attack by magic could hold few terrors!

"Perhaps you'd better stay hidden down here," Kelvin suggested to the
king. "Until after we see how things are above."

King Rufurt looked up the stairs and a set of stubborn lines appeared at
the corners of his mouth. "I'm still ruler."

"Yes, that's why we don't want you to fall into the hands of Rowforth
again."

"Rowforth and Zoanna. Damn Zoanna! My former queen!"

"We're all subject to sorcery," John Knight said soothingly. "Even those
of us who never wanted to believe it possible."

"I'll go check," Kelvin said, touching his belt. He rose above the boat
landing. In his right hand was the Mouvar weapon. Strapped on his left side
was his sword, while strapped between his shoulder blades was the lightweight sting the chimaera had given him. He was as armed, he thought, as a
human being had ever been.

They had brought King Rufurt back here through the transporter. Kelvin had been alert for any warning tingle from the gauntlets, but there had been none. Did that mean that Rufurt's surgically rounded ears made him eligible to use Mouvar's system, or was the prohibition against pointears a bluff? Maybe he should make Jon happy and bring her here, and see whether the gauntlets tingled for her. Her life must have been relatively dull, recently, far from the action, helping Heln prepare for the baby.

He nudged the lever forward with his finger, keeping the Mouvar weapon in his hand. He rose above the first flight, and then the second flight of dusty, ancient stairs. Finally he was at the hole that let in daylight to mingle with the softer radiance of the lichens. He accelerated and shot outside fast, in case someone was waiting there.

He paused in midair. Two men in guardsman uniforms sat at a block of masonry playing cards. One of them looked up with open mouth while the other played a card.

"Kelvin, you can really fly that thing!"

"Practice," Kelvin said. "You are waiting for me?"

"King's orders. You are to go directly to the palace, now that you're back. Your brother get married all right?"

"Yes, after some delays. Nice wedding. Everyone was there."

"Your father return with you?"

Kelvin hesitated. He didn't want to reveal too much to these guardsmen, good men though they were. His brother, he knew, would simply have lied, but somehow lying for him was not natural. "He's not with me," he temporized. That was true, as far as it went. John Knight and the genuine king had remained below, letting Kelvin scout the territory alone.

"We have a horse for you. Do you want to ride?"

"I thought I'd fly and surprise someone," Kelvin said. He reholstered the Mouvar weapon, placed his hand over his central buckle, and accelerated out of their sight.

What do I do now? he thought, looking down at blurring farmland. *Do I just go to the palace? I should have asked questions. Why didn't I think of that?*

Because he really wasn't a hero, he knew. He had all kinds of limitations and inadequacies. If it weren't for the magic and science devices he happened to have, he'd be nobody. Others might be fooled about him, but he didn't fool himself.

Down below was a troop of horsemen and men on foot wearing Kelvinia's grass-green uniforms. He lowered and hovered, while shouts went up and fingers pointed at him. No missiles followed, so he was still the Roundear of Prophecy as far as these men were concerned.

Cautiously he descended until his feet touched the ground. Soldiers who had been drooping from fatigue now ran forward with joyous and triumphant cries.

"He's back! He's back! The Roundear's back!"

Kelvin waited. Soon a man with what seemed a bad burn on his arm was pumping his hand and shouting loudly: "General Broughtner! General Broughtner! Someone get the general!"

In due course, after much handshaking and incomprehensible expressions on the part of the soldiers, General Broughtner was there. The pointed-ear general who had fought so valiantly in the war with Aratex drooped in his saddle and looked almost as though he had lost a campaign. Kelvin remembered that he had been a village drunk before the formation of the Knights and the Rud Revolution. It was possible, looking at him now, to think that he had regressed.

But when Broughtner spoke it was not with slurred speech, and no fumes of wine were on his breath. "Kelvin! Thank the gods!"

"I just got back," Kelvin explained. "From my brother's wedding."

"I know. Now we're saved."

"I don't know what has been happening. Has there been fighting?"

"Has there been!" Broughtner dismounted with the help of a private. He staggered over to Kelvin, shook his hand, and grabbed his shoulders. "Kelvin, we are at war! We've been losing, thanks to that witch! But now that you're back that will change. Now that you're here with that weapon."

Kelvin thought: *So Zoanna is fighting with magic! So she really is a witch that I have to destroy. Thank the gods Kian stayed behind!*

"See these burns?" Broughtner said, pointing. "Witch's fire did that! She's using witch's fire! What chance has an ordinary man against that?"

Kelvin looked at the scorched faces and arms. None had been fatal or even very bad, but maybe others were. The general was right, there was no way the ordinary soldier could fight against witch's fire.

"You'll burn her, won't you? The way you did with that witch in Aratex. Send her damned fire back to her. Burn her up!"

"I'll burn her," Kelvin promised. It seemed a dreadful fate to inflict on anyone. But then all that the Mouvar weapon did was send the magic back on the sender. If Zoanna was burning her one-time subjects then she deserved to burn.

"She's back behind the Klingland and Kance borders, way back to the twin capitals. She's got plenty of men fighting for her—Klinglanders and Kancians. If you don't stop her she'll take over Kelvinia!"

"I'll stop her," Kelvin promised again. His hands went to his belt.

"There's some of our own still fighting near the caps. At least there were. Take care. Witches can be dangerous."

"I know." Kelvin lifted off and cruised toward the border. He wished now that he hadn't slept through history class. He knew that Klingland and Kance bordered what had been the kingdom of Rud on its eastern side. He remembered that there were twin boys born on a once-every-four-years bonus day. The boy rulers were young in body but aged, thanks to a bit of prenatal magic, only one year for a normal person's four. But he had always heard the infants terrible, as they were called, were but mischievous perpetual boys. There was always something about a caretaker who had allegedly administered the calendar spell as they were born. But to the best of his recollection they were not bad boys, and their guardian mostly minded her own business. Certainly Rud had never fought with these lands, or had not fought with any other with the possible exception of Hermandy. If Zoanna had gone there with Rowforth seeking allies to get him a throne, then the situation was at least as serious as had been the affair with Aratex. Everyone seemed to think the witch was simply a guardian, but if Zoanna enlisted her as an ally then it was she who was hurling the fire.

Roads and hills and forests and rivers later he neared the caps. Down below he spied a dust cloud of battle, and in the sky was a ball of fire.

It's time to act! he thought, lowering himself to the ground. *It's time to crisp a witch as I crisped Melbah.*

He landed on a knoll, drew the Mouvar weapon from its hip holster, and prepared to intercept and turn back the witch's fire.

Charlain concentrated hard on the crystal as she guided the fireball. It was easier now. She had better control. No longer did she destroy men and horses with the witch's fire, but merely frightened them. If need be, she knew she would do more with it, deliberately.

In the crystal, men wearing the Kelvinian uniform were looking skyward as she danced the ball. Why didn't they give up? Why didn't they leave them alone? Was it because of magic Zoanna commanded, that sent them back? That must be it! They had no choice! It was the only explanation for these suicidal charges.

Below the fireball she knew there were men who were only boys. Perhaps that Phillip lad, and perhaps her own son-in-law. Perhaps big, hearty Mor Crumb who had so cheered her spirits the one time they had met. That had been after the wedding of Kelvin and Heln, and of Jon and Lester. She had been feeling sad because she knew there was so much more to the prophecy than just ridding Rud of its evil ruler. And now, now that evil ruler was back, so what actually had been accomplished?

"Charlain! Watch what you're doing!" Helbah was scolding; she didn't like it when her accomplice's mind wandered. Without intending to, Charlain had let the fireball drift past the invaders and over the forest. Helbah naturally wanted the fireball exploding where it would at least pose a threat.

Carefully, watching the crystal in the tree bole, Charlain brought the ball back over the troops. She knew that Helbah's look-alike, Melbah of Aratex, would have flung it right into their midst. Helbah was like Charlain herself in that she didn't really want to maim and destroy. The invaders had to be stopped, that was all, and if there was a way that would leave all intact, both favored it.

"Meow!" said Katbah, his dark paw touching the crystal over the men. "Meow!"

Oh, all right! Charlain thought, and exploded the fireball.

Phillip peeked cautiously out from behind a tree at the edge of the glen. He had stumbled about for days since running from his outfit. It hadn't been that he was scared, exactly, but Lester had been trying to make him go home and then those fireballs had started and all pandemonium had broken loose.

Now, having survived for some days on berries and a few bitter nuts, scared all the time that he would be caught, he had actually reached the glen. He had known something was going on here because he had seen the witch on the road walking slowly with a stick. He had wounded her properly once, he thought, but witches were notorious for surviving almost anything. Thus he had watched her and the cat from the woods, fearful that they would see, yet knowing that they had other things to think about. It had been luck that he had gotten into the woods and luck that he had remained undetected. With more luck still he might yet make up for the trouble he had caused.

There were *two* witches in that glen. He could not see them clearly there in the mist, but he knew there were two. He had been watching them while his belly growled from hunger and his arms and face smarted from their contacts with netishes and poison oavy plants. He would get her, he promised himself. He would get her.

Old witch Helbah was standing to one side of the tree, partially turned. The other witch and the cat were at the crystal. If he was very, very careful how he aimed he'd skewer old Helbah through the heart. After that he'd have to quickly kill the other witch and the cat. He didn't like it, but he knew it was necessary. How much mercy, after all, did a witch have? He remembered too well how Melbah, his nurse and mentor, had cackled gleefully while burning alive someone she had thought troublesome.

He cocked the crossbow carefully. Bolt in place, three others close at hand. Melbah had trained him in the art of crossbowing as well as in wood stealth and survival in the woods. Melbah had taught him well. Lester and St. Helens did not know how very much he had learned.

He rested the crossbow across a log, placed his cheek firmly against the stalk, and took infinitely careful aim. There would be but the one chance. This time he would get her right through the heart.

* * *

Blood! Mama! Blood! Blood!

Heln stifled a scream. It was the baby demanding that it be fed! That it be fed what was proper food for its growth and development and eventual birth.

"Heln, what's the matter?" Jon asked. She was bending near, almost asking for it.

Jon is my friend! Jon is my friend! Heln reminded herself. She thought for herself this time, hoping that the baby would understand.

Food, Mama, food!

HUNGRY! WAHHHHH! A second thought, different from the other in tone. How many babies drifted in her womb? What kind?

GRRRRRWWWWW! HUNGER! HUNGER! Gods, a third, and so unhuman!

"Heln, you're scaring me," Jon said. "Why do you look like that?"

They were only food sources, after all. Hunger of a superior life-form superseded everything else.

"Heln!"

She had to get her teeth into that luscious throat! Nourishment pulsed hot and red just beneath that vein. She was strong, very strong, her teeth would rip and tear into that luscious flesh, her tongue would lap up the steaming blood—

"Heln! Stop it!" The food source pushed at her head, holding her back, challenging her to use her full strength.

Food, Mama, Food!

Hungry, Mama, Hungry!

Gwrrrrrowth!

"Dr. Sterk!" Jon's voice rose suddenly in fear. "DOCTOR STERK! HELP!"

Kildom nudged Kildee in the ribs. "Come on!"

"What?"

"She's gone. Let's do what we said we'd do!"

Kildee followed his brother around the palace wall, worrying. Kildom was always getting him into things! He'd agree out of frustration from Kildom's challenging digs, and then he'd be hooked. This time he was really caught and he didn't like it.

Kildom ran right up to the dungeon guard just as they had planned. "Trom! Trom! They're coming, Trom! We just saw them run into the trees!"

"What are you two up to?"

"It's true, Trom," Kildee said, playing his part. "We saw three of them in the woods. Soldiers, wearing the Hermandy uniforms! I don't know how they got there, but—"

"Damn! If you're lying to me I'll hold you while Helbah soaps your mouths!"

"No, Trom, really. Enemy soldiers! Maybe slipping up to kill Helbah! Maybe to kill us, Trom! Trom, you've got to do something!"

"I can't leave my post," Trom said. "Even if I believed you I couldn't." He looked worried, Kildee thought.

"Trom, you go with my brother and I'll guard. Please, Trom, please."

"Oh, all right," Trom said. "But if anything happens here, you raise a shout!"

"I will, Trom, I will," he promised angelically.

Trom should have been warned by that, but he was distracted by the urgency of their message. "Come," said Kildom, taking off at a run.

Trom hesitated a moment more, then followed him at a brisk walk that became a trot. They rounded the corner of the palace and were out of sight.

Well, there was no helping it now. Kildee took the key he had surreptitiously taken from the guard's key ring and ran with it as fast as he could go. Down the dungeon stairs, to the dark, recently scrubbed cell.

"General Reilly, General Crumb, come quick! My brother and I have begun your escape!"

28 /

GOODBYE AGAIN

KELVIN'S FINGER WAS ALREADY tightening on the trigger of the Mouvar weapon when he noticed that his gauntlets were hot. Well, that was natural, wasn't it? The gauntlets warned of danger, and certainly that ball of fire was danger. So why did he hesitate?

He knew what would happen when he pressed the trigger. The witch's fire would return to its sender and destroy her. The Mouvar weapon was antimagic, as his father had deduced. By moving the little fin-shape on the handgrip he would simply counter the magic, wipe it out, as it were.

Was it really Zoanna hurling that fire? Or was it the other witch, the one said to live here?

No, No, Kelvin! Do not destroy the witch! Do not destroy her!

It was the chimaera's thought! The monster was still with him! He had thought Mervania long disconnected.

You think I don't want those berries? Leave it to you and you'll never get back with them! First you'll fool around fighting, then you'll go see your wife, and forget about what's important.

"But the fireball!"

Believe me, I know better than you!

But—

The fireball that was now ahead of the advancing army dipped groundward. Now was the time to act!

No! No, you fool inferior life-form! Don't you feel your gloves heating? You'll kill your mother!

That got him. He didn't know what the chimaera meant, but he knew a warning. Indeed, the gauntlets were burning; he had been concentrating so hard that he hadn't noticed, or had taken it to be from the radiation of the fireball. Quickly he moved the knob on his weapon so that it would simply counter the magic rather than rebound it on the sender. He started to squeeze the trigger, pointing the weapon skyward.

The fireball exploded spectacularly, sending down to the ground, just ahead of the troops, a golden waterfall of scintillating stars. The knoll shook, and his face hit the grass. He let loose of the weapon and for the moment he felt complete and overwhelming terror.

When he was able to look he could see the Kelvinian troops scattering, responding to the terror he'd felt. Behind them the fireball grew bright, sputtering like a dying fire. The fire hurt his eyes, creating afterimages that disoriented him and made him feel as if he were again in astral form. Then the images faded as the waterfall faded, and there was nothing but littered landscape and fleeing men.

Kelvin swallowed. "It—it could have killed, but it didn't!"

Now you know, Mervania said to him in his whirling head.

You said my mother! Kelvin thought back, dizzy.

Would I lie to you, when your mission for me is incomplete? Now you are soon to learn about your mother.

Phillip startled at the sound of breaking brush. His shot went wild and he heard the bolt thunk hard in the trunk of a tree down in the glen. He hadn't time to turn his head before he was grabbed hard from behind.

"YOU BRAT!" St. Helens roared. "You totally senseless nincompoop! Wasn't shooting her once treachery enough for you? Did you have to do it again and mess up our escape?"

Phillip was abashed. "I did it for you!"

St. Helens picked him up in very muscular arms and shook him. The face of this man who had meant so much to him since he had first accepted him as friend was terrifyingly red. St. Helens, he thought with shock, was about to kill him.

"You did it for yourself, you show-off brat! Don't you tell me otherwise! Don't you even think otherwise!"

Phillip bit his tongue, whether deliberately or accidentally he couldn't have said. He tasted salt and felt blood trickling from the far corner of his mouth as St. Helens quit shaking him. Maybe the blood would appease him, he thought. He gazed into those angry eyes and everything he'd thought to say vanished from his mind.

"She's a good witch, Son," Mor Crumb said behind St. Helens. He was as big and rough a man as ever lived, and one who had no reason to love witches. "She's the kind we can deal with."

"A witch is a witch is a witch," Phillip intoned. It was, he'd learned, since his kingship, a common saying.

"Not this witch, Son." Mor spoke firmly, fatherly, with a hint of reproach.

"She's a good woman," St. Helens agreed, the fire in his eyes dampening. "She'd have helped us out of our real difficulties when she and I first met. She's not the enemy. Our enemy's back at our home palace."

"Zoanna?" Phillip managed.

"Zoanna."

"But you—"

"Were bewitched. Had your mind twisted. We all did. Same's the bitch did to John Knight, long time ago. But now we know. We know it's her and we can manage to do something."

Phillip looked at Crumb's face and then back at his former friend. They were both serious. Was it that he had unwittingly let himself be used by Zoanna exactly as he had let himself be used by Melbah? A witch was a witch was a witch. But couldn't there be a good witch?

"You may be right, Generals Reilly and Crumb, but I was going by experience. A witch is treacherous, cruel, and unforgiving. That's how Melbah was. How could I think that this witch would be different?"

"You couldn't, Phillip."

St. Helens opened his hands and dropped him. He hit the ground and saw both men staring past him. He turned. There, standing before them, apparently unarmed and unprotected, was the witch who to his eyes looked exactly like the one who had raised him. Only not quite. Up close this woman was softer, with more agreeable lines, as if she had been known to smile sincerely.

"You did what you thought right," she said. "You knew that Melbah had always deceived you and that her word was not to be trusted. You assumed I would take advantage of General Reilly's trust. You are a boy; you thought as a boy does. Make a witch harmless and she will not harm you or those you love. It is an old recipe, long believed. To truly follow the recipe calls for the witch's complete destruction. In order to destroy a witch you have to believe in her malevolence."

"I—I did," Phillip agreed.

"And now you don't?" Her voice was soft, not unfriendly.

"I—don't know. I guess if you want to harm us, you can."

"I'm glad that you are not so certain. Come, the three of you. There is someone in the glen you will want to see."

"The other witch," Phillip said.

"Yes, you might say that," Helbah said agreeably. "But she is no stranger to any of you. I think, Phillip, that you are going to be surprised to learn exactly who she is."

Phillip got to his feet, wiped blood from his mouth, and followed Helbah. As his feet found their way he now and then looked over at St. Helens and Mor Crumb. These big men, these strong men, were at least as bewildered as he.

In the glen, near the large tree with the flat crystal set in its big bole, lovely Charlain stretched out her arms as though to long-lost children or her dearest friends.

Charlain? Kelvin's mother? A witch? Now indeed a lot about this mysterious roundear bubbled up from the bottom of his brain and drifted into place. The Roundear of Prophecy had a mother who had powers and was now using them to fulfill her son's destiny! But *against* Kelvinia rather than for? How could that be? Was she too bewitched?

"Phillip, St. Helens, General Crumb," Charlain said, "as you now must realize it is our old enemy that we have to fight. Zoanna and the man who appears to be but isn't King Rufurt now control Kelvinia. Every soldier, whether Kelvinia, Herman, or a mercenary from Throod, has been deceived. Each of you has been tricked similarly. Klingland and Kance are not the enemy, though they are the kingdom you fight."

"I know we were bewitched by her," Mor said. "But you, Charlain—a witch?"

"A necessary recruit, I'm afraid," Helbah said. "Charlain had the talent and I had need for it. Fortunately for all of us she learned quickly and well."

"There's something else," Charlain said. "My son Kelvin is here now, back in this frame and not far from where we stand. I saw him in the crystal."

"Then we're saved!" Mor Crumb said. "The Roundear will make everything right. He'll win this war, and—"

"You forget that the real war is inside Kelvinia," Helbah said.

"Yes, yes, of course," Mor said. "He'll get them out of the palace before you can say scat! Burn wicked Zoanna as she deserves! Burn the impostor king as well!"

"No," Charlain said. "Not immediately, anyhow. There's something more important he has to do."

"More important," Mor asked incredulously, "than destroying the former queen of Rud and the former king from the other place? More important than stopping the fighting?"

"Yes. Far more important. I have consulted the cards and the cards have never lied to me. There's a nodule, a crisis point. Either he fulfills this subsidiary task promptly and without fail or this fighting will not end and the prophecy will never be fulfilled. For the good of all of us and the eventual fulfillment of the prophecy he has to do what his mother tells him. Each of you, understanding or not, must help me to that end."

They stared at her, amazed, but hardly doubting her.

Kelvin, urged on by Mervania Chimaera's thoughts, walked slowly down the road that led to the glen. Ahead of him, prancing, flicking its tail, looking back with a come-along expression every now and then was a huge black houcat.

I'm getting into trouble, Kelvin thought. *I really can't trust the chimaera. It's putting me right into the hands of the witch!*

When have you not been in trouble, stupid mortal! Mervania responded almost affectionately. *And why would I want to have you in the hands of a witch?*

To make a deal, maybe. As you did with me.

And that you haven't yet delivered on! Be brave, little hero, and use some sense!

That's all right for you to think, Mervania. You don't have to face a witch!

You faced me, Kelvin. Do you honestly think a witch could be worse than I am?

No! Nothing's worse than a chimaera!

I'm glad you realize it. And remember, I'm right here in your thoughts, protecting my interests.

Kelvin wondered if he could possibly comprehend the chimaera's interests. He tried not to project the thought or call it to the chimaera's attention. The creature was a puzzle! Compared to the chimaera, dragons and witches were quite comprehensible.

Thank you, Kelvin.

Ahead he could see five people waiting. Two women, two big men, and one large boy or man like himself. Was one of those witches really his mother?

Do you doubt me, Kelvin? The thought had a tinge of menace.

Kelvin felt chastised. Focusing mainly on the houcat's constantly flicking tail he was only gradually becoming aware that the fog was lifting. He could have flown this distance in half the time with less internal agony, but the chimaera had decreed walk.

You may fly now, if you wish.

Thanks a lot! If the monster caught the irony, fine! He touched the button in his buckle, pressed it in and rose to the height of a horse's back. He nudged the forward lever and floated down the road, the houcat still ahead. He accelerated ever so little and he was there.

They were there. St. Helens in prisoner clothes, Mor Crumb in worn and filthy general's uniform. Phillip, the former king of Aratex, in filthy common clothes. A short, smiling woman who looked astonishingly like Melbah, the witch he had caused to burn. And, most surprising of all, a woman who appeared to be his mother.

"Come down, Kelvin," his mother said. "We have to talk."

It was as if she said "Come down from that tree" or "Get off from that woodpile." Could this be his mother, and wasn't there anything he could do that would surprise her?

Kelvin descended to the ground and deactivated his belt. This whole scene was strange, but his mother seemed to be the spokesperson here.

"Kelvin, we're all glad to see you. Come here!" Her arms went wide as he took a step forward.

Could this be some cunning illusion, designed to make him walk blithely into a trap?

If you don't trust your mother, trust me, Mervania thought with a certain amused disgust. *I want those dragonberries. Do you think I will allow you to be trapped before I get them?*

That satisfied him. A moment later Charlain was hugging him hard, as a mother long deprived must hug her son. He relaxed, all doubt gone that it was really her.

"What's this?" she asked, touching the copper sting on his back.

"A chimaera's sting, Mother."

"I thought it might be. Good, you hold on to that! Someday it may prove important."

Kelvin swallowed. Mom was so practical sometimes! No questions like "What's a chimaera?" or "How did you ever come by it?" Just instant, practical acceptance.

The other woman spoke—the witch who looked like Melbah. "Charlain, you must show him."

"Yes, I suppose I ought to. Come, Son, over to this tree, over to this crystal. Now what I'm going to show you may be a shock. Please be brave, Son; I know you can be."

"Mom, I just want to get rid of Zoanna and return home to my wife!" Kelvin protested.

Listen to her, you idiot! Mervania snapped. *You won't like this.*

Again, Kelvin found himself placing more credence in the monster than in his mother. He went with Charlain to the tree. What was going on?

Charlain's fingers stretched out and there was a tiny spark that danced between her fingers and then from her fingertips to the crystal. Suddenly the crystal was a window on a distant scene, as other magic crystals had been.

A madwoman stared and gibbered, crouching in a corner. On her wrists and ankles were chains. She was naked and grotesquely pregnant, as though she were set to deliver not a child but a colt. Her skin had a coppery sheen. Her dark, sunken eyes stared right at him. She screamed.

Why was this madwoman being shown to him? Why was she screaming like that, as though she saw him?

"KELVIN!" the imaged woman screamed.

She knew his name! This pathetic, mad, pregnant woman saw him and knew his name!

Suddenly the features of the woman became preternaturally clear. That chin, that nose, those facial contours, those round ears! "Heln!" he said incredulously. "Heln?" For how could such a horror be possible?

"Yes," his mother said. "That is she."

Kelvin felt the ground open under him. It was just too much. He sank down on his knees, his hands reaching out to the crystal. "HELN! HELN! NO, NO, PLEASE!"

In the crystal a raw piece of meat appeared. Impaled on a stick it waved before the face of the woman he tried not to believe was Heln.

The madwoman focused her glassy eyes on the meat. Her fingers curled. She licked her lips. Suddenly her neck shot out, fast, like that of a striking reptile. Her teeth sank into the flesh. Blood squirted, and ran from the corners of her mouth. Her chained wrists lifted and her clawed hands pushed the meat farther and farther into her savagely chomping maw.

"Kelvin!" the madwoman said between bites. "Kelvin!"

It couldn't be her! It couldn't be!

The picture in the crystal seemed to move back. His sister Jon came into view. She was holding the stick that supported the raw meat. It was evident that she did not dare come closer herself, lest her own flesh be attacked. Beside her, steadying her arm, was Dr. Sterk, the royal physician.

Kelvin thought he had seen horrors in the other frames, but none compared to this one in his own frame! "No, no, no," he said.

"Accept it, Son." His mother moved her hand and the magic scene vanished. It was now just a flat piece of crystal stuck in a tree bole.

"Mother, what can I do? Where is she? How can I—"

"She's in the royal palace."

"Good! I'll go there immediately, and—"

"No, Son. You must not."

"Not?"

"The evil queen is there, and will not be lightly subdued. In any event, there is no time for that. The queen put the spell on Heln, but cannot undo it. There is an antidote, and you must get it for Heln before she gives birth. That could be at any time, and that birthing will kill her."

Kelvin, noting the gross distension of Heln's body, understood. That birthing would rip her apart! "What antidote? Where?"

"Where you got your copper sting, Son. The chimaera has it."

"It has!" Had the chimaera held out on him?

No. I did not know about this until you entered this frame and contacted your mother.

"You know about the—?" he asked, amazed.

"The monster who speaks to you in your mind? Yes, the cards told me."

"But I have no idea what the antidote is!"

"Helbah here knows. There's a powder. A powder no chimaera can live without. It has an opposite effect in cases like this."

"What is this powder? How will I know it?"

I have it, Mervania thought. *I never thought I would need to give any of it away, but I see I do.*

Kelvin realized that there was a solution to this horror. If only he had known before, he could have gotten the powder and saved Heln before it got to this stage!

29 /

ANTIDOTE

JOHN KNIGHT WAS MUNCHING on smoked fish while waiting for Rufurt to make his move.

Rufurt leaned over the board and considered before moving a pawn. It might have been a troop movement or an execution.

"Good move!" Zed Yokes said.

The king nodded. A king's moves had after all to be approved. He took a swig of the appleberry wine and handed it to John. John shook his head and sipped from the water jar instead. That fish the old river man had brought was salty!

"So there's really a war on between Kelvinia and the twin kingdom," John mused.

Zed nodded, smiling his pleasant old man's smile. "The news comes to me on the river. It comes slowly, but it comes."

"So that must be what my son is up to—bringing it to a stop."

"Just so he gets the impostor," Rufurt said. "He and the queen."

"You still call her queen, Rufurt?" John inquired, amused. "After what she did to both of us, and the kingdom?"

"You know what I mean. Villainess is more like it! Witch will do."

John moved a bishop diagonally across the board. "Check."

Rufurt immediately took the bishop with his black queen. "Sorry to do this, John. Particularly with this piece."

John tried to smile, hoping to give the impression that he had sacrificed the bishop deliberately. Rufurt needed cheering. When Kelvin came back—and he didn't want to admit he was beginning to worry about that—there should be cheering aplenty.

"You think your son's a match for them?" Zed asked.

"He'd better be." John looked around the ruins of the old palace, remembering how the last revolution had been. "There's the prophecy, of course. I'm afraid I really believe in that."

"Now, you mean," Rufurt said. "You didn't believe in it in the old days."

"No, I didn't." How many times had he scolded Charlain for filling the boy's head with nonsense. How little had he known!

"But now you believe in prophecies and magic."

"In this frame I do! Some prophecies, some magic."

"Why is that, John?" The king put a bit of archness into it, knowing very well.

"The chimaera, for one thing. Other things we saw and experienced. I'll never again say with full certainty what can and can't be. In an infinity of frames I suspect anything is possible."

"Right you are, John. It's your move, isn't it?"

John concentrated on the board, difficult as that was for him. Finally he moved his remaining white knight.

Rufurt nudged the black queen onto the knight's square. "Sorry again, John. You're not concentrating."

"While you are." *Damn St. Helens for reinventing this game!*

"It's the experience of governing," Rufurt said. As usual he ignored the fact that he had lost his kingdom to Zoanna once and spent all those years in the royal dungeon.

"Hmmm," John said. If he moved his own queen down now he could take Rufurt's and checkmate his king in the bargain! He made the move. "Check!"

"Can't win them all," Rufurt said. He stood up from the block of masonry and stretched. His eyes scanned the skies. "There! Him, isn't it?"

John strained the eyes he hated to admit were less effective at distances than Rufurt's were. Something definitely was in the sky, and coming at them. It seemed to be the right size. "Yes," he said.

Within moments the figure was right above them. It descended, and hovered. Then, somewhat shrilly, it called: "Dad, Your Majesty, I'm going back to the chimaera's world. Wait here! I'll explain later!"

Kelvin started off again, then paused. "Mother divorced Hal. She's single now, and a witch."

With that John's surprising offspring dived rather than flew through the ruins and out of sight.

"Those young folk sure are in a hurry!" Tommy Yokes' grandfather remarked.

But John hardly cared about that. Charlain was single? Suddenly a wonderful new horizon lay before him.

Kelvin could hardly wait to reach the transporter. Very skilled now in how to hold his body while flying, he barely slowed before reaching the river ledge. Now was not the time to ponder the mysteries of the Flaw or of being. He opened the huge metal door with the help of the gauntlets and leaped inside. He barely took time to set the control for the chimaera's world, and was off.

After what his father had termed "special effects" he found himself in a somewhat more dusty chamber facing a froogear.

The froogear held out a small packet composed of one large folded leaf. Kelvin took it.

This is it? he demanded of the chimaera.

It is in there, Kelvin, Mervania's thought came. *Three little grains that will expand to a powder. Be careful you don't sneeze on them.*

Thanks, Mervania. I'll get back with those dragonberry seeds when I can!

I'll let you know about that, mortal! Hurry—you haven't much time.

Right! Clutching the packet, Kelvin leaped back into the transporter.

Mervania sighed. The sky was orange and cloud-filled and it was a good day to be working in the garden. Fortunately she could weed around the pumash and squakin plants while keeping a small bit of mind tuned to Kelvin.

Why was she helping this inferior life-form? Hadn't she paid her debt to it when she let it and its fellows go? An inferior life-form was after all an inferior life-form.

That's what I've been telling you, Mervania!

Mertin, you know that isn't nice, scanning my thoughts that way!

You're doing it with Kelvin and his kind!

Of course! They're inferior life-forms!

Foodstuffs.

If you will.

I knew we should have eaten them.

Groowmth! Grumpus added, tossing their dragon head.

What I don't understand, Mervania, is why you gave him the powder.

You know, Mertin. You know if you think about it.

You think about it for me.

I don't want to.

Do it anyway.

Oh, very well! Mertin was so vexing sometimes! Without giving it great attention she recalled the egg clutch they had laid just after dining on a stringy old wizard. There had been something wrong with it, as she soon realized. The eggs didn't have coppery shells, but were soft, and inside there was no more mind activity than from insects. Concentrating ever so little, she had gleaned that soft, single-headed beings were being formed that would closely resemble foodstuffs. The horror of producing monsters was too much, and the antidote, had it been available, had to be taken before the laying. There had been only one thing to do, and her body had a head for it.

Groowmth! Grumpus agreed, smacking his mouth. The memory of the eggs was still strong with it.

There. Satisfied, Mertin?

Not quite. The offspring of the foodstuff female will be like us, if she delivers while under the influence of the chimaeradrake root. It will have three heads and copper in its blood. In time it will grow a sting. Why destroy our own, Mervania? Why prevent its birth?

Dunderhead! Consider the horror! One of us raised by mortals! Cared for by the very inferior life-forms that are our food! Assuming they care for it at all; they might instead imprison or destroy it. No, any chimaera who comes into being must be here with us, in proper society, so as not to be stunted by regressive influences.

I understand, Mervania. Don't get so excited—you're making us ill.

I don't care if I do! Kelvin had to have the antidote, and I provided it! After she takes it the female won't lay an egg containing a superior life-form!

It'll be dead. The hatchling and the female. An inferior life-form won't adjust.

Possibly. I hadn't considered that. Mervania remedied that by considering it now.

At least there won't be a living superior life-form among inferiors, Mertin thought, satisfied.

If the antidote reaches the female in time.

Yes. But if that inferior female dies too, he may reconsider about fetching our dragonberry seeds.

But he made a deal!

He did. But inferior life-forms sometimes forget things when under stress. She pondered further, troubled. What could she do to ensure that Kelvin would not be distracted from his true mission of fetching the seeds?

Then she had it. She would have to be there, mentally, when the antidote was administered. Then, with a little guidance of precisely the right nature—yes.

A sound impinged on her thoughts. Someone ringing the bell at the gate.

She reached out mentally. A froogear was there, and in its arms was something that caused Mervania to start with surprise. This—why this changed everything!

As the sun was setting, Kelvin found his mother and Helbah waiting where they had promised outside the palace. He cut the speed of his belt, lowered his feet, and landed before them.

"You get it, Kelvin?" his mother asked worriedly.

"Right here," Kelvin said, holding up the packet. "The chimaera sent a froogear to meet me at the transporter."

"That's nice, dear. Now Zoanna and the false king have fled the palace.

Helbah is trying to locate them with her crystal. She's stronger now; she says
I've been a big help to her. Come now!"

"But—" Kelvin protested as he followed her. "The queen—"

"Oh, Helbah can counter her fireballs! Once it was two witches against
one, the queen was done for, and knew it. She won't want to give herself
away, but if she does, Helbah will be ready. Can you hurry?"

"Good idea," Kelvin agreed, and activated his belt. Scooping his mother
up in his arms—she weighed less than he did, now, which surprised him
somewhere in the background of his mind—he hopped-flew the remaining
distance. Actually the gauntlets made her seem even lighter, and they knew
how to support her; he would have bungled the job on his own, he was sure.
He carried her through the wall blasted open by Helbah. Through the twi-
light-lit throne room and the ballroom and down the halls.

"Here, this is it!" Charlain exclaimed, indicating the guest room that
Kelvin and Heln had once shared.

Kelvin never paused. With all the strength of his left gauntlet he shoved
in the door and paused, hovering in midair.

Dr. Sterk looked up birdlike and agitated at the bedside. Jon turned, her
mouth an O of surprise. On the bed, limbs chained to the bedposts, was a
bloated, misshapen thing of pure horror. This couldn't be Heln! His gentle,
lovely, loving wife! It couldn't be—yet it was.

"Kelvin! Mother!" Jon cried, gladness and horror mixing.

"She's having her contractions," Dr. Sterk said grimly. "But there's no
way she can birth it without destroying herself! I could cut, but—"

Kelvin swallowed. He thought he had come prepared, but his mind had
gone blank.

Charlain struggled in the grip of the gauntlets. "Let me down! Let me
down this instant!"

Oh. He touched down his feet and shut off his belt. He lowered his
mother to the floor. She started across the room.

Night fell in an instant. Lightning cracked outside, lighting the windows.
The oil lamps blew out. They were now in deepest darkness with Heln's
unhuman screams.

"Darn!" Kelvin heard his mother say. She snapped her fingers. Immediately a little ball of fire appeared near the ceiling and stayed there, brightening until it gave off more light than there had been from the lamps.

"Mother—?" Kelvin asked, his heart pounding. "What—?"

"That's my fireball," Charlain said. "The darkness is Zoanna's mischief.
She gave Heln the poison potion. Helbah may need a little help dealing with
the queen, and I'm going to be busy here. Why don't you go outside and find
her?"

"Mother, the powder!"

"Yes, and fast! Give it to me!"

He handed her the leaf packet. She held it near Heln's face. Heln drew in a breath to scream. Charlain touched the packet with a fingernail. The packet went POOF! and a cloud of pinkish smoke obscured Heln's face and head. From the midst of the smoke came an unhuman coughing and then a gasping, wheezing sound. The wheezing became a shrill whistle, as of an escaping gas. A heartbeat after that there was a choking from the midst of the pink cloud.

"Mother, she's—she's—"

Charlain raised a finger. POOF! and the cloud was gone. Heln lay there, sickly and pale, her eyes shocked and unbelieving. "Kelvin, Dr. Sterk, Mother Charlain—it's gone!"

"I know it is, dear. But your baby isn't."

"But—"

Then both froze for a moment, as if listening.

"What—?" Kelvin started.

Will you give over, oaf? Mervania's thought came. *The job is only half done. Let me concentrate on them; the situation is critical.*

Kelvin shut his mouth. Oddly, he felt better, knowing that the chimaera was present. He trusted Mervania's motive; she wanted this finished so he could go fetch her dragonberries.

"This is no ordinary delivery, Heln," Charlain said. "Now you know what is entailed. Are you strong enough?"

"I'll have to be," Heln said weakly.

"Then focus on the first, and bear down."

Heln's eyes rolled. Faintly she said, "I'll try." Then she lapsed into unconsciousness.

"Darn!" Charlain said. "Sorry, Kelvin, you shouldn't hear your mother swear."

"Is she—dead?"

"No, of course not. But we're all going to be if you don't get moving!"

"What should I do?" Kelvin had never felt more helpless. All he could think about was the stories of expectant fathers boiling water while the wife was in childbirth.

"How should I know?" his mother snapped in exasperation. "Go find Helbah!"

"But—"

"Your life and Heln's and all the others depend on it! Now go!"

Heln's eyes flickered open. "Go, Kel," she gasped. "You wouldn't like what happens here." She sagged down again.

Believe her, inferior form, Mervania thought.

Hardly realizing what he did, Kelvin left the palace. He knew that birthing a baby was difficult, but something more than that seemed to be in the offing. What was going on?

Outside a gust of wind struck him in the face and almost drove him back.

Rain spattered, hot and smelling of sulfur. Lightning cracked, luridly illuminating everything with an unnatural cast.

Where was Helbah?

"Over here!" her voice cracked.

There she was, hanging on to the gatepost. He activated his belt and flew over to her.

"Kelvin," she gasped weakly. "I need your help. I can't do it without you or Charlain, and your mother has her hands more than full. So it has to be you. I can't contain them."

"I—I'll do what I can." Kelvin knew that he was an inadequate substitute. "What can I do? Tell me, Helbah, tell me!"

A great ball of fire looped across the sky. Helbah raised her hands, and a smaller ball formed at her fingertips. The small fireball shaped itself into an arrow and shot skyward as though from a bow. Witch's fire collided above them, and there was a shocking thunderclap as both magically generated missiles imploded into nothingness.

"I'm getting weaker and she's getting stronger!" Helbah said. "With Charlain's help I had her beaten, but now I am alone, and her fireballs are getting closer before I can nullify them. I was shooting them down at the horizon, but now it's almost overhead, and soon I won't be able to stop them at all. I never thought Zoanna would recover so rapidly and well! If Charlain doesn't finish quickly with that chimaera so she can add her power to mine—"

"What?" Was Mervania attacking instead of assisting?

"Get that thing off your back!"

"The sting?"

"Of course the sting! What else have you got on your back? Get its butt down on the ground, way down, in contact with the dirt. Point the point east, where that fireball came from."

Numbly, Kelvin did as directed. He hardly understood any of what was happening, inside or outside. Some hero he was!

"There." Now Helbah's fingers lightly touched the sting and moved up and down its copper surface. Lightning flashes came from her fingers and were reflected by the copper.

"What?" he asked dazedly. "What?"

"Shut up! I've got to locate her and I can't use the crystal. When a fireball comes, you zap it. This is a case where science can counter magic, as with the Mouvar weapon."

"But I don't know how to—"

Helbah made a gesture. There was a poof of magic, and smoke. Lightning flashed in the sky. Where Helbah had been there was a large white bird resembling a dovgen.

Kelvin blinked, and then the bird—symbol of gentleness and peacefulness—was in the sky, flying, darting from side to side.

Another fireball appeared from the east. This one was smaller than the last, not much larger than the bird. It streaked for the bird, and Kelvin stared with opened mouth as his gauntlets tingled.

He grasped the top of the sting's shaft with his left hand and put his right hand farther down as far as he could reach. He tried to will lightning to stop the fireball.

Blue lightning crackled and snapped. A long, thin bolt shot from the tip of the sting and stretched out and upward. Above him the fireball sent by Zoanna was intercepted, pierced as if by an arrow. There was an improbable sizzling sound, a whiff of pure ozone, and the fireball vanished.

"I did it!" he exclaimed, astounded. "I shot down a fireball!"

Below where the fireball had been, a bird fluttered groundward in the fading light.

Kelvin's joy turned to horror. "No! No! No!" Without Helbah all was lost!

"Meow?" A blackness detached itself from the dark and reached up a paw.

The houcat! Helbah's familiar! Was it trying to tell him something?

Another fireball appeared. This one was larger than the last. Obviously Zoanna *was* gaining strength! Angry, determined, Kelvin put his hands on the copper sting and made the lightning jump. The bolt hit the fireball and the implosions all but deafened him. He gasped, almost knocked off his feet. Hot rain struck his face.

"Meow!"

He was getting weaker. He could feel it in his legs and arms. It seemed that it was his own life-energy that powered the shots. He was generating electricity from his body, just as the chimaera did, but his body was only a fraction the mass, and not adapted to this. How many bolts could he get from this sting? How many before he collapsed? Now he understood why Helbah had needed help!

He had to keep knocking out those fireballs. He thought the houcat was telling him as much. The familiar might be all that existed of Helbah, and that but for a time. If one of those fireballs hit the palace, it would be destroyed. It was up to him, then; he and the gauntlets and the chimaera's sting.

The chimaera! He tried thinking to Mervania, but got no answer; there was no indication that she was tuning him in now. What was going on within the palace?

"Meow!" Looking down in the moment of a lightning flash he saw every black hair standing up on Katbah's back. The animal's tail looked like a sharply bristled brush.

A phenomenally large fireball rushed with blurring speed across the sky. The queen was determined to finish them off now!

Concentrating hard, he threw the lightning. The ball seemed to accept the lightning and swallow it. There was an uncomfortable crackling that made his teeth ache and the blue lightning bolt snapped and cracked its full unnatural length from sting-tip to fireball.

Was this going to be the one that would destroy them?

"Meow!"

The little paw touch on the copper shaft felt like the blow of a hammer. The sting tipped. Remembering that Helbah had said the butt should make contact with the ground, he pushed down on it. Still the tip tipped, pointing more visibly, more directly at the fireball that was lighting the sky.

Lightning sizzled and there was a pop that might and might not have been in his ear. Streamers of fire faded rapidly. The lightning bolt vanished. Katbah, mewling as from singed pawpads, backed away.

How much longer could this go on? How much strength did Zoanna the witch now have? Was he going to weaken right out of the fight? Was it going to be the gauntlets and Katbah left to defend the palace?

No, he'd stay conscious, and he'd keep doing this, whatever it was. Eventually the wicked witch would have to weaken. Eventually there would have to come an end to night!

There was a horrendous roar from the palace. Katbah hissed. Kelvin turned, and saw a long low shape charge from the palace into the night. It looked a lot like a small dragon, but of course that couldn't be.

PLOP! A white bird, singed and sooty and apparently almost dead, fell beside Katbah. It lay there in the lightning's flash. Katbah sniffed it as all went dark.

"That was some trip!" Helbah groaned.

Kelvin swallowed. "You're—back?"

"Of course I'm back! For a dimwitted boy you ask the dumbest questions!"

"I—I'm sorry, Helbah. I thought—"

"You thought that fireball got me. That's what you were supposed to think! That's what Zoanna was supposed to think!"

"Meow."

"Yes, Katbah, you·did right. Can't depend on a hero for everything. Particularly one as inexperienced as this."

Considering all the adventures he had had in his relatively short life span, Kelvin did not feel he was inexperienced. But the need to get on with this was great.

"Helbah, what did you—?"

"Found them. Cave in the mountainside. Now it's up to you, me, and Charlain. Get that fireball, will you?"

Almost absently Kelvin directed the chimaera's sting to lightning out another approaching fire-bolus. The ground shook.

"But Mother is—"

"Here," Charlain said behind him. "And congratulations, hero, you are now the husband of a relatively healthy, loving wife, and the father of a healthy, squalling baby boy."

Kelvin's mouth dropped open.

"And a rather pretty baby girl," Jon said, emerging with a bundle.

The enormity of the change in his life hit him then, as did the ground before he had half realized.

30 /

DEFEAT?

"WAKE UP, HERO! WAKE UP!"
He felt her slapping him. Helbah. Then he felt the cat's tail under his nose and he wanted to sneeze.

"Does he do this often, Charlain?"

"I wouldn't know, Helbah. We'll have to ask his wife."

Wife! Heln! The baby!

Babies!

Kelvin sat up, then stood up. He was dizzy. There were stars in the sky, not all of his making. A moon, bright and coppery as a chimaera's haunch, lighting the grounds of the Kelvinian palace.

He made his way unsteadily to where Jon stood, holding his daughter. The baby's face seemed oddly familiar. The eyes were dark, almost coppery—

He froze. That face, after allowing for the difference in age—

Don't be concerned, Mervania thought. *All foodstuffs look alike to us too. She favors me only slightly.*

Kelvin reeled.

"What's the matter, Kel?" Jon asked, alarmed. "She's not ugly, she's remarkably pretty for a newborn baby, and so's her brother, Mother says. Nothing wrong with either of them."

"But—"

What your mother doesn't want to tell you, Mervania thought, *is that there were three. The dragon fled.*

But—

It was a very tricky disenchantment, Kelvin. You can't undo in a minute something that has developed for weeks. We saved your wife's life by breaking the chimaera into three: boy, girl, and dragon. You may keep the first two. That's fair, isn't it?

Kelvin's mouth was stuck halfway open.

682

Now go in there and see your wife, and be brave when they tell you about the third. It was the best that could be done, Kelvin. The two are completely human, except—

Except? he thought numbly.

They will be telepathic. Sorry about that; it just couldn't be helped. Now be on your way. I'll be on mine; I have business at home to hold me for a while. He felt her presence fade; she was gone.

Kelvin shut his mouth and started toward the palace.

"Uh, I know she wants to see you, but not just yet," Jon said. "It was a difficult delivery, and there's blood, and she's sleeping—"

"True," Charlain said. "And we do have other business out here. Stand by, Kelvin."

He stood by. Jon turned and walked into the palace with the baby girl. *They didn't know the whole story!* he thought. *They didn't know Mervania's part in it.*

"Later we must talk, Kelvin," Charlain said. "But right now we must deal with the queen, or all can still be lost."

Kelvin finally found his voice. "Yes. I'll help here."

"We have to get to work," Helbah agreed.

"The fireballs!" Kelvin said. "Are you watching? I forgot to—"

"She has quit sending them for the time being. It takes as much energy to generate them as to abolish them. I must admit I'm surprised at her strength. If you hadn't come out when you did we'd have been finished."

Kelvin refocused on the problem. He had managed, with the help of the chimaera's sting, to make witchfire arrows! Or at least the lightning to shoot them down. But indeed the battle was not over; not until Zoanna was gone. He stared into the sky. He'd never expected to see the moon out tonight; it had been so dark. But of course the storm had not been natural.

"Do you think they're trying to escape?" Charlain asked.

"I think they're planning something," Helbah said. "Zoanna swore she'd never give up. If that's so, we'll have to finish her."

"She'll come back if we don't, won't she?" Kelvin asked.

"Probably. One thing you can say for her, she's not a quitter."

"Nor is Rowforth. He's just as bad!"

"Fortunately Rowforth hasn't her magic. Let's go get them."

"To that cave?"

"As I told you, for a slow boy you ask the dumbest questions! Of course to the cave!"

"How will we—?" Helbah was clearly the general, he thought.

"Charlain and I may not need you there. Hand your mother the antimagic weapon. It won't crack Zoanna's barrier, but it just might help. You stay here with the sting and Katbah and watch for fireballs. Your former queen is just mean enough to try one final attack on the palace."

"I—I'll watch." He handed his mother the Mouvar weapon. Then he thought again and handed her the belt and short scabbard. She took these with as little surprise as though he had handed her a pot in her own kitchen. She strapped on the weapon, seeming not in the least curious about it.

"I'm sure you will," Helbah said. "Charlain, hop on my back!"

With astonishment that seemed lately never to cease, Kelvin watched his mother climb piggyback on Helbah's aging shoulders. Then, as the moon hid under clouds and it was as dark as the inside of a serpent, there was a whooshing sound. The moon came back and there was a white dovgen climbing into the sky with what looked like a small gray shrewouse clinging with tiny paws to its feathers.

The bird disappeared into the dark sky. There were no lightnings. No flaming balls of witch's fire.

"Meow." Absently he reached down and stroked the cat. He was back to the little-boy stage, he thought, waiting patiently for adults to accomplish adult business. All in all it wasn't too bad a place to be.

Katbah rubbed against him and purred contentment and wordless understanding. He was beginning to understand why witches had familiars; they could be a lot of comfort on dark nights.

No, not too bad a place for someone who had never wanted the hero mantle in the first place.

"Ohhh," Rowforth moaned. "Zoanna, you're taking too much of my life-force. It's flowing out and nothing is replacing it. Zoanna, you're draining me!"

"Can't be helped. You want to win, don't you? Quit your whining."

"But Zoanna, if you kill me in order to destroy them, where's my triumph? You don't want me dead." Then he paused, a new and not entirely pleasant thought occurring. "You don't, do you, Zoanna?"

Zoanna, now the complete witch, did not answer. She merely smiled in ever so enigmatic a fashion.

Rowforth, who had been merely uncomfortable, now found that he was thoroughly scared. He resolved that he would find some way of being useful to her other than at the expense of his life-force. To fail to do this, he strongly suspected, would cost him dear. It could, he knew in the depths of him, cost him his life.

John and Rufurt had ridden the plowhorse double half the way to the palace. John for his part was having second thoughts. True, the lights in the sky meant big things afoot, and probably danger to those he loved. But, and the thought jolted him worse than the plowhorse, the intelligent thing would have been to go back to Kian and get his help.

"Curse it," Rufurt said with disgust, "there's never an army around when you need one!"

Looking at the dancing lights in the sky and having his senses beset by implosive blasts, John had to agree with the former king's estimate. But he had to go on. Somewhere ahead there was Charlain!

Jon watched Heln nursing her firstborn and felt a stirring inside her that she had never honestly felt before. Possibly, just possibly, she herself was not completely devoid of maternal instinct. She looked down at the secondborn she held. She certainly was a cute baby! She had her grandma's coppery hair. But how were they going to tell Kelvin about the horrible third one?

Well, maybe they wouldn't have to. The thing had gained its feet immediately and scampered out before they could do more than stare. Heln, lapsing into unconsciousness again, hadn't seen it at all. Maybe nobody but Jon, Charlain, and Dr. Sterk ever needed to know of the horror that had been the remnant of the evil enchantment. It was safely gone.

"I'm sure they'll be all right," Dr. Sterk said, putting his beak of a nose almost in her face. "I wasn't certain. We physicians have so little training in magic."

"I'm sure that can change," Jon said.

"It will. It will have to. After all, magic is the basis of all healing."

"I've heard that all my life. From Mother, mostly." Jon looked at the window and was surprised how light it had become. The ball of fire Charlain had left had gradually grown dimmer until now it was about as bright as that of twin oil lamps.

"I'll light the lamps again, Doctor. I'm not certain how long my mother's light will last."

"Probably almost until morning," Dr. Sterk said.

Jon busied herself with the lamps. She hadn't a coal to apply to the wicks so she simply held them near the witch's fire and—not surprisingly, to her at least—they lit.

"Good girl, Jon."

"Doctor, do you mind if I go out and see what Kelvin and our mother are about? It has been a while."

"No indeed, Jon. I'm wondering about that myself." He took the baby from her.

Heln stirred, weak and wan in the bed. "Please Jon, find out about Kelvin."

"Don't worry about him," Jon said, patting the new mother's hand. How wonderful it was to have Heln back, instead of the monster she had become under the enchantment! "He's our hero and nothing bad will happen to him. He didn't come in before because I asked him not to. There was blood, and you were just about unconscious." *And we had to clean up the gory tracks of that horrible third birth!*

Heln sighed. "Of course. You're right, Jon. You almost always are." She closed her eyes. *And we didn't want to rouse you until that was done either,* Jon's thought finished.

Jon left the palace, sling in hand. She was wondering if what she'd told Heln was true. Prophecy or no prophecy, she knew she had on more than one occasion saved her brother's life.

Kelvin stood at the gatepost in the moonlight. His hands were on a copper something that looked a little like a dragon spear that she hadn't noticed before, in the mixed excitement of the birthings. The point of the spear thing was pointed skyward; was it some sort of new weapon? Why would he need anything different if he had the Mouvar weapon that had won the war with Aratex? And there, next to his leg, rubbing up against him, was a large, black houcat.

"Kelvin?"

"Jon!" he exclaimed, as if seeing her for the first time. "Is Heln all right? Are the babies—?"

"Calm yourself," she said with a tired smile. "They're all fine. Heln's asking for you. As soon as you finish here, you can go see her." What a boy Kelvin was, actually, she realized. How much more grown-up she and Heln were, and even her own Lester.

"I have to watch the sky for fireballs," he said. "Mother and our—" He paused, swallowed, and then went on: "Our ally, have gone to finish something."

"You mean the witch from the twin cities, don't you?" How naive did he think she was? Who else had been defending them from Zoanna and the false king these past days?

"Yes—yes, that's what I mean. Helbah thinks they're licked and that she can finish them."

"Isn't that a job for a hero?"

"I'm not complaining," Kelvin said.

Jon lightly touched his hand. "You've sent back Zoanna's fireballs, Kel?"

"This stopped them," he said, touching the copper spear.

"Why stop them? Why not send them back?"

"Witches erect magic barriers when they expect magical attack or counterattack. The returned fireballs might have bothered Zoanna but they wouldn't have crisped her unless she'd dropped her guard. She might even have been poised to bounce them back again, and that could have made it worse for us."

"She maintained that through magic?"

"Yes."

"Kelvin, why don't you go after them?"

"I'm supposed to guard the palace. If I neglect my post, and the queen sends one more fireball, we'll lose even if we kill Zoanna. Anyway, Helbah can handle it."

"Are you certain?"

He frowned. "Why?"

She bit her lower lip and tried to see off into the darkness, past the forest, to the mountainside. There was just the faintest of flashes there, first high up and then low down.

"Look, Kelvin," she said, directing his gaze, "isn't that a battle? Aren't the witches going at it hard?"

Kelvin's eyes squinted. "I don't see . . . I can't see past the forest."

"It is," she said. "The witches battling. Kelvin, I think you should go and help."

"They've got the Mouvar weapon."

"But it may not be enough. Zoanna can't take time to throw a fireball at the palace. Helbah and Mother have her occupied."

Kelvin frowned. "You really think I should—"

"Yes." She was really worried now.

"All right, then." He took up the copper spear and strapped it to his back. He did something to his belt and his feet left the ground, and he soared like an untethered cloud. He looked back once, and then he was flying through the moonlight in the direction of the mountainside.

Jon sighed. She hoped she had done the right thing. Her brother seemed so helpless sometimes!

"Meow?" The black houcat seemed almost to question her.

"Yes, kitty," she said. "Kelvin's off to be a hero, and I know that someway he'll save the day. Because he is guarded by the prophecy, while the others aren't. I wish I was going with him. I wish you and I could fly."

"Meow." Something stung her legs, like a jolt of what her father called static electricity but which she had always thought magic. The stars grew smaller and somehow the grass and the gatepost grew high. Ozone was in the air and there was a taste in her mouth that surely she had never tasted before.

She flexed her white wings. A black creature the size of a shrewouse climbed up between her shoulders and gently gripped her feathers with claws.

Jon flapped her dovgen wings and flew after Kelvin.

I'm off to join the witches! she thought as the fields and the trees slid by. Somehow she wasn't at all surprised.

Helbah sweated and strained to keep the barrier erected. She could feel it bulging inward, pushing at them, wanting to break. The heat from the steadily roaring flames was getting to her, and worse still, to her apprentice.

"Now, Charlain!" she said. With all their strength they pushed together, back, back. Who would have thought Zoanna commanded such power?

There was only one thing left to try, and she tried it. Hate technology though she might, there was such a thing as a mixture of technology and magic. She raised Kelvin's Mouvar weapon to point at the cliff, though where it pointed hardly mattered. She pressed its trigger.

The fireball receded from before them. It retreated to the cliffside and the entrance to a cave. It stopped there, held in check by Zoanna's barrier. If Zoanna should drop the barrier she would be consumed by her own bolide. If Helbah could now add her own witch's fire the barrier would surely disintegrate.

Unfortunately the Mouvar weapon recognized no distinction between Zoanna's fireball and her own. Should Helbah try a magical counterattack, it would rebound on her and Charlain.

She was weakening alarmingly fast. That treacherous injury she had taken on the battlefield still vitiated her strength; she needed far more recuperation time than she had gotten. She didn't know how long she could go on. If only Zoanna would weaken before Helbah weakened further. The Mouvar weapon held her in check for a breathing spell and then its power weakened and Zoanna's fireball was drifting back.

Now she regretted telling Kelvin to remain at the palace. She needed him here, with his copper sting! With that he might throw a nonmagical electrical bolt through the barrier. That would be the end of Zoanna and the worst of her many consorts.

THUNK!

The feathered crossbow bolt, definitely not magic, protruded from her arm. Blood started from around the shaft. She had only heartbeats left, if that, to maintain consciousness. Heartbeats to contain the barrier protecting them from the witch's fire!

She could deal with the wound, by focusing her magic on it, for it was not a critical one. But if she did that, there would be no barrier to Zoanna's magical attack. She had to maintain that barrier!

The wound burned horribly. Her arm seemed to swell to twice its normal size. She lost feeling in the extremity. Her finger loosened on the Mouvar's trigger. The weapon dropped, and she after it.

"Helbah! Helbah!" her apprentice cried.

Poor Charlain, Helbah thought as her senses faded. *I've failed you and the rest.*

"Good shot, Rowforth!"

"Nothing to it, my love." Despite his faking it, he could hardly stand. How he had gotten to his feet and aimed the crossbow was a mystery proving once again his remarkable endurance. "Better get them now, love, while you have the chance."

"I'm going to, sweetie. But I intend to savor my victory. Look who's there! Can you see him in the morning light?"

Rowforth squinted. "Kelvin!"

"That's right. We've got the entire bunch! At our mercy, only we have no mercy."

"Burn them! Burn them!"

"In good time." She sharpened her eyesight, a trick she had only recently learned. The thin, tawny-haired troublemaker and prophesied curse was definitely there. He was trying to help Helbah and at the same time he was looking up at them. Helbah was almost finished—and he was almost finished.

She began forming a fireball in front of the ledge. Slowly, slowly, slowly. No need to hurry. Big, big. Hot, hot. Oh, it was nice!

Rowforth gasped weakly and sat down. He was being drained beyond his tolerable threshold, but it couldn't be helped. This was the fire that counted!

Rowforth picked up his crossbow, tried to put another bolt in it, and tried to crank it taut. He fumbled with the cocking mechanism, then dropped it, too weak. "For the gods' sake, Zoanna, you're weakening me too much!"

"How much is too much?" she inquired indifferently. "This will be the fullest revenge, Rowforth. You didn't know I knew about the maid, did you?"

Even in the hot glow from the fireball, Rowforth's face was white. "I thought—"

"You thought you could be unfaithful. That was an error on your part."

"You were unfaithful!"

"Zoanna is Zoanna. My consorts are my consorts. You were only a consort, my sweet."

"Was?" Realization made his voice weak.

"Was, sweet," she said firmly.

Rowforth's eyes bulged above his big ruddy nose until his very face looked obscene. "Zoanna, you're draining me completely! You're killing me!"

"I am, Your Unfaithfulness. It's all part of my triumph. For my next consort I think I'll take a young and inexperienced boy. That guardsman who stole your prize mare and ran off and joined with that fool St. Helens, what's-his-name—Lomax. Yes, for a time he might be quite pleasant. With what I know now I can make him come to me. Come and perform, delightfully."

"ZOANNA! ZOANNA!" He could not even move his hand to draw the dagger he carried. All of what energy he retained went into his pleading, accusing shouts.

Feeling a bit smug about it she moved the fireball to where Helbah's barrier had been. Past the spot, to where Kelvin could feel the heat and not quite fry. The boy was now trying desperately to get the chimaera sting from his back. *Excellent, Kelvin! With that you really could destroy me!* Now his mother was helping him, pulling at a thong, guiding it off his shoulder with her fingertips.

"That's too easy for you!" Zoanna said. She nudged the fireball closer. Now they were burning their dainty fingers on the sting, as they tried, but failed, to point it at her. Like houcat and shrewous, this game!

One more little nudge and it would be all over. She was almost reluctant. Wait until they nearly had the sting grounded, almost pointing at her. Wait until the very last microsecond. Wait, wait, wait, savoring.

She glanced down at Rowforth's inert body. Too bad he was already out of it. He would have enjoyed seeing Kelvin die. It was appropriate: it was Rowforth's remaining life-force that was in the fireball, doing the deed.

She nudged the fireball just a tiny bit closer. There, let them fry, let them cook and steam before she burned them. Let their lungs burst, their hearts explode, their eyeballs melt. When she was done only their charred bones would remain.

Now, now, now was the moment! Now her triumph when all her enemies burned.

Throwing back her head, she vented a vengeful laugh of complete and final triumph.

Kelvin felt his skin blister. The stench of his own burning hair was in his nostrils. His hands and the leathery gauntlets protecting them were cooking on the copper surface of the chimaera's sting. Waves of continuous pain were making him nauseous. His mother was beside him but he had almost forgotten her. What magic she and Helbah had had was vanquished. There was no way, no way at all that they could survive.

Klunk! It seemed to be an irrelevant, meaningless sound to accompany their dying. The fire around them was somehow fainter. Then, remarkably, the fireball vanished and his eyes flashed with pain.

Was this death? No, it hurt too much!

"KELVIN! CRISP THEM!"

His sister's voice? It couldn't be! Delusion before death? He couldn't think.

The fire was gone now. Through streaming eyes he could see the cave above them. Two bodies were lying there. Zoanna's and Rowforth's. Were they dead?

"HURRY, KELVIN! HURRY!"

It *was* Jon's voice!

"Kelvin, I can't find another rock!" Her voice was close and unmistakably hers. "She's going to wake! Hurry!"

No time to question. He placed his hands on the copper, heard the sizzle, smelled the burning flesh. He was screaming, though hardly aware of it. He ignored the agony ballooning bigger and bigger and threatening momentarily to explode his heart. Only one thing to think about: lightning. Pure, sizzling lightning to cleanse and destroy . . .

"Kelvin, she's awake! She getting up! She's—"

CRACK! It was his bolt, scoring.

In the blue afterimage he saw two skeletons on the cave ledge. One stood upright with raised hands, but now all flesh was gone from it. Yet it remained vertical, unwilling to fall down. The very bones were shapely, retaining the outline of a beautiful woman.

Magical beings died hard. Maybe witches died hardest. Almost entirely destroyed, they could yet somehow return to life. Or so it seemed possible to believe, right now.

The figure moved. It didn't fall. Its arms came together over its head, as if shaping something between the bonefingers. Something like another fireball.

"Kelvin!"

Again he willed the lightning.

CRACK!

The standing skeleton crumbled, yet it remained intact. It landed on hands and knees, trying to break its fall.

CRACK! SIZZLE! CRACK! Lightning bolt after lightning bolt. He felt himself being drained, but he gave it his all. The bolts blasted the skeleton apart, and blasted the individual bones, and blasted the fragments.

Now nothing remained on the ledge or in the cave but ash. As he stared upward the ash stirred in a morning breeze and slowly lost all shape.

He tottered himself. Now he could die. It was done.

"Kelvin, did you get them?" Whispery and dry, it was Helbah. He had thought her dead.

"They're gone," Kelvin gasped. "Forever, I think."

"Good. Your mother—?"

He looked down at the crumpled heap that had been she who had borne him. "I—I don't know."

"She may survive. You may. I may."

"Yes." But unlikely, he thought.

"The war—will you surrender to me?"

War? Surrender? What was she talking about?

"Do it, Son. *Please!*" It was his mother, reviving, still able to speak!

"I'll do what you ask," he said, hardly aware of what he was promising.

"Your side won. Kelvinia stands defeated."

It was never my war in the first place! he thought. *Never Kelvinia's. Never mine.*

"In that case, I'm sure we will survive," Helbah said more briskly. "Charlain, hands!"

Charlain lifted her arms with difficulty and placed burned palms against Helbah's. There was a sizzle and the blackness disappeared from their hands. Both women grew rosy and visibly stronger. Burns and scorch marks disappeared. Firefrizzed hair lost tips of ash and became all dark and healthy. Helbah's shoulder wound stopped bleeding and she removed one hand from Charlain to start to pull out the arrow's head.

"Kelvin!"

Hands touched, gripped, firmed. Helbah held his right, his mother his left.

The agony faded. His heart resumed beating normally. Strength came back in waves that were positively exhilarating.

"There," Helbah said, dropping his hand. "We are now whole again, thanks to some help from a friend."

That was an overstatement, for she still had a crossbow wound in her arm. But now she was able to attend to it.

Jon appeared suddenly, breaking through some brush. In her arms was Katbah. Over her left shoulder hung the sling that had saved all of them.

"Kelvin, we did it!"

"We did, Sister," he agreed. He was thankful that Jon hadn't arrived a moment earlier, for then she would have seen what pitiful shape they were all in. How had she gotten here, anyhow?

"She inherited some of her mother's latent talent," Helbah said. "Katbah recognized it. Smart Katbah."

"It was awful!" Jon said, looking happy. "I looked for another rock after I changed, but I never found one. I knew all the time she'd only stay down so long. If you hadn't lightning'd her, Kel . . ."

Katbah, who had been contentedly snuggling in her arms, suddenly stiffened and jumped down. Every hair on the familiar's body stood out. The hair on Helbah and Charlain flared as well.

"There's a presence," Helbah whispered. "A presence whose energy I utilized."

Kelvin's heart resumed pounding. Did this mean Zoanna had somehow survived the lightning? Had they been cruelly tricked?

"Calm yourselves," a feminine voice said. It seemed familiar, yet strange. It wasn't Zoanna, or Helbah's or Charlain's or Jon's. Yet he knew that voice! It—

"Mervania?" Kelvin exclaimed.

"Perceptive!" Mertin's voice said. Then there was a growling, as of a dragon.

"But I *hear* you!" Kelvin said. "Why aren't you in my head?"

"Because I'm here outside your head, inferior life-form!" Mervania said.

"I came to tell you that you needn't bring those dragonberries. One of you planted some seeds, maybe accidentally. I've now got plenty of them."

The seeds they had carried with them and that Kian had lost? They had somehow come up in the chimaera's frame?

"You catch on eventually, human foodstuff."

"Then I won't need to return to your frame? Ever?"

"Don't say it!" Mertin said.

"No," Mervania said. "You won't have to return, Kelvin."

There was a growl of disappointment. "Damn it, Merv, if you'd kept your mouth shut he might have come, and we could have eaten him."

"I know, Mertin. But leave me my foibles. He's a cute boy."

Kelvin sighed, thankful. "You came all the way here, astrally, just to tell me that?"

"No trouble, Kelvin. Actually I thought I might give you some help, but you seem to have done well enough on your own. Not without the use of my present, though."

"Yes." A horrid thought hit him. "Will you stick around? Do you mean to stay here?"

"Calm yourself again, Kelvin," Mervania said, amused. "No, you won't see me again unless you come visiting, which I wouldn't advise. I want to find my own kind. In an infinity of frames there has to be one where an intelligent life-form is dominant. Where one of our kind may have hatched and survived in a civilized manner, instead of degraded by savages. Here the only intelligent beings are houcats and dragons."

"I . . . see."

"Unless your wife would like to visit."

"What?"

"Don't be concerned. We wouldn't eat her. But we could give her more of the powder, so she could birth one of our kind in a suitable environment. It's a rare talent, to be able to—"

"No!" Kelvin cried, echoed by Jon.

"Well, I did help her," Mervania said, sounding hurt. "Considering that I already had the dragonberries, I really didn't have to."

"You already had—when you—the birthing—?" he asked, stunned.

"Her and her damn-fool sentiment!" Mertin exclaimed angrily, accompanied by a similarly outraged growl.

Kelvin realized that Mervania had indeed been generous, by chimaera definition. She had no longer needed him for the berries, yet she had done him a singular favor. She had saved his wife's life.

"Well, actually, I did it mostly for the offspring," Mervania said. "This is no frame for a Superior Life-form."

"All the same, Mervania, thanks," he said sincerely.

"Now see what you've done, Merv!" Mertin said accusingly. "You've made him grateful. The mush is so solid you could bite it!" And the dragon growled with similar disgust.

"But he has such a charmingly foolish image of me!" Mervania said defensively.

All too true! Kelvin swallowed, then uttered a difficult truth. "I—I think my daughter *does* look like you, Mervania, and I—I don't mind."

"Why thank you, Kelvin," she replied, sounding genuinely touched.

"Goodbye, Mervania."

There was silence. After a moment he realized that the chimaera was gone.

The others were staring at him, but Kelvin didn't mind that, either.

Epilogue

IT WAS NOT A BIG, fancy wedding. Certainly nothing to compare with what Kian's had been. But when John took Charlain's hand, pushed back her copper hair, gazed into her violet eyes, and said, "Charlain, we are again wed. For always, you and I," and she replied, "Yes, John, always, you and I," there was not a dry eye in the ballroom of what had been Kelvinia's palace.

Later, after the formal reception and the shaking of hands of all well-wishers, the bride, groom, their family and closest friends sat together in the lounging room.

Jon still wiped at her eyes. It was apparent that she had been moved even more than she might have wished, and in more ways. Brave, tomboyish Jon, holding Lester's hand and trying valiantly to stem the tide.

"How come Easter's pregnant and I'm not?" she demanded in a whisper of Lester. "She's younger than I am!"

Startled, Lester turned to her. It was evident that a certain attitude had changed somewhere along the way. "We'll discuss that later," he whispered back.

"We'll do more than that!" she muttered. Then she looked around as if fearful that someone had overheard, or had noticed her tears. It seemed that no one had. At least, no one gave any sign.

Kelvin noticed, though. He was tempted to say something brotherly, but then thought better of it. He and his sister were getting on famously these days and he didn't want to wreck it. So instead of telling her that she had a right to weep, or whatever, and that the wedding made it legitimate, he turned to Morton Crumb.

"It was a nice wedding, wasn't it?"

"Yeh, very nice." Beside Mor sat his Mrs., fat and comforting Mabel, whom Kelvin hardly knew.

Kelvin turned to his wife. She had recovered so nicely during the past weeks. No nightmares, though he hardly understood how that was possible. Maybe it was the efficiency of the chimaera's powder. She sat there calmly nursing Charles, whose pink, chubby expression never betrayed what he might have been. Twin Merlain lay sleeping beside her. They were to be Knights, by mutual agreement, now that the marriage of their grandparents had been restored.

"You comfortable, dearest?"

"You ask me that so often! Yes, of course. But I'll be more comfortable once we're home."

Kelvin smiled. There was a type of comfort that he had not had recently that only she could supply.

"Well anyway," Rufurt spoke up from across the room, repositioning the crown on his head, "that's another two words of your prophecy. 'Uniting four' means Kance, Klingland, Hermandy, and Kelvinia. We're one confederation now, each with one vote, with brothers Kildom and Kildee having the power to veto all the rest of us. In all of history there's never been such an arrangement, but Helbah wanted it."

"It's for the best," Kelvin said. "I trust Helbah. Kelvinia never had any difficulties with Klingland and Kance that Zoanna and your look-alike didn't invent. And with those boys in charge you know Hermandy will behave itself."

"They already got rid of their dictator," St. Helens said. "I say hooray for them."

"I'm sure we all do," Kelvin said almost automatically.

"And Kelvin," his father-in-law said, leaning forward, "you know what's next for you. The prophecy says 'Until from Seven there be One / Only then will his Task be Done.' Well, there are still three kingdoms left for you to conquer."

Kelvin considered carefully before he spoke. St. Helens was not an evil man, though he did sometimes talk like what his father called a war hawk. Those two young fellows in the twin caps had many, many years to grow, and he was certain Helbah wouldn't let them declare war yet if ever. All in all, one pleasing solution as far as he was concerned.

"I'm glad it's only old words some people believe in, and that I'm not even nominally in charge," he said.

No one looked disappointed with his answer, not even St. Helens. They were all too polite to speak the obvious: as a hero, he was an inferior lifeform.

It was a great, fine time in Kelvinia and the confederation.

ABOUT THE AUTHORS

PIERS ANTHONY is the renowned *New York Times* bestselling author of fantasy and science fiction novels. With his longtime collaborator, ROBERT E. MARGROFF, they have created other popular fantasy novels, such as *Orc's Opal* and *The Ring*.